TOGETHER WE FALL

THE COMPLETE SERIES

KATIE MAY

EXPRESSO PUBLISHING, LLC

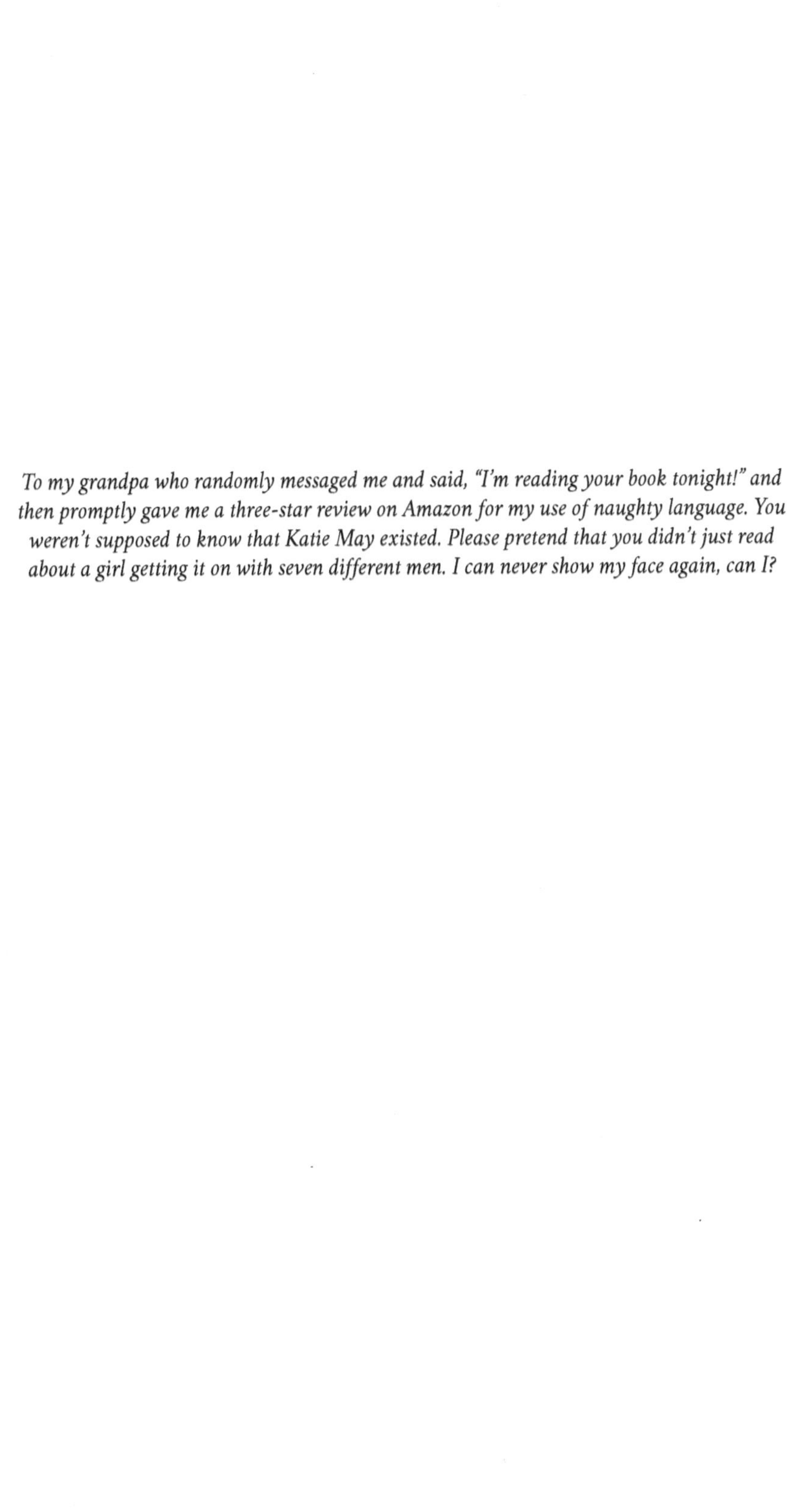

To my grandpa who randomly messaged me and said, "I'm reading your book tonight!" and then promptly gave me a three-star review on Amazon for my use of naughty language. You weren't supposed to know that Katie May existed. Please pretend that you didn't just read about a girl getting it on with seven different men. I can never show my face again, can I?

CONTENTS

THE DARKNESS WE CRAVE

THE LIGHT WE SEEK

THE STORM WE FACE

THE MONSTERS WE HUNT

THE CHRISTMAS WE SHARE

THE DARKNESS WE CRAVE

TOGETHER WE FALL BOOK 1

PROLOGUE

The only friend I ever had was killed.

You would think that I'd remember his death in vivid detail, but I didn't. At least, not consciously. My therapist said that it was my way of coping with the loss.

I did, however, remember the day I met him. Like a distorted tattoo, the details of that day had permanently imprinted themselves onto my brain. One could best compare our meeting to a fairy tale. There was a girl and a boy, a knight and a fearful child. You see, this was where our story varied from most others—he was weak, and I was strong. I had never been the damsel-in-distress type of girl, and he had never been the knight-in-shining-armor type of guy. Our pasts were too atypical to create such stereotypes.

The day I met him, the weather had been uncharacteristically cold, and the trees seemed to be cooperating, their branches leafless. If anything, it was beginning to look more like fall than the previous months had displayed. I was terrified my butt was going to freeze off, and I would be forced to poop out of my mouth—Nanny Number One had a huge imagination.

Daddy and Mommy had been fighting again. I remembered that detail, but I couldn't recall what the fight was about. I remembered that he called her a lot of nasty names, and she retorted with another guy's name, declaring that he was "better" than my father. Of course, my innocent brain thought she was talking about cooking or some shit like that. Well, in my defense, it turned out the other guy *did* know how to take care of a muffin, if you know what I mean.

My eyes flickered nervously between Mommy and Daddy, my small hands holding my favorite doll in a death grip. I wore a new outfit my nanny—yes, the one who told me I'd shit from my mouth—bought me a white, billowing number with a contrasting red bow. She had brushed and styled my hair into two braids, and I felt beautiful for the first time in my life. All I had ever wanted to be was a little girl my mommy and daddy actually loved and wanted around.

"Mommy! Daddy!" I pleaded, my little voice trembling. "Please stop fighting."

Daddy looked at me as if he'd just realized I was in the room with them. Instead of apologizing like I expected at getting caught in an argument, he appeared almost enraged. Even back then, he didn't like me interrupting him. He didn't like me doing anything, really, besides smiling like the pretty puppet he wanted when he sired me.

Before I could even think to scream, he grabbed one of my braids and dragged me outside.

My knees hit the grass, small rocks and other unsavory substances digging into my skin as my dress rode up. The poor dress itself was stained a deep brown and an almost garnet red.

Blood, I realized numbly. My blood.

And Dolly, well, Daddy hadn't been gentle with her. Stuffing covered the grass, mixing with the stream of blood from my legs. The sight would cause any psychopathic pedophile to orgasm.

I stared at my doll for a long moment, barely hearing my dad's cuss words and threats aimed towards his six-year-old daughter. I didn't even process it when he slapped me across the face.

No, my eyes remained fixed on Dolly. She couldn't be gone, not Dolly. Who would have tea parties with me or cuddle with me when I became scared at night?

I didn't cry as I stared at her maimed body. I was too numb for that, and still, somehow innately, I knew that she wasn't real. You couldn't mourn an inanimate object.

No, it would take a few more years, when I was thirteen, to understand what mourning meant. But I wasn't the savior during that point of my life. I was the murderer.

Looking back at my interaction with Dolly, I found it ironic that I lost something important to me the same day I gained the best friend I ever had.

Sniffling, I watched my dad's back retreat into the house until the door slammed shut, leaving me alone and outside as if I was nothing more than discarded trash. Maybe that was all I'd ever been to him.

It took me a few tries to scramble to my feet. My body shook from my dad's unexpected aggression. I suppose you could say that my dad's anger was the only constant in my life.

Piles of leaves littered the grass and sidewalk, crunching underneath my sock-clad feet. I wrapped my arms around myself, attempting to ease the sting in my arms. The chill from the howling wind caused goosebumps to erupt on my flesh.

With no purpose or destination in mind, I walked. All I knew was that I wanted to get as far away as possible from the two people who were supposed to provide me with unconditional love and support. Of course, these thoughts only came to me later when I was older. All I remember at the time was wondering why Daddy didn't love me. Why had he hit me? Did I do something wrong? Why was I a failure as a daughter, even wearing my beautiful new dress?

I wasn't aware how far I had walked until I stumbled upon a gated playground.

A school, I realized almost dumbly. Like where the kids on TV go.

I had never been to school before. For as long as I could remember, Daddy kept me in purposeful isolation and therefore, homeschooled. He didn't want me to have friends.

Kids climbed the jungle gym, played tag in a field, and swung on the swings. The sight seemed almost ethereal, and my little brain attempted to process everything at once.

For a brief moment, jealousy speared my chest. I was the girl who had everything, yet ironically, my isolation grew more pronounced in the presence of people. At least the people my parents *allowed* me to associate with, namely stuffy children of business executives.

I simply stared at the kids in awe. I didn't want to join them. I wanted to *be* them.

My searching eyes landed on a figure surrounded in a sandbox. She was bent over a toy truck, her dark hair cascading down to her knees. She appeared dainty compared to the boys surrounding her, and I couldn't see her face.

Moving along the fence line, I planted myself behind the sandbox, metal separating me from the elfin figure. I caught the end of the taller boy's speech.

"…freak. Why don't you choke on sand?"

"Hey!" I yelled before I could rethink my decision—because really, when did I ever think things through? I balled my hands into fists and banged them against the fence. The rattling sound, more than my voice, startled the bullies. The one I initially heard speak narrowed his eyes at me.

"What are you doing? You don't even go to school here!"

I tried to keep my voice strident, like my father always did. "Stop picking on her, and I'll leave!"

For some reason, my words sent the boys into another fit of laughter.

"See, freak? Even a stranger thinks you're a girl!" a new voice sneered, poking the long-haired figure in the back. In my mind, I referred to this boy as Short Stack. No reason, really, except for the fact that his face looked like someone had smeared syrup on it, stuck cement to said syrup, and then came and ripped the cement off his face. Yup, he was *that* ugly, and my nanny's vivid imagination had rubbed off on me.

It was when the sandbox child turned around to hit away Short Stack's finger that I realized he wasn't a girl, but a boy. He had decidedly masculine, if not slightly cherubic, features. His haunted eyes stared at me with such sadness and betrayal that my heart began to pound an erratic rhythm in my chest.

"Leave him alone," I said, proud I kept my voice steady. My eyes never left the long-haired boy's face.

"What are you going to do about it, girl?" taunted one of the bullies, but I didn't see which.

There was no way I could beat these boys in a physical fight, but I had one thing they didn't—an abundant knowledge of useless facts that no six-year-old should know.

"Do you know who I am?" I asked, straightening my spine. It did very little to add height to my short frame, but it made me feel somewhat imperious to these bullies.

"A girl?" bully one—let's call him Turd Wiper—asked, oh so original with his gibe.

"I am the world's youngest doctor," I lied, crossing my arms over my chest. Short

Stack snorted, but bully three—Not Relevant Enough to Name—looked slightly anxious.

"Bull crap," Turd Wiper said.

"It's true. And if you don't leave him alone, I will pull out your mitochondria and you will die."

That big word threw them off guard. Three sets of eyes flitted to my face with varying degrees of horror.

"Y-You can't—you can't do that!" one of them stuttered. I believed it was Not Relevant who spoke.

"The mitochondria are the powerhouse of the cell. If you don't have them, you'll die."

"But—"

"And I'll also give you hydrocephalus!" The boys shifted uneasily. "And your heads will explode."

Looking back, I didn't know if it was my nonsense words or my slightly sardonic smile that did it. Maybe it was the sincerity in which I threatened to murder them. Either way, the boys ran away as if a hound from hell was chasing them, nipping at their heels.

"You run away!" I yelled after them. "And don't let the swing hit you on the way out!"

I waited until they were out of sight, no doubt tattling to a teacher, before turning towards the boy.

"Are you okay?" I asked somewhat tentatively. I was afraid that he'd run from me too.

While he didn't run, he didn't address me either. He continued to stare up at me as if I was an exotic specimen, a zebra in a flock of sheep.

"My name's Adelaide," I said after a moment of uncomfortable silence. "What's your name?"

At first, I thought that he wasn't going to answer, but he mumbled something inarticulate under his breath.

"Ducky?" I asked, afraid I'd heard him wrong. When he didn't correct me, I smiled down at him. I'm sure I looked like a mess—what with my disheveled hair and bloodstained dress, I was probably giving out *The Ring* vibes—but Ducky didn't seem to mind. He actually smiled back at me.

"Well, Ducky, I would stick around, but I have a feeling those jerks will be back and get me in trouble."

Ducky's face fell as if he was disappointed that I wasn't staying. It suddenly occurred to me that I didn't want to leave either. There was such wistfulness in his face that I knew mirrored my own. We were both broken souls in desperate need of a friend.

"How about I come back tomorrow?" I said. "I'll meet you here?"

The smile that lit up his face was glorious.

That same smile haunted me for years after his death.

CHAPTER 1

$\mathcal{M}$r. Fuckadoodledoo Picklesucker Buttlicker was leering at me. Again. I mentally tallied the number of times I caught his penetrating eyes turned in my direction over the last hour. Fifty-two. He had eye raped me *fifty-two* times in a span of sixty minutes.

Stiffening in my seat, I attempted to pay attention to my father across from me and ignore Mr. Buttlicker. DOD—Dear Old Dad—had his peppered hair trimmed so it cascaded neatly to his shoulders, and he wore a gray suit that seemed to accentuate the blue in his eyes. Some might've considered him a handsome man, if they found ice-cold, asshole statues handsome. Seriously, the man was a dick. He even put Buttlicker to shame in the whole creeper-asshole department.

We had arrived at the restaurant only a few minutes earlier, traveling immediately from the conference room to the elegant restaurant in the basement of the resort. The only word adequate to describe such a room was 'golden.' I know, not the most eloquent description, but a golden sheen seemed to paint everything, from the intricately carved woodwork to the golden flowers canvasing the wall. It was almost nauseating.

"I appreciate you taking the time to meet with us," DOD said, for probably the billionth time that evening. I resisted the urge to roll my eyes. Buttlicker had as much choice in the matter as I did—needless to say, none at all.

"It's always a pleasure doing business with you," Buttlicker responded stiffly. His tone suggested, though, that he found it anything *but* pleasurable. Daddy tended to evoke fear in his clients.

"What looks good?" DOD asked, scanning the menu.

And cue…

"I can think of one thing." Buttlicker's gaze flickered appreciatively over my body, and I resisted the urge to shiver. He made me feel naked, despite the fact I purposefully wore a modest black number with a pearl necklace strung tightly across my neck. The guy also seemed to be forgetting the fact that he was thirty-some years older than my own age of seventeen.

A reminder, my friends, that pedophilia is a punishable offense.

My mother made a sound as if she heard Buttlicker's comment and found it as repulsive as I had… Wait, no. She was just ogling our waiter's backside while simultaneously touching Mr. Dickhead's—aka our head of security—knee underneath the table. Like, seriously? Did the woman not realize I sat directly beside her, clearly able to see her hand trailing upwards towards no-no land. Dear Lord. The woman was going to be the death of me.

As I thought this, Buttlicker gave me a smile that he must've thought was seductive but came across as more of a constipated grimace.

Correction. *He* was going to be the death of me.

The waiter, who my mother so shamelessly gaped at, stopped at our table, and my mouth nearly fell from its hinges.

The guy was gorgeous. Like, ridiculously gorgeous. His ash blond hair was disheveled, as if he'd run his hand through it one too many times. His eyes, a vibrant off-set blue that seemed to heighten an already arresting face, sparkled as if he was the only one privy to an inside joke. Even his cheekbones—oh sweet baby Jesus, those cheekbones—were chiseled and rose high on his face.

And. He. Had. Dimples.

My one weakness.

"Good afternoon. My name is Asher, and I'll be taking care of you this evening."

"Is that a promise?" My mother batted her eyelashes at him, and I felt my own eyes widen in horror.

"Dammit, Mother," I hissed. If it was possible, and I didn't think it was, DOD's expression darkened further. If he hated one thing, it was the attention his wife gave other males. Of course, DOD made an exception for Dickhead the guard, but that could've been because he was banging him too.

I touched my pearl necklace, a reminder of what I could gain with a little blackmail.

If only it could *rid* me of such nuisances, say the Buttlicker licking his buttlicking lips beside me.

I wanted to apologize to the waiter for my mother's crude, though unsurprising, behavior. However, I knew the gesture would be futile. DOD was not only the owner of this ostentatious restaurant, but the entire resort. And a few other not so legal enterprises that I probably shouldn't mention.

Gorgeous kept his smile pleasant, though his eyes dimmed marginally. He looked embarrassed by my mother's outburst, but how could he not? She basically implied that he was a prostitute to hire, despite the fact that he could only be a year or two older than myself.

"I'd like the chicken alfredo," I said quickly. A pathetic attempt, I'll admit, to ease the awkward tension, but it seemed to have the desired effect. DOD let out a breath I hadn't realized he'd been holding, and Mother's face contorted into a scowl. She really didn't like it when I interrupted her 'flirt sessions,' as she so liked to call them. Gorgeous's eyes flickered to me, his relief obvious.

And then they stayed there.

I knew what held his gaze. It was the same thing that everybody else saw, the same thing I saw when I looked into the mirror. A girl who was almost ethereal in beauty with brown, curly hair and a porcelain-like face. Bright red lips and a cute, button nose. And my eyes, a color that seemed to be a mixture of violet and blue, like the light at the crack of dawn where the sun had yet to set and the moon had yet to disappear completely.

Did nobody see how haunted these eyes were? How my lips were constantly turned down into a frown? How the makeup was barely able to conceal the bruises marring my perfect skin?

Did anybody care?

I knew that Nik did…

I didn't allow myself to think of my younger brother. Not now. Not ever.

Asher continued to stare at me, a blond brow lifting slightly. His mouth opened before snapping closed again. I couldn't understand the expression on his face.

Buttlicker also must've noticed the attention the waiter gave me, for he rested his hand possessively on my knee. I winced, shifting away from the man who made me squeamish. One reprimanding stare from my father had me cowering and leaning closer towards Buttlicker.

It was a choice between two evils. With Buttlicker, I knew that I would survive whatever he had in store for me. With my father, I could never be too sure.

Gorgeous's gaze hardened as he surveyed my father and then Buttlicker, but he didn't comment. Smart move.

"And what can I get you?" Asher asked sharply, turning towards the slimy man still gripping my knee as if his life depended on it. Yup. That was going to leave a nasty bruise there.

Great. Another one added to the inventory.

Mental me could barely contain her eye roll.

"Did you say something?" Buttlicker asked, turning his attention from Asher to me. This time I did roll my eyes, both physically and mentally.

If there was such a thing as rolling your eyes mentally, I wasn't exactly sure, but I pictured myself rolling my eyes inside my mind. Did that count?

"I didn't say anything," I said with a huff, glaring a hole into my menu. I had a tendency to speak my mind. Literally. Therapist One called it a defense mechanism for my traumatic childhood, whatever the hell that meant. Therapist Two said it was a way for me to express myself. Therapist Three just chuckled and called me an idiot—I didn't believe Therapist Three was an *actual* therapist—but Therapist Four admitted that it was not uncommon for trauma patients, when facing isolation, to find comfort in their own thoughts. Thus, my inner monologues and ramblings often turned into my outer monologues and ramblings. You could imagine how embarrassing it could be at times, especially with my tendency to create nicknames.

Asher continued taking orders around the table, and I half expected my mother to make a smartass comment along the lines of "I'll have you for supper" or something dumb like that. I was pleasantly surprised when she only made a passing comment about having "the Asher special for dessert." That was real progress for my mother.

I wonder if his last name is Gorgeous? Then I wouldn't feel as creepy calling him Gorgeous. Asher Gorgeous. Hmmm. Fitting.

It took me a moment to realize that all eyes were on me, including the stunning waiter, who directed his blinding smile at me.

I tried to recall what I'd just thought and obviously said, and my cheeks flamed with the realization of what transpired.

"Shit."

Kill me now.

"Tempting," DOD said, taking a sip of his water. His expression was as severe as his eyes. I had the distinct feeling that he wasn't joking. Great. Just what I wanted.

"So, about those Red Sox?" I interjected quickly. Though, in the middle of winter, I doubted that baseball had started up again. Sports. Sports were always a good topic of conversation with men. Asher, moving from our table to the next, smirked at me. He'd no doubt heard my comment and found it amusing. What could I say? I had that effect on people.

Conversation, thankfully, steered away from the whole me-dying-of-mortification thing and Red Sox to more work-related material. Taxes and employees and the whole stimulating shebang. They didn't talk about any of their, for lack of better term, *illegal* enterprises, not that I blamed them. I wondered how that conversation would go.

"I was wondering, how much you have been selling those illegal guns for?"

"The same amount as I've been selling my coke." Or pot. Or marijuana. Or whatever the hell they were up to these days.

DOD had insisted that I take part in the business.

"You're no longer a little girl," he'd told me sternly. "You have to start training to take over the family business."

I snorted. Family business made me think of a sweet, loving family who laughed as they fixed their shop and then came home to meals around the dinner table. I'm pretty sure that most *family businesses* didn't involve over a hundred shell companies, connections with the mafia, and a date with the drug lord of Mexico. Running the "family business" sounded about as appealing to me as stabbing my eye repeatedly with a rusted spoon would've been. Needless to say, it wasn't appealing.

Still, I behaved like the good girl, the good daughter, that my parents wanted me to be. It wasn't so much to please them as it was to protect myself. When I was good, when I listened and obeyed, they had no reason to punish me.

No reason to send people like Buttlicker to my room.

The mere thought made me tremble as if I had been electrocuted. My hand absently pulled at my sweater sleeves until they covered my hands.

It wasn't long before our meal came, though it was a different waiter from the one earlier who wrote it. Great. The *one* guy who I actually found attractive, my family had to go and scare away.

I shouldn't have been surprised. The longest romantic relationship I had…well, that had lasted approximately two days. In kindergarten.

You see, I had a little problem—yes, even more of a problem than talking to myself—and it involved people. More specifically, it involved my lack of talking. To some, I came across as a complete and utter bitch. To be completely honest, I kind of was. I didn't have friends, I had minions and wannabes who followed me around like lost puppies. I was the girl who every boy wanted and every girl wanted to be. The socialite constantly stalked by paparazzi with a slew of hookups in her wake. The trendsetter, the beauty queen, the diva.

I was everything but myself.

It was almost as if I were a playable character in a video game being controlled by a monkey on acid. I ran into walls, tripped over air, and ninety-nine percent of the time, looked completely lost and oblivious. I often wondered if my life were just a big joke and God and the angels sat up in heaven laughing at me.

Ha. Ha. Ha. Look at this mistake. You see? This is what a human shouldn't be.

It was *super* empowering.

"How is everything tasting?" Asher reappeared at our table, breaking me from my depressing reverie. His eyes flickered briefly over the other occupants before coming to rest on me. He offered me a crooked smile.

"It's delicious, thank you," I responded, chasing down a bite of my alfredo with a gulp of water.

"It's acceptable. The meat's a little dry, however. I would like to speak to the cook about that." DOD's eyes narrowed. Of course my dad couldn't go one freaking minute without acting like a complete asshole. And you wondered why I didn't have any friends.

Asher visibly stiffened, but he managed another serene smile.

"Of course. I'll go get him for you right away."

I wanted to tell him that it wasn't necessary, that I understood the restaurant was packed and taking away the head chef in the middle of the dinner rush was beyond idiotic, but I kept my mouth shut. I tried to convey with my eyes how sorry I was for…well, everything.

Something in my expression must've distracted him, because one second, he was staring at me, and the next, he was lurching forward. The plate of food he was carrying shattered on the floor, food flying through the air to land in Buttlicker's lap. Dickhead immediately jumped to his feet, surveying Asher as if he was a potential threat.

I felt my body grow cold.

It was obviously an accident, but I knew my father and the people he surrounded himself with. The best-case scenario would be the waiter getting a good old firing. The worst…

Thinking quickly, I threw back my head and let out a lilting laugh. Every eye at the table immediately turned to stare at me. The usual chatter in the restaurant diminished around us until all I could hear was Asher's pounding heart as he picked himself up behind me.

DOD pinched the bridge of his nose.

"What the hell are you laughing at?"

I smoothed my expression into one of icy impassiveness. I called it my bitch face, one that I reserved only for meetings like these. It was a part that I had long since perfected. Bitch me was almost like an extension of my personality.

"I didn't appreciate the way the waiter was ogling me," I said flippantly, scowling at Asher. He blinked at me, momentarily speechless. "So I taught him a little lesson about respect." I tossed my hair over my shoulder for effect. I'd seen girls do it in movies, so I figured why the hell not?

You got this, Adelaide. You're a bad bitch.

DOD's hands tightened around his cup until I could see his blue veins protruding from beneath his alabaster skin.

"You tripped him."

It wasn't a question.

"I just wanted to teach him some respect, Daddy Dearest. Isn't that what you always told me?" Yeah, so maybe now I was being a sarcastic bitch instead of just a mean bitch, but I couldn't help it. He always seemed to bring out the worst in me. Maybe I just figured that whatever punishment he dished out wouldn't change no matter how bad I was. I could murder someone, and it would be just as bad as if I were to cuss at the dinner table.

Not as if I'd ever murdered someone before, mind you.

For a moment, I thought he was going to yell at me in front of the entire restaurant. I even feared that he would throw his cup at me. Glass was a pain to get out of my skin and hair.

After what felt like an eternity, he released a breath while simultaneously releasing the cup. I felt like I could breathe again.

"We will discuss this tonight," he said sternly, turning back towards his meal. His eyes promised pain. Lots and lots of pain. Buttlicker, beside me, grinned like the deviant I knew him to be.

"If you don't mind me asking, sir, but I would be more than willing help you administer punishment."

My fork clattered against my plate, and my mouth dropped open.

God no. Please no. Not again. No. No. No.

"I believe we could come to an agreement," DOD said with a tiny smile. "If you, of course, agree to my original proposition."

Once again, the conversation turned back towards buildings and real estate and all that other fun stuff. I, however, felt as if I couldn't breathe. My body felt cold, as if someone had dumped a bucket of ice over my head. It was a numb type of cold. Painful almost, but dulling as the seconds dragged on.

I noticed that Asher hadn't moved from where he stood behind me, food covering his white shirt. Nobody paid him any mind as the conversation veered towards contract, not even my mother was staring at him any longer, but I could feel his eyes caressing my back. I tried my hardest to ignore him, tried my hardest to face forward, but the urge to turn around was almost unbearable. Finally, I couldn't resist any longer.

His eyes were anguished when they met mine. His thick, ebony lashes feathered against his cheekbones. Just as suddenly, the expression was swept away by a tidal wave of anger. His gaze turned towards my father, who seemed utterly oblivious to the penetrating gaze searing his skin.

I recognized that look. It was the same look I'd both given and received. That look promised pain and revenge.

It was also a look that made me, almost innately, hopeful.

CHAPTER 2

spen Resort was an immense structure located in the dead center of nowhere. Only the surrounding trees rivaled the log structure, their coniferous needles coated with a soft layer of fluffy snow. Besides the trees, occasionally splintering off to create a small enclosure for ice rinks and hills for skiing, the town of Aspen was devoid of anything that remotely resembled a normal city. There was no theater, no restaurant, no mall. Of course, there was no need for any of that, not with Aspen Resort.

I was all too familiar with the amenities that came with the tourist trap. It drew you in like a fly to a spider web, entangling you until you became stuck. And no, I wasn't being dramatic.

I really hated Aspen Resort, my home for the better part of my seventeen years.

There might've been a time, when I was an infant, where I lived a semi-normal life. I have a vague recollection of a petite house nestled in a suburban neighborhood. Of course, that could all just be a wistful fantasy I constructed from the various books I read and television shows I watched.

I only found one spot peaceful in all of Aspen Resort. It was a relatively small room when compared to the rest of the building, but it was my own. The diminutive pool room was usually abandoned. A couple of years ago, my parents had decided to create an indoor water park with an Olympic-sized pool near the lobby of the resort. That left the old pool, which I coined the 'wannabe beach,' all by its lonesome, a considerable distance away from the rest of the amenities the resort had to offer.

The wannabe beach consisted of nothing more than a few tables, decorated with colorful umbrellas, and a makeshift plastic sun in the far corner of the room. The walls were supposed to have haphazardly-painted palm trees on them, but they were beginning to fade away from years of neglect. I was honestly surprised my parents still allowed this room to exist in their perfect resort. I assumed they'd forgotten about it, just as they often forgot about their daughter.

I pulled my brown hair up into a disheveled bun. Surveying myself in the mirror, I bit my lip. When had I gotten so skinny? Even in my one-piece bathing suit, a stylish, black number with silver adorning the top, I could see the bones of my hips. The thought should've worried me. Once upon a time, it *would've* worried me. Now, all I felt was…empty.

There was no other word to describe it.

My gaze flickered to my arms, visible with my bathing suit. There was no way I could go to the pool like that, even if it was empty. The halls were always bustling with people. Sighing, I reached for the coverup inside my dresser. Long-sleeved, of course, and falling just above my knee.

My father would reprimand me for wearing such an outfit.

"A whore!" he would announce. "You shouldn't be showing so much leg."

My mother, on the other hand, would look me over with a critical eye and demand that I show *more* of my body.

"It's important for business, sweetheart." It was always the same tone with her, haughty and imperious, with a set to her chin that came from years and years of power. The type of tone that made me squirm just thinking about it.

Letting out an exasperated grunt, I grabbed my book off of my chair and tiptoed out of my room. I needed to be careful that I didn't alert anyone to my presence, from my parents, to the guards, to Mr. Buttlicker, whom I just knew I'd find lurking somewhere near my bedroom. It wouldn't be the first time my parents handed out such information, and it definitely wouldn't be the last.

Finding the hall empty, I stealthily crept towards the elevator, sighing with content when the light dinged. The wannabe beach was at the ground level, below even the lobby. It felt like years until the doors finally slid open.

Walking briskly past the occasional straggler—though what idiot would be up at this time of night? Wait. Me. *I'm* the idiot—I moved to the door at the end of the hallway. I was always wary about swimming laps, even when I knew the area remained abandoned most of the time. If one person were to walk in and see me…

If one person were to see my arms…

Boisterous laughter interrupted my musings. Frowning, I pushed open the door…to see the pool swarming with teenagers.

Those filthy sons of bitches…

I gritted my teeth together and resisted the urge to throw my book at the nearest person. I was really, really, *really* not a people person. And I was really, really, *really* looking forward to some time by myself.

Maybe if I shit in the pool…?

My mind ran through all the possibilities.

Oh God. I was officially losing my mind. Soon, I would be huddled in a bunker muttering about the old woman that dared speak to me in the grocery store.

I debated whether I wanted to escape back to my room. The option was *not* tempting. Knowing my luck, and my parents, I'd find Buttlicker waiting for me. I trembled with revulsion at the thought.

No, I would much rather take my chances with drunk teenagers than old perverts.

Spotting an empty chair in the corner, I hurried to sit down. I learned long ago how to ignore everyone around me. To drift away, to empty myself so I would feel nothing at all. It wasn't the safest coping mechanism, but it got me through the day.

Sort of.

I turned blindly to a page in my book, but my attention was fixed on the scene before me. I wondered if a school group was here. Usually, we only got old farts, rich families, and the occasional teenager coming up for their school break. Never this many, and never ones that all seemed to know each other.

Girls and guys were making out in the pool.

A group was playing a game of water volleyball.

Chicken fighting over in the shallow end.

A game of spin the bottle.

Two girls stepped in front of me, their attention as fixated on the pool as mine was. The two blondes wore the skimpiest bikinis imaginable. Seriously, the poor fabric looked as if it was straining against their considerable chests. I was not lacking in the chest department by any means, but those two girls put mine to shame. I scoffed.

They were too round and perfect to be real.

What type of high schooler was allowed to get a breast job? What type of parents would allow that?

I thought of my mother and her condescending smile. Ugh, that smirk. I hated that smirk. I wanted to punch that smirk off her face. She would most definitely be okay with me getting a breast job. Anything to help the family business.

"Do you see Ryder?" the blonde in the pink bikini asked, flicking her hair over her shoulder.

"Don't worry, Missy. He'll come," Purple reassured her friend. Pink—Missy, I assumed—glowered.

"He's probably off with Declan or something," Missy finally conceded, though she didn't sound convinced. They stayed silent for a moment, each one surveying the pool with predatory glints in their eyes.

"Do you think I look okay?" Purple asked suddenly, twisting to show off her purple bikini, the cause of her namesake.

"You look fine," Missy snapped. "And if you don't think you look good, change bikinis."

"But I only brought one bikini."

Missy's mouth dropped open. "Are you serious? I brought, like, three. But you're not a cheerleader, so you wouldn't understand."

Huh? I raised an eyebrow, thoroughly intrigued. This was ten times better than my book.

"But I do *dance*," Purple insisted.

What the actual fuck was happening?

"You only brought one." Missy sighed. She looked honestly upset by that prospect. Still sulking, she turned and walked towards the water volleyball game. Purple followed her like an obedient, besotted puppy.

"Oh my gosh, did you hear that? She only brought *one* bikini?" The voice came from beside me, making me startle. I turned with almost blistering speed and nearly fell off my chair when I met the laughing eyes of the person beside me.

Oh, sweet Jesus, have mercy...

He was hot. Like, sex on a stick hot. Bronze skin, amber eyes, tousled black hair with green highlights at the tips. And his body. It was a work of art. It would take me hours to fully appreciate every detail depicted across his abs, every intricately designed vine and flower and... Was that a unicorn? Somehow, that mythical creature etched into his skin demoted him from intimidating to approachable. I mean, seriously, any guy who was willing to flaunt a unicorn must've had serious balls.

Don't think about his balls, Adelaide. Don't think about his... Dammit, now I'm thinking about them.

"I can't believe it," Sexy continued, his voice rising a few octaves as he attempted to adopt a Valley girl accent.

I pitched my voice in a similar fashion to his. "I know, right? I brought, like, eight. One for dipping my toes in..."

"One for sitting at the pool in," he continued, fighting a grin.

"One for going waist deep. Only waist deep. And of course, I have one entirely made of satin." I dramatically flipped my hair over my shoulder to emphasize my point.

He looked at me in mock horror. "Only one?"

"I mean, you wouldn't understand. I have, like, hobbies and interests and stuff."

"And activities?"

"Oh my god, who does activities? Seriously?"

A laugh escaped his lips.

"What's your name, doll?" he asked, his voice dropping back to what I assumed was his normal tone.

Oh, and what a fine voice he has...

"I have a fine voice?" Sexy asked, raising a pierced eyebrow in my direction.

"Oh shit. I said that out loud, didn't I?" I questioned, not at all perturbed. You got used to it after a while. The number of times I'd said stupid stuff... Well, it was no wonder I had no friends and my parents hated me.

"I just don't have a filter, I guess. But I mean, you *do* have a nice voice. It's all husky and sultry and stuff. You'd probably be a good singer." I was rambling, my go-to move when confronted with cute guys.

Sexy stared at me for a moment before bursting into laughter.

"I would love to hear you say that in front of Ryder," he remarked. Before I could inquire, he turned towards me. "So am I going to get a name?"

Shrugging, I pointed towards the ditzy blond in the skimpy bikini I had seen earlier.

"I heard her name is Missy."

"Well my name is Ronan." He extended a hand, and I shook it after a slight hesitation.

"Nice to meet you, Ronan with the satin bikinis."

He smirked. "And the fine voice."

"How could I forget?"

Shifting in my seat, I turned back towards my forgotten book, effectively ending the conversation.

"I haven't seen you around. You don't go to Highwood Prep?"

I guess I *wasn't* effectively ending the conversation. Looking down the bridge of my nose, I smirked at him.

"How do you know?"

"Because I would've remembered someone like you." He gave me an appreciatory stare that made goosebumps break out across my skin.

"Maybe I was just hiding. From you."

Shrugging, I sprawled myself out in my seat and turned the page of my book. I felt him, almost as if he was charged with electricity, come up beside me.

"So, are you here on vacation?"

I hesitated, only briefly, before nodding.

"Yes."

I mean, what else could I do? Tell him that my parents owned this damned place? What a good conversation starter. *"My parents are members of the mafia, and you're staying at their shady-ass, illegal business and talking to their daughter."*

Ha.

Of course, most people didn't know that my parents were not…well, *normal* business entrepreneurs. But I knew.

"Are you going to go into the pool?" Ronan asked.

"Oh, that just sounds dandy," I drawled. I held up my book. "Because obviously I'm not in the middle of doing anything. Now shut up and leave me alone. I'm at a good part."

His silence lasted for approximately fifteen seconds.

"Whatcha reading?"

"Oh for the love of…" Before I could stop myself, I whacked him on the head with the book. It didn't hurt him because I was a weakling, but his eyes widened in shock.

"Did you just hit me with your book?"

"I told you, I'm at a good part," I pointed out, biting my lip to keep from smirking. Believe it or not, I liked talking to Ronan. He was one of the least douchey people I had met at Aspen Resort so far. It was always fun to flirt with the tourists.

I knew I was beautiful. Hell, I doubted my parents would keep me around if I weren't. My beauty served as both my shield and my sword. My defense and my offense. Today, I was on the hunt, not that I would let anything happen between the tourist and me, of course. I couldn't afford to let them get close, and I *definitely* didn't want them facing my parents' wrath.

But it was nice to pretend.

"You are a strange girl," Ronan mused, but he did so with a smile. I kept my attention fixated on my book as I turned a page.

"Still at a good part."

"Ronan! Baby!" a shrill, feminine voice cooed.

I set the book on my lap, pinching the bridge of my nose.

"I swear to God, Ronan, you have exactly five seconds to get rid of that voice before I castrate you."

Ronan nearly fell out of his seat from laughing so hard. I should've felt guilty.

After all, I'd just insulted a total stranger who obviously knew Ronan, but that voice was annoying. How did anyone listen to that…sound?

The girl that stepped up was beautiful. There was no other word to describe her. If Ronan was sexy and dangerous, this girl was flowers and cupcakes. A dewy face with emerald eyes, framed by thick lashes and silky hair that cascaded down her back. She also had a perfect, hourglass figure. I supposed she had to be beautiful to have a voice as annoying as that.

"Who's your little…friend?" Her eyes ran over me, the malice in them nearly suffocating.

I took back my early assessment.

She was most definitely *not* flowers and cupcakes. If anything, she was wilted flowers and poisoned cupcakes.

"Elena," Ronan said stiffly. His body was as taut as a string on a bow.

"I was looking for you," Elena hissed. That voice… I shuddered.

To Ronan, I mumbled, "Five seconds."

"Five seconds until what?" Elena asked with a huff, her penetrating gaze swiveling my way. I resisted the urge to stick my tongue out at her like a child. Or give her the finger like an adult. Either option appealed to me, honestly. Maybe I could do a combination…?

A smile ghosted across Ronan's lips before it contorted into a cold mask.

"I'll meet you by the entryway, Elena," he said evenly.

"But—"

"The entryway or not at all."

It was a contest of wills, his golden-brown eyes locked with her vibrant green ones. The air around them practically seemed to spark with electricity. Elena broke away first, scowling, before storming towards the door of the poolroom. She did *not* look pleased.

"Well, damn," I stated. "That was intense. I *felt* the tension. Or was that sexual tension? Hmm…I guess the world may never know. Actually, that's not true. If you guys start pawing at each other, then it was most definitely sexual tension."

Ronan stared at me with an unreadable expression.

"Trust me. That was the exact opposite of sexual tension."

"So it was platonic tension, then?" I pressed. When he didn't respond, I shrugged nonchalantly. "Dude, I feel ya. Platonic tension is intense. It makes you lose control. Like, you suddenly want a hug from your brother or something."

"What is wrong with you?" The question did not hold any malice. If anything, he sounded bemused, as if I were a puzzle he was struggling to solve. I considered his question thoughtfully before responding,

"A lot actually."

Sighing, I scooped up my book and folded my towel. I supposed I could always read in my room behind a locked door.

"Wait! Where are you going?" Ronan seemed confused.

I patted his cheek. "I told you already. I'm hiding from you."

Maybe I was slightly insane. Maybe I wasn't. At that moment, I didn't care. The way he looked at me made me feel as if I was the most beautiful girl to have ever existed.

Not sexy, but as if I was someone cherished. No one had ever looked at me like that—with awe.

"I never caught your name!" Ronan shouted after me. He sat rooted to the spot next to our chairs, hands outstretched as if he could pull me back to him.

"That's because I never gave you anything to catch!" I called back.

CHAPTER 3

$\mathcal{G}$iselle was muttering again.

She had two distinct types of mutterings. One I would often refer to as her annoyed mutters. They would be nearly inarticulate phrases hissed beneath her breath and accompanied by a small shake of her head. My least favorite, and the most frequent, were her pissed off mutterings. These would involve a lot of swear words and a lot of random statements sewn together. Once, I believed I heard her make up a pretty interesting curse concerning a monkey, a lawnmower, and plastic surgery, but I could never be certain. With the latter utterances, her face turned beet red and her eyes narrowed into slits. She'd always been a condescending woman, but with her eyes probing my scalp as if she could physically skin me alive, she became terrifying.

Fortunately for me, I had grown immune.

"Can't you do anything?" she snapped. The question was vague, though I suspected it was because she didn't expect an answer. Still, being the smartass I was, I made a show of considering her words.

"I can recite the alphabet backwards," I replied innocently. I held the coffee cup up to my lips and took a tentative sip. It was still scorching hot, but the cream helped to dampen the heat. I was always a bear if I didn't have approximately five hundred cups in the morning. Hell, I was a bear even *with* my coffee.

"I can also hold my pee in until the very last possible second," I continued, watching her face pinch together. "Let me see... Oh! I can put my toe in my ear. And I definitely have a talent with fire. On my last birthday alone, I lit my hair on fire... though I don't think that really counts as my fault. It totally was the candle's."

Giselle shot me a glare that could've withered grapes into raisins. If I could only use one word to describe my tutor, it would be mousey. Of course, she would probably whoop my ass if she ever heard me describe her as such, but the older woman just reminded me of a petite mouse. She kept her gray hair cut short around her small, elfin face. Her body was wiry, nothing more than bones and wrinkled skin.

Still, Mrs. Baldwin was a scary son of a gun.

"I don't even know why we do these lessons anyway," I said when it became apparent that she wasn't going to respond. Moving from my seat at the counter, I poured myself another cup of coffee. A girl needed at least twenty in an hour if she didn't want to become a murderer. "I already graduated high school and college. This is stupid and overkill."

I graduated high school when I was only thirteen, courtesy of Mrs. Giselle Baldwin herself. Online college followed immediately after. Heaven forbid that my parents let me attend a brick-and-mortar school…like Highwood Prep. Not that I wanted to go there or anything. Not this girl. Nope. Nada. Who needed social interaction with kids her own age or boys with unicorn tattoos across their chests? Definitely not me.

Giselle still didn't answer me, possibly too angry to speak.

With a roll of my eyes, I turned back towards the textbook she had laid out in front of me. Business Law and Relevant Cases. *Oh joy.* Because there was nothing else I would rather do than study business law cases.

"Are we done with lessons for today?" I asked in my sweetest tone, batting my eyelashes for effect.

We were in my suite, an immense, multi-room space located on the upper floor of the resort, entirely separate from my parents'. We currently sat inside the kitchen, which was nothing more than an open space with sleek, marble flooring and a wide, granite countertop. Off the right wall was my small dining room, though I barely used it. Why would I want to sit at a dining room table by myself? Even for me, a girl who talked to herself, *that* was entirely too depressing.

The living room was just as extravagant as the rest of the place, with a black leather sofa, a television mounted to the wall, and a collection of armchairs arranged into a makeshift semi-circle.

Overall, the place was devoid of any personalization. If it wasn't for the scattering of clothes in my bedroom, some might wonder if the suite was even occupied. I may be living here, but it sure as hell wasn't my home. It felt too cold, too empty, too lonely.

Despite feeling this way, the idea of moving in with my parents made my skin crawl. I was stuck in perpetual isolation. I could be around hundreds of people, yet my heart still ached as if it was just me. Maybe it was because nobody ever saw *me*. Sure, they saw the beautiful girl that my parents desired me to be, but nobody looked past such a superficial mask. Did they see my scars, both mental and physical? Did they understand that my sarcasm and wit were defense mechanisms?

Did they understand I was barely hanging on?

My hand went to my arm covered by my red sweater. Sunlight trickled through the kitchen window in soft beams, making the temperature in the kitchen stifling. Still, I knew I couldn't take off my sweater. Not with Giselle around.

Not ever.

"I suppose we can stop for now. Despite your obvious attention problems, you are far enough ahead that we can call it a day." Though her mouth was set into a thin line, her eyes warmed slightly. Giselle loved to brag about her teaching skills, but I would've been fine just learning the material myself.

I found it all easy.

I couldn't tell you how to change a tire, but if you asked me to configure data for a property, I'm your gal.

Taking another sip of my coffee, I opened my mouth to thank Giselle for my few hours of free time—I had to meet DOD in a couple of hours for a meeting—when something on the television caught my attention. Frowning, I hurried past my aging tutor and into the living room. The remote was where I left it, smothered between two couch cushions—totally intentional—and I quickly turned the volume up.

"...so far, only five casualties have been reported, though this may increase over time."

The footage switched away from the newscaster to what once might've been a pretty town but was now nothing more than piles of debris and broken homes. Everything was in shambles, and I couldn't discern one house from the next.

Frowning, I squinted my eyes at the screen to make sure I'd read the heading correctly.

FOUR TORNADOS HIT BRACKEN, ALASKA.

Alaska? Tornados? That was a rare phenomenon all on its own, but four?

The footage switched once again. The camera shook, obviously the work of an amateur, but it still managed to capture the moment the tornado touched down, a swirling sheet of dirt and debris. The camera panned away, and almost instantly, another tornado appeared a little bit away from the first. They seemed to dance around one another, tilting towards each other like forbidden lovers but never once touching. It happened a third time. And a fourth time.

The trees folded underneath the intensity of the winds. The houses, before my very eyes, began to collapse in on themselves like old, yellowing paper. The newscaster was speaking, but I couldn't hear over the roaring in my ears.

How awful...

"I agree. It is awful." I hadn't even realized that Giselle had come in behind me. I also hadn't realized that I had spoken aloud, not that I was surprised, mind you. "Your family has property up there. I hope there weren't any damages"

My hands fisted against my sides.

"That's what you're worried about?" I asked, barely able to rein in my temper. "One of our *many* properties? What about the houses that were destroyed? The lives that were lost?"

Giselle tilted her head to the side, silver hair appearing almost like starlight in the artificial lighting. I'd never considered my tutor cruel before. Mean, yes. A hard-ass, most definitely. But cruel? Evil?

Just now, though, she was looking at me as if *I* were the mistake. As if *I* had an issue.

When she spoke, her voice was uncharacteristically kind. "My dear, I prepared you so much better than this. There is no them. There is only you and us. Why be shoved when you can shove? Why be dead when you can kill? Why care when you're better than them?"

I resisted the urge to roll my eyes. That was Giselle for you—always spewing wisdom. And you wondered why I was a little fucked up?

~

I saw him a moment before he saw me.

How could I not notice him? He looked just as gorgeous as he was the first time I saw him. His blond hair was lightly tousled, as if he'd run his hand through it one too many times. His body was lithe and defined, muscles accentuated in the faded T-shirt he wore with blue jeans. His eyes brightened when he saw me, as if someone had lit a candle beneath the surface.

"I know you!" he exclaimed, walking forward. Sure, he was attractive, but I'd met a lot of attractive guys in my life. He was just another pretty face in a sea of...well, pretty faces.

I feigned impassiveness as I considered him coolly.

"The waiter, correct? Ashton?"

"Asher," he corrected. He remained silent for a minute, a blush staining his cheeks. "So, what are you up to?"

"Last I checked, I was walking down the hallway," I said dryly. "But I'm stopped now, so I suppose you could say I'm standing in the hallway."

His blush deepened, and he opened his mouth to speak, shut it, and then opened it again. He looked like a gaping fish. An adorable, blond fish, but a fish all the same.

I decided to have pity on the poor, unfortunate soul.

"I was actually going to the wanna—I mean, the pool. To read." I held up my book. "I didn't get a lot of reading done yesterday." The final statement came out as an annoyed grumble. Asher cracked a smile at that.

"Somebody annoyed you?" he guessed, sounding amused. I scowled.

"You could say that."

"Well, I just wanted to thank you for what you did the other night. Sticking up for me, I mean. Taking the fall so I wouldn't get fired." He let out a sigh, his hand running through his blond locks.

"It's fine," I said quickly, hoping he'd drop the subject. The last thing I wanted to do was discuss emotions and feelings and all that shit. I shuddered just thinking about it.

"Well, it was a pretty cool thing for you to do."

"Yup."

"And I just wanted to say thank you."

"Okay."

I was not the most eloquent speaker, was I?

Asher shuffled from one foot to the next. Judging from his scuffling and shifty eyes, he wanted to say something else to me, something important. But I needed to tell him something too.

I'd never warned anyone before. Did it make me a horrible person that I knew all of this information, yet I kept it to myself like a good girl? Did it make me a coward?

I didn't know why I told Asher what I did. Maybe it was the way he looked at me, his eyes the bluest of blues. Maybe the vulnerability and tenderness on his face made me do it. Or maybe, and this was probably the most likely explanation, I was just a sucker for attractive guys.

"Look, Asher, if you want my advice…quit your job. You're young, good-looking, and probably smarter than half of the people hired at this resort. Find a job modeling or something. Just don't work here. Ever." Asher's eyes widened at my assertion. He opened his mouth as if to ask me why I would say such a crude thing when I cut him off. Again. "Now, why don't you run along and listen to a chilling rendition of Celine Dion's 'My Heart Will Go On,' or whatever it is you boys do nowadays." He continued to stare at me as if I'd suddenly sprouted a second head.

Gah. This was why I didn't talk to boys. They annoyed me.

"Chop. Chop." I clapped my hands for emphasis. "Run along, Goldilocks. Go find yourself some porridge."

Still nothing. Not even a twitch this time.

"Sacrifice ravens and stain the trees with their blood?"

I got a mere blink. The transformation from a prowling, flirtatious tiger to this shell-shocked boy terrified me a bit. And provided a touch of entertainment, if I was so inclined to admit such a thing to myself.

"Play jump rope dressed as Humpty Dumpty? Belly dance around a volcano? No? Does none of that sound interesting to you?"

How difficult was it to please this man? Geez.

"I…" he finally said. I watched his Adam's apple bob as he swallowed. "I wanted to invite you to lunch with me and some of my friends. As a thank you."

My stomach growled at the mere mention of breakfast. Daddy insisted that I ration what I ate—read as, eat literally nothing in order to keep my figure, minus a few business-oriented dinners.

"Will there be coffee?" I demanded, raising an eyebrow. I had to get the important questions out of the way.

He still seemed stunned, maybe even a little scared. Who could blame him? I *was* a little crazy. Okay, maybe a lot of crazy.

"Yes?" The statement turned into a shaky question.

"Then why are we still standing here? Coffee awaits, my gentle knight."

Linking my arm through his, I practically dragged him down the hall. It was only when we arrived at the lobby that Asher came back to his senses.

"Um…we're going the wrong way."

"Right. Of course. I knew that."

I dragged him down another hallway.

"Still the wrong way."

I stomped my foot against the ground and pouted. Why was it so difficult for a woman to get her coffee?

I kept the game up for a few more minutes—opening up a random door, feigning obliviousness, and leading a very amused Asher to another section of the resort.

"Okay. Okay," Asher said with a huff after I dragged him towards a supply closet. "I'm too lazy to do all this walking. And I'm hungry. Exercise and hunger do not make a good combination for a growing boy."

At the first statement, I gave him a pointed once-over. The boy was fit, to put it bluntly, and could've easily run around the entire resort numerous times. It was *my* lazy, frail ass that was beginning to pant erratically. Okay, so maybe not my ass, because asses can't pant, but you get what I meant.

"Fine," I obliged, tugging on his jacket sleeve. "Let's go Little Miss Waiter."

"Miss?" he asked, eyebrow raised. I shrugged.

"You have very feminine, pretty features." When he continued to stare at me, I added, "And you sort of remind me of a girl PMSing. You know, the whole food thing."

He tilted his head to the side. I may have considered his expression thoughtful if not for the wicked glint in his eye.

"I can't say I've ever been compared to a female before." He didn't sound at all offended, only amused. "I can assure you that I'm all man, sweetie."

"Laying it on thick, Ash?" asked a voice, booming with laughter. "That was the most pathetic, ball-clenching pickup line I've ever heard before."

Asher's face turned a dark shade of red as he faced the newcomer above my shoulder.

Well, that was just rude.

Twinkling out a laugh a couple octaves higher than my normal voice and channeling my inner Elena, the bimbo from the pool, I placed my hand on Asher's bicep.

"Oh, Ashy! You have such a way with words." Another laugh.

It was so annoying, I almost wanted to slap myself.

"You totally know how to win over a woman." I took a strand of my hair and curled it around my finger. Lowering my voice, I added, "And if last night was any indication, please a woman as well."

If it was possible, and I didn't think it physically was, Asher's face went five shades redder. With a wink, I braced myself, turning to face the intruder who dared to insult Asher.

Okay, so maybe I came across as a territorial bitch, but Asher was the only semi-decent guy I had met and it was a shame that he felt embarrassed. Not that it wasn't cute or anything to see red blotches on his cheeks…

Nope. Nada. Totally hideous and not at all sexy to see a gorgeous man blush.

My breath left my body in one big whoosh when I faced the newcomer. Was every boy in this resort drop-dead, mouth-wateringly beautiful?

The new guy was gorgeous—there was no other way to describe it. While Asher sported more standard, boy-next-door good looks, this new one screamed danger. A sexy sort of danger, but danger all the same.

He had strong, broad shoulders, clearly noticeable in his fitted black tee. His defined cheekbones appeared chiseled, and his hair was cropped close to his head. His dark skin showcased several tattoos. Not as many as Ronan had, but enough to keep me intrigued. It was his eyes, though, that captured my attention. They were almost an amber color, bright and smoldering in an already arresting face.

Every fiber of my being wanted to fan myself like a blushing schoolgirl. It took incredible restraint on my part to keep my face impassive. Honestly, I was pretty proud of myself. If they handed out gold medals in the Olympics for resisting handsome boys, then I would receive them all. Gold medals, that is, not the boys. Okay, maybe some of the boys.

Focus, Adelaide. And stop drooling.

The new boy smirked, and I realized I had said that thought aloud. Oh well. You can't win them all, can you?

"And who might you be?" I gave him a dismissive once-over as if he were nothing but a pesky bug. I was sure that he could see through my apathetic front—hell, he would've been an idiot not to—but he didn't call me out on it. I appreciated his respect in allowing me to ogle him without admonishment

"The name is Ryder," he said, grabbing my hand and pressing a kiss to the skin there. Yup. He most definitely saw through my less-than-impressed attitude...or he was just a cocky bastard. I chose to believe it was the latter.

But his lips though...

I barely resisted the urge to roll my eyes. He went from sexy to cheesy in a span of five seconds. With a wicked smile, he kept a firm grip on my hand. I wanted to accidentally—but very purposely—knee him in the balls.

"And what might your name be?" he continued. "Probably a beautiful name for a beautiful girl?"

I couldn't help it. A laugh bubbled up from my chest before I could stop myself.

"Oh my god. That is so fucking corny. Does that actually work for you? Good grief, I need a shower now to replace the stench of shitty pickup lines." I giggled at Ryder's blank expression and slowly extracted my hand. The traitorous limb still tingled from his kiss. "Now run along and head back to your computer so you can look up better pickup lines. Go on. *Shoo.*" I waved him away with a flick of my wrist.

Ryder was silent for only a moment before he said, playing off of my word shoo, "Flipflop." Pause. "Croc."

I shook my head. "See? So freaking corny." A smile betrayed my amusement. "You remind me of a cat—constantly rubbing against everyone for pleasure."

"That's nicer than what she said to me," Asher interjected. "She called me feminine."

Ryder erupted into laughter. He practically fell over.

Good. I hope you choke on your laughter...that is, if you can choke on laughter. I meant your spit. Choke on your spit, you cocky son of a—

My inner monologue, which somehow became my outer monologue, only made Ryder laugh harder. Tears formed in his eyes, and he hastily brushed them away.

"I can't say that I disagree with her assessment," Ryder said after he collected himself. "I meant the part about you being feminine, not me choking on my laughter." He sidestepped the hit Asher aimed at his head.

Turning towards me, Ryder rewarded me with an indolent smirk. He really did remind me of a cat—a lazy, sprawling cat that expected the world to drop at its feet as nothing more than filthy peasants.

"But seriously, what's your name, Kitten?"

Snorting at the nickname, I ignored him and turned back towards Asher.

"So, are we heading to get food and coffee or not? You can't promise a girl food and renege. I've castrated boys for a lot less."

"Wait?" Ryder interrupted. "She's joining us for lunch?"

I frowned. "Wait? He's joining us for lunch?"

"You can't just copy me!"

"You can't just copy me," I mocked, lowering my voice to match Ryder's husky tone. I admit, I took a few creative liberties in my impression of him.

"Stop it."

"Stop it."

"Seriously, Kitten."

"Seriously, Kitten."

"Stop—"

"Will you stop acting like a child, Ryder?" Asher exclaimed, sounding exasperated. Ryder opened his mouth and then closed it soundlessly. He pointed to me like a reprimanded schoolboy passing the blame.

I decided that I liked Asher a little bit more.

Poking Ryder in the ribs, I smirked at him. "Come on, *child*, let's go get food."

I hurried ahead of them before he could retort. As I turned the corner, I heard Ryder mutter something about "favoritism" and "breasts." Oh well. Mama can't help what she was born with.

WE WENT to a small café on the outskirts of the resort. Styled after a seventies, red-seated diner, Rosie's House failed to mimic the opulence displayed elsewhere in the resort. I was honestly surprised that DOD allowed such a normal place to exist in his "prestigious establishment." His words.

I personally liked Rosie's House, despite no one with the name Rosie actually working there. Maybe it was because my dad hated it. Maybe I went only as a big middle finger towards DOD and Mommy Dearest.

I recognized the hostess as a young woman named Shannon. She spotted us immediately and batted her lashes at the two boys. Ryder straightened his spine. He was a lion that wasn't just out for the hunt, but for the kill.

He leaned against the host podium, smile sly. "And what might your name be? Probably a beautiful name for a beautiful girl."

I snorted, turning my face towards Asher to conceal my laughter.

The poor boy needed help. His skills were severely lacking. Fortunately for him, I had been told I was a great wingman. Wingwoman?

Schooling my features, I turned back towards Shannon and Ryder, the former of which was giggling and kicking her foot.

"So, Ryder was telling me about his modeling gig," I said cheerfully. Both Ryder's and Asher's eyebrows rose. I just winked. Something akin to understanding flickered across Ryder's features.

"Well, I don't want to brag..." he drawled, trying to act sheepish. I snorted yet again. Ryder didn't seem to have a modest bone in his body. Yes, he was attractive, but did he have to let the entire world know that he knew? Okay, so maybe I was biased—because for some reason, Ryder just seemed to piss me off—but he could've at least had *some* class.

I decided to up the ante, so to speak. Giving a shit-eating grin, I continued, "And tell her about your offer. Pro football? What was the team again?" I batted my eyelashes, feigning ignorance. Behind me, Asher burst into laughter, though he quickly tried to mask it into a cough.

"I...um..." I imagined this was one of the few times that the great Ryder got flustered.

"You play football?" Shannon asked dreamily. "I only ever date football players."

Yuck. Gag. Ew.

A "hump me now" sign would've come off as less desperate.

"Well, unfortunately for you, I'm not interested," Ryder said briskly. I gaped at him. His sudden change in behavior was surprising, to put it mildly.

Shannon seemed just as stunned, if not slightly pissed. Without another word, she spun on her heel and hurried in the direction of the kitchen.

I guess we weren't going to get seated after all.

Huffing with indignation, I put my hands on my hips.

"What the hell was that about? You are a horrible flirt."

Ryder shrugged, a beautiful grin touching his gorgeous face.

"She only dates football players." Tilting his head towards mine, so his breath caressed my cheek, he murmured, "I'm a musician."

"You're also an ungrateful swine. I totally could've gotten you laid. Never ask me to be your wingman again!"

He straightened. "I never asked you the first time," he pointed out. That stupid grin still graced his face.

"It was a gift! You...you...ass!" I sputtered in mock outrage, but inside, I was having fun. Talking to these boys, joking with them, helped me forget everything else transpiring daily in my miserable excuse of a life. So sue me, but I actually liked the cocky bastard. He kept me entertained.

"Now come on, Casanova," Asher said. "I'm hungry, and the others are probably getting impatient."

Ryder muttered under his breath yet again—I wondered if he even realized he was doing it or if he was like me—before he obediently followed Asher.

"Ha," I whispered, sidling up beside him. "So whipped." He shoved at my shoulder, and I shoved back. He, of course, only shoved me harder.

"Seriously? You can't go around hitting girls." Asher sounded moderately horrified. Ryder gave a small shrug.

"She started it."

Something Asher said previously struck me like a bolt of lightning all of a sudden. I froze midstep, barely registering when Ryder ran into my back.

"Wait. Others? There's more of you?" I wanted to add that two hot boys were enough but didn't want to risk inflating Ryder's already immense ego.

"Yeah," Asher said absently, leading us to a large booth in the back. "We're here on a school trip."

"What type of school takes a field trip to a resort?" I questioned, bemused.

"Ours, *obviously*," Ryder huffed. I was tempted to stick my tongue out at him. Instead of physical sarcasm, I settled for verbal.

"Okay, smartass, because obviously it's completely normal for an entire school to travel to the devil's balls for a field trip."

"Devil's balls?" Asher raised an eyebrow.

"Stop talking about my man parts!" Ryder said with a huff, and I couldn't help but chuckle. Dammit, Ryder was growing on me.

Conversation ended, though, when we reached the table in the corner. I gasped at the familiar face staring back at me.

"Ronan?"

"Princess?"

Asher rubbed his chin. Ryder looked annoyed.

"Do you two know each other?" he asked, eyes swinging from mine to Ronan's.

I answered, "No," just as Ronan answered with, "Yes."

"We met last night," Ronan supplied. "Though the little minx has yet to reveal her name to me."

"Phew," Ryder said, wiping invisible sweat from his forehead dramatically. "I thought it was just me."

"It *is* just you," I retorted.

He waggled his eyebrows suggestively.

"Are you saying I'm the only guy you see?"

Rolling my eyes, I turned away from Ryder to face the rest of the table. Two unfamiliar guys stared back at me, one appearing transfixed and the other almost angry.

The first one had brown, almost red, curly hair just reaching his shoulders. His features were boyish, with emerald eyes framed by thick lashes and a tentative smile. As I considered him, his cheeks tinted red.

The second one had a fauxhawk, a few shades darker than Boy Number One's. His eyes, unlike his friend's, were narrowed on me as if he could physically penetrate my skin. I didn't understand his animosity towards me, a virtual stranger, and it made me wonder if it was because I was intruding on bro time or their bro meal or whatever it was called. Was there a code for it? Was a female not allowed to eat during this sacred time? Either way, I found myself glaring right back. For the briefest of moments, a smile graced Glarey's features before he immediately masked it. With what, you might ask. You guessed it—a scowl. I'm pretty sure that was a standard emotion on Glarey's face.

"This is my friend Tamson," Asher introduced, gesturing towards the curly haired guy. "And this is Declan." This was directed towards Mr. Grumpy. Maybe the boy just needed food in his system.

Tamson offered a small smile, blushed, and then looked down at his menu. The back of his neck burned a bright red

So apparently, Mr. Tam was a blusher. There was a lot that you could do with that type of information.

"So, Princess, are you stalking me?" Ronan asked with a dramatic wink. I swear these boys never did anything half-assed. It was always with an elaborate flare, as if they were actors on stage.

"I prefer to say that I was following you without your knowledge," I deadpanned. Ronan threw back his head and roared with laughter.

"I like this girl. Can we keep her?"

"You like *every* girl," Asher muttered under his breath.

Ryder said, "I think Asher already called dibs. He spent the night with her." He sounded bitter at the prospect.

Declan's eyes whipped from where they were focused intently on Ryder's face to mine. If Ryder looked slightly annoyed, Declan looked positively furious.

Ronan sputtered, "What? Asher?" He pointed towards the boy in question. "Our sweet, innocent, virgin Asher?"

"Shut up!" Asher mumbled, whacking Ronan on the back of the head. "And no, we did not hookup."

At this, Ryder gasped in mock outrage.

"Did you lie to me, my little kitten?"

Raising my chin imperiously, I said, "First, don't call me that. And second, I decided I didn't like you, and so I wanted you to suffer."

Asher snorted, and Ronan laughed again.

"Why didn't you like me?" Ryder asked. He sounded oddly amused by my confession, as if he found me cute instead of serious. Men and their egos.

"You were cocky. Emphasis on the cock." I leaned forward to whisper conspiratorially. "It can't be that big for you to have such an attitude. You must be compensating for *something*."

For a moment, the boys stared at me, too stunned to speak. As one, they howled with laughter, garnering the attention of a few customers eating nearby. Even grumpy ole Declan cracked a smile.

"I can assure you that my ego is justified," Ryder responded smoothly. "So getting back to the matter at hand… If you're not dating Asher, does that mean you're single?"

Ronan thrust up a hand to interrupt.

"I would just like to point out that I saw her first."

Declan looked amused by this declaration, while Asher just appeared annoyed.

"That's not the way it works," he said with a sigh. "Besides, I technically saw her first."

I snorted. Guys were amusing…well, more amusing than girls who seemed to come prepackaged with drama. To be honest, I'd never actually had a girl best friend, someone to do my hair and paint my toenails and whatever else girls do together. I was ninety percent positive that it wasn't comparing dick sizes and harassing a poor female about her dating life. Hell, for all I knew, this was probably normal man-dude-bro-time conversation.

Smirking, I allowed my eyes to sweep over the men present. I would've liked to say that I was merely observing my prospective friends, but that would've been a lie. I was totally checking them out. How could I not? They were all hot, even Tamson with his reddening cheeks and disheveled hair. Why did they have to be so attractive? They were really testing my self-control.

Shame.

"I don't date," I answered at last, disrupting their argument. Ryder blinked. He looked as if he wasn't sure if he believed my declaration. After a moment, an incredulous expression contorted his features.

"Like right now?"

"Like ever." I ran my hand over the glossy menu, an absentminded gesture. "I don't want to be in a relationship."

Ryder seemed aghast, though I found that hilarious because he did not seem like the type of guy to do long-term relationships. More like one-night relationships, if you know what I mean. Men with their double standards and hypocritical judgements. As you could probably tell, I hadn't had the best track record with guys. I supposed that most of that could be contributed to DOD and his string of business partners. They saw girls as easy, and we lived in an unfortunate society where the perpetrator was victimized, and the actual victim was blamed. It wasn't my fault that I couldn't trust men, it was my father's.

"Why not?" Ryder asked, diverting my attention.

I shrugged. There was really no way for me to confess the truth to a group of strangers. How did one say that she was afraid of getting close to people because they could get hurt? That she didn't believe she was deserving of love?

Yeah, totally not first meeting conversation.

"You just haven't found the right guy," Ryder insisted, and my mind immediately flashed to Ducky. Declan's eyes almost reminded me of his, minus the whole stare-you-down-until-you-die sort of thing that Declan had going on. The two could've been related.

"Trust me. That's not the reason."

"Where's Calax?" Asher interrupted.

My body went cold at the strange name. How many people at this resort had that name? It was such a stupid name. An evil name...

"For the love of..." I muttered just as a strident voice demanded, "What the hell is she doing here?"

Plastering a pleasant—but fake—smile on my face, I turned towards the voice, already knowing that I would have to strain my head to make eye contact. Calax was a giant, a real monster of a man. His tousled brown hair shielded his eyes which were —unsurprisingly—narrowed on me, and he wore his customary scowl.

"Hello, Callie. Looking lovely as ever this fine day."

Calax pinched the bridge of his nose. This was his standard "trying to be patient with Adelaide" face. Well, excuse me. I *tried* to be nice.

"Addie, what are you doing here?"

There was an eruption of voices from the table.

"Your name is Addie?"

"*This* is Addie?"

"Well, shit."

I didn't look to see whose words belonged to which voice. Calax's eyes remained locked on mine in an unspoken battle of dominance, and I would be damned if I let him win. Calax was, admittedly, a scary man. If I were to see him in a dark alleyway, I'd probably piss my pants. With his shadowed face, black clothing, and towering frame, he could put even the strongest of people in cardiac arrest.

He was also my mortal enemy. Don't ask me why or how. He just was.

"*This* is Adelaide," Ryder sputtered. I didn't like the way he was saying my name— as if he was accusing me of something. Knowing Calax, that wouldn't be surprising. The entire table probably thought I was crazy. I mean, I probably *was*, but he didn't have to *tell* everyone.

"Judging by all the exclamations, I assume Callie told you many wonderful things about me," I said, subtly giving Calax the middle-finger behind my back. The bastard snorted.

"Trust me. We hear a lot about you," Ryder said, smirking at Calax. I didn't even have to turn my head to know that the mountain man was glowering. Calax only had two expressions—a scowl and a semi-scowl. Semi because sometimes, I could've sworn that he wanted to smile but was too stubborn to actually do it. Thus, a semi-scowl.

It occurred to me that, in just a matter of a few minutes, I had two people glaring daggers at me. That was a personal record. I really bring out the best in people.

"Calax is my nemesis," I announced after a moment. "Like the whole enemy, fall-and-crack-your-head-open sort of relationship going on."

Ryder and Ronan broke into laughter. It was Ronan who spoke first, wiping tears out of his eyes. He turned towards Calax.

"You didn't mention that she hated you."

"He's a very hateable person," I pointed out. Calax grumbled inarticulately but slid into the booth beside me. His thigh touched mine, and I poked him in his muscled chest.

"Move over, Big Guy. I don't want to catch your cooties."

He ignored me, as always, and pressed his leg even closer to mine.

"Aw. No fair. How come Calax gets to sit so close to Princess?"

"Princess?" Calax grumbled, seeming annoyed by the nickname. Declan appeared upset that Calax was upset. So basically, everyone besides me was upset. A note to all my readers—if you want to make friends, make them cry first. Trust me.

Declan and Calax seemed to be engaged in some kind of macho stare down. I would seriously never understand boys.

Smiling at Ronan, I said, "Calm yourself, Lucky Charms. I didn't ask for this big brute to sit by me."

"Did you just call me a big brute?" Calax asked, breaking eye contact with Declan.

"Did you just call me Lucky Charms?" Ronan added. He ran his fingers through his tousled green hair.

"You have to admit that you look like a leprechaun."

"That is insultingly adorable." To the rest of the guys, Ronan pleaded, "Please? If you don't want to keep her, I will."

Calax shifted even closer to me at Ronan's words, and Declan's eyes zeroed in on the minuscule movement. Ugh. Boys.

"Nobody's keeping me," I interrupted. "Besides, I don't date."

The waitress picked that time to come up to our table. She was an older woman who was, fortunately, immune to Ryder's charm. Not that he didn't try.

"Doris, looking as beautiful as ever."

In answer, she merely whacked him with her notepad. It was official—Doris was the grandmother I never had.

The boys ordered quickly, but I took my time surveying the menu. So many choices...

"Okay, I'll have a cheeseburger with extra cheese. Like seriously, five slices would be perfect. And some onion rings...yes, onion rings sound amazing. Hmm...let me try a slice of your cherry pie. And a chocolate shake. Are your French fries good? It doesn't really matter. I'll try them anyway. Do you have cheese sauce for them? I'll take some of that. And coffee. Lots and lots of coffee." I closed my menu happily and handed it to the amused waitress. The boys all stared at me as if I had just sprouted wings and flown around the restaurant.

"What?" I asked. "Have you never seen a girl eat before?"

Ronan mock whispered to Asher, "And all I ordered was a salad to try to impress her."

Calax snorted. "Addie eats enough for an army."

"Are you calling me fat, Callie?" I asked, narrowing my eyes playfully. He scoffed.

"If anything, you need more meat on your bones."

"Don't go dissing my bones, Big Guy." In response, Calax stabbed my belly with his finger. I was almost positive that his finger rested on my stomach a second longer than necessary before he pulled it back and crossed his beefy arms.

"You're too skinny."

"Surprising," Ronan injected, "considering how much she eats."

"Hey!" I said, stomping my foot on the ground. "I'm feeling verbally attacked right now."

"Well maybe you should—" Whatever Calax was about to say was cut off by a rumble. For a moment, I was frozen. What was that?

A violent tremor rocked my body forward. Glasses shattered, and somebody let out an earsplitting squeal. I would've liked to say that somebody was Calax, but that would've been a lie. It may or may not have been me. The table trembled, collapsing in on itself like old, brittle paper.

Before I realized what was happening—not a hard feat, mind you—Calax had pushed me to the ground, his muscled body covering mine. An assortment of dishes and wall decorations rained down upon us, but I was too stunned to move.

After what felt like hours, but was probably more like a couple of minutes, the shaking subsided.

"What the hell was that?" I heard Ronan ask, but my tongue felt like sandpaper in my mouth. I couldn't answer him, even if I wanted to.

We'd just survived an earthquake, that much was obvious. While earthquakes weren't unheard of in our area, they weren't necessarily common either. I could count on one hand the number of earthquakes I'd experienced while living in this resort.

"Is everyone okay?" Asher questioned.

A chorus of affirmatives sounded around us.

It suddenly occurred to me that I was still sprawled on the ground, underneath the table, with Calax hovering over me. His weight rested on his forearms.

Squirming, I turned onto my back so I could see his face. I couldn't understand why he'd protected me. Was it a chivalrous gesture? Or was he trying to smother me with his body and make it look like an accident?

Despite my wishes, the expression on his face didn't appear murderous. It could almost be described as...tender. That was one word I never thought I'd use to describe that giant of a man. His lashes feathered against his cheekbones, and his breath left him in a smooth exhale. Before I realized what was happening, his calloused hand reached down to brush my hair away from my face.

And there it was again. That *tenderness.*

"Are you okay?" he asked. That same hand curved around my jaw, thumb skimming across my cheek. His hand almost engulfed my entire face.

"I'm fine," I whispered.

This was a very strange moment for me. I didn't know how to behave, what to say. For as long as I could remember, Calax had hated me and I had hated him. We were Romeo and Juliet, but without the love or the whole dying thing. In a blink of an eye, we found ourselves balancing on a precariously strung tightrope. One wrong move, and we would both be thrown over the edge. I had to remember that Calax was my nemesis, even if his body elicited completely un-nemesis-like feelings above me. Non-enemy feelings that were getting harder and harder…

Scrambling out from under him, I tripped over a toppled chair in my haste to get some space. As he climbed to his feet, his hardened…um…manhood drew my eyes before they flickered back to his face. My cheeks burned.

Earthquake. There was an earthquake. And the salt and pepper shakers broke. Oh dear god, not the salt and pepper shakers. How could we continue on?

That, ladies and gentlemen, was deflection at its finest.

"Are you okay, Princess?" Ronan asked, his fingers grazing my arm to turn me towards him. Ryder appeared over his shoulder, his brows furrowed in concern.

"Of course I'm okay," I said with a scoff. "What about you guys?"

"We're fine." That came, surprisingly, from Tamson. He brushed dust from his slacks and pushed his glasses farther up his nose. I noticed, with some relief, that they weren't broken.

"Everybody stay calm!" an unfamiliar man called. I thought he was the manager, though I couldn't recall his name. "Somebody should be here shortly."

I resisted the urge to roll my eyes.

Great. Just freaking great.

CHAPTER 4

*R*yder suggested we move our party to the lobby. I couldn't help but giggle at that. I'd never been invited to a party—minus the elite affairs forced upon me by my precious parents—but I didn't think what we were doing constituted as a party. No, I was almost certain, based on my extensive Netflix research, that parties did not involve sitting on couches and chairs while eyeing one another warily.

"Is everybody okay?" Asher asked for probably the one-hundredth time.

"Fine and dandy," responded Ryder, flashing me a cheeky grin. "All of my organs are still in working order."

"Pervert," I muttered.

The only response came from the crackling flames from the fireplace. The heat it emitted was near stifling, but I wasn't brave enough to suggest moving the party elsewhere. See? Pun.

Spotting a familiar, gray-haired man hobbling through the expansive lobby, I jumped to my feet.

"Mr. Ackles! How is everyone? Are there any injuries?"

The resort's manager considered me with kind eyes. I always thought Mr. Ackles was too good to work at such a place, too kind to be under the thumb of my malicious parents. He had a way about him, whether he was fussing at me for running down his halls or reminding me not to do drugs, that reminded me of a grandpa. If I had a grandpa, because I seriously believed my parents were hatched from the eggs of the devil, I would want him to be like Mr. Ackles.

"I just heard back from Gavin. There was one minor injury, but nothing else has been reported."

I let out a relieved breath at the information.

"And you? How are you?" I asked, surveying his tiny form. For as long as I could remember, Mr. Ackles walked with a limp. He told me once that he'd gotten it from the war, and I knew that even the slightest bit of strain could cause him immense pain.

"I'm fine, darling." He waved his hand dismissively, though I didn't miss the slight wince as he attempted to amble back towards the elevator.

"You're not fine," I countered. "You need to rest. Go sit at the counter. Don't worry about anything besides getting yourself better."

"But your father—"

"I'll talk to my father. Go. Sit." Without breaking eye contact, I pointed towards the mahogany counter situated at the far wall of the lobby. I knew that there was a stool directly behind it, though very few employees dared to sit on the job. Daddy was a mean son of a bitch, and his employees were well aware of his temper tantrums.

Mr. Ackles gave me an undecipherable look before nodding his head. Relief was evident in his eyes as he hobbled back towards the desk. I made sure to keep an eye on him until he was safely seated and engaged in conversation with one of the many guests demanding an explanation. Though why people felt the need to reprimand the resort for a natural disaster was beyond my comprehension. Seriously, people were strange.

Turning back towards the boys, I saw them all staring at me with varying expressions of awe, though they quickly turned towards one another when they caught me looking. A tentative smile played on Calax's lips, but his eyes remained glued to Asher, acting as though he was paying attention to whatever the other was saying.

"Look," I began, sliding back into my seat between Ryder and Ronan—the R squared, as I liked to call them in my head. "Can we just admit that what happened in the diner was one big shit fest? A shest?"

"A chest?" Tamson parroted, peeking at me through his mane of curly hair.

"A shest," I repeated. "S-H-E-S-T. It's my word for shit fest."

"Do you do that a lot?" Ronan questioned. He brought his knuckles to his chin and sat his elbow on his knee as he surveyed me. "Make up words?"

"Yes," Calax, the bastard, responded for me. I threw a throw pillow at him, which he neatly dodged. Apparently undeterred by my anger, he continued, "Her mind is strange. I don't even understand what goes through her head half the time."

"First you call me fat, and now you call me dumb. Is this National Insult Adelaide Day? Because I'm pretty sure that day passed, like, two months ago. They had a whole parade and everything. I think my parents even got a piñata that looked exactly like me just so they could whack it with a stick without guilt. Unfortunately, no candy came out. Just guts. And blood. I think the piñata was alive."

There was a moment of stunned silence, and then Calax said, "See?"

The boys burst into laughter. If I wasn't a mature, young lady, I would've given Calax the middle finger and then threatened to burn him alive at the stake. Instead, I walked over, hit his head, and then sat back down. *Maturely*.

"So, want to tell me why you guys are here?" I said, attempting to change the subject. Calax was rubbing at his head, eyes narrowed on me, and Ronan was on the floor in peals of laughter.

"Well, as we said before, we go to Highwood Prep. It's a private school a couple of miles from here," Ryder began.

"There was a fire in our dormitories," Asher continued, "so we used our admission fee to pay for a section of the resort as a replacement until the repairs are completed."

"Highwood Prep isn't just a high school," Ronan continued, finally collecting himself enough to move back towards his recliner. "It actually goes all the way to college. I think the youngest kids are about thirteen and the oldest are...what? Maybe twenty-one or so."

That explains all the boob jobs.

"W-What?" Tamson sputtered, face a deep, burgundy red.

"Just...the girls...at the pool...they definitely had boob jobs. I was wondering what type of parents would let high schoolers get such a big boob jobs. Get it? Big? Anyway, it makes sense now that I know that some girls are over eighteen. They don't have to get their parents' permission. Not that I'm knocking a boob job or anything. I mean, some people can totally rock them, but some just look really..." I trailed off, unable to coherently express my private thoughts. This was exactly why some things needed to remain silent. "How old are you guys?" I asked, desperate to change the subject. Again. I really needed to stop getting myself into such awkward situations.

"Well, Tamson over there is the baby. He's only seventeen. Asher and Ryder are both eighteen. Calax, as you know, is nineteen along with Declan and I," Ronan said, pointing at each face as he went along, as if I needed a reminder of their names.

It was one of the final names that I got stuck on. Declan.

Before I could stop myself, because, really, I had no filter, I asked, "Why doesn't he talk?"

There was a moment of silence, during which Declan met my eyes with a smoldering stare of his own. For once, he didn't seem upset with something I said, only startled. His hand moved in a flurry of motion. Sign language.

"Do you think she's playing ignorant or does she really not know?" he signed, though the question wasn't directed at me. Calax immediately responded.

"Trust me. I've known Addie for years. She can barely remember where a wall is at. She's oblivious, not cruel."

Rude.

"She's hot though," Ryder signed. *"I say that we keep her."*

"I already called dibs," Ronan broke in.

"I don't trust her," Declan said. *"She's shady."*

Asher added, *"Well, this conversation escalated quickly."*

"She's hot though."

"Kind of stupid."

"Not stupid. Just naïve."

"A girl like her? Doubt it. And I doubt that she never had a boyfriend before. That was the worst way to put someone down I've ever heard."

Their words—excuse me, *motions*—blurred together so I had trouble keeping up with who signed what, too focused on their hands to notice. After a moment of letting them continue their insult Addie game, I broke in.

"You're right—Addie is seriously hot. And stupid. And kind of crazy, to be honest. And no, she has never had a boyfriend. Good grief, you guys are pathetic."

I finished my signing with a dramatic flip of my hair. The guys all gaped at me yet again. Even cold, unyielding, asshole Declan appeared sheepish and flustered. Good. Served him right for talking about me—damnit, *signing* about me.

"Now, if you guys are done being dick faces, I'm going to go. You know, do some shady shit and all that. I call it shat. Shady shit. And yes, that is an Adelaide original word. And no, you cannot use it."

Aware that their eyes remained on me, staring at me like fish out of water, I gave them the universal F-you sign. It made me feel better.

CHAPTER 5

I was exactly thirteen minutes and twenty-six seconds late to the meeting.

I know. I'm a smartass. Sue me.

From the glower DOD gave me, one would think that I was two days late and had arrived wearing a fedora dipped in the blood of my enemies. Okay, maybe Daddy would've appreciated the whole blood thing. He'd always been a sick, twisted bastard.

He held his hands in front of him, folded on top of his desk. To anyone that didn't know him, the gesture might've been considered relaxed. Comfortable.

But I could see the vein bulging in his forehead and the noticeable grinding of his teeth.

"I'm sorry," I began immediately once I entered his stuffy office. I'd learned at a young age that an apology was always the best first step when it came to my father. Correction, it was the *only* step. "With the earthquake and everything—"

"I don't want to hear your excuses," he snapped. "Sit."

He pointed to a plush, leather chair directly in front of his mahogany desk. As I made my way there, I noticed the occupant of the second seat. I recognized the receding hairline and beady black eyes instantly.

Buttlicker. He'd returned to lick more butts...my father's, I imagined, because DOD wouldn't allow him to kiss it.

Daddy stared at me, eyes penetrating, for a few seconds longer before turning towards Buttlicker. He then began discussing their contract, and I deflated in relief. Maybe, just maybe, he'd forgiven me for my transgression. After all, it wasn't as if I could control the weather. Not even my dad could, though I supposed that he wished it.

I realized the mistake of my earlier relief when the meeting concluded an hour later. I'd spent the time nodding occasionally, and the majority of what they discussed went through one ear and out the other. Oh well.

I'd just climbed to my feet, stretching my taut muscles, when I noticed two sets of eyes trained on me. One was darkened in anger, another with lust. I'm sure you could guess which eyes belonged to which psycho.

"You know that I hate tardiness, Adelaide," DOD reprimanded, his tone cold and calm. I hated when he used this voice—it was like the tranquility before a storm. Frankly, it was his shit-your-pants type of voice that instilled justifiable fear in anyone who heard it.

"I was on my way to the meeting," I lied, because who would want to show up an hour early? "I told you. It was the earthquake—"

The—not altogether unexpected—slap interrupted my excuse. I barely even winced when my head twisted sideways. No, I wouldn't give him the satisfaction of seeing me in pain. It was something that I could call my own. My pain. When did I start coveting pain? God, maybe I was sick.

"Don't lie to me." Spit flew from my dad's mouth. Buttlicker, still leaning back in the seat next to me, smiled smugly. "I have a source that said they saw you whoring yourself out."

For a moment, all I could do was blink in disbelief. "Whoring myself...?"

Slap.

I rubbed at my cheek. From the self-satisfied grin on Buttlicker's face, I could hazard a guess at the identity of that source.

You stupid perverted son of a bitch—

Buttlicker's face reddened, and I realized I'd spoken aloud. Buttlicker confirmed this when he leaned forward to slap my other cheek. Yay! At least I'd have matching bruises. It was all about symmetry, my friends.

It took considerable restraint to stop myself from cutting off Buttlicker's balls and feeding them to DOD. Heaven knew that DOD preferred the pickle over the muffin, if you know what I'm saying.

"Take off your clothes," DOD sneered. Knowing I was already in trouble, I figured it wouldn't hurt to poke the bear a little more. I had so many suppressed emotions, so much pent-up anger, whirling inside of me that demanded release.

"Wow. I knew you were a psycho, but I never imagined incest on your list of perversions. Is that how you came into being? Were your parents brother and sister?"

The following punch was hard, landing right in the stomach. I doubled over.

Yes. *More.*

I enjoyed the pain. It reminded me of what I often forgot—that I was alive. Sort of alive, at least. I mean, I knew that my heart beat and I continued to breathe, but I wasn't living. I couldn't even remember what that felt like. The closest I'd come to happiness was earlier today with the guys, the few times I'd talked with Calax, and my friendship with Ducky. All I had now was the pain, and though not ideal, I would take it over the nothingness I often wanted to succumb to.

I barely paid Buttlicker any mind as he ripped my dress off. His hands groped me, fondling my breasts like the pervert he was. Fortunately, he left my bra and underwear on.

From this angle, I knew my dad could see the scars marring the length of my arm. It was impossible not to. They etched themselves into my skin like an ugly tattoo. A few, the ones closest to my wrist, began to well up, blood rising to the surface, for the cuts had yet to heal.

My dirty little secret.

Without speaking, Dad grabbed my wrist and dragged me out of the office. We received a few stares from employees as I was dragged down the hall, through the breakroom, and into the backdoor of the restaurant.

The kitchen was bustling with activity. Chefs slaved over stoves and pans in an attempt to cater to the dinner crowd. A few waitresses and waiters lurked around, shouting directions at the cooks and grabbing plates. Even an earthquake couldn't stop the resort from running.

I spotted a familiar mound of tousled blond hair.

Please no. Not him.

I turned my head away, telling myself that if I couldn't see him, he couldn't see me. I channeled the stories I read when I was younger, the ones where the kid hid herself under her blankets to ward off the monsters—as if a fluffy blanket could repel a monster. Seriously, sleep with a knife like a normal person.

The kitchen quieted down, the chatter and strident voices diminishing almost immediately.

Keep talking. Nothing to see here. Just a poor, bruised girl about to receive her punishment. Completely normal.

I honestly couldn't tell you if I'd spoken that thought aloud. I'm sure the pitying expressions would've stayed the same no matter what I said.

DOD walked briskly over to an iron-top stove and flicked the dials to the highest settings. Buttlicker squeezed my arm, propelling me towards my father, while his free hand groped my bottom.

"What the hell, you pervert!" Asher yelled, trying to make his way to me, but he was intercepted by two cooks. Asher was young and angry, but he was no match for the two chefs that looked as if they ate more food than they made.

They knew what was going to happen. Hell, Chef Larry and I were old friends.

My dad merely stared at me without saying a word. I knew what he wanted.

Bracing my body, I placed my arms on the stove. The pain was immediate, blistering. My skin felt as if it was splintering from my body, shattering like cracked glass. I screamed in agony, instinct driving me to fight to remove myself from the source of the pain. DOD held my body tightly, refusing to allow me to budge an inch. I was trapped.

"Let her go! Stop! Stop it!" Asher screamed, pushing against the men that held him. More employees had joined the fray.

They all knew what would happen if they intervened, if they called the cops or told anyone what they witnessed. Once, a new waitress reported my dad to Child Protective Services... She was found dead the next day. A home invasion, the official police report read. But I, along with everyone else here, knew the truth. That was years ago.

Through my haze of pain, I felt something that resembled relief. Since that day, no one had ever fought for me. At least, no one cared enough to risk their lives to save mine. I always faced every trial alone. Turning my head, I met Asher's tear filled eyes and gave him a shaky smile. This stranger, this shy, sweet boy, was in my corner when everybody else had abandoned me.

His was the last face I saw before the world faded into darkness.

~

I WOKE up to someone sobbing.

For a moment, I thought the sound was coming from me. I didn't think I was crying, but who the hell knew anymore. Mixed with the whole sobbing symphony, I heard a steady beeping. Confused, I twisted in the bed, and the beeping noise began to sound at intermittent intervals.

Huh. A heart monitor.

The sound immediately began to slow itself once I came to that conclusion. Voices, though stunted by what was probably a door, floated to me.

"What the fuck are we going to do?" The voice sounded familiar, and it took me a second to place where I'd heard it before. Ronan, the unicorn tattooed, green-haired, leprechaun.

What was he doing here?

"I didn't know it was this bad," a choked voice added. I didn't even need to think to know whom this voice belonged to. Calax. He sounded ragged, as if...as if he'd been the one I heard crying.

I snorted at the ridiculousness of that thought. If he was crying, then it was probably because I survived. The bastard seemed to hate me more than my own parents did.

"You didn't see it," Asher said. I had to strain to hear his quiet voice. "The entire staff knew what was going to happen. They fucking knew, and they did nothing to stop it. They told me that shit like this happens all the time. Not a week goes by when she isn't covered in bruises or casts. Hell, they even told me her parents often send sleazy fuckers to her room at night—" His voice broke off in anguish, and my heart fluttered at his obvious distress of my situation. Sure, I knew my parents' treatment of me wasn't normal, but to hear someone else vocalize it, to condemn the people who repeatedly put me through hell, almost made me smile, like the twisted fucker they'd created. I could barely remember the last time anyone cared about me or advocated on my behalf. The feeling was strange but not entirely unpleasant.

An explosion of noise met Asher's confession. Something shattered, and I could only hope it was something expensive. Maybe a nice old vase.

"You were with her for years!" Ryder exploded at someone. I was assuming Calax, because he was the only one I knew before yesterday. "How could you not have known?"

Ryder was rewarded with a strangled sound.

"Enough!" This forceful voice surprised me the most, mainly because I didn't recognize it. "I know tensions are running high, but we need to keep our shit together. Now, how is it going with the police?"

My mouth—well, my mental mouth, because I totally wasn't going to move—dropped open when I finally placed that voice. The last few times I'd heard it, it had been nothing more than a timid murmur, but that husky timbre was unmistakable. *Tamson.*

Who would've thought that shy boy had a bossy streak?

Maybe he just behaved like that around me. After all, I was a girl. Or maybe, just maybe, I'd gotten him completely wrong. For all I knew, he kept a house full of play-girls bending over to please him. Literally. Because, you know, in this fantasy, Tamson was a kinky son of a—

Focus, Adelaide! I mentally scolded myself.

I concentrated once more on their conversation.

"...under their thumb," Ryder was saying, irritated. "The fuckers laughed when I called."

Laughed? Who did they call? Hopefully, it wasn't the police because they were—

"Crooked cops," Ronan sneered.

Yup. What he said.

I made the idiotic mistake of calling them once, after a particularly bad beating. My arm had been broken in more than two spots, and I'd had a punctured lung. The doctor of the resort, an aging, malicious man who was blinded by his loyalty to my parents, had announced that I was lucky to be alive.

As if it were *my* fault my dad decided to beat me.

So I'd called the cops. I was many things, but I wasn't stupid enough to take chances with my life. The conversation had started off simple enough, until I gave them my name and address. All at once, the operator declared there was nothing she could do to help me and hung up.

Not even an hour later, DOD punished me for attempting to get in contact with the authorities. At least it was me he punished and not Nik. At least my little brother was as far away from this world and my parents as humanly possible.

"I agree with Declan," Asher said. "I don't give a damn about our supervisors. We need to change the mission. All in favor?"

A chorus of "ayes" rang out.

What mission? And what supervisor?

I wanted to yell at them for not providing more information. What was the point of eavesdropping if you didn't understand half of the conversation?

But as my mind spun, drowsiness threatened to pull me under. The darkness was alluring and seemed to be calling for me.

I answered the call and allowed it to consume me.

THE NEXT TIME I woke up, I was actually able to open up my eyes.

The first thing I noticed was that I was in a hospital—the resort's hospital, no surprise there. The familiar white walls and pungent aroma of bleach made the room unwelcoming. How many times had I been here? It struck me deep when I couldn't recall the exact number.

The heart monitor still beat its annoying tune, and someone still sobbed nearby. *What the actual...?*

I twisted my head, a surprisingly painful movement, to see Calax in the chair beside my bed. His large frame looked awkward in such a cramped, tiny space, and I wondered if he'd gotten stuck.

He held his head in his hands and shook as sobs racked his body. It didn't make any sense. Giants didn't cry. He should've been smiling or licking blood off his fingers or lapping up intestines...

Calax's eyes flickered towards me.

Whoops. Must've spoken that aloud.

"You're awake," he said breathlessly. "How do you feel?"

"Like my dad beat the shit out of me and then burnt me over a stove like a pot of spaghetti," I teased with a light smile. Calax did not seem to find it funny. His scowl deepened.

"This isn't fucking funny!" As if his agitation demanded a physical response, he jumped from his seat.

"It's fine, Calax," I whispered. "This happens all the time. I'll feel better in a few days, tops. I'm used to it."

I had meant to comfort him—though I didn't know why because he hated me, and likewise, I hated him—but my words only appeared to make him angrier. A hundred different emotions flickered across his handsome face before settling on despair.

"You shouldn't have to get used to something like this." All at once, as if his legs couldn't hold his body up, he collapsed onto his knees before me. "Baby, I am so sorry this happened to you. It shouldn't... You shouldn't have..." Unshed tears glistened in his wide eyes. Somehow, that vulnerability made him seem less like an evil giant and more like a handsome young man. I had the irresistible urge to wrap my arms around his thick neck and cuddle against him.

Woah. Where did that come from?

I settled for awkwardly patting him on the head like a dog.

"Calax," I began softly. When my voice faltered over that one word, I cleared my throat and tried again. "Calax, you have to understand that there's nothing you or I can do about this. My parents are...well, they're powerful people. And obviously, they're not the good guys. I know—"

"You don't know shit if you think I'm just going to sit back and allow you to be tortured!" Calax snapped, his rage filled eyes meeting mine. I knew his anger wasn't directed at me, but I didn't like seeing him upset. Absently, I used two fingers to smooth over the furrow between his eyebrows. I moved those same two fingers to his lips, turning them up. He shivered beneath my touch, and I wondered if my hands were cold.

Of course, that meant I had to keep them on his face longer. For torturous reasons only. Nothing else.

Calax sighed deeply and turned his face into my palm. Was that...

Were his lips pressing against the skin there?

"I promise we'll figure something out, baby. You don't have to go through this alone anymore."

Somehow, despite everything, I believed him.

"I know, Big Guy. I know."

~

THE THIRD TIME I woke up—because third time's a charm—I realized males surrounded me. Hot males.

It's official. I must've died and gone to Heaven.

Deep chuckles greeted that statement.

Chicken shit. Butt groper, piece of—

"Princess, you're doing it again," Ronan said, still chuckling.

I huffed. "Oh please. You guys find it adorable."

"She's not wrong," Ryder pointed out and was simultaneously whacked in the head by the two grumps of the group—Calax and Declan.

"Ow!" he whined. "Addie! They hit me!"

His lower lip protruded out into a pout, and I nearly fell off the bed in my hysterical fit.

"You...look like...a constipated puppy!" I managed to wheeze out, very eloquently, mind you. The rest of the boys burst into laughter at my statement, even Declan. Ryder's face flamed.

"That face usually works on the females," he whispered to Asher, but that only made me laugh harder. Those females must've been blind or desperate. I said as much to Ryder.

The boys doubled over in laughter, and Ryder leaned forward to pinch my arm.

"You're such a little shit!"

"Hey!" Calax bellowed, grabbing Ryder by the back of his shirt. "Careful of her injuries!"

I rolled my eyes. "It's fine, Callie. It's not like a little pinch is going to cause internal bleeding."

He merely glared at me in response.

"So," I began, attempting to pull myself up into a sitting position. I probably looked like a dying fish on land for all the good that did me. Ronan, chuckling under his breath, finally helped me up and placed a pillow behind me. At least someone knew how to behave like a gentleman, minus the whole laughing thing.

Before I could continue my thought, though I honestly didn't know where I was going with it in the first place, Tamson piped up from the back. He had, once again, reverted back to the shy, sweet boy I'd initially met.

"How are you feeling? Do you need me to get the doctor?" At his words, the mood instantly sobered.

"I can grab you a water," Asher added. "Or would you like something to eat?"

Smiling cheekily, I said, "It's official. Tam and Asher are my two favorites. I mean, come on. Asher offered me food not once, but twice. How could he not get top honors? And Tam's just a sweetie."

Both of their faces turned bright red, which only reaffirmed the whole favoritism thing. I loved it when they blushed.

Ryder growled at my words.

"Oh, it's on, Kitten."

"Challenge accepted," Ronan added, cracking his knuckles.

"Whatever, drama queens...or in this case, leprechauns. Now back to my question…which I may have forgotten. Okay, so I never actually asked it to begin with, but it was important. Just give me a moment. One second."

"Is she always like this?" Ronan mocked-whispered to Calax.

Calax grunted an affirmative.

Snapping my fingers together, I was pleased with myself when I finally remembered what I was going to say. It was so obvious that I felt kind of stupid for needing to think about it. More stupid than usual, anyway.

"Why are you guys here?"

The boys blinked at me.

"That was the question you struggled so hard to remember?" Ryder asked in disbelief. I gave him the finger.

"This is why you're not my favorite."

"Nooo!" he whined. "I take it back, you intelligent goddess."

"Flattery will get you nowhere."

"It seems like she's immune to your charm," Asher muttered with a smirk. I, once again, nearly fell off the bed in laughter.

"Ryder doesn't have charm!" I gasped out, giggling. Ryder surged forward, probably to pinch me again, but Calax restrained him.

"Boys," I cooed, flashing a shit-eating grin in their direction. "Why don't you kiss and make up already?"

Calax and Ryder froze, exchanged horrified looks, and jumped apart as if their lives depended on it.

"Ignoring those shit for brains, why wouldn't we just want to spend time with you?" Asher asked. I stared at him incredulously.

"Uh…because you don't know me, and I'm certifiably insane."

The boys gave me a look for that one.

Huffing, I added, "Is this about the whole incident? Are you guys playing bodyguard now or something?"

If I expected guilt to appear in their expressions, I was sorely mistaken. They faced me with what I could only describe as resolve.

Well, fuck.

"Incident?" Ronan asked with a snort. "You can't really say what happened was only an incident. What those sick bastards did to you…"

"You can't get involved!" I hissed, not even caring when my voice came out in a desperate plea. "You don't understand what my family will do to you—"

"And you don't seem to understand what they do to you," Calax broke in. Before I could retort, he grabbed my hand. I expected his hand to feel rough on my skin, but despite his many callouses, his touch was unexpectedly gentle. "Or maybe you do understand," he murmured. His finger traced one of the many scars adorning my arm.

"Did you do this to yourself?" Asher asked, his voice sounding uncharacteristically loud in the sudden quiet of the room. Everybody seemed to await my answer with bated breaths.

My voice was just as low when I responded with, "It's none of your business."

This felt too intimate, too private, to share with a group of strangers. It was my pain, *mine*, and it was a secret I'd managed to keep for years. Didn't I deserve to have something all to myself? Something that was mine and mine alone? I was both terrified and angry that these boys had taken that from me.

From their anguished expressions, they were able to pick apart my words and uncover the truth.

Refusing to wallow in the pity party about to happen, I clapped my hands.

"Now, back to the important issues. You guys. And what I mean by that is you guys getting the hell out of here as fast as you can. No arguments? Good. Now leave. Pack your bags. I'm sure you can find a nice little hotel to house your sorry asses until your school is fixed."

The boys surprised me by chuckling. They actually chuckled, as if they found me amusing when I'd been deadly serious.

"Not happening, Princess."

"We're staying with you, Kitten."

"You're so adorable when you think we're going to leave."

I huffed, crossing my arms over my chest. There was a slight sting from the burns, now wrapped in bandages, but nothing I couldn't live with. The drugs helped to numb the pain. Speaking of drugs...

Maybe I could get my hands on a drug I could use to knock them out. Granted, it would be difficult to carry their fat asses—muscular, well-defined asses—out of the resort, but I had connections. I mean, it wouldn't count as kidnapping if I was doing it for their own good, right?

A hand waving in front of my face interrupted my musings.

Jolting back, I turned towards Declan.

His hands moved rapidly as he signed to me.

"You're an idiot if you think we'll leave you after everything that happened. Now quit your bitching and allow us to help you."

All I could do was stare at him, stunned. Slightly breathless, I said, "That was the longest sentence you've ever signed to me in my life. Does this mean we're best friends now?"

He rolled his eyes at me. Of course that meant we were best friends. Only best friends would roll their eyes at one another.

Totally nailed it.

"Do you ever take things seriously?" Tamson asked with sincerity. It threw me for a loop, and I paused to consider my response before speaking.

"Sometimes, but it hurts me more when I do," I admitted. When the guys gave me flabbergasted expressions, I hurried to explain. "I've spent my entire life failing to meet my parents' expectations. As you can see, I'm punished almost daily for these failures. Some days are worse than others. Because of this, I've never had any friends or anyone to confide in. Well, the one friend I did have was killed in a car accident." Tears burned my eyes at the memory, and I heard a sharp intake of breath. I didn't look to see which boy made the sound. "It was my fault. Everything is always my fault, because I bring it on myself—that's what my parents drilled into me. If I so much as sit the wrong way, I get beaten. If I talk to one of the residents, my father sends one of his business partners to my room..." I trailed off when I noticed how hard Calax gripped the hospital chair. His eyes were unfocused, his breathing ragged. None of the guys looked any better after my confession. Each wore varying degrees of anger, horror, disgust, and sadness. I was almost grateful when I didn't spot pity in their kaleidoscope of emotions.

I wouldn't be able to handle that.

Swallowing, I hurried to continue before I lost my nerve. "I think I just gave up. If I choose to take everything seriously, to drown in my sorrow, I may never get back up again. God, it feels like I'm dying almost every day. I can't breathe at points. But I accepted my life, and I accepted the mask that I must wear to survive it. Instead of breaking, I make it into a joke. It may be a twisted way of handling things, but it keeps me sane, or somewhat close to it. I wouldn't be able to smile without it."

I let out a ragged breath. I hadn't meant to share as much as I did. I couldn't even tell you why I had. The words just spewed from my mouth like a verbal freight train. Maybe it was some innate need inside of me, a need that I didn't fully understand, that craved human companionship.

Acceptance.

Maybe I had spoken because these were feelings I'd never dared put into words before because I had nobody to listen.

Or maybe, just maybe, it was because the last remaining grip I'd had on my sanity disappeared the moment my arms hit the stovetop.

"Addie," Ryder said. Tears welled in his eyes as he stared at me. "Nobody, and I mean *nobody*, should go through everything you did. You are so incredibly strong." His hand cupped mine, swallowing it whole.

"You don't have to worry about being alone anymore. We're your friends now, and we always look after our own," Asher added. I pushed back the tears that threatened to spill.

"You don't even know me," I pointed out huskily. I was an ugly crier, with snot and slobber and everything. They didn't want to see that. I didn't know how some girls could cry and still manage to look like freaking goddesses.

I bet Elena had a pretty cry, that bitch.

"I know you took the fall for me the other day at the restaurant, despite knowing that you would be punished," Asher whispered.

"I know that you're a stubborn brat who I want to learn more about," added Ryder.

Declan waved his hand once again to get everyone's attention.

"You can't blame yourself for everything. I know you believe that your friend—" Whatever he was about to say was cut off by a scream.

The boys all jumped to their feet and immediately surrounded my bed. The movement was so smooth, so rehearsed, that I had to wonder if they'd done it before. Or perhaps they were just telepathic and could communicate in one another mind to mind.

Calax and Ronan broke away from the group to press their bodies against the door, one on either side.

If they thought I was some damsel in distress in need of saving, they were mistaken.

Pulling the IV out of my arm and disconnecting the heart monitor, I ambled to my feet. The pain in my arms wasn't as bad now—nothing more than a dull ache that thrummed throughout my body. I had to thank the morphine for that.

Ignoring the guys' protests, I grabbed a scalpel off the table and steadied it in front of me. It wasn't the greatest weapon, but it was sharp.

I liked sharp things.

"Dammit, Addie!" Calax mouthed at me, but he didn't charge over and try to stop me. Progress.

My smug smile faded as another earsplitting scream echoed through the hospital. My muscles locked together at the horrendous sound.

Calax and Ronan exchanged a look that made words unnecessary. As one, Ronan moved to open the door, and Calax released a gun from his holster.

A gun? What in the actual—

Calax stood in the doorway, aiming the gun to the left and then to the right—you know, that thing cops did in movies before they announced that a room was clear—and did a weird gesture with his hand.

Apparently, that wasn't the come-out-and-follow-me signal, though you could've fooled me. So of course, I was the idiot who stepped out of the room and into the dimly lit hallway.

In my defense, I totally thought he was telling us to follow him.

The first thing I saw was the blood. Illogical as it sounds, I couldn't help but think that somebody had spilt cranberry juice on the hospital floor. There was no conceivable way that the mess before me could be blood. Did a human even have that much blood in their body?

Seemingly, the answer to that question was yes, yes indeed, for only a few feet away lay the mangled corpse of the resort's doctor. His stomach had been torn out, guts and other unsavory substances spilling out of him like cotton from a stuffed-animal. That wasn't the strangest thing, though.

That was horrifying, yes, and slightly bizarre, but it wasn't what caused me to tremble in fear. I had seen death before, and though gruesome, his body was nothing new.

No, what terrified me was the second figure leaning over Dr. What's His Name. From this angle—and it had to be the angle because the alternative was too disgusting to comprehend—it looked as if Buttlicker was eating him.

Three things happened in a very quick succession.

First, I must've made a noise, whether it was a gasp, an intake of breath, or a whimper, I couldn't entirely determine, but Buttlicker's head whipped in my direction.

It was him…but it wasn't him. His eyes were the color of garnet stones, an unnatural red that contrasted with the white surrounding his eyes. His face looked cracked, as if it was precious glass that had been dropped one too many times. The jagged lines curved steeply down each cheek in an asymmetrical design. The skin around his neck was red and bloody.

Before I could even think to scream, he charged.

I would like to say that what happened next, I'd done on purpose. I would like to say that I had been totally kickass and managed to defeat him with my ninja moves.

No, what happened was a complete and utter accident. The boys yelled out, with Ronan warning Calax not to shoot me by mistake, when Buttlicker pounced.

In my panic, I lifted my hands in a defensive maneuver, forgetting that I still held the scalpel. He fell on top of me, and the scalpel lodged itself in his throat.

I had to be the only human alive who could accidentally stab someone.

A disgusting black tar exploded from the exposed wound. Buttlicker let out a series of inarticulate cries, hands reaching desperately for me.

The boys pulled him off me, but I barely processed that snippet of information.

I had killed someone. I'd killed someone I knew. I didn't know how to deal with that knowledge. Instead of anger or guilt, I felt almost empty. I didn't like the feeling, the nothingness that promised pain. The urge to hurt myself hit me in a near palpable wave.

But what was that black substance oozing from his neck? And why was he still moving, still wiggling, even after I'd stabbed him? His eyes looked feral, enraged.

I'd never seen anything like him before.

"Are you okay? Princess, breathe for me. You need to breathe. Take deep breaths."

I complied with his instructions almost mechanically.

"Good job. Good job, Princess. You're doing just fine."

Through my erratic spurts of breath, I caught sight of Ronan's terrified eyes. Was he terrified of me? Because I killed someone?

The thought only made me freak out more.

"Guys, what the hell is going on over there?" Ronan asked the others, not taking his eyes off me. His hand rubbed soothing circles into my back as he occasionally reminded me to breathe.

Easier said than done.

"I don't know what the fuck this thing is." Ryder's strained voice came from somewhere in front of me, hidden behind Ronan's bulky frame. "This is *Walking Dead* level shit right here."

"We need to call this in," Tamson added, sounding shaken.

"I killed someone." The words left my mouth in a broken whisper. "I'm a murderer. Oh god. I'm going to vomit."

Before I even finished my sentence, said vomit exploded out of me like a volcano eruption. Ronan, for his part, didn't look away or even crinkle his nose in disgust. He continued to pat my back soothingly with one hand while the other hand pulled my hair out of my face. I was mortified to realize that my vomit had hit the unexpected bullseye…of his shoes.

"You didn't kill anyone," Ronan said softly. "It was self-defense, and he was still alive when Calax shot him dead."

Shot? Calax?

I hadn't even heard a gun go off.

"I don't think…" I gasped out, but then clamped my mouth shut when I realized I didn't know how to put my thoughts into words. I tried again. "I think he was sick or something. Did you see his face? His eyes? Oh god, what happened to him?"

Ronan's hand tightened marginally in my hair, the grip more pleasurable than painful. He released it with a heaving breath.

"I don't know. I don't know."

CHAPTER 7

The next few hours were a blur. One minute turned into the next, which turned into the next. I remained motionless as my father's security arrived at the medical center, guns drawn.

The boys moved into a protective circle around me. I was too weak, too numb, to tell them that they didn't need to baby me.

But maybe I did. After all, I could barely stand on my own two feet without collapsing. The only thing that kept me upright was Ronan's hand around my waist. It was both a mental comfort and a physical one. I was sure I would've fallen face first if he hadn't been there to hold me up.

My heart beat erratically as the body was removed and questions were asked. I don't remember what I said. Probably something stupid like "Buttlicker."

The doctors arrived shortly after the security. I didn't recognize them, but from the way they surrounded my father, I reasoned they must've worked for him. I was put into a room separate from the males, and the lady doctor asked me to strip off my clothes.

I felt immensely relieved that it wasn't some pervy old male attempting to cop a feel. That had happened to me once. Apparently, Dr. Johnson wasn't a real doctor.

After I washed off the blood, the lady doctor, who didn't provide her name, searched me for any injuries. She poked and prodded me to the point where I wondered if I'd been abducted by aliens. She rebandaged my arms, her brow furrowing with something akin to disapproval, but did not comment on the red, raised skin from the stovetop.

When she finally dismissed me, I saw Ryder sitting in the waiting room, playing on his phone.

"How are you doing?" he asked when he saw me emerge. I was still dressed only in a hospital gown, the flimsy material doing very little to cover my body, yet I didn't feel sexualized in any way—surprising, consider that this was Ryder. A look of tender anxiety softened his handsome face.

"Usually, I like stuff in my butt," I deadpanned. When Ryder began choking on his own spit, I added, "Too much?"

Despite my light words, I couldn't erase the image of Buttlicker in my mind. For some reason, it occurred to me that I didn't know his real name. I didn't know if it made me a horrible person or a sane one when I realized that I didn't want to know.

In my mind, I saw his eyes, the whites surrounding a red abyss. The feral snarl marring his features. The black, almost inky, blood pooling around him.

Had he felt any pain when he died? I imagined that his death hadn't been pleasant. He'd been stabbed and, evidently, shot. How long had he been alive before death finally claimed him?

Ronan assured me it wasn't my fault, but that didn't stop the guilt. It felt pronounced and all-consuming, as if something heavy was pressing on my chest.

Suffocating me.

Was this what it felt like to be buried alive? Was there any relief?

One part of my mind scoffed at that word. Relief. No matter what Ronan said, I stabbed a man and, unintentionally or not, killed him. A life had been cut short because of me. Did I deserve relief? No.

I'd caused Ducky's death and now Buttlicker's. I deserved whatever punishment the universe wished to inflict upon me.

I got separated from the guys once again sometime during the interrogation. That was okay. I didn't deserve their friendship or their comfort.

No outside help came during the investigation. There were no police officers, no doctors besides my dad's hired staff, no FBI.

The conclusion they came to was simple—ecstasy. He'd been on drugs, they told me, and wasn't in his right mind. I had questioned whether ecstasy could cause black marks on faces, cracks throughout skin, or blood red eyes. They'd just exchanged wary glances before assuring me again that everything had been handled.

Hours later, I found myself sprawled across my bed. My eyes were heavy, but I found that only nightmares greeted me when I slept. It was difficult to discern reality from fantasy. Both were hell.

I barely flinched when I heard footsteps pounding through my kitchen, heading towards my bedroom. When my door slammed against the wall, I didn't even blink.

You deserve this, a sly voice whispered inside my head. *Murderer.*

Ducky's face flashed through my head, and I stifled a sob. I was beginning to see his face everywhere again.

"What the hell did you think you were doing?" Dad demanded. Before I could even speak, he grabbed my foot and pulled me from the bed. My body clunked against the rail, head turning at an unnatural angle. Pain. I felt the pain. It broke through the hazy sheen like tiny, penetrating needles. More. I needed more.

"Stupid!" Punch. "Bitch!"

His hand fisted in my hair, pulling it back. The pressure made me whimper, but I quickly tried to keep it contained. My body ached everywhere. My back hurt from yesterday, my cheekbones stung, my scalp felt as if it was on fire—ironic, considering it was my arms which had gotten burned.

"He attacked me," I managed to wheeze out between kicks to my stomach. From the darkening of his eyes, I realized that was the incorrect thing to say. In his eyes, the man couldn't do anything wrong. It was my fault.

Always my fault.

After one more kick to my midsection, he sauntered away as if he had no care in the world. As if he didn't just beat the crap out of his only daughter.

The tears flowed down my cheeks now that I was alone and could be vulnerable. Would I cry in front of my dad? Hell no. Would I cry now that he was gone?

Well, if my snot was any indication, then yes. I couldn't always act strong, and I didn't want to. Just once, I wanted to fall and not worry that I would get stabbed by swords on the way down. An impossible feat, I was beginning to realize.

After drowning some aspirin to placate the pain, I changed into a pair of sweatpants and a sweatshirt. The clothing did nothing to obscure the bruises darkening my cheeks and neck, but it provided me with some semblance of a shelter.

Still, I couldn't hide my limp as I wandered down the hall.

I didn't know where I was going, nor did I care. Half of me wanted to go to my secret pool, but I didn't want to run into any more annoying boob ladies with their shrill voices and their…well…fake boobs that made me self-conscious. Damn tears trailed unchecked down my cheeks as I walked from hallway to hallway.

A few guests met my gaze before quickly turning away, and the employees couldn't even meet my eyes. It was always the same story with abuse—everyone was too much of a coward to do anything, myself included. It wasn't as if I was unused to surviving alone, but it still caused an uncomfortable lump to well up in my throat. For once, I wanted someone to stand up for me as Asher had done before.

Preoccupied with my admittedly depressing thoughts, I didn't see the person in front of me until I plowed into him.

Looking back, I wondered if it was chance or fate. Why else would we be happening to walk down the same hallway at the same time of night?

Sniffing, I turned my face up blindly to meet Declan's bright eyes.

His mouth opened, probably to call me out for not paying attention to where I was walking, but his expression shattered upon seeing me. He took a horrified step backwards, as if my appearance was a physical repellence.

I wanted to growl. I didn't need, nor did I want, his damn pity.

Dozens of emotions flitted across his normally impassive face until it settled on determination, if determination was even an emotion. If anything, his eyes looked as if they were made of steel, and his expression was almost angry. Not at me, but at the world.

Briskly, he made one motion with his hand.

Come.

I didn't know if I was more surprised at him for talking to me or me for following him.

We didn't speak as we walked down hallway after hallway, stopping occasionally to allow a guest to pass us. I appreciated it, since I didn't want any more people to see me than necessary.

When we finally reached our destination, I grabbed his arm to get his attention.

"The game room?" I questioned, glancing at the surprisingly empty room. "What are we doing here?"

He ignored me and proceeded towards an air hockey table in the center of the modest room.

Like the wannabe beach, this room had long since been abandoned in place of a high-tech, shiny arcade located a few halls down. I much preferred this room and its simplicity.

There was a ping-pong table against the far wall, adjacent to what looked to be a bookshelf but was severely lacking in actual books. On the other side of the room was a pool table.

Besides the games, it was a rather unremarkable room. Ugly almost, compared to the rest of the resort. The walls were painted a light blue that clashed with the dark blue of the carpeting. I wondered which designer decorated this room—and had no doubt been fired because of it. Why was it even still here?

"Air hockey?" I asked, my disbelief evident. When he ignored me yet again, I leveled a glare at him. "Are we playing?"

He gave me a look that made me question my sanity. Geez. It was just a question.

He bent over to put quarters into the machine, and I took the time to shamelessly admire his butt. I honestly hadn't meant to at first, but it had been right in front of me

Ha ha. But. Get it?

Realizing what I was doing, I focused instead on the peeling wallpaper at the very top of the walls. Declan wasn't a person to be objectified. I hated when it was done to me, so why would it be any different for him?

"I'm sorry," I blurted when he turned towards me. He raised an eyebrow in question. "For staring. At you. When you were bent over."

When he just continued to look at me strangely, I signed, *"Your butt."*

I expected him to be mad, I would've been, but he surprised me by doubling over in hysterical laughter. I had seen the other guys laugh, and I'd even caught a smile gracing Declan's hardened features, but I had never seen him outright laugh before. It did funny things to me.

"What's so funny?" I demanded. "Aren't you pissed that I checked out your...you know?"

Of course, that only made the idiot laugh harder. Tears dripped down his cheeks, and he held his stomach with one hand. Huffing, I crossed my arms over my chest and waited for him to regain control of himself.

After what felt like hours, the laughter diminished from his eyes to be replaced with what looked like respect. I rationalized that I must've seen it wrong. Who would respect someone as pathetic as me?

"I'm not upset that you checked me out," Declan signed. *"I'm flattered."* He paused his movements, head tilted to the side as he regarded me curiously. *"But thank you for apologizing though. Most wouldn't have."*

I snorted. "I just didn't want to give you a double standard. I just know that I hate when it's done to me."

His eyes clouded over with an undefinable emotion before he quickly nodded to the game. The puck was already sliding across the table.

"I'll have you know that I'm the Stanley Cup winner of air hockey, so don't cry too hard when I whoop your ass," I said, grabbing the…handle? Fetus hockey stick? Guard thingy? I mean, really, who actually knew the name of the thing you hit the puck with?

He placed his prong—because that was totally what I was going to call it—on the edge of the table so he could sign to me.

"You talk a big game. Let's see if you can back it up."

In answer, I made an exaggerated show of cracking my knuckles.

I managed to score once. I would've liked to have blamed my loss on my injuries, but the truth was, I sucked, and Declan was a freaking beast. He countered every one of my moves with a ninja one of his own. The only way I managed to score that one point was tackling him to the ground and slipping the puck in manually.

I was breathless from laughter by the time we finished the fourth game. I didn't know where Declan got all those quarters, but I was grateful. I didn't realize how much I had needed the distraction. It was dangerous for me to be alone with my thoughts.

Smirking, I pointed a finger at his chest. "The only reason you won was because I'm rusty. If we played another game, I would totally kick your ass."

"So how about one more game?" he asked, calling me out on my bluff. I feigned a dramatic yawn.

"I would, but I'm exhausted. Letting you win took a lot out of me."

Rolling his eyes, he plopped himself onto the table, feet dangling. He gestured to the spot beside him, and I eyed the table with distrust.

"Are you sure it will hold my weight? According to Callie, I need to slow down on the food." Which would never happen because food was the only thing that gave me joy.

Declan rolled his eyes at me yet again. Sighing, I sat beside him.

We remained silent for a few moments, both of us watching our feet swing back and forth. It wasn't uncomfortable, which surprised me greatly. This was Declan, after all, who seemed to hate me from the second he laid eyes on me. Maybe he'd been on a guy period or whatever and was PMSing.

He finally tapped my shoulder to garner my attention, and I turned towards him expectantly.

"What happened?" he questioned. It felt more like a request than a demand. He was giving me the choice to answer him or not.

He was a stranger, yes, but I'd been alone for so long that his sudden display of kindness left me confused. I craved more of it. If that required honesty, then I would give it to him willingly.

"My dad," I admitted softly. "Being a dick." I rubbed at my cheekbone almost absently, the pain from his hit only moderate when compared to the rest of my body. Declan didn't interrupt me as I did an assessment of my body. He just watched me with those wide, impassive eyes, seeing everything but giving nothing away.

"He blamed me for Buttlicker's death," I said, barely even processing my inadvertent use of his nickname. Declan seemed to know who I was talking about though, and he didn't ask for clarification. "So he hit me. I don't know. Maybe I deserved it after what I did—"

Now he did interrupt me, an erratic flurry of hand gestures.

"No. Don't say things like that. You don't deserve this. No one deserves this type of treatment, and don't for one second believe that you're worth less than what you actually are."

His words brought tears to my eyes.

"My worth," I scoffed. "What type of worth can someone like me have? I've done so many horrible things to good people. My own parents don't even love me."

I paused, a ragged gasp escaping my throat unbidden. I pressed my palms to my eyes to retain some dignity, but the sob escaped.

"Why don't my parents love me?" I asked, the question haunting me. "What did I do wrong? Am I not deserving of love? Am I being punished? Because I'm sorry for anything I may have done to deserve this." The tears came down faster, blurring my vision. Of course, that display of weakness only made me cry harder. I was pathetic.

I felt Declan's arm around my shoulder a second before he gently pressed me to his chest. His touch was light enough that I knew I could get away if I wanted to. He made sure I knew it was my choice with him. Always my choice.

He allowed me to wet his shirt for who knew how long. By the time my sobbing subsided, my head was pounding and my body felt drained.

I pulled my head up so he could read my lips.

"I'm sorry for slobbering all over you. Usually, I'm not so needy and emotional. God, I don't know what the hell is wrong with me." I covered my face with my hands, embarrassed by my mental breakdown.

Declan grabbed both of my wrists and tentatively pulled them away from my flushed face. He waited until my entire focus was on him before he signed.

"No person should have to deal with what you deal with. It's okay to cry once in a while, and it's okay to ask for help. I'm sorry that you've been alone for this long, but I promise that's going to change. Your parents are assholes if they don't see how amazing you are. They don't deserve your love. Besides, my group already adopted you. Those guys are practically my brothers, and we protect our own."

I smiled at the familiarity behind those words. Our own. I liked the sound of that. Hey, if they were stupid enough to take on a crazy, emotional teenage girl, then who was I to stop them? I craved the companionship they offered. Was it stupid and potentially dangerous to trust a bunch of strangers? Maybe.

But they were offering me friendship, nothing more. Sure, the friendship probably wouldn't last when they realized how fucked up I truly was, but I would enjoy the hell out of it while it lasted.

"So I'd be like your sister?" I asked. For some reason, Declan looked horrified by that proclamation. Maybe I'd misunderstood him. Maybe he didn't want to be my friend after all.

"No! Not a sister! But a friend that we look after and protect and keep away from other boys."

"So a sister?" He was making zero sense.

"Not a sister," he insisted. *"And stop saying that."*

"But we're going to be friends?" I asked softly, peeking up at him through my fringe of lashes. His smile was marvelous and slightly familiar. I could lose myself in a smile like that.

"Next week, the guys and I are hitting the slopes. I would like to cordially invite you to join us."

I giggled. "Well, how could I say no to a cordial invitation?"

He smiled back.

"Meet us in the lobby at eight Friday morning. And dress warm."

CHAPTER 8

I arrived at seven, like the over-eager dumbass I was. Of course, that meant I had to sit around awkwardly in the lobby until the boys arrived, making small talk with the bellhop.

Jared always came over to talk to me. No matter where I was, what I was doing, or whom I was with, he would find an excuse to sidle up beside me and start up a conversation.

I wouldn't consider him a friend, more of an acquaintance, but he seemed to want to become closer. If anything, he always asked me to go out to dinner with him.

Was that how friendships began? Should I take him up on his offer now that I was branching out, putting myself out there? Joining the whole "friend world"?

A growl interrupted my musings. A literal growl.

Jared looked up, startled, at the hulking figure towering over us.

I let out a heavy sigh.

"Hello, Callie dearest. What can I do for you?"

He grunted something unintelligible, continuing to glare daggers at Jared. The bellboy noticeably gulped.

Huh. Did Calax not want me to make more friends?

"Jared was just asking me if I wanted to go to dinner with him," I explained, remembering how only last week I attended lunch with him and his friends. Friends go to restaurants together, right?

So why did Calax look as if he couldn't decide if he wanted to vomit or punch Jared?

As if he felt my gaze on him, Calax turned towards me with a resigned expression.

"Do you want to go out with him?" he asked.

Huh?

"Well, I decided I needed to do the whole friendship thing. You know, friendship bracelets and the whole shebang. That's how I became friends with you guys... through food. Or at least, the rest of the guys. You're still my nemesis."

Both Jared and Calax appeared confused by my answer.

"Yes, but what he's asking is if you want to go to dinner as more than friends," Calax explained, which in turn, made *me* confused.

"Like as a sister? Because Declan made it clear last night that I couldn't be you guys' sister."

At my confession, Calax snorted, the grumpy expression leaving his face to be replaced with amusement.

"Princess!" a deep voice called from behind me. Before I could turn around, I was picked up and spun in a circle.

"Put me down!" I said, laughing. Ronan obediently placed me on my feet, eyes surveying my face. They darkened as they took in the bruises, only slightly better than they were a week ago when I'd last seen Declan. Gratefully, he didn't say anything, only brushed his thumb along my cheekbone. I imagined Declan had told them everything. I wasn't mad, mainly because I would've told any of the guys if they'd asked. Friendship included trust after all. Besides, it was only a body. And bodies were made to be broken and healed.

"Hello, Kitten," Ryder said, shifting his body to maneuver himself between me and Ronan. Ronan glared but backed away. "Did you dream about me?"

"Oh yeah. Woke up screaming too. Worst nightmare I had in months."

"That's my girl." He gave me a side hug, then allowed Asher to pull me away.

His words were quiet, meant only for me. "How are you feeling?"

"A little sore," I whispered back. "But I took some painkillers this morning, and they're starting to kick in." My arms were red and splotchy, the residual scarring of third-degree burns. Not horrible, and they no longer hurt as bad as they once did. The bruises looked worse than they felt.

He nodded his head and gave me a stern look.

"Let us know if you need to take a break or if we're moving too fast. I don't want you to feel that you need to hide your pain from us. We want you comfortable."

"I know, Ashy," I said, pinching his cheeks. He swatted my hand away, but a dusting of pink appeared on his cheekbones. It still pleased me that I could embarrass Mr. Gorgeous.

Declan gave me a nod in greeting, and Tam muttered a "hey" before looking down. I really wanted to learn more about the shy boy. He was the same person who'd spoken so dogmatically when he thought I wasn't listening. Who *was* Tamson...?

"Excuse me, Tam?" He glanced up, shocked at being addressed directly. "What's your last name?"

"My what?"

"Your last name."

He gaped at me as if he didn't know how to respond to the simple question. Seriously, these boys were so strange at times.

"Uh...Jameston," he admitted at last. Smiling triumphantly, I turned back to my inner musings.

Who was Tamson Jameston?

"Sweetheart," Asher said. "You said that aloud."

I risked a glance at Tamson to see the boy blushing furiously. Oops.

"I'm sorry," I said to Tam. "I didn't mean to embarrass you."

"It's okay," he mumbled, but the red refused to leave his cheeks. I felt awful. I wasn't an expert, but I was pretty sure embarrassing someone wasn't the best way to begin a friendship. Tamson seemed so innocent compared to even Asher, so naïve.

"Who's your friend?" Ryder asked. I turned to see his eyes zeroed in on Jared. The poor boy looked as if he wanted to shit his pants at the attention. I didn't blame him. The guys were big.

"He was asking our Addie out for dinner," Calax said, smirking. "She was debating on whether or not she should say yes. After all, our friendship started with food."

I couldn't understand what they found so funny. Did we or did we not eat food—well, order food before the stupid earthquake—to begin this unconventional relationship?

"She wants to become his sister," Calax continued.

Ryder was grinning ear to ear now.

"Was that what you intended?" he asked the smaller boy. "For her to become like your sister?"

Ronan barked a laugh, though he tried to conceal it with his hand. I elbowed him in the stomach, and he flicked my head in retaliation.

"I just thought it would be a good idea to make some new friends, especially since Declan said I can't be the sister to your group of brothers," I snapped, offended.

All the boys began chuckling now. Even Tam had a slight smile on his face.

"Is that why you asked her to dinner?" Ronan asked Jared. "For the friendship?"

I really didn't understand why it was so funny.

Laugh it up, bastards. Laugh it up.

Asher turned towards me, a brilliant smile lighting his face.

"I love it when you speak your thoughts. It's entertaining."

"Well, right now my thoughts are saying that you guys are all assholes!"

"At least that's better than being your brother," Ryder said, chuckling. Without sparing Jared a second glance, he stepped in front of him, effectively excluding him from the conversation.

Well, that was rude.

"We're sorry, sweetheart. We're not trying to be rude. It's just kind of funny… Okay, look. The boy isn't asking you out to become your brother, you do realize that, right?" Asher said.

When I looked at him blankly, he offered me a soft smile. "He's asking you out on a date. You know, like a boy and a girl going out, getting to know one another, then maybe becoming boyfriend and girlfriend."

He was…? Oh.

Oh.

I felt like such an idiot.

"If you like him like that, then ignore these big assholes and go on a date with him," Asher continued, ignoring the grumbling his assertion created. "If you don't, it's best not to lead him on."

Well, that was a no-brainer. I didn't date. Ever. Jared was sweet and all, and he might be considered handsome by some, but he wasn't for me. Even if I did decide I wanted to date, he didn't cause my heart to pound inside of my chest or my hands to sweat with nerves. We didn't talk naturally with one another, and he didn't cause butterflies to flutter throughout my stomach. I may be oblivious, but I knew what I felt for him wasn't strong enough to take that leap. Hell, I'd even been wavering on whether I wanted to be his friend.

My answer must've been evident on my face, because Jared walked away without allowing me to explain. It made me feel like shit.

"It's better you let him know now," Asher reassured me.

A new thought occurred to me, and I glanced at the boys with wide eyes.

"Does that mean we're on a date?"

Calax's eyes seemed to bulge out of his head. The rest of the guys looked equally perplexed.

"Huh?" Ronan finally said.

"Well, I'm a girl, and you guys are guys. We're hanging out, getting to know one another. And Declan already said I couldn't be your sister."

It made perfect sense in my mind.

"What? I...um..." Ryder sputtered. It almost looked as if he was blushing. "Let's go to the slopes!"

Before I could question his odd behavior, Declan and Calax each reached for one of my hands and practically dragged me out the door.

"Don't tell me you're afraid of heights?" Ryder taunted as the ski lift propelled us over the gleaming mountaintop. The snow glistened in the waning sunlight like tiny diamonds. It was glorious.

"Don't try to project your insecurities onto me," I said with a huff, shoving at his shoulder. The lift rocked unsteadily with the movement, and I laughed when Ryder's face paled.

He quickly schooled his expression.

"You're the one who didn't want to ride up," he countered. I had no argument for that—he was right. Granted, my reasons were different than what he assumed, but it was true that I'd argued profusely against taking the ski lift.

Why couldn't we stay on the ground like normal humans?

"I'm not scared of heights," I insisted again.

"Whatever you say, Kitten."

Smirking, I unclenched my hand that held a previously made snowball and pelted him in the face. I had the pleasure of seeing his expression turn incredulous as he glanced from me, to the melted snowball that now dripped down his chin, and back to me again.

I nearly died of laughter.

All at once, his expression sharpened with something I would almost refer to as wicked. A devious smile stretched across his face.

"Revenge, my little kitten. Karma's a bitch."

"Oh, I'm so scared," I mocked. "I'm shaking in my winter boots."

He continued to smile at me, and I knew that death was coming for me. It was so worth it.

The swaying cart stopped at the top of the mountain, and an overly helpful attendant practically carried me off. He must've recognized me as the owner's daughter. At the very least, the other skiers did not get offered foot massages.

Ryder was shaking with laughter by the time I politely excused myself from the enthusiastic young man.

"Don't even," I snapped as soon as he opened his mouth. I leaned against a wood pillar, my puffy coat restricting my arm movements. I meant to cross them over my chest, but I settled for awkwardly placing my hands in my armpits when I realized the coat wouldn't extend further. Ryder noticed my dilemma and nearly fell over in laughter.

Good. I hope he falls down the mountain and lands on his head.

I continued to glare at him as the rest of the boys arrived. My eyes flicked towards Tam immediately, noting his skin was tinged with a grayish sheen. I winced in sympathy.

"What's so funny?" Ronan asked, sidling up beside me and linking our arms. The movement was awkward, for our long skis prevented us from getting too close together.

"Ryder's being a dick," I said simply. When Ryder chuckled, I reached down, grabbed a snowball, and threw it at his face. The impact took him by surprise— though really, he should've expected that from me by now—and he stumbled over his skis. I smiled in satisfaction as he collapsed in an undignified heap onto the snow.

"Aww. Did little Ryder fall over his little skis?" I cooed in a baby voice.

"You do realize that I have to get you back twice now. To keep things even, of course. Don't think because you're a girl I'm going to go easy on you."

"I'm all about equality," I said in a singsong tone. "I'd like to see you try and take me down…RyRy."

His expression froze at the nickname, and Ronan snorted beside me. Calax flashed me a tiny grin, though he was eyeing his friend with an unreadable expression.

Ryder staggered to his feet, and I was only slightly disappointed when he didn't fall back down.

"I'll have you know—"

"Ryder!" a familiar voice screeched. Dear lord, that voice sounded like a dying bird giving anal while simultaneously taking a shit.

It took me a moment to remember the name that belonged with the voice, though my mental self often compared myself to her. And found me lacking.

Elena.

Looking as fresh and perky as she had before at my pool.

With her damn fake tits…

"You seem to have an unhealthy obsession with her breasts," Asher whispered from beside me. "Care to fill me in?"

He spoke softly enough that the other boys were oblivious to our conversation. Their eyes were instead fixated on Elena with varying degrees of annoyance.

"She makes me feel self-conscious," I whispered back, my hands instinctively touching one of my boobs. "Do you think I have nice tits?"

Asher groaned, pink smearing his cheekbones.

"Sweetheart, that is one question you cannot ask a man."

"But I thought we were friends?" I said, confused. "And friends talk about boobs and periods and stuff like that. Don't bother denying it. I saw it on Netflix."

Asher let out a pained grunt.

"That's not the way it works."

Ugh. I was already failing at the whole friendship thing. Note to self—don't talk about vaginas and boobs around males. Apparently, that's a no-no.

"I just wanted to check on my boys after the earthquake. Are you guys all okay?" Elena asked, eyes flashing from face to face with something akin to worry. Declan rolled his eyes, but it was Ronan who spoke.

"We're fine, Elena. And we're not your guys."

Her guys? Hmmm. Interesting.

Her face fell marginally before it was quickly replaced by a gorgeous smile.

"Okay, well, I just wanted to check up on you and remind you that my room is only a couple doors down." Her voice dropped, going quiet. "I miss you guys."

When none of the boys responded, Elena's face fell once again. It was then that she noticed me, dressed in my marshmallow suit behind Calax's broad shoulder. I lifted a hand that held one of the ski poles in an awkward wave. She glared back at me.

Rude.

"I see you have a new whore to share between you," she snapped. Calax's shoulders turned tense in front of me, and I bristled.

"I'll have you know that I am not a whore. I am their sister that isn't really a sister but a friend that apparently can't talk about boobs and vaginas. I think that makes me a…brother? Well, I would make a horrible brother, so they probably don't want me to be that either. Maybe I can—"

Declan's hand covering my mouth interrupted me. Apparently, Elena had left in the midst of my rant.

Wouldn't even let me finish my sentence. So rude.

"Sooo…" I drawled in my cutesy voice. "What was that about?"

The boys glanced at one another, blushed, and then immediately began discussing which hill they were going to conquer.

"Oh, hell no!" I said, laughing. "We are so having this conversation."

When the idiots refused to look at me, understanding clicked into place.

"Holy shit! Did you guys share her?"

Numerous "shhhs" were the response to my question.

"You did, didn't you? Was it serious? Did you have a calendar? This is freaking hilarious!"

"No!" Ryder hissed. "I mean, yes, but no. It wasn't a relationship or anything. It was just…"

"Sex?" I offered, pleased when the great Ryder turned flaming red.

"Look," Ronan cut in, "she was one of the girls we had…relations with."

"One?" I said. "You shared more than one?"

I was probably more intrigued than I should've been. But, hey, weren't friends supposed to be interested in the relationship of their other friends? Maybe this could be my redeemer for the whole boob thing with Asher.

"We wanted multiple partners so we didn't get attached," Declan signed. *"And so they wouldn't get attached to us."*

"Did it work?"

"Obviously not with Elena," Asher said with a smirk. "She fell in love with those idiots but was too blind to see the feeling was only one-sided. She thought she could be the one to tame the beasts, so to speak. To make the wild boys settle down."

I felt a pang of sympathy for Elena. Not empathy, for I'd never been in love, but a deep sense of kinship with the girl. How awful would it be to love someone and to know that they wouldn't love you back?

"Did you all share her?" I asked, glancing from face to face. From Calax's brooding expression, Declan's impassive one, Ryder's sultry grin, the twinkle in Ronan's eyes, the blush permanently staining Tam's face, to Asher's amused smirk.

"It started off with just Ryder, Tam, and me," Ronan admitted, somewhat reluctantly. My eyes widened in shock. Ronan and Ryder, I could expect, but Tam?

Apparently, the shy boy had a kinky side.

"Asher, as I said before, is our sweet, pure prince. He never wanted to involve himself in such activities with us peasants," Ryder added. He didn't sound as embarrassed anymore, as if he understood I wasn't judging him.

"Calax, of course, set his sights on only one girl," Ronan said, spiking my curiosity. Who was the mysterious girl that could capture the giant man's attention? "And Declan only joined the...*rotation*...after he broke up with his girlfriend."

I turned towards the man in question after hearing that. It was time for me to put my friend-cap on and kick some ass. Or save some ass. Or get him some ass. It was time for me to behave like a guy...like a sister that wasn't a sister but wasn't a brother. I could be a guy, couldn't I? All angsty and broody and shit. And what did guys do in this type of situation? Threaten.

"Is it the whole 'that bitch, how dare she' type of scenario, or was the breakup amicable? Do I need to drive to her house, serenade her, and hand-feed her chocolates for you to win her back? Because I totally will. Just let me know if I need to bitch slap a ho, bury a body, or write a two-hour musical."

The boys stared at me in a stunned silence before Ronan put his arm around me.

"Oh, Addie, everybody needs someone like you in their life."

CHAPTER 9

The resort looked…small.

From my perch on top of the steep hill, the once magnificent building appeared rather dingy and insignificant. Even the people hustling to and from the various structures resembled nothing more than ants. Faces blended together, colors seemed muted, and words were inarticulate.

Was that all I was? Something so small and insignificant that, from afar, I was barely noticeable?

"What are you thinking about?" Calax grunted out from beside me. He looked intimidating in his black winter coat and black hat. He'd always been enormous, but with the added fluff, he looked particularly terrifying. I wanted to point out that he resembled a burnt marshmallow, but I figured that I liked my limbs intact. The metal bulb in his eyebrow glinted in the sunlight.

"About the apparent insignificancy of our lives. How we're just one of billions of people attempting to put our mark on the world. How, in a couple hundred years, we're all going to be forgotten."

Ryder let out a low whistle from behind me.

"Damn, girl, and here I was, just thinking about what we're going to eat for lunch."

I snorted and turned towards the immense slope. It looked especially menacing from this angle, though I supposed that was the point with a name like Death Cross. I could see a few tire tracks in the snow despite the early hour. One of them appeared to swivel off course and into a tree.

Ouch.

Turning my back to the hill, I watched the guys discuss turns. I'd gone down that slope hundreds of times before. Hell, I'd even invented an original pathway—through two trees, over a precariously positioned rock, and a sharp turn to avoid face planting into an icy river. But…

"I'm going to the bunny slope," I declared, referring to the diminutive hill a short ski away. The slope was designed for children and beginners.

The boys' faces showed disbelief.

"Don't be a chicken, Addie," Calax said.

"Come on! It'll be fun!" Ryder pleaded.

I rolled my eyes at their antics.

"Since Tam's my current favorite, he gets to accompany me."

That, of course, set off a chorus of rejections.

"Don't argue with me," I said, skiing towards Tamson and linking my arm with his. He wavered under my added weight, nearly toppling into the snowbank. I immediately released him.

"We'll meet you back at the lobby in an hour! And then you boys can buy your sister that isn't a sister some coffee!"

The boys chuckled and waved me away, though they all seemed slightly disappointed.

I skied alongside Tam in silence, arriving at the small hill situated nearby a cluster of trees. With this positioning, you had to ski through the forest to arrive at the hill, but it also assured the skier that she wouldn't hit any trees when descending.

"Um...Addie?" Tam asked. I turned to smile at him, pushing with my sticks—I'd never learned the actual name of them—to glide down the hill. The movement felt natural, an extension of my own feet.

Upon reaching the bottom of the hill, I smiled up at Tam with contentment. He remained at the top, hands clenched over his own poles as he surveyed me.

Moving my skis into a V, I climbed back up the hill and skied towards Tam.

"You're obviously not a novice," Tam pointed out. "So why didn't you want to ski down the big hill with the others?"

I rolled my eyes.

"Because of you, of course."

"Me?" His eyes widened in disbelief.

"I saw your face when you were on the ski lift. You looked terrified. And then, when you were skiing towards the first hill, you looked more awkward than a baby penguin on steroids. No offense. Why didn't you tell your friends that you don't know how to ski?"

He continued to stare at me with the same incredulous expression, and I feared I had overstepped my friendship boundary. Maybe it wasn't appropriate for me to make such an assumption. Maybe I should've pushed him down the hill and made him take that leap of faith.

"Look," I said quickly. "I'm sorry if I did something I shouldn't have. You just looked scared, and I knew that you would never admit to the guys you didn't want to ski down that hill. I just didn't want you to be uncomfortable."

I shifted uneasily from ski to ski. *Gah.* Why was this apologizing thing so hard?

After a moment, Tamson shook his head with a timid smile on his face.

"I'm not mad. I'm actually grateful." He chuckled, a surprisingly seductive sound. "I guess I was too embarrassed to admit to the guys that I didn't know how to ski."

He blushed at the confession, though it could've been because of the cold. Yeah. It was totally because of the cold—said no one ever.

"Why?" I asked.

"Why what?"

"Why would you be embarrassed?"

At that, an almost exasperated expression contorted his features.

"Because they're…them. And I'm me."

"And?"

"They're all charming and athletic and outgoing," he admitted, his tone bitter. "And I'm not."

I let out a sigh.

"Why does it matter what they are? You don't have to pretend to be something you're not to remain their friend. Is that what this is about? You're afraid that you're going to lose them as friends?"

Tam's cheeks grew as red as his coat, and he plopped himself on the ground. His skis stuck out at unnatural angles in front of him.

"No. I mean, I know they wouldn't ditch me. But…it's hard, you know? Hating who you are."

I sat down beside him, maneuvering my skis so I didn't stab him in the eye. Without speaking, I unhooked my boots from the skis and then reached for his with a question in my eyes. He nodded in answer, and I began to remove his skis.

"I understand why you said what you said, but you're wrong, though." I removed his left ski, gently setting it to the side, before crossing over his legs to detach the right one.

"Just because you're not into the same things as your friends doesn't make you wrong or less than. Just different. I don't know you that well, Tam, but from what I see, you're a pretty great guy."

Tam's eyes remained fixed on his zipper as he began to fidget with it. Zip up. Zip down. Zip up. Zip down.

"Tell me, what do you like to do?"

He ducked his head down, that adorable blush rising to his cheeks yet again.

"I like to read."

I smiled conspiratorially. "So do I."

"And play video games."

"So do I."

"And…" He trailed off, and I nudged him with my shoulder.

"Don't be embarrassed. You can tell me."

"I like MMA."

"Mixed martial arts?" I asked in disbelief. I surveyed his lanky form, hidden behind layers of clothing, to his arresting green eyes. I wouldn't have pegged him for a fighter, but then again, how much did I really know about any of the boys? Even Calax, my enemy for numerous years?

I knew absolutely nothing about MMA fighting, but I decided, right then and there, that I would research everything I could about the sport.

"Are you good?" I asked eagerly. Now that he admitted it, I could totally see him kicking ass. Oh yeah. My little Tam had a fire in him.

Cheeks burning, Tam muttered, "I'm okay."

"Do you compete in comps?" I asked.

"I used to. I stopped after arriving at Highwood Prep."

"Why?" Before Tamson could respond, a snowball materialized out of nowhere and hit me in the face. I winced at the cold sting, and Tam jumped to his feet to protect me.

Of course, I didn't need his protection, mostly since I recognized that semi-hysterical laughter.

"You know I'm just going to get you back, RyRy," I said, turning towards the snowball perpetrator. He smoothly skied out of the forest, Declan right behind him.

"You can't get me back for me getting you back," he protested.

"Addie can do whatever she wants to do," Asher pointed out. "And if that means revenge, then more power to her."

I smirked as the boys approached.

"Maybe I'll get Calax to hold you down while I attack you. I wonder how long it would take you to become hypothermic."

Calax chuckled, and Ryder pouted.

"No fair! He's too heavy."

I gasped in mock outrage.

"Callie! I think Ryder just called you fat. That deserves a solid sitting on, don't you think?"

"If it's you sitting on me, I think we have a deal." Ryder waggled his eyebrows suggestively at me. Apparently, those were the words that unleashed the beast. Calax lunged towards Ryder.

"Wait!" I screamed, and the boys all froze, Ryder cowering and Calax in midstep. Once I was sure I had their attention, I gestured towards their feet. "At least take the skis off. My god, if we're going to fight, we at least should be classy about it."

The boys exchanged a glance, shrugged, and all began removing their skis, tossing them to the side.

Chaos erupted. Calax tackled Ryder, and Ronan leaped forward to help his fallen comrade. I was beginning to realize that R squared were almost always a team.

Declan joined the fray by jumping on top of Ronan and pelting him in the face with snowballs.

Asher and Tam both stayed beside me, one on either side.

"Those boys are crazy," I mused, watching Ryder shove Calax's face repeatedly into a mound of snow.

Tam and Asher exchanged mischievous grins.

"At least they're not fighting with actual bullets this time," Asher pointed out.

"That's actually a good idea!" I said, jumping up and down. "Not the bullets thing, but the shooting each other part."

"I never said anything—"

"We should go paintballing!" I squealed. My voice was loud enough to garner the attention of the four boys tangled up in the snow—and not the sexy tangled up either, though that would've been really hot.

Bad Addie. Bad.

"Have you ever gone?" Ronan asked, shaking snow out of his hair.

"Nope," I said, popping the P. "But I want to! And the teams can be all of us versus Calax!"

"Hey!" the giant in question snapped, gaze scathing. I noticed that he had a small bruise on his cheekbone, and I instinctively stepped forward to brush my gloved hand against it. He shivered under my touch.

"Are you cold?" I asked, concerned. He was two hundred pounds of pure muscle, wearing a bulky coat and more cumbersome gloves. How could a man like him be cold?

Surprisingly, it was Asher that snorted from behind me.

"He's not cold, sweetheart."

"Shut the fuck up, Ashley!"

"Language, Callie!"

I pinched Calax's cheek, and he smiled at me sheepishly.

"What are you idiots doing here, anyway? Too chicken to go down the Devil's Anal?" I directed that last taunt at Ryder.

"For one, I'm pretty sure that's not the name, though I do like your name better. Secondly, we all agreed that we much rather hang out with you than the snobs over at the hill. Nobody can compare to your beauty." He practically sang the last line, his lilting voice causing goosebumps to erupt over my arms.

Rolling my eyes, I stuck my tongue out at him.

"You're still so fucking cheesy, RyRy."

"Admit it. It's endearing."

"In the want-to-stab-you-in-the-nuts kind of way," I muttered. Turning towards the rest of the boys, I clapped my hands together in glee. I probably looked like a young schoolgirl instigating a game of tag on the playground, but dammit, I was excited. I'd never had people want to spend time with me, much less go out of their way for it. The feeling was exhilarating.

"What are we standing around for? Get your damn skis on, and let's have an adventure!"

❧

BY THE TIME we made it back to the lodge, sweat, dirt, and water from melted snow covered us all. Ryder, the bastard, felt the need to sit on me while pouring snow down my jacket. Calax intervened, and now Ryder was huddled near the fire, teeth chattering as he cursed my family and me.

"Dammit, woman! My balls are going to fall off! They're blue! How am I supposed to function with blue balls! They're little ball icicles now!"

My legs curling up underneath me, I rolled my eyes at Ryder's usual theatrics.

"Why am I getting the blame? I believe it was Callie that did the ball bluing."

Asher's face turned deep in thought.

"That sounded really sexual."

"Shut up, Ashy!" Ryder snapped. It seemed as if the boys were adopting my nicknames. At least the ones I said aloud. I didn't know how I'd have felt if they knew I referred to them as Gorgeous or Sexy or Grumpy in my head. "But shit, Addie! Don't rile Calax up like that!"

"You're fine," I said. "It's not like you're using your junk anyway."

Asher choked on his hot chocolate, and Ryder narrowed his eyes at me.

"Take that back, Kitten."

"Make me, Blue Balls."

"What the fuck did I miss?" Calax asked, reappearing from the small coffee shop inside the resort. When he saw my expression, he relinquished the second cup of coffee he'd ordered into my hand. Yum. He sipped from his own cup, his eyes narrowed at me over the rim. Black coffee, of course, just like his soul.

And no. I didn't have a flare for dramatics. Sheesh.

"Ryder has blue balls," Asher supplied, amused.

"They've turned into icicles now," he whined.

"At least they're prime for licking," I pointed out helpfully. All of the guys froze. "What? What did I say now?"

I seriously needed a rule book, something like *The Acceptable Words and Phrases to Use Around Your Guy Friends*. Maybe they should teach a class or something.

Who needs to learn about how to find X when you can learn how not to be a dick towards one another? Or when it's apparently appropriate to say "dick" around the male population?

"Why y'all so quiet?" Ronan asked as he walked up, Declan and Tamson following behind him like silent shadows. Tamson offered me a small smile, and I accepted it greedily. I got the distinct feeling that his smiles were few and far between.

"I don't know what their deal is," I said when it became apparent none of the idiots were going to talk. Ryder, still in front of the fireplace, shifted uncomfortably. When he caught my gaze, he quickly turned his body towards the blistering flames, neck turning red.

What the...?

"Ryder was talking about how his balls were icicles, and all I said was that they were now good to lick."

Silence.

Tam's cheeks were a flaming red, though I wasn't necessarily surprised. He was almost always red. What *did* surprise me, though, was the bulge I could see in the front of his pants. In the front of all their pants.

As if...

I replayed my words in my head. Licking icicles. Was there anything dirty with that? Was that slang for the nasty?

Licking icicle balls.

Licking...balls.

Well, shit.

"Shit," I repeated aloud. "Totally didn't mean to say that. Well I did, but I just didn't realize how sexual it would be. Oops. Is that why you guys are all getting boners? Are you thinking about me licking your balls?"

"Damn it, Addie!" Calax growled out before storming away. Declan and Ronan quickly followed him.

"Where are they going?" I asked, slightly hurt at their abrupt exit.

"They're...um...taking care of business," Asher said. He rubbed at his neck, obviously uncomfortable with this whole conversation. Of course, I knew what he meant by that—I wasn't a complete idiot, just a kind of idiot—but I wanted to tease them a while longer. Actually, I just wanted to tease Ryder. It was a shame that sweet Asher and shy Tam had to get caught in the crossfire.

"What do you mean by that?" I asked innocently.

Ryder, Asher, and Tam all exchanged a look.

"I need to, uh, go," Tam said before bolting towards the hallway. One down, two to go.

"What business?" I continued. "Like schoolwork?"

"Not that type of business, sweetheart." Asher's voice sounded strained.

"So? Are you guys going to explain?"

Again, the two boys exchanged an unreadable expression. Ryder shook his head in desperation, and Asher's eyes went wide with panic.

"Um..."

I burst into laughter, unable to handle their stricken expressions.

"I'm just fucking with you," I said, once I was finally able to breathe. Then, in a more serious voice, I added, "They're going back out to ski, correct?"

I, once again, had the pleasure of seeing two ashen faces. When I began giggling, Ryder leaned forward to whack my arm.

"You're such a little shit!"

"Your dick's a little shit," I retorted, because yeah, I was totally original.

"What the hell?" Asher said abruptly. I turned towards him in surprise, but he wasn't looking at me. His attention was on his phone.

"What?" Ryder asked, all traces of teasing vanishing from his handsome face.

"I just got a weather alert. There's a tornado warning."

"And that's a big deal because...?" Ryder asked.

"You don't understand. There's a tornado warning *here*. Right now. Only a few miles away from this resort."

"What the hell?" I exclaimed, jumping from my seat and running to peer over his shoulder. Sure enough, the weather station detailed a tornado that had been spotted only a couple miles from our location. "How is that even possible?"

"Does it matter? We need to get low. Does the resort have a basement?"

"Yes," Asher and I answered immediately.

"It's where the employees' breakroom is," Asher explained.

"Here!" I reached into my pocket and grabbed a key ring. Shuffling through the numerous keys, I settled on a small bronze one. "This key can be used in the elevator to head to the basement. Grab your friends and get down."

As I spoke, I began to shuffle away.

"What about... Where the hell are you going?"

"I'm going to go door to door and get everyone to safety," I said. "And then I need to find my parents."

CHAPTER 10

"Addie, wait!" Ryder reached for my arm. Not constricting, but as if he was reminding me that he was there.

"You need to get down to the basement," Asher said from my other side. I looked between the two boys with bemusement.

"I need to make sure everyone gets somewhere safe. Not many people have weather alerts on their phones, and even if they did, they wouldn't believe that a tornado is heading towards us. Hell, I barely even believe it."

As I spoke, I quickened my pace. I reached the front desk at my last word.

"Addie?" a young man, whose name regularly escaped me, asked with a raised eyebrow. He glanced between the two men gripping each of my arms and me. His eyebrows furrowed together with concern. "Are you all right?"

"There's a tornado in the area. Can you set an alarm or make an announcement to get everyone to the first floor?" I knew the safest place would be the basement—it was below ground and had numerous rooms with no windows—yet employees were the ones with the key to access that level, and only certain ones at that. I doubted even Asher had a key.

"Are you sure?" the employee asked in disbelief. I resisted the urge to slug him.

"I'm pretty damn positive based on the weather alert," I said with a huff. "Can you make an announcement or not?"

He still eyed me with skepticism, but he eventually nodded.

"Yeah, I can make an announcement over the intercom."

"Thank you," I said stiffly. I knew I was being a bitch, but I didn't care. Those seconds he spent arguing with me were precious seconds taken away from people finding shelter. Now how was I going to communicate with the people hitting the slopes? Hmmm…

"Now that you have that taken care of, let's go to the basement," Ryder said, grabbing my arm once again. He attempted to drag me towards the elevator, but I dug my heels into the carpet.

"What about the people outside? And the other boys? And my parents?"

"It looks as if security is handling the people outside." Asher nodded his head towards a group of men heading towards the resort's doors. They looked far too casual for the disaster that was about to occur if the tornado struck here. The bastards didn't believe me!

I was tempted to shove the phone in their snotty faces or maybe just hit them repeatedly until they gained common sense.

"I'm not sure that's the best idea," Asher mused. "We kind of need them conscious to spread the word."

"Get out of my head!" I snapped, slightly irritated. He snorted.

"Quit speaking aloud."

Damn him and his logic.

"I texted the guys," Ryder broke in. "They're meeting us here."

"They're meeting you here," I corrected. "I need to go find my parents."

The boys both looked at me as if I was insane. Well, more insane than usual because I'm pretty sure they already knew I was a few screws short.

"W-Why?" Ryder sputtered.

"Because they're my parents, and they're too stupid to move without me pushing them."

And them pushing me back, I thought but didn't say.

"Why do you even bother with them?" Asher asked, voice rising with disbelief. I shrugged. I didn't quite understand it myself, so I knew it was pointless to try and explain.

"They're my parents," I admitted at last. "The egg and sperm donor that made me into being. Sure, they're emotionally and physically abusive assholes, but I wouldn't be who I am today without them."

Their faces darkened at my words, but they didn't refute my claim. Mom and Dad may not have been family, but they were blood. That had to count for something, right?

Then why did the thought of finding them make my skin crawl?

I couldn't decide if that made me a horrible person or a smart one.

We walked down the hallway, Ryder and Asher on either side of me.

"Where are the others?" I heard Ryder ask Asher.

"I told them to meet me by the elevator," he responded. "If we're not there in ten minutes, I told them to just go without us."

Ryder snorted.

"Do you think Calax will listen?"

"Not likely."

"You know," I began conversationally, sidestepping a family that was hurrying towards the staircase. "You guys don't have to come with me."

Asher smirked, and Ryder actually began to laugh. Elbowing me in the stomach gently, Ryder said, "Not happening, Kitten."

"We already said that we adopted you," Asher added.

"But not as a sister," I pointed out. The two boys exchanged a quick glance—a bro glance, I surmised. It was impossible for me to decipher.

"Not as a sister," Ryder agreed at last. We reached a fork in the hall, and I led the guys to the right, through a door, and into the kitchen.

For a moment, I stood there, stunned. This was the same kitchen that, only days before, I had been tortured in, to my utter mortification. And that was what I felt—embarrassment and something akin to shame. These, I realized, were not natural emotions one should experience when dealing with abuse. I felt sick at the direction of my thoughts. I had grown so used to the abuse, the torture, that it had become nothing but second nature. It was odd for a day to go by where someone didn't attack me, either emotionally or physically. Instead of anger or sadness that one would expect, I felt nothing but a deep sense of failure. It had been my fault, it always was, and it always would be.

Asher, behind me, let out a gruff sound. It was apparent that he, too, was remembering that day.

"Why are we here?" Ryder asked with disdain. His eyes flickered towards the stovetop, as if he was visualizing my body erupting into flames on the surface. His brow furrowed, and he quickly looked away, as if he was in physical pain.

"I think my parents had a meeting today in the dining room," I explained, taking stock of the abandoned kitchen. A pound of lettuce was left unattended on a cutting board, and smoke was beginning to curl from the oven. The crew had obviously left in a hurry.

Almost absently, I turned off the oven. The last thing we needed was a fire on top of a tornado.

"At least everyone was smart enough to leave and get to lower grounds," Asher mused, obviously coming to the same conclusion I had.

"Hopefully, my parents were some of those smart people," I said, though I severely doubted it. Knowing my folks, they would be sitting in the dining room, alone, screaming for waiters that would never come. My parents were idiots. Smart idiots, but idiots. And not smart. But smart. But also kind of dumb. Could someone be a smart, dumb idiot? Or maybe a dumb smart—

"Focus, Addie," Ryder chided. I mentally cursed myself. Deciding whether or not my parents were dumb or smart was not productive in our current predicament.

"I'm trying, but I—"

My next comment was cut off by a two-hundred-pound body jumping on mine. Okay, I know what you're thinking. Again, Addie? Because, yes, I was being tackled to the ground, and no, it wasn't in a sexy kind of way. I would consider it more like the piss-your-pants-because-there's-a-guy-attacking-me way.

I screamed, lifting my hands to protect my face.

Why did this always happen to me?

I recognized the man as a chef, though I couldn't recall his name. His bulky body was visible through his tattered, bloodstained clothing. Dark veins marred his skin, as if he had some parasite crawling beneath the surface. The skin itself flapped with each of his movements, not properly connected to his bones, and his eyes glowed a vibrant red.

Before I could do anything, his body was ripped off me and pushed to the side.

"What the hell?" Ryder shouted, grappling with the heavier man. Chef screamed, a guttural sound, and tried ineffectively to bite at Ryder's face.

He was right. What the freaking hell?

Though Ryder was young, he was no match for the immense beast of the man. In a matter of seconds, Chef pinned Ryder underneath him.

Asher rushed forward and tackled Chef, a flurry of limbs and blood.

Me? I was frozen. Nothing seemed real. An almost surreal-like haze obscured my vision. Was I dreaming? Was this a nightmare?

Between my gasps of terror, one coherent thought spliced through my horror. Save them.

Almost mechanically, my hand closed on the handle of a pan. Yes, I know, a totally badass weapon. I probably should've grabbed one of the large knives that were still by the vegetables. I mean, that would've been smarter than a dumb pan, but my thoughts weren't on "which kitchen appliance would inflict the most pain." Nope, they were merely "fuck fuckity fuck" like a normal person.

I meant to aim for Chef's head, but my short stature restricted such a movement. Instead, the pan connected with his balls. Now how, you may ask, did I mix up a man's head with his manhood? That was a very interesting question, and it had an even better answer.

Which you will hear at a later time because, currently, I was meeting the wide-eyes of Ryder from where he had released the heavier man. He was panting, leaning against the kitchen counter with sweat beading across his forehead.

"Shit, Addie," he said, wincing in sympathy. His hand instinctively moved to cover his own balls, as if he was afraid my ball-clumsiness would lead to me hitting his. Did he have such little faith in me?

"It was kind of an accident," I muttered, slightly indignant. Whatever Ryder was going to say was interrupted by a rasping groan. Chef was ambling back to his feet, greasy hair matted down with blood and other unsavory substances. A pungent smell reached me as he took a step closer, hands outstretched. I raised my pan.

If that fucker wanted another swing to the penis, then I'd be more than happy to deliver.

Asher came from behind Chef, arms constricting around the other man's meaty neck. Chef buckled against his weight, but Asher held firm. It reminded me, vaguely, of a bull attempting to dislodge a rider. Chef's red, piercing eyes began to slowly close, as if he was incapable of keeping them open for a second longer. He slumped to the ground like a bag of rocks.

Asher and Ryder surrounded me immediately, each breathing heavily.

"Are you okay?" Asher asked between pants.

"I should be asking you that. All I did was hit him in the balls."

"Cheap shot," Ryder muttered, and I glared at him.

"Next time, I'll just allow him to eat your face off!" I was lying, obviously, but he didn't need to know that. I would never allow Ryder to lose his beautiful face. But a hand? He could survive with only one.

"We need to get down to the basement. Now," Asher said, grabbing at my arm. His fingernails dug into my sensitive flesh, but I barely even flinched. I was used to pain. I welcomed it.

"No!" I argued, wrenching my hand free. The attempt was futile, for Ryder merely grabbed my other arm and began pulling me in the direction we came from. "I need to find my parents and get them to safety."

"Something strange is going on," Ryder insisted. He ignored my protests as we moved down the now deserted hallway. I hoped that meant everybody had gotten to safety. I refused to think of the alternative.

The alternative being, hundreds upon hundreds of red-eyed, black veined zombies lurking through the resort. Was that what they were? Zombies?

No, that didn't seem right. There had been something resembling coherence in Chef's gaze, as well as Buttlicker's. It was hungry, almost feral, but it had most definitely still been human. I tried to recall the latest newscast, but my mind had been more focused on the inconsistent weather than on any strange viruses.

What the living hell was happening?

"That's what I would like to know," Asher muttered. He sounded uncharacteristically tense, and his muscles were held taut. For the first time since we'd started this mission, I reached for his hand and tugged him to a stop.

"Hey," I said, waiting until his eyes were on me. They were dimmer than usual, a mere reflection of his familiar vibrant gaze. "You have to understand that what happened with Chef wasn't your fault. He was going to kill us, and you merely defended yourself and us. Do you understand?" I didn't wait for him to answer. I understood all too well the pulls of self-pity. You could drown in it, bask in the sorrow as it formed an unbreakable barrier around you. I didn't want that for Asher. No, he was too gentle, too kind, to experience such a leaden, miserable feeling. If I could take some of the burden off his shoulders, then I would do so happily. "He's not dead, okay? He's only unconscious. He's sick, but he'll be fine. We'll send him to a doctor after the tornado dissipates, and everything will be okay."

I could tell he didn't fully believe me, but I didn't know what other words of comfort to offer him. Guilt speared my chest. It was my fault that Asher had been in the kitchen in the first place. The stubborn boy had chosen to follow me, despite my protests. If anyone should be blamed for what had happened with Chef, it should be me.

I didn't say any of that to Asher or Ryder. Instead, I squeezed the former's hand and led him farther down the hall, back towards the elevator.

I wasn't surprised to find the other boys waiting for us when we arrived. What were they, stupid? Why hadn't they gone downstairs?

"We were waiting for you," Declan signed in exasperation.

See? Idiots.

"We're not idiots," Calax grumbled.

Total idiots.

"Let's get down to the basement," Asher instructed. He touched my shoulder, urging me in the direction of the elevator. In retrospect, it probably wasn't the smartest idea to take an elevator when there was a tornado nearby, but we weren't thinking clearly. Could you blame us? We all just wanted to escape this hellhole as soon as possible.

Fortunately, we were able to descend to the bottom floor with minimal interruptions. I was pretty sure someone farted in the enclosed box, and I glared at Ronan, who was nearest to me. He quickly pointed an accusing finger in Calax's direction. Calax, of course, gave me a disapproving frown as if *I* was the one that had stunk up the elevator. Poor Declan, with his keen senses, looked as if he wanted to vomit as the smell assaulted his nose. He began cursing up a storm in sign language. I tried to nonchalantly hide myself in the background. They didn't need to know that the fart was mine.

Six sets of eyes turned to stare at me with varying degrees of shock.

"You tried to blame it on me?" Ronan asked, stunned.

"Addie," Ryder said, then tsked. "I didn't know you had it in you."

"Girls fart. Get over it."

"All that hot air has to go somewhere," Calax mused, and I gave him the finger. Jesus, you would think that they had never seen—smelled—a girl fart before. Of course, the only girl they'd introduced me to was Elena, and I was pretty sure there was only a stick up her ass. It made perfect sense that she had never pooped or farted or any of the above in her life.

The boys all chuckled, and I realized that I must've spoken my thoughts aloud. I also noticed that none of the guys contradicted my Elena theory.

Despite the brief lapse of tension, nobody spoke as we stepped out of the elevator. Calax and Ronan took point, with Declan and Ryder at my back. Asher and Tam walked on either side of me. Together, the boys formed a protective cage. I usually would've reprimanded them for treating me like I was a fragile little girl—hello, I was a ball whacking maniac—but I was too highly strung to say anything. I enjoyed the heat their combined bodies emitted, and for the first time in my life, I felt safe. It was an odd feeling to know that I had people fighting for me. I'd gone from having no one to having someone. *Six* someones.

I feared that they would abandon me once they realized what a mess I was. I knew the fear was irrational, a product of my depressing childhood, but it smothered me all the same.

The basement was a large assortment of rooms. The initial one we entered consisted of nothing more than supplies—a volleyball and net for the summer months, a collection of water equipment, and broken skis in need of repair. We walked through an archway and into a breakroom. It held a long table, a single microwave, and a time clock. I knew for a fact the resort had two breakrooms. The second one, and the one most commonly used, was on the lobby floor. Farther and farther, we walked through the maze-like basement, leaking pipes and moist walls causing the wood to become squishy. While there were no guests this deep, I spotted a few employees curled against a wall. Good. At least some people had gotten to safety.

One of the girls I recognized as Shannon, the hostess Ryder had rejected, and I gave her a small wave when our eyes met.

We finally stopped at a small room with minimal shelving and no windows. With a grunt, Calax handed me a hardcover book. He must've grabbed it from one of the other rooms. When I stared at him with a raised eyebrow, he rolled his eyes.

"To protect your head."

"I knew that." I totally didn't know that.

Calax distributed books and game board boxes to the other boys and then gestured towards the far wall. As I watched, transfixed, the boys sat facing the peach painted wall.

"What are you guys doing?" I asked.

"Didn't you ever have a tornado drill at your school?" Ryder questioned. "You grab something hard to cover your head, you go to a room with no windows, where no shit can fall on you, and you face the wall."

I didn't bother to point out that I had never been to an actual school before.

"But why the wall? That seems dumb."

"It's to... Just shut the fuck up and sit down."

I chuckled at Ryder's flustered answer but obediently sat crossed-legged beside him.

"Use the book to cover your head," Asher instructed. I frowned.

"What could possibly fall on my head?"

"Stop arguing," Calax muttered, and I couldn't help but chuckle at the giant beast of a man crouched in a fetal position with Candy Land balancing on his head. He glared at me, but a tiny smirk pulled at his lips. He found it as amusing as I did.

"So," I began conversationally. "How did your boner handling go?"

Beside me, Ryder sputtered.

"Boner handling?" he asked.

I pressed my forehead against the wall, allowing my eyes to flicker from face to face. While Ryder was on my right, Declan sat on my left. Calax was beside Declan, a crimson flush on his cheeks. I could've sworn these boys blushed more often than any girl I had ever met.

Granted, I'd only met like five girls, and I was only on a first-name basis with three of them—if you counted Elena, though she didn't even know my name.

"Boner," I repeated slowly, in case any of the guys were confused by the word. "You know, like when your dick—"

"We get it," Ronan said. Declan tapped my arm, and I turned my face towards him expectantly. Frowning, he raised an eyebrow at me, and I signed him our conversation.

His face paled, and he quickly turned towards the wall.

"First, I'm not allowed to talk about my breasts, and now, I'm not allowed to mention your boners?" I asked in disbelief.

"I'm just going to point out that our little Addie has had bare minimum human interaction," Ronan said, a smirk in his voice. To me, he said, "I take it you're not the most socially capable person?"

I scoffed. "I'm socially able to talk about dicks and stuff."

"Sweetheart..." Asher groaned. "You can't just... I mean...this is... Ugh! Does anyone want to take it from here?"

"No!" was the immediate response from the other five boys.

Ugh. Calax was such a dick.

"What?" the dick in question sputtered. "Why me?"

"Because you're my nemesis," I pointed out. "And I just felt like thinking of it."

There was a long pause.

"Not *your* dick," I hurried to explain, "but you *as* a dick."

"Are we ever going to hear the story of how you guys became enemies in the first place?" Asher asked. There was a laugh in his voice, and I reached over Ryder's head to slug him. I only felt moderately guilty for the action.

"Vicious," Ryder said with a smirk.

"I'm curious about that story too," Tam piped up. "What exactly happened?"

"Well," I began, stretching my taut muscles. My shirt unintentionally rode up with the movement, and I noticed both Ryder and Declan's eyes both zero in on the swath of skin exposed. Now, it was my turn to blush, and I quickly tried to compose my features into some semblance of control.

"Well?" Ryder pressed, knocking my knee with his own.

"I don't want to talk about myself anymore," I huffed. If there was one thing I didn't feel comfortable talking about, it was my first meeting with Calax. I could tell from the tightening of his features that Calax felt the same.

"Does our little princess have a secret with the big bad wolf?" Ronan cooed.

"He's more of an asshole than a wolf," I mused.

Calax grunted. "Why do you…? Okay, never mind. Moving on."

"Listen," I began hesitantly. I shifted from knee to knee, and Declan put a gentle hand on my arm to settle me. Realizing that I had his attention as well, I spoke aloud while simultaneously signing. "I'm sorry if I say stuff that's inappropriate or wrong or whatever. I've never…well…I never had friends before, guys or girls. My entire life, I've had no one. Sure, I have a spine made of steel *now*, but it was forged from countless battles I had to face alone. There was one point in my life where I was confined to my room with only my tutor as company. I don't know how to interact with people, especially guys. If I say something wrong or stupid, just tell me. My entire life experience has been from books and television…" I trailed off, suddenly feeling silly for my impromptu confession. The world should seriously invest in a manual for these types of things, like *Making Friends for Dummies*. Did they have something I could buy off Amazon?

"We understand, sweetheart," Asher said. "Nobody here is judging you, okay?"

"Except for maybe Calax because he's your nemesis and a bastard," pointed out Ryder smugly. I heard rather than saw said bastard hit Ryder upside the head. I couldn't help but giggle.

"I feel like you guys know everything about me, but I know nothing about you," I continued, desperate to steer the conversation away from my depressing childhood and into safer grounds. Friends ask friends questions about each other, right?

Then why did all the guys look uneasy?

"We don't know everything about you," Ronan pointed out. "We don't know your favorite color or your favorite animal."

"Or how you learned sign language," Tamson added softly.

"Green, but not a grass type of green but a yellowish-green. Kind of like Declan's eyes," I answered, and my mind flashed to a different set of eyes. Eyes that had haunted me for years now, but also gave me strength. The eyes of someone I once loved unconditionally and who had loved me in return. Biting my lip to keep from admitting all that, I said, "And a white tiger."

"The third question?" Asher prompted.

I shrugged. "No reason, really. Boredom? That seems right. It was one of those long months where I wasn't allowed to leave my bedroom. I learned French and some Russian as well." Before the guys could assault me with more questions, I hurried to ask, "And you guys? Tell me how you became friends."

They exchanged glances, seeming slightly wary, before turning towards me. Under their combined stares, I felt suffocated, but not in a bad way. One could relish in their attention.

"We go to school together," Asher replied oh so helpfully. I rolled my eyes.

"Kind of knew that. But how did you become friends? You're all so different."

At this, Ryder chuckled.

"Is that a bad thing, Kitten?"

"Just shut up and answer the question."

"To be completely honest, we were kind of forced," Asher said with a chuckle.

"Forced?"

If I wasn't mistaken, though I usually was, that did not seem like the ideal making of any friendship. Granted, I wasn't an expert or anything, but friendship should be a natural bond between individuals, not two dolls pressed together while a child screams "kiss."

"Yeah," Ryder said, taking over the story. I was beginning to understand that Ryder liked being the center of attention. I couldn't decipher if this was because of his vanity or something else. Something deeper. Perhaps he didn't even realize he did it, like an innate need inside of him to be seen and be heard. "At our school, we're put into groups based on our talents and goals. We work with these people throughout the years. It's kind of inevitable that we'd become friends."

I contemplated his words. What type of school did they go to?

"It started off with just Ashy and me," Ryder said, ignoring Asher's grumble not to call him Ashy. "We were already friends before they paired us up."

"We lived in the same foster home," Asher explained. I lifted an eyebrow but didn't ask him to elaborate. I understood too well about pasts—the good, the bad, and the macabre. I didn't know the reasons for such a placement, and I didn't ask. They would tell me if they wanted to. The more you pressed, the further you pushed people away.

"Asher was the annoying twat that always followed me around," Ryder said with a smirk.

Asher groaned. "You were bigger than me, and I thought that meant you were cooler."

I couldn't help but laugh with the rest of the guys. Asher was adorable, even when he whined.

"I still am bigger than you, at least in the departments that matter." Ryder wiggled his eyebrows.

"Was he a pervert as a little boy?" I asked no one in particular. I couldn't help but picture a ten-year-old Ryder hoping to catch a peek underneath a woman's skirt.

"I am not a pervert," he said indignantly, huffing. "I just like women."

"Too much," Tam muttered.

"Back to the story!" I said, clapping my hands together. I knew there were other things I should be thinking of, like the virus or drug or whatever the hell it was and the tornado that may or may not hit at any moment, but that all felt like a distant memory rather than reality. A nightmare. I was good at suppressing unwanted thoughts, though I knew how unhealthy that practice was. Fortunately—or was it unfortunately?—it seemed as if the guys had adopted the same defense mechanism.

"We were taught together," Ryder continued. "Worked together. Did everything together, pretty much."

"I don't understand how these groups work," I admitted. "Are they common in schools?"

"That's complicated to explain," Asher answered.

"But—" I was interrupted by the vibration of my phone. Startled, I practically leaped three feet into the air, an uncharacteristic squeak leaving my mouth. Ignoring the laughter of the guys, I pulled my phone out of my pocket. In all honesty, I'd completely forgotten about it. Why would I need a phone when the only people I had to call were my parents? For the most part, the piece of technology was left unattended and forgotten in a bedroom drawer. I'd grabbed it this morning on the off chance the guys wanted to exchange numbers.

Hearing it said aloud—or at least in my thoughts, which were probably still aloud—made me feel pathetic.

BASTARD: Where the hell are you?

"WHO TEXTED YOU?" Declan signed, attempting to peer over my shoulder. I flicked his ear.

"Don't be a nosey shit," I said, but my attention remained focus on the phone. Damn technology and damn my father. My lips turned down in a frown.

ME: There's a tornado. I'm in the basement.

BASTARD: Come to the lobby. I need to talk to you.

THE MALICIOUS "OR ELSE" hung unwritten in the text.

"I need to go," I said, pocketing my phone.

"Why?"

"In the middle of a damned tornado?"

"Don't be stupid."

"It's my father," I said, as if that would explain everything. For me, at least, it did. No one left DOD waiting.

"Screw the bastard," Ronan said.

I snorted. "Easier said than done. You're not his daughter." *And you don't have to face his wrath.* I didn't say those words aloud, but I could tell from the guys' frowning faces they understood the unspoken words.

"Is he trying to get you killed?" Calax exploded, his hand clenching into fists.

"Wouldn't be the first time," I muttered. Louder, I said, "I'll be right back. Besides, the tornado probably missed the resort, if it's even still, you know, tornadoing."

"Tornadoing?" Ryder asked in disbelief. He really needed to stop doing that. I didn't know how this friendship would work if he repeatedly questioned my word choices.

"She's right, though," Asher said quietly. "It was a tornado warning, yes, but from the weather projection, there was only a slim chance that it would hit the resort."

"Still—" Calax began, but I held up a hand to stop him.

"No, Calax. You don't get to tell me what to do. I don't need you to always protect me." I met his eyes over the top of Asher's head. In his gaze, I could see a swarm of emotions, some I couldn't entirely understand. One thing I knew for certain was that there was no hate in his gaze. I knew hate, I saw it in the leering gazes of business partners and my parents regularly. This... I didn't know what this was, but it wasn't something I was familiar with.

"Fine," Calax said at last. With surprising agility given his immense size, he lumbered to his feet. "I'm coming with you."

"No," I hurried to respond. "My parents—"

"Your parents are no longer just your problem. They're *our* problem now. I should've come earlier, I should've realized earlier, and I didn't. That's on me. But that doesn't mean that I won't help you now. I'll be damned if I let anything happen to you when I could've prevented it."

I knew the resolve in his gaze mirrored my own. There was no changing his mind.

"Fine, but only you. The rest of you," I leveled my glare on the rest of the boys, "will stay here."

Before anyone could protest, Declan nodded stiffly.

"Fine. But you better come straight back."

We exchanged a long look. I could tell that he disagreed with my decision to only bring Calax, but he respected it. We may not have been friends, he may have hated me, but we understood each other at that moment. My decision was for my own sake as much as theirs.

I wouldn't be able to live with myself if something happened to my new friends because of me. I was already putting Calax at risk, though there was nothing I could do about that. The bastard was more stubborn than I was.

And yes, he was still a bastard, even if he did look at me as if we were lovers instead of enemies.

Even if he did want to protect me.

It was safer that way, both for him and me. I didn't do feelings or emotions, and I didn't let people in. It was easier.

"Come on, Callie. Let's go see what my lovely parents want."

CHAPTER 11

I leaned my back against the fence, the ragged metal jarring the bruises on my spine. Still, I didn't dare grimace or allow any outwards expressions of pain. Ducky didn't—couldn't—know the truth.

"Do you have a date yet?" I asked him through the barrier that separated us. He sat directly on the other side of the fence. I could feel the fabric of his shirt against my bare arms.

I was fortunate that his school went up to eighth grade. The only other public school, the high school, was a couple of miles away, and I was too lazy to walk that far.

Though for Ducky, I would've.

"Tomorrow," Ducky answered, touching his cascade of long hair. He constantly grew his hair out, cut it, and then donated it to a foundation that made wigs for cancer patients. His mom had died of the disease when he was a young boy, and this was his way to honor her. Though his foster parents didn't necessarily agree with his decision—the teasing had escalated from taunts into fights—they left Ducky alone to do as he pleased.

I'd always envied his hair, both long and short. For years, I wished that my hair would grow as fast as his did. It looked like silk. With a desire that was only slightly irrational, I longed to run my fingers through it.

"So your thirteenth birthday is coming up," Ducky said conversationally. He absently scratched a drawing into the sand with a stick. The sun, peeking through the boughs of trees, illuminated his pale hand as he drew.

At his age, they weren't allowed to have recess anymore, which I found ridiculous, so we were forced to meet up before and after school. It was difficult, what with my parents and his foster parents, but we were able to see each other at least two times a week. I would've preferred that number to be higher, but beggars couldn't be choosers or however that saying went.

"Don't remind me," I answered, rolling my eyes to the heavens. While birthdays were grand affairs for some, mine consisted of nothing but formal dinners and the occasional wandering hands of my parents' "friends." I'd never received any presents from anyone other than Ducky, but I didn't mind. What could my parents possibly give me? An "I'm sorry I beat the crap out of you" T-shirt? Or an "I'm a sick bastard" coffee mug? They didn't know me, and they didn't know what I liked. I had long since accepted the hand the universe had dealt me.

"Are you doing anything?" he pressed.

"The usual—dinner at Holt's and then a long spiel about how age comes with responsibility and blah blah blah." I didn't bother to mention the beating I was bound to receive. He didn't need to know that part. It wasn't his burden to carry.

"What time?"

"Seven."

I'd thought he was only being inquisitive, as was standard with Ducky, but I should've known better. He was trying to be my friend, trying to show me something that my parents had neglected to show me for so long—love.

And it was his love for me that would cost him his life.

THE TORNADO HIT ONLY moments before we reached the stairwell.

We were in a small room that had once been a second restaurant. A long bar was against the far wall, glasses piled on shelves behind it. A dozen tables were left abandoned in the center of the room, many collecting dust from years without use.

I remembered this room. My mother had wanted a pub and took it upon herself to hire a designer to recreate a 1930s nightclub. Apparently, Mommy Dearest was having an affair with said designer, who mysteriously disappeared. Thus, the bar never came to be, and the basement as a whole had been abandoned for storage. Daddy was a vindictive son of a bitch.

For a moment, I thought it was another earthquake. The feeling was very similar —the ground almost seemed to vibrate, and glasses from the shelf rained down upon us.

Calax reached for me, but one of the shelves came loose and it plummeted down, hitting Calax in the head. The giant immediately dropped to the ground, blood pooling from the wound.

Ah. That was what the book was for.

I couldn't help my slightly incoherent thoughts as panic set in. I knew I couldn't stay in this room. There was broken glass everywhere, and large objects pelted me like hail. I knew all this, I did, but I couldn't leave Calax, and it was impossible for me to drag him out. I considered running back towards the guys, but I didn't want to put them in harm's way.

I did what instinct demanded—I threw myself on top of Calax. Being careful of the blood gushing from his forehead, I attempted to shield his massive body with my small one. I hoped the effort wouldn't prove futile.

Spreading my legs and arms farther apart, I tucked my head into his hair to avoid the worst of the onslaught. I felt something particularly heavy hit my back, and I let out a whimper.

Breathe, Addie. Breathe.

My therapist always told me that, in any situation, all I had to do was breathe. If I was still breathing, there was a chance that everything would work out.

So I breathed. I breathed through the pain that seemed to almost consume me. I breathed when a shard of glass impaled itself in my arm, eliciting a sob from me. I breathed even when a table landed on my leg, crushing the bone.

I knew, without a doubt, that it was broken.

The pain was immediate and intense. It wasn't my first broken bone, but it was definitely one of the worse. Tiny licks of fire erupted in my veins.

Breathe. Just breathe.

Why didn't that sound appealing anymore?

After what felt like hours, the wind subsided, and the air went still.

I trembled, still sprawled on top of Calax.

What the hell happened?

It was the middle of winter, the middle of *fucking* winter, and a tornado had just hit. This, along with the earthquake, was not natural.

"What the hell? Addie…"

I let out a noncommittal grunt.

"Shit! Princess!" I felt someone gently grab my arms, pulling me off Calax and onto my back. I let out an involuntary screech as the pain in my back amplified.

Shit. Fuck. Shit. Ball sucking dick.

"What the fuck happened?" I knew that angry voice, though I didn't think I'd ever heard it with that particular inflection. Tam. Why was he angry?

"It looks like she threw herself on top of Calax. To protect him." Ryder sounded almost furious with that assumption.

Another hand—Declan's perhaps—repositioned me so I was on my stomach. That felt better for my back but worse for my arm. The slab of skin that had been cut by glass was now pressed against the flooring. Shifting, I moved onto my back yet again.

Better. Not great, but tolerable. The lesser of two evils.

"Shit! Look at her," Ronan said.

"Her leg's broken," Asher pointed out.

No shit.

Someone snorted. Ryder. "At least she still has her sense of humor."

"I will always have a sense of humor," I whimpered. "Even in death." Wincing, I turned my head to see Asher now leaning over Calax. "How is he?"

"He's fine. The big galoot's just unconscious for now. He's going to be pissed when he gets up, though."

I tried not to let out a scream as Declan did something to my leg. I'm afraid I made a howling noise instead, because apparently, that's so much sexier than a cry of pain.

"Why would he be angry?" I managed to gasp out. "I saved his life."

At this, the boys all exchanged amused glances.

"That may be," Asher began. He seemed to choose his words carefully. "But Calax would've preferred for you not to risk yourself for him."

I let out another sound. A laugh, perhaps? I couldn't really tell. My mind was fuzzy, both from pain and the fact that Declan had taken his shirt off, using the material to make bandages for me. I couldn't help but appreciate the expanse of golden skin on display. If I'd somehow died, at least I was in heaven.

"You're not dead," Ryder said in exasperation. "And if you think he looks good, you should see me."

Another choked laugh escaped me at that. Ryder was such a cocky bastard, but he was growing on me. Like a fungus.

I was slightly disappointed when Declan only ripped off the hem of his shirt before throwing it back over his head. Shame. A body like his deserved to be on display.

"You don't care that I was just eye fucking the shit out of your friend?" I asked, raising one eyebrow in disbelief.

"Fortunately for the both of us, he's constipated," Ryder answered with a wink. It took me a moment to understand what he said, but when I did put it together, I threw my head back in laughter.

Luckily, Declan's attention was fixated on my injuries, so he couldn't read my lips. I had the feeling that he would either laugh at me again or turn back into Mr. Glarey. The verdict was still out on that one.

"Are all of you guys okay?" I asked. "Any injuries?"

"We're fine, Princess," Ronan said reassuringly. "You are by far in the worst shape."

"Gee, thanks. Way to make a girl feel pretty."

"Well, you're beautiful. You could never be just *pretty*."

I snorted, my standard response when it came to these men. Still so fucking cheesy.

"What else hurts?" Declan signed after he waved his hands to gain my attention. I frowned. The boys really should be checking on Calax. I was fine, more than used to the pain that seemed to emanate from every pore in my body. Pain was just that— pain. It didn't determine the severity of an injury.

"My back and arm," I admitted at last. "Some glass got stuck…and I think something landed on me."

Tam moved to my side, his tentative hands rolling up the sleeve of my shirt. They paused at first, as they ran over the old scars from my self-inflicted injuries. A tremor went through his body before he settled on pulling out tiny shards of glass.

"Shit!" I hissed after a particularly nasty piece was removed. Yup. Glass still stung like a bitch.

I twisted my head, and my pulse spiked when I noted Calax's prone body. Was he breathing? Oh god, what if he was brain dead?

"He's not brain dead," Tam admonished gently. He glanced towards me, blushed, and then refocused on treating my wounds. "He's just unconscious."

"Hey, lazy bastard!" Ryder cupped his mouth to amplify the sound. He landed a light kick to Calax's stomach. "Wake up! Kitten is worried about you!"

The giant didn't even twitch. My heart hammered in my chest.

Ryder kicked Calax again. "It's Addie! Calax, come quickly!"

At that, Calax's eyes snapped open. With surprising speed, he sat up, eyes casting a quick, panicked look around. They noticeably relaxed when they landed on me, only for alarm to set in when he took in my condition.

"What happened?" he asked, crawling towards me. Asher halfheartedly warned Calax against moving with his head injury, but it surprised no one when Calax ignored him. Once he was above me, a towering pillar that blocked out every other face, his expression calmed. His hand gently smoothed my blood-encrusted hair.

"What happened to you, baby?" he asked, so softly that I had to strain to hear him.

"You were unconscious," I explained. "I had to protect you."

He swallowed, his Adam's apple bobbing.

"Why would you do that?"

I didn't have an answer for that. Because we were friends? Because you were vulnerable, and I was capable of helping?

Because, for once, I wanted to save a life instead of end one?

I didn't say any of that. Instead, I just gazed up at him. His eyes looked incredibly tender. I half expected him to yell at me, call me stupid, but I only saw awe in his commanding gaze. Awe…and that other emotion that I shall not name.

I chose not to look too far into that. Another day. Another time.

"What about Shannon and the others?" I asked, breaking my gaze away from Calax's.

"Who the hell is Shannon?" Ryder questioned.

"The girl you were flirting with last week," I answered with a roll of my eyes. "Blonde hair? Hostess at a restaurant? Only dates football players?"

"Nope. Don't remember."

I smiled through dried blood.

"You're such an asshole sometimes."

"Yes, but I'm your asshole."

"You're not my anything."

"Let's discuss this later," Asher said, not unkindly. "Addie needs to get to a hospital."

"Is it safe to use the stairs?" Tam asked. I couldn't see the state of the room, but from their cautious expressions, I gathered it was not in the best shape. Shame. I rather liked the half-finished restaurant.

There was a shuffle of footsteps and what sounded like chairs being scraped against the wood flooring. I wanted to crane my neck to see, but I was in too much pain.

The ceiling was much more interesting, anyway. All cracks and…well, more cracks. And were those cracks inside of cracks?

"Please stop talking about cracks," Asher said. "Ronan's dirty mind is making him giggle like a schoolgirl." Said schoolgirl began to laugh harder.

"So apparently, Ronan is the pervert, not Ryder. Interesting," I mused. Ryder let out a gleeful whoop, while Ronan began to protest. While I listened to the boys argue, a new thought occurred to me.

How much did I really know about these guys? Sure, Ryder came across as a huge flirt, but what was he really like? And Asher, was he really the sweet, charismatic boy he appeared to be, or was there more to him?

"Um...I don't know how to respond to that," Asher mumbled, cheeks burning in my peripheral vision.

"And I am most definitely just a flirt," Ryder insisted. "No character, no substance. Just a pain in the ass."

"That's what she said," I muttered softly.

"A woman after my heart," said Ryder with a dramatic sigh, and I snorted. I was pretty sure he didn't think with that organ whatsoever.

"Entrances are blocked," Tam said, voice distant. I heard the shuffling of footsteps.

"What about the others down here?" I asked weakly. "Did you check on them yet?"

Ronan rolled his eyes with a huff, but there was a cheeky grin on his face.

"So needy."

I gave him the finger in response.

"Should we congregate with the others?" Calax asked anxiously. He hadn't stopped stroking my hair since he'd awoken. I would've yelled at him if it hadn't felt so nice.

I mentally berated myself for the direction of my thoughts. I wasn't supposed to be thinking about Calax in that way. 'Nice' wasn't a word I liked to associate with the beast of a man. Sure, he looked like a ferocious giant, what with his defined muscles, black clothing, and glowering expression, but...

But he was never like that with me. He was always so tender, as if I was precious glass he was afraid would break. Maybe that was why I classified him as public enemy number one. If I were to look at him in any other way, any other light, I would break.

For him? Because of him? Despite him?

The world may never know.

I shifted my attention away from Calax to Tamson. As if he felt my eyes on him, Tam looked up, blushed, and then quickly glanced back down at his feet.

If there was one thing I noticed about Tamson, it was his inability to make and maintain eye contact with me. The knowledge didn't hurt or bother me as it might've others. From what I'd gathered in our brief interactions, Tam was shy and often felt inadequate compared to his friends. I disagreed with his self-assessment, but I understood it. I'd lived my entire life under a spotlight, every detail, every word, every action frequently analyzed in extensive detail, while longing to lose myself in the shadows. Despite the amount of effort I put into it, I always came up short. Lacking. I understood Tam and his need to hide behind his curly hair. There were some times where even my hands didn't want to be seen.

So no, I didn't judge him for his timidity. If anything, I respected him for being who he was, anxiety and all.

I was actually *grateful* when his eyes had fluttered away from mine. I didn't want to make eye contact with any of the boys. Calax made me feel too much, too deeply, and I understood how dangerous that could be.

"I vote yes to the whole congregating thing," I said brightly, my attention fixated on a spot above Tam's shoulder. From this angle, still on the ground, I could just make out the peeling wallpaper and exposed wood frames. The depressing structure seemed to balance on the precarious few pillars that remained standing.

Good god. If this was the basement, how does the rest of the resort look?

"Probably not good," Asher answered solemnly.

"I just hope there aren't any casualties," I whispered. My heart hurt at the thought.

At times, I might have appeared callous when it came to death, but that was only when it involved me. It was entirely different when death concerned others. Perhaps it was selfish thinking, but I couldn't bear to witness any more death. After Buttlicker —I really should figure out his real name—I'd thought I could brave anything. After all, it was my fault he was dead. Even if I hadn't pulled the trigger, he, no doubt, was in the hospital looking for me. Did his unintentional death by my hand make me a monster, even if his intentions for seeking me out were malicious at best?

I chose not to look too closely at that answer.

"Once the fire trucks come and free us, we should gain a better understanding of what happened," Calax responded vaguely, his deep voice causing my skin to tingle. Like most things in my life, I chose to ignore the feelings that brewed inside me at the sound of his voice.

Safer. Easier.

Healthier.

"There's a bunch of people in the next room over," Asher said from above me. He pointed over his shoulder. "Should we head over there?"

"Is it a good idea to move Calax and Addie?" Tam asked.

"Is it a good idea to stay in this room, where the walls and ceiling look like they'll fall down on us at any moment?" Ronan countered. I didn't even have to look to know that Tam would be blushing.

Lifting myself onto my elbows, with only a slight grimace of pain—yay me!—I addressed the boys with a smile. "Would one of you gentlemen do me the honor of giving me a piggyback ride?"

"I'll do it," Calax said instantly, and I snorted.

"You shouldn't even be walking, let alone carrying my heavy ass."

He opened his mouth to retort, no doubt against my claim of being heavy, when Ronan bent down before me.

"Hop on, Princess. Your majestic steed awaits."

"Why thank you, kind knight," I said with feigned reverence. Ryder and Asher helped position me on Ronan's back, with extra care not to disturb the bone protruding from my leg or the injuries on my back. I clung to Ronan like a monkey, arms around his neck and my good leg wrapped around his muscular torso.

I could feel my pants dropping down, and I hoped I wasn't displaying the crack Ronan liked so much.

As if he read my mind—or heard me, more than likely—Asher leaned forward to whisper in my ear.

"Coast is clear."

"I'm not flashing anyone?" I asked, wanting to clarify. Asher blushed but shook his head no.

One small relief.

The procession to the next room was slow, mainly because of my occasional whimper of pain. I tried to suppress the sound, I honestly did, but specific movements would jar my body in a way that felt like licks of fire kissing my skin. The boys would halt at the sound, trying to reassure themselves that I was all right. I tried to tell them that they didn't need to coddle me, but that only resulted in a glare from Declan and a shake of the head by Calax.

"How long do you think we're going to be in here?" Tamson asked quietly. He was currently on rear duty, which I translated to making sure my ass didn't hit the floor. It was a surprisingly tricky feat. My arms were weak, and my body ached.

I thought I just needed someone to permanently stand behind me, holding my butt up so I wouldn't slide down Ronan's body. Not in a perverted way or anything, but in a completely normal and platonic, non-sisterly—

"What the hell are you thinking about?" Ronan asked me.

"My ass," I responded immediately before I could think things through. I mentally cursed myself when I heard groans mixed in with laughter. Dammit. *No butts allowed in conversation, Addie. We've been over this.*

"Anyway," Calax said gruffly, averting attention to him and away from me. I could've kissed him...but not in a sexual way. A friend way. A friend that wasn't a sister way.

Stop. Thinking. Addie.

"I think the *school* will send people as soon as they can. I guarantee you that Sarge is already here," Calax continued, ignoring my outburst.

I fixated on the way he said 'school,' as if it was in all capital letters. What could a preppy boarding school do against a tornado?

And another thing...

"Who's Sarge?" I asked. The boys tensed around me, even Ronan, though he tried to relax his muscles after I let out an audible squeak. I could see Calax's brow furrow, which meant he was thinking.

I hoped he didn't pass out from it.

"Sarge, Sargent, is our group leader," Calax settled on at last.

"For the school?"

Another hesitation. "Yes."

"Is that his name?" I questioned. "Or his title? Isn't it supposed to be sergeant?"

Before Calax could reply, a high-pitched squeal made my ears bleed. Okay, maybe my ears were already bleeding because of the whole tornado thing, but that sound wasn't really helping matters.

"Are you guys okay? I was so worried!"

We had entered a room where a large group huddled together. They all had pale faces but otherwise looked unharmed. With mascara streaming down her face like onyx tears, Elena ran through the crowd and threw her arms around Ryder.

I couldn't help but chuckle at Ryder's flabbergasted if not slightly horrified expression. With a practiced efficiency, Ryder disentangled himself from Elena's arms. Of course, Elena took that as permission to throw herself at Declan, who did not remove himself from her gently. He cast her a glare that would've made any sane person shit their pants. Hell, I wasn't even on the receiving end of it, and I stilled trembled.

Tamson, knowing that Ronan was out of commission since he held me and that he was next, quickly ducked behind Calax.

Elena glanced at Calax, gaze slightly hungry.

Same girl. Same.

I frowned at myself.

Nope. Not the same. Because I wouldn't ever stare at Calax hungrily. Nope. Nada. I was not hungry for Calax. I had already eaten...chicken. Chicken's better than a boy.

Ronan's chuckle clued me into the fact I had spoken aloud. Again. Calax looked oddly pleased with himself, as if my unintentional confession reinforced something he had suspected. What that was, I had no idea.

I hated Calax. Hated him.

"I see you're still with...*her*," Elena said with false cheerfulness. Her eyes glared daggers at me. Despite the pain and the dire situation we were in—you know, the whole being trapped underground thing—I felt something akin to glee rise up in me. I had never met a mean girl before. I'd watched movies, read books, but this was my first experience with a jealous bitch.

It made me feel...well, not normal necessarily, but less like a freak.

Yes, I realized there was something wrong with me, thank you very much.

"The name's Addie," I said, attempting to wave. Of course, that led to me nearly falling on my ass and Tam darting forward to help stabilize my clumsy body. Elena's eyes honed in on my leg around Ronan's body and Tam's hands on my hips.

"You could put her down now," Elena suggested in a snide tone, as if we were imbeciles for not thinking of that sooner. I glanced in dismay from my leg, still broken, to Elena, and then back to my leg. Nope, apparently not even mean girls could will my bones to mend themselves. Shame.

"Don't be ridiculous, Elena," Ryder snapped. Gone was the jovial, flirtatious boy I had grown so accustomed to. This boy looked almost dangerous.

I didn't believe he would actually hurt Elena, but a small pang of fear made my heart beat erratically. I had often been on the receiving end of such a tone, and for me at least, it always resulted in a beating.

"Shit, dude. Soften your voice. You're scaring, Princess," Ronan said, and Ryder's eyes shot to my face.

"Princess?" Elena questioned.

"You know I would never hurt you or Elena, right?" Ryder asked, his voice considerably softer. He looked almost scared, his normally jubilant eyes downcast. I held out my hand to him, and he took it, giving it a gentle squeeze.

"I'm sorry," I whispered, quiet enough for only him and Ronan to hear. "I know you wouldn't. It's just...hearing your voice like that..."

"Reminded you of your parents," Ryder finished for me, just as softly. His face paled. "I'm nothing like those sick bastards, you hear me?"

"I hear you."

"Does your new toy know that you used to fuck me?" Elena asked, disrupting our moment. I blinked at her in surprise. "Me and my entire team."

She gestured towards a group of girls huddled in the far corner. They all stared at our group with varying degrees of jealousy and hatred. Yup. The boys were apparently real winners in the female department.

"At the same time?" I whispered in Ronan's ear. "Like a seven-some?"

Ronan snorted in laughter, and Elena turned her glare onto him.

"No," Ronan whispered back, ignoring Elena. "Not like that." He hesitated. "But yes, all of those girls were on the rotation at the same time."

I frowned at the way he spoke so brashly about females, as if we were just commodities to go through.

"We don't think of you like that," he assured me, easily reading the tension in my body. "You're our friend."

"And Elena never was?" I found that hard to believe. Why would they pursue a relationship with someone if that person wasn't a friend? Didn't most relationships develop from a friendship?

Sighing, I glanced up from the crook of Ronan's neck to meet Elena's glare.

"Yes, I know all about your little nightly adventures with Tam, Declan, Ronan, and Ryder. This isn't show-and-tell, Elena. We don't need to talk about our conquests. Now scuttle away and leave the guys alone."

Elena sputtered, face turning red, but I continued to face her resolutely. There were far worse storms than her, and I'd encountered thousands of them. After a moment of heavy breathing, she smiled. It was a smile you would see on a demonic child, though I would never tell her that. Why make her feel self-conscious over her bitch smile? No, it was better for everyone involved if I mocked her silently.

"And Calax," she said smugly. "You're forgetting my nighttime adventures with him too."

CHAPTER 12

$\mathcal{T}$he air left my lungs in a whopping rush. I could scarcely believe what I'd heard.

Calax? And Elena?

No, that couldn't be true. I tried to picture it, tried to picture Calax cupping Elena's face as he had done so often with mine, but the image made me a little nauseous. I told myself the turmoil of emotion raging inside of me was pity for Elena and nothing more.

Why did it feel like my chest was tightening? Why did I have the sudden, irresistible urge to claw Elena's eyes out?

I knew the name of the emotion, but I refused to accept it. No, I was not the type of person to be jealous, especially over activities Calax may or may not have partaken in. The spastic, frantic energy I felt dissipated, leaving me with only confusion.

"Shut it, Elena," Calax hissed. He took a step closer to me, and Elena's smile grew. She knew she'd hurt me, and she relished in it. That…that…bitch!

"Good observational skills," Ronan muttered. I pinched his cheek.

"Shush."

"Don't listen to her. She's desperate for attention," Declan signed, making me chuckle. Elena's hair whipped in her face as she turned to glare at him before turning back towards me.

"What's he saying?"

"You're so 'in love' with him, and you didn't even bother to learn sign language?" I asked, smirking. How could she not be willing? Wouldn't you do anything, cross any oceans, for the people you loved? What she felt for these boys, I realized, wasn't love but infatuation. She was like me in that aspect—clueless about what love actually was.

"Whatever." Elena rolled her eyes as if a language barrier was only a minor inconvenience in a relationship. And then she glared at me. Again. Because apparently, it was my fault the boys brushed her off.

Maybe I was wrong. Maybe mean girls were not as fun as I initially thought. Didn't, in the movies, they get hit by a bus or something?

Well, I didn't see any buses barreling towards Elena.

"Hey, I know this girl!" another pig screeched. Excuse me, teenage girl said. This girl looked familiar though her name escaped me. Considering I only knew a few people, that was a surprise.

I guessed she hadn't been very memorable.

Ronan snorted beneath me.

"Bikini girl," he supplied.

"One bikini or ten?" I had to ask the serious questions here. Apparently, the number of bikinis you had determined the importance of a person.

"She was the one who had ten."

"The leather one..."

"The glass one..."

"She only wears the glass one in the sunlight. So it reflects," I murmured. "And only when she does activities and hobbies."

"Because she has interests."

The new girl, whose name I still couldn't remember, looked back and forth between the two of us, obviously unable to hear the conversation, and she seemed pissed by that prospect. I didn't know why her panties were in such a twist. If I remembered correctly, she'd been looking for Ryder, not Ronan.

I wasn't currently riding Ryder.

Hmmm. That was both a pun and a sex joke. I had to remember to recycle that one.

"Ronan, baby, what are you doing?" Bikini asked.

Baby?

Ronan?

He was most definitely not a baby.

"Thanks, Princess," said non-baby with a wink. I rolled my eyes.

"Wasn't supposed to hear that."

"Suck it up."

I leaned forward to stick my tongue out at him, but I accidentally leaned too far and licked his neck.

Licked. His. Neck.

Okay, so I might've just tapped his neck with my tongue, but still.

Fuck.

Ronan froze beneath me, a violent tremor running through his body. I heard him make a sound in the back of his throat—a combination between a sigh and a grunt.

Maybe if I just pretended it hadn't happened...

From the looks the boys and girls gave me—shock, disbelief, hatred, and jealousy—I figured that wouldn't work.

"Whoopsies," I said sheepishly.

"What the fuck was that?" Elena screamed. Literally screamed, as if we weren't standing two feet away from her.

"Um…an accident."

"How the fuck do you accidentally lick someone?"

"Easy, actually. Like, if you're walking and you mistake someone's head for ice cream. Or if you want to stick your tongue out at someone, but you trip and fall into them. There can be a lot of reasons for accidental lickings."

Calax, seeming to forget he was jealous, doubled over in laughter. Ryder and Asher were on the ground in hysterics. Even Mr. Grumpy had a small smile on his face.

Okay. It wasn't that funny.

"It really was, Princess," Ronan said with a chuckle.

Laugh it up, bastards.

"What the hell is wrong with her?" Bikini asked in disbelief. She exchanged a long, measured glance with another unfamiliar girl.

As one, the boys and I answered, "A lot."

Choosing to ignore the glares I felt piercing my skin, I nudged Ronan's stomach with my good foot.

"Put me down. My arms are sore. I'm weakening…" I said the last sentence as dramatically as possible, a poor impersonation of the Wicked Witch melting. Ronan chuckled at my theatrics but obediently lowered me to the floor. Ryder and Declan moved on either side of me to position me comfortably against the wall. I hissed at the pain ghosting down my spine but quickly tried to mask my frown when I saw Elena looking at me. I wouldn't show weakness in front of anyone, especially her.

"What even happened to her?" Elena asked. Though her tone was stiff, her eyes appeared to be almost worried. I must've looked pretty damn bad to get such a reaction from the ice queen.

"When the tornado hit, she threw herself on top of Calax," Ryder explained. He sounded slightly awed, as if he was describing a mythical creature's actions and not that of an awkward girl. His eyes were warm as they grazed my face. "Had some shit fall on her."

Elena bit her lip. She seemed to be debating something, but what, I couldn't discern. After a moment, she sighed heavily and dropped to her knees beside me.

"What are you doing?" Ronan demanded. He had, at some point during Ryder's explanation, dropped to his butt next to me. His hand currently kneaded at the muscles in my neck.

"Fixing her. You want her to keep that leg, don't you?" Elena said snidely. Turning towards me, she softened her tone marginally. "What hurts?"

"Besides everything?" I asked with a chuckle. "Everything."

Elena didn't smile, but she also didn't glare at me anymore. I took that as a win.

"Her leg got crushed," Calax said gruffly. "And I think some glass got stuck in her arm."

"And her back!" Tam added.

Elena nodded slowly, gaze piercing. She immediately began unwrapping the flimsy shirt-bandage Declan had constructed.

"I need something to brace her leg on. Two pieces of wood, maybe? A hardcover children's book? Whatever you can find."

When nobody made any effort to move, Elena snapped her fingers impatiently in front of Ryder's face. "Now!"

He glared at her but got up and stomped down a hallway. Asher, after a wistful glance in my direction, moved towards another.

"What about alcohol? Something to clean these wounds with?"

"The room we just came from used to be a bar," I supplied, nodding towards the general vicinity with my head.

"I'll go," Ronan offered. Before he left, he pressed a chaste kiss to my forehead. I was too stunned to do anything but gape after him like an idiot.

What. The. Hell?

It was because I licked him, right? The whole licking incident opened up a large can of worms.

Calax, muscles bunched together as he crossed his arms, glared down at us from above. He really was an impressive man, all muscles and chiseled bones.

"I'm not going to be able to work if you're glaring down at me," Elena snapped. Her hands were tentative as they assessed my injuries. "Go wait over there."

When Calax didn't budge, Elena removed her hands from me with a sour expression.

"If you don't move, I won't fucking help her."

If looks could kill, Elena would've been dead a thousand times over. After one more ineffective glare in her direction, Calax stormed to the corner. He leaned against the wall, eyes trained on me as if he couldn't bear to look away. The attention felt...strange. I didn't know how else to describe it. I couldn't decide if I enjoyed it or feared it. He disarmed me with his gentleness.

From the corner of my eye, I watched Declan sign to Tamson. I couldn't see the movements, but I saw Tam nod and get to his feet. Before I could inquire, Tam turned back towards me with a smile.

"I'm going to see if there's any water or something to eat. I'll be back."

It was one of the longest sentences he'd ever spoken to me. Though a delicate flush still dusted across his cheekbones and his eyes wavered from mine, I felt as if we'd reached a turning point. I didn't want to be someone Tam feared, whether that fear was irrational or not. To be a friend, you had to rely on one another with an innate loyalty formed from trust and compassion. I hoped I could have that type of relationship with the guys. I wanted this friendship to work, more than I was willing to admit.

"You know," Elena said softly, "I'm not trying to be a bitch."

I snorted. "Could've fooled me."

From the angle she positioned herself, she effectively blocked Declan from the conversation. I knew he would be furious that Elena was purposefully excluding him, but there was nothing I could do. It hurt like a bitch to move.

"I loved them...at least I believed I loved them. It was nice to have their collective attention, you know? To feel like I was the only girl in the world, even though there were other girls." Elena's eyes turned watery with tears.

I realized then that she really wasn't trying to be malicious. This was a girl driven by jealousy and her concept of love. In a sense, she'd had her heart broken. I didn't know her history with the guys, and I didn't know the guys as well she probably did, but I could see from her sorrowful expression that she once thought the world of them. I could also see that this feeling, this love, was one-sided.

"They made me feel beautiful, special. Protected. Hell, they even gave me cheesy nicknames, but you know what I'm talking about, don't you?"

My tongue felt like sandpaper in my mouth. I swallowed, but no noise escaped me. It had never occurred to me that the guys may have only seen me as a fuck buddy. I recalled the crude way Ronan had talked about Elena and the rest of the girls. Was that what was expected of me? Was this friendship a ploy for something else? Doubts niggled my mind. I didn't want to believe that I was nothing more than a toy to them, but Elena's words planted those pesky seeds of doubt.

They *had* been using cheesy nicknames, and they *had* made me feel protected.

From what I gathered, these were boys who didn't want to fall in love, didn't want to have anything real, out of fear that they'd be hurt. Why else would they go through women so quickly?

"I can see the wheels in your head turning," Elena said. "And I'm just warning you, from woman to woman, be careful of them. They've left dozens of broken hearts behind them, and I'd hate for the next one to be yours."

I couldn't ignore the sincerity in her voice. Damnit, whether it was true or not, Elena obviously believed it to be so.

Before I could respond, Ryder slid onto his knees beside me, two thin pieces of wood in his hands. They must've fallen from the roof.

"Will these work?"

"Yes," Elena sneered haughtily, ripping them from his hands. Gone was the vulnerable girl she'd revealed to me. I wondered if I'd imagined that entire conversation.

~

THE DAY WAS LONG.

I didn't know how much time passed, but it felt like months. With no natural sunlight, it was near impossible to decipher night from day. Declan had a watch, but I much preferred to be dramatic than to ask him the time.

Elena had bandaged my arm and back before bracing my leg. I'd heard her sharp intake of breath when she saw the burn marks on my arms, but she didn't say anything. After she'd finished, she went back to her corner, while we stayed in ours.

Tamson handed me a water bottle, which I gratefully took.

"How are you feeling?" Asher asked me softly.

"Better. I really wish this place had pain meds."

Ronan leaned forward to grin at me, teeth shockingly white in his brown face. "Don't be a wuss."

"Don't be a puss," I countered.

From the other side of Ronan, Ryder let out a loud snore. I couldn't help my giggle. I wondered how the great, sexy Ryder would feel if he discovered that he both snored and drooled when he slept. It was no wonder he never let girls spend the night—I'd be embarrassed about that too.

Calax chuckled. "Please tell him that when he gets up. It might knock him down a peg."

"Doubtful," Asher said.

I turned to smile at him, but my expression froze when I saw Declan. He'd been silent thus far, more so than usual, and I feared that he felt left out. After all, we weren't using sign language to communicate with one another.

I felt a stab of guilt at my negligence.

What type of friend does that?

I squared my shoulders resolutely. It was fine. I made a mistake, but I could be better. I had to be.

Waving my hand in front of his face to garner his attention, I began to sign, *"How are you feeling?"*

The sullen expression contorting his features softened when his gaze met mine.

"You don't have to worry about me feeling left out," he signed quickly. *"I'm used to it."*

"Doesn't it get lonely?" I signed back. Beside me, Asher seemed to realize we were having a conversation and skirted out of the way. When I smiled at him, he winked at me.

"I'm used to it," Declan said, motions brisk. From the tightening of his eyes, I knew that he was lying. Nobody could be used to loneliness.

"I'm truly sorry," I said. *"I'll try to do better."*

If that meant facing him continuously so he could read my lips, I would. I was determined not to screw this up.

Declan was silent for a moment. His hand tapped an irregular pattern against his dust-stained jeans.

"Tell me about your friend," he said at last.

"Friend?" In my surprise, I'd spoken aloud while simultaneously signing. I decided to continue speaking that way in order for him to understand me if I were to mess up a sign.

"You said that you killed your friend. What did you mean?" he continued.

Unwanted tears sprang to my eyes.

Oh, Ducky. And here was Declan, with eyes almost an exact replica of my best friend's. An immeasurable amount of loss and emptiness filled me.

"You don't have to talk about it if you don't want to," Declan hurried to add, taking note of my distraught expression.

"No, it's fine." My voice was shaky. "I didn't have a lot of friends when I was younger. For obvious reasons."

I could feel Calax turning towards me, and Ronan had a thoughtful expression on his face. I offered them a gentle smile, so they knew I was okay with them listening. Taking a steadying breath, I pressed on.

"My best friend in the entire world was named Ducky. I met him at the public school after I'd gotten into a fight with my parents." I scoffed at the memory. I remembered how scared I'd been at the time. Why were Mommy and Daddy mad at me? What had I done wrong?

Younger Adelaide was a dumbass.

"What happened?" Tam asked softly. I kept my attention on Declan as I continued.

"We became inseparable, at least in secret. I would come to visit him every morning and every afternoon that I could. He told me about his foster family and his dreams for the future. I told him about mine." I took another deep breath. "But I never told him about my parents. At least, not about their abusive tendencies. I thought it was my burden to shoulder, you know? I didn't want him to feel like he had to save me when he was struggling to save himself."

Another breath.

"On my thirteenth birthday, I told Ducky about the dinner my parents had planned for me. He showed up at the restaurant to surprise me." A small smile bloomed on my face when I remembered his slicked-back hair and black suit, two sizes too big. He'd looked so handsome.

My body seemed to be an epitome of contradictions, for a tear hit my turned-up lip. I instantly sobered with my next words.

"I was afraid Mom and Dad would hurt him, so I sent him away. I told him he meant nothing to me and that our friendship was just a pity party." I laughed, but it held no humor. "I suppose it was. He pitied me. Why else would he be my friend? I said some awful things, but you have to understand, I was terrified. I knew what my parents were capable of, and I feared they would hurt him just because I loved him. Ducky left humiliated, and I watched him go. I didn't try to stop him or call him back."

A shuttering sob left me, and a hand pulled me against a muscular chest.

Declan.

His gentleness threatened to break through every wall I constructed around myself. I wanted nothing more than to lose myself in his embrace.

I allowed him to hold me, to comfort me, for only a second before I pulled away. I had the distinct feeling that once they heard the rest of the story, they would want nothing to do with me.

The murderer.

"I watched him through the window. He was running, as if he could escape me." Another tear slid down my nose. "But he wasn't fast enough. The car came out of nowhere. I didn't... I can't..." I was sobbing now, reaching full-blown hysterics. "I killed him."

Declan reached forward yet again to gather me in his arms. I didn't understand how he could touch me. Wasn't he disgusted with me? I was disgusted with myself. I was a monster.

"It was an accident, and it wasn't your fault," Asher said. I felt him behind me, hand smoothing down my untamed hair.

"I shouldn't have sent him away," I cried. All the anguish and fear I felt came pressing down on me. I'd always suspected that his death was my fault, but hearing it said aloud, I knew it was. There was no doubt in my mind.

God, I hated myself.

It should've been me.

"Don't say stuff like that," Calax ordered in a harsh whisper.

Was this why I craved death? To compensate for my past sins?

"It wasn't your fault, Kitten," Ryder insisted. I hadn't even heard him wake up.

Declan pushed me away from him, and I figured that he'd finally had enough of me. He finally saw me for the monster I indeed was.

Instead of the horror or hate I expected, his eyes widened with an undefinable emotion. It was impossible to read.

"Ducky's not dead," Declan said. A tear trailed down his cheek, soon followed by a second one.

"What?" I asked, shocked. Out of everything I expected him to say, it hadn't been that. "You don't have to try to make me feel better."

"You need to—"

"I took away his future, Declan. His chance at life. At happiness. At love. He probably would've had a girlfriend named Sasha by now and lived in a cottage only two miles away from college. He would've been studying biochemical engineering, but his girlfriend would've been bitching at him to get a degree in nursing. They would've had two cats together, which they fought over after the breakup. They end up deciding on joint custody of the cats and—"

"Stop talking!" Declan signed, interrupting my incoherent rambles. I complied, clamping my mouth shut. I met Declan's smoldering stare, unshed tears gathering in my eyes. I mentally prepared myself for him to yell at me. To tell me he hated me and to go to hell, which I more than deserved.

His eyes were clear when they met mine, an endless abyss of honey woven with a light green. Familiar.

"I'm Ducky."

CHAPTER 13

I'd worn a light blue skirt and a white blouse to my thirteenth birthday dinner. I was always told that blue, particularly a light blue, could heighten the golden flecks in my eyes. Of course, I scoffed at such a cliché, but it still felt nice to believe, even for a moment, that I was beautiful.

The restaurant was a drive away from the resort, in a small town surrounded entirely by trees. It was an odd combination—tall, thick pines interspersed with an assortment of glass buildings and enormous skyscrapers. It appeared as if someone had plopped a random city in the middle of the woods.

The manager greeted us by name when we entered the exclusive dining room. A three-tiered chandelier hung low in the doorway, its bright light probably supposed to be welcoming. If anything, the intermittent flicker of the bulb made me think I was walking towards my doom.

Dinner started off par for the course—read as awkward small-talk between my parents as they both ignored me. I sipped from my water and stirred the soup idly with my spoon. I hated this restaurant. Despite the price, the food was bland, and the atmosphere was too pretentious for my tastes. My opinions, of course, didn't matter to my parents, and the fact it was my birthday wouldn't change that.

You might think it was odd that my parents, emotionally negligent and physically abusive, would remember something as mundane as my birthday. Well, it was also my mother's birthday, which was the entire reason for our celebration. They'd never remembered that it was my day of birth as well.

I always wondered if that was why mom hated me—because she had to share her special day with me. She'd once told me I was the worst birthday present she had ever received, as though it was my fault she couldn't hold me in until the next day. Sometimes, I wished she'd been pregnant constipated and incapable of delivering me. A twisted part of me wished I'd died in her womb.

The waiter arrived with our food—a steak for DOD, a lobster for Mommy Dearest, and a salad for me. Daddy told me I needed to maintain my figure in order to remain beautiful. At that age, I'd just begun developing curves. My body was no longer lithe and lightly muscled, but in the beginning stages of womanhood.

He'd noticed.

And he made sure to make me feel inadequate whenever the opportunity arose.

Taking another sip of water, though it did very little to subdue the ranch lathered lettuce's bitter taste, I turned towards the front door.

I couldn't recall what drew my eyes there. Was it something inside me, like an innate knowledge of what was to come? Or was it a plea for someone to save me?

Ducky stood in the doorway, a sliver of moonlight illuminating him like a giant spotlight.

He wore his long, dark hair braided away from his face, showcasing his high cheekbones. I noticed that he'd dressed in a black suit, though it looked as if it belonged to a kid twice his size.

No. No.

What was he doing here?

I felt myself begin to panic. A thousand solutions floated through my mind—pretend I wasn't here, ask to go to the bathroom and warn him away, hope that it was just a coincidence.

Before I could collect myself, Ducky walked towards our table, a bright smile alighting his face.

"Hello. You guys must be Adelaide's parents. I'm Ducky." He extended his hand, his eyes warm.

My dad and mom exchanged confused glances. At least at the moment, they didn't appear suspicious. They'd always been slow. As one, I could see understanding flicker across their faces, followed by surprise. I wasn't supposed to know "how to human," and this boy, this Ducky, proved that I'd broken that rule.

Protect.

I had to protect him.

Scrambling to come up with a reasonable explanation, I watched my dad survey Ducky with more contempt than courtesy. The too-long pants, the unruly hair escaping his braid, the birthmark on his pale throat.

"Addie," my father said with a deadly calm. "You never told me that you'd made a friend."

I blurted the first thing I could think of. "He's not my friend."

Dad lifted a manicured eyebrow, and Ducky blanched as if I'd slapped him.

"He seems to think you're friends," Daddy replied evenly. He cut into his steak, his eyes never leaving mine. Yes, because it was completely normal to play with knives while glaring at your daughter.

"Oh please," I said with an exasperated eye roll. "As if I would ever be friends with someone like him. Have you seen his clothes? Pathetic. And that hair? Maybe he's trying to be mistaken as a girl."

I knew I'd hit a sore spot when Ducky's face paled and his lower lip trembled.

Ducky, I'm sorry. Please forgive me.

Protect him.

"No, I'm not his friend. He was just a boy I took pity on. I was nice to him once, and suddenly, he thinks we're friends." I laughed. Did my parents not realize how fake that laugh sounded? How brittle and broken?

Turning towards Ducky, I sneered as if I found him repulsive. If anything, I found *myself* repulsive. At that moment, I hated myself.

Protect him.

"You can leave now. God, the creepy stalker look doesn't look good on you."

Dad clamped his lips together as if to hold in a laugh. Mother, however, had already turned back towards her lobster.

I watched Ducky's face fall, surprise giving way to betrayal. He looked at me as if I'd ripped his spine from his body, spat on it, and then fed it to my dog.

For as long as I lived, I would never be able to forget that anguished expression.

And then he was running. In his haste to escape, he stumbled into a passing waiter.

And I laughed.

I fucking *laughed.*

I watched him as he ran through the doorway, into the road. He glanced back, tears on his cheeks, and I resisted the urge to run to him.

I'm so sorry.

These were words I couldn't say.

Looking back, I sometimes wished that I'd accidentally spoken my thoughts aloud back then. That particular trait wouldn't pop up until a couple months later.

Ducky's face was still turned towards mine, so he didn't see the truck barreling down the street. He didn't see the driver slam on his brakes in a desperate attempt to avoid the small boy in the road. He *did* see my face, however, with my mouth opened in a scream he couldn't hear. His brow drew down, his head tilting to the side.

And then the truck plowed into him.

I screamed until my throat was hoarse, and I haven't stopped since.

I REPLAYED DECLAN'S SIGNS, sure I'd seen them wrong. He'd probably meant to say that he knew Ducky. Maybe he actually said, "I'm Lucky." That was a more plausible explanation than the one he gave me.

Ducky was dead. I'd seen him die. My parents had told me as much.

This man, this Declan, was not *my* Ducky.

"I don't know what type of fucking game you're trying to play, but I'm…" A sob broke through my chest. I knew Declan was icy, but I'd never suspected him capable of such cruelty. This was unforgivable.

Without taking his eyes from mine, Declan pulled down the collar of his shirt. Staining his tanned skin was a dark birthmark.

Ducky's birthmark.

No. No.

I hadn't even realized I was speaking aloud until Declan grabbed my hand in both of his. I shook my head, as if that action could somehow change what I just saw.

"Your name is Declan, not Ducky," I insisted. I could barely breathe. My heart, my damn heart, thumped in my chest like a sledgehammer. It dared to hope while my brain warned me against it.

"My nickname is Ducky," Declan signed after he released my hands. He, too, had tears in his eyes. At some point, the other guys must've left us alone. I no longer felt the heat from their bodies.

"No. This can't... You can't... This can't be happening."

I began to sob in earnest now, overwhelmed by the influx of information he tried to relay. He couldn't be Ducky, I knew that, but I couldn't ignore the facts slapping me in the face. No, they weren't just slapping me. They were full on bitch punching me while a train ran over my beaten body.

On closer inspection, Declan had the same bone structure as Ducky. High cheekbones, chiseled jawline, tapered waist. While Ducky had been lithe, Declan was muscled. While Ducky had had long hair, Declan had short, at least on the sides. While Ducky had been pale, Declan was tan by consistent sunlight exposure.

While Ducky could hear, Declan was deaf.

But...

But the birthmark. The crescent-shaped brown patch marring his skin. Ducky, too, had had that on his neck, almost caressing his collarbone.

Something made me lean forward to brush my fingers against Declan's skin. I didn't know what I was hoping for. For it to be makeup? For it not to be?

The birthmark was real, and the fact sent an undefinable tingle through my body.

Voice quiet, as if I was afraid anything louder would force him to laugh in my face, I murmured, "Ducky?"

"Addie."

And then he wrapped his arms around me, extra mindful of my injuries. I pressed my face into his neck, crying, relishing the comfort and heat he emitted.

This was Ducky. My Ducky. My best friend, and the only person I'd ever truly loved.

I pulled away from him, eyes bloodshot, to see he wasn't faring much better. His own eyes were glassy with unshed tears. With a trembling hand, he pushed a strand of knotted hair behind my ear.

I didn't care that I was in pain. I didn't care that I had a broken leg, a scarred back, and an arm that was losing feeling by the second.

All I cared about was the handsome boy in front of me.

"You're alive," I whispered. His eyes remained focused intently on my lips as he read my words.

"Yes."

"Why didn't you...why didn't you tell me?" I sobbed, my relief transforming into anger. I'd spent years—years!—believing I'd killed my best friend. I knew he'd been pissed at me for what occurred at the restaurant, I didn't even blame him for his anger, but this? Ignoring me after I witnessed him getting hit by a truck? Making me believe that the was dead? Having me mourn him? That was borderline torture.

"I tried!" Declan—Ducky—insisted. His eyes grew wide. *"Your parents said you didn't want to talk to me. They said you..."* His hands faltered as if he was unsure what else he wanted to say.

"They said what?" I asked calmly. Too calmly.

"They said you never once asked about me. They said you laughed when the truck came."

I exploded. "And you believed them? After everything we'd been through?"

I knew I was yelling, and I knew the effort was futile, but I couldn't help it—and yes, I understood the irony of yelling at a deaf guy. Ducky and I had spent years together. He'd been my best friend, and I, his. How could he just believe I would throw that away? That I'd faked it for all of those years?

"What was I supposed to think? After what you said to me?"

"I did that to protect you!" I screeched. Calax, on the opposite side of the room, looked as if he wanted to run towards me, but Asher held him back.

"I didn't know that." Declan's movements turned jerky, his agitation reflected in his sign language.

I didn't know what to do. One part of me wanted to burrow myself inside of Declan, relish in the familiarity of my best friend, while another part of me wanted to run in the opposite direction.

Despite my outburst, I knew my anger wasn't directed at him, but myself.

It occurred to me suddenly that Declan hadn't escaped the accident unscathed. He lost something when the truck came barreling towards him, more than just a pathetic friend. He lost his hearing.

It was all my fault.

I'd felt guilty before, every day since Ducky's accident, but this was a different type. This was something physical, something I could reach out and touch. Seeing Declan now, his attention riveted on my lips as he watched me speak, I wanted to cry.

Scream.

Hurt.

I wanted to hurt myself, and I hated that thought. I didn't like it when my mind went to such a dark, depressing place.

"Addie," Ducky signed, but then he moved his hands to his lap. He didn't know what to say, but that was good. I wouldn't know how to respond.

"I think I need to be alone for a moment."

"Addie, please, I need for you to know..."

"Please, Ducky. I just need to be alone." I met his eyes, so familiar and sincere, before placing my head in my hands. I wanted to wallow in my self-pity and self-hatred. I was so fucked up, I knew that. I just...I just needed someone, and I had no one.

Declan was silent for only a moment before he nodded slowly. As he scrambled to his feet, I watched, almost mesmerized, as he wiped soot and debris from his clothing.

It hurt to look at him.

God, did it hurt.

As Declan left, Calax came over. Without a word, he sat down beside me.

"I don't want to talk," I whispered.

He grunted. "I know."

And we sat.

~

WE SAT for over an hour in companionable silence. Anytime someone came near us, Calax would glare at them until they scurried away. I'd never been more appreciative of his asshole-ishness than I was at that moment.

Only Tamson dared to venture closer to me, and that was only to give me a can of beans he'd found and a bottle of water. I eyed the items with distaste.

I didn't deserve to eat. I deserved to waste away like the scum I was.

"Baby," Calax murmured, cluing me in that I had spoken that thought aloud. "I hate it when you think that way."

"I'm a horrible person," I said, squeezing my eyes shut in a desperate attempt to will the tears away. "How can you even look at me? I disgust myself."

"Don't say that." His hand clamped down on my good knee. "You're strong and brave and a fighter. I'm so lucky I've gotten to know you."

"How can you say that? Declan's your friend, and it's because of me that he's deaf." Saying the words aloud made them all too real.

"Did you know that whenever Declan would talk about the incident that took his hearing, he never mentioned it as the worst thing that happened to him?" Calax asked. I bit my lip but didn't reply. No, I didn't know that.

And I doubted that to be true. He'd lost his hearing—his ability to motherfucking hear—and Calax dared to say that wasn't the worst thing that had happened to him?

"When he talks about that day, he refers to it as the day he lost his best friend." Though his voice was gruff—I didn't think Calax was capable of anything else—he kept it gentle. His hand squeezed my knee in reassurance. "Of course, I didn't know he was talking about you, and I didn't know this mysterious friend was even still alive, but it was you that he talked about. He really..." He coughed, as if the words had gotten stuck in his throat. "He really loved you. *Loves* you."

I snorted. "He hates me."

Declan's hostility at our first meeting suddenly made perfect sense now. I was surprised he hadn't straight up stabbed me. I would've.

"He never hated you. He was heartbroken." Calax removed his hand from my knee, and I immediately missed its warmth. His hand grabbed mine.

"That was actually one of the reasons why he broke up with his last girlfriend. Because of you."

"Because of me?"

"Because he wouldn't stop talking about you. He loved you."

I wiped at my eyes, the gesture proving ineffective when more tears escaped.

"Why are you telling me all of this?"

Calax grew silent. If his hand hadn't tightened around mine, I would've assumed he hadn't heard me. His jaw clenched.

"Because I want you to be happy, Addie. You deserve all the love and happiness in the world."

"Including yours?" I didn't know what possessed me to say that. But staring up at his handsome face, his shadowed jawline and keen eyes, I found I couldn't regret it. There'd been something brewing between Calax and me for a while now. I'd never dared look at it too closely, but just then, I wasn't thinking clearly. I was consumed by an unbearable pain and the overpowering need to be loved and love someone back.

Calax's face softened. The change was drastic on him, as if he'd suddenly become an entirely different person. His large hand cupped my cheek.

Was he going to kiss me?

Did I want him to?

Someone began to scream, and I wrenched my gaze in the direction the sound came from. I recognized the girl running into the room, her eyes wide and fearful.

Shannon.

"Are you okay?" Asher asked, hurrying to meet her at the entrance. She let out a strangled sob.

"It's...it's Dave! There's... He's not... Something's happening to him. He's not acting like himself. He's..." Shannon leaned forward and vomited.

Black blood.

When she looked back up, her eyes no longer were the emerald green I remembered. As I watched, horrified, red began to eat away the original color as if her pupils were bleeding. Something black crawled beneath her pale skin.

"Shannon?" This came from Ryder as he hesitantly stepped up behind Asher. Shannon cocked her head to the side as she considered him.

"Now you pay attention to me?" she asked in a hoarse voice. Before Ryder could respond, Shannon pounced on him.

CHAPTER 14

Things I never thought I would see in my life—my dad smiling at me, Calax smiling at me, a crazy hostess lunging at my new friend with feral eyes.

Apparently, I was rocking a solid two out of three.

Like a switch being flipped, my mind turned off. I couldn't, *wouldn't*, watch Shannon hurt Ryder. Too much pain and suffering already consumed my life.

I squeezed my eyes shut as if that small gesture could keep me hidden from the world.

Why was the world such a desolate place? When did it start going to hell?

I slapped my hands over my ears to muffle the sounds. Despite this barrier, I still heard the enraged snarl.

Shannon.

I didn't know how, but I knew that sound had come from her.

What the hell was happening?

The only two solutions I could consider were a virus or a drug, both of which seemed scary beyond belief. The latter, though, raised more questions than answers. What type of drug would both Shannon and Buttlicker be taking?

Come to think of it, what did they have in common in the first place? If it was a virus, which I was beginning to believe it was, they must've come into contact at one point, right? Or maybe they came into contact with the same person?

And how was this virus transmitted? Air? Saliva?

My head began to pound with the number of questions piling on top of each other like dirt on a coffin.

I risked opening one eyelid, only one, before wishing I hadn't. I couldn't look away,

Shannon was looming over Ryder. Somehow, her small, dainty body easily incapacitated his much larger, more muscular one. Where did she get all that strength from?

I froze in shock, growing numb as I watched Ryder attempt to push her off. Seeming indifferent to his efforts, she bared her teeth in an aggressive display. Asher grabbed at Shannon, but she flicked him away as if he was nothing more than a pesky bug. He came back, muscles flexing and chest heaving from exertion, and grabbed underneath her armpits. It was obvious that both boys were trying their best not to hurt her.

"Shannon!" another girl cried. She was slightly older than me, mid-twenties if I had to guess, and wore the pink pleated skirt that identified her as a waitress at Rosie's Diner. "What the hell are you doing?"

Shannon's head whipped towards the intruding voice, her lips pulling back into a malicious smirk.

"Hannah," Shannon said stiffly, and then, with her attention fixed on the other girl, she attacked. Her teeth dug into Hannah's neck, and all I could do was watch, unable to move or help. Blood splattered the wall, Shannon's face, and the boy beside Hannah. I could see the white of the bones in the older girl's pale neck

Somebody began to scream, but that sound only seemed to spur Shannon on.

She turned towards the boy next to Hannah and began clawing at his face. Blood cascaded down his cheeks like tear drops, and deep gashes marred his freckled skin.

And Shannon...

Her face morphed into something I would never be able to forget. Gone was the flirtatious girl who occasionally said hi to me in passing. Her blonde hair, once a vibrant sheen, now had balding spots. Her porcelain skin rippled like a reflective pool of water, veins darkening and twitching beneath the surface. She barely seemed to process that her fingernails were getting pulled off with each desperate swipe at the now dead body. Blood pooled around them all, staining Shannon's uniform and skin. If you hadn't seen her attack, if you hadn't heard their screams, you might've believed that all three of them were lovers in an intimate embrace.

Transfixed on the macabre sight in front me, I barely registered another figure entering the dimly lit room. He, too, had flesh dangling precariously from his face, as if he'd pulled at the skin repeatedly. His hands twitched, curling into claws by his sides, and his blood-red eyes surveyed the room with a predatory-like awareness.

And then they landed on me.

Prime prey, all broken and pathetic against the wall. In truth, if I were a carnivore, I would've eaten myself a long time ago. If, of course, I could eat myself. Not that it was possible to do so without dying. But if I could live and eat myself...

Good god. I really was insane.

The new guy took a threatening step in my direction, and I attempted to press myself farther into the wall.

Nothing to see here. Just wall plaster. I'm just wall plaster.

I squeezed my eyes shut. If I was going to die, I really didn't want to see it coming. Why couldn't my death be peaceful? Was that too much to ask? It occurred to me that I deserved this horrific death. It seemed monsters like me got what they deserved in the end.

I heard the rustling of fabric, but no pain came to me. I dared to open my eyes, startled to see Tam planted in front of me, hands raised in a defensive stance.

The two men went at each other, a flurry of fists and snarls, the latter of which came from Mr. Zombie. I didn't dare even breathe, afraid that any movement or sound would distract Tam.

A rough hand grabbed my arm, and I jerked away.

"No time, Princess," a familiar voice said in a breathless whisper. Ronan.

Before I could gasp, he threw me over his shoulder in a fireman carry. My body, aching everywhere, hung like dead weight. Slightly irrational, I couldn't help but pity Ronan for having to carry my heavy ass. It wasn't that I was fat, necessarily, but the bandages and makeshift cast on my leg definitely weighed me down.

Not the time, Addie, I mentally berated myself, trying to ignore the intense, blistering pain that shot up my spine from the way Ronan held me.

Shannon had turned away from her victims, teeth bared as she faced the newcomer. Tamson was now face down on the ground.

I felt a moment of panic before I saw him twitch, and Declan helped him to his feet.

Ronan began to run down the hallway, but with the way he held me, I was still able to see the scene we were leaving behind. I watched Shannon attack the new zombie—because what else could he be? They clawed and bit at each other, blood coating their skin.

An older woman, who sat on the far side of the room, got up and attempted to walk around them. They paused mid-fight, and in unison, they turned towards the woman, grabbing and beginning to eat her. Actually eat her.

It was something that I didn't think could happen in real life, only in movies. Their teeth broke through skin.

Stop.

Please stop.

Try as I might, I couldn't get the words to leave my mouth. Large spikes of terror shot through me, drowning out any surprise I might've felt at their actions. Drowning out even the pain that was gradually diminishing with every passing second as numbness took its place.

I tried to process everything I'd just seen. I tried to put an emotion to the feelings churning in my stomach and the haziness clouding my thoughts. I needed to think coherently. I needed to understand what just happened.

Nothing made sense anymore.

Ronan led me into a new, unfamiliar room and carefully lowered me into a chair. I winced at the pain firing through my leg but attempted to tamp down on my urge to cry. There were more important things to focus on than my stupid injury. And besides, I was used to pain.

It was the one thing in life I could control.

The rest of the guys, and a couple of other people that had been in the other room with us, including Elena and Bikini, ran in behind us. Calax and Declan slammed and held the door shut while Ryder, with the help of Asher, pushed a fridge in front of it. The boys continued adding items to create a makeshift barricade that, hopefully, would keep out the rest of the world.

I didn't have high hopes.

I'd seen plenty of horror movies. Wasn't this where we all died? Trapped, confined in a small space, lacking resources, and the only light reliant on a faulty at best generator. I mean, at least I wasn't the bitchy girl. They always died first in those movies.

"Actually," Ryder said casually, sitting down beside me. Fuck. I must've spoken aloud again. "It's the black guy."

"I'll write you a eulogy," I deadpanned. Ryder tried to smile, but it was clear he had to force it.

With the most pressing, immediate threat neutralized for now, I took the opportunity to look around the room we hunkered down in.

There was a long table in the center, surrounded by miscellaneous chairs that didn't seem to have a set style—a lawn chair, a plastic one, and even a recliner. The room was relatively barren besides a microwave on the far counter and a fridge. A time-clock was on the opposite wall. There was an adjacent staircase, but with the amount of clutter, I didn't expect us to get out of there anytime soon.

It was the fridge the guys went to first, still pressed against the door. Empty, mostly, besides a water bottle and a juice box. Declan grabbed them both.

"What the fuck are we going to do?" Elena screamed. She was huddled together with the group of girls from earlier. She no longer was the calm and composed girl fawning over the boys. She looked absolutely terrified just then, her face streaked with tears and her hair matted with dry blood.

"I don't know," Asher responded, not unkindly. His answer, however, didn't placate Elena. She stormed over to him, tiny hands curled into tinier fists. Before I could react, she pounded said fists against Asher's chest.

"Cut that shit out!" I snapped, an almost incandescent fury burning through me at seeing Elena hurt Asher. Or at least attempting to hurt. I was almost positive Asher's chest was made of steel. "If we want to get out of this alive, we have to work together, and that means no petty fights amongst ourselves."

I glanced at each individual face as I spoke to emphasize my point.

Besides the guys, Elena, and Bikini, I didn't recognize anyone else in the room with us. There was a cluster of girls that I assumed was with Elena, and a young man wearing a white lifeguard shirt. An older couple held on to each other in the far corner, away from everybody else, and another man stood stoutly beside Declan, eyes scanning the room intensely. I felt momentarily relieved that there were no children with us.

I wouldn't be able to handle that pressure.

"Okay," I said, once I'd gathered everyone's attention. "Here's what we know. Shannon and another guy—"

"Dave," the unfamiliar man supplied. I nodded gratefully.

"Yes, Shannon and Dave are not themselves."

"They're fucking zombies!" Bikini cried.

"We don't know that," Tam countered immediately. "It could be a new drug in circulation or a simple virus that is somehow messing with their brain."

"We have to kill them," the man said, crossing his arms over his chest. From the black leather he wore, I guessed he was a part of the resort's security.

"We can't kill them, Brad!" Asher sounded aghast at the prospect.

"Those...*things* aren't Shannon and Dave anymore. For all we know, Hannah and

Liam could be like them now. We don't know what the hell we're dealing with," the man, Brad apparently, insisted.

"There must be another way."

"How long do you think it will be until someone comes for us?" I asked no one in particular.

"Knowing Sarge, there's already a group digging us out," Elena said with a huff. I blinked at the name.

The mysterious Sarge. Who was he, and how would he be able to gather the manpower to save us?

Instead of asking all of that, I nodded seriously.

"Maybe we should just wait it out."

Brad's hands clenched by his sides.

"For how long? We have no food in here and only one fucking water bottle! It might take them days to get us out, if not weeks! I vote we kill those bastards outside and grab our water supply!"

"Those bastards," snapped Asher, his voice sharper than I'd ever heard before, "are our friends. You heard them speak. Some cognitive function remains in their minds. I believe they can be saved."

Brad stepped forward until he was nose to nose with Asher.

"We're saving murderers now, boy?" he asked. He pointed an accusatory finger in Asher's face, but Asher swatted it away.

"Don't fucking act like you're so much better than me. What you're suggesting is murder. Would you kill someone if they were high on weed and acting crazy?"

"This is different, and you know it!"

"Enough!" My voice broke through their fight like the crack of a whip. Both men turned towards me, eyes flashing. "You two fighting isn't going to help anything."

Brad's expression turned almost thoughtful as he considered me.

"Why don't we use the bitch as bait? Allow the Ragers to munch on her while we grab the water and food we collected."

His proclamation was met with a chorus of threats. The boys immediately stood in front of me, a protective wall of muscle.

I couldn't help but think back to what he said. Rager? I supposed that description was fitting with what we saw. Shannon and Dave had appeared to be almost blinded by rage, as if their entire mindset was focused on the primal hunt and the hunt alone.

"Don't fucking look at her!" Ryder snapped, jarring me from my thoughts. The boys were still facing off with Brad. They all seemed to be trembling with barely suppressed anger.

"She's injured. Probably bleeding out if her arm is any indication. Why wouldn't we sacrifice her for the good of us all?"

"Do you fucking hear yourself?" Tam exploded. My sweet, shy Tam. I didn't like it when he was angry. Everything inside of me wanted to walk over to him and touch him. Soothe him.

"Which one would it be? Those monsters' lives or that girl's? You can't have both."

"You even try to touch her, and you'll fucking die," Calax threatened.

I appreciated him standing up for me, but...

"Maybe he's right."

Every head turned my way. Grimacing under their combined stares, I focused on the brace supporting my leg.

"We don't know how long we're going to be down here. What if it takes weeks for them to find us? I mean, does anyone know that we're here? Most people would go to the level just above us, because only a select few have keys to this one. Brad's right —we need the food and water we collected."

"No fucking way," Calax hissed.

"Don't even think about it, Princess."

Declan just glared.

"I'm injured, that much is obvious. I'll be lucky if I'm even able to keep this damn leg." Tears filled my eyes, but I refused, absolutely refused, to let them spill. I met each boy's stare before turning towards Declan. Towards Ducky. His face was impassive.

"I have done so many horrible things, some of which can never be forgiven. But I can do this. I can save lives. Maybe, just maybe, this will redeem myself enough so that I can die without hating myself."

For a moment, Declan continued to stare at me, face impassive. The first crack I saw in his front was the trembling of his lips. His eyes began blinking rapidly in an attempt to hold his tears at bay. I watched with rapt fascination as he fell to his knees in front of me.

And then he spoke. His voice was hoarse from years without use, but it was still a voice I loved dearly. It was Ducky's voice.

"No."

One word.

Like a domino falling over, the boys took that as indication to move. They surrounded me protectively, eyes throwing daggers at the other occupants in this room.

"No way in hell."

"Not happening, Kitten. You're stuck with us."

"We protect our own."

Brad sputtered. "It's her fucking choice whether or not she wants to." To me, he said, "Don't be selfish. You have to think about the others."

"Why don't you be the bait, then?" Ronan demanded. His muscles coiled tight under his shirt, like a snake preparing to attack. I put my hand on his bicep to calm him, and he deflated marginally.

"I'm not injured," Brad said with a sneer, his voice laced with indignation and irritation.

Calax took a menacing step forward. "We could change that."

"Enough, okay?" I snapped. I tugged at Calax's arm until he turned to face me. His wild eyes bounced all around me before finally resting on my face. They seemed to have trouble focusing. "Enough."

"She's right." This voice came from an unlikely ally. Elena stepped closer to Brad, head tilted to the side. "For now, we're fine. We'll see how long it takes the cavalry to come. Who knows? The situation might look different tomorrow."

CHAPTER 15

*T*he fever set in that night.

I tossed and turned, but it did little to smother the flames attacking my skin. Sweat beaded my forehead, dripping down my cheeks and seeping into my clothes. At some point, the power must've gone out. We used our phone lights for as long as we could before they, too, went dead.

It was dark, almost unnaturally so, like a spilt cauldron of ink. I couldn't even see my hands in front of my face, let alone the other occupants of the room.

"How are you feeling?" Tam whispered. He brushed his hand against my forehead. We previously had taken ice from the freezer in order to lower my fever, but our supply had long since dwindled.

My teeth clattered as I said, "Shitty."

"Calvary is going to be here soon, Princess," Ryder said from the other side of me.

Even I knew that was bullcrap.

My body alternated between fits of intense heat and a numb coldness. I tried to escape these episodes with drastic movements, but that only brought pain to my leg and arm.

From experience, I knew not to whimper. Whenever I outwardly expressed my pain, the boys would react with cries of their own. I wanted to spare them of this as much as I could.

Though I couldn't communicate with Declan at all, I felt his presence behind me. He currently had my head in his lap, gently stroking my hair away from my sweaty face. Calax had grown frantic, pulling at the barricade in front of the staircase ever since my fever set in. I could hear him then, mumbling under his breath and cussing at anyone who came too close to him. He was desperate for an escape, desperate to save me, but I knew the effort was futile.

"Tell me something about you," I said softly, squeezing Tam's hand. I wasn't sure if he would be willing to share, what with his shyness, but the silence was almost oppressive. Even Elena had stopped her bitching when my condition worsened. They all thought I was going to die.

But I'd dealt with worse, and I would be damned before something as insignificant as an infection and broken leg took me in.

"Well," Tam began hesitantly. I heard his teeth clench together, and I gave his hand another squeeze.

"You don't have to tell me anything if you're not comfortable."

"It's fine." He lowered his voice to a whisper. This was just between him and me, and everybody else faded into the background. "I didn't have the best childhood either. My birth parents abused drugs, and I was adopted by my grandma when I was five." He paused for a second, and when he spoke next, I could hear the smile in his voice. "She was the best damn mother I could've ever had. She made sure I wanted for nothing. I was…a shy kid, to put it mildly, but she never made me feel bad for being exactly who I was. She supported me and my decision to join MMA." I squeezed our connected hands when he paused again. From his shuddering breath, I knew that the next part of the story wouldn't have a happily ever after. "She died when I was twelve."

I wanted to tell him that I was sorry, but I knew he didn't want my pity. There was a distinct difference between sympathy and empathy. You never really understood something until you'd been through it yourself. The only death I'd experienced had been Ducky's, and apparently, that hadn't even been a real death.

"I moved into a foster home shortly after. They were nice and all, but I couldn't live there. They always stared at me with pity, with poor-parentless-kid looks. So I ran away.

"I was alone on the streets until I was thirteen when I came across two boys playing baseball at the local park. I asked them if I could play, but the dickhead said no."

"In my defense," Ryder said with a hint of a smile in his voice, "you looked fucking creepy."

"I was homeless, you ass," Tam said with a laugh, but then instantly sobered. "Yeah, the dick was Ryder and the other kid was Sarge. I got to talking with them, and they told me about their school. Sarge helped me apply, and the rest is history."

"So you got your happy ending," I said airily. He leaned forward to kiss the top of my head.

"Maybe."

We were silent, each lost in our own thoughts. Declan's fingers against my cheeks were the only constant.

Somewhere in the darkness, Calax let out a string of curses, and Asher muttered something in response. Probably trying to calm him. Someone on the opposite side of the room was rearranging furniture. Why someone would do that when it was pitch black was beyond my comprehension.

I was suddenly very tired, overwhelmingly so. My eyelids fluttered as I struggled to keep them opened.

"You can't go to sleep yet, Kitten," Ryder said. "You have to stay awake."

"I'm tired," I mumbled, my words an inarticulate mesh.

"I know, but you have to stay awake."

The boys began talking about random things. Funny stories from school, Ryder's crazy ex-girlfriend—though Ryder insisted that they had never really dated—and plans for when we escaped. Every once in a while, I felt Declan's fingers feather against my pulse as if to make sure I was still alive. After the tenth time, I felt slightly offended that he doubted my ability to survive.

"Nobody's doubting you honey," Tam said. "We're just worried."

"Don't be. I'll be fine." My voice came out hoarse, scratchy almost, contradicting my statement.

"Did you know what I wanted to be when I was younger?" Ryder asked me suddenly. I blinked at the abrupt change of topic.

"A musician who's a horrible flirt?" I offered, and I heard him chuckle.

"I actually wanted to be a realtor."

"A realtor?" I asked in disbelief. Most kids said something along the lines of doctor or astronaut. I had to admit that Ryder was one of a kind.

"My foster dad was one, and I wanted to be just like him when I grew up."

"And then you fell in love with music?" I guessed.

He agreed. "And then I fell in love with music."

"Do you sing?"

His hand lightly trailed across my collarbone, leaving goosebumps in its wake.

"I do."

"Could you sing me something?"

If I was going to die, I at least wanted to die listening to this man's beautiful, raspy voice.

"You're not going to die, but I do agree that my voice is beautiful."

And then he began to sing. It was soulful, magical, as if he was transporting me to another place and time. I felt each word like a knife in my heart. He sung of love lost and hope for the future.

I could've listened to him all day. I might've, if I hadn't felt myself start to doze off. I tried my hardest to resist the pulls of sleep, but my body was weak and weighed down.

And it was so tempting…

I only had a second to think that sleep might be a really bad idea before darkness consumed my thoughts.

I DREAMED I was thirteen again, watching the truck barreling down on Ducky. I watched his body flip, like a gymnast doing a complicated routine, before his corpse settled on the ground, a puddle of blood surrounding him.

Unlike my past self, I ran towards where Ducky was sprawled. Dropping to my knees beside him, I sobbed into his hair.

His eyes snapped open suddenly. His face gradually began to shift, skin tightening over his bones to rid himself of his baby fat. Dark brown hair, currently grazing his waist, shrunk back into his head until it resembled the hair I was now familiar with.

Declan.

"Why did you do this to me?" he asked, voice devoid of any emotion. There was no lisp to his words, no stuttering.

This was what Declan would've sounded like if he hadn't lost his hearing.

"I'm sorry, Ducky. I am so sorry."

"You deserve to die." His hand grabbed my wrist, and I let out a squeal as his fingers tightened. They were going to leave a nasty bruise.

"Declan, you're hurting me. Please."

"And you didn't hurt me? You deserve this. You deserve everything that's happening to you."

"I'm sorry."

His eyes narrowed on me.

"You're only sorry because you got caught."

I woke up to someone's hand over my mouth.

At first, I thought it was one of the boys, unintentionally being aggressive. But then the person leaned down until his mouth was by my ear.

"Don't say a word, or I'll cut the throat of your deaf friend."

Brad.

My muscles tensed up, but I managed a weak nod.

To be honest, that wasn't the first time I'd been awoken by a strange man. However, it was the first time that I could remember being more pissed than scared. Couldn't he have just let me sleep?

To my right, I heard the familiar roar of Ryder's snore. On the opposite side, Tam's breathing was nice and even. I didn't know where Declan was, but I thought I heard Ronan mumble something in his sleep near my head.

Before I could smack the dickhead that dared disturb my sleep, he lifted me into his arms. Whatever protest I might've conjured died on my lips when I felt the press of a knife to my neck.

Well damn. He was taking this kidnapping thing pretty seriously.

He walked with startling accuracy through the snoring crowd, only stopping once we reached whatever destination he had in mind. How he could see in the dark was beyond me, and I didn't dare ask. I mean, I wasn't in the mood to be knifed just yet.

I let out a whimper as he hoisted me to one arm, like I was a toddler getting carried around by her parents.

"Quiet," he hissed. Well excuse me if my cry of pain wasn't silent enough for you. *Bastard.*

I heard what sounded like a door opening, and then we were walking again. It suddenly occurred to me where we were going. This theory was only reinforced when he switched on his phone light, and I saw the familiar hall outside of the break room.

He was sacrificing me to Shannon and what's his name.

And he had light while we had been struggling in the darkness.

I honestly couldn't tell you which one pissed me off more. I fucking hated the darkness, probably even more than I hated getting sacrificed to zombies.

Deeming me capable of walking, he dropped me unceremoniously onto the ground. I let out a cry as my leg jammed into the wooden floor. The pain was immediate and indescribable. No words could articulate the flames of fire creeping up my legs, my nerves, burning me alive.

Damn him. Damn him to the deepest pit of hell.

"Keep swearing all you want, sunshine. I'm doing us all a favor."

"Which is what exactly?" I grunted out. My legs wobbled underneath me as I attempted to haul myself to my feet. The bastard had dropped me too far away from a wall to be able to use it to steady myself. Instead, I was forced to awkwardly crawl onto my good knee, unsavory substances and grit clinging to my hands. This position caused my weak, bloody arm to scream in protest, but I ignored it.

"Are you just going to leave me here?" I whispered harshly. Brad—Damn Brad— had stealthily moved to a branching hallway, the light from his phone suffusing his features in a yellow glow. The bastard had the nerve to smile at me.

"I'm going to wait until they're distracted and then grab the supplies. Are you really so selfish you can't see the good your sacrifice will bring?"

I rolled my eyes, because really, what more could I do?

"Are you really so stupid that you can't see the death that will come to you when the guys realize what you did?"

"They'll thank me in the long run. Once we survive." He paused. "I'm sorry that it had to be this way."

From the sincerity in his voice, I realized he was telling the truth. He was sorry, but in his mind, there was no other alternative. It was me or them, and he had obviously made his choice.

I couldn't say I blamed him. From his perspective, I was nothing more than some rich, bitchy girl. I had everything, while he had nothing. It was the same story, the same cliché, and there was nothing I could do to change his mentality. He was the hero in his story, and I, the villain.

It never really struck me how easily death could occur. It was just a word. How many times had I wished death would claim me? How many times had I wished that I would survive?

I supposed that I had an unhealthy relationship with good old death. It was my constant companion. I had gotten close to meeting him too many times to count.

I could admit that I was scared when the light was snatched away, leaving nothing but the familiar darkness. My heart thumped erratically in my chest, threatening to break free from my ribcage.

Somewhere in the darkness, I heard a growl.

Well shit.

The growl was immediately followed by a voice.

"Come out, come out wherever you are."

Okay, let me just give you all a word of advice. If a creepy zombie-like creature asks you to come out, you stay fucking put. Or you curl up in a ball and cry. Any of those are acceptable responses.

I didn't dare to breathe. Hell, I didn't even dare think, afraid that my idiotic mind would speak the thought aloud. It always happened when I was panicking.

And I was most definitely panicking.

Stay calm, Addie. Stay calm.

I wondered if I would feel pain when I died. I wondered if I would scream in agony or if death would be a merciful escape. I hoped for the latter but not for the most obvious reasons.

I was afraid that if I screamed, the boys would come running. If I was going to be sacrificed, those boys were going to reap the benefits.

They were my first friends, and they would be my last.

Depressing, even by my standards.

Something moved ahead of me. It sounded like fingernails dragging against the wall.

Okay, so that was slightly terrifying.

I squeezed my eyes shut and waited. That was all I could do—wait for death.

Exactly how I wanted to spend my Friday night.

My eyes were still closed when Shannon jumped on me. They remained closed as her teeth gnawed on my neck, ripping apart skin and tendons. They remained closed when somebody began to shout, and then gunshots fired.

I barely processed Shannon's dead body on top of mine.

People rushed to and fro. I heard a voice that sounded like Calax's, but it was weak at best. Two men hoisted me onto a stretcher, and I was carted up what seemed like a staircase.

A staircase?

Did help finally come?

I dared to open my eyes then.

The moon was the first thing I saw, followed by the red and blue flashing lights of numerous fire trucks and ambulances. It was the ambulance that I was led into, my weak body and even weaker mind trying to hold onto consciousness.

A woman touched my neck.

My leg.

My arm.

Voices.

So many voices.

Tired.

And then I slept.

CHAPTER 16

*T*he first time I almost died, I had been nine.

Surprisingly, the blow hadn't been delivered by Daddy or Mommy, but by a business associate of my father. His name had been Luka, but I would forever refer to him as Evil Bastard.

To EB, I was nothing more than a pawn to use against DOD. I'd tried to tell him that I meant nothing to the old fart, that the love he gave me was conditional at best. If, that was, you could even call it love.

That didn't matter to EB.

I remembered his hand, steady on the gun, as he lowered it towards my stomach. I remembered how I'd begged for my life, begged for this man to understand that I was innocent in this battle between families.

A battle that I had yet to fully understand.

That didn't stop the man from pulling the trigger.

For a moment, I'd been stunned, unable to fully comprehend what had just happened. Had he really shot me?

My body had lurched forward, and my hands had instinctively gone to my stomach. The fabric of my shirt was stained with blood.

There was so much blood.

~

My eyelids fluttered open, but immediately slammed closed again when a bright light blinded me.

Throbbing. My head was throbbing, as if someone was stabbing my brain repeatedly with a rusty knife.

I dared to open my eyes again.

The first thing I saw was the bright, pink cast on my leg. Turning my head, I noted the white bandages on my arm.

What the hell?

Taking in the rest of the room, I realized that I was lying on a small cot, with only a thin blanket wrapped around my waist. I must've moved at some point during my sleep. The pungent stench of bleach assaulted my nose. I always hated that particular smell, since it reminded me of the frequent beatings I'd been forced to endure and the numerous resulting hospital trips.

A hospital.

But not the resort's hospital. No, I didn't recognize this room with its opened blinds and assortment of medical tools.

For a moment, I remained motionless, listening to the steady patter of my heartbeat.

I tried to recall how I ended up in this sparsely lit room with its white walls and gray bedding.

Brad had tried to kill me, hadn't he? Yes, I remembered that vividly. The bastard had wanted to feed me to Shannon! Fury churned in my stomach.

And then what happened?

I vaguely remembered gunshots, and then nothing. What had happened? How had I ended up here?

"I see that you're awake," a kind voice said. This voice belonged to a petite older woman with light blonde hair and purple scrubs. Her expression appeared friendly enough as she checked my vitals on the screen.

"You seem to be doing better," she continued, flashing me a smile. She fiddled with something, my IV, before pulling back. "I'm sure you have some questions."

"Only a few," I said with heavy sarcasm. She smiled again, undeterred by my bitterness. Maybe she was just one of those people that always smiled, even when the world turned to shit around them.

"The doctor should arrive soon. Fortunately, we were able to operate in time to save that leg of yours." She nodded towards said leg, propped up by strings hanging from the ceiling. "We were able to stop the infection, and your wounds are healing quite nicely."

"What happened? What's going on?" I pressed my palm against my forehead, as if I would somehow be able to conjure memories back into my brain.

"The police should also be here shortly to talk to you," the nurse said, ignoring my questions.

Where are the guys? Did they make it out okay?

I didn't dare voice these questions aloud. I feared what the answer would be.

"Where are my parents?" I asked instead. Her expression darkened, eyes glimmering with sympathy.

"Unfortunately, they weren't able to stay. You've been unconscious for a while."

I hesitated, biting my bottom lip, before I blurted out what I really wanted to know. "Is there anyone waiting for me?"

Like six handsome young men?

Again, the nurse flashed me a kind smile.

"I'm sorry, hun, but with everything that's been happening..."

"It's okay," I said quickly, ignoring the bitter taste in my mouth. "I understand."

What I understood was that I was alone, again. What had I expected? For the boys to continue talking with me after they left the resort? I was a freak, a murderer, and it was no wonder they wanted nothing to do with me. Despite knowing the reasons, my stomach clenched with the loneliness that threatened to bury me alive.

I, once again, had nobody.

But hey, on the bright side, that was my longest friendship since Ducky. A solid week, give or take.

The doctor came in right after the nurse left and reiterated what the nurse had already told me.

Lucky blah blah blah leg blah blah blah infection.

I barely paid him any mind.

After he left, I fiddled with the remote connected to the bed by a wire.

I flipped through channels absently, though most of the stations featured the same story—mysterious virus and unpredictable weather.

I focused on a news story about this.

Virus continued to baffle scientists.

No cure found.

Tsunami hits the east coast, killing hundreds.

Death count in Kansas City reaches one thousand.

Paris reporting erratic behavior by citizens.

My mind swirled with the onslaught of information. Unable to handle it all, I switched the TV off and dropped the remote.

Nik...

The thought of my little brother made my throat close with panic, but I reminded myself that he was as safe as he was gonna be. That he was with a family who would die for him and loved him unconditionally.

Tsunamis.

Earthquakes

Viruses.

This couldn't be happening. This type of thing just didn't happen in real life. In books, maybe. In movies, sure.

But here?

Now?

I squeezed my eyelids shut in an attempt to rid myself of the images from both the resort and television. I felt nauseous. The amount of death and violence...

I wanted the ground to swallow me whole. Anything to escape the horrors of this world. It was hell. This world was hell.

Had my past sins somehow caused this? Was that why this was happening?

That hardly seemed fair. The world shouldn't suffer because of my past transgressions.

I wished that I was smarter, better able to fully comprehend what was happening and why. Taxes and business law classes were so helpful at this moment—said no one ever. Why hadn't I been able to study the environment or pathogens?

Sighing, I turned towards the sliver of sunlight that illuminated the room through the cracked blinds. The day looked beautiful, not at all like a tornado had struck. The sun rose high in the sky, making the morning dew on the grass shine. There were a few people in the hospital courtyard that I could see, but nobody I recognized.

I tried not to be hurt by that. I really, really tried.

❧

I spent three days in the hospital. Three days of monotonous procedures consisting of needles jabbing into my skin and my body being checked over thoroughly. I probably stunk something awful by the time they released me, since the damn nurse didn't allow me to shower. No, she insisted on something called a sponge bath, as if I was really going to let a complete stranger wipe me down.

The doctor gave me a wheelchair that my insurance paid for. I was supposed to remain in it for two weeks before I'd be able to move to crutches. I hated the wheelchair with a passion. It made me feel weak, like an invalid. I understood the need, of course, what with the stitches on my arm and back prohibiting me from using crutches, but I still complained as I was wheeled outside.

My parents hadn't even bothered to pick me up. No sir, they sent the limo driver to do that. The damn limo driver. It wasn't as if I necessarily wanted to see my parents, but anything would've been better than the impassive man whose name was never given to me. Couldn't I, at least for a moment, have people that loved me? Was that too much to ask for? I supposed the bitterness stemmed from the lack of love distributed to me by my parents. There was only so much a girl could deal with before she exploded. Or imploded, whichever one you prefer.

"Where are we going?" I asked the driver after I managed to maneuver myself into the leather seat.

"A hotel," he answered stiffly. I waited for him to offer up more information, but he remained mute. He worked for my parents, so I wasn't even surprised. The employees seemed to have a clause in their contracts that demanded they be a bitch to me, no matter the situation.

Apparently, nearly dying didn't change that mentality.

With nothing left to do, I fiddled with the lock on the door. Push in. Push out. Push in. Push out.

I pretended that I was heading home to a large, Victorian manor with sweeping pillars and a throng of trees surrounding it. I pretended that my family would be greeting me at the door, arms outstretched as they welcomed me. It was stupid, wistful thinking, but I couldn't help the daydream that I was going somewhere where I was wanted and not just tolerated.

Through the tinted windows, I watched the scenery change from rolling landscapes to toppled buildings and crushed houses. Debris coated the road, wind carrying it from its initial resting place. It appeared to be such a desolate place, I could barely connect it to the town I once knew and hated. The farther away we drove from the hospital, the more I noticed trees littering the ground and once-grand buildings reverted to loose wood and plaster.

Horror filled me at the destruction.

We drove for what felt like hours before the car pulled into a modest, three-story hotel with manicured grass and freshly washed windows. This hotel must've missed the majority of the destruction wrought by the tornado.

"Thank you," I said to the driver opening the door. He, of course, ignored me.

It was difficult to seat myself back in the wheelchair. Mr. Driver Asshole refused to help me, so I settled for awkwardly jamming my elbow into the doorframe and then accidentally rolling the chair down a hill.

Fun times.

By the time I finally made it inside, a suitcase of my belongings planted firmly on my lap, I had managed to run into three walls and two doors. How the latter had happened, when I only needed to enter one door, was a true testament of my skills.

In my defense, I hadn't known that the door wouldn't open automatically. Seriously. What was the point of the blue handicap button if it didn't work?

The manager of this hotel, employed under my father, handed me a room key. I didn't bother asking where I would be staying. I just didn't care anymore.

I didn't care about anything.

Wheeling myself into the elevator, I ignored the angry looks I received from the guests as the chair took up their precious space in the small box. Those lazy fuckers could've walked up the staircase. They weren't in a wheelchair.

The elevator pinged at the second floor, and I successfully maneuvered myself into the hallway. I heard one of my fellow elevator riders mutter something under his breath that sounded like "finally," and I flipped him off.

The sparsely lit hallway had horrible, flowered wallpaper and burgundy carpeting. Just looking at it made me want to vomit.

My room, of course, was the farthest one down the hall. I struggled to wheel myself around the corner, and then struggled yet again to actually fit through the doorway. Were doors always this small?

By the time I made it inside the room, I was utterly exhausted. On the bright side, I didn't need to work out ever again. Nope, this girl could eat all the chocolate she wanted to compensate for such a rigorous workout.

Yay me. Small victories.

I surveyed the small room, noting with glee the single bed on the plush carpeting. I wasn't ready to face my parents yet. I didn't think I would ever be ready. The room was simple—a desk, leather chair, mini-fridge, microwave, and a bathroom. The plainness of the room did not deter me as it would've my parents. I much preferred this lightly furnished room than the elaborate designs back at the resort.

This hotel, I knew, was part of a chain owned by my dear parents. I hadn't been to this specific one, but I had been to one similar.

Daddy called this his "dump." The employees were his "dumpers," and the guests were the "garbage." My dad was a very eloquent man, mind you.

Throwing myself onto the quilted bed, I allowed my mind to think over everything that had happened. Those thoughts only brought tiny pinpricks of terror, all surrounding six certain men. What happened to them? I'd jumped to the conclusion that they wanted nothing to do with me, but what if I was wrong? What if they had been hurt? Or died?

What if they were still trapped beneath the resort?

If that was the case, then that would make me a shitty friend. Friends didn't let friends get trapped beneath resorts. Wasn't that common sense?

Groaning, I pulled at my greasy hair in anger and frustration.

I didn't want to think about the guys. Either option was not pleasant. I would've much preferred the guys to have decided that they hated me than for them to still be trapped. I would've even preferred for them to decide that Elena would be better suited as their sister that wasn't a sister instead of me.

Anything was better than the alternative.

Muffling my scream with a pillow, I emptied my mind. It was easier that way.

I didn't want to feel the pain.

I did, however, want to feel the water from a shower. How to get there…?

"Fucking shit. Damn dick sucking bitch. Fuck."

Trying to move in a wheelchair is difficult to say the least. Trying to move in a wheelchair in the middle of the night is damn near impossible.

After many new bruises and curse words—and one near death experience involving a pool—I made my way to the back of the hotel.

I hadn't had a direction in mind when I began my aimless wander. I'd just wanted to get out. Out of the room, out of my head, out of my life. Somehow, my feet—wheels—found themselves at the back lot of the hotel, next to an abandoned basketball court and a playset.

It was creepy back here so late. The crescent moon provided very little light. But the air was refreshing, and the pungent smell of lilacs made me sigh in relief. Anything, and I meant anything, was better than staying in the stuffy confines of that room.

That was, of course, until a twig snapped in the distance.

I froze, hands clenched around my wheels. I may have been a speed demon, but dammit, there were too many walls for me not to hit at least one of them if I had to escape.

Now, you might've thought that it was completely idiotic to go outside when there was a mysterious virus or drug or whatever. In my defense, I hadn't expected anything to be inside the gates of the hotel.

And, to be completely honest, I never really planned through my decisions until after I was dealing with the consequences. It was only then that I would look back and realize that I had messed the fuck up.

Healthy, I know.

Slowly, so as to not to alert whoever was here with me that I was retreating, I wheeled myself backwards. Of course, an ear-splitting squeak erupted from the chair.

Of course.

Because things couldn't just go smoothly for once, could it? Get it? Smoothly? Because of the chair… Oh, never mind.

Maybe whoever was here, whoever was lurking in the shadows of the swing set, wouldn't see me. Maybe I could escape back through the door unnoticed.

Just as I thought this, a small figure hurled at me, hissing.

I squeaked, a decidedly pathetic attempt at a scream if I wanted someone to hear me, and used my arms as a protective shield for my face.

The fur ball jumped onto my lap and—

Fur?

I slowly lowered my hands and stared at the offending creature. The cat's fur was matted to its head, dark rivulets of blood cascading down its nose. One look, and I determined that the cat was a boy.

Pushing away my unease, I used my finger to scratch behind its ear. The cat purred.

"What are you doing out here? Where's your owner?" I cooed in a high-pitched voice that made me wince. Apparently, I turned into an Elena when it came to animals.

I felt along the cat's neck.

"You have no collar, boy. Where did you come from?"

I waited, actually waited, as if the cat was going to answer me. Sometimes, I really did question my sanity.

"You're filthy, do you know that?"

Suddenly, the cat lurched to its feet on my lap and turned towards the playset. The hairs on his back stood on end, and he began hissing yet again.

"What's the matter, boy?" I asked softly, petting beneath his chin. Unlike before, the cat did not calm with my touch. He continued to stare at the thicket of trees surrounding the playground. It was almost as if…as if…

As if there was someone there.

Like cold water had been poured down my shirt, I tucked the cat closer against my chest with one hand. With my other hand, I began to roll back towards the door.

I didn't dare look behind me, look towards where the cat was still hissing. I didn't want to see what was out there. I didn't even want to know.

Using my key card, I quickly scrambled back inside, the wheel from my chair nearly getting stuck on the rug.

The cat, now that we were inside, seemed to calm considerably. He kneaded my lap with his tiny feet before curling up into a ball.

I petted his back absently, but my eyes couldn't help but wander towards the window next to the door.

At first, I didn't see anything. I had thought maybe I'd imagined the whole thing. Just as I was about to turn away, something stepped into the thin shaft of moonlight.

Taking in its torn ear and the wagging tail, I realized it was a dog. A freaking dog. Suddenly, the cat's behavior made sense, and it made me feel like an idiot. I almost laughed at myself and my paranoia. I watched the dog take a few steps closer, now standing underneath the hotel's outdoor lights. The laughter died in my throat.

On closer inspection, I saw the dog's eyes were a bright, vivid red. Blood red. Something white was foaming at its mouth.

Well shit.

CHAPTER 17

I named the cat My Only Friend, or Mof for short. I was pleased to find, after an intense scrub down, that Mof had fur as black as night, like molten obsidian stones. I knew some people believed that black cats were a sign of bad luck, but come on. Have you ever seen one before?

They're freaking adorable.

Shaking out his wet fur, Mof made himself comfortable on the edge of my bed. I'd never had a pet before, and I didn't know the first thing to do with him. Should I search for his owner? Buy him a collar?

Feed him?

Yes, I should definitely feed him.

Reaching into my duffle bag, I grabbed my phone and charger. I hadn't looked at the damn thing in days, not since I received the text message from Dad instructing me to go to the lobby. I really sucked at owning a phone.

"Don't worry, handsome man," I said to Mof, scratching behind his ears. "I'm going to look up what I can and can't feed you until I'm able to get to the store and buy you kitty food. Does that sound good?"

Yes, I was talking to the cat. Yes, I knew it was pathetic. And yes, I most definitely did not care. As the name implied, Mof was my only friend.

I awkwardly leaned over the bed, as I didn't want to grab my wheelchair, to plug in my phone. I was pretty proud of myself when I didn't face-plant onto the ground.

"I think we're going to be good friends," I told the cat seriously. "I don't really have a lot of them. I thought I had some, but it seems I was mistaken. But you and me? We're going to be inseparable. You heard me right. Just you and me…"

I trailed off as Mof hopped off the bed and ran into the bathroom. Apparently, even the cat got tired of me.

Dejection settled over me like a heavy cloak.

Why did I have to feel this way? Where was the light at the end of the tunnel?

The ping of my phone interrupted my admittedly depressing thoughts.

I frowned at the intrusion. Who would be calling me?

That sound was immediately followed up by dozens upon dozens of more beeps. Text messages, apparently, and a lot of them at that.

My frown deepened as I listened to my phone go off. I knew for a fact that it wasn't my parents. They gave less shits about me than I did. Nobody else even had my number that I was aware of, except for maybe their head of security. But why would the dick call or message me?

Nearly tumbling off the bed yet again, I picked up my phone from where it lay charging on the ground. The phone cord did not quite reach my bed, so I was forced to lean over the edge, balancing precariously on my side.

Unknown: Addie, please respond.

I didn't recognize the number, but there were at least fifty from it. Mixed in were several other numbers, though I didn't recognize any of those either. Frowning, I scrolled through the onslaught of text messages.

Unknown 1: Calax gave me your number. Please text back.

Unknown 2: this is rider. R u okay?

Unknown 3: Princess, please message back. We're losing our shit over here.

The messages went on and on, each one more desperate than the last. I scrolled to the end of the chain, to the most recent messages and felt tears threaten to break free. The time stamp on the first I opened said it had been sent only five minutes ago.

Unknown 1: I don't know if you're getting these. I don't think so. I'm so sorry. Calax lost his damn mind, and Declan's turned into a scary mofo. I don't know if you're getting these and not able to respond, or if something else happened. I refuse to believe that something worse happened, so please respond. Please.

And the last text, dated only two minutes earlier.

Unknown: I love you, baby. I'm sorry.

A sob escaped me, and then I was crying, nearly hysterical. I was ashamed to admit that I wailed like a toddler as I read through the texts. Again. And again.

They cared. They honestly cared. And Calax—I knew it was Calax without a shred of doubt—loved me. My emotions were everywhere. I'd always wanted somebody to love me, to care for me.

And now I had Calax.

Tears burning my eyes, I scrolled up until I found the number that I identified as Tam's. He seemed to be the sanest, at least in the consecutive texts sent in the last few days. Even Asher's messages sounded frenzied the more time went on without a response from me.

Wiping the fallen tears from my eyes, I held the phone to my ear as the line rang.

It only took one ring for the phone to pick up, voice breathless over the line.

"Addie? Kitten?" The voice wasn't Tam's, but I recognized the raspy tone immediately.

"Hi, Ryder."

A strangled sound escaped him.

"Shit, Addie…we thought…we thought you were dead." His voice turned harsher, angrier, as if he was overwhelmed with emotion and couldn't decide which one to settle on. "Why didn't you fucking call? You can't just do shit like this and not call.

We thought you were fucking dead! Do you know what that did to us? To Calax and Declan? For the love of... Fuck! Kitten, you should've called!" There was what sounded like a scuffle on the other end of the line before a gruff voice spoke.

"Adelaide?"

I didn't recognize this new voice. I was positive that I had never heard him before. He was not one of my new friends.

"Yes?" I began hesitantly. My lip gnawed on my fingernail. It was a very nasty habit that I'd been determined to break.

"Give us your location. We'll be there soon."

There was a pause. Slightly muffled, as if his hand was over the receiver, the man said, "Calm the fuck down, Ryder. You'll see her soon. Go grab the others and try to find Calax."

Deciding quickly, I rattled off the hotel's address. I didn't give him my room number, in case he was a psycho murderer.

Or—wait for it—a cat burglar.

I looked down at Mof smugly as I thought of that pun.

"I'm not a murderer or a cat burglar," he said in exasperation. I didn't even know him, yet I knew his eyes were rolling.

Squeaking, I quickly mumbled a "bye" before hanging up. I threw the phone against the wall as if it was the phone's fault I was a fuck up.

Yup. Totally blaming the phone.

I let out a very girly giggle.

They cared about me. They actually cared. And Calax…

I thought about his text message. I didn't know how I felt about his impromptu confession. Doubt nagged me. Did he mean it, or were those words said in a panic? I didn't know which one I wanted to be true.

Did I love Calax? Maybe. After Ducky, I wasn't sure I was even capable of love. Calax was a grouchy bastard on the best of days, but he'd always been there for me. Since the first day we'd met, he had never given up on me, despite the awful things I said to him.

I hated him. I'd told myself that I hated him, yet my heart said something else entirely. I didn't understand what it meant, but I knew that I would be forever changed with this realization.

And that was why I didn't do feelings. They sucked.

After a few unsuccessful tries, I was finally able to scoop up Mof and wheel myself to the elevator. I decided to wait in the lobby for the boys.

It was nearly empty when I arrived, minus the front desk clerk I had met earlier. He eyed me with obvious distaste when I entered but seemed to realize I didn't intend to intrude on his phone time and lost his scowl. He didn't even reprimand me for having Mof, despite the hotel's no pets allowed policy.

Placing myself in front of the fireplace, I allowed the dancing flames to warm my frigid hands. It wasn't cold in the hotel by any means, but I felt as if my body had been plunged into the Arctic Ocean in the middle of winter. Chilled. I felt chilled, if not slightly numb.

At the swish of the door opening, my head snapped up, eager to lay eyes on the guys. I was momentarily disappointed when only a single, unfamiliar male stepped into the lobby. That disappointment morphed into curiosity when his gaze landed on me and he walked swiftly in my direction.

He was tall, almost as tall as Calax, with clearly defined muscles displayed in a fitted black T-shirt and black sweats. His shoulder-length, brown hair was pulled back into a ponytail, and he had the prettiest brown eyes I had ever seen. Normally, I wouldn't think brown eyes were pretty. The color reminded me too much of mud. But his eyes were different, almost as if they were infused with gold. They stood out against his tanned skin.

He was ridiculously attractive, and he was staring right at me.

I stupidly looked over my shoulder to see if there was someone behind me before focusing again on the tall man before me.

"Adelaide?" he asked, voice clipped. I, once again, looked around. Nope, no other Adelaides were offering themselves up.

"Yes, and you are?"

He didn't offer me a hand, and I didn't offer him mine. We continued our stare off, the air around us practically crackling with electricity. I refused to look away first.

"Fallon," he answered. Again, briskly.

I raised an eyebrow.

"And that name is supposed to mean something to me because…?"

Before Fallon could speak, a figure ran through the doorway and threw himself at my feet. Mof hissed but settled down when the newcomer didn't come near his resting place on my lap.

"Don't you dare do something like that again!" Ryder began, a flurry of emotions distorting his features before he finally settled on relieved. "You scared the shit out of me, Kitten. Why didn't you call and tell us you were fine? Were you trying to give us a damn heart attack? Shit, you can't do stuff like that—"

"Calm down, Ryder," Fallon said gruffly. Ryder glared at the other guy.

"Fuck off, Sarge."

Sarge. So this was the mysterious Sarge. The group leader. The guy capable of rescuing his team after a tornado trapped them underground.

What made him so impressive?

His cold eyes narrowed on me.

Oops. Must've spoken aloud.

Ryder let out a sound that was a cross between a chuckle and a sob. He looked as if he wanted to hug me but wasn't sure where he could touch me with all the bandages. I probably resembled a mummy.

"Did you get ahold of the others?" Fallon asked, turning away from me to level his glare on Ryder. Unlike me, Ryder seemed unperturbed. Perhaps he was just used to it.

"I found Tam. He's tracking down the others right now. I haven't been able to talk to Calax yet."

"Calax?" His name caused my heart to beat unevenly. "Why wouldn't you be able to get ahold of him? Where is he?"

I wanted to talk to Calax more than I'd ever wanted to talk to anyone in my life. I didn't understand these emotions, but I didn't shy away from them. I wouldn't—

couldn't—after everything that had happened. Death, and the consequential loneli-ness, changed my perspective on a lot of things.

"We'll explain everything," Ryder said. His hand reached forward as if he wanted to touch me, before he quickly dropped it back onto his lap. I hated seeing Ryder so tentative, so unsure. I grabbed his wrist and brought his hand to my face.

I didn't understand his need to touch me, only that he did. A slight tremor went through his body, and his eyes shut. His thumb stroked my cheekbone.

"Come on. We need to get back," said Fallon, eyes fixed on Ryder's hand. An almost contemplative expression crossed his handsome features before it hardened yet again.

"Will you come back with us?" Ryder asked me. His eyes remained closed, but a tranquil smile made him look years younger. I liked this Ryder more than the other one, the cocky, flirty one. There was something real and vulnerable about him that had been absent in our previous interactions.

I hesitated as I considered Ryder's request.

"Please." His eyes snapped open. "Calax needs to see you with his own eyes. And Declan... Please?"

It was the final 'please' that did me in. I was a sucker for puppy dog eyes.

"Fine, but only if Mof can come too."

He titled his head in confusion.

"Who the fuck is Mof...and when the fuck did you get a cat?"

CHAPTER 18

*S*arge was not a talkative person.

I realized that as we piled into a black sedan. Despite the available front seat, Ryder insisted that he had to sit beside me. He kept touching my hand and shoulder, as if he was reassuring himself that I was there and alive.

At first, the constant contact made me almost uncomfortable. Maybe uncomfortable was too strong of a word, but it wasn't something I was used to. I'd only ever had bad experiences with physical contact, making it difficult for me not to shy away.

After the fifth touch, I realized that I enjoyed his hand in mine. It brought me comfort, something that I'd been severely lacking for years now.

"What happened?" I asked as Sarge—Fallon—pulled out of the parking lot. "How did we get out?"

How did I survive? I thought but didn't say.

Ryder idly played with my fingers as he spoke, his voice steadily becoming more excited as the story continued. He reminded me of an energetic little boy bouncing around, though I would never dare call him a little boy to his face.

"Well, Sarge here realized we were still in the resort when it collapsed. He hoped that we would be smart enough to make it to a lower level. They found the majority of the people on the level just above ours. But Sarge didn't give up. No, he got an entire crew to help dig us out. They came in guns blazing."

Ryder paused, a forlorn expression marring his handsome face. Fallon merely grunted. I figured that the man, the Sargent, had talked himself out with our earlier conversation. All he managed now were noncommittal murmurs and growls. A man of few words, I guessed.

"How many casualties were there?" I asked softly, though I dreaded the answer. Ryder squeezed my hand.

"Thirty-seven."

I told myself that the number wasn't that bad. That it could've been higher. It felt wrong to think like that, but I knew I would fall apart at the seams if I allowed myself to think of the people that had died. Right now, I could compartmentalize the losses. They were nameless characters with no stories. I didn't want to know any details about them. I couldn't bear the truth.

"What about the people with us? Elena? And..."

I couldn't say his name, but my mind conjured up an image of a cold man with cropped hair and a heated glare.

Brad was a monster straight from my nightmares. Ironically, I couldn't help the thought that the only beings that had ever hurt me were humans.

Monsters did exist, and they too often took the forms of the ones we thought we could trust the most.

"Brad didn't make it," Ryder said, eyes dark. Both relief and dread filled me at that proclamation. On one hand, I was grateful I would never see his murderous face again. On the other, he was still a person with a story and a life, possibly a family. He might've had a wife and children. He for sure was the son of someone, perhaps even a brother.

And now he was gone. Another person in this fucked-up world that ceased to exist.

"How did he die?" The words came out before I could censor them.

Ryder simply answered, "Shannon."

I didn't ask what happened to the blond waitress. I had a feeling I already knew the answer if the tightening of Ryder's jaw was any indication.

We rode for a while in silence. Ryder would occasionally glance over at me, as if he was assessing how I was holding up.

"Have you eaten anything today?" Ryder whispered after a moment. "Besides hospital food?"

I considered lying to him, but there didn't seem to be any point.

"No," I admitted back, just as quietly.

Before I could add that I wasn't hungry, which would've been a lie, Ryder leaned over the center console.

"Can we stop and get some fast food? Kitten here is hungry."

My cheeks blushed at the nickname, especially when Fallon's inquisitive eyes met mine in the rearview mirror. I had the distinct feeling that this man missed nothing.

He did what I'd come to expect from him—grunted an affirmative.

Taking a road that curved steeply up ahead, Fallon pulled the car in front of a familiar restaurant. The golden arches were easily recognizable.

Despite only being nine o'clock, not a single light was on. The parking lot was empty of any car besides ours.

"That's odd," Ryder said, echoing my thoughts. Without a word, Fallon pulled back onto the road.

Since we were now off the highway, I was finally able to see the town that we were in. It was odd, but it appeared to be almost abandoned. No restaurant or store was open, and the houses, nestled between businesses at intermittent intervals, had the blinds drawn closed and lights off.

It suddenly occurred to me how few cars were on the road. Even at this late hour, there should've been more than the handful I'd spotted.

An uneasy feeling made the hairs on the back of my neck stand on end. My hand tightened in Mof's fur. The kitten continued to snuggle in my lap, completely oblivious. What I wouldn't give to be a cat right about now.

"I'm not that hungry," I hurried to say. I felt unreasonably frightened, though by what, I couldn't discern.

Fallon made a noise, but he maneuvered the car back onto the highway. I counted, in the time it took us to get to wherever we were going, five cars in total. Five cars on the highway.

The uneasy feeling transformed into full on terror.

Something wasn't right.

"Where are we going?" I asked, relieved when my voice didn't tremble over those few words.

"Since the resort's out of commission, we've been staying at Sarge's," Ryder supplied, offering me a sympathetic smile at the first part of his statement. I realized then that I should've been mourning not only the loss of life, but the loss of my home.

I found that I couldn't even summon a single tear for the damn place. The bad memories far outweighed the good ones.

"You have a bunch of teenage boys staying with you?" I asked Fallon, focusing on the last part of Ryder's statement. "No wonder you don't talk much. I would be a brooding asshole too if I had to deal with these idiots twenty-four-seven."

"Hey!" Ryder said in mock-offense, but I thought I saw a hint of a smile cross Fallon's impassive face.

It was small, but it was there. I would call that a win, especially since Fallon didn't strike me as a smiling type of person. More like a murder-you-in-your-sleep type person.

He was a scary motherfucker, that was for sure.

I didn't know what I'd expected his house to be like, but a modest, two-story home with a white picket fence wasn't it. It was the type of house you would expect a suburban family to live in.

Unless...

"Holy shit! Do you have kids?" I asked Fallon in disbelief. He didn't look that much older than me, mid-twenties at most, but who was I to judge the accuracy of the sex organ? He might've hit bullseyes every time, for all I knew.

"You did not just say the accuracy of the sex organ," Ryder said with a groan. I shrugged in response. He didn't have to listen to my inner mumblings.

Another one of those diminutive smiles graced Fallon's features.

"No kids," he answered.

I eyed him quizzically.

"Girlfriend? Wife? Boyfriend? Husband? Come on, man, this is such a soccer mom home."

Ryder broke into laughter at my description, and Fallon looked towards the heavens. He wouldn't find the patience to deal with me up there. I was more associated with the other place.

"I think she's calling you a granny," Ryder said to Fallon between fits of laughter. To me, he said, "I've been trying to tell this bastard that his house isn't a suitable bachelor pad, but he doesn't ever fucking listen to me."

Ignoring him, Fallon walked to the trunk and grabbed my wheelchair. Unlike the asshole limo driver, Fallon and Ryder both helped me settle into the chair before pushing me up the gravel driveway. Fallon grabbed Mof for me, and the cat snuggled into his arms. I smiled at the sight of a muscular, scary ass man cooing at a kitten.

My smile grew when I spotted rows of perfectly planted perennials along the edge of the house.

Yup. Totally a granny house. All it would need next was some cherub statues to complete the old person feel.

Ryder sent me an amused glance at my ramblings while Fallon glared.

I noted, with some satisfaction, that the glare didn't hold near as much contempt as it previously had. Instead of full on hating me, he appeared to rather full on tolerate me. Trust me. There was a big difference.

Ryder and Fallon were forced to carry me and my chair up the front steps. He really should invest in a ramp. Hell, the entire world needed more ramps. We should just have ramps everywhere. And—

Getting off track again, Addie.

"Yup," Fallon muttered.

Fuck off.

The interior of the house was in sharp contrast to the exterior. Here, the resemblance to a granny-pad ended. Leather couches made up the living room, complete with a large flat-screen and a few gaming devices. The kitchen, to the right, was surprisingly clean, save for a few pizza boxes discarded on the counter.

All in all, it wasn't what I expected a bachelor pad to look like, especially sharing it with six other guys.

"Addie!" a jubilant voice cried. "Princess!"

Ronan appeared from the top of the staircase, a towel around his shoulders. He was wearing low-slung shorts that showed the irresistible Adonis belt I found so attractive on guys. Like the first time I saw him, his unicorn tattoo was on display, large and proud. I had to wonder about the meaning of that tattoo.

"Hi, Lucky Charms," I greeted him as he jumped down the remaining steps. His arms immediately engulfed me, and I resisted the urge to wince.

Fallon, however, must've noticed my discomfort, for he grabbed Ronan by the arm and jerked him away from me.

"Careful of her injuries," he barked. He reminded me so much of Calax in that moment that I couldn't help my smile. That smile instantly faded when my heart began pounding. I felt...anxious to see him again. Anxious and something else, something new.

Shaking my head to clear my muddled thoughts, I smiled up at Ronan to show that he hadn't hurt me, and I wasn't mad. "Where are the others?"

"We're here."

The voice belonged to Asher, the first, excluding Calax and Ducky, of the boys that I had met. The sweet, shy boy that had seemed so flirtatious that night at the restaurant. Now, he just stared down at me with wide, glossy eyes.

"I'm glad you're okay, sweetheart," he said softly. Tam, behind him, took a step towards me and squeezed my hand. He didn't make eye contact with me, and he didn't speak any words, but that was okay. I understood all that he tried to convey in that single gesture. I had been worried about him too.

"Where's Ducky and Calax?"

"Declan's in the dining room, and we don't know where Calax is," Ronan said.

"How do you not know where he is?" I asked in horror. A thousand scenarios ran through my head, each one worse than the next.

Asher rubbed my shoulder reassuringly. "Don't worry. We'll find him." He paused, considering his words carefully. "But you should talk to Declan. He...well... You should just go talk to him."

With that, Asher gave my shoulder another squeeze and nudged my chair in the direction of the dining room. When none of the guys moved to follow me or push my chair, I realized this was something I had to do alone.

What would I even say to him? Ducky had been my best friend, but Declan was a virtual stranger. How much of the long-haired, shy boy still lingered in the bitter man?

Shoving away my doubts, I tentatively rolled through the archway and into the dining room.

Declan sat at the table, profile to me. His eyes remained fixated on a single spot on the faded wallpaper.

For a moment, I sat and inspected the boy before he could see me.

The expression on his face, that distraught, horrified expression, was all Ducky's. I would remember that face anywhere. It was the same one he gave me the night of my thirteenth birthday. The night everything changed for both of us.

I honestly couldn't tell you how I felt about the realization that Declan was Ducky. I was surprised, sure, but I was also wary. A lot had changed in those few years. I had changed, and I knew Declan had as well. Would we still be compatible as friends? After everything I did, would he even want to be mine?

That last thought haunted me. If I were to admit it to myself, that was a driving factor in my hesitance to pursue a friendship with Declan. A part of me felt I didn't deserve his friendship, despite his reassurances that I did. Guilt was a funny thing.

I also didn't know if I was supposed to be mad at him or not. He left me believing he was dead, but in his defense, he'd thought I hadn't cared. I believed that fact hurt me most of all. How could he not know how much I loved him?

Moving slowly, so as not to startle him, I rested my hand on his bicep. Declan jerked under my touch, eyes coming up to glare...

Only for a mask to fall over his face, becoming completely unreadable.

For a moment, he simply stared at me. His eyes traced each of my features as if he wanted to commit them to memory.

And then he began to sob. Mr. Glarey, the boy I'd once believed to be nothing but an asshole, began to cry in earnest. His hands fumbled, reaching for my own, and I grabbed onto both of his in both of mine. I didn't know how long we sat there holding one another, but it didn't feel like long enough.

We had years to catch up on, and I was determined not to lose any more time with him than I already had.

CHAPTER 19

When nightfall came and Calax still hadn't arrived, I felt myself panicking. Where could he be?

I could tell by the tense faces of the other guys that they, too, were worried.

Okay, let's think this through, Addie. What do you know about Calax? He likes control, that much is obvious. And what else? He likes you. Correction, he loves you. Think, Addie. Think.

"Don't knock yourself out," Ronan said from where he was sprawled out on the couch. I leveled at him my best glare. Sadly, my glare resembled Mof's glare more than anything scary.

"He thought you were dead, sweetie," Tam said gently, and I blinked at the term of endearment. He hurried on, "Do you know where he would go to feel close to you?"

I thought that through. If what he said was true, if Calax was grieving over my supposed death, then it would stand to reason that he would want to feel connected with me somehow. Where would I go if I wanted to remember Calax?

The answer came to me easily, and I could've facepalmed myself for not realizing it sooner.

"Of course," I hissed. Ignoring the questioning looks from the other guys, I turned to Fallon. "I think I have an idea where Calax went."

"Care to share with the class, Princess?" Ronan asked.

"Where we met. His house."

DESPITE THE BOYS' protests, Fallon refused to allow any of them to accompany us. I could tell that didn't sit well with any of them, especially Declan. My old best friend glared at Fallon with an almost elemental fury. I was not wrong in my initial assessment that Declan was a scary motherfucker when he wanted to be.

Ignoring him—and Ryder, who insisted that we were car buddies—Fallon wheeled me to the sedan. Unlike before, I was able to claim shotgun.

"So, Sargent," I mused. "Like the army guy?"

"That's sergeant," Fallon said roughly. "And yes, I am that as well, but my last name is, ironically enough, Sargent. Spelled S-A-R-G-E-N-T." He glanced at me as if I were an idiot. But really, how was I supposed to know his last fucking name was spelled differently when it was pronounced the same way?

I didn't bother with small talk after that as we curved through the winding roads of the town. I knew Sarge wouldn't be receptive to any communication outside the occasional grunt and snorts. I had to admit that it took a very special person to create his own language.

Fallon snorted beside me, case in point, and I realized I must've spoken aloud. Oh well. You win some, you lose some.

After what felt like hours, but I knew was only a few minutes, Fallon pulled the car into an apartment complex that looked as if it had seen better days. Though not completely destroyed, a tree leaned precariously against the white siding, and glass now took up residence in the once thriving garden. I would know since I was the one who'd planted it.

Long story.

"He's probably not up in his room," I mused to Fallon who, of course, didn't respond.

At least I hoped Calax hadn't been stupid enough to climb up three sets of stairs to his room. That building looked as if it was going to fall apart at any moment, and I really didn't want to get trapped again.

Or sacrificed. I didn't want that either.

Fortunately, I spotted the silhouette kneeling near the pond. I wasn't surprised to find him at that particular spot.

After all, it was where we'd had our first, and only, kiss.

"Stay here," I instructed Fallon. He glared at me, not used to taking orders, but remained where he was after he helped me into my chair.

The headlights from the car illuminated the paved trail down to the pond. Despite this, I still managed to get my chair stuck on a rock and face-plant into the granite. Okay, so it may have been more of a pebble than a rock, but that shit hurt! Fallon, laughing like the bastard he was, got out of the car, helped me back into my chair, and then retreated to lean against the bumper.

"Go away!" Calax bellowed as I got near. "I don't want to talk to any of you!"

I'd never heard his voice sound quite like that before. I'd heard him growling and I'd heard him upset, but I had never heard him sound so...empty before. From the hunching of his shoulders, it almost appeared as if he'd given up.

I didn't like that.

Calax was supposed to be the brave and fearless leader, for that was what I'd always perceived him as. The sudden change from a prowling tiger to a shriveling boy scared me a little.

"If you wanted me to leave, you only had to ask nicely. No need to be an ass," I snarked, coming to sit beside him. His head whipped in my direction, back towards the pond, and then towards me again in a dramatic double-take. It would've been comical if there hadn't been tears in his eyes.

"Addie?" His voice was so soft, I almost didn't hear it. "Baby?"

"It's me, Callie," I said.

Instead of the relief I expected, Calax began to laugh. Like full on, clutch your stomach and fall to the ground type of laughter. Way to make a girl feel wanted. He needed to up his game.

"What's so funny?" I demanded. I really didn't appreciate being the butt of the joke. I much preferred the face of it.

Focus, Addie.

"You still speak your thoughts," he said, wiping tears from his eyes. "I didn't think my imagination would be that creative."

Imagination? Oh, hell no.

"I'm not your imagination, Big Guy. I'm flesh and blood. I'm a real girl now. The girl Pinocchio."

He chuckled again, turning his head to stare at me directly. From this position, the moonlight illuminated his features in a pale glow.

He looked like shit, and not the sexy kind either.

Not that shit could be sexy. But Calax could, and I'd always claimed he looked like shit, so I supposed…

Stop. Thinking.

Even in the semi-darkness, I could see the deep bags under his eyes. His face held the evidence of a beard, dark like his hair and prickly. I wondered when he'd last shaved. Or showered. Or did anything, really, besides mope around and hallucinate me.

I wondered if he jacked off to my image. I wondered if he—

I really needed to just get a new brain. That would be much easier.

"Did I die?" Calax asked. "Is this Heaven?"

I couldn't help but smile. I was flattered that he thought of being with me as the equivalent to Heaven. Flattered…and a little scared. Not of Calax, but of the feelings he brought out in me.

"Trust me. You wouldn't make it there," I teased, swatting his shoulder. "Now what do I have to do to convince you that I'm real?"

"You're dead. I saw your body as the paramedics took you away. I saw—" He broke off, dropping his face into his hands. I hated seeing him like this. He was my grouchy giant, not my depressed one. Gah. Even in my not-real-death, he still found ways to irritate me. I really wanted to decapitate Calax with a piece of paper at this moment. It would've been one hell of a papercut.

"I'm not fucking dead, you idiot! But you're going to be if you don't calm down."

He still looked doubtful, face pensive, so I did the only thing I could think to do.

I kissed him.

For a moment, he froze beneath me, and I wondered if I'd read his text wrong. Maybe he meant that he loved me as a sister, and I was performing, in his mind, some serious incestual action here. Maybe the text wasn't even meant for me—

His large hand cupped the back of my neck, tangling in my hair. He lips moved hungrily over mine as he thoroughly ravaged my mouth. Tiny licks of fire danced across my skin with each and every stroke of his hand. His tongue tentatively touched my bottom lip, demanding entrance, and I happily complied.

His arms were incredibly gentle as they rested on either side of me in the wheel-chair. It reminded me of the way my parents regarded fine chinaware—something precious and extremely valuable.

His kisses turned soft, light brushes of lips to mine.

"Addie." He said my name reverently. Total ego booster.

"Callie."

"You're alive."

"No shit." I couldn't stop the dorky smile from taking over my face. "And you *love* me."

I had the pleasure of watching as pink tinted his cheeks. One of his large hands went to rub the back of his neck. "Not the most romantic way to confess your love for someone, but I suppose I'll accept it just this once," I teased.

At this, another smile graced his handsome features. "Are you planning on a lot of boys confessing their love to you?"

I shrugged. "You never know. I'm a very lovable person."

His eyes suddenly turned serious, all previous traces of teasing gone.

"Addie," he said, and I held my breath. "I love you. I've loved you for years. God, I just...I love the shit out of you, baby."

I opened my mouth to say it back, I honestly did, but the words got stuck. It wasn't because I didn't feel them, but more so because the thought of laying myself out there, making myself vulnerable like that, terrified me. Calax had the ability to completely shatter my heart, and with it, the last of my humanity. I wouldn't be able to survive another heartbreak.

"You don't have to say anything right now," Calax murmured, hand smoothing down my hair. "I don't expect you to."

"You have to understand that it's not because I don't feel the same way," I whispered, ashamed of my cowardice. "It's just..."

"Scary. I understand that."

How was it possible that someone was able to make me feel the way he did? I felt so much love towards this man before me, so much affection. Ducky may have been my first friend, but Calax had always been my sun. The darkness would've consumed me long ago if it hadn't been for him.

"Who the hell is that?" Calax said suddenly, glancing at something over my shoulder.

"Fallon probably," I responded, but Calax was already shaking his head.

"It's a group of people. I don't recognize them."

I finally looked over my shoulder at what Calax was seeing. It appeared to be a group of at least twenty people, all running in our direction. I couldn't make out any individual faces, but the man in front appeared to have dreadlocks.

"We need to go!" Fallon shouted suddenly. He materialized behind Calax, frantic eyes scanning our surroundings.

"What's going on?" Calax asked gruffly. Gone was the teary-eyed man that had kissed me with so much passion and love. This boy was much more familiar. A predator. I was grateful that my Calax was back. As much as I enjoyed the attention, I much preferred his asshole-ishness.

"The virus! Those things are coming!" Fallon gestured towards the mob growing nearer. Their movements were jerky, as if they weren't quite used to walking. The only word appropriate to describe it would be a lurch. They were lurching towards us, propelling themselves off the balls of their feet.

"The Ragers," I whispered, horrified.

"Ragers?" Calax questioned but seemed to decide we had more important issues than my choice of words. "Come on! Go! Go!"

We moved back up the hill at a brisk pace. After my wheelchair got stuck for the third time, Calax scooped me into his arms and began to run. The poor wheelchair was left behind.

Fallon began accelerating before the door of the sedan was even fully closed. I fell forward, wincing as my head hit the back of his seat. Calax grabbed my body and held me firmly against him.

"Faster," he growled. Fallon didn't respond, but the car jerked forward yet again as he pressed down on the gas.

The group had finally caught up with us. The car headlights, though dim, could clearly showcase each one of their disfigured faces. Red eyes. Black veins. Peeling skin.

I watched in horror as two Ragers began fighting each other. I didn't know what set them off, but I couldn't look away once they started. They clawed at each other's faces and bit any bare skin available. Even when blood dripped from open wounds, they didn't stop fighting.

The apparent leader, Dreadlocks, jumped onto the hood of the car. His feral eyes roamed over each of our faces before settling on mine. His lips pulled back to reveal blood-soaked teeth.

"Sarge," Calax warned darkly. The mob was surrounding our car now. Their grotesque faces were smushed against the window as their hands grappled desperately with the door handles. Even through the steel barrier, I could still hear their cries.

"Come out!"

"Feed us!"

"We're hungry!"

A horrified shudder shook my body, and Calax's arms tightened around me. It would've been painful if I hadn't been in desperate need of the comfort.

"Sarge!" This was said sharply.

Squeezing my eyelids closed, I heard and felt, rather than saw, the car drive over bodies.

Drive over fucking bodies.

The sickening crunch made my insides tighten.

Oh god no.

No. No. No.

The guttural screams became more and more distant the faster we drove, but it still wasn't enough. There would never be enough distance between them and me.

CHAPTER 20

RONAN

I glanced anxiously at the door for the third time in the last minute.

What the fuck was taking them so long? I hoped Cal would stop being such a brooding asshole and get the fuck back here. I was worried about Princess. It wasn't safe for her to be outside for so long.

Sarge had been able to get ahold of the base a couple of days ago. Apparently, they were just as clueless about everything that was happening as we were. That realization did not sit well with me. Hell, weren't the powers above supposed to be almighty and all-knowing? Fuck them. And fuck Calax.

I resumed my nervous pacing, bare feet wearing a hole in the carpet. I'd never been one to sit still, and that was especially true whenever I experienced any strong emotion.

Damn Calax. Why did he have to go and run off? Didn't he realize how much danger he was putting her in?

I told myself that my concern for her was normal. After all, we were friends.

I'd always wanted to meet the beauty that had tamed the beast. Calax would not shut up about this girl who'd stolen his heart. Now that I'd met her, I understood why.

She was beautiful, sure, but Elena was beautiful. Beauty wasn't all there was to a person, despite Ryder's claims. Addie made me laugh. I couldn't remember the last time I'd laughed before Addie came into my life. Believe it or not, it wasn't often. I was usually considered even grumpier than Calax.

But she...

She understood my weird sense of humor. Not even Ryder, my best friend and half-brother, fully understood my sarcasm and dry wit.

The devil himself was currently perched on the edge of the sofa, hands strumming absently on his guitar. If I paced when I was nervous, Ryder played. Music that was. Or females.

I didn't like the attention he gave Addie, and I didn't entirely understand why. I told myself it was because of Calax. He'd been in love with her for years now, and we would not get in the way of that.

It could've also been because I knew my brother. To him, females were nothing more than playthings to use and discard. I didn't want that for Princess. The mere thought of it pissed me off and made me sick to my stomach at the same time.

She had suffered so much in her short life. She deserved love and happiness, not the fuck over Ryder was bound to give her.

I had to make sure he understood that she was off limits. She was Calax's girl, and in theory, that made me her…brother?

I shuddered at the word. No, most definitely not her brother. Most brothers would go to jail for having thoughts about their sister like I often had for her.

Friends. We were just *friends*.

Friends protected other friends from dickbag brothers.

And I also had Declan to think about. From the way he'd talked about her, worshipped her, I knew that Calax was going to have some competition in the romance department. It was a shame that they had met her first.

"Sarge will fucking kill you if you break his rug," Ryder said absently. His hand plucked at a few strings. He used to write his own songs until that bitch Liz came into his life. She sure did a number on him.

"You can't break carpet," I retorted, resuming my pacing. His hands strummed yet again, the song unfamiliar. That was especially odd, since I knew his entire set.

"Don't tell me what you can and can't break," he snapped back. Geez. Someone was in a shitty mood. I had to wonder if it had to do with his precious "Kitten."

The bastard probably wanted to fuck her.

"I hear a car!" Tamson yelled before I could respond to Ryder. Both of us rushed towards the door. Fucking Ryder looked like an energetic puppy waiting for his owner to arrive home. Pathetic. Granted, I probably looked the same way, but at least I had *some* class.

Declan came out of whichever room he was sulking in, for once not scowling. His face warmed with relief.

It was Ryder that opened the door, bouncing from foot to foot.

"Addie!" he said before the door was even fully opened. See? Puppy.

And then he froze. I could see the muscles in his back bunch together. His body thrummed with tension.

"What the fuck, Ry?" I questioned, pushing past him.

A group of people stood in the doorway. Most I didn't recognize, but the two standing in front of the crowd were impossible to ignore.

Our target for the last few weeks. Our whole reason for being at the resort in the first place.

And the two people I hated more than anyone else in the world, including Liz surprisingly.

The man took a step forward. With an arrogant set to his chin, he looked like an entitled dick. I wanted to punch the smile off his face.

How the hell did he even know where to find us?

"We're looking for our daughter," he said sternly, indicating the woman next to him as if we had trouble understanding the "we." Ignoring the scowl I aimed his way, he continued, "We're looking for Adelaide."

BONUS SCENE

RONAN

She stared off into the distance, apparently oblivious to my presence. I didn't like that. Not one bit.

I'd been with a lot of girls throughout my years of life, but there was something about her that captivated me. She demanded my complete and utter attention. Maybe it was because I recognized the pain she seemed to emit in palpable waves. Maybe I recognized her pain…because I saw it in myself.

"Oh my gosh, did you hear that? She only brought *one* bikini?" I whispered in her ear, smirking jovially when she jumped, startled. She spun around so fast, I was afraid her head would fall off. And fuck…

She was even more beautiful up close.

Her brown hair hung in loose curls around a cherubic face. Lush lips, currently curled upwards in a mischievous, almost devilish smirk, demanded my complete and unwavering attention. My eyes traveled over her exquisite body, an ache reverberating through me. What I wouldn't give to touch her. Own her. Make her mine.

The intensity of my thoughts made me pause. Never before had I felt so strongly about a girl, let alone one I just met. Who was this strange, fascinating creature with the haunted eyes and pained smile?

"I can't believe it," I continued on, my voice rising a few octaves as I attempted to adopt a Valley girl accent. I'd be the first to admit that I took some creative liberties.

Her smile grew, practically cleaving her face in two, as she pitched her voice to match mine.

"I know, right? I brought, like, eight. One for dipping my toes in…"

"One for sitting at the pool in," I continued, fighting a grin. Fuck, who was this girl? And where had she been my entire life?

"One for going waist deep. Only waist deep. And of course, I have one entirely made of satin." She dramatically flipped her hair—her glorious, brown hair that I yearned to wrap around my fist—over her shoulder to emphasize her point.

I stared at her in feigned horror. "Only one?"

"I mean, you wouldn't understand. I have, like, hobbies and interests and stuff."

"And activities?" I queried, cocking a pierced brow.

"Oh my god, who does activities? Seriously?"

A laugh escaped my lips.

"What's your name, doll?" I asked, dropping the pretense. I needed to know who she was more than I needed air to breathe.

"Oh, and what a fine voice he has…" she murmured, eyeing me strangely.

"I have a fine voice?" Yeah, that made me feel good. Immensely good. Ryder would be so fucking jealous if he heard.

But why was she talking about my voice?

"Oh shit. I said that aloud, didn't I?" she questioned, not at all perturbed. "I just don't have a filter, I guess. But I mean, you *do* have a nice voice. It's all husky and sultry and stuff. You'd probably be a good singer."

I stared at her for a long moment before bursting into laughter.

"I would love to hear you say that in front of Ryder," I remarked. Maybe I should've been the musician in the family. "So am I going to get a name?"

Shrugging, she pointed towards the ditzy blonde in the skimpy bikini. Ugh. I made the mistake of fucking her once, and she'd been hooked on me ever since. I seriously couldn't get rid of her, no matter how hard I tried.

"I heard her name is Missy."

"Well, my name is Ronan." I extended a hand, and she shook it after only a slight hesitation.

Win!

"Nice to meet you, Ronan with the satin bikinis."

I smirked. "And the fine voice."

"How could I forget?"

Shifting in her seat, she turned back towards her forgotten book, effectively ending the conversation.

But fuck, I didn't want that. I actually liked talking to her, more than I cared to admit. If my brothers could see me now, they would call me pathetic.

"I haven't seen you around. You don't go to Highwood Prep?"

She froze, lips pursing, before she turned towards me and looked down the bridge of her nose. Her mouth twisted into a smirk. That shouldn't be as sexy as it was. It really, really shouldn't be.

"How do you know?" she asked lightly.

"Because I would've remembered someone like you."

Oh yeah. I most definitely would've.

"Maybe I was just hiding. From you," she quipped, once more turning towards her damn book.

"So are you here on vacation?" Yeah, I was desperate. Sue me.

She hesitated, only briefly, before nodding once, the slightest dip of her head. "Yes."

"Are you going to go into the pool?" I asked when silence ensued.

"Oh, that just sounds dandy," she drawled, waving her book in my face. "Because obviously I'm not in the middle of doing anything. Now shut up and leave me alone. I'm at a good part."

My silence lasted for approximately fifteen seconds. It was a bad habit of mine. Terrible, really. No wonder I only had a few friends.

"What'cha reading?"

"Oh for the love of…" As if she couldn't help herself, she whacked me on the head with the book. It didn't hurt me or anything—three of her dainty arms made up one of mine—but it still made me widen my eyes comically.

"Did you just hit me with your book?"

"I told you, I'm at a good part," she pointed out, biting her lip to keep from smirking.

"You are a strange girl," I mused, but it wasn't a bad thing. No, not a bad thing at all. Normal was overrated, anyway.

"Still at a good part." She flipped a page in her book, lips compressed in a thin line as if to contain her laughter.

"Ronan! Baby!" a shrill, feminine voice cooed.

Oh, fuck. No.

"I swear to God, Ronan, you have exactly five seconds to get rid of that voice before I castrate you," the girl announced, and my name on her lips made my cock twitch in my swim trunks.

And what did she just…?

I nearly fell out of my seat from laughing. Because, yeah, I completely agreed. That voice was annoying.

"Who's your little…friend?" Elena questioned, her tone about as pleasant as a feral dog. Her bark was just as nasty as her bite—I should know.

"Elena," I said stiffly, my body tensing.

"I was looking for you," she hissed.

My new fascination murmured, "Five seconds."

"Five seconds until what?" Elena asked with a huff, her penetrating gaze swiveling her way. When the new girl didn't cow, didn't even react, I felt a smile ghost across my lips before I quickly contained it.

"I'll meet you by the entryway, Elena," I said evenly. The sooner I got this conversation over with, the sooner I could get back to stalking the gorgeous girl beside me.

"But—"

"The entryway or not at all."

We glared at each other, hatred emanating from my eyes, while hers were still lovestruck, even after all this time. After a moment, she turned on her heel and stalked away, fuming.

"Well, damn," Beautiful stated. I really, really needed to learn her name. "That was intense. I *felt* the tension. Or was that sexual tension? Hmm…I guess the world may never know. Actually, that's not true. If you guys start pawing at each other, then it was most definitely sexual tension."

I stared at her for a long moment, just barely containing my grimace of disgust.

"Trust me. That was the exact opposite of sexual tension."

"So it was platonic tension, then?" she pressed. When I didn't respond, she shrugged nonchalantly. "Dude, I feel ya. Platonic tension is intense. It makes you lose control. Like, you suddenly want a hug from your brother or something."

"What is wrong with you?" The question didn't hold any malice. She was a puzzle I was dying to put together. Something new and strange and ethereal. Something I wanted to make mine.

"A lot actually."

Sighing, she scooped up her book and folded her towel.

"Wait! Where are you going?"

Was she leaving? Already? Fuck, would I ever see her again?

She patted my cheek. "I told you already. I'm hiding from you."

"I never caught your name!" I shouted as I stared at her retreating back. My hands were slightly outstretched, as if I could physically pull her back to me. I wasn't sure if I would ever let her go once I caught her though, and that mindset scared the shit out of me.

"That's because I never gave you anything to catch!" she called, a smirk evident in her voice.

Fuck, who was that girl? And why did I desperately want to see her again?

BONUS SCENE

CALAX

"You just haven't found the right guy." Ryder's voice reached me as I stepped inside the modest diner in the resort. Red vinyl booths, a jukebox, squeaky bar stools, and checkered white and black flooring gave the restaurant a seventies vibe.

The hostess—Shannon, if I remembered correctly—smiled at me, but a well-placed scowl her way had a frown marring her features as she all but ran away.

I bit down on my lip to contain my grin, knowing that I was being an asshole but unable to stop myself. After all, there was only one girl I was interested in. One girl I would only ever be interested in.

One girl that I could've sworn I heard speaking at that moment.

"Trust me. That's not the reason."

Addie? What the fuck was she doing here?

I quickened my pace, ignoring the curious stares my hulking size got me, and finally spotted the back of Tamson's head. Declan was sitting beside him, but across…

My heart pinballed around my rib cage like errant fireworks as my gaze locked on Adelaide.

The love of my fucking existence…

Who currently hated me.

And who was also currently smiling at my best friends, all of whom were staring at her with the same doe eyes I knew I gave her daily.

She brushed a strand of her silky brown hair behind her ear. When she smiled, her porcelain face lit up as if there were a candle burning beneath the surface. She was, in a word, perfect.

Jealousy uncoiled in my gut like a malevolent, insidious snake as I watched her with them. Was this the girl Ronan was talking about? The girl who'd captured his attention?

I moved around the table before she could see me, so her back was now towards me, unable to do anything but stand there and gape. Desperate need coursed through me, something primal and foreign. A need to claim.

"Where's Calax?" Asher questioned, and his words broke me out of my bitter spell. I charged forward, my eyes hurling daggers at my friends' heads before my gaze drifted towards Addie, who now sat ramrod straight.

"For the love of…" she muttered, sighing.

"What the hell is she doing here?" I demanded my best friends, my brothers, as I gazed around the table. What I meant to ask was…

What the hell is she doing here with you guys?

Did I sound as jealous out loud as I did in my head? Probably, but I found I didn't give a single damn. They knew how I felt about her. That I loved her. That I needed her. That my fucking world revolved around her.

So why were they fucking staring at her with lovestruck eyes? How could they do this to me?

She slowly turned her head to stare at me, and the hatred in her eyes brought me physical pain. There was no greater torture than knowing the woman you loved would never love you back…

And that she actually hated you.

But maybe I deserved her hate, her ire. Until I could prove to her, and myself, that I was worthy of her affection, I needed to keep my distance. Though it was getting harder and harder every damn day.

Fuck, I loved her. I loved her so goddamn much that I could barely breathe.

But instead of taking her in my arms and kissing the shit out of her, as I yearned to do, I scowled. Because apparently, I had problems and trouble expressing my emotions. A therapist would have a field day with all of my baggage.

"Hello, Callie," she greeted in a saccharine sweet voice. She blinked innocently up at me, even as her smile turned malicious.

I pinched the bridge of my nose at her antics. I both loved and hated that nickname, but she would never hear me admit it. "Addie, what are you doing here?"

My friends all stared at me with varying degrees of shock before horror filled their faces.

"Your name is Addie?" Tamson all but squeaked.

"*This* is Addie?" Ronan asked, his mouth dropping open and his expression filling with guilt.

"Well, shit." Asher forked his fingers through his blond hair.

"*This* is Adelaide?" Ryder sputtered. He knew more than anyone how much she meant to me. Just the other day, I got wasted and confessed my undying love of her to him…thinking he was her. Not my finest moment.

"Judging by all the exclamations, I assume Callie told you so many wonderful things about me," Addie said, and behind her back, she tossed me a middle finger. I snorted.

"Trust me. We hear a lot about you." Ryder smirked at me, and I glared at him in warning. The last thing I needed was one of these assholes admitting the truth to Addie. She would run for the fucking hills if she knew the extent of my obsession.

"Calax is my nemesis," Addie announced after a moment, sounding as happy as could be. When I glanced at her profile, I saw her lips twitch in the beginnings of a smile, and the ice encasing my heart began to thaw at the expression. "Like the whole enemy, fall-and-crack-your-head-open sort of relationship going on."

Silence.

And then…

Ryder and Ronan broke into laughter, those bastards. Ronan wiped a tear from his eye before turning towards me, amusement dancing in his gaze.

"You didn't mention that she hated you."

I totally wanted to punch him.

"He's a very hateable person," Addie pointed out.

I mumbled something about beautiful, infuriating women before sliding into the booth beside her. My thigh touched hers, heat migrating from that menial connection, and she began poking my chest in irritation.

"Move over, Big Guy. I don't want to catch your cooties," she said with a huff, but I ignored her, purposely pressing my leg closer to hers, until my thigh practically engulfed her skinny one. What I wanted to do with those thighs of hers…

I had the sudden, vivid image of her ankles on my shoulders, my hands gently parting her legs, and—

"Aw. No fair. How come Calax gets to sit so close to Princess?" Ronan whined, and I snapped my head in his direction. Why the fuck was he giving her cute nicknames? The little green monster, otherwise known as jealousy, reared its ugly head.

"Princess?" I grumbled. Out of the corner of my eye, I watched Declan fold his arms over his chest, seemingly annoyed with Ronan's blatant flirting.

What the fuck was his problem?

I stared him down, but he met my gaze in that cold, disdainful way of his.

Addie's voice penetrated the green haze clouding my vision. "Calm yourself, Lucky Charms," she told Ronan, and I smirked at the nickname. With his green hair, the nickname was definitely fitting. "I didn't ask for this big brute to sit by me."

"Did you just call me a big brute?" I asked, reluctantly breaking eye contact with Declan.

"Did you just call me Lucky Charms?" Ronan added with a broad grin. He ran his fingers through his tousled green hair.

"You have to admit that you look like a leprechaun," she pointed out with another belligerent smile.

"That is insultingly adorable." Ronan swiveled his head to plead with us. "Please? If you don't want to keep her, I will."

I shifted even closer to Addie, resisting the urge to clamp my hand down on her porcelain thigh and growl, *"Mine."*

"Nobody's keeping me," Addie interrupted, waving her hands in the air. "Besides, I don't date."

I had to lower my head to hide my smirk.

You don't date?

Challenge accepted, baby girl.

BONUS SCENE

DECLAN

I stared at her intently, my confession settling between us like a bloated storm cloud. Any second, it would erupt, releasing torrents of rain on the unsuspecting population.

Her lips opened, closed, and then opened again as she struggled to articulate her thoughts.

"I don't know what type of fucking game you're trying to play, but I'm—" Her lips shut abruptly as tears welled in her eyes. Though I couldn't hear her, I watched as she fell apart, desperate sobs shaking her thin body.

I knew she didn't believe me, and I couldn't blame her. Without proof, I wouldn't have believed it myself. She believed me to be dead, she'd mourned me, and one confession from a guy she barely knew wouldn't change the years of pain and heartache.

Maintaining eye contact, I pulled down the collar of my shirt, revealing the birthmark coloring my skin.

I could see the exact moment that realization twisted her features—horror, hope, and anger all battled for dominance.

"*No. No.*" Her lips repeatedly formed that one word as she gripped her brown hair, pulling at the silky strands. I hated to see her like this, hated to know that I was the cause of her breakdown.

"Your name is Declan, not Ducky," she insisted, hope blossoming in her gemstone eyes, though she quickly stomped on it.

"*My nickname is Ducky,*" I signed. Fuck, I was beginning to cry as well. Staring at her face, staring at the only woman I ever truly loved, I felt something shatter inside of me. Something fragile.

"No. This can't... You can't... This can't be happening." She began to cry harder, and a demented part of me was grateful I couldn't hear the desperate sobs. I was afraid that I would fall apart with her, that I would lose myself to the pain.

She leaned forward and brushed her fingers against my skin. Fuck, her touch was heaven. I just barely resisted the urge to shiver as her fingers traced the edges of my birthmark. They were shaking, but her eyes were bright with determination. I'd never been prouder of her.

And I never loved her more.

Tilting her head back and peering at me through a fringe of sooty lashes, she asked, "Ducky?"

"*Addie,*" I signed immediately.

And then I wrapped my arms around her, extra mindful of her injuries. She pressed her face into my neck, her tears wetting my skin.

Fuck, I'd missed her. I hadn't even realized how much until that exact moment. For so long, I'd held on to my bitterness and pain. My heartache. Her words from years ago echoed in my head, each one a continual stab to my heart. Knowing that she didn't truly mean them, that she loved me as much as I loved her, soothed something inside of me. Soothed the savage beast.

She pulled away from me, her eyes bloodshot, and I knew I looked similarly disheveled. With a trembling hand, I pushed a strand of knotted hair behind her ear.

Addie. My Addie.

"You're alive," she said, pulling back to face me. I focused on her lips as she spoke, though I wasn't thinking about the words she was saying. I was picturing leaning forward and kissing her senseless. What would she taste like? What would she feel like? Would she even want my kisses?

"*Yes,*" I signed.

"Why didn't you…why didn't you tell me?" she sobbed, and her relief transitioned into anger. I could see her lips straightening into a grim line and her eyes narrowing slightly. Red splotches erupted on her cheekbones as she glared at me, her eyes spewing vitriol.

"*I tried!*" I insisted, hands moving rapidly in my agitation. "*Your parents said you didn't want to talk to me. They said you…*" I didn't know how to finish that sentence. The pain still cut too deeply.

"They said what?" Her expression smoothed over instantly, like the calm before the storm.

"*They said you never once asked about me. They said you laughed when the truck came.*"

My heart broke as I signed those damning words. Both because of the remembered pain from that time…and because I believed them in the first place.

Addie exploded. "And you believed them? After everything we'd been through?"

"*What was I supposed to think? After what you said to me?*" I knew I was being unfair, I knew it, but years of pain had piled up on me, suffocating me.

"I did that to protect you!" she seemed to screeched.

"*I didn't know that.*" My movements turned jerky. Fuck, did we have to fight? All I wanted was to hold her and never let her go. Never again. Addie owned me, heart and soul.

Something shattered in her expression, something I couldn't name, but I knew it didn't bode well for me. Familiar tendrils of self-loathing appeared in her beautiful eyes.

"Addie," I signed before sighing and dropping my hands to my lap. I didn't know what to say, how to help her. How could I tell her that I never blamed her for what happened to me? That my pain stemmed from her cruel words at the restaurant, not the accident that took my hearing? That I cared for her more than I cared about anyone else?

"I think I need to be alone for a moment," she said, her eyes vacant.

"Addie, please, I need for you to know..." I wasn't above begging. She couldn't leave me, not again. Not after we'd just found each other.

"Please, Ducky. I just need to be alone." She met my eyes before dropping her head into her hands.

I could give her that. I could leave her alone for now.

But Addie needed to know that I was never letting her go. Not again. She was mine, and I was hers.

She'd left me once, and I'd be damned if I allowed her to leave me again.

THE LIGHT WE SEEK

TOGETHER WE FALL BOOK 2

CHAPTER 1

ADDIE

I squinted my eyes against the blinding sun, lifting my hand to create a visor. The building my parents had led me to was small, smaller than even the lobby of the resort, with bushes lining the walls and the beginnings of a garden near the front entrance. A long trail dipped down a slope towards a pond. The translucent water glimmered like diamonds in the sunlight.

It might've been a beautiful sight if I had been in any other company.

Mother and Father tended to suck the joy out of things.

Smoothing down my black, pleated skirt, I followed my parents up the stone staircase. A woman, red hair piled high into a bun, greeted us at the doorway. She exchanged a hug with my mom and kissed my father's prickly cheek.

I couldn't help but notice that her lips lingered a second longer than appropriate. I also couldn't help but notice that Dear Old Dad grabbed her ass.

Yup, that was my father for you. A cheating whore. At least he was classy about it.

Read as, my mother had been looking away at the time.

I pondered this new blackmailing material when the woman stepped up to me.

"Adelaide," she cooed with a stiff smile. The woman didn't like me just as much as I didn't like her. Even though this was the fifth time I had met her, I'd never bothered to learn her name. What was the point? "You've grown into a beautiful young woman. How old are you now?"

"Fifteen," I answered automatically, but then winced when DOD gave me a penetrating glare. Apparently, I wasn't allowed to talk, even when asked a direct question. That also meant I wasn't allowed to think either.

You see, I had a little problem with my inner musings. As in, they became outer musings, *due to my good old friend, trauma. My therapists had told me that my need to literally speak my mind stemmed from my past, or more specifically, the death of my best friend, Ducky.*

"It's turning out lovely, Rachel," Mommy Dearest exclaimed, extending her arms to encompass the entire lobby of the apartment complex. Rachel, the owner, grimaced at being addressed by the "other woman."

Oh boy. She was one of those—one of those women who thought DOD would leave his wife for her. I didn't have the heart to tell Rachel that Daddy had approximately twenty other side hoes, both men and women.

How could he even handle that many relationships? I could barely handle one. Not that I had one, mind you, but if I did, I wouldn't be able to handle it.

My love life was seriously depressing.

"I can give you a tour of the upper levels," Rachel said, purposely turning her back on my mother to talk to my dad. I noticed Mommy Dearest slyly checking out Rachel's ass.

Yup. Both parents enjoyed dabbling outside of their sacred marriage.

"What have you added?" Dad asked. If he saw his wife's blatant ogling, he chose to ignore it.

"Well, in the upper suites, we put in new bathrooms, new flooring, and repainted the walls. I'm sure you'll be quite pleased with how they turned out."

Before DOD could respond, the front door opened and a tall boy walked into the lobby.

The first thing I noticed was how huge he was. Seriously, he was easily a foot taller than my own five feet. His body seemed to be made entirely of muscle, and he had broad shoulders, chiseled cheekbones, and mop of dark hair. Currently, he was scowling.

At me.

What the fuck did I do?

Without a word, he brushed past me, his leather-clad jacket cold against my bare arms.

"He lives on the second floor," Rachel explained as we watched his retreating back. "He's been emancipated for a couple months now."

Conversation steered away from the angry boy to other matters. I didn't think twice about him and his scowl...only once.

I mean, who wouldn't think about a boy as attractive as him?

It would take me a month to discover that the stranger's name was Calax.

My HEART POUNDED ERRATICALLY in my chest as I glanced out the window.

Despite being miles away from the Ragers, I couldn't help but feel as if we were being watched. My hands were clammy as they desperately gripped Calax's. Right now, I needed his comfort and support more than I needed to pretend to be brave.

"What the hell was that?" Calax asked, his voice a breathy exhale. His arms tightened around me marginally, as if he was terrified I would be taken from him again. Considering he spent the last few days believing I was dead, that fear was valid. "Have you heard anything from headquarters?" This was directed at the driver, an intimidating man with shoulder-length hair and tanned skin.

Fallon glanced at us through the rearview mirror.

"Nothing new," he said. "They're just as confused as we are."

"Headquarters? Does that have something to do with your school?" I knew that

Calax and Fallon both went to a special boarding school, and the school had visited my parents' resort. It was actually how I met them. After a fire destroyed their dormitories, the students had rented out rooms in my parents' resort. Through chance, I was introduced to Calax's "team," whatever the hell that meant. All I'd been able to gather so far was that their school was not like any other school. They apparently took a heavy interest in orphans and foster care children—not at all shady. For the most part, I didn't bother asking.

They had their secrets, and I had mine.

"Yes," Fallon answered briskly. Though I'd only known him a couple of hours, I had quickly realized that Fallon—or Sarge to the others—was a man of few words. He much preferred grunts and snorts to get his point across.

I couldn't say I blamed him. I would love to not have to interact with other humans.

Minus maybe Calax.

And possibly Ducky—Declan.

And the other members of Fallon's team.

Besides them? Nope. I already had to deal with Elena, their scorned ex-lover, and I really didn't want to invite any more people onto the "Adelaide talks to" train.

I mean, I used to talk to Shannon, but...

My hands clenched into fists instinctively. I didn't want to think about Shannon or the last time I saw her. Eyes red, veins darkened, a feral glint to her normally semi-kind expression. She had turned, there was no other word to describe it. The restaurant hostess had become something that no longer held a shred of humanity, just like the throng of people that had chased us out of the apartment complex. Something other.

A Rager.

That was the name Damn Brad had used to describe the virus-infected—or perhaps drug-induced—humans.

As you could probably tell, I didn't like Brad. He'd tried to sacrifice me to the ragers, and I really didn't like being a sacrificial offering.

That had all happened when we'd been trapped underground for a day or two after a tornado struck. Yup. You heard me right. Brad had decided that I needed to be killed after only a few fucking hours.

And people said I was messed up.

The three of us were quiet as we drove back to Fallon's granny house. I didn't think there was anything we could say. How could we possibly begin to process everything that had happened? I much preferred my oblivious bubble than the crap fest that was my reality.

"What the hell?" Calax mumbled, glaring out the window. We'd arrived at Fallon's modest, two-story country house. In the driveway, which had been empty only hours before we had left, were three cars.

"Friends of yours?" I asked Fallon hopefully, though I already feared his answer.

With how little Fallon talked, I didn't think the bastard had friends.

"Rude," mumbled Fallon, parking the car behind a silver SUV.

I shrugged. He really shouldn't have expected anything else from me.

Unfortunately, I no longer had my wheelchair. That bad boy had been left behind when we were forced to flee from a group of Ragers. That meant, of course, that Calax had to carry me.

Normally I would've been fine with the physical connection, especially after he'd just confessed his love to me, but I felt myself cringe when I met the keen eyes of my parents in the entryway.

It was odd seeing my parents in such a diminutive, cute house. They'd always had a surplus of money, which meant that they were able to live in luxurious apartments and on tropical islands. The two of them almost looked uncomfortable as they leaned against the photo-framed wall.

"Addie," DOD said stiffly. His nose was crinkled as if the house had a particularly pungent smell. "It's time for you to go."

"She's not going fucking anywhere with you," Calax growled out. He hugged me closer to his muscular body, arms trembling with tension.

"He's right," I said, attempting to appear more confident than I actually was. That was surprisingly difficult, given that I was being held like a baby. "I'm not going with you."

"You are seventeen. You don't have a choice," Daddy snapped, and I resisted the urge to roll my eyes. Knowing him, he probably looked up my actual age before arriving. Heaven knew that he hadn't known it before today.

He referred to me as his thirteen-year-old daughter last week.

Last fucking week.

Mother ignored the conversation, as was usual with her. Her eyes were fixated on the boys glaring at her from the living room.

My friends were attractive, there was no way to get around that, but did my mom have to stare at them as if she was imagining them naked?

"I'm not going home with you," I repeated to my dad stubbornly, crossing my arms over my chest. Or at least I attempted to. The wrapping and sling around my arm prohibited such movement.

"Do you think you have a fucking choice?"

The men my father came with, his security detail, all stared at me intently. Their hands inched towards the guns I knew were in their holsters. Right thigh. A few centimeters below the waist.

I would know because I'd been shot by one of them before.

Not something I would recommend.

Uncrossing my arms and raising them in what I hoped was a placating gesture, I said, "Could we talk about this privately?"

"Fuck no!" That outburst came from Ryder, a flirty musician who I was just becoming friends with. I gave him a reassuring smile, grateful that he was protective of me but knowing I had to do this alone.

His face was grim as he met my stare.

"Drop me off in the kitchen, Callie," I said, patting the big guy on the shoulder. "I need to have a word with my parents."

ADDIE

Calax dropped me gently onto the kitchen chair. With a scowl aimed at my parents and a gentle kiss on my forehead, Calax reluctantly left the room.

And then there were the three of us.

Daddy remained standing, as was his usual intimidation technique. He always needed to be the tallest, most imposing figure in the room. I suddenly wished that the chair was on the table just so I could be taller than the condescending bastard.

I figured that would've looked a little weird.

"You wanted to talk, so talk," Daddy said bluntly. A scowl marred his handsome face.

"I'm going to be eighteen in a couple of weeks," I began, folding my hands and placing them on my lap.

"And? Do you think that gives you the right to leave the family?"

Well yes, actually, but I figured that wouldn't go over well with DOD.

My birth giver considered me thoughtfully, his hand absently rubbing at the stubble on his chin. I didn't understand why he felt the need to do that. Did it really help his thinking capabilities?

"You're right," he said at last, surprising the shit out of me. I was a lot of things to my father, but right was never one of them. Maybe he had turned into a Rager. Maybe the virus actually flipped your personality. That would make more sense than whatever the hell was currently happening.

I thought I would have to beg, cry, threaten. I thought I would get beaten down before I would be able to rise back up. Life, particularly the one my parents had given me, had taught me as much.

A sly smile touched Dad's lips.

"We could always ask Nikolai for help."

Just like that, the smile was wiped from my face. Something icy slithered down my spine. I'd been fearful before when facing the Ragers, but this was something entirely different. Deeper.

I'd never experienced such an intense fear before than I did at that moment.

"Leave Nik alone," I whispered, stunned that they were even daring to bring him into this. Tears welled in my eyes, but I stubbornly held them in. "Please."

When had "please" ever worked? Monsters didn't listen to pleas; they used that desperation to their advantage.

Still, I was frantic enough to try anything.

"Please don't."

My entire life, my parents had owned me. There was no escaping them, no running away. I should've realized that the monsters would always come for me.

"If you don't want to help us..." DOD trailed off ominously. I knew exactly how he wanted to finish that sentence.

If you don't want to help us, Nikolai will.

And just like that, they owned me again.

I COULDN'T MEET any of the boys' eyes as Fallon helped me out of the kitchen, the door swinging shut behind us. My dad entered after, looking so damn smug that I had to resist the urge to punch him. In the nuts. With a sledgehammer. While throwing monkey shit at his head. While he was tied to a train track with me driving the train.

Now, where to buy a monkey...

"Are you okay?" Calax asked immediately when he caught sight of me. His gaze flickered from my face to my parents', and his expression darkened. I couldn't decide if it was because of my stricken expression or my father's contented one. "No. No, damnit, no."

Before I could respond, Calax kicked at the wall. The plaster crumbled.

"Calax," I whispered, indicating for Fallon to put me on the couch. He complied, and Calax immediately sat beside me. I reached forward to cup his face with my hand. He was trembling beneath my steady fingers. In the last few hours, I'd seen him more distressed and panicked than I had ever seen him before. I knew that I was to blame for that change. "I have to leave with them."

"No, baby, you don't have to. You can stay with me." His voice was a mere whisper. I leaned towards him, our foreheads touching, and could almost pretend that it was just the two of us. My curtain of hair provided a barrier between us and the outside world.

"Addie, we need to leave," Daddy snapped, and I knew I was going to be punished for saying goodbye to Calax.

"Please stay," Calax pleaded. Even as he spoke, I felt strong arms lift me up. It wasn't my father, thank God, but one of his security members. Calax's hand gripped my shirt sleeve ineffectively before he was forced to let go. It was either that or risk hurting me more than I already was. My parents were never letting me go now that they had me, so Calax had to bend.

"Addie!" Calax lunged forward, but both Ryder and Ronan grabbed him and held him down. I was immensely grateful for them. I watched them whisper something to Calax, and though Calax still stared after me with a distraught expression, he wasn't fighting against the two boys anymore.

It was only as we were leaving, the security guard all but dropping me into the car, that I saw a face pressed against a window.

Ducky.

He'd been my best friend when we were young, and I'd thought him to be dead for years. Apparently, he was still alive. And his name was no longer Ducky, but Declan.

A member of Calax's team, Declan had been an asshole to me when we'd initially re-met because he believed I had ditched him after he became deaf. I was still dealing with his abandonment, and he was still figuring out where, exactly, our friendship would head.

His eyes were dark as they watched the car pull out of the gravel driveway. If I didn't know Ducky as well as I did, or at least thought I did, I would've been terrified by the expression on his face.

~

DECLAN

I watched Addie until the car disappeared, just barely resisting the urge to run downstairs and show her parents exactly what I thought of them.

Hands clenched into fists, I hurried down the staircase and into the living room, where the other guys had convened.

I knew, from the frantic hand motions, that Calax was yelling at the others. I couldn't hear what was being said, but I imagined that it was similar to what I was currently feeling.

How could you have let this happen? What were we going to do?

I'd only just gotten her back. I couldn't lose her again.

She'd been my best friend, and she always would be. Despite the friendships I developed with the guys, my brothers, nothing could compare to what I felt for her.

She was the first woman I'd ever loved, in a way that only a young teenager could.

Stepping around Tam, I planted myself in the center of the living room, waiting until I had everyone's attention. I didn't care that I was glaring at my closest friends. I didn't care that Tam actually shrunk away as if my eyes could physically penetrate his skull.

What I did care about, however, was the girl forced to go back to her abusive parents. Even if it wasn't Adelaide, even if it was a complete stranger, I would still fight for her.

The world needed more warriors.

I turned towards Sarge, our team leader, with narrowed eyes. He was currently holding Addie's black cat, Mof—My Only Friend. My girl was a bit dramatic.

"What's the plan?" I signed. I saw Sarge's chest rise and fall as he sighed.

That was universal Sarge language for he had no fucking clue.

I ground my teeth together.

"We have to come up with a plan," I added when it became apparent that Sarge wasn't going to respond. Somebody must've said something over my shoulder, for Sarge's eyes flickered there. He nodded at whatever the person said.

To me, he said, "We'll get her back."

Calax came to stand beside Sarge and clapped his shoulder.

"We protect our own."

CHAPTER 3

ADDIE

I stared at my true love with hungry eyes.

You know how people claim that someone, somewhere, held the other half of your soul? Well, I'd found mine.

Hot, steamy, delicious.

Smiling contently, I took a sip of my coffee. The heat burned going down my throat, but it was worth it.

Coffee was life.

I stared up at the sinewy man, blinking my eyes innocently when he cocked his hip out. George Farman was two hundred pounds of sass in an eighty-pound body.

"Are you even listening, or are you too busy orgasming?"

With a huff, I put my precious coffee cup down on my bedside table.

"Of course I'm listening."

"Then what did I just say?"

"You asked me if I was listening or orgasming," I replied innocently, and George rolled his eyes. Surprisingly, I didn't hate the therapist my parents had hired for me. He was a sarcastic asshole, sure, but he wasn't cruel. I actually enjoyed our sessions together, though I had yet to talk about anything of importance.

The last few weeks had consisted of cat videos, stories of my bladder, and relationship advice. George listened to it all with only the occasional snort of complaint.

I would call that a win.

"I heard that your new physical therapist is arriving today." He nodded towards my leg, now free of the restrictive cast. Despite the doctor assuring me that my body had healed, at least as well as it could've, I found that I was unable to walk without help. Daddy had believed that it was my own stubbornness prohibiting such a movement, thus the need for a therapist.

That could be true. My depression had worsened considerably since I'd left the guys. Though I still texted them every day and visited them when my parents were away, I felt an unbearable loneliness that threatened to eat me alive. Depression was a fickle fucker.

It had been two and a half weeks since I was forcibly separated from the guys I was beginning to consider my only friends. My parents had moved us into a large villa, adjacent to the lake. My room, unchanged from when the previous owner had occupied it, had coral painted walls and light blue furniture. My bedspread was a tacky pink. It was this hideous bed that I was currently lying on, arms crossed stubbornly over my chest. So far, George had been smart enough not to ask me about my feelings. I might've killed him if he had.

"So are we done now?" I asked, once again ignoring whatever he'd been saying. George narrowed his pinprick brown eyes at me, so dark, they were almost black.

"Yes," he snapped at last, moving to his feet. "We're done."

Without another word, he stormed from my bedroom. That was pretty standard with him. I would say something to piss him off, and he would run out of the room with a few choice words.

It was a very healthy relationship.

Sighing, I turned towards my bedside table. It honestly held my entire life, since it was immensely difficult to move anywhere without the help of someone. My phone, coffee—heaven's gift to mankind—and an assortment of chocolate that the guys had snuck through my window resided there.

It was the phone I grabbed, scrolling through the messages with a tiny grin. I couldn't help the instinctive schoolgirl giggles that erupted from me as I read through the thread.

Ryder: Kitten! Ronan Beijing mean.

Ryder: *being

Ryder: stupid autocorrect

Ronan: the ugly asshole locked me in a fucking cage

Ryder: He's farting on my face until I pass out!

Ryder: it smells

Tam: Do I even want to know?

Calax: u r children

Addie: Ryder, don't lock people in cages. It's not nice. Ronan, don't fart in people's faces. Calax, please learn proper English grammar, or I'll have to break up with you.

I smirked at my phone as a flurry of text messages came through.

Calax: I do apologize, my fair lady. I will work diligently to text the way you prefer, my beloved.

Ryder: so whipped.

Ronan: whipped

Calax: idiots

Calax: I meant to say that those two are hooligans in desperate need of a life and a good, old-fashioned courting.

Ryder: courting? What the fuck?
Ronan: language brother. And he meant a lay. We need to get laid.
Ryder: ohhhhhh
Fallon: turn on the tv

I blinked at my phone, surprised at seeing a text message from the elusive, sullen group leader. Frowning, I grabbed the remote for my television.

I didn't even have to change the channel. I imagined this story was covered on every possible station.

Yellowstone National Park's volcano had erupted earlier this morning.

The sky in the surrounding areas had turned a dusty gray, soot and other materials thickening the air. The death count, according the news, had reached the thousands. There had been no warning, no alarm, just destruction. It was difficult to hear the news relay what had transpired. It was too surreal, like I was watching a commercial for a movie instead of a live broadcast. It was horrifying.

I'd thought that the world was going back to normal. Scientists, according to the media, were working tirelessly to find a cure for the virus XHJKM. I had no idea what those letters stood for, but it sounded terrifying. They still had yet to discover what caused the virus and how it was transmitted.

It didn't transfer from a bite like it did in the movies.

Nerves fraying, I switched the TV off and settled back into bed. I didn't want to think about the molten lava on screen turning black the farther it slithered away from the mountainous base. I didn't want to think about virus ABC or whatever the hell it was. Not dealing was my way of not feeling. I could bury the emotions inside me until they threatened to rise from the grave. No, what I wanted to think about were…the pillows. Why did a bed need so many pillows? Was it to smother someone in their sleep? Were they for pillow fights?

"Why are you thinking about pillows?" a familiar voice questioned. A moment later, a blond head peered into my room.

I squealed happily. If I could've, I would've run to him and given him a big hug. My excitement quickly turned into panic. Asher couldn't be here. He couldn't be in my home, where my parents could see him. They would destroy him as they had destroyed Ducky and tried to destroy me.

"Asher, what are you doing here?"

The boy in question smiled brilliantly.

"I'm your new physical therapist."

I blinked.

"Say what now?"

He looked exactly how I remembered him, though it had only been two days since I'd last met up with him and the others for lunch. I was, admittedly, a bit dramatic when it came to them. His blond hair was tousled, framing an arresting face of high cheekbones and blue eyes. He wore slacks and a button-down shirt, rolled up at the elbows.

Why did he have to be so mouthwateringly handsome?

Asher blushed, indicating that I had said that thought aloud. Typical.

I wondered if I should've felt guilty for noticing Asher's good looks. After all, I was sort of, but not really, dating Calax. I didn't know what to call the two of us anyways. Was he my boyfriend? Friend? Lover? Enemies that occasionally kissed and confessed their love to one another?

Why was I so clueless about this life thing?

Shaking my head to clear the cobwebs, I turned my stare onto Asher.

"I thought you were a waiter?" That was how I had first met him, actually. He had been waiting on my table, much to my mother's pleasure, and had accidentally fallen. I, being the awesome friend that I was, though I didn't know him at the time, took the blame.

"I do a lot of things," he replied, flashing me an official looking ID. I imagined he stole it, or at least made one on a computer. There was no way that Asher, only a year or two older than me, could be a licensed physical therapist.

"I put my ad online," he continued, "with a picture and brief description. Your mother called me."

Of course. For eye-candy. I would not be surprised if she was lurking somewhere nearby, waiting to pounce. Please, for the love of all that was holy, have her be wearing clothes.

When Ryder came to the house as the hired "electrician," Mother had decided that it was appropriate to walk around in her birthday suit. I'd never seen Ryder look more scared than he did then. He had taken to hiding in my bedroom, pretending that it was a circuit in my wall that had caused the power outage, though how he managed to turn off the power in the first place was beyond my comprehension.

"You're allowed to walk around naked anytime," Ryder had flirted with a wink. I'd elbowed him in the stomach.

"So are we actually going to do physical therapy?" I asked Asher now, planting my feet on the carpet. I wobbled slightly, but Asher immediately helped steady me. Smiling gratefully, I attempted to amble around the bed. My leg dragged uselessly behind me.

"Let's do some exercises," Asher suggested. He instructed me to lie face down on my bed, legs dangling over the side. He began bending my leg, instructing me to push and pull against his grip.

"How has it been?" he asked, fingers tentative on my ankles. "Push against my hand."

I did as he said, considering how to respond.

"The usual."

"Anymore…" He trailed off. I knew what he wanted to ask me though. Anymore beatings?

"No," I answered truthfully. "They want me to heal, and that would be kind of difficult with another broken leg." I tried for humor, but Asher didn't laugh.

Geez. Tough crowd.

"You're going to be eighteen soon," he stated, and all I could do was nod. When it became apparent that I wasn't going to speak, he pressed, "Why aren't you getting out of here? Is it because of money? Do you need a place to stay? I know you might not feel comfortable staying with a bunch of guys, but Sarge would be more than happy to let you stay with us."

I didn't know what to say to him. How could I explain Nikolai? Until I knew he was safe, I had to remain quiet.

"It's complicated," I admitted with a shrug. Asher smiled sadly.

"It's always complicated with you."

Ignoring him because I didn't know how to respond, I kicked my foot towards the television.

"Did you see the news?"

"About Yellowstone? Yeah, I was listening on the radio."

"It's absolutely awful," I whispered. "I can't even imagine. Did you know anyone in the area?"

"Thank God, no. But I think Fallon's parents lived near there."

"Are they okay?" I asked, sitting up in alarm. "Has he been in contact with them?"

Asher patted my thigh reassuringly. "They're fine. I already asked Sarge, and he said that they called him an hour ago."

I sagged back into the bed with relief. I may not have known Fallon that long, but he had saved my life. Calax and I would've been attacked by Ragers if he hadn't warned us. He was still a grumpy bastard, but I believed he was warming up to me. After all, the last time I'd seen him, he gave me two full sentences and only glared at me three times.

Progress, my friends.

~

"WHAT THE FUCKING hell is this shit?" Ryder held up the offending material with an expression that bordered between a scowl and a grimace.

I rolled my eyes and snatched it from his hand.

"Don't just dangle it for the whole world to see," I hissed, throwing it back in the bag.

It had taken us two hours to find a shopping mall that was actually open. Even then, only a handful of stores actually had their lights on.

Ronan and Ryder had insisted on taking me out shopping. Apparently, Ryder had a thing—*cough* fetish *cough*—for clothes, and Ronan was there for damage control.

"Somebody needs to rein my brother in," he'd told me. I had laughed, doubting that Ryder could be as bad as Ronan had claimed him to be.

I was right—he was worse.

"Who the fuck pays seventy dollars for a bra?" Ronan added, loudly enough to garner the attention of the two other shoppers in the small clothing store.

"Shush," I hissed, maneuvering through the collection of clothes. I'd insisted that the boys wait outside while I picked up some undergarments, but my suggestion only held weight for approximately twenty seconds until they got bored and followed me inside.

Now, they were providing commentary about every single fucking movement I made and item I grabbed.

"It's so tiny." Ryder held up the offending thong yet again. "Does it even, like, cover stuff?"

"Of course it covers stuff, you noob!" Ronan snapped.

"But why would you pay so much for so little?" Ryder seemed to be struggling to wrap his head around this concept.

"Oh my god! Shut up!" I slapped both boys on the head, one after another. Nothing I did seemed to deter them. I wondered if they'd made it their life mission to humiliate me.

"Maybe they accidentally put the wrong price tag on this…thing." Ryder held the thong between his thumb and pinkie, an expression of distaste marring his handsome features.

Despite the fact that I'd long ago moved away from that section and was now looking at pajamas, the boys wouldn't let it go. It was almost as if they took the price of the underwear personally.

"Underwear is always that expensive," I said with a sigh.

"I can get like twenty pairs for this price," Ronan said in horror. "This is so wrong."

"You should see the price of our feminine products," I muttered.

"The volcano eruption?" Ryder asked, aghast.

"The river of red?" Ronan added.

"Devil's birthday?"

"Cranberry juice?"

"Enough!" I said, throwing my hands into the air in exasperation. There was only so much I could take from these boys before I lost my mind. "You guys can discuss my period. I'm going to the changing room."

"Here! Try this on!" Ryder said before I could escape, tossing a pair of jeans into my arms. I put the items I'd picked out for myself down on a display rack and grabbed the jeans Ryder wanted me so desperately to wear.

They looked as if they were made for a Barbie doll. Did people seriously wear jeans that small? I didn't know if I should feel flattered or appalled.

Ronan, thankfully, came to my rescue. "Those won't fit her, you idiot! Here, Addie, try these on." He'd been browsing the same collection of designer jeans Ryder had and found the same pair in a bigger size.

Ronan was officially my favorite…

Until I looked at the jeans in question.

They looked as if they could fit two of me, if not more. I gritted my teeth together, resisting the urge to curse both of the boys to hell and back.

It was official—I hated them both and was denouncing this so-called friendship.

Shoving the jeans back at Ronan and Ryder, a scowl aimed particularly at Ronan for his unintentional implication, I stomped towards the dressing room.

Stupid guys. Stupid, sexy guys. Stupid flirtatious leprechauns.

Stupid—

I was so lost in my thoughts that I didn't see the girl until I plowed right into her. I squeaked, dropping my collection of clothes.

"Oh shit! I didn't see you there! I'm so sorry!" The girl quickly bent over to gather my fallen items.

"It's my fault," I said quickly. "I wasn't paying attention to where I was going."

Handing me back my clothes, she flashed me a smile. I noticed immediately that she was beautiful, a type of ethereal beauty that made me look like a hobbit in comparison. Her long, black hair cascaded down around her like an onyx waterfall. She had cheekbones I would die for and beautiful, vibrant green eyes. Standing next to her godliness, I felt small and ugly. My hands instinctively wrapped themselves around my waist.

It was a defense mechanism, something I hadn't done since I was younger. It allowed me to believe I could hold myself together. Though the gesture was physical, it provided me mental comfort.

"Again, so sorry," the girl said brightly before sashaying away. My hands were sweaty, and I tried to inconspicuously rub them against my jeans.

Why would the guys ever be friends with me when there were girls like her around? She seemed nice enough. There were probably a thousand girls in this city alone that weren't screwed up by their pasts. They were probably better, brighter, prettier than I could ever hope to be.

I allowed myself, for only a moment, to wallow in my self-pity. I felt as if the walls of the changing room were pressing in on me, burying me alive. The despondency inside of me was consuming, similar to how it felt before I befriended the team. It wanted me to suffocate.

It wanted me to die.

I tried to ignore the pulls of my own self-pity, but they were relentless. For just a moment, I would allow myself to succumb to the darkness.

Only for a moment.

Just for one moment…

CHAPTER 4

ADDIE

"What do you mean he didn't show up?" DOD snapped into his phone, body vibrating with an almost elemental fury. This had become more and more common, not just with my parents' company. Stores and restaurants, especially those that were family-owned, had shut down due to a lack of workers. With the disease sweeping across the nation and the world, according to the news, more and more people preferred to stay huddled inside. The president had issued a statement last week addressing this problem. She had pleaded for the country to come together and carry on like we had before.

She seemed to have trouble understanding that nothing was like it was before.

Storms still ravaged the east coast, and the west coast was still dealing with the after effects of the volcano. Ragers ran rampant on the street, forced to be shot down by officers.

"Well, fire his sorry ass!" DOD snapped.

I shrank further down in my seat as his anger grew. With nowhere to go and no business to run, Daddy had taken up his second favorite activity—hurting me. I had just barely escaped his fit of rage unscathed last time.

Unfortunately, I had to finish this dinner before I could even think of escaping. I was quite certain that my death would occur if I didn't.

Stirring my soup, I dared a peek through my fringe of lashes at the other occupants. My parents had invited Mr. Julius and his son, Lorenzo. Enzo, as he liked to be called, was a handsome boy with naturally tanned skin and a shock of dark hair.

Too bad he was a masochistic dick.

The only saving grace for this shit fest dinner was the catering crew, aka the guys. How my parents failed to recognize that the same person was a physical therapist, a chef, and an IT programmer was beyond me. Considering my mom flashed each guy at least once, her obliviousness and stupidity was a blessing in disguise.

The guys had apparently decided to completely immerse themselves in my life. I couldn't say I minded. The darkness that had always seemed to consume me was receding into the crevices of my brain and not nearly as overwhelming as it once was.

I felt relief with their continual presence. Despite everything, they weren't giving up on me.

"So, Adelaide," Mr. Julius said stiffly once my dad ended his phone call. "I heard that you were a fan of the ballet. Maybe Enzo could take you sometime."

Two things.

First, I absolutely hated the ballet. They bored me, and ninety-nine percent of the time, I would fall asleep. Secondly, I would rather sit through twenty hours of the ballet than go anywhere with Enzo.

Ryder, posing as a waiter, scooped potatoes onto Enzo's plate with more force than necessary. When he got to me, he was much more gentle, and he slipped something into my hands.

A note.

I smiled giddily, thinking of the other collection of napkins and papers he'd given me this evening.

What a prick.

I'm bored.

Crinkle your nose so I know you're reading these.

Glancing from my left, where Mother sat, to my right, where Enzo was lounging, I unfolded the new note Ryder had given me.

Fallon accidentally set your kitchen on fire. Whoops.

Though I hadn't seen him, Ryder had told me that Fallon was acting as a chef. Asher was his helper. All of the boys tried to visit me at least once a week, minus Calax, whose face was too recognizable. Of course, that pissed him off to no end. He hated not being able to see me constantly, not being able to protect me. I'd put him in charge of Mof, my tiny feline companion. Though he complained constantly, I knew the little furball was growing on him.

The boys had paraded around my house as cleaners, kitchen staff, computer experts, and more. It would've been almost comical if I hadn't been genuinely concerned about the idiocy of my parents.

I snorted as I read Ryder's note, ignoring the inquiring glance Enzo threw my way. Folding it up, I shoved it into my sock.

"How does that sound, Addie? You and Enzo at the ballet," DOD asked, sipping daintily from his wine glass.

What it sounded like was torture, the slow and painful kind. Of course, I couldn't say so to my dad. It wasn't appropriate dinner conversation. Not the torture part, that was fine, but the me having an opinion part.

Instead, I said, "I'm pretty sure that the ballet had been canceled, Father."

Along with everything else.

DOD glared at me but refused to acknowledge my insubordination. At least not at that second.

Ryder reappeared again, filling drinks this time, and dropped another note into my lap. I waited until he exited back into the kitchen before opening it.

Have to go. Something came up. I'll miss you, Kitten.

I tried to smother my disappointment. I enjoyed Ryder's company more than I cared to admit. He, Tam, and I were currently on level twenty-seven of some new video game. I'd never played it before, but apparently, I was a natural. I enjoyed the nights Tam and Ryder would sneak through my window to play games with me.

Frowning into my soup, I tried to focus yet again on the conversation. DOD was bitching about his employees, and Mr. Julius was nodding his head enthusiastically, as if my dad actually gave a damn about his opinion. Mother had her shirt unbuttoned, revealing a hint of lacy bra and cleavage, and I noticed Enzo's eyes glued to that exposed swath of skin.

Same old. Same old.

After dinner, we convened inside the family room.

I'd always hated that term. There was nothing "family" about the room at all. With the black leather sofas, and stark white walls, the place was devoid of any trinkets or photographs. It was the type of room that you would see in a home interior magazine—pretty but cold.

Shuffling to my usual seat, a leather recliner opposite of the couch, I frowned when I noticed Enzo walking in the same direction. There was a reason I picked this chair. It was away from everyone, away from any wandering hands or thighs pressed too close to mine. It was my sanctuary. I couldn't help but snort at the thought that something as mundane as a chair could provide me relief, yet it was the truth.

There was no escape in my house. I just had to learn to hide in plain sight.

So why the hell was Enzo sitting down beside me?

The seat was not necessarily small, but it definitely wasn't large enough to fit two people comfortably. His big ass thigh was half on top of mine, the weight crushing. He casually threw his arm around my shoulders as if we were a couple instead of virtual strangers.

I shuddered instinctively. There was something off-putting about Enzo, something menacing. I had the irresistible urge to burrow myself into the ground and never return.

Who the fuck did he think he was?

For the first time in a while, I felt alone and utterly spent. The boys had left earlier, after dinner had finished. I had gotten used to the consistent laughter and jabs of the guys that this tensed, charged silence made goosebumps breakout on my flesh. I didn't want to be here, and I didn't want to act like I was okay with the physical contact Enzo was giving me.

What could I do? Did I dare push him away? Move to a different seat?

This was just another example of how trapped I actually was. The chains were invisible, but they were so impossibly heavy.

Conversation steered in the direction of "worthless employees" and "new locations." I could barely concentrate on anything that was being said. No, all I could focus on was the pungent smell of sweat assaulting my senses and Enzo's fingers idly playing with the tips of my hair.

"Addie dear, why don't you give Enzo a tour of the house?" my father asked suddenly. Tears sprang into my eyes.

I knew exactly why DOD wanted me to give a tour. I knew exactly what he expected of me.

Why was I so weak? Why couldn't I just say no? Why couldn't I leave?

Because of Nik, I thought. If I had to choose between me or him, I would choose him.

Every. Single. Time.

So I managed a forced smile and gestured towards the hallway.

If Enzo wanted a tour, a tour he would get.

The man's face was bright with expectation as I lead him down the small hallway, pointing out various rooms as we walked.

"This is a bedroom, but not just any bedroom. No, in 1965, a family was murdered in there. Blood splattered walls, missing heads, the whole shebang. And here we have bathroom number two. A man hung his wife in that shower. He then drowned his baby."

How to kill the mood? Talk about death.

Ryder had drilled this lesson into my mind.

I was feeling quite proud of myself when we neared the backdoor. Though Enzo's face was set into a customary scowl, he hadn't made any inappropriate comments or attempted to grab me. I was mentally giving myself a pat on my back when his hand wrapped around my waist, pulling me against him.

Oh hell no.

His lips moved to my neck, brushing against my skin as he spoke.

"You're so beautiful. So perfect. You've been driving me crazy, girl. I know you feel the tension too."

What I felt was the irresistible urge to stab him in his Tic Tac sized balls.

So I did just that. Barely processing what I was doing, I lifted my foot and slammed it into his nut sack. Did I feel guilty? No. I was a certified ball cruncher, at least according to Ronan and Ryder, since I may have accidentally hit a Rager in the nuts with a pan.

Feeling slightly triumphant, especially when he keeled over in pain, I grabbed him by the scruff of his neck.

"Don't ever fucking touch me without my permission again. For that matter, don't ever touch another girl again." Releasing the pathetic creature, I smiled down at him malevolently. I felt...wicked, as if I'd finally found my element and that element was kicking a guy in the balls. Did that make me a psychopath? Maybe.

"If you tell anyone about this, I will hunt you down and kill you."

Groaning, he sputtered, "Y-You wouldn't."

"No?" I feigned innocence, blinking my eyelids. "I have enough money to buy myself an alibi, and I am sick of putting up with filth like you."

With that, I stormed towards my room.

My heart was beating erratically, threatening to break free from my chest. Had I really just done that? Had I really just said that?

Who was this girl, and what happened to the shy, timid Adelaide?

I couldn't say that I minded the transformation. I was done being weak and frag-ile. I wasn't glass that could shatter anymore.

I told myself that I was stronger, better. I told myself I could deal with the conse-quences of my actions.

I just hoped that wasn't a lie.

$$\sim$$

RYDER

I parked my car a little ways down the street, out of sight from my destination.

My hands were pale where they gripped the steering wheel—pale for me at least —and I could feel sweat beading my forehead.

I couldn't believe I was doing this.

Actually, I could believe it. It was time that I finally put an end to things.

Throwing my jacket on, I marched through the high weeds and decaying flowers. It was apparent that the owner had neglected the yard's upkeep. The house itself, made up of chipped yellow paint and unwashed windows, seemed pernicious in the darkness. It was a house that held bad memories, a house that would forever haunt my dreams.

I hadn't bothered to tell the others about my little trip. Ronan would shit bricks if he discovered where I was heading, and the rest would quite literally murder the person inside if I told them the reason why I was here in the first place.

I shoved my hands into my pocket, half to ward off the frigid chill and half to keep from strangling the home's occupant, then rang the doorbell with my elbow.

It only took a few moments for the door to open and a familiar girl to stand in the entryway.

"Ryder!" she cooed, throwing her arms around me. I stiffened under her toxic touch but didn't dare pull away. No, it was smarter if I pretended to play nice, at least for the moment.

Elizabeth looked as if she had just woken up. Her black hair, like onyx stones, hung just past her waist. She wore a skimpy nightgown and a translucent robe that indicated she must've been sleeping...or pleasing someone. When her eyes feasted on me, she pushed her chest out and flittered her eyelashes.

She was beautiful, I'd give her that, but I much preferred brunettes.

Shoving her aside, I strode into her living room. Fortunately, if she had a guest, he was occupied upstairs. I wasn't in the mood to vomit on my new shoes.

"Ryder," she said in what she thought was a sultry voice. To me, she sounded as if she was pushing out a particularly large shit. "To what do I owe the pleasure?"

"You know why exactly I'm fucking here," I snapped, unable to handle any more pretenses of nicety. She didn't deserve that.

Eyeing me with feigned innocence, she shrugged a shoulder, the strap of her nightgown sliding down with the movement. It gifted me with more skin than I ever wanted to see on her.

"Whatever do you mean?"

"I got your message."

Smiling serenely, Liz folded her legs.

The bitch wasn't wearing underwear.

Ugh. And I was trying not to vomit.

"I swear to god, if you threaten her again—"

Liz cut me off with a lilting laugh.

"You'll what? Tell me, Ryder, what would you do?" She clasped her hands together, the perfect image of a composed, calm woman. It was for that reason alone that the world failed to see the psychopath lurking beneath the exterior. She wore her mask effortlessly.

"I don't want to play games anymore, Ryder baby. I looked the other way when you fucked around with Tallia, Lacey, and Elena, but I'm afraid I can't turn a blind eye towards this one. What makes this girl so special? Why do you go out of your way to see her so often?"

"Leave Adelaide the fuck alone," I snapped before I could rein in my feelings. I paused, afraid that my outburst would reveal more to Liz than I'd intended to. Instead, the crazy bitch merely laughed.

"Ryder, I accept your apology. Now come up to bed." Without another word, she sashayed back towards her staircase. She might've thought she was being sexy, but I only had eyes for one girl now.

A girl I would never be allowed to have, but one girl all the same.

"Liz, we have never and will never be a couple. Stay the fuck away from me, and stay the fuck away from Addie."

With that, I stormed from her house. It was a solid ten on my dramatic exits scale.

Only when I was back in the car, did I replay the entirety of my conversation. Shit. Had I made things worse by talking to her? Should I have just stayed away? Should I have told someone?

I told myself that whatever happened next, I could handle it by myself. Never again would I drag my brothers into the shitstorm that was Liz.

CHAPTER 5

ADDIE

I pounded my fist into Ronan's bicep.

"You." Hit. "Stupid." Hit. "Cheater."

Ronan, not even wincing at my feeble attempts to murder him, fell off the bed in a fit of laughter. His ass hit the ground, and he sprawled out along the floor. Still, he didn't stop laughing.

"How the fuck is that even possible?" Ryder asked, still in shock. Ryder was attractive, there was no denying that. With his dark skin and darker hair, he was the epitome of male hotness. His muscular body had a few distinctive tattoos that ran up his neck.

Still blinking rapidly, he dropped his cards into his lap. The expression of disbelief on his face would've been comical if I wasn't so pissed off at Ronan. Stupid unicorn loving leprechaun...

The idiot burst into giggles. Actual freaking giggles like he was a little schoolboy. Why did he have to go and be so adorable when I was mad at him?

Scowling, I stared down at my own UNO cards.

Apparently, Ronan, the bastard hellspawn, decided that it would be hilarious if he cheated at UNO. How does one cheat, you ask? Well, it involves numerous Draw 4 cards hidden up your sleeve. People have gone to war over a lot less.

Would he still think it was funny when I murdered him and fed his body to the sharks?

"You wouldn't be able to carry me to the sharks," Ronan taunted, leaning back on his elbows. He glanced up at me with hooded eyes. "You're a weakling."

That was it. The final straw.

Smiling maliciously, I pulled out my phone. "I guess I'll just have to call Fallon and tell him you cheated. Let's see what he says." I'd realized early on that their team leader, Sarge, was able to instill fear into all of the boys. All I had to do was text Sarge that they were being mean to me, and then voilà, problem solved. He was a tactical weapon.

My weapon. My…Sarge? My threatening Sarge. My weapon threatening—

What the hell? I seriously needed to see a therapist. Well, I needed to actually talk to my therapist about my issues instead of my bowel movements. Not that my bowel movements weren't an issue…

Stop. Thinking. Addie.

"What the hell, Kitten?" Ryder asked in amusement, and his smile only grew when Ronan blanched at the threat.

"Don't even joke. Last time you tattled on us, Sarge made us run seven laps. Seven!"

I snorted. He deserved that. He and Ryder had convinced me that I'd eaten Mof. Granted, that hadn't been their intention, but the end effect was still the same.

"I think that's enough games for a while," Ryder said. He leaned back in the bed, and Ronan moved to lie down on my other side. I was still pissed at him, but I chose to be the bigger person and not push him over the edge. I suddenly found myself sandwiched between two very hot men.

Excuse me. Cold men. Not hot. Lukewarm at best.

"Pshh! I am a sex god. How you offend me," Ryder said with a scoff. "Lukewarm. Geez."

Ignoring him, as was my standard response when it came to these two men, I settled comfortably against my stuffed dog. Ryder had gotten it for me for my birthday.

Despite the boys' insistence that I have a big party to celebrate, I chose to keep things small. After all, my birthday held nothing but bleak memories. Even after the miraculous return of Ducky, I found that I couldn't get into the birthday cheer, so to speak. That didn't stop the guys from getting me presents.

I named the dog Doggy, much to Ryder's chagrin. I didn't dare admit that the only reason I named him that was because I knew it pissed him off. Ryder and Ronan were quickly becoming my best friends. As best friends, it was my job to make sure they were safe, happy, and moderately pissed off at me. What type of friend would I be if I didn't annoy them at least half of the time?

"What movie do you feel like watching?" Ryder asked, sliding his arm beneath my shoulders. I took the hint and rested my head on his muscular bicep. Ronan immediately twisted towards me, arm wrapping around my waist.

"Doesn't matter," I said through a yawn.

"Something with blood," Ronan suggested, and I rolled my eyes.

"Okay, psychopath."

He immediately jabbed a finger into my stomach, damn well knowing that I was extremely ticklish there. Squealing like a demented pig, I thrashed in Ryder's arms. Ryder didn't release me, but he also didn't join in on the tickle fight—or slaughter, as the case might've been. He began to flip through channels.

My laughter died in my throat when a familiar city was mentioned.

"Wait!" I yelled, sitting upright. Both Ryder and Ronan froze, identical expressions of concern crossing their faces. I grabbed the remote from Ryder's hand and turned up the volume until it was almost earsplitting.

"…plans?" somebody, the news anchor more than likely, was asking. The camera zoomed in on another man, white hair pulled into a low pony and keen eyes zeroed in on the camera.

"We don't have any answers to what started this outbreak," stated the man, which the screen identified as Dr. Colvin. "All we know is that the entire city has been evacuated after the virus began to spread."

"And what about the ones that hadn't been evacuated? The ones infected by the virus and the ones being attacked by the infected? Any word on them?" the anchor pressed. Dr. Colvin's lips went into a thin line.

"As of right now, that number is unspecified…"

"You have to have some answers," the news anchor said. "How many of those people are dead?"

The conversation continued like this for a while. The news anchor would ask a question, and the doctor would immediately deflect. He didn't have to say the words. I could read between the lines easily enough.

From the government sanctioned evacuations, to the immense army presence on the border, it was startlingly apparent—Atlanta had fallen.

Atlanta, a city I'd never visited but had heard numerous stories about.

A large city, home of some football team that I couldn't remember the name of.

The home of Nikolai.

My heart began hammering in my chest. Before I realized what I was doing, I had crawled from between Ryder and Ronan and was grabbing my backpack.

I needed clothes. And food. And water. And something to protect myself with. And—

"What are you doing?" Ronan asked in alarm. He came to stand up beside me. I barely processed his words.

I had to hope that Calax could continue looking after Mof until I could come home. Would he be mad? Would he—

"Addie!" Ryder snapped, his use of my name breaking me out of whatever trance I was in. Still trembling, still feeling as if my heart was breaking, I grabbed his hands.

"I need to go to Atlanta. I need to go see that he's all right."

How could I have forgotten about him? What type of person was I? He should've been the first, the only person, that I thought of when the world went to hell. Heaven knew that my parents wouldn't. They barely even remembered I was alive, let alone him. And, if for some reason they did bring him up, it was only as a means to make me do their bidding.

He was a ghost. Forgotten and hidden away.

But he was mine.

My person, my responsibility.

"Okay, calm down. Let's talk this out."

Tears, unbidden, formed in my eyes.

"I can't. I need to go. I need to leave right now."

Ronan and Ryder exchanged a long look that normally would've pissed me off, but now only proceeded to bring more tears to my eyes.

The way they understood each other...

Nikolai and I never had that. We never wanted to have that.

Why couldn't I be more like these two amazing brothers?

Straightening his shoulders in what looked like resolve, Ryder turned from his brother to face me.

"Can we at least discuss this with Sarge? I promise you, if you want to leave, no one will stop you."

It was impossible to doubt the sincerity in his voice. With a nod as my answer, I finished packing my bag, throwing Doggy in there for added comfort, and followed the boys out the door.

They could try to stop me all they wanted, they could plead and grovel and cry, but I would be going after Nik.

I would be going after my brother.

◇

SARGE WASN'T HOME when we arrived at his house, but Calax was.

The giant of a man immediately engulfed me in his arms. His dark brown hair was longer than I remembered it, and a light scruff was beginning to form around his lush lips. Normally I wasn't one to get all hot and bothered by facial hair, but with Calax, I had to make an exception. It could've been because I you-know-what him—that L-word that should never be said—or it could just be that my taste in men was expanding greatly. After all, I found all of Calax's team ridiculously attractive in different ways.

Resting my head against Calax's beating heart, I allowed myself to believe everything was okay. I was okay, Nikolai was okay, and these boys I had come to count on were okay as well. Didn't I deserve this one win? Wasn't it about time I got a happily ever after instead of a kick in my nonexistent ballsack?

Glancing at the other two guys, Calax pulled me away from them and into the kitchen. I was too stunned to do anything but allow him to drag me along like a strung up puppet.

"Callie, I need to talk to you."

Well, that was what I tried to say anyway, but the words never left my mouth because said mouth was suddenly preoccupied.

Calax's lips were bruising on mine, hard and demanding, just like the man himself. I melted in his arms as I kissed him back, his large hands holding me as if he never wanted to let me go.

He loved me. He'd admitted it to me only weeks earlier and had made sure to remind me every chance he had. It wasn't just in words that he expressed his adoration towards me, but in his gestures and expressions. He would do anything for me, cross any ocean, face any hardship.

He loved me, and I lo—

Nope. Even though I felt it, I couldn't think the cursed word.

Smiling contently, I made a little mewling sound in the back of my throat. I could die like this, wrapped in Cal's embrace as he kissed me and kissed me and kissed me.

A gasp made both Calax and me spin around.

Declan stood in the kitchen door frame, hand white from where it gripped the handle. A thousand emotions flittered across his face—sadness, hurt, anger, helplessness, and then finally, jealousy.

Declan was jealous? Of what? I tried to meet his eyes with my own, but he purposefully looked at his feet. For some inexplicable reason, I felt guilty, as if I'd been caught doing something I shouldn't have.

Why should I feel like this? Declan was my oldest friend, sure, but we had never been a couple.

Still, the pang in my heart refused to go away.

Motions brisk, Declan signed, *"Sarge is here. Meeting in ten."*

Without another word, he hurried from the kitchen. Calax's arms were still wrapped around me, and he peppered kisses across my cheekbones. I loved his kisses, loved being in his arms, but a wicked part of me craved another set of arms— or five or six.

I ignored that selfish voice and twisted in Calax's arms. Smiling, I planted a kiss to his lips.

"Let's go talk to Sarge. There are some things I need to say."

~

MY ANNOUNCEMENT WAS MET with silence.

I glanced from face to face, trying to decipher each of their emotions. Asher, my sweet friend, looked anxious. Tam also wore a similar expression, though I was beginning to think that was his natural face. Ryder and Ronan exchanged long, eloquent glances. Declan was glaring at the wall, and Fallon merely stared at me, unblinking. Only Calax looked unconcerned, almost relaxed, as he leaned back on the sofa. Normally, I would've been cool with the whole supportive boyfriend thing, especially when his girlfriend was a vindictive psychopath, but now, it only made me nervous.

"Is there a particular reason why you wish to travel to Atlanta?" Fallon asked, almost conversationally. I would've thought he was fine if I hadn't seen his fingers tapping against the armrest of his chair. That seemed to hint at whatever emotion he wished to keep hidden.

I pulled my lip through my teeth, surveying each face. Not even Declan or Calax knew about Nikolai. It wasn't that I was ashamed of him or anything, but fear was a fickle thing. He was something whispered about in the dead of night. Safe. Protected.

"Nikolai," I whispered at last. The boys blinked at me, various expressions crossing their faces. The general consensus seemed to be confusion.

"Who's Nikolai?" Asher asked gently. I swallowed, images of my brother flashing through my mind.

"He's my brother," I answered at last. "My younger brother." I pulled at the frayed edges of the couch as if I suddenly found it very interesting. "He's autistic." Taking a deep breath, I began to tell the story for the first time. "He was six when he was first diagnosed, and I was ten. Nik had always been a strange boy, but I always attributed it to shyness more than anything. He didn't talk often, and he always had head-phones over his ears. He worked with a specialist named Nancy." I paused, watching my fingers unravel the bottom of the couch. Life was just as fragile. It was a thread, and one pull could completely destroy it.

"My parents were so embarrassed of him. I remember they would always keep him locked in his room whenever they had friends over. They eventually decided that he would be better somewhere else, with someone else. He went to live with Nancy and her family in Atlanta." I wiped at the tears escaping my eyes. "I would get to see him on holidays, and I would talk to him on the phone whenever I could, but it wasn't the same. We grew apart. But you guys have to understand that he's my little brother, and I would do anything for him. So I'm going to Atlanta, and I'm going to find my brother and bring him home."

The boys were silent yet again as they absorbed my story. Tam was biting on his fingernail, an indication that he was distressed by the story he had heard. I had the distinct feeling that Tam himself suffered from a mental illness, though he'd never actually admitted it to me and I didn't press. Every morning, if I were to arrive before the sun fully rose, I would catch Tam in the kitchen counting the cups in the cupboards. Every morning, he would count every cup. Every night, he would count every brick on the wall.

He didn't think I noticed. I would never tell him differently.

Fallon's expression was grave, no doubt thinking of the implications of my announcement. He must've seen the resolve on my face, the determination. There was no changing my mind on this issue.

"You look fucking comfortable," Ryder sneered to Calax. "How are you not freaking out?"

I'd wondered that same thing. Calax, out of all of them, was the most protective of me. I didn't know if it was because of our relationship, or the fact that he felt the need to atone for the years of suffering I endured under his nose, not that I blamed him. Either way, his sudden impassiveness was startling.

In answer to Ryder's question, Calax shrugged.

"It doesn't matter to me. Whether she goes or not, I'm staying with her."

I blinked.

"What? You can't come with me! It could be dangerous!"

Reports were continually coming in. The death count had been steadily increas-ing, and the number of infected had also increased.

"And you think I'm going to let you go alone?" Calax asked in disbelief. He snorted. "Please."

"Callie…"

"No, baby girl. You don't get to argue about this. We'll go together, and we'll get your brother back. I love you. I would never leave you alone."

Ronan, who was sitting beside me, stiffened at something Calax said. I wondered if it was because he said we would go together, or if it was because Calax had admitted his love to me. I noticed that Declan's eyes had narrowed on Calax's face as well, hands clenched.

"You've given us a lot to think about," Fallon said at last. He folded his hands in his lap, thought better of it, and rested them on the armrests. "Calax, are you sure of your decision?"

Calax nodded.

"And, Addie? Are you sure?"

I nodded as well. It seemed as if we were doing the silent, brooding routine.

"Okay." Fallon clapped his hands together, ignoring the protests from the other guys. "Calax, why don't you and Addie grab some food. There's some things we need to discuss as a team."

I met Calax's stare, but he looked just as baffled as I felt. What could they possibly be discussing? Were they going to stop me from going?

There would be a lot of asses getting kicked if that was the case.

Frowning, I rose from my seat and grabbed Calax's hand. I would use Calax as a shield if the need arose.

~

DECLAN

I watched Addie and Cal walk into the kitchen, fingers interlocked.

Addie's announcement echoed in my mind. A brother? Why hadn't I heard of him before? She had told me everything, but she never mentioned Nik, the most important person in her life.

Did she not trust me? The realization made me feel sick to my stomach.

If Addie was going to Atlanta, I sure as hell was going with her. I'd already lost her once. Never again would I let her walk away from me.

My mind unwillingly flickered back towards the kiss I witnessed between Cal and Addie. I should've been happy for them. Addie was my best friend, and Cal was practically my brother. Instead, it felt as if my heart was breaking free of my chest.

Jealousy. I wasn't familiar with the emotion, since it had never before applied to me. Even with the girls I occasionally shared with my team, I'd never felt jealous of who they spent their time with. They spent the night with Ryder? Good for them. Went out to dinner with Tam? Hopefully, he paid.

Everything felt different with Addie. I felt too much for her, too deeply.

I couldn't help but imagine my own body in Calax's place. Her hands wrapped around my waist, her lips on mine, my fingers tangled in her hair.

Sarge's sudden movement captured my attention.

He was speaking to the group, continuing a discussion I must've missed in my wistful daydream. He turned towards me, as if he felt my eyes on him, and signed.

"What's your vote?"

About what?

Sarge would be pissed at me if he discovered I'd zoned out during a meeting. My confusion must've been evident on my face, though, for his own features hardened.

"Do you want to go with Adelaide to Atlanta?"

Did he even have to ask me that? I didn't even need to think about my answer.

"Hell yeah."

Sarge nodded as if he already expected my answer. Knowing him, he probably did.

"Then it's settled. We'll all pack up and go with Addie to Atlanta."

Wait, what?

CHAPTER 6

ADDIE

*D*espite my protests, all of the guys insisted on coming with me.

"It'll be a mini vacation!" Ryder had said eagerly.

Ronan added, "Hopefully, that means you'll wear a bikini."

I think those two would've blown a nut if I told them that I'd never worn a bikini before in my life. I had too many scars, too many horrors that I preferred to keep hidden behind long sleeves. It had only been recently that I felt comfortable enough to walk out of my house in a tank top. The boys never judged me, and they never questioned the collection of scars on my wrists. They knew what they were from, and they helped me overcome it.

"You guys don't have to come with me," I said for the millionth time. We were in the living room of Sarge's house, an assortment of suitcases littering the small room. Mof, much to his displeasure, was in a small cage. I could hear his hissing from across the room.

The boys continued to talk over me, discussing transportation. Growling, I grabbed my own suitcase and walked out the door.

It took them a solid five seconds to realize what I was doing.

"Where are you going, Princess?" Ronan asked, sounding way too amused for the situation.

"I'm leaving. By myself."

"No, you're not," Asher said. He, too, sounded like he was on the verge of laughter. That bastard was supposed to be on my side!

"I'm ignoring you," I said with a huff.

Fallon's house was in a small neighborhood, each house more stereotypical of a grandma's house than the next. White picket fences, yellow siding, elaborate garden displays.

Yup. I would never not make fun of Fallon's taste in bachelor pads.

"Are you just going to walk there?" Calax called.

I saluted him with my middle finger.

"Adelaide!" Fallon's strident voice made me stagger to a stop. Frowning, I glanced at him over my shoulder. He must've been following me while the others stayed at the front door, as I nearly ran into his stomach when I turned.

Stupid Fallon. Stupid Calax. Stupid everyone.

Scowling up at him, I crossed my arms over my chest.

"It's not safe for you guys to go," I said, low enough that the boys' prying ears wouldn't be able to hear.

"And it's safe for you?" The question wasn't said meanly, but as an observation.

"No," I admitted. "But I don't want anyone to risk themselves for me."

He was silent for a moment, his handsome face deep in thought. "It's your decision whether or not you wish to go, right?"

Nodding, I smiled gratefully.

"Exactly. My decision."

"And is it not also their decision on whether or not they wish accompany you?"

His question threw me off balance. I opened my mouth, closed it, and then opened it again. Damn. Why did he have to go and use logic?

"But..." I floundered to come up with a legitimate excuse. "But did everybody agree?"

I didn't want people to feel obligated to go because others on their team were. I'd lived my entire life with a very vague perception of freewill, and I hated to think that I was depriving the boys of it.

"They all agreed," Fallon assured me. "They all want to go with you because they care about you."

His voice was unexpectedly gentle. This development in character was new to me. Fallon had always been the gruff, unwavering leader. His display of tenderness was unusual but not unwanted.

Blinking back tears, I took a step closer to him. His shoulder-length brown hair was down today, instead of in its usual ponytail. A loose strand curled around his eye, and I absently brushed it behind his ear.

"Thank you," I said. His eyes were soft as they traced my features.

"You're welcome."

"Are we leaving yet?" Ryder called from the front porch. "My suitcase is heavy!"

"That's because he's too shallow to allow the suitcase to touch the ground," Asher said.

Ryder gasped in mock outrage. "It's designer!"

Rolling my eyes, I smirked up at Fallon.

"I call whatever car Ryder is not in. I don't think I have the stomach for a five-hour lecture on the importance of elegant luggage."

Fallon shuddered. "Sometimes, he's a very effective torture tool."

～

UNFORTUNATELY, neither Fallon nor I got our wish.

We found ourselves in a large white van. The boys played rock-paper-scissors to determine seating arrangements. At first, I thought they were arguing over who would get shotgun, but when Asher won with a whoop, he immediately crawled into the seat beside mine. Ronan had also won, and he took the seat on my other side.

Grumbling, Calax reluctantly took the front seat, and the other guys crowded in wherever they could fit. Tamson was on Mof duty. The cat seemed to have picked Tam as his favorite, only allowing the shy boy to pet him and carry him. Fallon declared that he, and only he, would drive.

"I don't want a repeat of last time," he had said, giving Ryder a pointed look. I never did figure out what happened, but from the shudders of the other guys, I reasoned that it wasn't pretty.

I was overcome with fatigue only a couple of minutes into the drive. Yawning, I rested my head on Asher's shoulder.

"Comfy," I murmured sleepily.

"Go ahead and sleep, sweetheart," Asher said. "We have a long drive ahead of us."

I was more than happy to oblige.

I OPENED my eyes to see that I was no longer in the car, but a field. The grass was a vibrant green, manicured to perfection. The sky, a light blue with a yellow tint from the sun, smiled down at me. The sight was peaceful, serene, as if I'd stepped into an entirely new world.

A new life.

Somewhere in the distance, children began to laugh. The sound made goosebumps erupt on my skin.

Pulling myself onto my elbows, I surveyed the scene before me.

I was underneath a single tree, the boughs protecting me from the punishing sun. Everywhere I looked, a rolling landscape greeted me. It seemed to go on and on forever, an endless carpet of green. Wiggling my bare toes—what the hell happened to my shoes?—I allowed myself to relax. Despite the strange location, I didn't feel threatened. If anything, I felt awfully calm, as if I was where I was meant to be.

"Hello?" I called, scrambling to my feet. It might've been a dumb idea to call out in this unfamiliar place—hello, I'd watched enough horror movies with Asher—but the sudden silence was disconcerting. Weren't there children earlier? I could've sworn I heard laughter.

Wiping dirt from my pants, I turned in a circle, taking in everything. There wasn't a single soul besides me and the tree. That is, if trees even had souls. Who was I to judge their worthiness to have a soul? I wasn't the soul judger person thing—

Focus, Addie.

It was almost annoying that I couldn't stay on topic for more than five seconds before my brain wandered.

I made one more circle, expecting to see the same empty grassland as before. Instead, I was moderately shocked when I saw a small girl standing a few feet in front of me.

Her back was towards me, but I could see that she had long brown hair and pale skin. She wore a simple white dress with a red bow around her waist.

Little girl appearing out of nowhere? Hell no.

Taking a step backwards, eyes still latched onto the demonic child, I tripped over a loose rock. That was why I didn't multitask. One couldn't walk backwards and keep an eye on the creepy girl at the same time.

I tried to fall quietly, but my clumsy ass landed on the ground with a bang. I may or may not have also let out a string of unladylike curses.

Yup. Exactly the words a young girl needed to hear.

She turned towards me, head tilted to the side thoughtfully. Whatever I was about to say became caught in my throat when I caught sight of her young, elfin face.

Cupid-bow lips, small nose, large eyes framed by thick, dark lashes.

I was staring at myself. Albeit, a younger version of myself, but myself all the same.

Gaping, I scrambled back to my feet.

"What the hell is going on?" I whispered to the younger me, taking in her sweet expression. Had I once been that innocent? Had life made my features harder, my eyes colder? I longed to go back in time, before I was abused and forgotten by my family. I wished I'd remained this girl.

This better version of myself.

She continued to smile, unaware or ignoring my growing panic. Tentatively, she ventured a step closer. Her smile began to contort with each movement.

Eyes flashing a garnet red, she bared her teeth at me. Black veins, almost like worms, began to crawl beneath her pasty skin.

I held my hands up in surrender.

"Please," I whispered, a second before she pounced.

~

I woke up in a cold sweat, heart pounding.

Sometime during my slumber, I must've sprawled over both Ronan and Asher. My head was nestled on the latter's chest, while my feet were on Ronan.

To my mortification, a small puddle of drool darkened Asher's light shirt.

Whoops. Learned something new every day.

"Good morning, sweetheart," Asher said once he saw that I was awake. His hand tenderly brushed some of my sweat soaked hair out of my face.

"It's actually afternoon," Ryder pointed out from somewhere behind me.

Yawning, I tried to recall my strange dream, but my brain turned to liquid the more I tried to concentrate. I could never remember my dreams once I woke up. Bits and pieces, maybe, but never the overall image. It was like a puzzle that was missing too many pieces to accurately figure out what it was supposed to depict.

Frowning, I stretched my sore muscles.

"How long have I been asleep?" I asked, blinking the last remains of sleep from my eyes.

"A couple hours, give or take," Tam answered. He'd released Mof from his cage and was absently stroking his silky, black fur. My heart warmed at the sight. "We haven't moved an inch in the last fifteen minutes though."

"And we probably won't move any farther for a while," added Fallon gruffly. "It's been this way since we've driven onto the main highway."

I finally sat up to see what Fallon was referring to, and my jaw practically popped from its socket.

There were cars everywhere. Parked in every available crevice, the road was a collection of color. Now that I was paying attention and no longer in my sleep muddled daze, I could hear the beeping of horns and the chatter of people. It seemed as if the majority of drivers were outside of their cars, resting against the hoods and enjoying the last rays of sunlight before night fell.

"Is there an accident up ahead?" I asked, leaning forward to get a better view out of the windshield. "Or construction?"

"No road signs for construction," Fallon said. Then, almost as an afterthought, he muttered, "I should've expected this to happen during a panic."

I nodded, fully accepting Fallon's explanation. After all, it was what we were doing. I didn't know these people's stories, I didn't know if they were running from a weather ravaged home or a virus infected city, or if they were trying to get to a loved one. I supposed it went back to the fight or flight response active in all humans. The response, for these people, appeared to be flight. Were we any different, despite the fact that we were running towards danger and not away from it?

Casting another glance around, it became apparent that we were trapped.

A few of the other cars must've come to the same conclusion, since I saw them attempt to maneuver their vehicles onto the median dividing the lanes. How they expected to get past all the cars and the people was a mystery to me, but I applauded their efforts.

"Does this mean we get to play car games?" Ryder, my energetic puppy, asked eagerly.

"No!" came the immediate response from the other guys. I didn't have to look behind me to see that Ryder's expression would have fallen, lip protruding in a pout like a now dejected puppy.

I really had to stop comparing Ryder to a dog.

Ronan and Asher, on either side of me, burst into laughter. Ryder reached over to pinch my arm.

"I am not a dog," Ryder growled out, and I couldn't help but think he sounded like an angry dog just then. Of course, that sent me into another fit of giggles. Ronan and Asher began laughing again as well.

"You're one to laugh, stupid leprechaun and feminine man!"

Oh yeah. I may have accidentally, in my attempt to compliment Asher, referred to his features as feminine. It wasn't my fault. He truly was a beautiful man, with his symmetrical face and shock of blond hair. How was I supposed to know that it wasn't socially acceptable to call a male feminine?

Ronan rightly deserved his title as a leprechaun. Even in the months that had gone by, he still maintained his green tipped hair.

A sexy leprechaun, but a leprechaun all the same.

"Maybe I'll let you sing a song," I cooed. When the guys groaned, I added, "Just one. I don't feel like dying just yet."

"It wouldn't be you that they murdered, Kitten," Ryder said, voice tinged with amusement. I rolled my eyes.

"Fine. I don't want you to die just yet either. Give it a couple days."

"How you flatter me," Ryder said with a cheeky grin.

The sound of a propeller stopped me from retorting. Pushing past Asher, I pressed my face against the glass window.

There, up in the sky, was a helicopter. A US military helicopter. No, that wasn't right.

There wasn't just one, but two.

No, three.

No, ten.

I watched, transfixed, as the helicopters flew by us.

Where were they going, and what could possibly require ten helicopters?

CHAPTER 7

ADDIE

*I*t happened just before nightfall.

The sun was low, not yet completely devoured by the horizon. Pale pink light filtered through the car windows.

Fallon was right—we hadn't moved an inch in the hours we'd been here. Getting off the highway wasn't an option, so we were forced to sit in the car and partake in Ryder's ridiculous games.

At least I was having fun, though Calax looked as if he was seconds away from strangling the other man. For that, I wanted to strangle Calax.

I blamed it on the platonic tension I'd talked to Ronan about when we first met. Just the normal, non-sexual tension between seven brothers and one non-sister.

Like I totally didn't notice Asher's thigh pressed against mine, and I didn't pay attention to Ronan's hand lightly holding my own as he drew on my arm.

Nope. Not me.

Was I allowed to feel attracted to Calax, my almost-but-never-clarified boyfriend? Was I allowed to feel it for his friends as well?

"When we stop for the night, I want you to start self-defense classes," Fallon said suddenly, snapping me out of my less than sisterly thoughts. Cheeks burning, I tried to smooth my features into a careful mask. The last thing I wanted them to know was that I was thinking about the sexual tension reverberating through the car.

"S-Sexual tension?" Asher stuttered, and I stuck my tongue out at him.

"Hadn't meant to say that aloud."

"But it's cute that you did," Ronan said, still bent over my hand. I hadn't been able to see what he was drawing. Whenever I tried to peek, he would swat my head away with a reprimanding "No."

Ignoring them, I turned my attention back towards Fallon. He met my gaze in the rearview mirror, eyes smoldering.

He really was a scary man. Attractive, yes, but there was something innately dangerous about the way he moved and talked. He was a man of few words, but when he spoke, you knew that the only option was to listen and agree.

"What type of self-defense?" I asked. "I only know the fall-on-my-ass maneuver."

Fallon rolled his eyes, his standard response to my quips, but I thought I saw a hint of a smile gracing his features. I wanted to pat myself on the back.

"Tam will teach you," Fallon said simply, and the man in question blushed scarlet. Tam had once told me that he was an MMA fighter. I found it hard to believe that my sweet, shy Tamson was able to fight another human being, but I'd seen his skills firsthand when he fought a Rager to protect me.

Granted, he'd lost, but it was the thought that counted.

"Have the phones started working yet?" Calax asked, effectively changing the subject from my soon-to-be ass kicking. It was something we'd noticed almost immediately when we began our journey—none of our phones had a signal. At first, when I tried calling Nik's foster parents from Fallon's house, I'd assumed that I just had bad cell reception. This theory was quickly debunked when the rest of the boys began to complain as well.

It didn't get better the farther we drove. No, it was apparent that the connection was dead everywhere.

"Nope," Ryder said, popping the P.

Declan made an annoyed sound in the back of his throat, and I threw him a small smile.

"Hey, lazy pants. Did you sleep well?"

He looked adorable post nap. His hair was tousled, and the seatbelt he'd been using as a pillow had indented itself onto his cheek. His tired eyes flickered from face to face before resting on the immobile traffic.

"Yeah," I answered his unspoken question. "We're still stopped in traffic. Haven't moved an inch."

"That's not true!" Ryder protested halfheartedly. "We moved approximately two point eight inches a half hour ago."

I chuckled softly at his weak attempt at a joke. The mood had grown increasingly somber, as if we all realized we were living on borrowed time.

There were too many things we needed to do, too many people we wanted to save, and we couldn't afford sitting around doing nothing. Everywhere I looked, people were indolently lying outside their vehicles. A couple groups had a grill going and were selling cooked meat for a decent price. Others had set up makeshift tents, and one even had a campfire blazing.

"This is fucking ridiculous," Calax said. "Isn't there a way we can get off this fucking highway?"

"Freeway," Fallon corrected absently. "And language."

I snorted as Calax's face turned red.

Tuning out the argument I knew was about to transpire, I peered over Asher's head. We really were trapped, I realized dumbly. With our car squeezed into the middle lane, there was no way we could escape.

Unless, of course, we ran over other people and their cars.

Even the cars on the far right were trapped by a steep decline that led to a forest. Though some of the cars could easily break apart the railing, the drop itself had the capacity to be deadly.

On the other side of the freeway, across the median, were even more cars. An adjacent forest blocked any access to and from the cluttered road.

My eyes were locked on those trees, leaves beginning to form on their once barren branches and the remains of fallen snow melting at their bases, when I saw the figure. He moved stealthily from behind the throng of trees, face obscured by haunting shadows. As I watched, transfixed, another person exited the tree line, coming to stand beside the first. Their hands were restless by their sides, twisting and untwisting as if they were desperate for something to do with them. My heart hammered as even more people emerged, stalking towards the oblivious people both inside and outside of their cars.

I told myself that there was no reason for me to panic. Logically, I knew there was no rational reason for me to believe these people were anything other than wandering travelers. Perhaps, like many others, they'd gotten bored with sitting in their cars. Perhaps they had taken a walk, explored the woods, and abandoned their cars farther down.

But there was something almost recognizable in the way they walked. Each movement was clunky, as if they were unfamiliar with walking or were forced to carry a heavy weight with them. Though I couldn't see any facial features, their heads whipped from side to side with an almost startling intensity. It was only as one of them stepped farther from his hiding spot, coming to stand beside a silver sedan, that I knew I wasn't looking at a sane human.

I was staring at an horde of Ragers.

"Guys," I whispered huskily, unable to tear my gaze away from the horrific sight before me. People were finally beginning to realize what was happening.

I saw flailing arms, heard bloodcurdling screams, and watched the Ragers cut through the assembled people.

I didn't need to say anything else. All of the guys had their faces pressed against the glass windows, varying expressions of horror turning their faces pale.

"Holy shit," Calax said, mouth agape.

Before I'd even processed what was happening, each of the guys pulled out a gun.

A freaking gun.

My mind was incapable of focusing on anything at that moment, let alone the weapons held expertly in each of their hands.

"Ronan, stay with Addie," Fallon said before sliding out of the driver's seat. I was too stunned at first to say anything as he walked towards the fight instead of away.

Everybody else was screaming, lunging back towards their cars with a blistering speed. I heard many locks click into place. Some were attempting to escape their car prison, but that only results in smashed car fronts and bumpers.

"What the hell are you guys doing?" I yelled, watching the rest of the guys exit the vehicle.

"Take care of her," Asher warned, ignoring me, and Ronan nodded seriously.

They aimed their gun at the nearest Rager, now across the median, and fired. A half dozen bullets spliced through the Rager's body, but he continued to run. It was only when Fallon raised his gun and shot directly at his forehead that the monster fall.

My mouth felt impossibly dry, and my stomach churned.

Before I could warn him, I vomited across Ronan's shoes.

That was the second time I'd thrown up on him.

"Who the hell are you guys?" I said, my mind reeling. It suddenly occurred to me that I didn't know the guys I was traveling with. Not really. I knew Calax, or at least I thought I did, and I knew of Declan. The rest? They were enigmas. What type of people carried guns around with them and knew how to shoot them so effortlessly? What type of people would run into the face of danger instead of screaming in the opposite direction?

I couldn't focus on the mysteries surrounding the boys though, because my attention became stuck on a woman being mauled by a Rager. His long fingers dug into her neck as he swiped desperately, erratically. Blood and skin flew everywhere, darkening the white of a nearby car.

"Ronan," I cried, shaking his arm. He glanced from where he was perusing the opposite window, body tensed and hand tight over his gun, before he turned in the direction I was pointing.

He let out a series of curses. Indecision crossed his face.

"Go!" I screamed, shoving him towards the door. I knew the only reason he was considering waiting was to keep an eye on me. "I'll be fine! Go!"

Stiffly, he thrusted a pocket knife into my hand.

"You only use this if it's an emergency. Don't exit the damn car."

Before I could protest that I wasn't a child and that I wanted to help, Ronan had run towards the direction of the woman. I hoped he made it in time, but by the grotesque positioning of her arm and blood-splattered face, I found that doubtful.

My heart was heavy, and I yearned to do something besides sit like a pathetic princess. I didn't want to have to wait for the knights to return. I was stronger than that.

Or at least I wanted to be.

Despite my thoughts, I knew it would be idiotic to leave the confines of the car. I wasn't capable of defending myself adequately enough to help in a fight. I would only get in the way, and the boys would get hurt trying to protect me.

Or worse, others would get hurt because the boys weren't around to protect them.

I pressed my hands to my ears, trying to ignore the gunshots. It appeared as if other people had joined the fight. A few dozen men and women, some that I'd noticed before as being our car neighbors, were also taking shots at the ferocious Ragers. Those that didn't have guns were using any weapon they could find—a bat, pepper spray, their own bodies.

My hand clenched around the knife. I was desperate to help, desperate to feel useful. I didn't want to remain hidden behind a shield anymore.

It took every ounce of my self-control to remain seated, even as Ragers moved closer towards my car.

I couldn't see the guys anymore.

Even Ronan, who'd only been a few cars away from me, had become lost in the fray. I prayed that they were all right.

Bodies were sprawled along the highway. Blood coated every available surface with a deep, garnet red. I couldn't tell how many of the fallen were Ragers and how many were innocent people. In death, they all looked the same.

Was it wrong that I was relieved that none of the fallen were the boys? Was it wrong that I rejoiced at an unfamiliar shock of red hair on a body that looked similar to Asher's?

From my other side, I heard a scream. I immediately turned towards the source, despite knowing what I was going to see.

The scream, though unfamiliar, was octaves higher than a normal person's. This theory was only reinforced when I saw a small boy pinned down beneath an immense Rager.

For a moment, fury blinded me. I could barely think straight, let alone see clearly through the red haze clouding my vision. All I could think about was Nik.

Nik getting attacked. Nik being torn apart. Nik.

Before I realized what was happening, I was charging from the car, knife raised. Mof made an unhappy squeal from where he paced in his cage, and I paused briefly.

"I'll be right back," I promised the cat, though I knew the promise was intended for the others more than the diminutive creature. The boys were going to freak if they discovered I was gone.

But they had to understand. This was a child.

Even if he didn't have a strong resemblance to my brother, I would help him anyway. There was nothing else I could do.

Up close, I saw that the Rager was a female. Or had been. The verdict was still out on that one.

Her brown hair was falling out in clumps, black veins twitching beneath the surface. Her red eyes, as red as the blood covering her face, were fixated on her prey. It didn't seem to matter that the person she was holding down was a little boy. It didn't matter that he was pleading with her, tears coating his chubby cheeks.

And it didn't matter that he cried her name, voice anguished.

"Mamma! Mamma, stop! Please!"

I faltered.

This woman was his mother?

But there was nothing resembling recognition in her feral gaze. No, his mother was gone, and in her place was a monster.

I grabbed the woman by the hair, pulling her off of her sobbing son. I ignored the boy's pleas not to hurt his mother as I pushed the Rager onto the ground.

I knew that it was an opportune time to stab my knife into her head. I knew that I should've slashed her neck.

I knew all this, but I also knew that I could never do it. How could I possibly live with myself knowing that I killed this woman? A mother?

I was still holding onto hope, through frail, that a cure would be found. When the world was finally saved, I wanted to be able to live with myself and my actions. I wanted us to be a race worthy of being saved.

I extended a hand towards the prone kid, still a sniveling mess on the ground. The boy merely began to cry harder, and I let out a grunt of annoyance.

"Come on! We need to get out of here!"

The boy blinked rapidly and hesitantly began lifting his hand towards mine.

Something hard hit me in the back of the head, and I tasted blood. Spinning so fast I no doubt got whiplash, I met the snarling face of the mother Rager.

"Tommy, don't listen to this stranger. Come with Mommy." Even her voice was distorted, a low growl that was more animal than human.

"Yeah, I don't think that's the best idea, Tommy," I muttered. I leveled my knife at her chest, but I was utterly inept at using it. In only a matter of a seconds, she was behind me, hand gripping my hair in a tight fist.

I winced at the pain, scrambling to free myself from her prying fingers. I let out a slight scream as her hold deepened, tilting my head back in a way that made my neck crack.

I desperately propelled my body backwards. I hoped that it would catch her off guard. It seemed to work, as she released me with a grunt. I swiped at her stomach with my knife for good measure, nausea threatening to take me down when blood welled.

Please don't make me hurt you. Please don't make me hurt you.

Unfortunately, I must not have been saying those thoughts aloud because the Rager lunged again. I squeaked, swinging my knife yet again in what I hoped was a threatening manner.

If I was being honest with myself, I probably looked more amusing than threatening.

"Come on! Let's go!" The little boy, Tommy apparently, was tugging at my arm. I turned towards him, stunned, and the Rager took my momentary lapse in concentration to pounce on me. My head cracked as it hit the concrete, and I felt something metallic in my mouth. Blood. My blood.

In my fall, I must've dropped my knife. I was alone, with a Rager on top of me, and no way to defend myself. I'm sure this would've been a lesson on what *not* to do in Tamson's self-defense class.

"You stupid bitch," the Rager purred, echoing my own sentiment. She leaned down, breath caressing my neck. I squeezed my eyes shut.

Maybe, just maybe, my death would be painless. Maybe, just maybe, I would finally atone for all of my sins.

There was a sudden gurgling sound, and my eyelids flew open.

The woman was still on top of me, but her eyes were unfocused. Distant. Her mouth was open, blood dripping down her pale chin.

And it was then that I noticed the knife protruding from her head, the copper handle familiar.

It was the knife Ronan had left me. But how did it end up in her head?

That question was soon answered when I saw Tommy, trembling like a leaf, pulling the knife out from where it was lodged in her skull.

She fell.

The darkness around us seemed to consume the continuous onslaught of screams.

CHAPTER 8

ADDIE

What words could you possibly say to comfort a little boy that was forced to kill his own mother?

What could anyone possibly do to make this very wrong situation right?

Tommy's hands were trembling, and the knife clattered to the ground, slick with blood.

"I killed her," he muttered. "I killed her. I killed her."

He held his shaking hands out in front of him as if he didn't recognize them. As if they belonged to someone entirely different, someone capable of stabbing his mother in the head. My heart ached for this boy, for the innocence that was so brutally taken from him.

I knew, without a shadow of doubt, that he would never be able to forget this day. This wasn't merely an obstacle that he could grow from. No, this was something much darker.

Angrier.

"Tommy—your name is Tommy, right?" I asked, scrambling to my feet. My head hurt furiously, and blood burned my eyes. I swiped the red, thick liquid away in annoyance.

"I killed her," Tommy repeated numbly. Only his lips moved. His eyes stared vacantly at the fallen body of his mother. His hands were still held out in front of him.

"Tommy, we have to go." I leaned down to pick up the knife he'd dropped. I tried my hardest not to look at the blood smearing the shiny blade. I told myself that if I didn't see it, it wasn't real. I repeated this mantra until the words became meaning-less. Even I—the Queen of Shitty Childhoods—knew that this was something neither of us could ever come back from. I just had to hope that Tommy was strong enough, stronger than I'd ever been, to face the storm raging ahead.

"Tommy." Without waiting for him to respond, I grabbed his hand and began walking in the direction of the car. I stopped in mid stride when I saw the Ragers surrounding the van's tinted windows.

"Shit," I cursed, immediately changing direction. There were bodies everywhere, and gunfire ricocheted through the air. I much preferred the gunfire over the screams.

It allowed me to pretend that we, humanity, were winning.

"I killed her," Tommy muttered shakily.

I didn't know what to say or how to comfort him. I'd never been the greatest with children, especially ones that had gone through so much tragedy. In a sense, I could relate to Tommy on an almost spiritual level. I didn't know if that connection made it harder to talk to him or easier.

Sidestepping a snarling Rager, I tightened my grip on Tommy's hand. We'd reached the edge of the road, towards the decline that was only separated from us by a metal fence following the length of the highway. Behind us, the Ragers tore apart people as if they were nothing more than discarded dolls.

Vaguely, my mind brought up an image of my childhood doll, smartly named Dolly. Dad had destroyed her, ripping her arm clean from her body.

These people, these humans, reminded me of her.

My stomach twisted as I scanned the sea of dead bodies. There were still people fighting, but the growing darkness made it hard to discern who was friend and who was foe. I didn't see any of the guys, and I tried not to panic.

They were resourceful and obviously skilled in weaponry. I had to believe they would be safe.

For my own sanity.

"Okay, Tommy, we're gonna have to jump."

He didn't even glance my way, his face a pale sheet.

I read in a psychology book that it helped if you repeatedly used your patient's name. Apparently, it allowed the person to feel a sense of security and familiarity. Or some bullshit along those lines.

I really hoped it was working now.

"Tommy," I said again, squeezing his fingers. His wide, terrified eyes landed on my face as he turned towards me. I hated the anguish in his expression. When he spoke, his words were almost mechanical.

"Yes. Jump. Yes."

Pleased with the response, I released his hand. He immediately let out a cry at the loss of contact.

"It's okay. I'll be just a moment," I said, trying to soothe him. Putting my hand to my forehead, I used my blood as a makeshift paint.

Demented? Yes.

Effective? Also yes.

Quickly, aware of the Ragers fighting behind me, I drew a picture on the railing. It took only a few seconds, shorter than what it would've been to spell out my name.

"Are you ready?" I asked Tommy as soon as I finished. I held out my hand, not the bloody one, and he immediately engulfed it in his own.

I had no time to think about the people I was leaving behind or the lives lost. No, I would lose my mind if I was to focus on such a depressing detail. I had to get Tommy to safety, first and foremost. He'd saved my life at the expense of his mother's, and it was time to return the favor.

Would I be willing to hurt someone I loved to help a complete stranger? Was this young boy twice the person I could ever be?

I didn't know the answer to either of those questions.

Holding my breath, I stepped off the ledge.

And down we fell.

Let me make something perfectly clear to you. Never, and I mean never, is it a smart idea to throw yourself off a bridge.

It hurts like a bitch, especially when you tumble down the side of a hill.

Loose pebbles and sharp rocks jabbed themselves into my side as I fell. My head, still roaring from the hit the Rager had inflicted, whacked itself against a jutting tree stump.

Sometime during my tumble, I must've let go of Tommy's hand. The boy was no longer beside me.

I was relieved when I heard his cry of pain. At least he was alive.

For now.

When I finally stopped falling, I was a panting, broken mess on the forest floor. A few painfully sharp twigs jutted from my arm, and I ripped them out with a small growl.

Why did this shit always have to happen to me?

"Tommy!" I cried hoarsely, though I doubted my voice carried over the screams from above.

It wasn't like in the movies. I didn't just fall and transport myself into an entirely different reality, free of monsters. It didn't all of a sudden become deadly quiet, the silence broken apart by the intermittent song of crickets.

Nope, I still heard every scream, every snarl, every gunshot. I still saw the blood coating my fingers, cascading down my cheekbones like teardrops.

The silhouettes of Ragers captured my attention from their perch high above.

Had I really fallen that far down?

Of course, I realized that question wasn't necessarily important, but it was all I could think about. I refused to think about the boys I'd left behind or the creatures that could be lurking in my new resting place.

"Are you okay?" a timid voice asked. Tommy. He dropped to his knees beside me.

"I'm fine. How about you?"

He looked okay, at least on the outside. I knew, mentally, that the wounds inflicted could be fatal.

"I'm fine. There's a house up ahead." He pointed towards a particularly dense thicket of trees. I wondered what he'd seen during his tumble that led him to believe that because I saw jack shit.

"You sure?" I asked.

"Of course I'm damn sure!" Tommy snapped, and I blinked at the little boy.

Choosing not to comment on his language—he deserved to curse up a storm, after all—I allowed him to help me to my feet.

The world momentarily began to spin as I struggled to maintain my footing. Once I was positive that I would be able to stand without puking or falling over, I nodded for Tommy to lead the way.

I couldn't help but glance over my shoulder, just once, at the highway. Flames of fire licked the sky, though I wasn't sure if it was coming from the cars or an out-of-control campfire. The farther we walked, the quieter the screams got until I could almost imagine they were a figment of my imagination.

Almost, but not quite.

I could still feel the blood on my hands, a real, tangible liquid.

I could still hear the screams, though faded, in the distance.

My stomach churned angrily.

I couldn't handle this world anymore—the injustice, the senseless violence, and the feeling that, somehow, I could've stopped it all.

I wondered if Tommy blamed me for his mother's death. Heaven knew I blamed myself. This little boy had chosen me over a woman he loved. How could he stand holding my hand? Where was the resentment? The hatred?

We stopped in front of a modest house with peeling paint and torn shutters. The floorboards of the front deck creaked beneath our combined weight.

Hands trembling, both in fear and anticipation, I knocked on the door.

Silence greeted me.

Feeling desperate, I rapped my knuckles against it again.

And again.

And again.

I didn't dare scream for fear that Ragers were lurking nearby. Was there anybody home?

Were they merely asleep, unable to hear my persistent knocking? Were they ignoring us?

I refused to think that they were dead, though a tiny voice in my head warned me that we might not be coming home to live bodies.

All I knew for certain was that we couldn't be out here any longer than necessary.

"Stay behind me," I ordered Tommy, turning the knob of the door. It opened easily.

The house was dark. After an ineffectual swipe at the light switch, I realized that the power was out.

My phone battery was nearly dead, but I flicked on that light anyway. Immediately, the room was suffused in a yellowish glow.

The light was so small that it did little to penetrate the shadows. Something, anything, could be lurking in this darkness.

One hand holding my phone, the other my knife, I ventured cautiously farther.

I didn't like this feeling, not at all. I'd always been afraid of the dark, even when I became older. There was no rational explanation for this feeling. I knew that there was no such thing as monsters, but the fear paralyzed me all the same.

I checked the living room first in a thorough sweep that included crouching on the floor to look under the couch. The kitchen and dining room were also clear of any ragers or dead bodies.

Tommy continued to hold the back of my shirt like a lifeline.

"Stay here," I whispered, putting a foot on the bottom step.

"Alone?" Tommy asked, voice trembling. "In the dark?"

"There's nothing down here," I assured him. "I'm going to check upstairs too."

Because knowing my luck, they'd be hundreds of Ragers wearing "Kill Adelaide" T-shirts. When had anything ever been this easy for me? Because escaping an horde of Ragers and jumping off a highway were most definitely easy.

I tried to put as much warmth into my smile as I could muster. I'm afraid the end result made me appear more constipated than anything else.

After one last glance at Tommy, I moved towards the staircase.

Please don't let there be anything up there. Please don't let there be anything up there.

I really didn't want to be one of those too-stupid-to-live heroines I'd always seen and laughed at in horror movies. I mean seriously, what made the final girl so deserving of life? Was it because she was pure and a virgin? Because she was nice? Scoff.

The nice girls never win in real life.

My hand was white where it gripped the stair rail, but I was pretty proud of myself when I didn't pass out. I quite was literally, and shamelessly, shitting my pants as I climbed farther into the darkness. I hated the dark. Hated it.

The beam of my phone's light did very little to help me conquer this fear. If anything, the added glow only created more shadow monsters, more places they could hide.

Now a stupid person would say into the darkness, "Hello? Anyone there?"

A smart person, like me and deserving of life, would instead trip over a toy truck and fall onto her ass.

Yup. Totally final girl material right here.

The first two rooms were devoid of any dead bodies or nasty zombies. My body practically sagged in relief by the time I got to the last room.

A child's nursery.

From the painted walls and collection of dolls, I figured that the room was made for a baby girl. I prayed that the family had gotten away, that the little girl wasn't the food in her mother's stomach.

Vomit threatened to escape me at the thought, but I pressed it down.

A single picture was on the dresser of the room, the gilded frame immediately illuminating in my thin shaft of light. Despite knowing I was wasting precious phone battery, I picked up the picture and trailed a finger over the happy family. A mom, a dad, and two kids. An older boy, about five, and a baby girl. They were all smiling at the camera, even the infant.

Why couldn't I be that happy?

Had I ever, in all my years of existence, been that happy?

I was just setting the picture down when something outside caught my attention. The blinds were open, revealing a gray backdrop steadily turning darker as the sun fell. My eyes narrowed at the figure ducking behind a tree.

A Rager?

My heart was hammering, brain turning to liquid, as I stared intensely at the unknown figure. The unknown variable.

Who was he, and what did he want? Was he friend or foe?

But the figure never showed his face—or her, I wouldn't discriminate—and I wondered if I'd imagined it.

Maybe I really was losing my mind.

With a shaky breath, I walked back down the staircase. Tommy was where I had left him at the foot of the stairs. I could hear the sobs emitting from his body.

"It's safe upstairs," I said, deciding not to mention the person I may have or may have not seen outside. There was no use worrying Tommy more than necessary.

Absently, I shone the flashlight into Tommy's tear-stained face. It was then that I noticed something that I hadn't seen earlier.

I'd assumed he was a young boy, maybe eight or nine, but on closer inspection, he looked older. The baby fat hugging his features took off a few years.

"How old are you?" I asked, and then mentally winced.

His mom just died, and you're asking him his age? Good going, Addie.

"It's fine," Tommy said. Though his eyes still looked dazed, I was pleased to discover his voice was more coherent than earlier. "I'm thirteen." Before I could respond, he continued, "And Addie's a pretty name."

I reached for his hand and gave it a squeeze. We remained like that for a few moments, each lost in our own thoughts. It was Tommy who broke the silence first, voice pensive and lower lip trembling.

"I really killed her, didn't I?"

I didn't think he wanted me to answer, so I instead said, "I'm sorry."

"Don't be," he said bitterly. "That wasn't my mother. No, my mom died the second that worm entered her."

I was about to comment on his way of handling things, which was surprisingly bravely, when something he said stuck with me.

"A worm?"

Tommy nodded absently. "Yeah. Just before she…changed, I saw something crawl into her skin. It looked like a little worm. A little black worm."

CHAPTER 9

CALAX

The first time I met Addie, I thought she was a pretentious, stuck-up rich girl. How could I think anything different? Her hair hung in perfect ringlets down her back, and she wore a headband in her hair. A fucking headband. Combined with her pleated skirt and white blouse, she was the exact replica of every schoolgirl fantasy I'd ever had.

Of course, I didn't think anything of the beautiful girl with the plush, red lips and alabaster skin. Not only was she the daughter of some rich fuck, but she had an air of imperiousness that could only be achieved by a sense of entitlement.

Looking back, I realized that so called "entitlement" was fear and an unrealistic pressure to be perfect.

It was only after the second time I met her that I couldn't get her out of my mind.

I'd been riding home with the girl of the day, some chick with the name of a stone. Emerald, maybe? Ruby? It had been my day with her. Ryder had taken her the night before, and Tam had her before that. I remember positively nothing about that girl. Hair color? No clue. Race? No freaking idea.

Yet, I remember every single detail about Addie. There had been a streak of dirt on her left cheek, right under her eye. Her hair had been in a ponytail that day, loose strands cascading around her perfect face.

The girl I was with—let's call her Diamond—hopped off my bike with a sway to her hips. Normally, I would've been entranced, or at least as much as I could be knowing that this girl had screwed my best friends only hours earlier. Not that it bothered me, necessarily, but I never looked at these women as anything other than a meaningless fuck.

I only wished they'd felt the same.

My attention, however, wasn't on my "date" but on the girl who was kneeling over a plot of dirt. As I watched, transfixed, she wiped sweat from her forehead and pursed her thick lips.

"What the hell is she doing?" Emerald—shit, Diamond asked in disbelief. The girl, whose name I hadn't learned at the time, turned towards us with a smile. Seemingly undeterred by Diamond's scowl, she waved.

"Well, hiya. I'm planting a motherfucking garden."

There were so many things wrong with that sentence...and so many things right with it.

Addie turned back towards her rather depressing garden, mumbling something about sexy bikers under her breath.

And yes, I may have smiled smugly and puffed out my chest. I was a conceited bastard.

"Come on, pookie," Jasmine cooed. "Let's go to your room."

I absently waved her away.

"You're planting a garden?" I asked Addie in disbelief. "You okay up there?" I pointed to my forehead to emphasize what I meant.

She snorted.

"Are you okay down there?" she countered, staring pointedly at my manhood. And damnit if I didn't get a little turned on by her teasing.

"So why the hell are you planting a garden at an apartment complex you don't live at?"

Because I definitely would've remembered her if she had moved in.

"Because my parents are little shits who don't think that this apartment is pretty enough." She made a face. "When they're not happy, I'm not happy."

Almost instinctively, I took a step closer to her. Ruby was not happy.

"I thought we were going upstairs," she sneered. I gave her an annoyed look. Had she always been this irritating?

"You go ahead," I said. I didn't bother to add that I would meet her there. I had the distinct feeling I would want her gone after all this was over. "Or you could call Ronan and have him pick you up."

Her face immediately perked up. I didn't bother to tell her that Ronan was currently on a date with another girl. With Ronan, the more the merrier.

"So your parents are tough, huh?" I asked, turning back to Addie. I was such a fucking idiot back then. How could I have not seen what she was enduring?

But she hid everything so well. When she turned towards me, flashing me a singularly beautiful smile, I didn't detect anything besides the normal annoyance one would feel towards her parents.

"Are any parents not tough?"

I chuckled.

"Wouldn't know. I never had parents."

I had a deadbeat dad in between stints of foster parents. Never someone to kiss my knees when I fell or hold my hand or tell me that monsters didn't hide in the dark.

No, they just proved to me that monsters lurk in the fucking daylight.

"Lucky bastard," she responded, and I'd thought that she was being a tad bit dramatic. She had a life that others would kill for. Beauty queen. Rich. Parents. What more could she want?

But there was something familiar in her eyes, something that called to me in a way no other girl ever had before. I would almost call it haunting, as if she'd seen too much for her young age. Those were eyes that held thousands of secrets.

And I stupidly wanted to learn each one.

"Well, do you need any help planting your dumbass garden?" I asked, smirking when she glared at me.

Yes, I was an asshole, but so was she.

"It's a smartass garden, by the way, and no. I don't want your pity help."

"Pity help?" I asked with a raised eyebrow.

She groaned, putting her head into her hands in a movement that indicated her exasperation. That led to more dirt being smeared across her face. Somehow, that only heightened her ethereal beauty.

"I'm good at reading people," she said at last, voice muffled from her hands. "You think I'm a nutcase."

Kind of.

"What else can you tell about me?" I asked, genuinely curious. For some undefinable reason, her answer mattered to me. I wanted her to like me.

Hell if I knew why I wanted to make a good impression on this crazy girl.

"Well," she began, tilting her head to the side thoughtfully. "You were planning on fucking that girl." She nodded her head towards where Diamond—Ember?—was arguing on the phone. No doubt Ronan had refused to pick her up. He never liked being with the same girl twice in the same week.

He was a bastard like that.

My mind was fixated on her use of the word "fucking." I'd have been lying if I said it didn't do something funny to me.

"Well, that's enough gardening for today," she said, standing up and wiping her hands against her jeans. "I need to start heading home before it gets dark."

"Wait? Did you walk here?"

I didn't know where she lived, but I knew this apartment complex was in the middle of fucking nowhere.

She shrugged nonchalantly.

"No biggie. I needed the exercise."

At that, I raised both my eyebrows. With some girls, I could tell they were putting themselves down in order to get attention and compliments, but I only heard sincerity in Addie's voice. That struck me as...wrong.

She was as thin as a twig, almost unhealthily so.

"What's your name, doll?" I asked, realizing that I hadn't asked her. Damn, I really was a bastard.

Instead of answering, she smiled. The smile was both sultry and devious, as if she had perfected wicked seduction in the mirror.

And yes, I said wicked seduction.

As I watched, mesmerized like a lovesick fool, she walked away. I couldn't look away as her lithe figure retreated down the street.

Who the hell was that girl, and where had she been all my life?

Emerald came up to me, bitching about Ronan, but I barely processed her words. I couldn't stop thinking about the strange girl planting a garden in an apartment complex she didn't even live in.

She hadn't left my mind since.

~

Nothing could compare to the panic I felt when I arrived back at the van to discover Adelaide was missing.

There were no possible words to describe the way I felt, the tightening of my chest, the sudden difficulty I had breathing, the haze coating my vision. My hands clenched and unclenched at my sides as I stared at the blood smeared white exterior of our vehicle. There must've been a battle here, as the ground was covered in bodies.

Tam, who'd arrived before me nursing a bruised rib, was holding Mof. The damn kitten had not stopped crying, as if he knew…as if he knew something had happened to his owner.

I didn't know whether or not I wanted to scream or cry. I'd been feeling pretty good about myself, as I was able to take out at least a dozen of Ragers.

Eliminate the threat. Protect what was mine.

The mantra, to some, might sound masochistic, but I could assure you that was the furthest from the truth. Addie owned me, heart, body, and mind.

I didn't want to think about a world where she was no longer in it. I'd thought it before, after she'd been taken from the collapsed resort, and it had completely destroyed me. This, especially after knowing how she felt about me even though she couldn't say it, was ten times worse.

I finally knew what it was like to be truly loved by a girl like Addie. By anyone, really. I'd never been loved before.

"Where the fuck is she?" Ryder demanded, eyes wild. He looked as if he were getting ready to tear the world apart.

It was then that I realized something that was so blatantly obvious. How had I not noticed it before?

He was in love with her.

I couldn't focus on that, however. Not with Addie missing and possibly—

I couldn't even think that word. She couldn't be dead. I would be able to tell.

Declan, pacing, had rounded on Ronan. His hands were a flurry of undefinable movements. I was too tired, too dead, to read what he was signing so dogmatically.

Ronan blanched, face paling.

"You were supposed to be fucking watching her!" Ryder exploded, storming towards his brother. Before Sarge could intervene, Ryder's fist connected with Ronan's face. Bones cracked, and Ronan tumbled over the gruesome body of one of the fallen. I couldn't decide if it had been a zombie or a human.

At least it wasn't Addie.

Ronan allowed Ryder to pummel his face, not bothering to raise a hand to defend himself. He looked lost and forlorn, a mere shadow of the cocky bastard I knew and occasionally loved like a brother.

An idiotic brother, but a brother all the same.

"Enough!" Sarge screamed, grabbing Ryder by his shirt. "I said enough! This isn't going to help anything!"

"You fucking left her alone! You had one fucking job to do! One!" Ryder lunged for Ronan again, but both Asher and Sarge held him back. Sarge looked, as always, cool and stoic, but I saw him continually clenching and unclenching his jaw. He was worried about Addie too, and I tried not to think about the reasons why. "You better hope we fucking find her! You better fucking hope!"

Ronan was staring at his brother, and I watched as realization slowly dawned on his face. He apparently hadn't been aware of the extent of his brother's feelings either. I saw his expression morph, surprise giving way to unreadability.

Ronan's eyes flickered to something over Ryder's shoulder, and his expression froze.

"We have to start looking for her. If she's alive, she couldn't have gone far," Sarge was saying.

"She's fucking alive," I snapped. The alternative was too horrible to think about.

"Guys," whispered Ronan, face tightening.

"Where could she have gone?" Asher questioned. He glanced at the bodies, and I knew he was searching them for any signs of her familiar dark curls. He wouldn't find her down there, I was sure of it. My baby was a fighter.

"Guys," repeated Ronan.

"You better make sure her damn cat is alive," Ryder continued, either oblivious to his brother or choosing to ignore him. I was beginning to believe it was the latter. "When she gets back, she'll skin your nutsack if something happened to him."

"The cat is fine," Tam said dizzily. He grimaced in pain and grabbed at his stomach. The crazy son of a bitch decided to fight a Rager by hand after his gun ran out of ammo. It was a miracle that he was still alive.

"Guys!" Ronan's voice broke through our conversation sharply, a contrast to his normally indolent tone. Sarge's eyes narrowed on his face. He hated being interrupted, especially by his subordinates.

But Ronan wasn't paying our group leader any mind. No, his trembling finger was pointing towards the edge of the highway where a metal gate separated a low forest from the highway.

"I painted that on her hand," he mumbled. I turned to see what had captured his attention.

Across the silver railing, painted in a bright, cranberry red, was a haphazardly drawn crown. A single "A" rested above the design.

Only one person would be stupid enough—or smart enough—to draw a design instead of writing her name. Why the hell did she feel the need to be so secretive?

Addie.

Baby, hold on. We're coming for you.

CHAPTER 10

ADDIE

The food in the fridge was spoiled.

Pulling the door open, I made a face as the pungent smell of moldy cheeses and meats assaulted my senses.

"That smells like shit," Tommy said from behind me where he was going through a cabinet. My phone, staying at a solid five percent the last hour or so, was resting on the table, light facing up. I watched as Tommy held a can to the light, made a face, and then put it back.

"I hate cheese broccoli soup," he muttered. I snorted.

"Is it the cheese part you don't like, or the broccoli?"

He gave me a look that said he seriously questioned my intelligence.

"Besides," Tommy continued, pulling out cans and pasta boxes at random. "The soup requires milk."

The only milk around was a chunky, off-white mess that I had immediately thrown outside. It smelled something awful, putting even Mr. Cheese to shame.

"Touché," I said, turning back towards the fridge. I hoped that there would be at least one redeemable food item, but my search was futile. The only eatable or drinkable item I found in the fridge was a gallon of water that Tommy and I had both used to clean ourselves off. We probably should've saved the water for drinking, but both of us felt sick with the blood coating our skin. No, I would rather dehydrate myself than live another moment with flesh under my fingernails and blood smeared over my cheekbones.

"Yes!" Tommy suddenly yelled, voice triumphant. I turned towards him in surprise, only to see him lovingly holding a box of chocolate Pop-Tarts. He stroked the box. "Come to papa, you nasty thing."

"Talking dirty to food, I see?" I kept my voice light, attempting humor. In the last hour or so, color had steadily returned to Tommy's cheeks and his eyes no longer looked so despondent. There was still fear in his eyes, still self-hatred, but it didn't seem to consume him any longer. I knew that he needed a chance to grieve, but I also knew that now was not the right time.

He was brave, I had to give him that. Stronger than me.

"Don't diss my true love," Tommy retorted.

"Are just Pop-Tarts your lover, or is it food in general?" I teased.

A door opening and closing cut off whatever Tommy was going to say.

In a blistering speed that surprised even myself, I ran towards my light and flicked it off. Darkness immediately descended.

Tommy let out a shaky breath, and his hand grappled to find mine. I took it, giving it a squeeze.

I tried to control my breathing as the footsteps came closer. The last thing I needed was a panic attack.

But I freaking hated the darkness. Hated it.

Instinctively, my hand curled around the knife in my waistband. If I had to, I would stab a motherfucker. Or kick him in the balls.

I was pretty good at that too.

The footsteps were coming closer, pounding against the linoleum tiles of the kitchen. The hair on the back of my neck stood on end...

And then the footsteps retreated. I heard the front door opening and closing, and then I heard nothing.

Tommy's hand was a vise in mine.

I heard him suck in a breath as if to say something, but I gave his hand a moderately painful pinch.

Not yet, the eloquent gesture said. Wait.

"Who the hell was that?" Tommy asked, after we stood silently in the kitchen for fifteen minutes. His tiny voice wobbled over the words.

"I don't know." I fumbled with my phone, flicking back on the light. The kitchen was yet again bathed in a pale, yellow light.

Nothing seemed to be missing. The food remained where we'd left it.

Was it a Rager? The owner of the house?

But why would someone walk into a dark room without doing anything? Granted, I had often walked into a room, forgot what I was doing, and left, but I'd thought that society was smarter than me.

My terror spiked at the normality of the kitchen. Nothing, and I mean nothing, was different. Had the person wanted something to eat? Had it been someone who'd escaped from the highway?

I strained my ears to hear if they were still in the house. Maybe they needed a place to sleep for the night. After all, this was the only house we could find in the dense thicket of trees.

The number of questions I had were staggering. Even more staggering was the lack of answers.

Moving nimbly, I pushed back the curtain.

There was only a sliver of moon tonight and a handful of stars, so not enough natural lighting to see clearly. I watched the forest, muscles coiled, but saw no movement.

Whoever had come must've gone.

"We should get some sleep," I said to Tommy.

Tommy nodded, though he still looked as if he wanted to piss his pants.

Same, kid. Same.

We found some spare blankets in a linen closet and settled down on the couch and chair. It would've felt odd to sleep in someone else's bed. I knew Tommy agreed with my sentiment.

I placed my head gingerly on the pillow, angling my phone towards my hand.

The design Ronan had drawn was beautiful—an elaborate crown that looked surprisingly realistic. Though it was made in pen, each jewel seemed to pop as if they were actually implanted into my skin. I wasn't surprised that Ronan was an artist. After all, his brother was a talented musician. It would only make sense for him to be good at art as well.

I stared at it, illuminated by the thin shaft of light, before my phone died.

I whimpered as the house was completely plunged into darkness.

I WOKE up to a light shining in my face. Squinting, I glanced from side to side. It was still dark outside, and Tommy, in the chair beside me, was snoring softly.

There were two figures leaning over him, each one holding a gun.

Before I could scream, strong arms grabbed me around the waist. I bucked, cussing, when a familiar voice broke through my panic.

"Oh my god, baby! I thought we told you to stay in the fucking car!"

I went limp in his arms. His familiar, comforting arms.

"Callie?" I whispered softly, and then I was kissing him. Or he was kissing me, though I'm not sure that there was a difference. We became nothing more than a flurry of gasps and tongues and clashing lips.

"Princess, is that really you?" Ronan asked softly.

"Of course not," Calax said with a scoff, pulling his lips away from mine. "I'm just kissing a random stranger."

Ronan pushed Calax aside, wrapping his arms around me and pulling me onto his lap. His body shook with silent sobs, and I felt his lips touch my hair. The contact made me shiver.

"Are you guys all okay?" I could see seven distinct silhouettes in the darkness, but I still wanted the reassurance.

"We're all fine, sweetheart," Asher said.

I turned in Ronan's lap, tracing his indecipherable features with my fingers.

"And the woman?"

I remembered the person he'd been trying to save. Her body had looked so broken, nearly unrecognizable as a human.

My fingers touched Ronan's lips as they turned down simultaneously with the slight shake of his head.

No. She hadn't made it.

I tried not to feel too upset by that verdict. After all, I didn't know that woman. I told myself that I shouldn't cry over the death of a complete stranger.

Despite this, tears welled in my eyes.

A soft meowing grabbed my attention, and I turned towards where Mof was curled up in Tam's arms.

"My baby!" I cooed, and Tam set the squirming cat into my own arms. I was immediately assaulted with sandpaper-like kisses.

"Who the fuck are you guys?" a tiny voice screamed. "And why the fuck are you aiming guns at me?"

Tommy bolted upright in the chair, his blanket falling off his body. His tired eyes went from me to them and then back to me. He raised an eyebrow, slightly sardonically. He must've noticed the position I was in—sprawled on Ronan's lap, with Calax's arm still wrapped possessively around my waist, and Mof happily licking my face to death.

"Friends of yours?" he asked, amusement evident in his voice.

"Guys, this is Tommy. Tommy, these are my friends."

Tommy blinked, grabbed his blanket, and closed his eyes yet again.

"Save the introductions for tomorrow. I'm fucking tired."

Without another word, he began to snore again. The two men holding the guns—Fallon and Ryder, I realized—slowly lowered them with identical puzzled expressions.

"Who the hell is he?" Fallon asked.

Ryder added, "*What* the hell is he?"

～

AFTER ASSURING myself that they were all right, I set out to find medical supplies for Tamson. He'd been the most injured, though he promised me that he would live. I was beginning to realize that Tam thought that I was a tad bit dramatic. Just a tad, like Shakespeare level.

I'd spotted a first aid kit under the sink in the upstairs bathroom, and I pulled that out now. Calax had let me borrow his phone for a flashlight.

I was scrambling to my feet when I spotted the figure in the mirror behind me. I nearly screamed, spinning around so fast, I was afraid my head would fall off.

"Ryder, you scared the crap out of me," I hissed.

He didn't respond for a moment, expression drawn. His eyes wouldn't meet mine, despite my repeated attempt at eye contact. He stared at his unlaced shoes, the burgundy shower curtain, the dirt his shoes had tracked in.

Everything besides me.

His lashes flickered against his prominent cheekbones.

"Ryder, are you okay?" I asked tentatively. Still, Ryder didn't answer. His hand continually tapped out an unfamiliar rhythm against his jean-clad legs. Before I could ask him again, he glanced up, eyes wild with an undefinable emotion.

"I'm really glad you're okay," he said at last. I offered him a small smile.

"I'm glad you're okay too."

He looked as if he was going to say more—I wanted him to say more—before he glanced back down at the floor. His hands were clenched into fists at his sides.

Without another word, he left the bathroom. Escaped from the bathroom would be a better description. He ran as if he wanted to be anywhere else but there with me.

I tried not to feel hurt.

Grabbing the red box I'd unintentionally dropped, I headed back towards where I'd left Tam. Unlike me, he had no such qualms about sleeping on someone else's bed. He said that all the bed needed was a fresh pair of sheets, which we found in the closet.

"How is this any different from a hotel?" he'd asked me with a gentle smile, and I couldn't help but smile back. Everything about Tam was gentle and kind. His smile, though rare, was contagious.

When I arrived back at the room, he was lying in the bed with his shirt off. Fallon was there as well, but I barely processed him.

Skin. So much skin.

I wouldn't have thought that Tam would be so muscular, though I shouldn't have been surprised since I knew he did MMA. It was a glorious sight of chiseled abs and dark red hair, trailing down his toned stomach—

"Did you get the stuff?" Fallon asked, breaking me out of my not-so-sisterly thoughts. I blinked like an imbecile.

To be honest, I wouldn't have been surprised if my jaw was popped open and drool was coming from my mouth.

Fallon smirked, as if he knew exactly where my thoughts had headed, before grabbing the first aid kit from my hands.

Tam looked up at me, blushed, and then attempted to hide himself underneath a blanket.

The boy didn't have to hide. He was perfection in human form.

Tam's face turned even redder, and Fallon coughed to cover up his laugh.

Shit.

Wincing, I perched myself on the edge of Tam's bed. "Sorry. I hadn't meant to say that aloud."

"It's okay," he muttered, ducking his head. That only made me feel worse. The last thing I ever wanted to do was embarrass my sweet friend.

"Seriously, Tam, I'll try to control my perverted mind."

At that, a tentative smile touched his lips.

"You'll probably need training to undertake such a hard goal," he teased, and I gently shoved his shoulder, being careful not to hurt him further.

"Asshole," I said, smiling. Tam offered me a smile back.

And Fallon? He was watching both of us with a contemplative, if not slightly thoughtful, expression. Shaking his head as if to clear his thoughts, he began bandaging Tam up.

"You picked a creepy as hell house to stay at tonight," Fallon said at last, voice gruff.

"Why is that?" I asked, though my mind immediately conjured up a whole list of reasons.

Creepy abandoned nursery? Check.

Stereotypical broken picture frame? Double check.

Vacant house in general? Triple check.

"Was that blood on the wall in the living room?" Fallon continued. "Or red paint? What type of creepy fucker lived here? That's what I want to know."

"Blood?" I asked, raising my eyebrow. I must've heard him wrong.

"Didn't you see the blood on the wall when you arrived?" Tam asked. "We all noticed it right away."

Even before he'd finished speaking, I was shaking my head.

"No, you must be mistaken. There was most definitely no blood when I got here."

Fallon froze, hand hovering over the first aid box. His eyes were trained on my face.

"Are you sure?" His tone frightened me. He almost sounded...well scared.

And Fallon was never scared.

"I'm positive," I said at last, confused by the urgency in Fallon's normally apathetic expression. He exchanged an unreadable glance with Tam.

"We need to leave," he said at last, putting the bandages back into the box. Turning towards me, he said, "Tell the boys to grab everything they can. All the food, any water bottles, and put them in the duffle bags we found. We have to walk until we can find a car that isn't stuck in traffic."

"But..."

"Don't argue with me, Adelaide," he said, sounding extremely young just then. Tired, almost. It suddenly occurred to me that Fallon wasn't that much older than I was. He'd always seemed older, but that was because of the responsibility he assumed. The weight of the world seemed to press down on his shoulders, aging him in a way I couldn't even begin to understand.

"Okay," I agreed softly, biting my tongue to avoid the thousands of questions I wanted to ask.

It only took me a minute to find the rest of the boys. They were all convened in a spare bedroom. When I told them what Fallon had said, they nodded once without any argument.

I couldn't help but think over Fallon's strange behavior. The blood. What blood had he been talking about? I immediately thought about the person who'd entered the house before I'd gone to bed. Had he done something?

I discovered the answer to that question the second I stepped into the living room. Across the peach walls, in bright red, someone had written a message.

A message that hadn't been there earlier.

I'M COMING FOR YOU.

CHAPTER 11

ADDIE

"It was probably just a prank, right? It had to be just a prank."

No matter how many times I repeated it, the boys refused to agree with me. They were uncharacteristically tense as we trudged down the stretch of road. We had chosen—well, Fallon had chosen—not to take the highway back. Between the army flying overhead and the Ragers, we unanimously agreed to take back roads.

It was eerie, to say the least. We'd been walking for over an hour, and we had yet to see another human being or vehicle. The houses were all dark, the driveways were empty, and the only sounds were the animals scurrying through the bushes.

"A prank?" Tommy snorted in disbelief. "Yes, because it's completely normal and fucking hilarious to sneak into a house, that they didn't even know was fucking occupied, and write an ominous warning with blood. Ha. Ha. Ha."

"You're a sarcastic smartass, aren't you?" I asked innocently, and Tommy glared.

"Fuck off."

"Language!" Fallon scolded, and Tommy rolled his eyes. He was less than impressed by my friends, and he made sure to bring that little fact up every other minute.

Sidling up to me, he leaned forward to whisper, "I still vote we leave the assholes. We can easily survive without them. So they're big and have guns? We're badasses."

He made a point to whisper loud enough for the others to hear. Ronan made a face, and Calax rolled his eyes. I noticed that Ryder didn't make any comment, which seemed entirely unlike him. That would've been a perfect opportunity for him to talk about his "big gun," if you know what I mean.

Choosing to ignore his odd behavior for now—I would address it when we were alone—I said, "Anyway, it's not like anyone hurt me. If they wanted to murder me, they had the perfect opportunity, right? So it was just a prank."

Tommy huffed out his chest.

"I probably scared him off."

Ronan gave Tommy a less than impressed once-over.

"Sure you did, kid."

Before Tommy could retort, Fallon cut in.

"It's better to be safe than sorry."

"Yeah. Yeah. Yeah," I said, waving my hand dismissively. "Save the fortune cookie crap for later, and let's find a car. The sooner we find a car, the sooner we can get to Atlanta."

I hadn't allowed myself to think about Nik since we left. To be fair, I hadn't had a lot of time. The last few days had been a hectic whirlwind that had left me struggling to breathe. I was drowning, pushed under by consistent waves. When I managed to find a pocket of fresh air, all I could think about was my brother.

I missed him something fiercely. My chest tightened at the mere thought of him. Was he still with Nancy? Was he alone? Did he miss me as well? It may have been selfish to think the latter, but I couldn't ignore the doubt nagging me. What if when I got there, he didn't want to go with me?

I wouldn't be able to handle his rejection. That would completely destroy me.

I knew for a fact he wasn't dead. No, I had a sixth sense when it came to my brother, and I most definitely would've been able to tell if something bad had happened to him.

I had to hold onto hope, though feeble, that my brother would be alive and well.

"A penny for your thoughts?" Asher asked, coming to stand beside me. He had a backpack over his shoulders and a duffle bag slung over his arm. I'd offered to carry more than the one backpack they gave me, but the guys insisted that it wasn't necessary.

Their macho act didn't fool me.

"My thoughts are worth at least a dollar," I joked. "Though you guys have been getting them for free recently."

He smiled good-naturedly. "It's not my fault you like to speak your mind."

"Involuntarily speak my mind. There's a difference."

Asher lightly hit my shoulder with his own.

"No, seriously. What's up? You look down."

I took a deep breath. "Just thinking of my brother," I admitted at last. "I miss him."

Asher was silent for a second, but it wasn't uncomfortable. Asher could never make me feel uncomfortable or uneasy. It just wasn't in his nature. He was as bright as sunlight, despite that statement being such a cliché. Even in my darkest of times, I knew that he would be around to brighten it.

God, I was such a cheese ball.

Seriously, that stuff was Hallmark card worthy.

"What is he like?" Asher asked, and I appreciated the fact that he didn't use the past tense "was."

I smiled as I thought of sweet Nik. "Smarter than me, for sure. He always saw the world as a thousand shades of gray, instead of black and white. I always joked with him that he was the better half of me." I didn't bother to add that, half the time, the joke went over his head and he would take my statement literally. "He loves his music," I continued. "All kinds. You'll always find him sitting somewhere with these big, red headphones covering his ears."

My smile grew the more I pictured it, the more I pictured him. I couldn't even express how much I missed him. Talking to Asher helped relieve the ache his absence had left in my heart.

"Your brother sounds like a good kid," Asher said, squeezing my hand. I smiled up at him.

"The best."

It was then that I realized how close we'd gotten. Asher was significantly taller than me, not a hard feat considering my petite frame, and all he had to do was lean down a few inches and his lips would be touching my skin.

I didn't know why that thought both terrified and excited me. Half of me wanted him to kiss me, while the other half warned me that I was treading in too deep water. One wrong move, and I would be pulled under. I would drown.

Why did that suddenly sound so appealing?

Before I could properly analyze my strange, conflicting thoughts, Ronan had turned on his heel and was stomping back towards us. His face was red with fury.

"What's your problem?" I asked, stunned by his sudden change in behavior.

"My problem," Ronan hissed, "is the little bastard threatening to neuter me!" He pointed an accusatory finger at Tommy, who was conversing with Fallon. Fallon's face was set into a scowl, but I couldn't tell if that was his normal resting bitch face or an expression Tommy had brought out of him.

"That kid is halfway in love with you already," Asher admitted, and I snorted.

"If anything, I should be the one in love with him." At the boys' incredulous expressions, I lowered my voice to a whisper. "He saved my life. His mom had turned into a Rager, and he killed her to stop her from attacking me."

The boys seemed stunned at this proclamation. Asher blinked furiously.

"He killed...his mom?" He seemed to have trouble wrapping his head around the concept. I squeezed our still joined hands.

"To save me. A stranger in need of help." I glanced back at Tommy, his reddish hair wildly disheveled and a long scar distorting his chubby cheeks in a jagged, raised line. I hadn't noticed the scar being that prominent last night, but I knew it wouldn't go away with time. He now had a physical scar to accompany the mental one. "I'm just waiting for him to break down. He hasn't had a chance yet."

And that breakdown would happen. Of that, I was certain. Tommy wasn't impassive, and he wasn't made of steel. What he'd done was emotionally damaging. It was a wonder he could even talk or walk at all.

So no, I wasn't going to complain about his treatment of the guys. If insulting them helped ease the guilt and pain he felt over losing his mother, then I would support him until we could find a more healthy way for him to cope.

"Well damn," Ronan said. "I guess I can't hate the little shit anymore."

"Speaking of little shits," I broached tentatively. "What's going on with Ryder?"

The boy in question had a continually dazed look to him, as if he was seeing something that wasn't there. He'd insisted on carrying Mof's cage, and I'd caught him, from time to time, absently mumbling to the cat. Had he lost his mind? Or had something happened during the fight?

In response to my question, Ronan shrugged, though I thought I saw a flicker of unease cross his features. It was there and gone before I could question it.

"He probably just needs to get laid," he answered at last.

That was more than likely true. From what I'd gathered, Ryder was most popular with the ladies. Being as handsome as he was, as well as the lead singer for a band, meant he had no problem getting and keeping any woman he desired.

"What about one of you guys?" I asked, before I could think it through clearly. "Could he do the dirty with one of you?"

Asher looked as if he was on the brink of laughter, while Ronan just looked sick.

"Unfortunately, sweetheart, none of us swing that way, if you know what I mean."

"I really don't."

"We're all straight," Asher cut in, sounding amused at Ronan's flustered answer. "We all like girls."

"I mean," Ronan continued, shaking himself out of whatever funk my question had put him in. "My brother and I would sometimes make a girl a sandwich if she was into that sort of thing."

I couldn't help but think how thoughtful they were for doing that. I would imagine that one would get hungry after continuous sex, though I struggled to understand how the topic of food fit in with my question.

"What type of sandwich?" I asked. I wasn't really curious, but what was the appropriate response to your guy friend talking about post sex food? A question seemed the obvious choice.

Both Asher and Ronan were staring at me with matching indecipherable expressions. Was that hunger I saw in their gazes?

Lust?

What the ever-loving hell?

"We usually prefer white meat," Ronan said. I'd never heard him use that voice before. It was sultry, almost like Ryder's singing voice, and it did very strange things to me. Very strange and bad things that I no doubt shouldn't feel for Calax's best friend.

"And dark bread," Ronan continued. "A little burnt."

I raised an eyebrow. "Wouldn't that be disgusting?"

I knew there were people who liked their toast burnt, but I personally found it gross. And what type of white meat was he referring to? Chicken?

At my comment, the lust cleared from Ronan's eyes.

"Disgusting?"

"I mean, I guess that it depends on the girl," I continued. "I, personally, would like a peanut butter and jelly sandwich."

Asher's eyebrows crinkled adorably.

"Peanut butter and—" As if something suddenly occurred to him, Asher blushed a bright crimson. "You think we're actually talking about sandwiches, don't you?"

Ronan also seemed to have come to the same realization as Asher, for he, too, began to blush. I'd never, in all the weeks I'd known him, seen Ronan blush.

Before I could question their strange behavior, Asher released my hand and hurried to the front of the group. The back of his neck was on fire.

"What's his problem?" I asked, worried that I would have to speak privately to Asher as well as Ryder.

Ronan cleared his throat, uncomfortable at the direction this conversation had headed. I really couldn't understand him.

He was the one who'd brought up sandwiches. Was I just missing something? Why would the talk of sandwiches cause Ronan to look at me with such lust and wanting and—

Oh. My. Fucking. God.

I squeaked. "What the hell, Ronan?"

My outburst was loud enough to garner the attention of the rest of our party. Even Ryder had stopped his sulking to stare at us with bemusement.

"You should've said you made her *into* a sandwich, not that you made her a sandwich!"

Now it was my face that was blushing furiously.

"What the hell is she going on about?" Tommy asked curiously. Asher, who was closest to him, shook his head viciously.

"Don't ask. Please, for the love of all that is holy, don't ever ask."

It was Fallon who killed the next Rager.

It had come up behind us, its footsteps masked, despite the collection of twigs and pebbles snapping beneath our own feet.

I'd been in the back, singing softly under my breath, when rough hands had grabbed me. I screamed.

The boys turned.

And then the Rager had fallen. In his head—I could discern by his features that it was, indeed, a male—was a gaping hole. Black blood oozed from the wound, staining my hands. I scrambled backwards.

Fallon stood before me, the gun held steadily in his hand.

Since we don't know how the disease—virus, parasite, worm, whatever the hell it was—was transmitted, the boys insisted that I wipe all the goo from my skin. They averted their eyes respectfully as I eagerly stripped off my leggings and jacket, the cold air biting on my sensitive bare skin.

I used water from our pack to scrub my skin raw. I wanted to rid the blood staining me, coating me, consuming me.

It had only been minutes. Mere minutes for a life to be lost. Fallon hadn't hesitated to shoot him in the head.

Would he, if I were to turn, not hesitate to shoot me as well?

CHAPTER 12

ADDIE

Outside of an old farmhouse, we found a large silver van that would fit all of us comfortably. Despite the obvious age, the house was in relatively good condition with a fresh coat of paint and neatly trimmed hedges.

"Wait at the end of the driveway," Fallon instructed. "I'll talk to the owner about buying the car from him."

The boys all agreed immediately, even Tommy. It seemed as if my young friend had fully accepted Fallon as the leader.

I held up my hand like a schoolchild waiting to get called upon. Fallon let out an exasperated groan.

"Yes, Adelaide?"

"Don't you think I should go with you?" I asked. "I mean, you're a scary motherfucker, and I'm a sweet, innocent girl."

Calax, beside me, snorted at the adjectives I used to describe myself. He could take his snort and shove it up his ass.

Fallon opened his mouth, to no doubt protest, but I cut him off with a wave of my hand.

"Don't argue with me. You'll scare the crap out of them before we can even ask about the car. Besides, you know the saying—two is better than one."

Once again, Fallon rolled his eyes at my cheesy quote. I wanted to hit him. My reasoning was sound, and he was just being overprotective. I would be the first to admit that the whole alpha male thing was attractive, but it was also immensely annoying. I couldn't even pee without someone in hearing distance. Freaking pee. Do you know how awkward it is to have your sort of boyfriend listening to you tinkle?

"Where did your mind go?" Fallon asked, now sounding amused.

"I was thinking about pee," I said before I could stop myself.

Cue seven simultaneous groans. Only Tommy, my new best friend, didn't stare at me like an imbecile.

"Fine," Fallon said, changing the subject from bodily fluids. "You can come."

I let out an excited whoop complete with a handclap and a little jig. And these boys thought I was childish? Grown ass mature woman right here.

Skipping up the long driveway, I admired the carefully planted tulips creating a path towards the door. The sloping roof was held up by two white pillars, and the wooden porch was wrapped around the entire building.

Fallon gave me a pointed look as I jumped up the small staircase.

Don't do or say anything stupid.

In response, I stuck my tongue out at him. He who had so little faith in me rang the doorbell, and the two of us waited impatiently. The first thing I heard was the shuffling of footsteps, and then I saw the front curtain being pulled back slightly. I barely caught a glimpse of a blue eye before the curtain fell back into place.

In agonizing slowness, the locks of the door snapped open.

I found myself staring down the barrel of a shotgun.

Well…shit. That wasn't what I was expecting.

The man behind the shotgun was old, probably in his mid-sixties if I had to guess. His white hair was receding at the top, showcasing his bald, shiny head. His face was covered in wrinkles, but his blue eyes were surprisingly sharp as they locked onto my face.

"What do you want?" he asked. I noticed that he didn't release the deadbolt. How many locks did this man have on his door?

It was Fallon that spoke, his voice placating, despite the question being directed at me.

"We just want to talk."

"Get the hell off my property," the man hissed.

I would've responded, I would've tried to appease the tension, but there was a fucking gun pressed to my forehead. Not really conversation material.

I could hear the guys shuffling closer behind us, still out of view from the man's penetrating eyes, but Fallon held up a fist to stop them in mid stride. I imagined that Calax would be glowering. He really didn't like people holding guns to my head.

Not that I could blame him. I wasn't the biggest fan either.

"Are you one of them?" he continued. His voice was scratchy, as if it had been used continually. Or, and this seemed the more likely scenario, as if he'd screamed it dry. Why my mind went to that, I would never know, but there was something almost haunting in Mr. Shotgun's face. He looked…fearful. Somehow, that vulnerability cracking through demoted him from scary to somewhat approachable.

"Please sir," I said, trying to control the waver in my voice. "We're not one of those creatures. We just wanted to buy your van off of you. Our own car got stuck on the highway a few miles back."

He did not lower the weapon, but his finger moved from where it was poised over the trigger. Small reliefs.

"What do you have to offer?" he asked stiffly, and I nodded for Fallon to continue the conversation.

"How much money do you want?" he asked in his no-nonsense voice. The old man actually laughed at that. Cackled would be a better description. I eyed the man like he'd lost his mind. It would be just our luck for us to ask a psychopathic serial killer for help.

Laughter still evident in his voice, he said, "I don't want your fucking money. What supplies do you have? Any food? Medicine?"

I blinked. No money?

It suddenly occurred to me that the world was changing rapidly. What else had changed in the last few days?

No, I suppose the more accurate question was what else would change?

The thought sent pinpricks of terror down my spine. If we changed the way we behaved, changed the societal norms for humanity, then we were screwed. People would do anything if they became desperate, including acts they once had deemed atrocious.

Putting those demented thoughts to the back of my mind, I listened attentively as Fallon spoke.

"No medicine," he said easily, though I knew that was a lie. We'd raided the house we had previously been at, taking two first aid kits and all the pill bottles we could find. It never made sense to me in movies for the main characters to only grab the specific medicine they needed. What about in the future? I was determined for our group not to fall into the stereotypical horror movie roles. If that meant grab all the medicine, then we would grab all the fucking medicine.

"But," Fallon continued, "we have a bag full of food."

That was also a lie. We had at least six bags full.

Fallon nodded his head towards me, and I obediently slipped off my backpack and opened it for the man to see. It was the lightest pack of the bunch, only consisting of twenty or so cans and half as many water bottles.

As the man surveyed the contents of my bag, I couldn't help but compare this exchange to that of a drug movie I had seen.

"Do you have the money?"

"Yeah, man. I have the money. Now where's my drugs?"

Okay, so they may not have spoken like that, but you got the idea.

After a moment of indecision, the man nodded stiffly.

"Fine," he said at last. "It's not like I'm going to use that vehicle. But I want the backpack as well."

"Deal," Fallon responded immediately, taking it from my hands and zipping it back up. He handed it to the man who, in exchange, handed us a set of keys.

"The tank is almost completely full. I haven't driven the thing since I heard about the attacks." The man was silent for a second. His keen eyes seemed to slice through my skin, seeing something that I had yet to fully understand. I wondered yet again how he'd gotten such a haunted look in his eyes. "I'd recommend getting somewhere safe as soon as you can," he said. "These roads aren't safe, especially at night."

"At night?" Fallon asked. The old man's words sounded like a horror movie cliché, but I knew there was more to it than an ominous warning.

"The monsters are active during the day, sure, but it's at night when things really hit the fan."

"What do you mean?" Fallon asked, echoing my own thoughts. His fingers absently twirled the key around and around. I noticed, somewhat dizzily, that he had numerous rings adorning his fingers. I wondered why I'd never noticed them before.

The man hesitated yet again at Fallon's innocent question.

"There are many types of monsters," he settled on. "Just make sure you're inside when the sun goes down."

With those parting words, he slammed the door into our stunned faces.

~

It was as we were walking back to the car, sun burning down on us, that I felt the eyes on the back of my neck.

There was no logical reason for me to feel like somebody was watching me, yet my entire body clenched in terror. My breathing became stilted, and the whole world seemed to tilt on its axis.

Someone, somewhere, was watching me. Of that, I was almost sure.

"Are you okay?" Tam asked softly. He glanced wearily over my shoulder as if he was looking for the unseen threat.

I scoffed at how ridiculous I was behaving. Between the message at the previous house and the old man's words, I was becoming paranoid. I knew there was no one watching me, I knew that, but my heart still hammered inside my chest like a sledgehammer.

"Yeah," I answered with a smile that I hoped looked genuine. "Just tired."

"We've been walking for a while," Tam said in understanding. I flashed him a small smile in appreciation.

"Yeah."

We loaded up the van, me sitting in between Declan and Tamson. Tommy refused to release Mof to me, so the cat was bundled in his arms a row behind me. I heard the cat's purr of contentment.

The boys immediately began joking with one another, talking about plans for the journey and wondering if we should get a hotel for the night. I listened half-heartedly, but I couldn't quite shake the feeling that someone was outside the van.

Watching me.

Always watching me.

~

DECLAN

There were only five cars on the backroads the first twenty or so miles. I counted.

What else was there to do?

Sure, the others around me were partaking in conversation, but with their faces turned away from me, I had trouble reading their lips. I tried not to let it bother me.

Normally, I didn't allow my deafness to hinder my ability to live life. It was a burden, yes, but one that I was easily able to jump over. I'd dealt with it for years.

So why did it suddenly make me feel as if I were less than a man?

The answer came to me quickly when the sleeping beauty beside me put her head on my shoulder. She seemed to mutter something before twisting slightly in her seat, eyelashes casting shadows on her perfect cheekbones. My arm automatically came out to hold her to me, and I couldn't help but notice how good she felt in my arms. How right. It was almost as if she were made to be here with me.

That wasn't necessarily a surprise. Even when I was younger, I knew we were soulmates. I just didn't expect the feelings to return so suddenly and so staggeringly after all of those years apart. I didn't blame her for what had happened. I'd never blamed her, even after years of distancing myself from her. Those years had been torture, but I'd been under the impression that she wanted nothing to do with me. I knew that I was wrong for believing the lie so quickly—when had Addie ever left me any reason to doubt her?—but her hurtful words echoed through my head, continuous stabs to the heart.

Sarge parked the van in front of a motel.

It appeared as if I'd missed out on the plan. No surprise.

Seeing my befuddled look, Sarge quickly signed, *"We're going to stop for the night."*

I nodded, though I didn't agree. I wanted to get to Atlanta as soon as possible.

Addie had her reasons for going, and I had mine.

Though I couldn't admit my reasons to anyone. Not yet.

Sarge brought Asher, who'd been sitting in the passenger seat, inside to reserve us rooms. After about thirty minutes, they returned with matching perplexed expressions.

"What's going on?" I signed. Somebody behind me must've said something, no doubt along the lines of what I just said, for Sarge's eyes flickered in that direction.

"There's nobody in there. No employees. No guests that I could see. We're probably going to have to break into rooms tonight."

Normally, those words would instill fear and something akin to excitement in my heart. We weren't criminals, but with our jobs, we had to do some pretty shady shit. What was the world coming to that those words now sounded normal? Would we ever go back to the way things were?

We parked in the back parking lot, away from the street and any wandering eyes. Sarge's recollection of the old man's warning was worrisome. Was he trying to threaten us?

Unfortunately, we were left with more questions than answers.

Ryder made quick work on the locks. With modern technology upgrading from actual keys to key cards, breaking into a hotel was nothing like in the movies. We would separate ourselves into two bedrooms, the bigger of which would contain Adelaide. Despite the fact that those in her room would have to cozy up on the opposite bed or sleep on the floor, every person volunteered. Even that annoying fuck, Tommy, though he assured us it was only to make sure we kept our "wandering, perverted man hands off of her." I couldn't decide if his fascination with her was hero worship, some morbid type of love, or something else entirely. It didn't bother me since he was way too young for her, but it did make me feel slightly bad for the little bugger. He would not take it well when we ultimately parted ways.

After a brief discussion, it was decided that Tamson, Ryder, Asher, and Tommy would sleep in one room. The rest of us would sleep in the bigger room with Adelaide. None of those guys seemed happy with the arrangement, and I noticed a particularly fierce scowl on Ryder's face. What was his deal?

I couldn't help the smug smile on my own face as I stepped into the modest bedroom with two queen-sized beds. I would happily sleep on the floor if it meant I could stay with Addie.

I'd learned long ago about the monsters in the world. Those monsters were, unfortunately, growing and expanding. Evolving, almost, into entirely new beings. I hadn't been able to protect her then, but I'd be damned if I let anything happen to her now.

No monsters would get to her as long as I was breathing.

CHAPTER 13

ADDIE

I woke up…in a bed?

My stupid, incoherent mind immediately thought that I'd dreamt the last few months. The whole Ragers attacking thing and the hot boys taking care of me. I honestly couldn't tell you which one sounded more illogical.

But…

But I knew, even as my mind slowly started to piece the last few days together, that it was only wishful thinking to believe that the horrors we'd faced, the horrors the world had faced, were only nightmares. No, this was very much real.

I heard the sounds of shuffling beside me.

"Where are we?" I mumbled sleepily, turning towards where Ronan was getting comfy in a chair. His dark hair was longer than I remembered, the green strands cascading almost to his eyes. He brushed them away, as if he knew where my mind had gone, before placing his chin in his hand.

"We stopped for the night," he said back. He sounded tired. Not physically tired, but emotionally. I couldn't see his expression that well in the waning moonlight, but I imagined it to be drawn.

"Where is everyone?" The small room, which on closer inspection appeared to be in a hotel, was devoid of any bodies beside mine and Ronan's.

"Sarge told them that they had to have a meeting in the other room," Ronan explained.

"And you got stuck on babysitting duty?" I asked softly. For the first time since we'd begun the conversation, a smile tentatively touched Ronan's lips.

"It's such a chore, but someone had to do it." Rolling my eyes, I tossed a pillow into his face.

"So what's wrong?" I asked suddenly. He blinked at me, surprised by my line of questioning.

"Huh?"

"You look like someone killed your puppy. Tell me what's wrong." Though it may have sounded like a demand, I hoped that Ronan knew he had a choice whether or not he wanted to share with me. He could always tell me to fuck off, and I wouldn't think anything less of the green-haired leprechaun. I wasn't trying to be nosy. He was my friend, and I wanted to know everything about him. The good, the bad, his fears, and his goals. I didn't like seeing such a despondent expression on his face. I told myself that I would remedy that the first chance I got.

Sighing heavily, Ronan rubbed his hands against his thighs. My eyes were instinctively drawn to the movement. He was wearing a pair of sleep shorts and no shirt, and the moonlight accentuated every tattoo across his broad chest.

How had I not noticed that before?

The poor boy really should put a shirt on if I was going to concentrate.

Another smile graced Ronan's features, clueing me in that I'd spoken aloud.

"You always know how to make me smile, Princess," Ronan said softly. His hands played with the edge of his sleep shorts, and I almost thought he wasn't going to respond. "But it's Ryder," he admitted at last.

"Ryder?"

"I'm worried about him. He hasn't been the same since the attack on the highway. I don't know exactly what went down, what happened to him, but he's become more subdued than before."

I nodded slowly, thinking about Ryder's strange behavior. He hadn't made one inappropriate joke since we'd begun this journey. His smile? Nonexistent.

"I noticed that as well," I admitted. "I could try talking to him."

"No!" Ronan snapped before I could even finish my thought. I winced at his abrupt refusal. He must've seen the hurt on my face, since he hurried to elaborate. "I don't think you should be around him when he's like this. I'm his brother. It's my job to figure out what's wrong and fix it."

"That sounds like a lot of responsibility," I pointed out. Ronan and Ryder were only a few months apart in age. According to the latter, they had the same father but different mothers. They hadn't known the other existed until they were about thirteen. I didn't know the full story, but I knew enough to gather that they both hadn't received the childhood they deserved. Ronan, for some undefinable reason, had appointed himself the caretaker to Ryder. Something had happened in their pasts, something tragic enough to create such an innate need for Ronan to protect his younger brother. I'd never asked.

They would offer the information when they were ready.

"He's my brother," Ronan said, as if the answer was obvious.

I surveyed him, really looked at him, before coming to a conclusion.

Without another word, I hopped from the bed, grabbed the blanket, and placed it over a chair.

"What the hell are you doing?" Ronan asked in disbelief. I didn't answer him as I shoved another corner of the blanket underneath the TV.

"Addie..."

Once every corner was weighed down, I crawled underneath my makeshift fort with a handful of pillows. And then I waited.

It only took a few moments for Ronan to crawl in as well, an eyebrow raised as he considered me.

"This is our fort," I explained. He just continued to stare at me as if I'd completely lost it. "In this fort, there are no responsibilities. No pain. No outside world. There's just us and pillows." I held up said pillow for emphasis. "For just a little bit, we're going to pretend that the world isn't a big shit fest—a shest—and we're going to be happy. Can you do that with me? Can we be happy?"

Something changed in Ronan's expression. I didn't know how to describe it, but it was like a cloud moving away from the sun.

He cleared his throat. "I would very much like that."

For the next half hour, there was just us, the fort, and silence.

I WOKE up a second time at the butt crack of dawn.

Rubbing sleep from my eyes, I practically crawled from the hotel room to the van. My precious kitty, Mof, was snuggled in Tommy's arms, and I immediately reached for him.

"No," Tommy hissed, turning his back to me and effectively cutting off my view of the cat. "He's mine now."

I was too tired to argue with him, though I contemplated hitting him upside the head. Hopefully, that would knock sense into him.

He couldn't just steal my cat and expect to live.

"You look cranky today," Fallon mused, coming to stand beside me. His muscles bulged as he lifted his suitcase into the trunk of the van. And yes, in my sleepy state, I did admire his sexy muscles longer than appropriate. Sue me.

"Fuck off," I answered instead. Why couldn't they have just let me sleep? Did they want me to go on a murder spree?

I didn't even get my damn coffee.

Fallon smirked, obviously amused with my attitude, before nodding towards my clothing.

I gave him a confused stare before glancing down to see what had captured his attention.

My shirt was on backwards, the tag tickling my chin, and my jeans were unbuttoned. Oh well. At least I'd actually remembered clothes.

The temperature outside was in that awkward in-between stage where you didn't know whether it was acceptable to wear a tank top or a winter coat. Currently, the wind was frigid against my arms, creating a trail of goosebumps in its wake. The sun was just barely peeking over the boughs of trees, but I could tell that it promised a sweltering heat.

Damn bipolar weather. Couldn't it just decide to be warm or cold without all the drama?

Tam was near the front of the car, checking underneath the hood. His brown, disheveled hair was hanging limply in his face as he leaned forward. I noticed a smudge of grease over his cheekbone.

Absently, I licked my fingers and gently wiped at the smear. His eyes snapped up in alarm, a blush dusting his cheeks, but he didn't pull away.

"Whatcha doing?" I asked in my cute voice. I figured if any of the guys could tame the beast that was me in the morning, it would be Tam. He was probably the only guy that I didn't feel the need to snap at or curse to hell. How could I? He was sweetness personified, though I doubted he would take kindly to me telling him that.

"Making sure the engine's running smoothly," Tam said, shutting the hood. He wiped his dirty hands on his jeans. "We're hoping to drive a while without stopping."

"You know about cars?" I asked, unable to hide my disbelief. I shouldn't have been surprised that my Tam had more secrets hidden up his sleeve. After all, my lanky friend was an experienced MMA fighter. Anything was possible with these boys.

"Yeah. I learned a lot when I was younger."

"Really?" I asked, intrigued. I didn't know a lot about Tam's past life, but I knew he'd been homeless after his grandma had died. It was by mere chance that he met Fallon and the others, quickly becoming implemented into their team.

"Fallon actually taught me," Tam explained. His attention was locked onto the hood of the car, as if he found it riveting. I didn't take offense to his lack of eye contact. With Tam, any conversation at all was a small blessing. I watched his finger tap against his legs, a break in his normally timid front.

He tapped the same pattern continually as he talked.

"He knew I needed to learn a skill, something to make me valuable to the team." Tam shrugged as if it was no big deal, but his eyes sparkled with affection for the team leader. "He became the big brother I never knew I needed."

I smiled gently.

"I'm happy that you got your family," I said, tentatively placing my head on his shoulder. He stiffened momentarily before his muscles relaxed. He pressed a kiss to my forehead.

"These guys are my brothers, and you are..." He trailed off.

"Your sister that isn't a sister?" I suggested coyly. He snorted.

"A sister that isn't a sister," he agreed. Before he could say anything else, there was the sound of a gun going off. Ironically, I hadn't been familiar with that particular sound until the last few days.

Now, it seemed to be the only constant in my chaotic life.

Tam immediately pushed me to the ground, then his lean body covered mine.

I tried to tell him that I didn't need or want his protection. I tried to remind him that I wasn't made of glass.

Instead, all I was aware of were pinpricks of terror running through my veins and making me incapable of speech.

The rest of the boys had been standing near the entrance of the hotel, away from us and the van. Through my sprawled position on the ground, I could only see their feet.

And...more feet?

"Put your hands where I can see them!" a strident, unrecognizable voice demanded. "Let me see your fucking hands!"

I didn't know what was happening, but I thought that was a blessing. While half of me wanted to run to their rescue, the other half of me noted how futile that endeavor would be.

Especially since I didn't know what I was up against.

Tam finally rolled off of me, motions silent, to peek around the side of the van. He let out an inaudible cuss before putting a finger to his lips.

"Is this all of you?" the new voice demanded.

"Yes." Ryder. I would recognize his husky voice anywhere.

"Grab the backpacks off of them," someone demanded, and I heard what sounded like a struggle.

"Stay on the ground or I'll shoot you!" the first voice screamed, and I winced, praying that the boys would listen.

If someone was holding a gun to you and demanded that you stay on the ground, you stayed on the fucking ground. If you pee your pants, more power to you.

Ignoring Tam's glare of protest, I popped my head around the wheel of the van.

My breath left me in a whooshing rush.

My boys sat on the ground, their hands raised in the air. Each one looked livid as they surveyed the figures above them. Even Tommy was scowling, though I'd be the first to admit that he looked more like Barney on crack than anything remotely scary. His hand was still absently petting Mof.

The men—and from their large stature and broad shoulders, I assumed they were, in fact, all men—stood around the guys, each holding a gun. They had white masks obscuring their features and wore all black clothing, the stereotypical bad guy attire. I counted at least six of them.

Great. Just frickin' great.

After the last backpack was roughly grabbed from Fallon's shoulders, the leader— Red Eyes, I coined him in my head, based on his painted mask—turned his attention towards Mof.

"And what is this sweet thing?" he cooed, reaching down to pet the kitten. Mof, like the perfect cat he was, hissed and burrowed himself further into Tommy.

"Fucking hell!" Red Eyes said with a laugh. He swiveled his head to face his goons. "I don't think the cat likes me much!"

"Has some good meat on it," one of the others mumbled, and I felt my body go cold.

I was the type of girl that, in movies, if the main character was to get killed off, I wouldn't shed a tear. The second an animal died? You better grab a fucking boat because the waterworks would create an ocean.

How dare this bastard threaten my cat, a sweet, defenseless creature?

My intention to kill, or at the very least maim, must've been written all over my face, because Tam grabbed my shoulder and pulled me back behind the van. He shook his head viciously.

"No," he mouthed.

I could feel hysteria rising through me. Mof was my pet, my responsibility, and it was my job to look after him. I'd failed my parents, I'd failed my brother, but I would be damned before I let anything happen to my kitten.

I lunged forward, intending to take the bastards off guard, but Tam pulled me back. His hand wrapped over my mouth, and I debated whether or not I wanted to kick him in the nuts.

A nut kick to anybody, good guy or bad guy, was an effective means for you to get your way.

But I didn't want to hurt Tam. No, the people I wanted to hurt were the bastards threatening my friends. I secretly hoped that Fallon had a plan—a plan that involved these dumbasses being neutered for messing with my family.

"We're not eating the cat," a new voice said, and I decided I hated him slightly less than the other ones. "Let's just grab the bags and go."

Yes. Go.

I closed my eyes, face wet with a single tear that cascaded down my cheek.

I hadn't allowed myself to realize how scared I'd been before that moment. I feared for the boys and Mof and myself. This world was evil, and by default, the people were turning evil as well. When would it end?

I was so lost in my thoughts, so preoccupied by the people in front of me, that I didn't hear the footsteps until the gun was pressed to the back of my head. From Tam's startled expression, he, too, had failed to realize that there was another asshole lurking around. His eyes met my wide ones, and in them I could see his desperation and panic. He immediately lunged for the man, but he'd yet to fully recover from his earlier injury. After a quick hit to the head, he dropped like a bag of rocks.

"Well, what do we have here?" This voice was colder than the others, devoid of any feeling or compassion. I couldn't pinpoint the accent, but it sounded as if he was from down south. Texas, perhaps?

"I found their bitch!" the boy said, roughly grabbing my arm and propelling me to my feet. My boys all turned to stare at me, panic similar to what I'd seen on Tam's face evident in their expressions.

"Don't be so crude, Kyle," one of the men said. He sounded wary.

The asshat holding me—Kyle, I presumed—gave my arm a shake.

"Have you seen her? She's hot!"

Calax jumped to his feet, and five guns were suddenly trained on him.

"Don't you fucking touch her," he yelled, spit flying.

"Get your ass down," Red Eyes sneered. He kicked the backs of Calax's knees, and the big man crumbled with a few choice words.

I was frozen, incapable of speech beyond nonsensical muttering and squeals. Fear threatened to suffocate me. Darkness. Darkness descended over my vision, and it took me a moment before I realized that it was because I had closed my eyes.

I didn't want to see Kyle's hands under my armpits. I couldn't see his expression through the mask, but I imagined it would be a leer. People like him were scum. They were worse than the dirt under my shoes, the fungus on the walls, the mold growing on old cheese. I'd dealt with his type for far too long, and I wanted nothing more than to escape.

Him, myself, and my life.

"She's cute, isn't she?" Kyle said. I felt his hands—his slimy, disgusting hands—curve around my stomach.

"Get your hands off of her." I'd heard Fallon mad before. I'd even heard him cold before, as if he were wearing a mask. Never, in the months I'd known him, did I hear him sound so furious, so incensed. His breathing was heavy.

"Is she your girlfriend?" Kyle asked. "Or is she that big guy's? Or does she just fuck all of you?"

"Shut the fuck up!" Ryder snapped, and Kyle let out a manic laugh, as if his outburst only reinforced what he'd already suspected.

The traveling hands went higher, towards my breasts, and I couldn't stop the involuntary whimper as he squeezed.

This couldn't be happening. Not again. I thought I was supposed to be safe with these guys. They'd promised me that I would be safe.

"We're going to kill you," Ronan seethed. I still didn't dare open my eyes. I didn't want this moment to be more real than it already was. I also didn't want to give any of these horrible men the satisfaction of seeing me cry.

His wandering hand went underneath my shirt, touching the bare skin of my stomach, and I squeezed my eyes further shut.

I ignored the guys' growls. I ignored the heavy panting of the pervert behind me. I ignored the growing hardness jabbing into my back.

Fighting the urge to vomit, I prayed to whatever God was listening that I could make it out of this unscathed. My life had never been fair, but this? This was positively awful. Nothing could compare to this, the shame I felt, the guilt that it was somehow my fault, the disgust.

All I was capable of was a pathetic, "Please."

I felt another body come up in front of me. I felt someone lick the lone tear that had escaped my traitorous eye.

Somewhere to the side, there was the sound of a shuffle. A gun went off. Something fell.

But those were distant sensations, ones that I couldn't entirely focus on.

Screams. I was aware of screams.

The ground began to shake around me, and at first, I thought it was my own horror manifesting itself as a physical reality. Maybe I had truly lost my mind.

The bodies that were on either side of me were pulled away. The world continued to tremor around me.

I couldn't stand. I didn't want to stand.

Darkness, mercifully, consumed me.

~

THEY WOULD TELL me later that it was an earthquake.

It started off as a simple crack, like an egg that had been dropped but not completely destroyed, before the entire earth broke apart like a gaping mouth opening up to swallow. They said that the hotel caved in on itself, debris and asphalt joining the cars in the newly formed hole.

They said that Kyle and his friends "accidentally" found themselves inside the hole as well.

They wouldn't tell me who pushed them, but I had my suspicions. After all, my guys did enjoy doing things as a team.

They thought I would be disgusted, horrified, angry at their blatant disrespect for life. And I did feel all those things, but for entirely different reasons than what the guys initially assumed.

I felt horrified that men like Kyle existed. What if he'd found another girl, a younger one, who didn't have the protection of seven amazing guys? How many victims had he had before me?

I tried not to dwell on that nauseating fact, but bile still managed to rise up in my throat. I didn't want to think about what happened. I didn't want to reminisce about how close he'd been...

No. I wouldn't think about that. I would push all my memories behind an immobile barrier. There would be a time when I would reflect on these thoughts, recollect on these daunting memories, but now wasn't that time.

I had to be strong.

Forget. That was my motto. There were so many thoughts pressing against the forefront of my mind, but I ignored them all.

I knew that if I responded to the darkness's seductive call, I would be lost. Already, I could feel my control slipping away.

I just had to bury those feelings until they were forgotten.

Always forgotten.

CHAPTER 14

ADDIE

We didn't talk about what happened
I didn't talk about what happened.

It wasn't possible for me to put into words all that I was feeling. I was like a volcano ready to burst. Without a shred of doubt, I knew that I would burn everyone in my general vicinity when I finally did decide to erupt, as if I had a conscious choice in the matter of my eventual mental demise.

We were all broken. All of us. Tommy had yet to fully comprehend what he'd done. Ryder was dealing with something unknown to the rest of us. Ronan and Fallon both felt the weight of their responsibility. Fallon's extended towards all of us, and I didn't know how far Ronan's went. Did he just feel responsible for his brother? For me? Tam, Asher, and Calax dealt with their guilt over what had transpired, though I did not blame them.

And me? I was tearing apart at the seams. My life was shattering around me, swallowing me whole, and I was helpless to escape. My mental pain seemed to mani-fest itself into physical aches. I found breathing difficult.

How could I go back from this?

So we didn't speak about it, about anything. We all remained mute as the van—which had miraculously survived the earthquake—thumped over cracked streets.

I was afraid that we wouldn't be able to hold ourselves together that much longer. One wrong move, one wrong direction, and we would completely shatter.

And my cynical mind had to wonder if that wouldn't necessarily be a bad thing.

WE MADE an impromptu stop at a grocery store.

There were a few other groups already milling about when we arrived inside the pungently smelling building. They, too, were grabbing all the food they could carry, loading it into their cars. There were no workers manning the checkout lanes, yet I couldn't ignore the stab of guilt I felt as we began grabbing items at random as well.

Wasn't this considered stealing?

I had to wonder if there was anything left in this world that was even remotely humane. It seemed as if laws, rules, and social decency had all gone out the door the second shit hit the fan.

Sighing heavily, I listened as Fallon broke us apart into groups. I would go with Ryder and Tommy to gather any and all medical supplies. Again, he didn't give us anything specific. He merely handed us a duffle bag with vague instructions to "grab it all".

And of course I would be stuck with Mr. Silent and Mr. Sarcastic. I'd hoped I would be able to talk with one of them, at least, but no such luck. We walked to the medical section of the store in silence.

We'd been doing a lot of that lately. Silence. It made the air seem almost thick, as if it could swallow us whole.

I was slugging pill bottles into the bag when I got my hand stuck on a surprisingly sharp edge of the shelf. My twisted mind welcomed the pain, welcomed the distraction...and then I lost it.

I absolutely lost it. The volcano erupted.

There were casualties.

"Fuck! Fucking shit! Fuck this and fuck all of you!" I didn't know who my anger was directed at, but it felt good to let it out. The relief made the stricken expressions on Ryder's and Tommy's faces seem almost worth it. Almost.

"Kitten?" Ryder asked hesitantly. He took a step closer to me, arms outstretched, and I flinched. I didn't want anyone touching me. People only brought me pain, immense, unbearable pain that left both mental and physical scars.

"I can't do this anymore," I sobbed. My body felt weak, and my legs couldn't support my weight. "It hurts. It hurts so much. Why does it hurt so badly?"

"Kitten..." His voice was hoarse as he, too, slid down to his knees. He looked as if he wanted to touch me but decided against it.

"Damn it all! Damn it!" I smashed a fist into the shelf, ignoring the throbbing pain that erupted in my knuckles. I was a hysterical mess, tears mixing in with my snot. A few unfamiliar faces glanced down at me, expressions pitying, before quickly hurrying away. I didn't doubt that this was the first girl they had seen break down in a supermarket.

"You don't get to fucking act like this!" Tommy exploded.

And another volcano erupted.

"I saved you! I chose you, and you're acting like an ungrateful little brat!" Tommy jabbed an accusatory finger into my face.

"Watch it!" Ryder snapped.

"I chose you over my own mother! I chose you, and that doesn't give you the right to fall the fuck apart! I chose you, and you have to live!"

I wiped the tears from my eyes angrily. "Fuck you, Tommy. I didn't ask you to save me."

He gave a snort of disdain. "You're right—I should've let you get eaten by my mother. At least then she'd still be alive."

His face smoothed over a second before his expression shattered. It was then that I saw it, the moment where he realized what he had done, and my stomach twisted almost painfully. On his young face, his anguished expression made him look centuries older. We stared at each other, and I knew that the horror in his expression was reflected on mine.

There was no comparison to our pain, despite what people may believe. You couldn't possibly look at someone and deem that their pain was somehow less than yours. That wasn't how pain works.

It was in that grocery store, in the medicine aisle, where we eventually broke down. I was distantly aware of Ryder holding me in his arms, my face in his neck and my tears wetting his dark shirt. Fallon must've come, no doubt hearing our blubbering, but instantly left with whoever he came with. Nobody else bothered us after that, but I could feel the guys' presence around me.

Always watchful. Always vigilant. It helped to know that they were near, though I didn't know how to articulately express such a sentiment. All I could do was hold Ryder tighter and hope that I conveyed my thankfulness for him through that eloquent touch.

It was Tommy who stopped crying first. His chubby hand touched his cheek where his prominent scar protruded from his flesh.

"I have a scar," he whispered. I grasped his hand and gave it a squeeze.

"So do I."

~

We departed Freddy's Supermarket more somber than we'd arrived, a feat I didn't think was possible. Nobody attempted to engage me in conversation, and for that, I was grateful.

Tommy hadn't stopped crying since his initial outburst. He curled into a ball in the backseat, nearly inaudible whimpers escaping him. None of the guys coddled him or sat near him—another thing I was thankful for. I knew Tommy would not want their pity or even their sympathy.

It was only after an hour on the road, Fallon expertly maneuvering the vehicle between cars and trucks that had been abandoned, when Calax broke the silence. He was sitting beside me, his hand on my thigh, and leaned closer so his words would only be heard by me and me alone.

"You okay, baby girl?" he asked softly. His hand was tantalizingly soft against my bare leg.

"Besides the fact that I had a complete mental breakdown, feel emotionally exhausted, and want to curl into a fetal position and cry myself to an early grave? Just peachy."

His eyebrows furrowed, but he didn't respond to my twisted perspective of life. All he did was hold me tighter, as if he never wanted to let me go.

Mof, in my lap, was getting antsy. I tried to recall the last time the cat had peed or even ate, but my mind came back blank. I'd been a terrible owner. Fortunately for Mof, he had the guys looking after him, or else I was pretty sure he would've been dead.

Speaking of bathroom breaks…

"Can we stop at the next rest area, please?" I called up to Fallon. The scary man in question met my gaze in the rearview mirror and let out something that could probably be taken as a yes. It was a strange mixture between a grunt and a growl—Fallon speak, I called it. He had his own language.

We'd barely grazed the state border, so the rest area we stopped at was just as chilly as where we'd come from. The sun had long since descended behind numerous trees leaving nothing but an icy wind.

Fallon had fortunately found a highway that hadn't experienced the same pileup that the previous one had. There were still abandoned cars, of course, but traffic moved surprisingly easily. According to Asher, who was on map duty, the new route put us a few hours behind schedule.

The rest area had only a few cars and a couple of trucks when we pulled up. I noted a family leaning against their bumper—a mom, a dad, and three children. My mind immediately went back to the house with the framed photographs, and I once again wondered what had become of that family. Either way, I was grateful for them for letting us use their house, despite their obliviousness.

"Thank the Lord!" Ryder said eagerly. I was pleased to see that he was gradually turning back into his old self. I adored the serious side of him, but there was something charming about his flirtatious half that I couldn't ignore. "My butt was beginning to fall asleep."

"Your butt can't fall asleep," I said absently, though I wasn't entirely sure if that was true. It just seemed easier to tease Ryder than admit to him being right, even over something as insignificant as butts.

"All you have to do is look at my butt to see," Ryder said, wiggling his eyebrows at me. "I hear little snores coming from my asshole."

"Quit farting then," I retorted.

He glared playfully at me, and I hadn't realized how much I'd missed him until that moment. He hadn't been gone, necessarily, but he hadn't been himself. I still didn't fully understand what had happened during the highway attack, but I knew that he'd been changed because of it.

I could only hope that the change was for the better, not the worst.

Linking my arm with his, I walked towards the diminutive brick building surrounded by nothing but forest on one side and a highway on the other. A few cars drove by as I watched, each one rapidly approaching one hundred mph on the speedometer. There would be no cops to stop them.

"I missed you," I said to Ryder absently. He nearly tripped over the curb at my confession.

"I've been here," he said.

"Yeah, but you've been so quiet. I know you probably don't want to talk about whatever upset you, but I just want you to know that I'm here for you. Whenever, if ever, you'd like to talk about it."

He glanced down at me, eyes inscrutable. His teeth gnawed at his bottom lip, as they often did when he was in deep thought.

"It's nothing bad," he admitted at last. He cast a quick look over his shoulder, towards where the guys were discussing plans, before turning back to me. "I just realized something."

"Would you like to talk about it?" I didn't know what else to ask him. I didn't want to demand information from him, despite my concern. He would choose to tell me if and when he was ready, and I wouldn't force him.

His smile was dull on his handsome face.

"It's not something I can talk about," he admitted at last. "It's something that I need to stop thinking about, though I'm beginning to believe that it's impossible."

I blinked at his cryptic words but didn't ask him to elaborate. Whatever realization he'd come to made him sad. Pensive. And though a part of me wanted to shake him until he revealed all of his secrets, another part of me understood his need for privacy.

Changing the subject, I blurted the first thing that came to mind. "I need tampons."

Because I was just that smooth.

Ryder stared at me before breaking into roaring laughter.

"It's not funny!" I huffed, slapping him across the chest. "I bleed!"

That, of course, only made him laugh harder.

"You're not a girl, so you wouldn't understand."

My cheeks flaming with embarrassment, I practically ran into the women's bathroom. I could still hear Ryder's laughter echoing from the lobby.

I used the bathroom quickly, pleasantly surprised when the water actually ran, before drying my hands on a paper towel.

I frowned at my reflection in the mirror. God, I was a mess. Hair greasy, eyes shadowed, dirt smeared across every available swath of skin. Ugh. How was one supposed to remain beautiful and perky and all that during a freaking zombie invasion? That was one thing movies got really wrong.

A girl walked into the bathroom and flashed me a smile.

She was pretty with long, dark hair braided back from her face. For some reason, I thought she looked slightly familiar, though I couldn't place where I knew her from.

"Rough day?" she asked, moving to splash water on her face.

"You could say that."

She was silent as she grabbed a paper towel and scrubbed the invisible dirt from her body. Seriously, she made me look like I'd taken a mud bath and then decided to roll around in shit for a little extra fun. Stupid pretty girls and their pretty faces.

"Did you see the guys outside?" the girl said, attempting conversation no doubt. "They're hot."

Something twisted inside of me at her description of the guys. They were hot, yes, but I didn't want her to notice it. My possessiveness and jealousy surprised even me. What the hell was happening?

Without responding, and probably appearing to be a psycho bitch off her meds, I hurried from the bathroom.

I couldn't understand why my stomach ached so badly at the thought of her checking out the guys...or the thought of them looking at her back. I knew that it was inevitable that they would find a girl, but for a while, I enjoyed it being just us. Of me being their girl, and of them being my guys. Did that make me selfish?

I couldn't say.

Correction, I didn't want to say. If I looked at it closely, if I tore apart the motives behind my actions, then I would have an answer.

A gunshot shook me out of my thoughts.

I immediately began running towards where I'd left the guys. I didn't know if Ryder had already joined them or if he was still in the bathroom. I hadn't even been certain that the gunshot came from one of the guys, yet...

I knew.

My feet slowed of their own accord when I spotted Asher with his gun still raised. He had it pointed at a small creature, and for a horrible, nauseating second, I thought it was Mof.

I let out an audible sigh of relief when I spotted my cat curled in Fallon's arms.

No, the creature that had been shot down was a squirrel.

"Don't get too close," Tam warned me as he saw me sneaking towards the fallen animal. But I didn't have to get closer to see the squirrel. Even from a distance, I could see its wide eyes staring blindly ahead. Blood red. Familiar white foam, almost like whipped cream, came out of its mouth.

I realized then that what I'd seen previously with the dog hadn't been a fluke. The disease was, apparently, transferring itself to animals as well as humans. If I didn't think we were screwed before, I definitely had a change of heart.

For a brief moment, I wondered if it was worth going to Atlanta. I knew, without a shred of doubt, that I still had to go, but the others?

My brother wasn't their responsibility. Hell, I wasn't even their responsibility, despite their claims otherwise.

I had to talk to them. I had to make them see reason. This was my journey, and I wouldn't let them come with me.

Nobody else would get hurt if I had my say in it.

CHAPTER 15

CALAX

he first time I realized I was in love with Adelaide was the same day she decided she hated me.

I had, without fail, met her outside at the garden every evening, excluding the few days I was sent out on a job with my team.

They'd noticed my strange behavior, particularly my decision not to date any females during that time frame. Ryder had asked me if I was gay, Asher had questioned my sanity, and Sarge had just stared at me with this knowing look. It was fucking annoying.

Every day, I would talk to the strange, elfin female who'd slowly and surely weaseled her way into my heart. Sometimes I would help her, and other times, I would tease her relentlessly. She'd often join me in my apartment afterwards for a glass of lemonade.

I found myself entranced with every word she said. She was effortlessly funny, and I loved hearing her laugh. I made it a mission to get that laugh out of her as often as possible.

So it was no surprise when I fell. It wasn't like falling asleep. It wasn't a gradual process that I could understand. It happened fast, and it happened hard, like a bag of rocks dragging me down into the ocean. That wasn't to say that it was bad, but it was definitely different. I found that I could barely breathe when she was around.

The day everything changed, I was shrugging into my jacket in an effort to beat her to the garden. I'd hoped to ask her out—hoped being the important word there. I knew that she would more than likely laugh in my face, but I was determined to wear her down.

I'd never tried this hard for any girl. To be completely honest, I'd never had to. Girls flocked to me, and I was never the type to turn them away. They helped fill this emptiness inside me that I couldn't quite explain, if only for a moment.

But Addie...

With her, I had completely forgotten that I was alone in this world. She was something bright and warm and vibrant, slowly melting away the walls around my heart and setting me free.

Damn. I sounded like such a cliché.

Stupid Addie, and stupid love.

I'd just stepped out of the elevator when Adelaide came barreling towards me, face pinched. I smiled immediately when I saw her.

God, how did I get lucky enough to meet a girl so perfect?

My smile disappeared when she hit me.

Okay then.

"What the hell is your problem?" she asked, face turning redder with each word.

"A lot?" I said, though my answer turned into a question. I didn't understand her sudden hostility towards me. She teased me, yes, but she'd never been outright cruel before. I couldn't understand the change.

"You're such an asshole," she hissed. Before I could respond, she stomped away from me.

Looking back, I realized that it hadn't been anger in her eyes. Sure, she was upset, but her eyes were not dark with fury. She was scared. Terrified. I hadn't understood then that she feared her parents' reaction.

What had I done to garner such an intense reaction from her? I was pissed.

For once, I hadn't done anything wrong.

I spent that night with two other girls, one of them the same bitch that had the name of a stone. Emerald or something.

It was with her that I discovered why Addie was so furious—someone had destroyed the garden. All of the plants had been trampled, the dirt overturned, and the bricks outlining the garden had been shattered.

Emerald, who'd been outside when Addie had arrived, told her that I'd done it.

The stupid bitch had been jealous of Adelaide and was determined to end our relationship.

I should've been mad at Addie for believing the lies so easily, yet I only began to love her more.

I was not a small guy by any means. My tall frame, broad shoulders, and defined muscles were an assurance of that. Despite everything, Adelaide had stood up to me. She'd looked me in the eye, tilting her head back to see me fully, and had called me out. There had been no fear that I would retaliate or hurt her. No, despite being pissed as hell at me, she trusted me implicitly.

I couldn't say the same of others. I may not have ever hit a female—though I sure wanted to with Emerald—but my size and strength often intimidated members of both sexes. They stared at me as if I was a monster.

Addie stared at me as if we were equals.

That was the last time I'd even touched another girl before that kiss with Addie at the pond. Nothing, and I meant nothing, could compare to her. She was my everything, and I would do everything in my power to get her to understand that.

∼

I PULLED myself out of my thoughts to focus on the matter at hand.

Never, in all my years of existence, did I think I would see Ronan getting attacked by a squirrel.

I mean really, what the hell?

I was discussing the plan for the trip with Sarge—we would try to keep our stops to a minimum in an effort to get to Atlanta at a reasonable time—when I heard Ronan let out a string of curses.

That didn't surprise me. The green-haired bastard swore like a sailor. What surprised me, however, was the bushy tailed squirrel climbing up his legs.

Letting out a rather girly squeak, he began shaking his leg erratically. The squirrel clambered off of him, foaming at the mouth, before charging yet again. I caught a glimpse of the creature's beady red eyes before the gun went off.

The first time I'd heard a gun, I had instinctively brought my fingers to my ears, as if that could somehow block out the rest of the world. Now, I barely even stumbled. Barely. A time or two, the sound would catch me off guard.

This was one of those times.

Asher stood, panting, his hand steady as it held the gun. The rabid animal had a gaping hole in its head, black blood splattering across the asphalt.

"Don't get too close," Tam said. My head snapped up towards the impending footsteps, and I gave Addie a quick once-over, cataloguing any injuries. Fortunately, she seemed to be fine.

I hadn't allowed her to see the momentary anxiety I'd felt when she'd left. I knew she was with Ryder, but I didn't like having her out of my sight.

The memory of her death still haunted both my waking moments and my dreams. It was something that I didn't know how to come back from.

"What the hell happened?" Addie asked, running up to Asher and inspecting him for injuries. Ronan let out an annoyed snort.

"I was the one that got attacked, yet Asher is getting all the attention. Geez." Though his words were somewhat teasing, I caught something in his eyes that he tried to keep hidden. Something akin to jealousy.

I didn't like that.

I had the distinct feeling that my brothers thought of Addie as a little more than a friend.

"Ronan!" Addie finally seemed to notice the blood smearing his pants. She ran towards him, cupping his face in her dainty hands.

My stomach tightened at her display of affection towards him. I told myself that I had no right to feel so possessive towards her since we'd never clarified what our relationship was, but I couldn't ignore the hammering of my heart.

She was mine…but she was also theirs.

I didn't know how she fit in with our team, but I had a feeling that it was going to change everything. I glanced at Sarge's contemplative expression and knew that he thought the same.

I was going to have to talk to him about me and her. *Us* and her.

I didn't care if they had feelings for her too, but I wasn't backing away. I wasn't giving her up.

"What the hell is that thing?" Asher asked, finally lowering the gun. He slipped it back into his holster.

Ronan was now on the ground, his pants rolled up as Fallon and Addie tended to his wounds. Well, Fallon did. Addie merely hovered over him like a pestering, albeit very cute, vulture. I noted with relief that he hadn't been too injured in the squirrel attack. Only a couple of scratches marred his skin, red and raised. It would leave faint residual scarring.

Sarge methodically applied antibiotics to the cuts, and Ronan hissed.

"The animal had the virus," Tam murmured. Despite the gravity of the situation, he sounded almost excited. No doubt was he thinking about grabbing the carcass and studying it in detail. My friend was a little strange in that respect.

"I'm fine!" Ronan protested to Sarge, mitigating the damages. He had always been a baby when it came to pain. Even with something as simple as a scratch, he would act like his entire leg had been amputated. I could tell he was trying to play it cool now, trying to impress Addie no doubt, but a low hiss escaped his clenched teeth. Addie, hearing the sound, tightened her hand over his.

"When I was at the hotel, before I came to you guys, I saw a dog. He had red eyes and was practically foaming at the mouth," Addie said softly. Her eyes were wide, lost in a memory that only she could see. "So you think the virus is spreading to animals?"

Sarge's face was hard. I could tell he was pissed that she hadn't bothered to share that information earlier.

Indignation on Addie's behalf reared its head, but I smothered my protective instincts. Addie didn't need me running my mouth to defend her honor.

No, my girl was strong all on her own.

"I hadn't thought anything of it," Addie said, voice cold. "I would've told you if I thought it was important."

It became a contest of wills. Sarge stared down at her, trying to intimidate her, and Addie stared defiantly back at him. My mind transferred back to when I'd first realized the extent of my feelings for her.

She'd stood up to me that time too—without fear, without shame.

It was Sarge who looked away first, a fact that nearly had me stagger over my own two feet. Never had he allowed another to display their dominance over him. He always had to be the alpha.

For Addie, he was willing to submit.

He muttered something under his breath, his version of an apology, before strolling back towards the van.

I exchanged bemused glances with the other guys, and I could tell we were all thinking the same thing.

We didn't bother to question his strange behavior, mainly because that made us hypocrites. This girl was making us all crazy.

CHAPTER 16

ADDIE

I slept on and off during the car ride, the level plains slowly being replaced by immense, towering mountains. Fog had settled over the road, creating an ominous presence that sent goosebumps up my arms. There was something almost malevolent about the abandoned road and the heady layer of fog obscuring my vision.

The next time I woke up, it was to the clap of thunder. I jolted upright and probably would've banged my head against the front seat if Ryder hadn't put his arm around me.

"Easy there, Kitten."

Rain pounded against the window, and diagonals of lightning cracked in the sky. It lit up the forests on either side of us like a giant spotlight before the light was snatched away and darkness returned.

"The weather's getting bad," Asher said from where he was navigating in the passenger seat. Fallon mumbled an affirmative, twisting the steering wheel so that we were parked on the side of the road.

"We're getting low on gas," he added gruffly.

"Any gas stations open?" I asked, though I already knew the answer. Every building and store on this stretch of road had been closed down. We had been able to find a couple of abandoned cars discarded on the side of the road and siphoned gas from them. Illegal? Absolutely. Did we care? Not anymore.

Still, Fallon answered my question in resignation. "Nothing opened most likely. We're probably going to have to get a new vehicle. We're for sure going to have to sit out this storm. Is there a hotel nearby?"

Asher fumbled with the map, paper crinkling as his finger traced a dark line.

"Wait a minute! Is that…?" He trailed off and turned towards Ryder behind him. Ryder released me to lean forward.

Peering at the map, a scowl contorted his features into something almost unrecognizable.

"No way in hell," he huffed. He crossed his arms over his impressive chest.

I raised an eyebrow at him, but he didn't look my way.

"No. We'll find a hotel."

"The next hotel is still a long ways away," Asher said placatingly. "This is our best option."

"What is he going on about?" Ronan asked. He was sitting on the opposite side of me. At first, when I'd discovered the seating arrangements, my mind had immediately conjured up images of a brother sandwich, as Ronan so eloquently stated before. I couldn't ignore how appealing that idea sounded…or how flustered I became.

Asher handed Ronan the map, pointing to the same road he'd shown Ryder. Like his brother, Ronan's expression darkened.

"No."

Another gunshot of thunder reverberated through the night air. Lightning streaked overhead, a vivid light show in the dark sky.

"Do you even think they'll let us stay there?" Ronan continued. His eyes flickered anxiously my way.

I couldn't ignore my unease at his reaction. What the hell were they talking about?

"They'll let us," Fallon said, voice subdued. He seemed to be contemplating something. What, I had no clue. Coming to an apparent conclusion, Fallon expertly drove the car back onto the road. "We'll spend the night there."

The boys all groaned, even Tam, who I'd thought was asleep.

"Where are we going?" I asked. I didn't know how comfortable I felt going to a location that brought out such a reaction from the guys. Surely there was a better option, right?

I had to tell myself that the guys would never let any harm come to me. It was inconceivable to believe that they would bring me to a place where I could get hurt. Calax loved me, and I knew the others cared for me as well.

Still, my anxiety threatened to boil over as we drove down the dark streets.

When we finally stopped, the darkness was so thick that I had trouble deciphering the features of the building before us. It appeared to be a tall Victorian manor, walls painted a light color, though that color was unknown, even with the intermittent flashes of lightning. Rain immediately consumed me as I stepped out of the car. My clothes became plastered to my body like a second skin.

Clinging to the back of Calax's shirt, I followed the boys up a staircase to a small porch built beneath a drooping alcove. It was Fallon who rang the doorbell, completely at ease, despite the taut postures of his team.

Who lived in this house? Why did I have the distinct feeling that we were trading one hell for another?

I remained huddled behind Calax's broad back. Declan was behind me, his hands seeping warmth into my shoulders. He gave them a reassuring squeeze.

Ducky had always been able to sense my unease.

The door swung open suddenly, the barest whoosh of sound, but I couldn't see over the tall men blocking my path.

"Hello, ladies," Fallon said politely. "We were wondering if we could stay here for the night."

I could've snorted. The bastard was never that polite with me. No, he seemed to hold a constant "Adelaide's an idiot" mentality whenever he was forced to address me. For some reason, his reverence towards these strangers caused jealousy to churn low in my stomach.

That jealousy only increased when a familiar voice spoke up.

"Of course! Anything for you guys! Come in! Come in! Let me get you something hot to warm you up." Nobody could miss the suggestiveness of that last statement.

When the guys stepped into the house, I finally caught sight of the familiar, beautiful girl.

Elena.

Standing beside her, smile coy, was Bikini.

I tried to tamp down my jealousy, especially when Elena rubbed her hand against Ryder's bicep, but I couldn't ignore the stabbing pain in my heart. I needed to bury this jealousy. I couldn't allow these nonsensical feelings to hurt my relationship and friendship with the guys.

Plastering a large smile on my face, I stepped into the porch light. It appeared as if this house was one of the few with electricity. I had to wonder if they had a generator or something.

Elena's smile instantly fell when she saw me, being replaced by a cool glare.

Without any greeting, she turned on her heel and stomped back inside. Bikini, after one last wistful glance at Ryder and Ronan—she, no doubt, was thinking of a sandwich—followed after her.

"You didn't say we were going to be spending the night at the devil's house," I whispered to Calax, and he snorted.

It was hard for me to ignore the cruel way Elena had treated me. She'd been a stereotypical mean girl, driven by jealousy and a desperate need to be noticed and wanted by the guys. I knew she was in love with them, but I also knew that they didn't hold the same sentiment towards her. According to the boys, they had shared her long ago, along with a dozen other females. And despite knowing she was one of many females they'd shared, she'd thought their relationship was something special, while they'd looked to her for sex. I couldn't help but think that my boys were the bad guys in this scenario.

I did not want my relationship with the guys to become anything like Elena's. Despite her hostility towards me, I pitied her. It must've been hard to love someone who would never love her back.

And she'd saved my life. I couldn't, wouldn't, forget that. She could've left me to die after the tornado trapped us underground, yet she spent the time to fix my injuries.

I had a feeling there was more to Elena than what met the eye.

My socks sloshing with water, I followed the boys into the living room. A group of girls were spread out between the couch, the loveseat, and the floor. They all glanced up when we entered.

"Ryder!" an annoyingly chipper voice said. A petite figure immediately wrapped her arms around his narrow waist. Surprisingly, Ryder looked uncomfortable with her display of affection, especially when she pursed her lips in an awaited kiss. Side-stepping around her, he flashed a small smile.

"Afternoon, ladies," he said. I couldn't help but notice the appreciative stares the girls gave the guys. *My* guys.

Once again, I had to rein in the green monster threatening to explode. I'd never been the jealous type before, or the possessive type, but I'd never had anyone I actually cared about.

I half expected one of the guys to take up the offer that each girl was silently giving. I wouldn't blame them, as each girl was almost ethereal in beauty, all different body types and colors. They instantly made me feel like a damaged Cabbage Patch Kid.

I knew my demented thoughts were only my depression speaking. I honestly knew that, but it didn't change anything. The world could be a dangerous place when your own mind was against you.

I felt moderately better when the boys remained standing beside me, arms crossed and expressions fierce, though I wasn't naïve enough to believe they were doing it for me.

Elena appeared from the side door, a pair of pajamas in her hands. Without making eye contact, she thrust them at me.

"I don't have anything for the guys, but I figured you wouldn't want to sit around in wet clothing."

My heart swelled. "Thank you, Elena."

She glanced up, only once, before moving swiftly to an empty seat on the couch.

"Don't worry about it."

"Fallon! You never introduced us to this young woman! What's her name?" a strident voice demanded. It belonged to a surprisingly elfin figure with blond, flowing hair and emerald green eyes. She was sitting on the lap of another girl, this one equally as stunning with dark locks and smoky, exotic eyes.

Fallon looked away, properly chastised.

"This is Adelaide," he said briskly. He didn't even bother to point at me. Bastard.

The blonde girl's face turned up into a glorious smile.

"Hello, Adelaide. I'm Samantha, and this is Lilly." She nodded towards the girl beneath her, and Lilly gave me a two fingered wave.

"Those ladies over there are Michele, Tally, and Monica. You probably already know Lacey, Missy, and Elena."

She spoke the names so rapidly that all I could do was blink like an idiot. Yeah, there was no way I would remember any of them.

"Come on!" Samantha jumped to her feet, and Lilly got up as well. "You can tell me all about your adventures with these hooligans while we get you changed. I'll make you a hot cup of cocoa."

She practically skipped towards the living room. Fallon grabbed her shoulder just as she was in front of him.

"Off limits," he muttered, and she rolled her eyes. I wondered what that was about.

Sending a pleading look at the boys, which only served to make them more amused, I was dragged into the kitchen by an eager girl who seemed to have five hundred pounds of muscles despite her one-hundred-pound frame.

"So, spill!" Sam said as soon as we were in the kitchen. "I'll get the hot chocolate started as you change!"

Lilly leaned against the counter watching Sam with an amused, if not slightly annoyed, expression. Sam must've caught my nervous glances towards the door, for she softly said, "The guys are not going to be coming in if that's what you're worried about."

Shrugging, I peeled my shirt over my head. The material stuck to my skin as I tossed it on the counter. Gross. My jeans hadn't fared any better, dirt smearing across the cuffs.

I quickly peeled off my underwear and bra too. I hadn't wanted to get completely nude, not wanting them to see all of my scars, but it didn't seem worth keeping my disgusting undergarments on.

I had so many scars. They practically made a map on my body. How could anyone ever think that I was pretty like this? Each scar seemed to tell an entirely different story. I'd used to be so ashamed of my body, I would constantly hide my arms away behind long sleeves. Why should I be ashamed? I was becoming stronger, healing, and that deserved some recognition.

The kitchen door swung open, and I squealed, attempting to cover my body with my hands.

Fallon stood, arms folded over his chest. He didn't seem to notice my lack of dress as he glared at the girls.

"Are you almost done?" he asked. "What the hell are you guys doing?"

It was then that I noticed the hungry stares Lilly and Sam were giving my naked body. Fire flared in my cheeks when I finally understood the warning Fallon had given them.

Oh.

Oh.

"I'm sorry." Sam sounded honestly horrified. "I hadn't meant to stare. You just have a lot of scars."

I didn't bother to tell her that none of those scars were on my breasts, the place her eyes were currently locked on. I didn't have a problem with my nudity. I was confident enough in my sexuality to flaunt what God had given me. I knew that I was only attracted to men, but it didn't deter the ego boost I had at seeing the heat in the girls' gazes.

Fallon finally turned towards me, no doubt to reprimand me, when his eyes flared with a sudden heat. He caressed my body through look alone, eyes lingering on my peaked nipples a second longer than necessary, before landing back on my face. I couldn't ignore the desire in his eyes even if I wanted to. As if suddenly aware of what he was doing, his cheeks turned a bright red and he hurried from the kitchen.

Shifting uncomfortably, I quickly dressed in the pajamas Elena had picked out for me.

"If I would've known that you were attracted to girls, I wouldn't have stripped naked in front of you," I said. My body felt alight by the attention Fallon had given me. He'd stared at me as if I were the only girl in the world. As if it pained him to tear his eyes away. I should've been more self-conscious that he'd seen me naked, seen all of my curves and scars, but I trusted Fallon.

And he looked at me as if I was beautiful.

Sam and Lilly seemed equally as stunned by Fallon's reaction.

"I've never seen him stare at any girl like that," Sam said at last. Turning towards me, she said, "I'm truly sorry, Adelaide. You're just really pretty, and obviously I'm attracted to girls. I kind of thought you realized that with the whole sitting-on-lap thing." She looped her arm around Lilly's waist and planted a kiss on the other girl's cheek. "But please don't think I'm a crazy stalker or a lesbian freak."

She sounded honestly terrified that I was going to judge her, but I understood completely. I had, more than once, given the boys an appreciative once-over when they were shirtless. It was human nature to stare at the sex you were attracted to.

I smiled at the girls to show them that I wasn't mad. "I'm actually flattered." They still looked anxious, so I gave them a wink. "Apparently, I still got it." I gave a stupid hip shake, and Sam burst into laughter.

"There's always this stigma with us that we can't be friends with other girls because we want to jump their bones," Lilly said sullenly.

"But we want to be friends with you," Sam hurried to add. "The guys talk about you all the time. They're practically our brothers, and we were dying to meet the mysterious Adelaide."

"Though I don't know how you put up with them," Lilly added. "I can only deal with those boys in small doses." She shuddered delicately, and Sam whacked her girl-friend's butt. I had to admit that they were a cute couple. It made me slightly wistful to have something like that of my own. Maybe I could talk Calax into wearing matching couples' outfits...

"So, spill," Sam said, placing her elbows on the counter and her head in the nest they created. "How did you end up with Fallon's team?"

I thought it was strange how she phrased it—Fallon's team. Not friend group, not family, but team.

Did they go to the same school that the boys went to?

"I knew Declan when I was younger," I began hesitantly. "And I met Calax two or three years ago. The others I only met a few months ago. They're my friends." I chose to keep the details of our meetings to myself. Though they seemed nice, I didn't know these girls. I'd be the first to admit that I had trust issues.

"How long have you been dating Fallon?" Sam asked. She handed me a steaming cup of hot chocolate, covered with whipped cream and marshmallows. If I hadn't already forgiven her for staring, I would've then. She was officially my new best friend.

Taking the cup eagerly, I took a tentative sip. Damn. Too hot.

And then I thought about her question, and the hot chocolate flew from my mouth.

"Fallon?" I asked in disbelief. "No, you got it wrong. I'm not dating Fallon. He actually kind of hates me." Maybe hate was too strong a word. I'm pretty sure we'd progressed from hate to a strong dislike with the occasional need to strangle.

Both girls stared at me dubiously.

"I don't know about that," Lilly said at last. She exchanged a knowing look with Sam, and Sam giggled.

"Honey, the man looks as if he wants to eat you alive. Trust us when we say he doesn't hate you."

Now it was my turn to stare at them in disbelief. Sure, I may have been slightly dramatic when describing Fallon's feelings for me—or lack thereof—but I knew for a fact that Sam was pulling my leg. I definitely would've been able to tell if that was the case. And if he did want to eat me, it was probably because he was a cannibal who'd gotten sick of my talking.

"So what about you guys?" I asked, changing the subject. "How did you two meet?"

They began to tell me how they were put onto the same team, Elena's team, and were assigned a job in Japan, whatever that meant. While they were on a mission, they both fell in love with a French tourist there, as well as each other. Apparently, the duo was actually a trio.

"Lance is away right now," Sam told me. She exchanged a worried glance with Lilly. "We haven't seen him since everything went down."

"Where is he?" I asked. I could see how difficult it was for them to talk about. They obviously loved this man, this Lance, and it pained them to be separated from him, to not know what had become of him.

"Down in California," Sam supplied. "We're still trying to convince our team to go down there with us."

"They say it's too dangerous." Lilly rolled her eyes.

"But we're going there with or without their help."

I smiled at them. It had only been a few minutes, but I was already beginning to like Sam and Lilly.

"Please be careful," I said. "And I hope you find him."

The two girls were silent, each sipping their own cups of hot chocolate. Elena came in at one point, grabbed the other cups we'd made, and walked back out. I could hear the guys thanking her before the door closed.

"You know," Lilly began. "You don't seem too weirded out about us being in a three-way relationship."

Sam nodded her head in agreement. "Even our own team freaked the fuck out when they first found out. They told us it was wrong." She rolled her eyes. "As if I would listen to them when they were fucking four guys at the same time." Noting my wince, she added, "Sorry."

"Does it really not bother you?" Lilly asked.

I shrugged. "I'm not one to judge who you can and can't love. I mean, people fall in love all the time. Why can't you be in love with two people at the same time? It's not as if a widow is only ever going to love her deceased husband, though that may be the case. No, the most likely scenario is that she will fall in love again. Does that mean she doesn't love her old husband? Not at all. She would probably always love him. Her heart just expanded to make room for her new husband."

Sam and Lilly exchanged another one of those looks, the type of look you could only have when you innately understood your partner. It was Sam who spoke next, thin lips curving into a wicked smile.

"I would keep that in mind, Ms. Adelaide. Sometimes, it's important to follow your own advice."

I smiled back at her, though I honestly had no idea what she was talking about. That wasn't necessarily a surprise.

I tended to get confused a lot.

CHAPTER 17

ADDIE

"*Y*ou don't choose the cat. The cat chooses you. So you can't touch the cat unless—What the fuck did I just say?"

Still holding my hot chocolate, I raised an eyebrow at Tommy. The boy was sitting between Lacey and Elena, the former of which was attempting to pet Mof.

Tommy glared at her outstretched hand.

"You don't touch the cat unless you want to lose a finger. We clear?"

In that moment, it became clear to me that Tommy was kind of a psychopath. At least he was my psychopath. I couldn't imagine having that boy as an enemy.

"Don't be so dramatic, kid," Elena said haughtily. She was now wearing shorts and a tank top that displayed way too much cleavage than what was socially acceptable.

"I'm not a kid! I am thirteen fucking years old!" Tommy protested, staring down his nose at her. Elena blinked, gave him a once-over, and then blinked again.

"Bull crap."

"My sex appeal is, admittedly, years above my time," Tommy said seriously. "It's nothing to be intimidated by."

I snorted, drawing the attention of the other occupants of the room. Lilly and Sam slid around me, reclaiming their chair against the wall. I noted with some satisfaction that, minus Elena, Bikini, and one other girl, the other females had already retired for the night. I also noticed that all of my guys were still present.

Almost unwillingly, my eyes met Fallon's. They were dark in his face, lust dilating the pupils. Warmth pooled in my lower belly.

I truly wasn't embarrassed of my body. After I'd gotten over all of my scars, I decided to embrace what I had kept hidden for so many years. I'd grown accustomed to men looking at me with lust. After they saw my bare skin, that lust would transform into disgust. Horror. Pity.

The heat in Fallon's eyes, however, never faltered.

And it wasn't just lust in his expression. No, there was something else too. Something akin to reverence.

I didn't know if I would be able to handle Fallon's undivided attention. I imagined, like the man himself, it would be overwhelming.

Shaking my head, I refocused on the conversation.

Elena was handing out room assignments.

"Unfortunately, we don't have enough spare beds for all of you. Most will have to sleep on the couch or the floor." She smiled suddenly, pushing her ample breasts out. "Of course, I'm more than willing to share my bed."

"Me too," Bikini added. The third girl, whose name I couldn't recall, merely smiled sultrily.

"That won't be necessary," Fallon said sternly, and I ignored the pointed looks Lilly and Sam threw my way. I resisted the urge to roll my eyes. Him refusing Elena's offer was not evidence that he was "hungry for me." He might've just been stuffed. Maybe he would be hungry later for females. Maybe he would be—

Asher, beside me, gave me a long look, and I blushed when I realized I'd spoken aloud.

"Maybe for you," Elena said, unperturbed by Fallon's rejection. "You can't speak for the group."

Fallon sighed heavily. "It's their choice."

When nobody spoke up, Elena's face darkened.

Bikini just appeared crestfallen.

It was Thirdy who spoke, expression livid.

"So are you guys just going to take turns fucking your little slut?" She gave me a scathing look.

"Don't talk about her like that," Ryder snapped.

At the same time, Asher said, "That's horrible to say."

Even Fallon looked as if he was about to blow a nut.

But it was Elena that surprised me the most.

"Don't be a bitch," she snapped, turning towards her friend. Thirdy opened her mouth, closed it, and then opened it again. "Ignore her," Elena said to me.

We all gaped at her.

Tommy, my sweet friend, absently placed Mof in Elena's lap.

"You've earned the right to hold the cat."

The next few minutes were awkward. I didn't know what to say or how to act. Elena, who hated me with a passion, had defended me? Had hell frozen over? Had she turned into a Rager?

Or was she someone that I could potentially become friends with?

I'd never had a girlfriend before. It had always been an elusive fantasy, so close but just out of reach. For the longest time, I hadn't even considered it a possibility. Maybe I could become friends with Elena. Maybe with Lilly and Sam. Maybe with...

My brother's face flashed through my mind, almost as intense as the thunder rumbling outside. The sheer strength of it made me topple over my own two feet.

How could I possibly be thinking of friends when my brother was in danger? He could be dead.

Hysteria bubbled inside of me. The change was so sudden, so dramatic, that I keeled over.

The pain. There was so much pain.

My brother had been at the forefront of my mind for so long. Was it wrong for me to crave a bit of normality? Did he have to be the main character of every one of my thoughts?

Did it make me horrible if, for only a second, I forgot about him?

I was dimly aware of someone's hands rubbing my back. Voices, sounding as if they were coming through a funnel, reached my ears.

Oh god. I couldn't breathe. I couldn't think.

"Princess, breathe for me. You're okay. You're fine. You're having a panic attack." The soothing voice was familiar. Where had I heard him before?

"Keep breathing. Just like that. Good."

Ronan.

And it was Asher patting my back. I recognized his spicy scent.

Slowly and surely, I began to get my bearings.

One of my therapists had told me to focus on my surroundings if I had a panic attack. I decided to do that now.

I was in a house, Elena's house. I was sitting on a couch. The air was pungent with the smell of chocolate. My hands were warm.

And I was alive.

I repeated that last sentence numerous times. It seemed important to remember that. While these attacks weren't frequent, they were debilitating. I had to remember that I was stronger than them.

I had to remember that I was alive.

Taking a staggered breath, I gave Ronan's hands a reassuring squeeze.

"I'm okay," I said gently. Then louder, "I'm okay."

Somebody handed me a glass of water, and I glanced up, shocked, to see the manicured hand belonging to Elena.

"What was that?" Fallon crossed his big arms over his chest. His expression was impassive as always, but I saw the slightest tightening of his eyes.

"A panic attack," I said. "But I'm fine now."

They still didn't look as if they believed me, so I offered another timid smile.

"Seriously. I promise."

"The girl says she's fine!" said Sam, clapping her hands together. "You guys all need to stop crowding her."

Cue seven penetrating glares in her direction.

"That's it," Calax said suddenly, jumping to his feet. He looked enormous in the dainty living room, his body made entirely of muscles and skin. He pushed through the guys and extended a hand towards me.

I eyed it warily.

"Did you finally decide to murder me?" I asked. "Because I promise I'm not a good victim. And I don't taste good either. I'm too skinny and white. Ryder would probably taste better, you know, with the dark meat."

"Racist," Ryder mumbled. I stuck my tongue out at him.

Calax rolled his eyes. "So dramatic." Without waiting for me to retort, he grabbed my hand and tenderly pulled me to my feet. I would've never expected Calax to be as gentle as he was. He always touched me as if I were fine silk he longed to purchase.

"What are we doing?" I asked. Now that my initial panic had ebbed, I felt slightly embarrassed by my earlier outburst.

Calax's smile was almost devious. Well, as much as my giant could be.

"We're having a date."

Tommy gave him a long look.

"I don't know how comfortable I feel about that," he said at last. "What time will you have her home? I need a location and your mother's name."

Ryder furrowed his brows. "You're a strange little man."

"Bite me, Ryley."

"Ryley?" Ryder appeared even more confused, and I had to turn my face away to hide my brewing laughter.

"Ry. Ryley. Same thing." Tommy waved his hand dismissively, and Ryder frowned.

"My name's not Ryley. It's Ryder."

Now it was Tommy's turn to look bemused.

"That's not what Addie told me."

The laughter I tried to keep silent bubbled out.

Fallon folded his arms over his chest, expression amused.

"What exactly did she tell you our names were?"

"Ryley, Callie, Ashley, Tammy, Rowena, Destiny, and Felicia." He tilted his head to the side thoughtfully. "I mean, I wasn't going to judge you or anything. You be you, man."

The six men turned to me, expressions murderous. With a squeal, I ran from the room, laughing my ass off.

∼

My first kiss had been with Calax.

I had been touched before—violated, some would say—but I'd never been kissed.

I remember that night vividly. The humid, scorching air, despite the absence of sun, a multitude of stars breaking up the monotony of darkness, the singing of crickets.

My parents had been furious with me that day. No reason, really, besides the fact that I existed.

They hadn't noticed the garden, and if they did, they hadn't cared. I realized that my reaction to Calax may have been a tad overdramatic, but he'd hurt me.

That girl, that beautiful girl with ebony skin and luscious hair, had introduced herself as his girlfriend. I hadn't realized until that moment the extent of my feelings for the grouchy man. Her words were a stab to my heart.

So I had reacted, as I always did when faced with immense stress, and I'd watched him drift away from me. He didn't know that I'd remained after our fight, hoping to apologize. He didn't know I'd seen him leaving only to return with two females.

I wouldn't ever tell him that.

Surprising even myself, I stared up at the apartment complex. Why had I come here?

I didn't have the answer. Even if I did, I didn't want to look at it too closely.

Resisting the urge to run up to Calax's room, I changed direction and walked down to the pond.

The moonlight reflected off the tranquil water, yellow combining with pale silver. It was a beautiful sight, but I couldn't focus on it.

I couldn't focus on anything besides the pain in my stomach from where my dad had hit me and the knowledge that, somehow, it was my fault. I could come up with no other reason why my parents would continually torture me. Surely, I did something wrong.

"Addie?" a surprised voice said, startling me, and I spun around on the bench. Despite the darkness obscuring his features, I would recognize his broad silhouette anywhere.

"Hey, Callie," I said absently. I turned back towards the water, watching a few flowers sway over the surface.

"What are you doing here?" he asked gruffly. I heard rather than saw him take a seat beside me on the wooden bench.

"Thinking," I answered. I didn't really know how to elaborate. There were some things that I couldn't tell him. How does one say that she's consistently getting beaten by the very people who are supposed to love her? How would he even respond to that revelation?

We were silent for a few moments, each lost in our own thoughts. I didn't know what he was thinking, but the moonlight illuminated an almost contemplative expression on his face.

"I fixed it," he said at last. His voice was uncharacteristically quiet.

"Fixed what?" I still didn't turn to look at him, and he didn't turn to look at me either.

"The garden. I fixed it."

At that, I whipped my head towards him.

"Why would you do that?" I asked. Why would he have broken it, only to fix it again later? The only solution I could come up with was that he was psycho...or that girl had been lying.

"I stayed up all night." He let out a heavy sigh. "I made it bigger than before, added a few more flowers and a couple of pumpkins."

I repeated myself. "Why would you do that?"

In answer, he leaned forward and kissed me. It was my first kiss, and tiny pinpricks of heat raced up and down my spine. His lips were soft over mine.

But I didn't want soft. Not then. I was consumed by this need to feel loved and cherished instead of just wanted. Trust me. There was a difference.

My tongue touched his lips, demanding entrance, and he easily complied. His gentle kisses turned into ones that emitted a feral hunger. He kissed me like he wanted to devour me. He kissed me like he would never kiss another girl again.

His hand twisted in my hair on the back of my neck, pulling my head up to reveal my neck.

Oops. Apparently, I needed to breathe.

My panting was embarrassingly loud. Calax didn't take his lips away from my skin, however, as I struggled to control my erratic breathing. They merely traveled to my neck to kiss a line to my collarbone. He alternated between nips, sucks, and a soothing flick of his tongue.

Yes. More. More.

His hand reached forward, almost hesitantly, and hovered over my breast. I pushed myself into his waiting hand, giving him permission.

I'd been touched there before, but never like that. Never reverently.

His hand cupped my breast through my shirt, and I groaned, eagerly gripping his face to bring his lips back to mine.

It was then that I realized something that should've been blatantly obvious. I felt too much for him.

I felt too deeply.

For my entire life, I was told how dangerous it was to have feelings and to have those feelings reciprocated. My mind flashed to Ducky.

I couldn't lose another person I cared about.

So I pulled away from him, still breathing heavily, and ran towards my car.

As I was driving home, tears dripping from my eyes, I decided that if I were to feel any emotion towards Calax, it would be hate. Hate was easier to deal with, easier to understand.

And I emptied myself of that damning emotion. It was safer that way.

I STARED at my face in the mirror in Sam's bathroom.

Makeup cluttered the countertop, courtesy of Sam and Lilly. I eyed the foundation with distaste.

To be honest, I wasn't overly familiar with makeup or anything remotely connected to "prettying myself up."

But I could do it. That blush? I would make it my bitch.

Pinching my cheeks, I applied the bare minimum to my face, excluding any and all eye makeup. I didn't feel comfortable using any of the girls'.

Once I was satisfied that I looked semi presentable, I walked back into the adjoining bedroom. Sam and Lilly were lying on the bed, talking, but they both looked up when I entered.

"Well..." Sam trailed off, tilting her head to the side as she eyed my half-hearted attempt at makeup.

"It could be worse," Lilly finished.

I snorted but didn't respond.

I'd never been on a date before. Never been asked, though I wasn't sure I would've said yes to anyone besides Calax.

I appreciated his attempt to divert my attention from Nik. It would do me no good to wallow in self-pity, especially when I wasn't physically capable of leaving the house to search for him at that moment. The storm still ravaging the petite house was brutal.

And another part of me felt giddy at the thought of going on a date. With Calax.

Or with any of the boys, if I was being completely honest with myself.

"You're probably too tall to fit into my clothes," Sam was saying. She turned towards Lilly. "Do you still have that cute black dress from last year? That would probably fit her."

"Wait. Wait. Wait. Hold up. A dress?"

I'd worn dresses, of course, but I much preferred the pajama combination I had on now, courtesy of Elena. Comfort over beauty or however that saying went.

"You're going on a date," Sam said, rolling her eyes in what appeared to be exasperation. "You have to dress like it."

"Our date is consisting of a dirty garage and canned food," I pointed out. "Not exactly romantic."

Lilly smirked. "The location doesn't matter. What matters is who you're with." Her grin widened when I blushed.

Desperate to change the subject from my love life, I blurted, "So you guys like vaginas?"

What. The. Fuck.

If I thought Lilly and Sam were going to be offended, I was sorely mistaken. They both erupted into uproarious laughter.

"Shit," I muttered, searching my scrambled brain for something more appropriate to say. Because, really, when was talking about vaginas ever appropriate? Ronan still reprimanded me to this day for an earlier incident involving my speech concerning female body parts. Long story.

"So you guys all live together?" I decided on. The house was small, only slightly larger than Fallon's own granny home. I'd assumed that most of the girls would have to share a room, but being able to have guest bedrooms? I wondered if there was a wardrobe to Narnia or something that I wasn't aware of.

Sam, still snickering, said, "Lots of vaginas in this house."

Lilly fell off the bed in peals of laughter.

"Most of us prefer to share a room," Sam said once she'd gotten her own laughter under control. "It helps encourage us to remain communicative with the team instead of receding into our shells."

"Believe it or not," Lilly added, "I share a room with Lacey, not Sam."

"And I share with Missy," Sam said.

"Again, it's to encourage family bonds, not just romantic ones."

I supposed that made sense, though I was still confused over this ominous "team" mentioned so often. I'd have to drill the boys for information at a later date.

Conversation turned from them to me, much to my chagrin. They questioned me on my relationship with each of the guys. A gasp escaped Sam's lips when I told her that I was only dating Calax, my nemesis who wasn't really my nemesis.

"Not the others?" she asked, brushing back my hair. She'd insisted on styling it, despite my protests that my hair was fine down. Apparently, girls did other girls' hair. Or something. I still struggled with the whole friendship concept. I mean, Ryder had bitched up a storm when I painted his toenails, so how was I supposed to know what was acceptable and what wasn't?

"I doubt that," Lilly added from where she was sprawled on Sam's bed. "This was the first time that they refused to take any of the girls to bed. They didn't even consider it. And you don't see them look at you when you're not paying attention."

I rolled my eyes at their dramatics, though my heart stuttered unhappily at the thought of them taking another girl to bed. As before, I told myself that my possessive and jealous response was unfounded. They would've been disgusted if they heard my thoughts.

I knew that I felt strongly for Calax, but the rest of them?

Stop. Thinking.

Lilly left the room once to grab me a black dress. It hugged my upper curves deliciously, swooping out at the bottom to give my ass breathing room.

It was an instant win in my book. Anything that allowed the crack to fly free was a miracle.

Sam handed me back my undergarments, now washed, and I tried not to grimace in disappointment. So what if my nipples showed? They could make a surprisingly good weapon against any Ragers.

Deciding against the bra, I grudgingly put on the underwear. They felt like an ass prison.

Seriously, I might never wear underwear again now that I knew how freeing it was to have the cheeks hang out.

"Normally I like your thoughts, but today, I'm just confused as hell," Ryder stood in the doorway, face reflective as he considered me.

Lilly and Sam had long since left, and I'd found myself surveying my reflection in the bathroom mirror.

"I like going commando," I said, before realizing that those words probably shouldn't have left my mouth. I was a verbal freight train at times, derailed and barreling towards a heavily populated city. Once I had a thought, you couldn't stop me.

I met Ryder's smoldering stare in the mirror. He'd somehow snuck up behind me, his body warming mine, even with the distance between us.

"You look really beautiful." His words sounded choked. "Calax is a lucky man."

Before I could question his eccentric behavior, he hurried from the room. My eyebrows touched my hairline, betraying my confusion.

Note to self—after date, confront Ryder about his strange behavior.

And check in with Tommy. I had a feeling if I was even a second late past the "curfew," he would come charging into the garage with a shotgun.

CHAPTER 18

ADDIE

The garage was barely recognizable.

Before, it had been a collection of dust and debris, surprisingly empty of any vehicles. Instead of cars, the entire expanse had been cluttered with box upon box.

Now, the gray walls were adorned with twinkling lights. A thick blanket was laid out, surrounded by a collection of pillows. Candles were spaced evenly along the perimeter of the room.

Calax sat in the center of the blanket, an anxious expression on his face and a picnic basket before him.

Tears sprang to my eyes, and I tried to stomp down the emotions threatening to leak out.

"Do you like it?" Calax asked. He clasped his hands together, unclasped them, and then put them behind his back. His timidness was adorable.

"It's perfect," I breathed, slightly awed. And it was. It was everything I had ever dreamed of. The girls were right—it didn't matter where I was, as long as I was with someone I cared about.

Someone I, dare I say, loved?

The strength of my feelings dropped me to my knees on the pillow. Before I realized what I was doing, I leaned forward and kissed him. It was a light kiss, the barest brush of lips, but I felt him tremble beneath my touch as if I were straddling him naked. The feeling was empowering.

"Thank you," I murmured against his lips. I felt, rather than saw, his lips turn upwards.

"I would do anything for you, you know that, right?"

I was going to tell him. I was going to tell him that I would do anything for him as well because I loved him. The realization didn't come as a surprise. I knew it from the very first kiss. He was mine, and I was his. The rest of the world faded away when he was with me.

But the words couldn't leave my lips. It wasn't just because said lips were occupied, though they were, but more so a fear that held me back. Three words. Eight letters.

Why couldn't I say it?

"I would do anything for you as well," I settled on, like the coward I was.

Sitting backwards, I watched Calax unpack the picnic basket. A can of peaches, already opened. Peanut butter and jelly sandwiches. Two cupcakes with vibrant red frosting.

Calax's cheeks tinted pink as he surveyed the food. His hand absently rubbed at the back of his neck.

"I know it's not the greatest spread…"

I shut him up with a quick kiss.

"I love it." *And I love you.*

We were silent as we ate, though it was not uncomfortable. He placed his muscular arm behind my back, and I leaned against it as I stuffed my face. I was famished.

Outside, lightning streaked against the windows, and rain continued to plunder the vaulted roof.

Inside, we were in our own peaceful cocoon. Safe.

Calax told me stories about his childhood, skimming over the bad and focusing on the good. He told me how he joined the school, how he befriended the guys, and the moment he fell in love…with his apartment.

At my pressing, he told me more about his parents. His dad had been a drunk and emotionally abusive, but not physically, and his mother had left them when he was a baby. He hadn't heard from her in years. While his dad wasn't necessarily a horrible parent, he was often neglectful of his son and used harsh words as a form of punishment.

Calax told me that he had felt like an inept failure when he'd lived under his father's roof.

He explained how he decided to get emancipated, and his father had eagerly agreed, relieved to rid himself of his only child. His team helped him throughout the process.

And then he mentioned the first day he met me.

"I loved you from the second I saw you," he said wistfully. He smiled down at me, and I rolled my eyes up at him. We were currently leaning against a stack of pillows, my head on his chest and his fingers absently tracing an invisible pattern on my bare arm.

"No you didn't," I said with a scoff.

"You don't believe in love at first sight?"

"Of course not. It's infatuation and lust, not love."

Calax smirked. "What about Romeo and Juliet? I'm pretty sure that they were a love-at-first-sight type of couple."

"And look how well they turned out."

Calax was silent for a moment, absorbing my words. Finally, he nodded slowly.

"You're right. I think the first time I realized I loved you was when you stood up to me. I was a whole foot taller than you, and you still made me cower in terror."

I smiled at first at the memory, but that smile immediately morphed into a frown.

"You never did tell me why you destroyed my garden in the first place."

I felt him stiffen underneath me, his hand stilling on my skin.

"I never told you?" he asked in disbelief. My frown deepened.

"Never told me what?"

"I didn't destroy your garden. That girl, Emerald, did."

I considered his answer.

"Well, why did you let me yell at you?" I asked, embarrassed. I turned my face so my flaming cheeks were hidden by his chest. "Why didn't you just tell me the truth? Why did you fix it for me?"

His hand resumed its gentle caress.

"I already told you. I did it because I loved you."

And damn it if my heart didn't grow even more. I loved this man. I loved this man with my entire being.

"Diamond," I said at last.

"Huh?"

"The girl's name was Diamond, not Emerald."

He chuckled, the sound reverberating through my body. It was the most glorious form of music. His lips moved to my ear, and I felt his teeth nibble on the sensitive lobe. I shivered in delight.

"I don't like redheads," he told me.

"She had black hair."

"She did?" He sounded honestly confused, and I smiled against his chest.

"How do you not remember the girl you used to date? Are we that forgettable to you?" Though I tried to sound teasing, my voice betrayed my hidden insecurities. How long would it be before Calax grew tired of me? Before he decided that I was too damaged to deserve his love? He had a new girl every day. What made me so special?

Seeming to pick up on my fears, his arms tightened around me. His lips parted on the top of my head.

"*She's* that forgettable to me. You? You're everything."

Before I could answer, the lights flickered once before completely plunging the house into darkness.

～

Using one of the candles, Calax guided us back into the house. I heard harsh whispers coming from the kitchen. Though most of the house were already asleep, the few that were awake had convened around the table.

"What happened?" Calax asked as soon as we entered the room. He placed his candle on the table, illuminating the faces around us.

Ryder and Fallon were sitting on one side, identical scowls on their faces. Asher was leaning against the marble countertop.

Tam, Declan, and Ronan must've already gone to sleep. An irrational part of me hoped that they went to bed alone.

Tommy also was noticeably absent, and for that, I was grateful. After his emotional breakdown, the boy needed his beauty sleep.

And I may or may not have missed the "curfew" he'd tried to enact. I would not put it past him to shoot Calax in the nutsack for keeping me out late.

"The generator ran out of batteries," Elena answered. She was sitting on the opposite side of the table, golden flames accentuating the bags under her eyes.

"Well, shit," Ryder said dryly. "There goes my hot shower."

"Addie?" Asher said calmly. In response, I walked towards Ryder and hit him on the back of the head.

"Ow," he whined dramatically. "So abusive."

Snorting, I said, "You know you love me."

Even in the darkness, I saw the heat in his eyes at my words.

What the hell was that all about? I was ninety percent positive that I hadn't said something with a sexual innuendo.

"So, do you guys need a new battery?" Fallon asked Elena. Elena shook her head slowly, answering Fallon's question despite her attention fixated on me and Ryder.

"We're probably going to leave this house soon. Head west."

"Is that safe?" Asher asked, concerned. I myself felt slightly anxious at her proclamation. We hadn't been able to get into contact with anyone, and we weren't able to see what was happening outside of where we traveled. The phone lines were down, the internet was down, and the television showed nothing but static. The disconnection felt like a repeated kick to the gut. I didn't like feeling so alone, so disassociated. Anything could be happening.

Elena shrugged, finally turning her attention away from me and Ryder to face Asher.

"Lilly and Sam are planning on going, regardless of whether we come with them or not. We're a team. We could never leave them alone."

The boys nodded as if that answer was completely acceptable. I supposed, to them, it was.

"Why are they even heading west?" Calax asked. "Do they have family out there or something?"

"Lance," I answered for Elena. "Their boyfriend lives out there."

"And they love him." Elena's voice took on an odd quality. "You would go anywhere for someone you love. But, of course, you guys already know this." She gave Calax, Ryder, Fallon, and Asher a pointed look. "You would even go across the country."

Asher shifted uncomfortably, though I didn't fully understand what Elena was attempting to imply.

"Well, we'll be out of your hair by tomorrow at the latest," Fallon said, changing the subject briskly.

"To go to Atlanta?" she questioned, amused.

Fallon gave her a penetrating glare.

"Yes."

Her smirk grew as Fallon's scowl deepened. I glanced back and forth between the two of them, unsure what had caused their intense standoff.

"Well…" I drawled, stretching my arms. "I'm going to head to bed. I'm tired."

Fallon finally broke his staring contest with Elena to address me. The annoying part of me was tempted to ask who'd won, but I figured that I wanted to keep all my limbs intact, thank you very much.

"We saved you a guest bedroom upstairs. Third door on the right."

"You didn't need to do that. I could sleep on the couch, easily. You're giants, and I'm a little pixie creature."

Fallon gave me a cold stare. "Don't argue with me, Adelaide."

Glaring right back, I huffed and grabbed the candle from the table.

I really didn't think it was practical to give me a bed. All of the guys were bigger than me, and I would've been perfectly comfortable on the sofa or floor. Despite this, I knew arguing with Fallon was futile, especially when he had his scary face on.

You didn't mess with Fallon when he's wearing his scary face.

"I'll come with you," Ryder broke in, jumping to his feet. At his announcement, Calax's head whipped in our direction. Something undefinable fluttered across his hard features.

It almost looked like fear.

What did Calax have to be afraid of?

"You don't have to leave on my account," I said with a sigh. I was feeling more and more like a little girl whenever they babied me. What would be next? Would I be able to piss without one of them standing guard?

I really had to have a talk with them about the whole macho-male-alpha-caveman thing they had going on.

"I was going to go to bed anyway," he answered. I eyed him suspiciously but eventually nodded when I saw only sincerity in his expression.

We were leaving the kitchen, heading towards the living room, when I heard Elena question Calax about the remainder of the candles we'd used on our date.

"I swear to Satan if you burn my house down, I will end you."

I decided I liked Elena even more.

As we walked through the living room, I instinctively gripped Ryder's arm. The last thing I wanted was to face-plant into a chair because I lost my footing. At least by gripping him, I could throw him down first so he would catch my fall.

Yeah. Totally stellar logic.

"Did you speak to Ronan yet?" I pressed as we reached a fork in the hallway. I knew one direction would lead towards the bedrooms while the other would bring us to the bathroom and study. Ryder paused there, holding the candle away as he turned to stare at me.

"Ronan?" he asked, blinking rapidly. He looked confused, but I could clearly see beneath his apathetic front. Ryder had a tell—whenever he was anxious, he would tap out a song on his thigh. The song was always different, though lately, the pattern seemed to be similar. I wondered if he even realized he was doing it.

I watched his fingers pound erratically against his jeans as he played a song only he could hear.

"He's worried about you," I explained. My hand itched to take his. I didn't like seeing him distressed. It made me want to do something, want to say something, to take his pain away.

"Why would he be worried?" he questioned.

Tap. Tap, tap. Tap.

"Because you're his brother, and he loves you."

His hand stilled against his jeans before turning into a claw and bunching up the fabric. It was then that I did reach for him, smoothing out his fingers and tracing gentle circles on his palm. Ryder needed gentleness. I didn't know how I came to that particular conclusion, only that I knew it was true. He could hide his pain all he wanted behind his bad boy, rock star persona, but I knew the truth.

Ryder craved love. It was for this reason that he indulged himself in a different girl every night. He craved the power, the control, the break in reality, if only for a moment.

"You should talk to your brother," I continued softly, tilting my head up to meet his smoldering golden eyes.

"Yes." He glanced down at me, and the same undefinable expression I'd seen earlier flickered over his face. My heart began beating rapidly inside my chest.

Something was happening between us, something I didn't entirely understand. I knew that I loved Calax. I loved him with a ferociousness that surprised even me, but my heart was big.

I thought about what Sam and Lilly had talked about in the kitchen.

About how the heart could expand to make room for more people. The love you felt for others didn't diminish. No, the love was able to expand.

I didn't know what to do. I didn't know how I felt. I was confused and frightened and terrified I was going to do something wrong.

I wanted Ryder to kiss me.

I wanted Calax to kiss me.

Hell, I think I even wanted Fallon and the others to kiss me.

Briefly, I wondered if that was how my mom felt when she surrounded herself with adoring men. The last thing I wanted to do was turn out like her.

That thought immediately dissipated in a storm of fury. I wasn't like her. She'd never loved anyone, and I loved everyone. Maybe love wasn't the correct word, yet, but I knew that I felt strongly for every one of the guys. I'd told myself I never wanted to fall in love. I did everything in my power to protect my heart, since it had bled enough.

But now?

Now the traitorous bastard was eagerly snatching up boys like a kid in a candy store.

"Ohh, look! I want that one! And that one! And why not try a little taste of this one over here?"

Ryder's eyes suddenly glazed over, dark lashes feathering on his even darker cheekbones. Before I could respond, he slumped forward and fell to the ground. I tried to catch him, staggering under his muscular weight, but my arms were leaden.

I was barely aware that there was a figure before me. A figure in a black hoodie holding a metal pan.

The pan connected with the side of my head, and I, too, descended into darkness.

CHAPTER 19

*M*other and Father stared down their noses at me. I hated when they wore that particular expression—so haughty, so imperious. I wanted to yell at them, to tell them that they weren't better than me, no matter how much they believed otherwise.

As usual, the words got stuck in my throat.

Nikolai sat at the table beside me, absently doodling on a piece of paper. His familiar headphones were around his neck, but his eyes were entirely focused on his art. The world could've fallen into shambles around him, and he wouldn't have noticed.

He wouldn't have cared.

DOD opened his mouth, and I waited impatiently for him to berate me. It wasn't uncommon for him to point out my flaws and failures. I could never be good enough in his eyes.

Did I even want to be?

Instead, the scowl softened on his face, transforming into something that resembled a smile.

A smile? I'd never seen my father smile before in his life. He had three expressions—a frown, a sneer, and a grimace, as if he'd eaten something disgusting. Never a smile.

At least never directed at me.

"Addie," he said softly, reaching across the table to place his calloused hands on mine. I couldn't remember the last time my father had touched me, but I definitely knew these hands didn't belong to him. He'd never worked a day in his life. "Your mother and I would like to say how proud we are of you."

Tears sprang to my mother's large eyes as she watched me. Smiling shakily through the tears, she nodded.

"We love you so much, darling."

I resisted the urge to flinch and pull away. I'd never heard those words leave my parents' mouths before. Love. Proud. Those were a foreign language to me.

"Are you feeling okay?" I asked, finally gaining the nerve to release my hand from my father's grip.

Their smiles were brilliant. It made them look younger, almost. Happier. Beautiful. They were the faces I would've seen if life hadn't chipped away at their innocence. It occurred to me that this was what my parents would've been like if we'd stayed in our tiny, suburban home, away from the damning influences that had destroyed us all. Monsters weren't made. They were created.

"Mom. Dad." I didn't know what to say to them. Words failed me at that moment. Despite knowing that this wouldn't last, I wanted to cherish the precious moments I was given.

They smiled at me, and then directed their affectionate smiles at my brother. Nik didn't look up from his painting, but his ears tinted red at their undivided attention. He, too, had only ever wanted to be loved by them.

The feeling of love was intense, intermingling with wistfulness. I'd never realized what I had been missing. Love and acceptance, being the main ones.

The images in front of me blurred. It was as if I was looking into a funhouse mirror, their faces distorted and hazy. I glanced from them to Nik, alarmed, but my little brother's face was surprisingly tranquil as he watched me. By the time I looked back at my parents, they were gone, replaced with a familiar group of individuals.

The boys stared back at me, eyes bright with love.

"Princess, why do you have tears in your eyes?" Ronan asked. His green hair was tousled, and his unicorn tattoo was visible over the neckline of his shirt.

"These are happy tears," I said, choked.

Fallon tilted his head at me.

"Why are you happy?"

"Because I'm loved."

Calax smiled warmly. "Yes you are, baby."

"You have always been loved, sweetheart," Asher added. "You just haven't realized it."

"You're loved even more now, Kitten."

Declan made a familiar gesture that I recognized instantly.

"I love you."

Tears welled in my eyes.

"All of you?" I asked, barely able to believe it.

"Of course," Tam said, cheeks flaming. He met my eyes, looked down, and immediately began counting the cracks on the table.

A part of me wanted to believe them, the part of me that had been denied love for years. Another part of me realized how irrational it was to think that these perfect men would ever feel anything for me besides friendship.

My brain was going haywire as the fantasy took hold.

I wanted to feel loved. I wanted to feel loved and love another in return.

Or others. I didn't think I was physically capable of only loving one person. My heart was eager, and it latched on to every available person like an annoying parasite.

Fallon's face suddenly darkened, a cloud moving in front of the sun.

"Why are you acting like such a whore?" he snapped.

I blinked, stunned by his sudden outburst.

"What?" I whispered.

"Seriously, are you trying to lead us all on?" Ronan sneered. And then he added, in a voice that held more contempt than kindness, "Princess."

"She's a bitch," Declan signed dismissively. He turned towards the others. *"We should just ignore her."*

"I can't believe I kissed that whorish mouth." Calax gave me a look akin to disgust. "How many others has she kissed with it?"

"A lot, apparently," Asher said. My kind boy sounded furious. "You all heard the rumors about Adelaide. A new man every night."

The tears, once brought out by happiness but now by a smothering depression, cascaded down my cheeks. I brushed them away, ashamed by my weakness.

"You know I didn't have a choice," I said. "They didn't take no for an answer."

Tam abruptly stood from his seat, eyes blistering as they met mine.

"You must've done something wrong. What were you wearing?"

"Huh?"

I couldn't believe what I was hearing. The tears were falling faster now, a physical representation of my heartache. My self-hatred.

"I would just end it if I were you," said Fallon.

"End it," echoed Calax. My love. My rock.

My enemy.

"She's too much of a pussy," Ryder said.

A razor blade materialized in front of me. I glanced up from the keen weapon towards the boys who'd quickly become my entire world. Their stares were unrelenting as they met my eyes.

Fallon, the stoic leader, nodded towards the blade.

"Use it."

The pain threatened to consume me. I was drowning in it.

Hand trembling, I grabbed the razor and held it up to my wrists. The guys watched me impassively.

And then I began to cut.

∼

TAMSON

Her hand was tentative as it touched my arm, fingers tracing the corded muscles of my bicep.

I groaned in my sleep, rolling over to face her more fully.

The hand was soon replaced by her lips, and the erotic touch nearly made me come undone.

My brain was fuzzy, still fighting the remains of sleep, but my body was alert. Wanting.

Wanting her.

I turned into her expectant lips, heart hammering.

How many times had I imagined kissing her? Touching her? I'd thought it was nothing more than fantasy.

"Addie," I groaned against her mouth.

"Addie?" a strident voice demanded, abruptly pulling away from me. The belligerent sound of it cleansed the last tendrils of sleep that clung to me.

That voice…

It wasn't Adelaide's.

Popping my eyelids open, I turned to stare at the figure leaning over me on the bed. It was dark, surprisingly so, considering the fact I'd left the bedside lamp on, but the moonlight and flashes of lightning allowed me to see her asymmetrical face and blonde hair.

Lacey.

Scrambling backwards with revulsion, I pinned her with an annoyed glare.

"What are you doing in my room?" I asked darkly.

It was then that I noticed what she was wearing. Actually, what she wasn't wearing would be a better description.

Absolutely nothing.

Her breasts bounced as she crawled towards me, and before, I might've thought she was attractive.

Now? I just felt disgust.

I'd be the first to admit that I used to have a relationship with Lacey, as did the rest of my brothers. She was pretty and never seemed to want a commitment from us.

The perfect girl.

Any other day, I would've eagerly claimed her body. I may have been what some considered shy, but in the bedroom, I became a completely different person.

"Come on, Tammy," Lacey purred, and I blanched at the nickname. I supposed she thought it was seductive to use Adelaide's nickname for me, but it only proceeded to make me furious.

"Don't call me that," I snapped. Her hand moved down my thigh, still covered by the blanket, and I hit it away. "And don't touch me."

"What the hell, Tam?" Lacey asked, voice brimming with disbelief. And then she began to laugh. It was a laugh that made me involuntarily flinch. "It's because of that girl, isn't it?" When I didn't answer, she took my silence as confirmation. "Holy shit! You have feelings for her, don't you?"

I began to blush. I hoped she wasn't able to see my flaming face in the darkness. My fingers twitched against my thigh, and my eyes automatically wandered to the bricks surrounding the windowsill. It was all I could see in the darkness.

One brick.

Two bricks.

Three bricks.

"Don't be such a pussy," Lacey sneered, grabbing my chin roughly to turn my face back towards her. I felt the familiar claws of panic begin to take hold. I had to—no, I needed to finish counting the bricks. "She would never look twice at you. You're a fucking freak. You're good for nothing but a quick fuck. It's the only thing you're good at."

Her free hand trailed up her stomach, towards her breast, and she pinched her nipple.

Yet all I could see were the bricks out of my peripheral vision.

One brick.

Two bricks.

Three bricks.

Four bricks.

"You're such a fucking cunt," Lacey sneered. Her hand still fondled her own breasts as if she thought that might turn me on. Before, it probably would've. It was only recently that I'd begun to notice someone's true beauty.

And I knew she was right—Addie would never feel the way for me that I felt for her, and I would never get in the way of Calax's happiness. He'd loved her longer than I had.

But I knew what I wanted now. I knew my standards. I wanted somebody like her in my life. Not a quick fuck. Not a string of girls every night.

From downstairs, somebody began to shout, the noise startling enough for Lacey to drop her persistent, wandering fingers from my chin.

It wasn't a scream, necessarily, but more like a battle cry.

With a blistering speed, I jumped out of bed, threw a shirt on, and headed down the stairs. Lacey followed behind me, still as naked as the day she was born.

I hoped Addie wouldn't see her and assume the worst.

The doors around me opened, and the guys came hurrying out. The girls followed behind from their own rooms, their paces decidedly slower.

Lacey thrust her breasts out into Ronan's face, the man closest to her, but he barely paid her any mind.

We entered the kitchen where Elena was standing, sopping wet. Her eyes were wild, flickering from face to face without sticking on any one person.

"Tell us what happened, Elena," Fallon was saying. His arms were crossed, but he didn't look concerned. It was apparent that she hadn't said anything yet.

"I was heading to bed," Elena said. "I saw Ryder and Addie talking in the living room."

I exchanged a look with Asher. That wasn't surprising, but from Elena's petrified expression, that wasn't all she saw.

I tampered down my jealousy at the thought of what they could've been doing besides talking. I had no right to be jealous.

Turning my attention towards the fridge, I decided to count the magnets. It calmed me.

"I headed to the bathroom for a second, the one near the kitchen."

Again, I had no idea where she was going with this.

From the other boys' irritated expressions, I concluded they felt the same.

Elena began to cry in earnest now.

"I followed the car as long as I could. I promise you. I got the license plate, but… I'm so sorry. I couldn't stop them."

"What the hell are you talking about?" Calax exploded, his already thin patience splintering. Elena looked up, sniffling, and met his gaze unflinchingly.

"I only saw the end. But it's Addie and Ryder."

"What about them?" Fallon asked, stiffening. Elena rubbed at her eyes once again.

"Somebody took them."

CHAPTER 20

ADDIE

I woke up groggily, barely able to remember where I was, let alone what my name was.

I'd been at…Elena's house. Yes, I briefly recalled the cute manor. The garage had been lit up with flickering lights. Calax had kissed me so tenderly, so reverently.

And then what happened?

The power had gone out. I'd talked to Ryder.

And then something.

What that something was, I couldn't remember.

I seemed to be lying in a bed. The mattress was rough, and I did not have a blanket. The latter discovery was the most shocking. I always—repeat, always—curled myself up in a blanket. All of the guys knew that. Whenever I fell asleep at Fallon's house, one of them would drape a blanket over me so I could create an Adelaide-cocoon. Unfortunately, I didn't transform into a butterfly until after I had my coffee. Before? I was a man-eating worm on a quest for vengeance.

I tried to stretch my taut muscles, but something restrained the movement. I tried again to no avail.

Flicking open one eye, I turned towards my arm. I blinked furiously at the sight, certain I was seeing it wrong or jumping to conclusions.

But nope.

Even as I attempted to lift said traitorous arm, I knew the effort would be futile. I was literally tied to the bed by thick ropes. Both wrists and both ankles.

Okay, if this was Calax's way of letting me know he was into kinky shit, then I was gonna take a hard pass. He could find another girl to tie up.

Actually, no. Only me.

"Cal?" I asked wearily. My body felt heavy, and my eyelids continually threatened to close. I blinked again, desperate to stay conscious.

There was something I had to remember. Something important…

My memories were foggy, but one face continued to sneak along the edges of my memory.

"Ryder?"

The rope burned where it dug into my skin, leaving hideous red gashes that seemed to deepen whenever I struggled. I lifted my head, the movement surprisingly difficult, and stared at the unfamiliar room.

Was I still in Elena's house?

It appeared to be a bedroom, yet it was utterly devoid of any pictures or memorabilia. A desk was pushed against the far corner, and a closet, empty of clothes, was opened directly in front of me. While moonlight filtered through the shut blinds, and artificial lighting greeted me from the propped open door.

Apparently, this house had electricity.

Hadn't the generator run out of batteries?

My head throbbed, though I couldn't decide if it was from the beginning of a headache or the end of one. There was also another reason why my head hurt so badly.

The realization had me gasping in alarm.

The hooded figure. The pan. Ryder.

Oh my.

My mind, bordering between hysterics and fear, latched onto the second word almost mechanically. A damn pan. Why did they have to use such a cliché? Seriously, did they have no originality? I'd already used a pan, so they weren't allowed to as well. The pan betrayed me.

And then I thought of Ryder. I thought of the blank expression on his face before his eyes fluttered shut. I thought of his body hitting the ground, my own helpless to stop his fall.

I should've screamed, but I hadn't been thinking rationally.

I was one of those girls that, in a movie, you would've been throwing popcorn at because of her stupidity. Why didn't you scream, bitch? Did you want to be taken by the bad guy?

Well excuse me, assholes, but you try thinking clearly when you're in the midst of getting kidnapped!

There was no flight or fight response just then. There had only been numbness and fear.

I yearned to touch my head, if only to see if the damage matched the pain, but the rope restricted such movement. I growled in frustration.

Think Addie. Think.

I was in a room that may or may not have been in Elena's house, though I was definitely leaning towards the not. The guys would never let me be tied up, even if they were into the kinky stuff.

Somebody had hit me. Had it been only one person? More than one?

Male or female?

I tried to recall the body type of my captor, but the bulging sweatshirt masked the gender. It could've been either, and I would've been none the wiser.

Ryder was more than likely in a different room than me. I refused to believe that he'd been killed or even seriously injured.

No, Ryder was nearby, no doubt, attempting to heroically rescue me like a dashing prince. I would be willing, for him, to play the damsel in distress.

From behind the door, I became aware of footsteps pattering in the direction of my room. Though I longed for them to be Ryder's, I wasn't naïve enough to take that chance.

I immediately snapped my eyes closed and attempted to steady my breathing.

The door creaked open, unsurprising given how old and rusty it looked, and the footsteps stopped right near the head of the bed.

Despite my prevalent fear, I didn't succumb to the panic. My breathing remained controlled, even as the unknown figure leaned forward, rancid breath dusting against my neck.

I felt a hand touch my cheek. My hair. My nose.

I barely even stiffened when the hand trailed lower.

It didn't lag behind on any particular body part, and I had the distinct feeling that the touch was not sexual. More…questioning, as if I were being examined by a doctor.

I heard what sounded like a disgruntled sigh, and then the person slapped me in the face. My head whipped to the side, hair covering the visible side of my face, and I allowed myself to open my eyes in shock.

What the hell?

My face stung from the hard slap, but my body remained unresponsive.

"You little bitch," the voice hissed. It wasn't anyone I recognized, but it was decidedly female.

I tried not to cower as something heavy hit my stomach. I groaned, an instinctive response, but kept my body still, lashes fluttering against my eyes despite the need I had to see the figure inflicting so much pain onto me. I hoped that she thought I was unconsciously making these sounds in my sleep.

Who was she?

Though I couldn't see her face, I was almost certain I'd never met her before in my life. I knew very few people, and only a handful of them were females. The unrestrained hostility she displayed towards me, a stranger, was startling. This felt almost personal.

I kept my eyes squeezed shut, even as her footsteps retreated to the door. Even as the sound faded, indicating she'd moved farther away.

No, I didn't dare open my eyes.

If I kept them closed, I could almost pretend that this wasn't real. I sometimes hated reality.

~

"Get up, bitch!" the cold voice demanded, accompanied by another slap to the face. I didn't bother pretending to still be asleep anymore.

I was determined to meet my assailant's eyes as she attacked me.

Glaring at her with all of the anger I could muster, I asked, "Who are you?"

She appeared to be around my age, dark hair pulled back into a simple braid. She might've been pretty if she hadn't had such a disgusting scowl on her face or if she hadn't decided to use my face for her bitch-slap practice.

"I've always thought you looked like a whore," she said in answer. Well, okay then. I guessed I would just call her Whore. "What's so special about you?"

Her voice held so much contempt, so much animosity, that I couldn't help but glance away. The hatred in her eyes was a brutal reminder of all the other times I'd been stared at angrily. It was the look I'd receive right before the abuse began.

As if she knew what I was thinking, her fist connected with my jaw. The ring she was wearing slashed my face, as piercing as a knife. I whimpered, unable to contain the pathetic sound. Of course, if there was one thing I knew about bullies and abusers, it was that they orgasmed at the slightest show of pain. Of weakness. I could not afford to show such vulnerability.

Gasping from the pain, I schooled my features into a fierce scowl. The pain was manageable. I'd dealt with worse.

If only she hadn't been wearing the damn ring…

Feeling my eyes upon it, she fluttered her fingers in front of my face. It was a silver ring, set with a glimmering emerald directly in the center.

"Do you like it?" she asked coyly. She seemed to forget that she hated me and liked hitting my face. Now she wanted to engage in girl talk?

"Like what?" I feigned annoyance, glancing from her finger to her eyes as if I had trouble understanding what she was referring to. Yeah, it may not have been the smartest move, considering the bitch was psycho and I was tied to a bed, but she was really beginning to piss me off.

"The ring," she snapped. She jabbed her finger in my eye, as if that would somehow get me to see better.

Yup. Could totally see better with the water dripping down my face from my suddenly irritated eye.

Unperturbed by my lack of response, Whore Bag Psycho Eye-Stabbing Bitch leaned backwards with a sly smile.

"My fiancé gave it to me," she answered, as if I really gave two shits where she got it from. She could tell me she got the ring from the President of the United States, and I would still stare blankly at her.

Again, she seemed undeterred by my lack of response. I imagined she spent a lot of time talking to herself. She probably even proposed to herself.

You know what they say—you have to love yourself before you can love others.

I think she might've taken that saying to a new extreme.

"I would like you in attendance for the wedding," she added suddenly. "As my maid of honor."

…the fuck now?

There were two things I could do—play along like a good little captive, or tell her to go fuck herself. Which probably was completely normal to her. She might even take it as a compliment, or she might get pissed that I was meddling in her love life.

My mind weighed the pros and cons of each solution, though neither seemed stellar or viable for the long haul. My main focus was Ryder. Before I could even think of escape, I had to find him and make sure he was okay.

I could only pray that he'd been left behind at Elena's house, though I knew that was only wishful thinking.

Face searing with pain, I smiled deviously up at the psycho. "I would love to be your maid of honor."

Bitch.

~

IF THERE WAS one thing I learned about Whore, it was that she needed to be the prettiest girl in the room.

You might think that would be normal for a petty teenage girl. Most girls had an abundant number of insecurities. But her?

I, at first, wore a pink dress. She'd undone the bindings around my arms and legs, had me change into a dress, and then immediately tied me to a chair.

Big improvement.

After studying me with a critical eye, she decided that I looked too much like a "raging slut," which was unsuitable for her wedding.

"Can't have my future husband looking at other girls," she said lightly. And then she laughed. Actually fucking laughed, as if we were two girlfriends enjoying one another's company until the big day.

Instead of changing my outfit, she grabbed scissors out of a drawer and cut the bottom of the dress.

Despite the jagged lining, she only proceeded to make the dress shorter and more revealing.

To fix my face, she decided to decorate it in black and blue. Yup. The bitch bruised my entire face, her deranged laugh causing goose pimples to rise on my arms.

Once she was satisfied that I looked hideous enough, she left to get herself dressed.

Okay. Think, Addie.

I considered the repercussions if I were to break the chair. On one hand, I might've been able to sneak away before she returned. On the other, I still had no idea where Ryder was, and I sure as hell wasn't leaving without him.

Also, it was surprisingly more difficult to break out of a chair than it appeared in the movies. You couldn't just push your body backwards, your fat ass causing the chair to shatter. Oh no.

Trust me. I tried.

And how were these characters magically able to untie their hands now that their bodies were no longer connected to the chair? Hands tied together have no correlation to bodies tied to chairs, unless you're in need of a few basic anatomy lessons. Seriously, if you couldn't do it sitting down, you sure as hell couldn't do it standing up. And the wooden stake miraculously created by the broken chair?

Snort. Fairy tales.

It hadn't occurred to me until that moment how trapped I was. How alone. How pathetic.

Shifting through my options quickly, I decided that the safest method to ensure my safety, as well as Ryder's, was to play this out. I'd find Ryder after Whore's wedding, and we would be on our merry way. I wouldn't mind punching the bitch in the boob first.

In this case, a boob shot would be completely justified.

But there was a voice nagging me to remember. Something at the edge of my consciousness, something important.

It hit me so suddenly that I nearly stopped breathing.

I was wrong before—I did know that girl.

She'd been at the mall that day with Ronan and Ryder, and again at the rest stop.

Why was she following me?

CHAPTER 21

*I*t was the freaking wedding of the century.

Seriously. I don't think anything could compare.

What was probably once a living room was now devoid of any couches and TVs, instead set up with row after row of folding chairs. In each chair, blind gazes fixed eerily on the front of the room, were stuffed animals.

And no, I was not kidding. Actual stuffed animals.

I didn't know whether I wanted to pity Whore or hate her even more. There was obviously something severely wrong with her brain, but hello. I was kidnapped and tied to a chair. And beaten. You couldn't forget that little tidbit of information.

Instead of untying me, Whore Bag merely dragged me down the hallway. She didn't seem to care if I ran into a wall or if the chair got stuck in the carpeting. I could've sworn that she did it on purpose, especially when she let out a lilting laugh whenever I groaned.

Apparently, my pain was amusing…?

I wondered if she would still find it amusing if I put my foot up her ass.

Glancing around the room, I realized suddenly that my throat was parched. I couldn't remember the last time I'd had a sip to drink. Probably during my date with Calax, which seemed like eons ago.

Calax…

My mind conjured up images of his handsome face the last time I'd seen him. Dark hair grazing his eyebrows, in desperate need of a cut. Muscles clearly defined beneath his dark T-shirt. Low-slung jeans that revealed a tiny swath of golden skin whenever he stretched. My heart ached something fierce when I thought about him.

He, no doubt, would've realized that I had been taken. At least, I hoped that was what he would conclude. I didn't want him to think that I would ever abandon him.

I'd considered it, briefly, but I knew the bastard would only follow me.

I thought of Fallon next. His impassive face contradicting with eyes that always seemed to hold a boatload of emotion. His golden-brown hair messily tied back into a ponytail.

Tam. My shy, sweet boy. His hair constantly covered his face as if it was an actual shield between him and the outside world. I envisioned his finger pressing his glasses farther up his nose. What had happened in his life to make him so shy, so timid, so afraid? I longed to break through his walls as he'd done to mine.

Ronan was my leprechaun. Protective of those he cared about, he still never failed to make me laugh. There was so much I yearned to learn about him. Why did he have a unicorn tattooed across his chest? Why did he dye his hair green?

Declan was another enigma, mainly because I couldn't help but compare him to my childhood best friend. I knew that the man no longer resembled the boy, but I thought I saw glimpses of Ducky in his expression. When he smirked? Ducky. Blushed? Ducky. But his features had hardened, time and space chipping away at the sweet boy I remembered. I longed for the relationship I once had with him, but I knew I had to look forward instead of backwards. Ducky was gone, but Declan was still around. I just had to decide if I liked the new man as much as I'd loved the boy.

Asher had always been my sweetheart. He had this innocence about him, this compassion, that put others to shame. He was too good for this world. Too good for me. I tried not to allow that realization to pain me as much as it did, but I felt tears spring in my eyes.

Maybe it would be better for everyone if I just stayed away.

I knew for a fact that Calax would finish my mission for me. He may not have known about Nik, but he would do anything to ensure my happiness. By association, Nik was now his brother as well.

My heart thumped painfully in my chest at the thought of never seeing any of them again.

I thought of Tommy, my little friend with sass that put even mine to shame. What would he do now that I was gone? Would he allow his depression and grief to consume him?

I could only hope that the boys would keep an eye on him. They may have claimed that they hated him, but I saw their eyes sparkling with amusement on more than one occasion. They considered him a little brother, just as I did.

I told myself that if I were to get out of this shest—shit fest—alive, I would tell Calax the truth about my feelings for him. And then I would go on to explain how I also had feelings towards the other members of his team. He might hate me after my confession, but he deserved my honesty. I would also make sure he understood that I didn't love him any less. My heart was growing, expanding, making room for these men that had somehow snuck their way past my defenses.

I didn't love them all. I knew that.

But I also knew that I couldn't imagine a life without them in it. Actually, I could, but the world without them in it was so bleak and depressing that I didn't want to even consider it. The emotions I felt towards them were confusing and terrifying, but also kind of exhilarating.

Music began to play from the speakers, and I flinched instinctively at the strident voice singing about first love and all that shit.

Whore Bag stood in the doorway, wilted flowers in her hands and a long white dress clinging to her curves. I had to admit that the dress was gorgeous. The bodice appeared rather snug, but the skirt cascaded around her legs like blankets of snow on a mountaintop. Her dark hair was twisted into an elaborate braid, and she'd applied a light coat of makeup onto her face.

She would've been beautiful if her eyes hadn't been shining manically and her lips were pulled into something other than a sneer. Even a frown would have been preferable.

Her eyes trailed over her "audience" distastefully before resting on me, then her expression brightened marginally.

"Come up here with me!" she said, waving her arm enigmatically. "My maid of honor has to stand by me!"

I didn't bother to point out that she was the one who'd brought me into this room in the first place. If she wanted me over there, she could've put me over there.

Oh no. She had to go and blame the tied-up girl.

Geez.

No respect.

Grunting in irritation, Whore Bag dragged my chair to where the wedding ceremony was apparently taking place. There appeared to be a podium, though I had no idea how she'd gotten that, and even more flowers swimming in their own bug-riddled refuse.

I scrunched my nose at the repugnant sight.

Seemingly satisfied that I was in the right position, Whore Bag smiled at me coyly.

"I'll be back in a little bit. I need to grab my fiancé." She snorted. "He's getting cold feet."

Well…could you really blame him?

I was momentarily grateful that she didn't react to my thought. I was afraid my stupid mind would speak aloud again, and I really wasn't in the mood for another beating.

Smiling up at Whore Bag, I said, "You look positively beautiful. Radiant."

My compliment seemed to please her, as pink tinged her cheeks.

"You mean it?" she asked, almost shyly. I kept my smile firmly in place, even when my emotions fully settled on pity. I still felt anger towards her, of course, but that anger was steadily receding. She was mentally and emotionally unstable. She needed help, first and foremost.

I kind of wished I knew her name. Maybe I could do what I did with Tommy— appeal to her humanity and her need to be loved.

"Of course I mean it!" I replied to her question after an awkward length of time. "Absolutely stunning."

She let out a squeal of happiness and then excitedly began chatting about her beauty process. I wanted to point out that she needed to grab her groom so that they could get on with the wedding. I had to find Ryder and get out of here.

I had the distinct feeling I wouldn't be able to do either until after the wedding was over.

"So…" I began casually. I hoped that she would indulge me with more information, now that her lips were loose. "You're an awfully skinny girl." She preened. "How did you manage to get me out of the house?"

That question had been bugging me. She may have been taller than me, but I knew it would've been immensely difficult for her to get both me and Ryder out of the house without being seen.

I hoped that she was the stereotypical movie villain, evilly cackling as she revealed all of her villainous plans. A girl can dream, all right?

Instead of answering, she merely glared at me. "I had help," she answered stoutly.

Okay then. Evil sidekicks? Apparently, a touchy subject.

I watched as she turned on her heel, white dress twisting like water between her legs, and headed down a hallway that I assumed housed her fiancé.

Or a mirror. I still wasn't entirely convinced that this mysterious person existed.

Alone once again, I allowed my mind to wander.

Why did I always find myself in these messes? It just wasn't fair.

My head was throbbing, a combination that I was certain stemmed from dehydration, stress, hunger, and my good old bruised face. Blood continually cascaded down my cheeks, a waterfall of garnet. Yeah. Yeah. I know. A cliché. But could you really blame me for not being the most eloquent at that moment?

I considered the room once more.

Sometime during my capture, the storm must've stopped. It was still dark outside, the stars breaking through the monotony of blackness. The room itself had peach colored walls, a warm and inviting color that clashed greatly with the dark carpeting.

Whore Bag had gone all out for this wedding. Twinkling lights were wrapped around the two pillars creating the hallway's arch. I was pretty sure I saw posters of Ryan Gosling taped to the wall, though my position hindered my ability to see clearly.

No wedding could be complete without the inclusion of Mr. Gosling.

I wondered if he was still alive.

The world would be a sad place without that beautiful human being.

I was pulled from my thoughts by a grunt, followed immediately by an onslaught of curse words. All male.

My body immediately tensed at the masculine voice, and my hands clenched into fists, despite the bindings. I knew that I wouldn't stand a chance, but the movement helped relax and calm me. It gave me hope that maybe, just maybe, I could get out of this situation. Alive, preferably, and in one piece. I wasn't greedy, though. If fate felt like I had to lose a hand to survive this shest, then I would've been more than willing to cut it off.

Whore Bag stormed back into the room, hand curled around a dark, thin fabric.

A leash, a tiny voice in my head told me.

Why would she have a leash?

That question was immediately answered when the "groom" came into view.

His short hair was slicked back, and he wore a tuxedo that seemed two sizes too big. Even with his dark skin, I could see the gashes on his face. A particularly jagged cut slashed across his temple, the puffiness of the edges and the red shadow hinting that it would leave behind a nasty scar. His arm hung crookedly by his side.

His eyes flickered towards me, wide with panic, and I felt my own instinctively tearing up.

Whore Bag pulled on the leash, and he staggered farther inside. The movement propelled him off his feet.

I would never forget the anguished cry he made as he landed on his broken arm.

I no longer pitied the psycho bitch. I hated her. The intensity of my emotions blew me away.

"Shall the wedding begin?" she asked sweetly, seemingly oblivious to her "fiancé" lying in a heap by her feet. Or maybe she just preferred him in that position.

I glared at her.

"You bitch," I hissed. I wanted a reaction from her. I wanted her to direct her anger at me instead of him. It was torture to see him so broken, so vulnerable. He tried to hide it, but I could see the tears falling down his cheeks. I could see the horror, self-pity, and disgust, all masked behind an apathetic exterior.

What did she do to you? I questioned silently. I tried to convey it with my eyes, but he didn't look up.

No, Ryder was merely a shell of the man I remembered.

CHAPTER 22

ADDIE

*E*very good memory I had was tainted by a bad one.

When I was five years old, we moved out of our quaint, Victorian manor. I remember how diminutive that house seemed, at least in comparison. A yellow painted building with dark shingles, a brick chimney, and windows stretching the expanse of the back, it was the epitome of "cute."

We hadn't moved into the resort at first. No, instead, my parents moved us into a hotel, owned by one of their shell companies. While the hotel was large, it lacked any warmth. With the white painted walls, leather couches, and bleached linoleum flooring, it was immensely unwelcoming.

Father had been happy that day. I wouldn't be able to tell you why, though I imagined one of his deals had gone through. He'd lifted me up, spinning me in a circle, tears in his normally piercing dark eyes. I'd never seen my father so happy before, so energetic. He made it feel as if he had the world at his fingertips, and I, by association, did as well. Planting a sloppy, wet kiss onto my forehead, he had called me his "angel" before gently setting me down onto the floor.

I was elated by his show of love. For the first time, I succeeded in bringing happiness instead of inflicting pain. You may believe that's demented thinking for a child, but I'd lived my life under this constant pressure of being perfect and having my surroundings behave perfectly as well. It failed to reach my parents' attention that I had no control over the world. I wasn't like my father. I couldn't just snap my fingers and have the world fall to its knees.

Only an hour after that initial spurt of happiness, the anger began to brew, like a bloated storm cloud teetering at the edge of the sky. It hadn't quite concealed the sun yet, but the slow-moving storm would eventually consume it.

I prepared myself for the darkness.

When it came, I held my hands up to protect my face. Only, instead of rain, it was fists. Instead of thunder, it was screams. Instead of lightning, it was a blistering sharp slap to my cheek.

The deal had fallen through. I didn't know the logistics, but for some reason, he took the blame out on me. An innocent.

That was my first trip to the hospital. The doctors had examined me with raised eyebrows, but no questions were asked. My father spun his web, and they became stuck in its binding. They were nothing but insects to him, a food that could easily be devoured.

I'd never felt so helpless before, so empty. The world was crumbling around me, yet all I could do was watch it fall. I was balancing precariously on a ledge, and a part of me wanted to take that leap. Would it hurt if I fell? Would anyone care?

I could see, now, all of those emotions in Ryder's face as the girl leered down at him. There was so much pain.

Nobody could live through that much pain.

I longed to reach out to him, to comfort and touch him, but there was nothing for me to do but watch. Watching, I realized, was nearly as agonizing as being the one tortured. I would rather face a thousand of my fathers than see that helpless expression even once on Ryder's face.

Was that love? Or was that merely human decency?

"You don't have to do this," Ryder gasped, slowly climbing to his feet. The girl watched it all with an amused expression.

"Why wouldn't I have to do this? This is the only way for us." She sounded so young just then, so full of hope. She stared at Ryder as if he held the moon. Awe, longing, love.

"Liz, please…"

The girl, Liz apparently, yanked on the leash, and Ryder stumbled forward. On closer inspection, I saw that his eye was completely swollen shut and blood smeared the roots of his hair. What had the bitch done to him?

Smirking, she lowered her voice in a poor of impersonation of Ryder's. "Liz, please," she mocked. Then, in her normal, singsong voice, "Don't you want to be my husband?"

"Of course I do!" Ryder said quickly. Too quickly. If Liz noticed or suspected, she didn't say anything. Instead, she continued to stare up at him with her doe-like, innocent eyes. Eyes that had the capability to penetrate skin like millions of tiny knives. It was always the innocent looking ones that were the most dangerous. Liz was no exception. "I just don't understand what she has to do with anything." He nodded his head towards me, refraining from making eye contact. His hands were clenched tightly, the only indication that he was anything other than fine.

"Her?" Liz glared at me over her shoulder. "My partners have more interest in her than I do. But I do need her at our wedding. The other woman." Her face contorted into its customary sneer, but all I could focus on were her first words.

Her partners? Who were they, and what could they possibly want with me? But I couldn't afford to focus on that right now. I had to focus on the now, on the current problem.

Liz.

Ryder, however, narrowed his eyes at the petite bride.

"What do you mean? Who's after her?" His entire body was considerably more taut than it was moments before, as if the threat against me trumped the current threat against him.

Oh Ryder…

"Why do you care?" Liz hissed. "She's nothing to you. I'm your wife!"

Taking a deep breath, Ryder relaxed his features. The change was startling. Instead of the pissed off, brooding boy, he looked oddly calm. Loving.

"Liz, my love, of course she doesn't matter to me. She's just a hoe." He stumbled over that word, but Liz remained oblivious. I wanted to tell him that I understood, that I didn't care what he called me, as long as he remained safe. I tried to convey all that and more in my eyes.

Call me a bitch. Call me a whore. Say that you hate me.

It would only make me love you more.

The words couldn't leave my mouth, but I felt them. I most definitely felt them.

"I just want to make sure our ceremony won't be interrupted," Ryder continued.

"It won't be." Liz waved her hand dismissively. "We have a deal."

"A deal?"

But Liz was apparently done talking about me, the other woman, as she abruptly turned towards the wooden podium.

"Come. I don't want the cake to get cold."

When her back was turned, Ryder finally, finally, met my eyes. In his, I could see a terrible loneliness and hopelessness that made me sick to my stomach. Ryder, my flirtatious rock star, shouldn't look like that.

Taking a deep breath to steady myself, I turned away from Ryder, towards Liz. I didn't know what I intended to do until I did it. All I knew for certain was that I wanted Liz's attention off of Ryder. I could deal with her anger and fits of rage in a way that most people couldn't.

"Hey, Lizzy," I cooed sweetly, barely registering Ryder's quick shake of his head. His eyes had widened in terror. Terror for me, I realized. I ignored him.

I waited until Liz had turned towards me fully, eyes clouded with contempt.

Still giving her my shit-eating grin, I said, "Were you aware that your fiancé has been screwing me behind your back?"

If she wanted to play a game, I could play.

And bitch? I never lost.

Liz's face turned red with anger. She spun on her heel and put her face inches from mine.

"What the fuck are you talking about?" she asked slowly. Her eyes could've made me drop dead.

"She's just kidding," Ryder said. "She's just trying to get a reaction out of you."

"Oh, am I?" I asked with a light laugh. My laughter seemed to only infuriate her further. Her lips were pursed as if she were eating something sour. Before I could add anything else, her fist connected with my face.

Ryder let out an anguished gasp, but I kept my face impassive, even as it began to ache.

"Is that all you got?" I teased. "No wonder Ryder seeks me out. He does like it rough."

Another punch.

My head jerked to the side, and I tasted copper in mouth. Spitting out the excess blood, I gave Liz a toothy grin. I was vaguely aware of Ryder screaming at Liz, begging her to stop.

I mentally berated him. He had to stop acting like he cared. Couldn't he tell I was doing this for him?

"I wrote you a song!" Ryder shouted, and Liz paused, fist pulled back as if she wanted to punch me yet again. At his proclamation, she dropped her arm and smiled brilliantly at him.

"You did?"

"Yeah!" Ryder was nodding his head animatedly, but I could see his hands shaking. He was terrified.

"You haven't written a new song in years," Liz said dreamily. She perched herself on one of the many folding chairs, ignoring the stuffed turtle already residing there, and gestured for Ryder to continue.

He cleared his throat uncomfortably.

"I don't have my guitar or anything…"

"That's okay. Just sing it."

He closed his eyes, lashes feathering against his high cheekbones, and opened his mouth. I stilled as the familiar, raspy voice assaulted my senses.

"When I first saw you, I never wanted to look away. There's so much I could've done, but I just wanted you to stay. You may be crazy, but I would love you just the same."

The song continued, melancholic yet hopeful lyrics about the girl that had captured his heart.

About being trapped together, in a brand-new world, only for this girl to quickly become his world.

About her tendency to speak her thoughts, which only made him fall for her harder.

About the adventures they'd been on, and the adventures yet to come.

Tears sprang to my eyes as the meaning became clear. I wasn't completely stupid, despite my admittedly airheaded moments.

Ryder loved me.

He looked at me over Liz's shoulder. The air around us seemed to crackle with electricity, warming the stagnant air.

He loved me, and I loved him.

And I loved Calax.

I would have to deal with it, all of it, at a later point. Right then, I had to work on getting us out of there.

There was no other option.

We would escape, Liz would get help, and then I would focus on the emotions thing.

Yup, completely acceptable goals.

CHAPTER 23

I'd never understood the concept of falling in love.

Of course, I'd seen it done before in movies and television, but never in real life. My parents hadn't loved each other, at least not the type of love I yearned to experience myself. Their marriage had been one of convenience and necessity. Maybe, at first, they'd felt love towards one another. Maybe they'd believed their relationship would have a fairy-tale happy ending. Maybe they'd believed their love would conquer all.

Maybe the world was harsher than they'd expected, numerous obstacles prohibiting them from reaching that finish line.

Love, I'd come to realize, wasn't perfect. You couldn't just bottle up all of your feelings into a nice, diminutive box. No, that would be too easy.

They said that love hit you when you least expected it, barreling down on you like a ton of bricks. I supposed that analogy was true. Depending on where you were when that love hit made a difference on whether or not you survived it. Standing in water? You would drown. Standing on land? Maybe, just maybe, you'd be strong enough to carry the weight across the finish line. Some people believed that you had to do it alone, but I knew that wasn't true. Your partner would be with you every step of the way, shouldering the burden that you were unable to carry.

Once you realized that, once you fully grasped that concept, you would finally be able to receive your own happily ever after.

I thought all that as I maintained eye contact with Ryder. I didn't want him to have to face this alone.

I'm here, I thought. *I'll always be here.*

I continued to stare at him when Liz clapped her hands gleefully, raving about his new song, and I stared even when she kissed his neck. He shuddered, and while she'd mistaken it for lust, I understood what it really was.

Disgust.

"You want to move straight to the honeymoon, don't you?" Liz said in a voice that she no doubt thought was sultry. Ryder's face paled drastically at the implication.

"The wedding first," he rasped.

I stared when Liz's face contorted into a pout before a devious gleam entered her eyes. I stared when her hands traced patterns across his shoulders, down his stomach, and into the waistband of his pants. Ryder winced, squeezing his eyes shut.

It was only then that I looked away. I couldn't save him from what was to come, but I could give him the privacy he wanted. I knew, without having to be told, that he didn't want me to see him like this.

I planted my gaze firmly on the three-tiered chandelier. Bright, artificial lighting made the room seem almost golden. Cozy. It was one word I wouldn't ever associate with the disgusting room.

No, not cozy. Horrifying, maybe.

But the room was like Liz in that sense. The beauty hid a darker, malevolent entity. I'd never be able to forget this beautiful room with its intricately carved woodwork and freshly painted walls, just as I'd never forget Liz's face. She would haunt my nightmares, right alongside my mother and father.

I was brought out of my thoughts by the slash of a knife across my cheek. I let out a cry, an instinctive sound, and whipped my head in the offender's direction.

The copper handle fit perfectly in Liz's hand, the penetrating blade dripping with blood. My blood.

"Stop! Please stop! I'll do it! I'll do it!" Ryder screamed.

I didn't want to know what he'd agreed to.

But, somehow, I already knew.

I continued to look away, continued to grant him this one relief, as Liz let out a loud moan. I kept my eyes fixated on the chandelier as Ryder began to cry, horrible desperate pleas.

I knew I was crying as well. I could taste the tears in my mouth, feel them on my cheeks.

It was too much.

Ryder's sobbing cut off abruptly, and I dared peek over at the two of them. Liz was still sitting on top of Ryder, head thrown back in ecstasy as she ground against him, but Ryder's face was utterly impassive.

I could see the tear stains on his face, but his eyes were vacant. He didn't notice me, Liz, or anything else in the room. He had retreated into his own mind.

I didn't want to talk about everything I saw. I didn't want to talk about the silent tears cascading down Ryder's face or his mouth opening in a silent scream that no one would hear.

I screamed. I struggled against the bindings. I threatened.

Nothing stopped Liz. She took what she wanted, without a care to those around her.

And Ryder? He was forced to carry that burden alone.

~

THERE WAS NO WEDDING.

After Liz had finished, she'd deemed herself too tired to continue with the festivities. Then she'd dragged my chair back into the bedroom and pulled Ryder into her own.

Ryder hadn't even fought. He'd just stared blindly ahead as if the world was crushing him. Suffocating him. Killing him.

As if the world had forsaken him.

I shoved my face into my pillow, and I cried. For Ryder. For me. For the boys left behind.

My sobs made my body shake, but I couldn't stop them. I wouldn't.

It was the only thing I could give Ryder, my beloved. I couldn't save him, but I could offer him my prayers and empathy. I understood what he was going through, and I also understood that comfort was not always wanted. There were no words I could possibly offer him to mend what was broken.

The sun was just beginning to rise, painting the room in palest green and pink, when the bedroom door opened.

I turned, the bindings now around my waist, making the movement immensely uncomfortable, to see a silhouette in the doorframe.

I would recognize him anywhere.

"She's in the bathroom," Ryder said simply. His voice was different than I'd ever heard it before. Devoid of feeling. It was as if he was merely reciting a fact instead of discussing the monster that had assaulted him.

"You shouldn't be here," I replied shakily.

Ryder didn't respond. Instead, he merely walked into the room and gathered me into his arms.

Only for a moment, did he allow himself to cry. He kissed my cheek, my nose, my neck. Sniffling. Sobbing.

Only a moment.

Just as quickly as he arrived, he left.

I heard Liz's shrill voice, and I heard Ryder's soft rumble, the exact words inarticulate.

With nothing else to do, I cried myself back to sleep.

~

I WOKE up to the smell of coffee. Not an unpleasant smell by any means, but my hackles became raised as I peeled open my crusty eyelids.

Liz stood at the foot of my bed, hand warmed by a steaming cup of the delicious liquid.

"Good morning," she said cheerfully. All I could do was glare at her.

There were no words that could adequately describe my anger and hatred towards her. The loathing I felt just staring at her elfin face suppressed anything found in the dictionary. Normally, I wouldn't have minded my lack of eloquence.

Just then, though, I wanted to bombard her with every horrible word I knew. I wanted her to understand pain, even if it was only in the form of words.

Silence was the next best thing.

Seemingly unperturbed, or able to fake indifference better than I could've, Liz set her coffee cup down on my bedside table.

"I was hoping you could join us for breakfast today," she said, smiling happily. "My best friend and my husband."

She really was delusional. As before, the tiniest stirring of pity churned in my stomach. I quickly dismissed such an emotion with a tidal wave of anger. I could feel nothing for her except hatred. Maybe I could've forgiven her for what she'd done to me—bruising me, hurting me, scarring my face with her knife. But for what she did to Ryder and still continued to do to him? I could never forgive that.

Still, I managed an amicable nod at her request, despite the clenching of my teeth and the tightening of my jaw.

A plan quickly formed. Okay, it wasn't a plan, necessarily, but an idea. An idea that could potentially free us from this hellhole.

As I watched, Liz diligently began untying the rope from where she hooked it on the side of my bed. My hands clenched beneath the quilt as she began to talk about Ryder. About his love for her. About his lovemaking.

Still, I held my tongue.

The rope finally came undone, sliding off my body with a light pull on her end. Finally, I could move my arms.

She moved down to the rope around my legs, still chattering excitedly. I didn't listen to a word she said.

I wouldn't—couldn't—hear those words. The way she degraded Ryder.

Stealthily, I inched my hand towards the bedside table as she continued to undo the knots around my legs.

Slowly. Ever so slowly.

"There!" The second rope fell to the floor just as my hand connected with her coffee cup. She turned towards me, a singularly beautiful smile alighting her face, and I smiled back.

Just before throwing the coffee at her.

She let out a scream, dropping her head into her hands. Coffee sizzled where it connected with her skin, and shards of glass got caught in her disheveled hair.

Without waiting for her to recover, I slammed a fist into her face.

There was nothing satisfying about seeing her tiny body drop to the floor. I was too numb for anything like that. This girl, this monster, needed help.

I told myself that I would find her that help as soon as I escaped.

For now, though, I wasn't going to leave her here unattended. That was a novice move. Grabbing the rope from the ground, I made quick work in tying her to the bed.

I hoped, slightly sardonically, that she would tremble with fear, with the knowledge that she was trapped. The rope almost seemed to be a physical manifestation of her continuous torment. With them on, I knew that I was restrained. Captured.

Hers.

Ignoring the pain in my body—the raw skin brought from the rope, the cut on my face, the bruises no doubt a hideous combination of blue, yellow, and black—I shuffled down the hallway.

I wouldn't be able to tell you what it looked like, how many pictures hung on the wall, or how many doors ran the length of the space. All I could focus on were the barely audible sobs from the door farthest down the hallway, adjacent to an open bathroom.

Without hesitating, I threw the door open, blinking my gaze against the piercing sunlight blinding me from the window.

"Go away!" Ryder cried.

He was lying on the bed, back to me, wearing only a pair of shorts. His dark skin was covered in gashes—both, I suspected, from knives and fingernails.

"RyRy," I said softly. Tears welled in my eyes.

At the sound of my voice, Ryder's head snapped my way. He stared at me for a long moment, expression indecipherable, before he jumped to his feet.

His strong body collided with mine, the momentum nearly propelling me off my feet. He held me tightly against him, his nose in my hair as he inhaled my scent.

"Kitten," he breathed. As if a thought suddenly occurred to him, he pulled away from me, pushing me behind him and standing guard in front of me. He cast a predatory look in both directions, muscles tensing.

"She's not coming," I said, keeping my voice gentle. "I took care of it."

He didn't ask me to elaborate, and I didn't offer any more information. I honestly didn't think he could handle hearing her name, let alone seeing her again.

The tension drained from his body, and without looking at me, he collapsed to the floor. I reached down to comfort him, but I immediately withdrew my hand when he flinched away.

"How do I...?" He trailed off with a sob. "How do I deal with this?"

Keeping each of my movements slow so as to not startle him, I sunk down onto the plush carpeting. This time, he didn't move away from me as our thighs touched.

"Sometimes, you can't deal with it," I answered honestly. "Some days are worse than others. It doesn't matter where you are or who you're with. You remember, and it feels like you're drowning. Again. And again. But then you reach the surface, and you're finally able to breathe. Ryder, the world is so beautiful once you're above the water. It sucks when you're drowning, but you have to hold on. You have to wait until you can breathe again, because it's an amazing feeling. It's...relief."

I didn't know if my words registered in Ryder's head. I hoped they did, but I was a realist. It would take time for him to go back to the boy he once was, if he ever would. It didn't matter to me either way.

Something inside Ryder broke, like a dam exploding. He cried in earnest, leaning into me. I wrapped my arms around him from behind, holding him to me as if I were physically able to hold together his broken pieces.

I would hold him until the day I died if I had to.

CHAPTER 24

ADDIE

"I met Liz a couple of years ago," Ryder said, breaking the silence I'd grown accustomed to. His head was in my lap as my fingers ran through his soft hair. I knew that we had to leave—the boys were probably worried sick, and both of us were severely injured—but I couldn't find the strength to move from the ground.

"She went to school with us, but I never really talked to her, you know? I thought she was hot and everything, but I was warned to stay clear of her. Apparently, she was batshit crazy."

Ryder let out a humorless laugh, and I squeezed his hand, wordlessly encouraging him to continue.

"For one of our classes, we were paired up together. It was a dumbass class, to be completely honest. I don't remember a single thing that was taught.

"I invited her over to my apartment to work on our project a couple of times, and I visited her house as well. I didn't think anything of it until one night, I got completely drunk. We slept together." His eyes flickered up towards my face anxiously as if he was afraid I was going to judge him because of his confession. All I could do was smile lovingly at him.

No words. I didn't have words to console him, nor did I think he would accept them. All I could do was listen to his story without judgement.

"I was stupid. I didn't understand that my actions had consequences, and it was my responsibility to pay them. I looked at Liz like I looked at every other girl—an easy fuck. She looked at it differently.

"The next day, she told me that she loved me. I laughed, of course, because I thought she was teasing. I couldn't even recall her full name, yet she was in love with me? It didn't make any sense. Besides, everybody at school knew my reputation. I didn't love anyone, and I sure as hell didn't do relationships."

He was silent for another long moment. Again, I had the distinct feeling he was gauging my reaction. Tilting my face upwards, I noticed a fan swirling above us providing the room with much needed circulation. On and on, it spun. Never stopping. Never starting.

There was no endpoint, no starting point, just the repetitive swirl of the propellers. I didn't know why my attention had become fixated on such a mundane object. Maybe it was because I recognized Ryder for what he was, a kindred soul, and the onslaught of emotions that accompanied that revelation made my head pound in tangent with my heart.

Still, my hand continued to play with his hair in a feeble attempt at comfort.

"She became obsessed with me. She would show up at my doorstep at random times, demanding that I take her out. She was jealous of my friendship with the guys and the other girls.

"One day, she showed up to my band practice. She was babbling incoherently about how I'd cheated on her. She told me she was going to kill herself if I ever left her. She told me..." Ryder broke off with a sob, and I wrapped my arms tighter around him.

"I didn't know how to deal with it. With *her*. I didn't love her like that, but I felt obligated to be with her. After all, it was my fault she was so fucked up. If I would've just kept my dick in my pants..." He trailed off yet again, this time with a resigned sigh. I could tell he blamed himself, but I knew that the blame wasn't warranted. It wasn't his fault that she was mentally ill. He may have been a catalyst for her behavior, but he wasn't the reason.

"I was diagnosed with depression shortly after that incident. Sarge talked to Liz's parents, and I honestly thought we had it all figured out. She would get the help she needed, and so would I. I hadn't talked to her in months. A few weeks ago, she reached out to me again."

When the silence became more pronounced than any of the previous ones, I tentatively asked, "What happened a few weeks ago?"

"She saw me with you, and she knew that it was different. That you were different." His hand squeezed my thigh, grip almost painful. "I hadn't realized that she still felt...so strongly for me. She texted me and demanded that I meet up with her. She threatened you."

My hand paused its ministrations.

"Threatened...me?"

"She knew how I felt about you, or at least she suspected it. Either way, she suddenly had leverage over me that she never had previously. I told her to fuck off." He laughed again. "Wrong move apparently."

We sat in companionable silence for a few long minutes. I honestly thought he'd finished his story, so his next words surprised me.

"She told me that I had to like it. She told me that she would hurt you if I didn't. I wasn't allowed to cry or scream. I wasn't allowed to fight." His body shook with sobs, and all I could do was hold onto him tighter. Feeling helpless to end his suffering, I pressed a kiss to his forehead.

"You don't have to explain," I whispered.

"But I want you to know that I wouldn't have touched her. I didn't want to touch her." He curled himself further into me. And then he said it, in a house that held nothing but bad memories and with our tormentor tied up only a few doors down.

"I love you."

He cried harder, hands clenching and unclenching where they wrapped around my leg. It was a desperate attempt on his part to hold on to something tangible.

"Please say that you love me back," he sobbed. "I don't have anyone anymore. You're all that I have. I love you. I love you."

I didn't answer him, though it wasn't because I didn't feel the same. Those were not words I could say in such a desolate place. No, when I finally said them, I wanted the moment to hold nothing but good memories instead of the pain we were both feeling. They shouldn't be spoken in a house that reverberated with the horrors we'd endured.

Ryder was lost in his own thoughts, his own guilt, and any words spoken would've gone over his head. I hugged him a little tighter, though, in the hopes that my actions would convey my own feelings towards him.

Ryder was lost, I knew that. He needed to be found by someone. I wasn't sure if that person would, or even could, be me. I didn't know how to love, nor did I know if I was capable of it. But I would try.

For Ryder and Calax and all of the other boys weaseling their way into my heart, I would try.

I COULDN'T TELL you how long we sat there. It might've been hours or even minutes. Ryder, at some point, must've fallen asleep. He was lightly snoring, his head still resting on my lap.

Shaking his shoulder with more gentleness than I knew I had, I whispered, "Ryder, we should get going."

The ominous mention of Liz's "partners" hadn't left my mind. So far, we hadn't seen anyone else in the house. Where were they, if they even existed? It wouldn't have surprised me if Liz had imagined them, but it still didn't change the fact that someone had helped her kidnap Ryder and me. It stood to reason that, at least on one matter, she had been telling the truth.

It begged the question—what the hell did they want with me?

Ryder blinked, fatigue evident in his blind gaze, before finally nodding. He maneuvered himself into an upright position, wincing at the pain in his shoulder and arm. I knew that he would need a sling sooner rather than later.

"Wait here," I instructed, easing reluctantly to my feet as my body detached itself from Ryder. He let out a small cry, hands feebly reaching for me. Heart clenching at his anguished expression, I crouched down in front of him. "I'll be right back."

Moving quickly, I first checked the room I'd left Liz in. She was still unconscious on the bed.

She looked so peaceful when she was asleep, so tranquil. How could someone so angelic in appearance hold so much evil? Shaking my head to clear my thoughts, I moved from room to room, quickly grabbing supplies and anything that I could use as a sling. Liz, fortunately, had hoarded a large collection of medical supplies, including some pills and bandages. I threw them all into a duffle bag I'd spotted beneath the bed.

Grabbing a shirt from the drawer, I marched back towards Ryder and began treating his numerous injuries. They weren't as bad as I'd initially suspected. Aside from a couple of cuts and bruises, his arm was in the worst condition. After I wrapped his arm up in a makeshift sling, I catalogued the remainder of his injuries with narrowed eyes. I wanted Liz to pay for every slash on his skin, every bruise on his face. The need for vengeance was palpable. My chest constricted at the thought, and my hands turned clammy.

Still, I kept my face impassive as I pressed a kiss to Ryder's bloody cheek.

"What's the verdict, doc? Am I going to live?" Ryder asked, a bit of his usual sass returning to his voice. I snorted.

"Probably not. Don't worry, though. I'll make sure to eat everything besides your head."

His eyes gleamed. "Evil woman." Turning towards the medical supplies, he grabbed a wipe and a bandage. "Now you."

Grunting, I obediently allowed him to dab at the cut on my face. I heard his sharp intake of breath as he surveyed my bloody and bruised form. I knew that I would be scarred, but I also knew that I didn't care. My scars always served as a reminder of all that I'd endured and eventually conquered. I was a warrior, and the scars only accentuated that.

Ryder's fingers were gentle as they traced my swollen cheek, down to my lips, and across my collarbone. Pain and guilt darkened his amber eyes.

"I'm so sorry this happened to you," he choked out. "If it wasn't for me—"

"If it wasn't for you, I wouldn't laugh as much as I do," I said, cutting him off. "If it wasn't for you, I wouldn't have found my comfort zone, and then broken through it. If it wasn't for you, I wouldn't be as happy as I am now."

His hand stilled under my chin, breath leaving him in a whoosh at my confession.

I brought my own hand up and gently traced the shape of his face. The high cheekbones, the light stubble, his luscious, full lips, the bruise just below his jaw. We stared at one another, and the world around us seemed to still. Stop.

There was no Liz. No Ragers. No storms.

It was just us and the feelings that we both struggled to understand. I realized then that I didn't have to face this unfamiliar territory alone. It was new to Ryder as well, and we would juggle the obstacles together.

It didn't change the way I felt about Calax. He was my rock, my sun, and my love. What I felt for Ryder was different. He made me laugh when I felt like crying. He understood me in a way that no one ever had before.

I loved him. I loved them both.

I could only hope that they wouldn't hate me when I told them the truth.

"Come on. Let's go," I said at last, breaking eye contact. I held out a hand for him, and he took it eagerly. "We need to get the hell out of here."

"But first…"

Before I could ask what he meant, Ryder pressed his lips to mine. It was a short kiss, only a second, but it made my stomach clench and heat rise to my face. He pulled away, looking happier than I'd ever seen before. His smile was glorious, and his eyes, though still shadowed, radiated an inner light that had been missing for a while.

"Let's go," he echoed.

Without another word, we moved towards the front door of the house. We didn't know what awaited us, but I knew we would face it.

Together.

ADDIE

When we stopped at the front entrance, I looked in one direction and Ryder another. The forest was still. Silent.

I hadn't noticed our surroundings when I was confined within the house, but we appeared to be in a stretch of woods. Only the house broke through the endless canvas of trees that stretched out in all directions.

I waited, breath held, but could hear nothing besides the scuttling of animals and the crackle of fallen leaves.

"I think we're clear," I whispered to Ryder, and he nodded.

Still on guard, we ran the short distance to the truck Liz must've transported us in. The paint was fading and beginning to rust in places, but it would have to do.

I had no idea how far away we were from the guys. From any civilization, if I was being honest with myself. How long had I been unconscious?

Hours? Minutes?

The terrain was unfamiliar to both Ryder and me. After a quick search through the glove compartment and dashboard, I found a map. It was crinkled, repeated use wearing and yellowing the paper in certain areas, but it would have to do.

Ryder recited the address of our prison. The house wasn't Liz's, I realized. She must've raided it and claimed it as her own some time recently. Probably the same time we arrived at Elena's.

"We have to get onto Cherry Street," Ryder said, tracing a road with his finger.

"Direct me where to go," I instructed, sliding into the driver's seat. I couldn't remember the last time I'd driven. Pathetic, I know. For years, I'd relied on drivers to get me to and from any locations I wished to go to. Of course, I didn't have a lot of options. The line was rather short for the whole "hang out with Adelaide" ride, and I had no reason to travel to any store. I had all of my clothes and food delivered directly to my room.

Sticking the keys into the ignition, I listened to the purr of the vehicle. There appeared to be a half tank of gas. Hopefully, it would be enough to get us to our destination.

We didn't speak as I clumsily drove the car down the driveway. Ryder's face was unnaturally pale, and his hand was gripping the handle above his head tightly.

I called it the oh-shit-you're-going-to-die handle.

And from Ryder's petrified expression, I had no doubt he was feeling exactly that.

"Why didn't you tell me that you didn't know how to drive?" Ryder said as the car came dangerously close to a tree. Oops.

"I know how to drive!" I defended. "I have my license."

Ryder snorted but didn't argue with me. Probably because he was too busy pissing his pants.

After only about fifteen minutes, the car pulled out onto a long road. Cherry Street, I believed was the name. It was devoid of any stores and only held the occasional house. The trees towered over us, thick branches obscuring the sun.

Ryder finally seemed to relax now that the road was bigger and the trees farther away. He still glanced warily at the impending tree line as if he were afraid I planned to drive the car into it. I mean, I wouldn't do it on purpose or anything.

On accident? It was good for him to be cautious. Hell, even I wanted to hold the oh-shit-I'm-going-to-die handle, and I was driving.

After miles of forested road, we emerged into a small town. The buildings were unfamiliar, despite Ryder's insistence that we were in the right area. Our truck got stuck on more than one occasion due to the flooded streets. Trees littered the road, providing impenetrable barriers that we struggled to avoid. Roofs were collapsing, and the buildings themselves had broken windows and tattered siding. Cars were beginning to corrode away, as if something acidic had attacked the paint.

I wondered what the town had been like before the storm ravaged it. Before hell claimed it.

I imagined that it had been cute. Not busy, necessarily, but bustling with regulars and the occasional tourist. Small towns like these always had a certain charm.

The truck suddenly began to spin.

Ryder gripped the handle.

"What the fuck, Addie?" he yelled, accusatorially.

"It wasn't me!"

I glanced through the rearview mirror, towards the road we'd just traveled on, and I cursed when I noticed the tiny spikes protruding from the ground.

"Shit!"

I attempted to regain control of the car, but I knew that the effort was futile. I couldn't determine how many tires were blown. One? Two?

Either way, we were screwed.

Just as I thought this, the back window exploded. That was the only word I could think to describe it. One second it was fine, and the next, glass was shattering everywhere.

"Duck!" Ryder screamed. Using his good hand, he pressed my head down.

A gun rapidly began to fire, the bullets dinging the siding of the truck.

I screamed, wildly turning the wheel in a desperate attempt to escape. I tried to stare over the top of the dashboard, I tried to see where I was going, but fear kept my head between my legs.

The car lurched to a stop, the momentum making my head bang against the steering wheel.

I heard Ryder beside me, asking if I was okay, but my tongue felt like sandpaper in my mouth. My body was shaking.

Lifting my head, I noticed the car had slammed into the side of a brick building. Smoke emitted from the hood.

Besides a trickle of blood on Ryder's forehead, there seemed to be no new injuries that I could see.

That relief was only short-lived when I realized the predicament we'd found ourselves in.

Shit.

We were alone, injured, with at least one shooter hunting us down. Was this the partner Liz had alluded to? Or were they another group of people like the ones we ran into before?

I didn't know if my sanity could deal with anymore Kyles.

Ryder shook my arm gently, rousing me from my stupor. I turned towards him, wide-eyed, and saw my own panic reflected in his gaze. I couldn't even begin to think of how we were going to get out of this situation.

Ryder's hand reached for my own, squeezing tight.

All I could do was hold my breath and wait.

I heard the footsteps, heavy boots crushing debris and leaves, but I kept my eyes locked on the off-set brown bricks. I was trembling, my body unable to help its instinctive reaction when facing danger.

Ryder's grip was iron around my hand. Still, I held on. That was all I could do.

"Addie?" a voice called in disbelief. A familiar voice.

Turning my head so fast, I was afraid I would get whiplash, I met Fallon's dark, incredulous eyes. I knew my own had filled with tears.

"Fallon?" I whispered.

"Sarge!" Ryder cried.

Before I could say another word, the door was flung open and I was in his arms. I sobbed into his chest, relishing in the comfort his strength gave me.

"We've been looking everywhere for you guys," he whispered into my hair.

"Wait a minute…" I tried to take a step back from the tall man, eyes narrowed in accusation, but he kept his arms firmly around me. "You shot at us!"

Fallon blinked rapidly, as if coming out of a daze, before focusing fully on my face. He raised an eyebrow, the eloquent gesture worth a thousand words in Sarge-speak.

"Why the hell did you shoot at us?" I continued. My eyes automatically flew to the bulge in his pants. I knew it wasn't just a happy-to-see-Adelaide type of bulge. Stupid bastard with his stupid bastard gun and his stupid bastard—

"We get it," Ryder said, placing his hand on my shoulder. "Sarge is a stupid bastard."

Turning towards the man himself, Ryder's eyes filled with tears.

"Thank you, brother," he said. Fallon's eyes warmed as he considered the younger member of his team. I didn't know what Ryder was thankful for, but I figured it had to do with the fact that the team hadn't stopped looking for us.

I hoped Ryder understood that he was loved by more than just me.

It was then that Fallon finally got a good look at us. The bruises, the blood, the makeshift slings, the knife cut across my cheek.

"What the hell happened?" I'd never heard Fallon use that voice before. It was a voice that promised revenge and death. I had no doubt that he would storm back to the house and finish off Liz for us. Fallon was terrifying when you hurt those he cared about.

I knew he cared about Ryder. They were brothers in every way but blood.

Me? I'd thought he merely tolerated my presence.

So why was he holding me so tenderly, as if he couldn't bear to let me go? Why did his lips brush against my hair?

If Ryder noticed his leader's strange behavior, he didn't say anything. Instead, he took my hand and propelled me forward. With Fallon on one side and Ryder on the other, I found myself sandwiched between the two men.

Totally would've enjoyed it more if I hadn't been bleeding out.

"I'll tell you what happened," Ryder said, helping me into an unfamiliar vehicle. I figured it was Fallon's car, or at least the car he'd stolen. "But I don't want you to tell the others everything."

His voice was raw. Bleeding. Desperate. He needed this privacy, this promise from Fallon that his secret would remain safe.

Despite the pain searing down the length of my body, I rested my head on his shoulder. He wrapped his good arm around me, holding me close.

I squeezed my eyelids shut as if I could somehow erase the memories of that house. Of Liz. Of everything she put us through.

As Ryder began to speak, I risked peeking at him through my fringe of lashes. His eyes were glassy, and he took a shuddering breath between words.

We were survivors. I wouldn't let Ryder shoulder this burden alone.

WE ARRIVED BACK at Elena's house only an hour later.

Ryder gave a full recap of the events with Liz. He purposely left some details vague, but Fallon was smart enough to read between the lines. His face was an icy mask by the time Ryder had finished his version of events. He looked positively livid when I told him mine.

Fallon explained what happened after we'd been discovered missing. Elena, apparently, had followed the car in the rain for as long as she could. She'd gotten the license plate information as well as the car details. Both the boys and girls had split up, each taking a radio with them. The boys, minus Fallon, went to the nearest town. The girls, excluding Sam, went to another. Sam had stayed home, just in case we came back.

Fallon had decided to go rogue, so to speak. From what I gathered, he didn't really have a plan. He instead went from door to door, kicking butt and taking names.

Nobody fucked with Fallon's team. And me. Because I was their sister that wasn't a sister, so that made me an honorary member of the team.

It would've been sweet of Fallon if, of course, he hadn't freaking shot at me.

"I didn't know it was you," Fallon said, for probably the one-hundredth time. His hand was feather light on my arm as he helped me from the car.

"I'm still pissed at you."

"I saw a car with the same license plate and description Elena gave me. I didn't know you were in it."

"Shut up, Meany Butt."

Ryder snorted at my eloquent nickname for his fearsome sergeant. I was happy that Ryder was smiling again. They weren't as frequent, but he would get there with time.

The house was quiet as we entered. All of the blinds were pushed back from the windows, allowing natural sunlight to illuminate the room.

A flurry of footsteps came around the corner as soon as we entered.

"Did you find—Oh, Addie!" Sam threw her arms around me, but immediately pulled back when I winced in pain. She turned from me to Ryder and gave him a small smile. I could tell she wanted to hug him as well, but refrained due to his injuries. "I'll radio the others to tell them you're back."

While she hurried to do just that, Fallon helped me to the couch. Ryder sat beside me with a heavy sigh.

We both looked like shit.

"I don't look like shit," Ryder said, responding to my thought that I must've said aloud. "I look like a sexy beast. You look like shit."

"Your mom looks like shit," I retorted.

"Your mom fucked your dad!"

It felt so natural to fall back into our easy banter that I found myself laughing semi hysterically. Ryder, after a moment of disbelief, began laughing as well. Soon, we were both laughing, and Fallon was staring at us as if we were insane.

Once the laughter subsided, Ryder turned towards me, wiping tears from his eyes.

And abruptly began laughing again.

"We were kidnapped by a crazy bitch!" he wheezed out.

"She beat the shit out of me!" I managed between fits of laughter.

"Fucking shit!"

Ryder and I laughed until the pain became too much.

We were a mess. We were broken and fucked up. So we laughed. We laughed because it was the only way to hide the scars.

We laughed because we weren't okay, and we probably never would be.

We laughed because we were two tortured souls who just happened to find each other.

We laughed because we longed to be happy again.

And the laughter actually kind of helped.

CHAPTER 26

ADDIE

I woke up to scorching heat.

For a moment, my incoherent mind couldn't remember where I was or how I'd gotten there. Was I back in my room at the resort? DOD really had to invest in new air conditioning. After a moment of my inner inarticulate ramblings, the memories came flooding back, nearly drowning me in their intensity.

Liz.

Ryder.

Fallon.

Those were the only names I could think of. Names and faces. Not actions. Not words. My mind couldn't handle reliving all of the details, so it kept everything broad.

But that still didn't explain why I was so hot.

Twisting in what appeared to be a bed, I discovered my answer.

I was surrounded by men. Well, only two men, but still.

Ryder slept on one side of me, snoring softly, our legs intertwined. Calax was on the other side of me, his arm resting gently on my waist.

His eyes were open, staring at me with love and relief. Before I could ask him how long he'd been awake—and staring at me like a creeper, I might add—he crushed his lips to mine. I moaned at the taste of him.

"Wait," I whispered as something occurred to me. Calax pulled back at once. His expression was so tender, so loving, that I wanted nothing more than to burrow inside of him and forget the last couple of days. But there was someone else to think of and something that needed to be understood by both of them. "Ryder…"

I saw the flash of pain in Calax's eye, and I hated myself for putting it there. I could see that he was retreating from me. Not physically, at least not yet, but mentally. He loved me, and I'd broken his heart.

He had to understand.

"I love you," I blurted, stunned by my own forwardness. Calax blinked. Apparently, he hadn't expected me to say that. A joyous, wondrous expression crossed his handsome face, and then he was kissing me again. He was showing me all of his love, and I, in return, was gifting him mine. I'd thought the words would feel unnatural, that I wouldn't be able to say them, but they felt so right. I was unsure about a lot of things in life, but my feelings for this mountain of a man wasn't one of them. "Wait!" I said again, slightly louder. I quickly worked to lower my voice. The last thing I wanted to do was wake Ryder. He needed his sleep, both because of his mental injuries and his physical ones.

"I was so scared, baby. I thought that I'd lost you...again. Do you have any idea how much I love you?" His fingers so incredibly gentle, he brushed my hair behind my ear. I shivered delicately at the sensations his mere touch created. His calloused hand caressed the bruises on my face, tracing the curve of my scar. If I thought he would look at me any different, I was mistaken. He still regarded me as if I were the most perfect woman to have ever existed.

I didn't deserve him.

"I love you, Callie. So fucking much. But..." Tears filled my eyes. Nodding towards Ryder, I said, "I love him too."

I watched Calax's jubilant expression shudder, like blinds being drawn. That only made me cry harder.

"You don't understand," I sobbed. "I love you, and I love him. I don't know how it happened, and I'm so sorry. I'm a horrible person. I wouldn't blame you if you hated me, but you need to understand. I don't love one more than the other. I love you both the same. You each hold my heart in different ways. God, I disgust myself. I'm so sorry." I rubbed at the snot and tears dripping down my face. I hated myself right then.

For hurting Calax, the man I loved.

For inevitably hurting Ryder as well.

I was going to lose them both, I knew that, but they deserved my honesty.

Calax's expression was still guarded, but his eyes were soft as they grazed my face.

"You love us both?"

"I'm so sorry," I cried.

I felt lips on my hair, and I jumped, startled. The movement brought about another round of pain, but I quickly smothered the whimper that threatened to break free.

Ryder was behind me, his good arm wrapped tightly around my waist.

"Why are you sorry, Kitten?" he asked, his lips brushing my ear. "For loving both of us? Why would you be sorry for having such a big and beautiful heart?"

"Baby." Calax took my hand in both of his. "I'm not mad. And I'm not letting you go."

"W-What?" I stuttered. Calax used one of his hands to wipe away a few stray tears.

"I love you. I always have and always will. I'm yours, and you're mine. But you're also his."

I didn't understand what he was saying. All I could do was stare up at him like an imbecile, hoping that his words would begin to make sense. Maybe if I stared at him hard enough…

Nope. I just looked like a freak.

"I already told you how I feel about you," Ryder said from behind me. He turned his face into my neck, breath causing goosebumps to erupt on my skin. "I love you, and I'm not letting you go either."

"I don't understand."

I shook my head, scarcely believing what I was hearing. It was almost too much for my heart to handle.

Calax and Ryder exchanged a long look over my head.

"We've shared girls before," Calax began, neck turning red as he blushed.

"But never any that we actually cared about," Ryder finished.

My stupid heart began to go into overdrive. I was ninety percent sure I was about to go into cardiac arrest.

"What we're saying…" Calax pressed a big palm to his face and dragged it down. He let out a grunt as words failed him, taking a page out of Fallon's book, *No Words Language 101*.

"What we're trying to ask you," Ryder cut in, "is if you would be our girlfriend?"

"Your. Girlfriend?"

Apparently, I was only capable of mechanically parroting words back to them. My brain had stopped.

Adelaide broken.

"So dramatic," Calax muttered, smiling. Still smiling, he leaned in closer to me. "We would be your boyfriends, and you would be our girlfriend."

"Like an open relationship?" I asked, stunned. I wasn't sure how I felt about Ryder and Calax seeing other girls. Actually, I was sure how I felt, and I hated it. The mere thought made me see red.

Ryder chuckled. "No, Kitten. Like a relationship. I would only be dating you, but you would be dating both of us."

I frowned as I considered his words. "That doesn't seem fair to you guys."

Because I got two boyfriends out of that arrangement, and they only got one slightly psychotic girlfriend that they had to share between them. I was pretty sure I was the winner in this scenario.

Calax leaned forward and brushed his lips against mine. I tensed, aware that Ryder was behind us, no doubt watching us intently, but he just continued to play with my hair as if it wasn't a big deal.

It was a big fucking deal.

"We don't want anyone else. We love you and only you. You love us." Calax shrugged as if it made complete sense.

"It might not be the most conventional relationship in the world, but we can make it work. There are actually a lot of polyamorous relationships in the world. Look at Sam and Lilly, for example. They have a loving, consensual relationship with a third person."

I glanced between Calax and Ryder.

"So would you two be lovers as well?" I asked seriously, still attempting to wrap my head around everything. And there was a lot to wrap my head around. They both broke into laughter.

"Don't swing that way, Kitten," Ryder said, chuckling.

Calax just continued to laugh.

"It would only be you," he said at last. There was so much love in his eyes, so much awe, that it was impossible for me to doubt his sincerity.

Still, I had trouble accepting what they were offering. Why would Calax be willing to share me? I wasn't that special. And Ryder was a flirt. He couldn't possibly be satisfied with only one girl, let alone one he had to share.

"Baby, Ryder needs you right now. I need you. Please just consider it."

Well I didn't have to consider it. If what they were offering me was true—though I still believed that they were going to laugh in my face and tell me it was a joke— then I would accept. I would do anything to keep the two men I loved with me.

Anything.

If that meant managing my time to ensure both of their happiness, then I would do it eagerly.

My voice was shy when I spoke next.

"Yes, I'll be your girlfriend."

The next few seconds were a flurry of cheers and kisses. I felt thoroughly loved… and very horny. Having two boyfriends was going to do wonders to my previously non-existent sex drive.

Calax's face was brilliant when he smiled. Beautiful. Ryder looked like I'd offered him the world. After everything he'd been through, he deserved to smile like that.

What did I possibly do to deserve these men?

"Two boyfriends," I said at last, a yawn distorting my voice. I'd never expected to even get one.

Calax exchanged another look with Ryder, and Ryder chuckled.

"I have a feeling that it's going to be more than that," Calax murmured. Before I could ask him what he meant, sleep claimed me.

I fell asleep nestled between two boys who loved me and whom I loved back.

LIZ

I was going to kill that bitch.

She took what was mine, and I would make her suffer.

Mine.

He was mine.

I knew she thought I was unhinged, but how could she not see the connection between Ryder and me? We were soulmates, meant to be together, and she was just the whore in our way.

I mentally planned how I was going to kill her. Stab in the neck? No. Too painless.

Suffocation? A possibility.

Dismemberment of her limbs?

A smile curved my lips upwards. Ding. Ding. Ding. We'd found ourselves a winner.

Footsteps from downstairs interrupted my musings. Of course, I couldn't greet the intruder, given the fact that the bitch had tied me to the bed.

I wondered if they'd come back. Not they, as in Ryder and the bitch, but the other they. The they that made my wedding possible.

They would be pissed that I lost Adelaide.

Oh well. She was a skank anyway.

The footsteps came closer, and I pressed my lips into the singularly beautiful smile I'd perfected. I puffed my chest out for added emphasis.

If they wanted to take me while I was tied to the bed, then I wouldn't complain.

The mere thought made me wet.

But when the person came into the room, eyes fierce on his handsome face, I felt my smile falter.

"Fallon?" I asked. "Did you come to save me?" I made my voice sound as weak and pathetic as possible. I even added a couple of tears. No guy could resist the tears.

Fallon crossed his muscular arms over his chest, and I licked my lips instinctively. That man could ride me any day. I would totally be his whore. Hell, he could even call me Adelaide if he wanted.

"Your partners," Fallon said. "What are their names?"

I sniffled dramatically.

"Aren't you going to let me go first? These hurt!" I tugged against the rope in clar-ification.

Fallon's face remained impassive. He could've been carved from an icicle.

"Names," he repeated.

Realizing that my innocent act wouldn't work on him, I spread my legs farther apart. It was difficult to do with the bindings, but somehow, I managed. I offered him a coy smile.

"I think we could make a deal."

I wanted his gaze to roam over me lustfully. I wanted his eyes to spark with love. And of course, I wanted Ryder to walk in, become jealous, and then decide to join us. My nipples hardened at the fantasy.

But stupid Fallon didn't remove his eyes from mine.

"Names."

Blowing out a breath, I said, "I don't know their names. They came to me with information about your little whore. They helped me follow her and grab her. They told me I would have a couple hours with her before they took her back."

My tone turned bitter. Why did everybody want Adelaide? What made her so special?

Oh wait. It was because she was a hoe. Duh.

"What did they look like?"

What was this? Twenty questions?

Sighing, I began to recall everything I knew about them. Which was nothing at all. They wore masks—not at all creepy—and had fake names. The leader was Red Eyes and his muscle was Lion. I couldn't recall the other two's names.

"So there's four?" he asked in confirmation. I nodded.

My body was stiff from being in the same position for so long, and my wrists were red from the rope.

Stupid bitch.

"They were supposed to be here a while ago. I don't know where they went. I told you everything I know. Can you let me go now?"

Fallon considered me thoughtfully. There was something in his expression that I didn't entirely understand. Something dangerous.

"Did you know that there were two Ragers outside your front door when I arrived?" he asked conversationally. I blinked up at him, unsure where he was going with this. "They followed me inside. I believe they're currently in your living room."

I felt the beginning of panic start to set in.

"Are you going to let me go?" I struggled against the ropes. "Fallon! Let me go! Fallon!"

But he was walking away.

And he left the door open.

"Fallon!" I struggled in earnest now. Sobbing, I screamed his name again. "Fallon!"

Two figures ran into the room, but neither of them was Fallon.

I screamed for him. I screamed when their teeth dug into my neck. I screamed when they tore apart my body, one clawed fist at a time.

The pain.

So much pain.

Then nothing.

BONUS SCENE

RYDER

"What the fucking hell is this shit?" I held up the tiny, lacy thong, unsure if I should feel arousal or horror. Because the thought of Addie in this scrap of a thing? Yeah, my cock was harder than granite. But the price? I swore my balls shriveled in on themselves like fucking raisins or some shit.

Addie rolled her eyes and swapped it from my hand.

"Don't just dangle it for the whole world to see," she reprimanded, tossing it in the bag. A delicate blush stained her cheeks, as if she was honestly embarrassed that someone might have seen the underwear she was thinking about buying. Though underwear was too…tame a word.

"Who the fuck pays seventy dollars for a bra?" Ronan tossed in, staring intently at a colorful collection and garnering the attention of a few curious on-lookers. He twisted his head to stare at Addie before lowering his gaze to her hands. He, too, was glaring at the shopping bag intently, and I wondered if he was also imagining Addie posing for us in that sexy lingerie. Hmmm. Maybe I should suggest a fashion show…

"Shush," Addie hissed as she sifted through a rack of clothes.

"It's so tiny." I dug the thong back out of the bag and held it delicately between two fingers. "Does it even, like, cover stuff?"

Not that I was complaining. The less it covered, the better.

"Of course it covers stuff, you noob!" Ronan snapped, and I couldn't help but snort. Noob? Really? Fucking asshole. He really needed to work on his insults, though I understood he was trying to censor himself around our new, beautiful friend.

"But why would you pay so much for so little?" I just couldn't wrap my head around that. Was this what girls dealt with daily? I was even more happy than usual that I had a dick dangling between my legs. A dick that was rapidly hardening when I thought about Addie in that fucking thong.

"Oh my god! Shut up!" Addie slapped both of our heads, one after the other, but our grins only broadened. There was nothing we loved more than seeing a feisty Addie.

"Maybe they accidentally put the wrong price tag on this…thing." I held the thong between my thumb and pinkie, almost as if it were covered in acid and I had to quickly bring it to a containment room.

"Underwear is always that expensive," she sighed.

"I can get, like, twenty pairs for this price," Ronan interjected, his face etched in horror. "This is so wrong."

"You should see the price of our feminine products," Addie mumbled absently, already moving to a new section.

"The volcano eruption?" I queried.

"The river of red?" Ronan added. A shit-eating grin erupted on his face.

"Devil's birthday?"

"Cranberry juice?"

"Enough!" She threw both of her hands up into the air as my brother and I grinned. "You guys can discuss my period. I'm going to the changing room."

Addie? Changing into that fucking thong?

What I wouldn't pay to be a fly on the wall…

BONUS SCENE

I didn't like the way Samantha was staring at Adelaide—as if she were a toy to be stolen, a treasure to be coveted. I'd never considered myself a jealous man before, but just then, possessiveness reared its ugly head. My hands clenched into fists as I watched Lilly and Sam drag her into the adjacent kitchen.

Stiffly, I moved to lean against the far wall. I crossed my arms over my chest and surveyed the scene before me with glacial attachment. Elena was sitting beside Ronan, so close that their knees were touching. Ronan, for his part, looked immensely uncomfortable with the attention. He was already squeezed so far to the side of the couch that he was practically spilling over the armrest. When she placed a manicured hand on his knee, he jumped as if he'd been electrocuted.

I knew that this was a bad idea. I didn't know why I'd agreed to do this in the first place. There were only a few people I could handle, and Elena and her crew were definitely not any of them.

I felt a hand touch my bicep, and I tensed instinctively.

Don't panic. Don't panic.

I repeated that in my head like a mantra. I wasn't like the other guys. Hell, I didn't know anyone who was like me. Needless to say, I didn't like being touched. Pinpricks of aversion danced across my skin. My muscles were coiled and ready for a fight. I was not against breaking a girl's hand if she didn't respect my personal space.

Don't panic. Don't panic.

"Lacey!" Asher said with a wide smile. He maneuvered himself so he was between the blonde and myself. Though his smile was forced, he wrapped an arm around her shoulders and led her to the couch. After a moment, he sat beside her.

I'd never been more grateful for my brother before. Asher had a way of innately reading me—of reading everyone. He must've seen that I was nearing a breaking point.

Lacey, either oblivious to the grimace on Asher's face or choosing to ignore it, began to paw at his arm. Calax hid his laugh behind a large fist.

My patience was splintering. Where was Addie? How long did it take her to get changed? My mind unwillingly conjured up images of her. What if a Rager had captured her? What if Sam had seduced her? What if...

Before I realized what I was doing, I charged towards the kitchen.

The first thing I noticed was Lilly and Sam leaning against the counter. I crossed my arms over my chest and leveled them with my most penetrating glare.

"Are you guys almost done? What the hell are you guys doing?"

"I'm sorry," Sam said, though her eyes weren't on me. "I hadn't meant to stare. You just have a lot of scars."

I swiveled my head to see what had captured and entrapped both of their attentions.

My breath left me, and heat flowed through my veins.

Addie...

Her body was a canvas of art. Scars adorned her porcelain skin, each one telling a different story. Her brown hair was pushed behind her ears, leaving her breasts on full display. She didn't hide behind her hands as other girls might've. No, she merely met my heated stare with a defiant one of her own. I couldn't help but envision my mouth sucking on one of those perfect, pink nipples. My body dominating hers...

What was wrong with me?

I didn't like touch. I didn't do girlfriends or relationships or any of that shit.

And yet...

Heat ran straight to my groin, and I felt myself harden in my jeans. The urge to take her, to claim her, was nearly overwhelming.

Before she could say anything, I turned on my heel and practically ran from the kitchen. Still, her body was etched into the backs of my eyelids whenever I closed them.

"Sarge?" Ryder asked, watching me with a quirk to his brow, confusion swimming his gaze.

"Fallon..." That annoying whine came from one of the girls. I was too far gone to see, or even care, which one.

Pushing past them all, I ran up the stairs and into the nearest bathroom. I gripped the sink and panted. God, that perfect body...

Before I realized what I was doing, I had my pants unzipped and my cock in my hand. My body trembled as I once again envisioned her silky skin, her perfect breasts, the mound of curls leading to her...

I pumped myself faster, my breathing nothing but shallow gasps. The image changed. Now, she was on her knees before me. Instead of my hand stroking my cock to oblivion, it was her plump, pink lips. I allowed that image to take me over the edge, and I came with a barely muffled grunt.

Damn it. Damn her. Damn everyone.

Was I going to go to hell for jacking off to the image of her naked body? Probably. Did I care?

Well…maybe hell wouldn't be too bad.

THE STORM WE FACE

THE DARKNESS WE CRAVE BOOK 3

PROLOGUE

ADDIE

I stared at the place I'd last seen him. I stared at the place where he'd made his final stand, where he'd gone out in a blaze of glory. He had always wanted to die like that—a hero.

I let out a scream of anguish, but the sound was lost in the cries. One cry couldn't be distinguished from the thousands of others.

All I could do was stare. I'd loved him, and he was lost to me. Love, I began to realize, was dangerous. It only brought unbearable pain, a pain that could not be put into words.

I wondered, as I stared at a splatter of blood darkening the carpeting, if my love had inevitably led to his death.

CHAPTER 1

ADDIE

He was going to kill me. Of that, I was sure. He was going to kill me and enjoy it, like the twisted psychopath he was.

I leveled a kick at his stomach, but he easily sidestepped it. It felt almost like a dance. Each one of us performed a separate part, a separate move, utterly in sync with one another. Okay, so he was in sync with me. I was floundering in too deep water, trying my hardest to keep my head above. Unlike him, I *didn't* know the moves to this dance. I tried, I failed, but I tried again, ever persistent.

He grabbed my arm, twisting it behind my back, and I let out a grunt of pain. He really was going to kill me. Before I could scream, he flipped me over his shoulder. My back thumped painfully against the grass, and I stared up into my attacker's brown and gold eyes.

"I am going to kill you in your sleep. No, better than that, I'm going to cut off your balls, feed them to you, then kill you in your sleep," I said from my spot sprawled on the ground.

The bastard in question merely stood over me with an amused tilt to his lips.

I was only going to refer to him as Bastard. I'd made up my mind about that yesterday, when we first began. He didn't deserve a first name.

Or a sexy nickname.

Not that he was sexy or anything. Well, I mean, he was, but...

Bastard's smile had grown, hinting that I might have spoken aloud.

Oops.

"Sarge!" Ronan, bless his soul, called from the doorway. "We need you for a sec."

Bastard, aka Sarge—or Fallon, but it was whatever—offered me a hand. Over his broad shoulders, I could just make out the dusting of sunlight slowly disappearing behind the boughs of trees.

"Get your dumbass hand away from me," I hissed. "I'm content to just stay here."

He raised an eyebrow at me.

"Let me die in peace, please," I added. He smirked but obediently jogged towards the back porch where Ronan was waiting impatiently.

The bastard decided I needed to "train." Apparently, getting kidnapped by one of my boyfriends' psycho ex-girlfriend made it clear how weak and frail I actually was. Thus, Bastard decided to put me on a strict diet and even stricter training regimen.

I'd argued profusely when he first suggested it. I had to get to Atlanta ASAP to see my little brother, Nikolai. I haven't heard from him since the world went to hell, and worry constantly niggled me.

But we weren't able to leave. The boys insisted that we had to collect more supplies since most of ours were lost in an earthquake and Ryder needed time to heal. I hadn't argued after that, especially when I considered Ryder's empty gaze.

Yes, he most definitely needed time to heal.

I myself hadn't fared any better from the kidnapping. My face would always hold a reminder of what that bitch did to us. The scar sliced down my cheek, starting just below my eye and ending near the top of my lip. I didn't know how I felt about it.

I'd always paid tribute to my various scars. They were a reminder of all I had conquered and all that I wanted to conquer. This one was no different, yet I could see Ryder's haunted expression whenever he stared at the line disfiguring my face.

Blame. Guilt. Shame. Something akin to embarrassment.

I understood the expressions he wore all too well. I tried telling him what Liz did wasn't his fault, but he always pushed the subject away with a stupid joke or a sarcastic remark.

He was like me in that way—using wit to hide his pain.

A large figure stood above me, effectively cutting out the sunlight once again. His silhouette would've been almost ominous if I didn't know who he was.

Only one person was that big

"Is this what death feels like?" I asked dramatically, flinging my arms out on either side of me for emphasis.

Calax snorted.

"Don't be so dramatic and get your ass up."

Yup. No sympathy from my giant. If it was Asher or Tamson, they would offer me a massage or a hot blanket. But Calax?

Apparently, I had to suffer through it. Ugh. He was lucky I loved him.

His dark hair was extremely tousled just then. He always had a tendency to run his hand through his hair when he was anxious or upset. Planning our day-long, if not longer, trip to Atlanta would most definitely put anyone in a sour mood.

"Carry me?" I asked weakly, holding my arms up to him. He chuckled but obediently scooped me into his arms as if I weighed nothing more than a baby. Smiling, I nuzzled his neck.

"I knew there was a reason I kept you around."

He turned his face towards mine, and his lips lightly brushed my own. They were as soft as a moth's wing. Tingles of electricity ran through my body at the contact.

"Is that the only reason?" he asked. I enjoyed this side of Calax—the light, relaxed side that remained hidden from the rest of the world. I loved his grumpiness and his protectiveness, but I adored his teasing. It reminded me of when we first met, when I decided I hated and loved him. He was still my mortal enemy, but I figured it wouldn't hurt if we kissed…and confessed our love to one another. Yup. No problem with that.

Bastard.

Smug, sexy, infuriating—

"You're talking aloud again," the smug, sexy, infuriating Bastard pointed out. In reply, I stuck my tongue out at him. His eyes turned heated.

"I can think of better things you could use that tongue for."

Before I could reply—or jump him like I was a dog in heat—the sliding glass door that led to the backyard opened, and Ryder stepped out.

His dark hair had been freshly washed, no doubt from the nearby stream, and he wore a pair of jeans and a white shirt. The shirt itself greatly contrasted with his dark skin and showcased the many tattoos circling down his large biceps.

He was sex on a stick.

And mine. Did I mention that already?

Not trying to brag or anything…

"Don't hog our girl," he said to Calax lightly, and my heart fluttered at the words. Our girl. Swoon.

I would never get over the fact that these two perfect men decided I was worthy enough to be in a relationship with. To share, some may say, though I didn't like that connotation. It would imply that I'd split my heart and body between the two men. I loved them both equally, as if I had two entirely separate hearts beating inside of my chest. One for each.

Ryder brought out the playful side in me.

Calax was my rock.

And for some miraculous reason, they decided I was deserving of their love and affection. Of course, that meant I had to actually be a girlfriend to these two men. I thought that meant I had to feed them or something? Maybe take them out for a walk? It was a learning curve.

Ryder, seemingly unperturbed that I was in Calax's arms, kissed my cheek tenderly. I glanced under my fringe of lashes, assessing Calax's reaction, but he appeared unbothered by his brother's affection towards me.

Despite declaring his love for me, Ryder had yet to actually kiss me. You know, like *kiss me* kiss me. He gave me a chaste brush of the lips when we were in hell— okay, Lizzy's house, though they were basically the same thing—but never a toe-curling, tongue-humping make out. I was honestly afraid that he didn't want to or something. The boy had kissed a lot of girls, yet he somehow hadn't been able to kiss me?

Puh-lease.

I tried to ignore these insecurities. Ryder was mine in heart, soul, and body, and I was his. I knew that he loved me, yet the child in me recollected all of those times I'd felt vulnerable and unloved.

Used.

Discarded.

Ryder's hand was still resting on my cheek when we heard the door behind us open. He immediately pulled away from me as if he'd been burnt.

I blanched, though not for the obvious reasons. I wasn't hurt or upset that Ryder hid his affections towards me. We'd agreed to keep our unconventional relationship a secret from the rest of the team.

A team that I may or may not have feelings for.

Yup. I was a nutcase. Apparently, my demented mind decided that two perfect guys weren't enough. Oh no. I had to develop feelings for the other five members of their team as well.

I wasn't in love with them, at least not with all of them, but it was something undefinable that caused my heart to clench painfully whenever they were near. It was lust, yes, but something so much more than that. They each brought out a different side of me, a better side of me, that I had thought didn't exist. They made me want to be better.

My breath left me in an exhale when I saw only Tommy standing on the porch, his eyes narrowed suspiciously.

Tommy was my child. Not literally—I was only eighteen, and he was thirteen— but at least mentally. I didn't think he would appreciate that sentiment though.

"What are you assholes doing?" he asked, cocking his hip to the side and glaring at us through his large glasses. I was pretty sure that he didn't actually need glasses, but had found them inside one of Elena's drawers. His sass was just another reason I loved him. And his penchant for pink, sparkly eyewear. "Not you, Addie. You're not an asshole." He took a step towards us in what he probably thought was a threatening manner. I'm afraid that it was impossible for him to look dangerous standing at five feet with his face bloated from baby fat.

He was honestly kind of adorable.

Raising his eyebrow, he gave me a long look.

"You okay, Addie?" he asked me, voice considerably more gentle. He leveled a glare at Ryder and Calax, both of whom towered over his tiny frame. "If I discover that you two are taking advantage of her, so help me god, I will—"

I cut him off before he could end his threat.

"I'm fine, Tommy. Promise."

If I thought of Tommy as my surrogate son, he thought of me as his daughter. It was an odd relationship, but it seemed to work.

After one more glare aimed at the guys, he stomped towards the door, calling over his shoulder, "Sarge called a meeting."

"That kid is getting on my last nerve," Ryder muttered. I merely planted a sloppy kiss onto his cheek.

"You're just jealous."

He snorted but didn't contradict me.

Still in Calax's arms, we walked into the living room of Elena's house. The couches were now moved to form a small semi-circle. Tamson and Asher were sitting on the couch, both wearing small smiles. Tam, my timid friend, met my gaze, blushed, and then immediately glanced down at his feet. I hated that I made him feel self-conscious, but I also didn't know how to stop it.

Talk to him?

I doubted he would be receptive to that. Asher offered me one of his brilliant smiles, his shaggy blond hair brushing his eyes. It was in desperate need of a cut, but I secretly loved his disheveled look.

Ronan was on the loveseat, his legs kicked over the arms. His green hair was stylishly spiked and his unicorn tattoo peeked over the edge of his shirt. I still wondered about the purpose for that particular tattoo, but there had never been an appropriate time to ask.

Declan was leaning against the doorframe, muscles straining against his black T-shirt. I had a complicated relationship with Declan. Complicated because I used to love the shit out of him, but now I barely knew him. I hoped that we could rekindle the friendship we once had. Years had gone by with me believing he was dead and him believing I hated him. It was hard for anyone to get past that.

I waved my hands to garner his attention.

"You're doing a mighty good job of holding up that wall," I signed. *"Whatever would we do without your help keeping the house from falling?"*

His lips pulled into a tiny smirk, but that smirk instantly disappeared on his face when he took in the position I was in. Namely, still wrapped in Calax's arms.

I knew that he, as well as the rest of the team, was aware I was dating Calax. I was also aware that they didn't necessarily agree with that decision, though I couldn't discern if their disdain came from annoyance or something else entirely.

I wondered what they would do if they discovered I was dating Ryder as well.

Knowing Ronan, at least, he would want to join.

Not that I would object...

Pinching Calax's arm, I indicated for him to drop me on my feet. At first, I thought he wasn't going to listen as his arms tightened around me, like an impenetrable fortress between me and the outside world. His arms were a heavenly place where I didn't have to worry about pain. Heaving a heavy, if not resigned sigh, he set me down.

"Where is the bastard anyway?" I asked. Said Bastard was noticeably absent from the meeting he'd apparently called.

Such a bastard.

"Really, Adelaide?" a cold voice asked, accompanied by a raised eyebrow. I folded my arms over my chest and glared at him as he walked through the archway. His hair was pulled back into a knot on the nape of his neck, a few strands escaping and curling around his ears.

"I'm pissed at you," I retorted oh so wisely. To emphasize my point, I rubbed at my sore shoulder. He merely rolled his eyes at my dramatics before turning towards the rest of the group.

His team.

Fallon refused to sit, though that was no surprise. He always had to be the tallest, most imposing figure in the room. With his broad shoulders and penetrating eyes, he most definitely succeeded.

"Excuse me!" I said, before he could speak. I waved my hand in the air. Fallon pinched the bridge of his nose and closed his eyes.

"You don't need to raise your fucking hand, sweetheart," he muttered. "We all know you're just going to talk anyway."

I frowned.

He may be right, but still. Dick.

His smile grew, hinting that I may have spoken that insult aloud. Again.

"I have a few topics I would like to bring to the committee's attention today," I said seriously. Ronan coughed to cover up his laugh. "The first one is concerning Atlanta. I don't believe that everyone should go with me. I vote that I travel by myself."

I should have really considered a career in politics. I was a damn good diplomat.

Before anyone could protest, I held up a hand. "Calax can come with me, for obvious reasons. And Ryder can come to…sing me to sleep. Not any other reason." I knew that it would be wishful thinking on my part to believe that they'd let me go alone. Damn them. At least I nailed the whole subtlety thing concerning Ryder. The assholes would never suspect we were dating. Singing a person to sleep was a completely valid reason for coming with them on a dangerous journey across the country. Right?

"And Ronan will probably want to go because his brother is going, so I guess he can come too." I paused, considering my words thoughtfully. "Fallon is probably going to want to go, but I doubt Fallon would leave the rest of them behind. Declan, of course, is welcome to come. Tamson can come too, since his ninja skills would come in handy. If they all come, I'm going to need Asher to calm myself down. Heaven forbid that I'm stuck with all of these assholes without Asher. So yeah. Only those people can go."

I blinked innocently, glancing from one face to the next. Fallon raised a dark eyebrow at me.

"Kitten," Ryder said softly. "You literally just invited everyone."

"No, I didn't!" I protested, but my mind immediately replayed my monologue.

Damnit. That was a fail.

Fallon, still looking too damn amused, clapped his hands together.

"Now that Adelaide has given us all permission to join her, shall we move on?"

"I didn't mean to do that." I crossed my arms over my chest with a huff. Sometimes I wondered if it would be best if I glued my mouth shut. I had a serious case of word vomit.

The whole goal of my spiel was to convince the boys *not* to follow me. Obviously, I hadn't succeeded. I really sucked at the whole people thing, despite my repeated attempts at practice.

"The second thing I would like to address is your team and school. I'm not stupid. I know it's more than a normal boarding school. I want answers, and I want them now. I can't keep living in the dark. I mean, I'm a ride or die type of person, but I want to know where we're going and why we have to die." I leveled each of them with my best glare. The guys exchanged rapid glances with one another before Fallon released a heavy sigh. His thick lips were pursed as he considered me.

"You're right," he admitted at last. "You deserve to know everything."

Calax's hand tightened over mine, and Ryder turned to stare at me pleadingly, begging me to understand what I was going to hear. I had the distinct feeling that these answers, the answers I wanted so desperately they were almost a physical ache, were going to change my life.

"We should probably start at the beginning," Fallon said.

"The beginning?"

"There was a reason we were at the resort to begin with."

"Which was?" I was beginning to become irritated. Fallon had a tendency to give me vague answers. The more he talked, the dizzier I became. Crossing my arms over my chest, I waited for him to collect his thoughts.

"For your parents," he admitted after an excruciatingly long moment of silence. I shifted. Whatever I'd expected him to say, it wasn't that. What did my parents have to do with a boarding school?

My confusion must've been evident on my face, as Fallon released another heavy sigh. His hand crept up to pinch the bridge of his nose.

"I suck at explaining this," he mumbled beneath his breath, and I resisted the urge to make a very inappropriate joke about sucking.

"Look, Addie," Ronan interrupted, turning to stare at me. He leaned forward so his elbows rested on his knees. "We don't actually go to a normal school. We were chosen because we each displayed a unique set of skills that made us valuable." He ran a hand through his green-tipped hair. It was beginning to grow out, and I could admit to myself that I would be upset to see the green dye leave his dark hair entirely. Granted, he would always be my leprechaun. What could I say? I was a sentimental bitch. "What I'm trying to say is—"

"What he's trying to say is that we work—worked for the government," Tam broke in. "We work for the government, and we came to the resort in order to investigate, and eventually arrest, your parents."

What.

The.

Fuck?

CHAPTER 2

I stood there, staring at the men who'd quickly become my entire world. They gazed back at me, eyes earnest, if not pleading. I tried to process Tam's words, tried to understand the implications of such a simple sentence.

Arrest.

Parents.

Government.

Nothing made sense.

"Kitten," Ryder said. "Say something."

I blinked at him.

"I don't know what to say."

Because my world has just been turned upside down. All of our interactions had been a lie. Had they even wanted to be my friend, or was I just a mission to them? That thought made my heart squeeze painfully as if held together by iron clamps. I remembered my first meeting with Ronan, the first time I rested my eyes on Asher.

I remembered my conversations with Calax. How he'd conveniently moved into an apartment complex my parents owned.

Oh god.

"Addie, I see the wheels in your head turning." Calax almost sounded desperate, an emotion I doubted he was familiar with.

I only managed to croak out one word. "Explain."

It was Fallon who spoke, finally regaining his cool. He straightened his spine and leveled me with a penetrating stare. It felt as if he was seeing through my layers of clothes and into my very soul. I couldn't help but squirm at the scrutiny. My soul was dark and tarnished. I feared that if he looked any closer, he would see how broken I actually was.

"Your parents were believed to be involved with an international drug cartel, among other things. Human trafficking, for one. Murder." He continued to stare at me, eyes assessing. I shifted in my seat, both at his words and his unflinching eyes. "We were investigating a particular case. A Mexican drug lord named Jose Hernadez."

"Papa Jose?" I asked, stunned.

"Huh?" Ronan broke in, eyebrow quirked.

I knew exactly who he was referring to, and I may or may not have known that Papa Jose wasn't a grade A citizen. Don't judge.

"He told me to call him Papa Jose," I filled in helpfully. Tam and Asher exchanged startled glances. "I liked him. He would give me candy when he came to visit."

"Addie…" Calax began in his usual reprimanding tone. "How many times do I have to tell you? Don't take candy from drug lords."

"Bygones be bygones." I waved my hand dismissively. They were investigating my parents? Papa Jose? Again, that thought didn't unsettle me. It was surprising, yes, but somehow, I'd already suspected as much. I knew that the boys weren't the standard, all-American high schoolers. They were so much more than that.

"So…" I trailed off, unsure of how to phrase my next question. On one hand, I didn't want to offend any of the guys, especially Ryder and Calax. But…you know what they say. Curiosity killed the petty bitch. "Was anything true? Our friendships? Our…" I glanced between Ryder and Calax, too quickly for anyone to notice. "Relationships?"

I saw hurt flash in Calax's normally impassive expression, and I hated myself for putting it there in the first place.

"I didn't know who you were when I first met you," Ronan offered at last. "I knew they had a daughter, but you were not my assignment. Actually, it was Elena's team's job to get close to you. To become your friend."

A snort escaped, unbidden.

"That turned out well."

"No shit." Ronan's lips quirked. "All I knew was that you were a strange, slightly crazy girl that I had to get to know better."

"None of us looked at you like a mission, Kitten," Ryder said softly. He reached forward to squeeze my knee. "Sure, we wanted to protect you and care for you, but that had nothing to do with the case or your parents. That was solely because of you. We wanted to be your friend because of who you were as a person, not because of who your parents were."

My heart swelled at hearing his words. I offered him a brilliant smile, and he immediately met it with one of his own. Calax, however, was *not* smiling. His scowl was firmly directed at the wall above Fallon's head.

Well shit. I sucked at this girlfriend thing.

Food. I needed to offer him food.

Reaching into my pocket, I shoved a granola bar into his large, calloused hand. Tamson had given it to me earlier that day to eat after training. I was happy that I had saved it though. Calax glanced from the bar, to me, and then back to the bar again. Tentatively, he peeled back the paper and nibbled on the edge of the bar.

Finally, *finally*, he offered me a small smile. A breath of relief instantly escaped me.

Best. Girlfriend. Ever.

I turned back to the conversation, aware that I had missed the ending of Fallon's spiel. From the amused glint in his eyes, I figured he was aware of that as well.

Another thought swirled through my head, gaining traction the more I thought about it. I bit my lip, staring at each of their beautiful faces. The question continued to niggle at me, and I finally dared to ask.

"Do you know?" I whispered.

"Know what?" Ryder asked.

"What started the end of the world. Do you know?" My voice was soft. It might've given the impression that I was calm, but I was anything but. My thoughts were running rampant and unsupervised through my mind. I felt betrayed, angry, upset.

I felt it all, and it almost consumed me.

I didn't expect them to answer. If anything, I expected them to deflect.

"Global warming," Fallon said at last. His fingers drummed a pattern against his jean-clad legs. I watched the rhythmic pattern of his fingers, utterly entranced. The golden bands of his rings glistened in the candlelight.

"Global warming?" I repeated stupidly. Wasn't that the answer to everything? Was he joking? Was he trying to be funny?

I couldn't help but snort. Fallon? Funny? Good grief. Hell would freeze over before that day would come.

"That's a theory," Tam continued. His face lit up, as it always did when he discussed something that interested him. I yearned to see that brilliant smile on his face every day. Hell, I yearned to be on the receiving end of such a smile. I mentally scolded myself, breaking out of the wistful fantasies that held me hostage and focusing on his words. "When the ice caps melted, it released a parasite that had been stuck in there…well…forever. It can survive both in water and on land."

I turned over the information Tam had given me. While I'd studied biology, I was never an expert in it. My parents much preferred my curriculum to be math and business based. So this? I had no idea how plausible of an explanation it was. It could've been bullcrap for all I knew.

Ronan continued, "It enters a host—us—and takes over a section of the brain."

"The limbic system," Tam filled in. "The part that makes you want to fight or flight. It helps you understand stimuli and act accordingly. This parasite? It messes with that. The only option you have is to fight. It makes you behave with an uncontrollable rage. A rage that is almost primitive in nature…" Tam trailed off, face contemplative.

"You were told all of this?" I asked, turning from face to face. Asher appeared almost sheepish at my accusation, and Calax's scowl deepened when I turned towards him.

"By some of the top scientists," Fallon said, nodding. "I'm friends with some people high up."

This was almost too surreal. I wasn't supposed to receive the answers like this. I'd thought there would be trial and error before I would be able to come to a conclusion. It felt almost cheesy, in a sense, like a badly scripted scene in a B-rated movie. Everything was a coincidence, I realized. It was one of the numerous facets that pieced together fate. Maybe we were fated to come together. I was the mission, and they were the team. I had the questions, and they had the answers. Fate had a mind of its own, and it made you its bitch more often than not and squished you like a bug beneath stiletto heels. Still, my stomach churned almost violently as I leafed through all of the information given.

I felt betrayed. I was running down this race blind, and I'd dumbly assumed they were doing the same. It struck me deep to realize I'd been alone this entire time. They hadn't trusted me with their secrets, yet they'd expected me to offer up my own. And I had, like the desperate, scared girl I was.

I knew I should be grateful that they were finally telling me the truth, yet the sly voice in my mind wondered if they still would've told me if I hadn't asked. The voice said no.

Not Calax. Not Ryder.

Not Ducky.

"I need a second," I muttered, standing and walking towards my designated bedroom.

"Addie," Ryder called after me, and I flinched at the use of my name coming from his mouth. I wasn't Kitten at that moment. Just Addie.

And I hated her.

"I need a damn second," I snapped. Before he could respond, I threw myself inside my bedroom, my back to the door.

Fuck them.

Their secrets. Their lies. Their avoidance of the truth. I was beyond furious. They had betrayed me, and the scars cut deep.

"You look pissed," a voice said, and my head snapped up. Elena stood in the room, absently grabbing duffle bags off of the top shelf in the closet. Her blonde hair was braided back from her stupidly pretty face, and she wore a baggy T-shirt and ripped jeans.

"I am pissed," I said before I could stop myself. It was very easy to overlook the fact that Elena hated me with a passion. Sometimes, she almost seemed to be…nice. I knew that she was jealous of my relationship with the guys. She loved them, and it pained her that they never felt the same way. Her hostility towards me was somewhat understandable, if not completely uncalled for. You couldn't pick and choose who you loved. It just happened, a natural part of human nature.

"They told you?" she guessed, and I bristled. It may have seemed petty, but I didn't like the imperiousness in her tone, as if she thought she knew them and the reasoning behind their actions better than I did.

"Yeah," I said, deciding to play civil. "They told me. I just don't understand *how*. How are they privy to such classified information? How do they know everything they do?"

It just didn't make any sense. Even if they were "agents," something I wasn't entirely sure I believed, they wouldn't be told such important classified information.

I doubted every FBI and CIA agent knew what was happening with the world and why.

Elena's voice was almost mocking when she spoke next.

"It's because of Fallon's daddy," she cooed.

"Fallon's daddy?" I repeated. I really didn't like those two words coming out of her mouth—Fallon and daddy.

"Well not technically his dad, but his uncle." Elena turned back towards the closet, scanning the numerous bags adorning the shelf. "He's the Secretary of Defense."

I blinked, unsure if I'd heard her right. Secretary of Defense? Fallon's uncle?

If that was true, then it explained a lot.

And if that was true, I was going to skin Fallon alive.

I understood the need for secrecy, but after everything we'd been through, why hadn't they told me? My anger was primarily directed at the group leader. It was his secret and his secret alone. Like any coveted object, he chose what he wanted to do with it. Apparently, I wasn't trusted enough to be in the know of such a life-changing secret.

But Elena was.

"What are you doing anyways?" I asked, attempting to divert my attention off of Fallon and onto something else. Anything else.

Elena smirked.

"Supply run," she said. "We're heading to the mall a town over to gather supplies before we leave for California."

Two members of Elena's team, Sam and Lilly, had a boyfriend in that state. The girls were desperate to get their man back, and the team had reluctantly agreed to follow.

"Supplies? Can I come?"

I knew the guys would be pissed, and that only added fuel to the fire. But I couldn't just wait around until we decided to leave for Atlanta. I felt utterly helpless and inept. I wanted to prove myself to not only the guys, but to myself.

I would be worthy of their trust. Of that, I would make sure.

"Are you sure your babysitters will allow you to go? This isn't a twenty-person assignment. You won't be able to bring them all."

My lip thinned.

"I don't have a babysitter, and I don't need their permission," I snapped. Was I being irrational? Most definitely. Did I care? Not in the least.

I was hurting, and the only solution I could come up with was to prove myself. The team had to know I wasn't just a pretty face. I'd always been a fighter. I would kick ass and take names.

"Well then..." Elena stepped forward, two bags slung over either arm. "Welcome to the team."

∼

"No way in hell."

"Not by yourself. We'll come too."

Their reactions were better than I'd expected, meaning nobody tried to kill me.

Once I'd given my spiel on how necessary it was to gather supplies, the team had agreed. Once I added that I intended to go, all hell broke loose.

Calax, ever my supporter, allowed me to go on the condition he could come with.

Allowed. And cue the mental eye roll. I wasn't a fucking child in need of their permission. I was an equal member of their team. At least in spirit.

Physically, however…

I could shoot a gun, somewhat expertly—okay, a Nerf gun, same thing—and I was also pretty handy with a bow and arrow, if I did say so myself. A knife? Not my area of expertise. I knew that the pointy end went into the body, but besides that, I preferred to stay away from the keen weapon.

Don't get me wrong. I understood why they wanted to come with me. The world was dangerous, and I was, admittedly, somewhat weaker compared to them. But I was resilient and had a will to live that spanned years.

More importantly, I needed space. For just a moment.

"I'll be fine," I insisted. I stared at each face before turning fully towards Fallon. I glowered at the man, hoping he could see all of my pent-up anger and frustration. "Let me be fucking useful for once."

His eyes softened, at least as much as his eyes could. He considered me, eyes assessing, and finally nodded. Before anyone could protest, he held up a fist.

"Would you be willing to take one of us with you?" Fallon asked. "A compromise."

A compromise.

That I could do.

"Fine," I said, and I saw Calax straighten his shoulders expectantly. Poor Callie. Did he not realize I needed a day free of boyfriends? I loved him, but he'd lied to me. Yeah. Yeah. Yeah. I probably should get over it. But I was angry, petty, and vindictive. "I choose Tam, the ninja."

"Tam?" Calax said, brows furrowing. Ryder just gaped at me.

"He's the only one I'm not pissed at. Well, I'm not mad at Asher, but I want a ninja covering my back."

Tam blushed, and I could've sworn he mumbled, "Not a ninja," beneath his breath.

Without waiting for them to respond, I stormed towards my bedroom. I wouldn't have been able to tell you what I was doing. Was I running? Hiding? We all had a tendency to run, me more than anybody. I wasn't a fighter, and my flight response nearly overwhelmed me.

My breathing was ragged, shallow almost, as I pressed my forehead against the wall. There were so many emotions inside of me at that moment, but I was unable to detangle them all. It led to a combination of hurt, anger, and disappointment. The latter emotion was aimed at myself. I wanted to be someone they could trust and count on, someone like Elena. I'd spent my life hiding in my parents' shadows, and I was desperate to snatch the first available drop of sunlight. I wanted to feel needed, a juxtaposition I didn't entirely understand. The more I thought about it, the more I corrected myself. No, I *needed* to feel needed.

The door behind me opened, and I looked up, expecting Ryder or Calax. I was pleasantly surprised to see Declan standing in the doorway.

Staring at my best friend, my heart began beating almost painfully. He stared back at me as if time and space hadn't diminished our feelings towards one another, our seemingly unbreakable friendship. He stared at me as if I still held the stars to his darkness.

But I, too, suffered from the delusion of believing that no matter what, no matter how far I drifted from a person, we would always find our way back to each other in the end.

Even in the dissonant chaos of reality.

"Are you mad?" he signed, eyes carefully surveying my face. Every twitch of my lips, every blink of my eyes, every hand gesture, I knew would be analyzed. I expected nothing less from Ducky.

"Yes. No. I don't know." I immediately turned towards one of the drawers—Calax's. He'd taken to sleeping in my room most nights.

I grabbed one of his long black shirts and the smallest pair of jeans I could find. Elena had insisted that we needed to dress as guys. Being a woman had always been dangerous, but that danger only seemed to increase with time. The world was rapidly spiraling straight into the pits of hell. All we could do was hang on for the ride.

Eyes trained on the clothing despite my face, and lips, aimed at Declan, I continued, "I don't know how I'm supposed to feel. I'm mad and upset that you guys lied to me. And I'm disappointed in myself that you guys can't trust me."

I felt him in front of me a moment before he tapped on my shoulder. I glanced up, eyes watering.

"We trust you," he signed, but I was already shaking my head.

"If you trusted me, then why did you lie to me? Why did you keep everything you knew a secret? And don't you dare say it was to protect me."

Declan stared at me helplessly, and I knew that he wasn't able to answer that question. I also knew what his answer would be, what all of their answers would be —to protect me. I hated that they felt the need to keep me cocooned in bubble wrap and buried in obliviousness. I'd always strived to be strong, to be courageous, to be *worthy,* and I suddenly felt as if I was a timid child. In their minds, I was weak. I didn't know if that conclusion came from my gender or my background, but I would prove them wrong.

"I'm not mad…" I repeated, trailing off. I didn't know how to eloquently express what I was feeling. Declan seemed to understand that, for he merely nodded. I glanced down, towards my bag, and spoke in a whisper.

"I just want to be worthy of your love."

I would've never said those words if I knew he could hear me. They were too personal. I hadn't even admitted them to Calax or Ryder, the constant insecurity and doubt plaguing me. How long until they decided I wasn't worth such an unconventional relationship? How long until they left me for girls like Elena and Bikini?

I scrubbed at the tears welling in my eyes. I prayed Declan hadn't noticed my break in composure, but I shouldn't have been surprised when he pulled me into a hug. He noticed everything.

In his strong, familiar arms, I made a promise to myself.

I would prove myself to these men who'd slowly wormed their way into my heart.

Or I would die trying.

CHAPTER 3

RYDER

*K*itten was angry.

I'd learned long ago how to discern her different types of anger. She was a treasured book in my collection, and I was an avid reader. My favorite type was her petty anger. It was adorable when she pouted. And then there was this one—the dark one.

She was furious, and I wasn't sure if she would, or even could, forgive us. Forgive me. We'd not only lied to her, but betrayed her trust. Trust was difficult for her to give, I had come to realize. She'd lived a tough life, constantly under this pressure to be perfect, and the fact that she was willing to love and trust a demented soul like me was beyond incredible.

But of course I had to ruin it, like I ruined everything.

Pinpricks of fear ran up and down my spine. I didn't know what I would do with myself if she decided she wanted out of this new, precarious relationship. I supposed I could love her from afar, the way she deserved to be loved.

But could I live with myself knowing I'd had her love and lost it?

My emotions ranged from self-loathing to fear.

What had this girl done to me?

She'd turned me into a romantic sap. I used to laugh when I saw men like that, men like me. I didn't believe a love like that could even exist—an all-consuming love where your entire being and happiness depended on hers. I lived for those moments when she smiled. I could sing songs forever about her laugh, though my own music failed to accurately portray such a beautiful sound. The way her face lit up when she was animated. The furrow to her brows.

Perfect.

She was the epitome of perfection.

I stared at her closed bedroom door, unable to garner the courage to knock. What if she sent me away?

Man up.

Steeling myself, I rapped my knuckles against the door. When she didn't immediately answer, I let myself in.

And froze.

She was standing beside her bed, surveying the clothing items she had set out. Her hands were on her hips, and her brown hair cascaded around her shoulders.

She was also wearing nothing but a black bra and red, lacy panties. Normally, I wasn't much for mismatched lingerie, but with her?

I could've sworn my brain malfunctioned.

All of that silky, alabaster skin on display…

My cock began to throb painfully.

"Shit," I managed to say at last. "Sorry."

"Why are you sorry?" she asked, laughter in her voice. "Did you need something?"

There were so many things I needed. So many things.

Every speech I had planned was completely forgotten. I couldn't even remember why I'd come into her room in the first place.

"I…"

She was so perfect.

So beautiful.

And she was mine.

It was that final thought that gave me the courage to surge forward, hands curving around her tiny waist. She stared up at me, eyes hooded and mouth parted. That indolent expression on her face…

I shivered, bringing a hand up to trace the curve of her cheekbones. Her lips puckered underneath my inquisitive finger, and I immediately imagined her mouth opening like that for another one of my body parts.

"I thought you were mad at me," I whispered huskily. She might've thought I was using that voice to seduce her. Hell no. That woman had me wrapped around her itty-bitty finger. It was a wonder I could even speak at all.

"Not…um…mad…um…" Her eyes were fixated on my moving finger. I felt a surge of power that it was my touch that caused such a reaction from her.

With a sly smile, I ducked my head to capture her lips with mine. She groaned beneath me immediately, hands reaching up to twine around my neck. Her body folded into mine as if it were made specifically for me. I'd thought, after what Liz did to me, that I wouldn't be able to be with a woman ever again. That bitch had broken what little hold on sanity I had left. But Addie?

All of my worries diminished just by being in her vibrant presence.

I pressed a kiss to the corner of her lips.

"I love you."

Another kiss went to her neck, arched to allow me better access. We moved, our bodies as one, until she was on the bed. Her back arched, those glorious breasts on display like my own, personal show.

"I love you."

She mewled, hands clawing at my back.

"I love you."

My hands paused when I reached her bra strap, and I waited with bated breath. Her eyes were heated when they met mine, and she gave a tiny nod of her head.

Slowly, to give her the chance to change her mind, I undid the strap with an expertise I was ashamed to have. I watched the material flutter to the ground before raising my gaze to the perfect sight before me.

I'd seen many breasts before. Never had I seen a pair so perfect.

I lowered my head to suck on her pink nipple, my other hand fondling her other breast. I swirled my tongue around the peak, enjoying the moans of pleasure she made. I could die listening to those sounds.

"I want to taste you," I whispered, kissing the crevice between both her breasts.

Her voice was breathless when she spoke next.

"What do you mean taste? Because I immediately think of cannibalism, and I'm pretty sure that's not what you mean."

I couldn't help but laugh into her chest.

Only Adelaide could say something like that with as much sincerity as she did.

"I'll show you what I mean. You can tell me to stop whenever."

She made a pleading noise in the back of her throat.

"Don't you dare stop," she hissed, and I chuckled yet again.

Putting one knee on each side of her body, I planted kisses down her stomach, sticking my tongue into her belly button when I reached that point. She giggled, the sound musical.

Finally, I reached the waistband of her panties. My dick twitched when I realized they were the same pair she'd bought when shopping with Ronan and me.

"Don't forget you can tell me to stop," I whispered, hesitating. She merely leveled a glare in my direction.

Smirking, I gently tugged at her underwear with my teeth. Unfortunately, that process, though sexy, was too slow, and I quickly changed to pulling it down with my fingers.

Finally, *finally*, her perfect pussy was revealed to me. She was a delicious five-course meal…

…what the hell had happened to me?

Even my thoughts were cheesy, romantic movie lines.

But as my tongue attacked her mound and she squirmed underneath me, I realized it was completely worth it.

～

ADDIE

It was ten times better than cannibalism. Not that I had ever eaten another human, mind you, but if I had, it would've failed to replicate such a pleasurable feeling.

Okay, so I really needed to stop comparing cannibalism to having an orgasm.

But as Ryder completely destroyed me, it most definitely felt like he was eating me alive.

Licks of pleasure thrummed through my veins. I moaned, coming completely undone beneath his talented tongue. All coherent thoughts left my mind, and all I could focus on was him. His tongue. His lips. His love.

There was something empowering about having a man like Ryder on his knees for me, loving me so thoroughly.

One of my hands tangled itself in his black hair, while my other hand grabbed my breast, tweaking my nipple.

I tried to tell him that I loved him, but my mouth was incapable of releasing anything but indecipherable moans and grunts.

I closed my eyes, allowing my body to succumb to the absolute pleasure Ryder was giving me. He began to suck on my clit, and I just about died.

Was that possible?

To die of love and pleasure and lust?

I thought I would combust from the heat running rampant through my body.

I opened my closed eyelids, my hand still fondling my breasts. My eyes locked on a pair of dark ones in the doorway.

Ronan stood, silhouetted in the candlelight from the hallway. His eyes were hooded as they met mine, dark with lust, but indecision still flickered across his handsome features. I hadn't even heard the door open, and from the way Ryder devoured me, I figured he hadn't either.

I didn't know if it was because I was lost in the moment. I didn't know if it was because there was something in his expression, something that went beyond lust.

And something I no doubt reciprocated.

Still holding his eye contact, I pinched my nipple, groaning at the sharp sting.

Ronan's eyes glowed as if someone had lit a candle beneath the surface. Gaze still locked on mine, he reached into his pants and grabbed his rock-hard cock. He slowly began to stroke himself, each movement sensual, as if he was performing.

I supposed that, in a way, he was.

My thoughts were an inarticulate mess. All I could think about was the word cock. Why was it called a cock? It made me think immediately of a bird, though I didn't know why. Maybe I should refer to cocks as birds. He was stroking his…bird?

These men had destroyed me.

The way Ryder ravaged my pussy combined with watching Ronan's leisurely stroking made me come completely undone. My orgasm shattered, and I let out a scream, quickly muffled by Ryder's lips. I tasted myself as our tongues danced.

"That was…" I trailed off. I had no words to describe what we'd just done. What he'd done for me, *to* me. I glanced at the tent evident in his jeans. "I can take care of that for you."

He easily moved away from my hand, and I pouted like a child.

"This was about you, Kitten," he whispered, kissing my cheek sweetly. "I'll be fine."

My frown deepened. I didn't like that I hadn't been able to please him the way he'd pleased me. He must've seen something on my face, as he pressed another kiss to the corner of my lips.

"You need to get ready to leave. Don't worry about me. It'll go away."

"It looks painful," I muttered, eyes glazed.

He laughed in answer.

"I love you so fucking much."

He wrapped his arms around me, and I buried my head in the crook of his neck. Over his shoulder, I glanced at the doorway. The door was now closed, and I wondered if I'd imagined Ronan in the first place.

CHAPTER 4

ADDIE

"*B*e vigilant. Be smart. And always stay with Tam," Calax lectured after I appeared in the living room. The rest of the guys, including Tommy, had already dispersed—no doubt preparing for our trip to Atlanta—leaving me alone with my brooding boyfriend. Ryder had left with Ronan to steal maps and pamphlets from the local gas station. My cheeks flamed as I thought about what had transpired only moments earlier. Ryder's expert tongue inside of me. Ronan's hand slowly stroking the length of his impressive cock.

Had I been cheating?

It hadn't felt like that, but my emotions were running rampant within me. I didn't necessarily know how Ronan fit into the equation that was my love life, but I couldn't deny that he was a crucial and inevitable piece.

It was impossible to discern what Calax saw on my face. Guilt? Lust? Pain? His expression considerably softened as his eyes grazed my features.

I opened my mouth to confess God only knew what but was silenced by a calloused finger against my lips.

"I know, baby girl," he said softly. My eyelids fluttered rapidly, both at his addicting touch and his words.

"W-What?" I finally managed to sputter out. He removed his finger from my lips and wrapped his other arm around my waist. I could've melted at the warmth he emitted. I was close to him, but suddenly, I wanted to be even *closer*, both mentally and physically.

"It's okay if you did stuff with Ryder." Despite the accepting words, his jaw ground together. "I don't want to hear about it, but I understand. He's your boyfriend too."

Guilt instantly consumed me.

What the hell was wrong with me? I had two amazing boyfriends, and yet my traitorous body still responded to the other members of his team. My guilt was washed away by self-loathing, nearly as staggering. I found that I couldn't breathe as both disgust in myself and guilt at my actions battled for dominance. As before, Calax read my face easily. His thumb traced my cheekbones and brushed lightly over my parted lips.

"And it's okay if it's not just with us," he said softly. Carefully. His brow was furrowed as he considered his words.

Horrified, I glanced up at him. "Do you want me to have sex with other people?"

Like a prostitute?

Before the thought could fully form, Calax was shaking his head.

"No." He ran a trembling hand through his hair in agitation. "I suck at explaining. Okay, look, baby… I know for a fact that Ryder and I aren't the only people who have feelings for you. And I also know that we're not the only two whom you have feelings for."

I was afraid to admit that I squealed like a pig.

Feelings? For more than just Ryder and Calax? Puh-lease.

And yet…

All I managed to do was gape at him like a raving, albeit cute, lunatic. Calax smiled at the disbelief evident on my face before leaning forward to press a kiss on my forehead.

My forehead. Not my lips.

Did that mean I was in girlfriend timeout? Would it involve a spanking? Not that I was against it or anything…

"These men are my brothers," he continued. His breath blew across my forehead, and delicious tremors vibrated down my spine. "And I want them to be happy. I want *you* to be happy." He paused to tenderly brush a strand of hair behind my ear. "Do you understand what I'm saying?"

"That you don't want to spank me?" I blurted. "I'm not exactly clear on the whole spanking thing."

A thousand emotions flitted across his face in a span of seconds.

"Where the fuck did you get spanking from?"

"Like bare-handed? Or with a paddle? Usually, I wouldn't be down for it because of my past, but I trust you."

He blinked furiously before rubbing a hand down his face.

"No," he said through gritted teeth. "There will be no spankings." His voice fumbled over that final word.

"Then why do you have such a raging boner?" I asked innocently.

Because the hardness pressing into my stomach definitely contradicted his words.

"Tam!" Calax bellowed, pulling away from me as if I were acid. I tried not to be hurt, tried not to feel as if he were somehow rejecting me. "Don't look at me like that, baby," he pleaded. "God, the things I want to do to you…"

"Spanking?"

I couldn't deny the heat in his eyes. An almost voracious hunger, both primal and carnal. Before he could respond, however, Tam appeared, shrugging a backpack over his broad shoulders. His eyes flickered from my burning cheeks to Calax's lustful, if not slightly glazed, stare. His own cheeks turned crimson, and he ducked his head.

"You ready to go?" he mumbled behind his disheveled brown curls. Peeling my attention away from Calax, a surprisingly difficult feat, I saluted Tam.

"Yes, sir."

And now *Tamson* has a mother-effing boner. I wondered if it was the "yes" or the "sir." Or both. I couldn't understand what had warranted such a strong reaction.

Before I could inquire, Calax wrapped his arms around me from behind and kissed the top of my head.

"I love you," he whispered in my ear, quiet enough that even Tam couldn't hear him. I was fine with that. This conversation was between Calax and myself. Nobody else was privy to it.

"Love you more," I responded, just as softly. I would never get tired of saying those words, words that I'd neglected speaking for so long. My entire life, I didn't think they could possibly apply to me. I was a broken, discarded toy, undeserving of being loved and loving someone in return. Through my relationship with Calax and then Ryder, I was beginning to realize that I was a work in progress instead of something incapable of being mended. Time had chipped away at my innocence but not my capacity to love. Maybe, just maybe, I could make myself whole once more.

Calax reluctantly released me, and I skipped over to where Tam stood, linking my arm through his. He glanced up, shocked at my instigation of contact, before once again focusing his attention on the floor. Following the direction of his gaze, I tried to note if there was anything particularly exciting about this swath of carpeting. Not even a fucking blood stain.

Such a disappointment.

"I'll see you later, Calla-gator," I quipped. I'd expected him to crack a smile—after all, my jokes were amazing—but he instead leveled serious eyes in my direction.

"Please be careful," he said. His hands clenched and then unclenched at his sides as if he wanted to grab me and make a run for it. "And come back to me."

I understood where he was coming from. Fear. It was nearly as strong of an emotion as guilt. There were a lot of things that Calax feared, the biggest one being losing me. The mere thought of anything happening to any of these men made me nauseous. Hell would freeze over before a single hair was harmed on their big heads. So I understood it. He would always fear for my well-being in this new world, just as I would his.

"Always," I responded. And I would. Somehow, someway, we would find our way back to each other again. The alternative was too inconceivable to even consider.

Arm still linked with Tam's, I hurried into the foyer. I had a feeling that my carefully constructed resolve would crumble if I had to spend another second looking into Calax's anxious eyes.

Passing a mirror on the wall, I paused to consider myself. I was wearing a baggy shirt, courtesy of Calax, and ripped jeans. My brown hair was tucked away inside of a baseball cap. Though my features were still undeniably feminine, even I had to admit that the disguise was good. From a distance, I could be just another man.

"You'll be fine," Tam whispered. "I'll be there to protect you."

With any of the others, I might've scoffed at the notion that I needed protection. I hated the fact that they thought of me as somehow lesser, and I hated that I was restricted to the sidelines when I wanted nothing more than to defend what I perceived as mine. The guys? My twisted brain had claimed them all.

However, there was nothing but sincerity in Tam's voice. It practically oozed from him in waves, an innate comfort that only Tam was capable of evoking from me. I had no doubt that he would throw himself in front of a blade if the need arose. The mere thought of him getting hurt at my expense made my stomach churn with a leaden, miserable feeling. The strength of my conviction frightened me, my heart racing in tandem to the swirling of my thoughts.

"Are you guys coming?" my friend Samantha called from where she was perched on the hood of the car. Like me, she was dressed completely in men's clothing. I felt a pang akin to jealousy when I recognized the shirt as belonging to Asher, but I immediately quelled such a ridiculous response. It was just clothes.

Just clothes.

But when Elena appeared from the passenger side, Ronan's white tank top and jacket covering her ample breasts, I saw red.

Tam, oblivious to my inner turmoil, gave my shoulder a reassuring squeeze.

"Let's go and get back before Calax murders everyone."

I had the distinct feeling that he wasn't joking.

CHAPTER 5

ADDIE

The car ride was silent.

Not awkward. Just silent.

I would've almost described the silence as companionable, my cheek pressed against the car window and my thigh only inches, if not centimeters, from Tam's. The heat he emitted was almost palpable, a physical entity I longed to snatch and make my own. There was something about my shy ninja warrior that called to me in a different way than the others. The smile on his face that I yearned to see more often. The rapid flutter of his long lashes. The blush tinting his cheeks.

Confused by my own thoughts, I focused instead on the world passing before us. The procession of cars consisted of Elena and Bikini in a Jeep ahead of us, and Lilly and Sam in the van behind us. Tam and I rode with two girls whose names I'd already forgotten. At first, they'd attempted to engage us—read as Tam—in conversation before quickly dismissing us in favor of gossip. Of what they could be gossiping about when the only girls around were their team members and me...

Oh wait.

The landscape changed quickly from cypress trees to industrial towns. There was nothing noticeably uncanny about the town, no peeling paint or chipped sidings or vandalism, but it just felt *wrong* the second our cars pulled into it. I quickly discerned that I felt this way because it was empty. No moms pushing strollers down the streets. No businessmen hurrying towards their nine o'clock meeting. The lack of both people and sound brought goosebumps to my flesh. Fear, a tangible manifestation, churned low in my stomach.

My hand instinctively rested on Tam's knee, gripping so hard, I had no doubt it would leave a bruise. He glanced at me out of the corner of his eye, expression unreadable.

Without breaking eye contact, he pulled something out of his jacket pocket. The waning sunlight caught the keen tip of a knife.

"Use it," Tam whispered. "If we get separated, don't be afraid to use it. Pointy end goes into flesh. Got it?"

His expression was uncharacteristically grave. My stomach twisted even further, tightening in tandem to my hand still on his knee.

I tried for humor, my go-to defense mechanism. "Pointy end in flesh. Got it. Shouldn't be too hard, right?"

Flashing him a smile that he didn't reciprocate, I swiveled back towards the window. It was cold for this time of year, and my breath fogged the glass.

It was only then that I saw her. Him. It. The pronoun was inconsequential. All I could focus on was the gruesome sight before me, something pulled straight out of a horror movie.

There was a body lying on the side of the road—what was left of a body, anyway. Its face was distorted, blood and bruises making the face entirely unrecognizable. Sitting on its chest, was a girl. At least, I assumed it was a girl. She had cascading blonde hair, nearly down to her feet, and wore a tattered purple dress. Her face, however, was contorted into a deranged, almost maniacal, smile. Black lines marred her skin, twisting and convulsing with each of her erratic movements. And her hands…they were curled into claws as she tore at the dead human's face. Neck. Chest.

Blood.

Dripping in rivulets down his body and running into the rain drain.

A strangled sob escaped my throat, and Tam's hands landed on my shoulders, twisting me away from the horrific scene.

"Don't look."

I went to Tam willingly, my arms wrapping around his shoulders and my face burrowing into his neck. He stiffened at first, muscles rigid, before relaxing against me. His arms tightened further, and I was greeted with the heavenly scent that was uniquely Tamson's—something almost sweet, like sun-soaked honey.

His hands rubbed soothing circles into my back.

"Shh," he whispered. "Shh. It's okay. You're okay. I won't let anything bad happen to you."

The chatter up front diminished completely once the first word had escaped Tam's lips. Normally, I would've felt self-conscious, but I couldn't bring myself to care. I needed the comfort he was willing to provide me.

After a moment of relishing in his embrace, I attempted to pull back. His hands immediately touched the back of my head, securing me more firmly against him. He gently massaged my scalp, his hand tantalizingly soft.

"Don't look yet," he breathed into my ear. My body responded to the sound instantly. Goosebumps that had nothing to do with my initial fear pebbled on my skin.

I heeded his warning, my eyes fixed firmly on a freckle visible on his neck. I could still hear, however, even though the sounds were muffled through the car.

Cries. Screams.

Fists pounding against the windows. Begging for sanctuary. Food. Clothes. I couldn't distinguish between the cries of the ragers and the cries of normal humans.

The girl driving let out a curse.

"Shit! This is really getting out of hand."

Tam squeezed me as if he wanted our bodies to physically meld into one another. I tried to lift my head marginally, if only to glimpse the town over his shoulder, but his hold restrained me.

"Trust me. You don't want to see this."

And I trusted him. There were only so many things I could endure, so many things I could witness, before I completely fell to shreds. Despite his shoulder obscuring my vision, I had a good idea of what I would find in the once quiet town.

Ragers.

Survivors.

Dead bodies.

Blood.

So much blood.

My mind mentally depicted images of what could be happening behind my closed eyelids, each one more vivid than the last. I didn't know if I would be able to handle any more death.

God, I was so stupid. Why did I believe I would be capable of handling this by myself? Why did I think myself to be strong when I wanted nothing more than to be weak? I wasn't a fighter, and I didn't think I ever would be. Trembling in Tam's sturdy arms, I felt young and forlorn. Nothing more than a vulnerable child kicked out of the house and forced to face the world on her own.

It could've been hours. It could've been minutes. Time seemed to drag. I felt as if I were teetering on a pinnacle of discovery. All I had to do was open my eyes. Look…

Tam's warning flashed through my head.

No.

Don't look.

I couldn't decide if that made me weak or smart.

Finally, Tam's unrelenting grip on me loosened. He reached for my baseball cap lying on the car seat beside me.

"We're here," he said softly. And, surprising me even further, he pressed his lips to my forehead. The chaste gesture caused my body to shiver instinctively. I couldn't help but lean further into his embrace, even as he pulled away.

Reluctantly, I removed myself from his lap and faced the unremarkable building before us. It appeared to be a super store, though I didn't recognize the name. There were a few cars in the parking lot, but overall, the place looked deserted. A few white painted signs indicated that there was a grocery section, a technology section, a pharmacy, and even an area specifically designed to sell top-notch camping gear.

"I thought we were going to the mall," I said to no one in particular. I twisted my hair around my wrist before shoving it all into the cap. One of the girls from the front—I really should remember her name—spun around to face me. Unlike the others, she didn't regard me with distaste, merely curiosity.

"This is a hidden gem," she explained. "Everyone knows about the mall. It'll be too crowded…too dangerous. Only the locals know about this beauty."

I frowned, resisting the urge to interrogate her further. Honestly, I was confused, though that wasn't necessarily a surprise. I tended to get confused a lot. Did it make me a masochist if I admitted I was a too-stupid-to-live type of heroine?

Why would it be dangerous if there were other people? Wouldn't we all want to band together?

I supposed it stemmed down to human nature and whether humans were inherently good or bad. My knowledge of the subject matter was extremely biased. Experience after experience had led me to the conclusion that humans were evil, diabolical beings.

On second thought, I totally understood why they didn't want to involve themselves with others.

"Pointy end," Tamson muttered under his breath. He reached across the leather seat to squeeze my hand. Butterflies fluttered in my stomach for two entirely different reasons.

Fear.

And something else.

"Pointy end," I agreed.

With a shaky breath, I exited the car.

CHAPTER 6

RONAN

*T*he last newspaper was printed a month ago. Scanning the words quickly, I deduced that people were as idiotic then as they were now.

Zombies.

Viruses.

And earthquakes.

Oh my!

The president had officially declared a state of emergency. According to the article, similar phenomena were occurring across the globe. The faded paper included a diminutive image of a town completely cleaved apart after an earthquake destroyed half the city. Another picture showed two tornados leaning towards one another as if in a romantic dance.

Fuck.

It was official—the world was ending.

Or had already ended, depending how you wanted to look at it.

Ryder materialized beside me suddenly, a handful of maps and brochures in his arms. It was something that was often overlooked in movies and TV shows. We relied so often on technology and electronics that nobody ever considered what would happen if we no longer had them. They were something we'd taken for granted, myself included, to the point that it was almost inconceivable to imagine a world without them in it. But it was important to know where we were going, which places we would stop at, and the safest routes to take.

Survival 101—learn how to read a fucking map.

"You ready to go?" Ryder asked.

"We need to wait for…"

I trailed off as Tommy exited the bathroom, wiping his hands on his pants. His eyes narrowed into thin slits when he caught me staring at him.

"What are you looking at, Ass Hat?" he snapped.

Ass Hat?

The kid really hated me. Honestly, I couldn't understand why he decided to go with us and not his hero, Fallon. But the little shit insisted on traveling to the rest area and then the gas station with Ryder and I instead of the grocery store with the others. There was something in his penetrating gaze, something I would almost describe as *knowing*.

His words had been, "I need to keep an eye on my son-in-laws."

What the fuck of the fuckity fuck?

I wasn't one for swearing, but seriously. Fuck.

I wondered if Tommy knew what I knew—that Addie wasn't only dating Calax. She hadn't realized I'd been nearby the day she returned from that bitch Liz's house. Calax and Ryder had both told her that they loved her, and then they'd decided to become one big happy family.

Without me.

But then…

My body turned to flames as I envisioned her the last time I saw her. God, I hadn't been able to think of anything else. That vision was on a loop in my head. Over and over again, each one bringing me to the highest peak of pleasure.

Her brown hair cascading over her shoulders.

Her pink lips parted, a breathy moan escaping.

Her tits bouncing as she rocked her hips, each nipple sharp and beaded and just begging for attention.

Damn that woman.

It was impossible for me to think of anything or anyone else.

"I just took a monster shit," Tommy shared helpfully. Ryder pinched the bridge of his nose.

"How interesting," he said through gritted teeth.

Tommy's eyes narrowed even further. They looked like pinprick orbs behind his thick glasses.

"You're supposed to be nice to me. That's the bro rule. I read the rule book. I have the soundtrack. I effing invented the Broadway musical."

"There's a Broadway musical?" Ryder stage-whispered to me.

"At least he's cutting down on the swearing."

Fallon had gotten on his ass more than once for his crude language. He had called it "barbarian," which was hypocritical because Fallon himself swore like a sailor.

"Suck a motherfucking dick, RyRy," Tommy snapped, and Ryder bristled at the use of Addie's nickname for him. I had to agree—it did not hold the same appeal coming out of a young psychopath's mouth.

Without waiting for a response, Tommy shouldered past us and headed to where we'd parked the Jeep.

"I get shotgun!" I yelled to the tiny devil.

Tommy merely gave me the finger and said, "I licked it, so it's mine!" Silence. "Bitch!"

I watched him go with a chuckle and a small shake of my head. Tommy was definitely a strange little man. I supposed that was why Addie and him got along so well.

"Why do we put up with him again?" Ryder asked from beside me.

"Because Addie loves him and we love her, so by default, we have to tolerate the little shit." I crossed my arms over my chest as I watched Tommy pointedly rub his ass against the passenger side door, as if he was staking his claim.

"Love?" parroted Ryder, eyebrow quirking.

I frowned. The words I'd said earlier played in my head on repeat.

We love her.

We love her.

Shit.

"I meant…like a friend. Of course." I let out a breath of laughter, rubbing a hand through my green-tipped hair.

My brother eyed me with an inquisitive raise to his brow. His eyes—a burnt amber color two shades darker than my own—seemed to see me more clearly than I saw myself.

Sometimes, it was difficult to believe he was my brother. I'd been alone for so long that the prospect of having a family eluded me. Even now, staring at his face with striking similarities to my own, it felt completely surreal.

But I knew my brother's expressions as well as I knew my own.

"Friend," he said dryly.

"Friend."

"Who are you lying to?" he continued. "Me or yourself?"

I didn't understand what he meant. Did he know about my feelings for her? No, he couldn't have. I kept them safely hidden under lock and key.

Ryder's words, however, filled me with an almost incandescent fury. My hands clenched into fists as I resisted the urge to punch him in his smug face.

"Oh please. You're one to fucking talk. I know that you're with Addie also. I know that you share her with Calax. How does that work? Do you get her on alternating weekends? Is it a joint-custody agreement?" Laughing humorlessly, I took a step closer to Ryder and jabbed a finger into his chest. "I'm surprised that you, of all people, are willing to be in a relationship. How long until you get bored of her? I'm honestly surprised you lasted this long and didn't cheat—"

Before I could finish my thought, Ryder exploded. That was the only word I could think to describe it. One second, he was mere inches in front of me, trembling with unsuppressed rage, and the next, he was on top of me, leveling punch after punch to my face.

"Don't talk about her like that," he seethed between blows. "I." Punch. "Love." Punch. "Her."

Breathing heavily, he rolled onto his back. My face ached something fierce, but I knew I deserved it. I didn't know what had possessed me to say what I had, only that I regretted it immediately once the words left my mouth.

"You don't know shit," Ryder said after a moment, wiping spit out of the corner of his mouth.

I remained silent.

"I would never do anything to hurt her," he continued. "I love her, and I think you love her too. Hell, I know you love her. I'm not a fucking idiot."

Still, I kept my mouth pressed into a thin line.

How did one respond to that? What type of sick bastard did it make me to be in love with my brother's girl? Ryder would hate me if he discovered the extent of my feelings. It wasn't just lust I felt for the eccentric if not slightly crazy brunette, but something deeper. Something that made my stomach clench painfully whenever she was in the room. When she smiled at me?

Well…

I was a goner before I even knew her name.

"I'm not dumb. I see the way you look at her…the way everyone looks at her. And I see the way she looks back." Ryder's voice was uncharacteristically soft, and I wished I could see his face. Instead, I focused on the water stains darkening the white tiles of the ceiling. "Calax and I agreed that she's a good fit for our team. She's the missing piece we hadn't realized we needed. And that girl needs all the protection she can get. Of course, we haven't discussed it yet with the whole team—"

"What are you saying?" I asked, breaking into his speech.

But Ryder never responded. Trying to taper my annoyance, I rolled onto my elbow to face him. I paused when I noticed the predicament he'd found himself in. There was a gun aimed at his face.

Holding the gun, expression positively gleeful, was a girl about our age with blonde curls and bright blue eyes.

"Hello, boys," she purred.

I was distantly aware of someone coming up behind me. Before I could even move, something hit me on the side of the head and darkness consumed me.

❧

ADDIE

Guy me had a distinct walk.

A sort of swagger, I would say, that included both hip shakes and long strides. As a guy, you had to account for a lot of things. More muscles. Larger feet. And a penis.

Did a penis impact the way a guy walked? I couldn't even imagine having something hanging between my legs, swinging in the breeze.

I had to think of a guy's name.

What was a good name for a guy with an invisible, metaphysical penis? I was almost positive that there wasn't a baby name category for that.

"What are you doing?" Tamson asked me as we moved to the front entrance of the store. I attempted to lower my voice in a poor impersonation of a man's.

"Sucking titties."

Because that was what men said. Obviously.

Tam blinked, seemingly unable to decide if I was certifiably insane and needed to be committed or if he should just let me be me. He eventually decided on the latter with a slow shake of his head.

"You know you don't have to act like a guy, right?" Driver Girl said.

"But what's the fun in that?" I kept my voice low and gravelly, thumping my chest for emphasis. I immediately winced as a shooting pain reverberated through my breasts. "I'm…Antwonia."

Tam made a strange sound in the back of his throat, a combination between a gasp of disbelief and a laugh.

"Actually, I need to come up with my gangster name. Because that's a real thing we need to take into consideration. How do you feel about Lil' One Punch? I see real merit in a name like that."

Tam snorted, quickly bringing his hand up to cover his laughing mouth.

Frowning, I added in my normal voice, "Never mind. Being a guy is too hard. I only had a fake penis for a minute, and I'm already exhausted trying to keep it limp. I like tits way better." I grabbed my breasts for emphasis. "On me that is. I like penises on men."

"What is she even saying?" Driver Girl whispered to Tam. Tam shook his head at her, unable to articulate an answer, but kept his eyes trained on me. There was something almost carnal in his heated gaze. It took me a moment too long to realize I was still holding my boobs like they were a freaking life preserver. Dropping my hands to my sides, I marched into the darkened store.

"Let's go shopping, bitches!" And then, because I could, I added in a deep voice, "Let's get some shopping done, home dogs."

Nailed it.

CHAPTER 7

ADDIE

*B*eing a boy had its perks. For one, I could slap mannequins on the ass without getting weird looks. Secondly, I could caw like a bird without judgement. And finally, I could refer to Tamson as my "bro-mate" and "bro-bear." Things would've gone down differently if I was a female.

After my third bird call, Tamson rubbed at the skin between his eyes.

"You are a very strange person," he said, but there was no malice in his voice, just awe.

"The strangest," I agreed without preamble. The cutest blush curled up Tam's neck, darkening his cheeks. When he caught me staring, he quickly glanced down at the ground. His reddish-brown hair obscured his features.

"Why do you do that? Why do you hide?"

He peeked at me through his fringe of thick lashes. I'd never realized how beautiful his eyes were before. The splatter of freckles accentuated the green in his eyes and the length of his lashes.

"You're beautiful," I blurted. If it was possible, and I didn't think it was, his cheeks reddened even further. "I know it's weird, but it's true. And I don't like it when you look away. It makes me think you're sad, and I hate when you're sad."

As I spoke, I did what was instinctive—I took a step closer. His breath fanned over my face as my hand tucked a curl behind his ear. His eyes flickered from my lips to my eyes and then back to my lips.

Was he going to kiss me?

Did I want him to?

I remembered Calax's words from earlier. He told me, for lack of better words, to follow my heart. I knew that if I was to kiss him, neither Calax or Ryder would consider it cheating.

His head lowered…

"What the fuck are you two doing?" a strident voice demanded. Tamson jerked away as if he had been slapped. His eyes flickered towards the figure over my shoulder. Turning, despite already knowing who I would see, I flashed Elena a singularly beautiful smile.

"Hey, home girl," I said in my rather impressive, if I did say so myself, man voice. Her nose wrinkled in distaste.

"Whatever. Just hurry up and come help us load."

Tam, chin still touching his chest, hurried after Elena. I might've thought he was running from me if he hadn't stopped mid-step, taken a shuddering breath, and then extended a hand back towards me. For some reason, I thought that this moment was a turning point in our relationship. Something monumental, like crossing an ocean.

Heart hammering in my chest, I took his hand and followed him through the cluttered store.

~

THERE WAS NO ELECTRICITY. Instead, we relied on the thin shaft of light from the flashlight Elena held. I knew Tam had one in his pocket as well.

I tried to tell myself it was the flashlight I felt when I had been pressed against him. Just the flashlight.

However, I completely understood. I, too, experienced the issues caused by a phantom dick. Those things were impossible to control. Seriously. Trying to tame an imaginary penis was a struggle.

The rest of the girls were convened in the camping department when we arrived, Tam's fingers interlocked with mine. A few girls, one in particular that I recognized to be either Lacey or Missy, glared at our connected hands, but when Tam didn't pull away, I didn't either. Instead, I kept an imperious set to my chin.

I was a bad bitch.

Bad…man.

Bad boy. Bad boy.

"You're singing," Tam whispered out of the corner of his mouth.

"I'm channeling my inner male criminal," I responded.

"What does that even mean?" Bikini interrupted, rather rudely, if you asked me. She wasn't privy to our private conversation.

Keeping my expression and voice serious, I said, "I stab bitches."

Tam made another one of his strange noises, and Bikini turned on her heel with a dramatic huff.

The next hour passed smoothly. We gathered camping supplies, including tents, sleeping bags, and flashlights, and what was left of the food. The pharmacy had unfortunately already been picked through. Nothing remained besides an adhesive wrap and something labeled for lessening diarrhea.

We stopped in the clothing section to grab a few outfits. I fingered the lace of a rather revealing nightgown.

"So what did you do before?" I asked Tam, who was trailing behind me. I grabbed a pair of jeans that looked to be in my size and slipped them over my arm.

"Before what?" He perused a couple of sweatshirts still left on the rack, grabbed one, held it out in front of me, and then placed it back down when he decided it wouldn't fit me.

"Before everything went to shit," I supplied.

"Well…you already know my history." He considered a large, pink zip-up sweatshirt before eventually deciding on it. He tossed it over his shoulder.

"I meant on the team. What did you do?"

He gently removed the jeans I'd grabbed from my arm, placing it on top of the sweatshirt on his shoulder.

"I went on missions. Recon, usually. Traveled the world. Went to parties." He shrugged nonchalantly, but I stopped to gape.

"You? At parties? The world really has ended." I chuckled softly, and a small smile flitted across his handsome features. My breath caught. He really was beautiful, but when he smiled, he was positively radiant.

"World ended," he mocked, tossing a pair of leggings in my face. I caught the offending fabric before shoving it back in his face.

This was a Tam I was unfamiliar with. Carefree. Joking. It was almost as if he were an entirely different person from the shy and timid one I'd grown accustomed to. The change wasn't bad…just surprising.

I spotted Bikini over Tam's shoulder, walking towards us. Despite wearing a hat and loose clothing, she was still ethereal in beauty. I couldn't ignore the self-consciousness that rippled within me, permeating the air.

"We're waiting in the cars," she stated bluntly. Her eyes flickered appreciatively over Tam, resting on his ass. He went positively rigid, expression glacial, but refused to turn around.

Without another word, Bikini hurried towards the front entrance of the store. She rewarded us with her signature hair flip, which was hilarious because her hair was hidden beneath a cap. Instead, it translated into a weird hand gesture.

Tamson met my eyes, and we both erupted into giggles. Well, I giggled like the manly man I was, and Tamson simply chuckled softly.

"Shall we go?" I asked dramatically.

Tam mimicked Bikini's hair flip with the jeans still wrapped around his shoulders.

Giggling yet again, I nudged him with my shoulder. "I like this side of you. Don't get me wrong, I like both sides of you, but you should let fun, carefree Tam come out to play more often."

As expected, he ducked his head and blushed. I couldn't help but smile at the change. I had been wrong in my initial assumption. They weren't two separate men, but one man in desperate need of confidence. I had the distinct feeling that I was only just barely scraping the surface of everything Tam could be.

The eruption of thunder made me jump. This was immediately followed by rain pelting against the vaulted roof. It came down in torrents so heavy, it was impossible to see the cars in the parking lot.

Bikini was glaring out the window, her arms crossed under her perky, perfect tits. Her per-tits, as I referred to them.

Tam frowned at the aggressive weather before gently wrapping the pink sweatshirt he had grabbed around my head. It would do little to quell the frigid air, but hopefully it would protect me from the rain.

"Are you not going to offer me one?" Bikini snapped. When Tam merely ducked his head, I pointed towards the clothing section.

"There are sweatshirts in aisle one."

She sputtered, indignant, before pushing open the doors and charging straight into the storm.

It only took a few seconds before the screaming began.

Loud, earsplitting screams. Cries of anguish. Agony. Pain. Torture.

Only a few feet away from the glass door, I could see everything. Her skin turning red as the rain relentlessly pelted down. Her hair coming out in clumps. Blood mixing with rainwater.

I immediately ran forward with a shout, but Tam put a restraining arm around my stomach, holding me back. Once I was secured behind him, he grabbed the sweatshirt off of my head and secured it over his own. My pulse was hammering.

"Be careful!" I cried, knowing and fearing what he was about to do.

Before he could exit, however, a familiar Jeep pulled up. I recognized Elena's face instantly.

Her horror-struck eyes went from Bikini's unrecognizable body to us. Indecision marred her pretty face.

"Elena!" Tam yelled. His arm wrapped around my shoulders, now pulling me with him instead of away.

I could see the moment Elena's decision was made. Guilt briefly flashed in her eyes, there and gone too quickly for me to be certain I'd gauged it correctly. Tam noticed it too.

"Elena!" he screamed, lunging forward. But her car was already pulling away, followed quickly by the two vans. The last one happened to go right over Bikini's body, the wheel...

I vomited onto the floor.

Bikini was dead. The rain was poisonous.

And we'd been left behind.

CHAPTER 8

I hurled a thousand insults into the rain. Thunder continued to clap overhead, and lightning streaked across the sky like a giant spotlight being switched on. Just as quickly, the light was snatched away and darkness returned.

"Shit!" I screamed. Tam's hands still wrapped around my waist were the only thing that restrained me. My stomach clenched and tightened as I considered the body on the ground. I couldn't look away, the grotesque sight capturing and holding my attention. How could Elena just leave her teammate behind? How could she have left *us* behind?

And Lilly and Samantha. My friends. How could they have left us?

At least, I had thought they were my friends.

"It's fine, Addie. Everything will be fine," Tam said, pressing his face into the back of my neck. During my struggles, the baseball cap must've fallen off, and my long hair cascaded over my shoulders. "As soon as the storm ends, we'll go to the parking lot and check to see if any of the cars are working. It'll be fine."

"Fine?" I said, scoffing in disbelief. "Tam, there are so many things that can fucking kill us if we don't have a working vehicle. Ragers. Weather. Acid rain." My body began to tremble, a stark contrast to Tam's sturdy one pressed against mine.

"Addie. Look at me. Look at me." With a whimper, I reluctantly turned to face him. He captured my face with his large hands, his eyes begging me to remain calm, to trust him and his ability to get us out of this situation. Taking a calming breath, I nodded slowly.

Yes.

He was right.

All we had to do was wait for the storm to pass, and then we could check to see if any of the cars were working. Even if none of the cars worked, we could just wait for the guys to discover we were missing and come for us.

At the thought of my guys, panic once again threatened to consume me. Shit. I knew that they were traveling as well. What if they got stuck in the storm? What if something had happened to them? My throat closed, and tears welled in my eyes at the thought. If anything were to happen to any of them, even Tommy, I would lose it.

More than I had already lost it, that was.

"You're not calm," Tam pointed out, and I couldn't stop the bark of laughter that escaped my dry lips.

No. I was most definitely *not* calm.

With a resigned sigh, I placed my head on his shoulder. He dropped to his knees, still holding me, and I followed.

And then we sat, our arms wrapped tightly around one another, as the storm continued on.

ASHER

I saw my first dead body when I was seven.

And I killed my first person when I was eight. Granted, the killing could be considered self-defense, but that doesn't make a difference. Once a person was dead, he stayed dead. No more breathing. No more talking. No more living.

Lights out.

You might think that by this point, I would be immune to death, but I was not. It was entirely impossible to desensitize yourself to the pungent smell wafting from a decaying corpse. To shield your eyes from the gruesome body mere inches from your blood-soaked shoes.

To see the life bleed from their eyes in tandem to the blood dripping from their wounds.

I held the knife in a light grip, not palmed or tightly grasped. It was like holding a flower with barely applied pressure to the stem. Squeeze too tightly, and the flower would die. Squeeze too lightly, and the flower would slip through your fingers. The way one held a knife was a common misconception. It should balance on the tips of your fingers in order to slice through skin cleanly. A knife was a deadly, powerful weapon, despite the apparent insignificance of its appearance.

Wiping my knife on my pants, I turned towards Fallon expectantly. His brows were furrowed as he stared at the dead body before us, thousands of emotions flickering in his normally apathetic eyes. I couldn't help but notice that not one of those emotions was regret.

"He didn't talk," I said, slipping the knife back into my waistband. I didn't need to explain—Fallon had been present for the entire interrogation.

Arms crossed over his burly chest, Fallon took a step closer to the man.

Hunter something. I didn't catch a last name. Unimpressive in appearance with dark red hair, the beginnings of a beard, and muddy brown eyes. Right then, however, his features were nearly unrecognizable. Bruises marred his face, and lines carved from my knife distorted his skin.

For a moment, I almost felt bad. The man was fucked up, his body and face entirely unrecognizable. Just as quickly, I remembered the reasons why I'd had to interrogate him, and the pity was swept away in a tidal wave of anger.

When Fallon had first instructed me to keep an eye on the house Liz previously occupied, I'd thought it would be a complete waste of my time and skills. That all changed, however, when this assface arrived. He'd come for one reason and one reason only—Adelaide.

The lion mask still sat on the ground near his tied-up feet, discarded.

Who do you work for?

What do they want with Addie?

Those were the questions I'd asked repeatedly, all of which he replied to with a stubborn shake of his head. I had to give him some credit—the man was loyal to a fault. I might've let him live if his very existence didn't threaten the life of the woman I loved.

Shame.

"What do you want to do with the body, Sarge?" I asked, and our team leader's expression turned contemplative. On some, it might've been a serene expression. On him, it just appeared terrifying.

"Throw him outside. The Ragers will take care of him."

Nodding my agreement, I hauled his heavy ass to the sliding screen door. A demented part within me sort of wished he were still alive, if only to feel the pain of Ragers tearing apart his flesh.

At least that bitch Liz got what was coming to her. There were some people that I merely hated...and some people that I wanted to see torn apart and then peed on by rabid monkeys on acid. Liz fell into the latter category.

After depositing the body, I waited for Fallon to climb into the car. My mind immediately began to wander, as it always did after an assignment.

"Why are you such a failure?"

The words were the only constant in my life. That, and the press of a boot against my stomach. Shivering on the cold basement ground, I could only look up at my father with wide eyes. He didn't seem bothered by the fact that his one and only son was staring at him with undisguised disgust and terror. No, the man was utterly oblivious to anything but his own self.

As he kicked me yet again, tears gathered in my eyes. I'd failed him. I'd failed my father.

Bad son.

Bad Asher.

All I'd ever wanted was to be good. Now, I had trouble discerning what was right and what was wrong. What was good and what was bad. Why was there no clear distinction? The world was just a fucking contradiction leaving nothing but a murky shade of gray.

Kick.

My body ached, and I curled in on myself like old, yellowing paper. I thought that if I could somehow make myself smaller, then maybe he would stop.

My eyes rested on the handle of a rusty hunting knife...

Kick.

Kick.

I was pulled from my thoughts by the driver's side door slamming closed. Trembling, both from the suddenly chilled air and my own fear, I turned my face towards the window. Bloated, grey clouds hung low in the sky threatening rain. It was such a contrast to the sunny sky earlier this morning.

The car ride back was silent. We passed only a few Ragers, all of which ran after the car. They became bored after only a minute, resuming their endless wandering.

Ragers.

My heart hurt when I saw their distorted, grotesque faces. They'd been human once. Wives, husbands, fathers, and mothers. Children. Brothers and sisters. Now, they were nothing more than monsters.

Was that what human nature had resorted to? Was that evolution transforming us all into our true selves? The caveats of a human being were impossible to ignore. Perhaps we were all monsters. Perhaps this was a sign from God or whoever ran the universe that we were in dire need of change. Perhaps this was a punishment.

I knew that I was a monster. It was something I'd accepted long ago. Addie may have believed that I was a sweet, innocent boy, but her perception of me was wrong and tainted by situations she couldn't have possibly begun to understand. Sure, I may not have engaged in as much sexual activity as my brothers, but I was anything but innocent. My soul had long since been darkened by both my actions and my past.

Despite wanting her for myself, I knew that it could never be. I didn't want my own darkness to tarnish her vibrant light.

We didn't talk during the ride back to the house, though that was hardly surprising. I didn't think Fallon liked me very much. To be fair, the surly bastard didn't like anyone. Besides one petite female with dark brown hair.

Hell, she was the only one who'd ever made him smile.

Turning once again towards the window, I watched the fields flash by before subtly transforming into dense forests. The beginnings of rain pounded against the roof of the car. Thunder roared in the distance, the sound deafening.

"Weather's getting bad," I mused. Fallon, of course, merely grunted in response.

We pulled in front of Elena's cute Victorian manor. There were no cars currently in the driveway, a fact that made my blood turn to ice. Ryder and Ronan, at the very least, should've been back by now.

Fallon's lips twisted slightly, the only indication he was anything but impassive. His eyes roamed over the empty driveway and the darkened windows. Not one candle flickered in the house.

Clouds continued to release their torrents of rainfall, each one piercing into the roof of the car with a penetrating force. It almost felt as if the sky was crying. Falling apart, piece by piece. Tear by tear.

Fallon put the car into park, but continued to sit behind the wheel. His long fingers tapped an unfamiliar pattern, the first crack in his apathetic exterior.

"Why isn't anyone home?" he asked. Despite his question being spoken aloud, I didn't dare respond. Fallon, like Adelaide, had a tendency to speak through his thoughts. Any response from me would only serve to annoy him.

I felt immense relief. The last thing I wanted Addie to see was me, walking into the home with bloodstained clothes and a feral look in my eyes. I didn't want her to see me as someone dark and broken. No, the further I could remove her from my other identity, the happier everyone would be.

The good guy. The sweet guy. The loving guy.

I could be all of those things. Hell, I *wanted* to be all of those things.

Shaking my head to clear my muddled thoughts, I tossed open the passenger side door.

It was my hand that the rain hit first.

I let out a cuss of pain, instantly pulling myself back into the car.

"Shit. Shit. Shit."

The skin was turning red, a stark contrast to my usually pasty tone. Fallon's eyes widened as he took in my hand. Before I could say anything, he grabbed it and held it up to his face. His grip, combined with the blistering pain from the rain, was enough to make me hiss through clenched teeth. Damnit. The man didn't know the meaning of the word "gentle."

"Shit," he agreed after a moment of surveying my reddened hand. He released me as if I were toxic, and I allowed my hand to drop limply into my lap.

Shit was right.

And where were the others?

My mind conjured up images, each one more horrific than the last. Adelaide trapped outside, her skin reddening like a ripe tomato. Screams reverberating through the darkened sky, nearly overtaking the steady pound of raindrops. My brothers, lying in a pool of their own blood. Adelaide, her features nearly indistinguishable. I squeezed my eyelids shut as if that could somehow alleviate the mental anguish I felt. If anything were to happen to her, to any of my brothers, I would lose my mind. There was only so much mind I had left to lose.

Fallon's face was pinched as if he'd eaten something particularly sour. His eyes were narrowed on the door of the house. What was going through that calculating head of his? Was he willing someone, anyone, to exit? Was he envisioning Adelaide smirking at him through the window? Or, and this seemed to be the most likely option, was he planning someone's murder? Unfortunately, you weren't able to kill the weather. Shame.

Seeming to make up his mind about something, he put the car back into drive.

"What the hell are you doing?" I asked. Without bothering to respond, Fallon dropped his foot on the gas. I let out a curse as we flew over loose pebbles and broken cement. I could see the gray door of the garage looming ominously ahead of me. Closer and closer and closer...

Bracing myself for the impact, I turned my face away. The car crashed straight through the closed garage door. Glass shattered, keen shards barely missing my covered face. I felt a few lodge themselves inside of my arms, the pain barely registering over the blood roaring through my ears. My breath left me in a swooping exhale, even as my heart continued to pound erratically inside of my chest. I glanced at Fallon out of the corner of my eye. The burly bastard didn't seem to notice, or care, that he had slivers of glass in his hair and face. Bourns of blood cascaded down his face.

Without a word, Fallon climbed out of the car and stormed towards the door. I quickly scrambled after him.

I could feel his fear and worry as if it were a tangible being. It made the air almost stifling hot and sent goosebumps racing up and down my arms.

"Adelaide!" Fallon roared, striding down the hallway. And that was the only word adequate enough to describe his tone—a roar. Hints of panic seeped through. "Adelaide!"

"What's going on?" a tired, gravelly voice mumbled from behind me.

Calax stood in the doorway of one of the spare bedrooms, his face silhouetted in shadows. Even then, I could see his sleep tousled dark hair and his massive outline. He let out a yawn, his fist coming up to block the sound.

"Where's Addie?" I asked, not wasting any time with pleasantries. I didn't have the patience to be pleasant when her life was in danger. I thought about the dead body that I'd left to rot. No, I most definitely did not have the patience. When someone or something threatened the people I loved, I was willing to destroy the world. It would fall into shambles. Burn away.

Hell if I cared.

At the mention of her name, he stepped closer. Lightning streaked overhead, highlighting his cold face. His brow was furrowed, and his lips were turned down.

"What's going on?" he repeated.

I grabbed a flashlight out of my waistband and flipped it on. Holding it up to my red, blotchy skin, I allowed him to see for himself. For a moment, he merely looked confused. His eyes tightened, surprise giving way to confusion and annoyance. After another long second, that confusion morphed into horror.

"The rain?" he asked. Despite the fear evident in his facial expressions, his voice was devoid of any feeling. He could've been reciting a fact. I knew, from experience, that this was a defense mechanism. It was the slow churning lava before a volcanic eruption. The calm before the storm. "It did that?"

"Acid rain," I responded, nodding once in confirmation.

Calax, to some, resembled a monster. With his hulking frame and dark, intrusive eyes, he could've been one. I'd never considered him scary until that very moment. His eyes turned glacial, and his hands clenched into fists. Like Fallon, he wore an expression that only screamed one thing—murder. For the first time in all the years I'd known him, I was terrified. That, combined with my already overwhelming fear for Adelaide and my brothers, was an intense emotion. My body began to shake as both adrenaline and distress warred for dominance.

"Calax…" But he was already charging down the hall and into the kitchen.

The rain was acid.

Three of our brothers were missing.

And the woman we loved, the glue that held us all together, was facing the storm.

CHAPTER 9

ADDIE

I didn't have a lot of toys when I was younger. Besides Dolly, there wasn't a lot that I wanted. I was once caught playing with plastic cars, and DOD screamed at me for behaving like a boy. If I were to use fake medical tools I stole from the infirmary to play doctor, Mother would whack me upside the head. No reason besides the fact that she was a bitter woman. That was the reason for all abuse, I had come to realize—bitterness. It took years of therapy for me to understand that I wasn't to blame for the actions of my parents. They were the monsters, and I was the victim.

I bounced the red ball once more against the linoleum tiles. I allowed the motion to soothe me, to ease my inner turmoil. Up and down. Up and down. It was surprisingly easy to focus on the ball, only the ball, and to block out the rest of the world. Up and down. Up and down.

Tam sat behind me, his body heat almost stifling. Unlike me, his eyes were drawn to the gruesome display through the translucent window. The body. The dead girl.

The girl who'd been alive only an hour earlier.

No. I couldn't think about her. Pinpricks of terror sent my veins alight. Fear strangled me in an iron vise.

Up and down.

Bounce.

There was no word to describe the sound the ball made as it ricocheted off the white tiles. A plop, perhaps? Surely it couldn't be called a "bounce." The sound most definitely did not have that quality—

"Addie..." Tam murmured. I felt rather than saw him inch closer to me. His arms came to wrap around my waist, pulling me against his surprisingly firm and muscled chest. "You're thinking aloud again."

"Sorry," I said automatically. He rubbed his nose into my scalp.

"Don't apologize."

"Sorry."

He chuckled, his hands tightening. Despite the horrors of our situation, my heart gave a wild thump at his initiation of contact. Once again, I was reminded of the two faces of Tam—the shy, timid boy who used his hair as a shield, and the MMA fighter who exuded confidence. I didn't know what had changed within him now that we were alone, only that I liked it.

I liked *him*.

Both sides of him, that was. I liked him, and I didn't know how I felt about that.

"Why are you touching me?" I blurted before I could think my words through. I inwardly winced when Tamson's body went ramrod straight behind me, and his hands dropped from my waist. My body cried out at the loss of heat.

I didn't even have to look to know that his face would be a bright crimson and his head would be ducked down. What the hell was wrong with me? I was a verbal bullet—once I was let loose, I hurt everyone in my path. Words escaped my mouth before I could reel them back in.

"No. No. No," I said, reaching for his arms and rewrapping them back around my waist. "That's not what I meant. I just meant... Ugh. Words are hard and annoying. Why can't we just telepathically communicate? That would make things ten times easier..." I trailed off, my teeth gnawing on my lower lip. Tam, behind me, remained stiff and unresponsive. I worried that whatever progress we'd made had completely shattered by my big mouth.

I changed position so I was now facing him, still in the confines of his legs. As expected, his head was lowered and his cheeks were tinged pink. However, unlike the last few times, his eyes remained fixated on mine.

"I'm sorry I'm such an idiot," I mumbled. My hand tightened on the red ball, my fingernails leaving idents.

His lips quirked upwards.

"Stop apologizing."

"So now that we're here..." I trailed off. There was no reason for me to clarify what "here" I meant. "Tell me more about yourself."

He blinked at me, his lashes long and full. Beautiful. Framing eyes that were chips of emerald.

"I already told you," he said softly. The blush had receded from his cheeks the more I talked, and his head had gradually begun to raise. Hand trembling, he reached to tuck a strand of my curly hair behind my ear. "I lived with my grandma up until she died, and then the guys found me."

"But you never told me what your life was like between that," I pointed out. When his expression shuttered, I hurried to add, "You don't have to tell me if you don't feel comfortable."

There I went again, fucking things up. I was the equivalent of autocorrect—you put up with me, but I pissed you off more than I helped you.

Tamson's expression turned thoughtful, almost contemplative. He grabbed my free hand and absently began to trace patterns on the sensitive skin of my palm. Goosebumps covered the entirety of my body, but the feeling was pleasant.

Amazing.

"People do desperate things when they want to survive," he said at last, voice quiet. Broken.

I thought of Elena's stricken face as she stared at her fallen comrade. That was the same girl who'd run in the rain in a futile attempt to save me. But now, it was about survival. Who survived and who died. It was apparent from her hasty retreat that she'd made her choice, and we all suffered the consequences.

But would I have behaved any differently? If I had to choose between me and a stranger?

I thought of Tommy just then. He'd sacrificed someone he loved for me, a girl he didn't know. The bond forged from that decision was stronger than anything I'd ever experienced before.

Hero. Survivor.

Was it possible to be both, or did you have to choose? Which decision was the correct one?

Tamson's finger continued to idly draw shapes into my hand. Each touch was electric.

"I did bad things, both to myself and others. It was a choice between survival and my body. My integrity. I chose survival."

Tears sprang to my eyes at his words. He'd been a kid at the time. No kid should have to make such an impossible decision. I felt immense relief that he'd been discovered by the others, that he'd been molded into the man he was today.

"I realized something," I said quietly. One of my hands was still clenched around the ball, while my other was being stroked by Tamson's long fingers. I focused on the patterns he drew into my skin, envisioning his finger as a paintbrush.

"We went through all this shit, but look at how we turned out. We're fighters, all of us. The shit we've been through only made us stronger. I wish that my life had been different, but at the same time, I'm grateful. Who knows what type of person I would've been if I hadn't overcome all of these obstacles? Look at you! Kind, caring, strong. God, why did it take me so long to realize? I refuse to let my past chain me down. I'm so much stronger than I was before, and I will only continue to grow in my strength." As I spoke, I gained more conviction and animation. A smile broke my face apart. For so long, I'd seen myself as a victim, but I wasn't that. Not really. I was a survivor. The trials in my life may have been a burden, but my own interpretation of those events were the chains holding me back. For the first time, I felt free.

Tamson was staring at me with an unreadable expression. Before I could inquire, he closed the distance between us and kissed me.

A quick, hard kiss. Merely a whisper of what a kiss from Tam would feel like. One second, his lips were on mine, demanding and persistent, and the next, he'd scrambled away from me. His face was red, and his eyes flickered from his boots, my legs, the ball, anywhere besides my eyes.

My lips tingled from his sudden yet unexpected kiss. I wanted *more*. I wanted him. The intensity of that emotion was startling.

"Tam..." I said helplessly.

"I'll be… I'm going to look around."

Without another word, he was gone.

~

THERE WERE ONLY SO many times I could throw the ball against the wall. My thoughts were a whirlpool of various and contradicting thoughts and emotions. One part of me remembered the feel of Tam's lips on my own. How soft they felt. The taste of him. The other part of me felt nothing but guilt as I envisioned Calax's and Ryder's faces. And then I remembered Calax's words…

Gah. I was so confused. The more I thought about it, the more confused I became. What a shest. What a shit fest.

Between all of that, I couldn't help but feel self-conscious. Why had Tamson left so abruptly? Did he not want to kiss me? Were my feelings for him one-sided? I knew it was irrational to believe that all of the guys felt for me as I felt for them, but the wistful voice inside of me couldn't help but hope.

So stupid.

Because of your idiotic decisions, you're going to end up alone.

Wallowing in my own self-pity, I didn't notice the car until it was directly in front of the store.

I let out a squeal. They'd come for us! I knew they would, but I hadn't expected them already. I could only hope that they'd taken the necessary precautions to assure their protection. My excitement waned when four figures emerged from the car, silhouetted in the blighted sunlight.

They were all large and covered in thick, black clothing. I couldn't recall the name of such an outfit, but it looked to be military level. If anything, the rain cascaded off of their black armor.

Confusion turned into fear as they marched towards the glass door. One of them stopped at the fallen body and kicked at her chest before continuing forward. Rain continued to pelt them, though they moved as if they weren't affected in the least. Slung over their shoulders were large guns.

"Tamson!" I cried.

They were moving closer.

Black visors.

Black armor.

Black guns.

"Tamson." This was nothing more than a pathetic whimper.

Tamson materialized behind me, one hand covering my mouth and the other pulling at my waist. I went limp in his arms, allowing him to pull me farther and farther into the store.

Behind a clothes rack.

Out of sight.

I heard a door opening, followed by what I would almost describe as jovial laughter.

"Shit, man," someone exclaimed. This was followed by words too soft for me to decipher. My body trembled, and my heart hammered.

Could they hear it? My heart?

Fear pooled low in my stomach, churning the contents of my breakfast until I wanted to expel them onto the floor.

Tamson moved to drag me even farther back, and it was then that I unintentionally released the ball I had forgotten I'd been holding. The sound was deafening. Tam froze behind me.

Silence, surprisingly pronounced, charged the air like an electrical current. For a moment, I thought no one had heard the ball. I thought that I hadn't just made an idiotic mistake that could cost us both our lives. I thought that the thunder and rain had somehow masked the ball as it rolled across the white tiles.

But then, breaking through the silence, came a voice.

"Who's there? Come out, come out, wherever you are."

CHAPTER 10

ADDIE

"There's no one there, Shawn. Leave it alone," a cold voice, not belligerent but not necessarily kind, said briskly.

"You heard it, right?" the man I assumed was Shawn exclaimed. I held my breath, pressing my body even further into Tamson's. If it was physically possible, I would have merged with him right then and there until we became one person. One body. One heartbeat. I could feel his own heart pounding though his expression remained calm. For my benefit, I imagined.

"I hear the rain, dumbass," a different voice sneered. There was what sounded like flesh connecting with flesh followed immediately by a howl of pain.

"Grab what you can."

Tamson very gently squeezed my upper arm. Once he garnered my attention, he nodded towards a set of double doors that led to a separate hallway. A neon sign hanging from above announced it as the bathrooms. Nodding to show him I understood, I pulled my arm away from his. He reluctantly released me and began to stealthily move towards the desired destination. I was not as subtle as him, nor as sneaky, but I made it to the long stretch of hallway without any incident.

Tamson grabbed my arm once again, pulling me inside the nearest bathroom. The female's, I realized vaguely.

"Are you okay?" he whispered, once we were shoved inside the largest stall. He checked over my body, touch as light as a feather, for any injuries. I captured his wrist and held it gently between my two hands.

"I'm fine. They didn't see me." He let out a relieved exhale.

I couldn't bring myself to feel the same relief. All I felt was bitterness and something akin to self-loathing. Because of my clumsy fingers, they'd heard us and at least suspected that we were there.

Stupid.

Idiotic.

"Hey." Tam captured my face with both of his palms, his thumbs rubbing soothing circles into my cheekbones. "It's not your fault."

I didn't know how he'd been able to read me so easily. Was my face really the opened book he made it out to be? Or did he just know me better than I thought?

"I know," I said softly. I didn't want to talk about my mistake anymore. My mind and body felt heavy, the combination turning my legs into jelly. A leaden, miserable feeling settled heavily in my gut. I pressed my forehead against Tam's chest, and his arms, after a moment of hesitation, came to wrap around my waist. I pulled back as a sudden thought occurred to me. Tamson must've seen the panic on my face, as his hands came up to tentatively rub at my shoulders in an attempt to alleviate the pressure there.

"Please don't tell me we're going to split up," I pleaded in a harsh whisper. "I see movies. I know what happens, and the shy guy *always* dies. Always. I know I'm final girl material and everything, but I really don't want you to die. So we aren't going to split up. Promise me?"

I was aware that I was babbling, my fear manifesting itself into verbal vomit, but I couldn't make myself stop. My body trembled in his hands. All I could think about was Tamson's body lying in the parking lot, his skin melting from his face in red, blotchy streaks. Bloody tears cascaded down from his eyes. Teeth falling from his mouth, clattering against the asphalt. I closed my eyes to rid myself of such horrid images.

No. Tamson was okay. He was here, with me, and safe.

Everyone was safe.

I had to believe that.

I didn't know if he picked up on my own mental anguish or if he just knew I needed the comfort. Either way, he held me a little tighter, a little closer, a little longer. I could feel each shuddering breath reverberating through his ribcage.

It occurred to me that he was scared. Not only scared, but terrified. How could he not be? We were trapped in an unknown location with at least four hostiles only feet away from us. Guilt once again threatened to consume me.

If only I hadn't dropped that stupid ball…

If only I hadn't insisted on coming in the first place…

If only…

If only…

Those thoughts, too, were swept away in a tidal wave of anger. I couldn't focus on them. Not now. No, what I could focus on was waiting out the storm in Tamson's warm and comforting embrace.

Together.

We would face the storm together.

I cowered, turning my face against Tamson's chest and inhaling his sweet scent. It was different than Ryder's or Calax's. Something sweeter, like the man himself. I could relish in the pungent, yet wonderful, smell.

I didn't ask for much. Hell, I didn't even want much. But I could have this, right? Right?

Just as that thought occurred to me, the bathroom door banged against the wall. Tamson tensed, his muscles flexing beneath me. I heard a boisterous laugh followed by a slew of curse words.

I held my breath, waiting.

One.

Two.

Three.

It was a trick my old therapist taught me—hold your breath when you're anxious or scared. Apparently, it had calming qualities. I didn't know for certain if I agreed with that, but just then, it seemed applicable.

My teeth bit down on my lip so tightly that I tasted blood.

Why was he here?

How did he know?

I told myself that it was merely a coincidence. Maybe he needed to take a piss. Guys pissed. My days as Lil' One Punch taught me as much. Maybe he had a baby that needed a diaper change. Thousands of scenarios danced through my head, each one more gruesome than the last. The general consensus was death. Death for Tamson and me.

He paused right outside of our stall. I could see his thick, black boots poking through the tiny crack in the bottom of the door. My heart was racing, erratic butterfly wings pattering against my ribcage and demanding release.

For a moment, the man didn't speak. He just stood there, his presence as ominous and heavy as if he'd been screaming. Finally, after the tension was thick enough to cut through with a knife, he spoke.

"I know you're in there."

Tamson remained silent, but I felt his body shifting slightly to push me behind him. I was no longer wearing the baseball cap that hid my true identity as a female. Instead, my brown locks hung untamed down my back. I remembered Elena's words from earlier.

The world was a dangerous place for a woman, now more so than ever.

I tried to channel my inner warrior, but I was scared. And to be frank, I *wasn't* a fighter. I couldn't kick ass, no matter how much I wished differently. Instead, I had to rely on Tamson and the small dagger resting heavily in my waistband.

Stab with the pointy end.

Shouldn't be too hard.

"Are you going to come out?" the man thundered, and I flinched instinctively. The power he displayed seemed to innately command my respect. It was such a contrast to Fallon's quiet demeanor or even Ryder's eccentric presence. This was a man who knew what his place was in the world and demanded to be treated as such. "Or do I have to come in?"

～

DECLAN

The dream started off as it always did. My eyes fluttering open and facing a room with stark white walls and an overwhelming aroma of bleach. I glanced to the tiny needle protruding from my skin, leading towards a long tube. The heart monitor screen showed a steady rhythm of waves, yet no sound emitted. No beep beep beep *that would normally drive me insane.*

The room was utterly silent. Even with the opened door, I couldn't hear any excess noise drifting from the hallway.

Numerous flowers adorned the windowsill, a sort of demented offering. My brows furrowed, and my frown deepened. I hated flowers and the false condolences they evoked. People sent flowers to act like they gave a damn.

It was comical, really. Only one person actually gave a shit about me. At the thought, I sat up farther and glanced from the cracked open doorway to the garden of picked and artificial flowers. I strained to read the names, but none of them were familiar. Hell, one was from an Aunt Laura that I'd never met before.

And where were my parents?

My thoughts were interrupted by a figure moving in my peripheral vision. I turned, startled, to see a familiar man. His salt and peppered hair was cut short, heightening an arresting face made of chiseled bones and dark eyes. Those eyes were currently trained on me, as if his mere gaze was capable of physically penetrating my skin. I gulped at the intensity. This man was someone who was born to be feared.

Not respected. There was too much coldness in his face, his eyes, his taunting smirk.

I sat up straighter. My body ached something fierce, and I noticed, to my dismay, that my hair had been cut short. It was no longer placed into its customary braid.

The man opened his mouth and began to speak. At least, I assumed he was speaking. Instead, his lips moved and no sound emerged. I tilted my head to the side, surveying the person I knew to be Addie's father.

But his words were indistinct. On and on he talked, his hands moving more erratically and animatedly as he spoke.

When it became apparent that I couldn't hear him, a cruel smile broke upon his face. It wasn't a smile that evoked warm feelings. It wasn't a smile you should see on a man who called himself a dad. I felt my body grow cold at having such a smile directed at me.

It would be later that I understood what he had been trying to tell me—Addie hated me. She wanted nothing to do with the poor, lonely deaf boy.

The dream shifted.

I saw Addie's face, years younger, staring at me through the restaurant window. I'd dressed to impress her and her family. My father had lent me an old, black suit, and I'd brushed my long hair back.

My fingers twisted the wrapped present I'd bought her with what little money I had. It wasn't gold or silver, but it was from me to her. From a boy who loved a girl.

I wondered if she would like it. After all, a best friends necklace was beyond cliché.

And yet...

I envisioned her face as she opened it. She would be so excited! It was that thought alone that gave me the courage to march forward. Towards her.

Once again, the dream world dissipated and transformed. I was in a bedroom, the brown bedspread and clean floors indicating it as a room in Elena's house. My body was sprawled out on the bed, naked. My cock was throbbing. The feeling bordered the precarious line between pleasurable and painful.

Addie stood above my bed, an angel in the flesh. She was dressed in a lacy, black nightgown that accentuated her large breasts and tiny hips. Her brown curls hung loose down her back. God, what I wouldn't give to run my hands through them. Would they be as soft as they looked?

Eyes never leaving mine, she licked her lips, and I followed the diminutive movement like a man possessed. She was perfect. Absolutely and almost absurdly perfect.

She knelt down and took my cock between her plump lips. I groaned, my body arching upwards instinctively. Her tongue traced the vein running the length while her hand fondled my balls. My fingers dug into the comforter.

She alternated between long sucks and gentle kisses. I felt her everywhere.

On my cock. My lips. My chest. Teasing my nipples.

She was everywhere.

I was going to explode in her mouth. At that thought, I grabbed her hips and held her still. I wanted my cock to spill its seed over her perfect breasts. I wanted to mark her as my own—

I WOKE up to someone shaking my shoulder. The movement was so sudden that I jerked backwards as if I'd been slapped. Glaring, I turned towards the man who dared intrude on my sleep. My cock strained against my jeans.

The panic in Fallon's eyes stopped me short, and any lust I had diminished.

"Are you the only one here?" he signed, movements erratic. I'd never seen the man look so unkempt before. His long hair was out of its ponytail and hung in a disheveled heap over his shoulders.

"Just me and Calax," I replied. When he didn't immediately respond, I signed, *"What's going on?"*

"Acid rain."

Those words made my blood turn to ice. The implications.

No...

"Are they back yet? Is Addie back yet?" I signed, moving to my feet. The wooden chair fell to the floor with my movement.

The despondency in Fallon's eyes was all the answer I needed.

Though I was worried about my brothers, I knew they were more than capable of taking care of themselves. Addie, on the other hand, was oblivious to the horrors of this world. Maybe oblivious wasn't the correct word, but naïve. She understood that there were monsters in the world, but she failed to recognize them until they were directly in front of her. She would mistake a gun for a flower until the bullet had shot through her heart and killed her. There was no distinction between black and white. Instead, she perceived the world as shades of grey.

I feared that her innocence would lead to her death.

And her death, more so than anything else, I would not be able to survive.

I'd already decided *I* wouldn't live past Atlanta. What I had to do...

Shaking my head, I focused on the three figures before me. Asher was coated in blood—not his own, I knew—and Fallon looked positively feral. He was a scary man on the best of days, but just then, he appeared murderous. A beast trapped too long in a cage.

They were talking amongst one another, but I didn't bother trying to read their lips.

Tamson was with Addie, I knew that. And he would protect her with his life. Ronan and Ryder were together. I was even worried about the little bastard, Tommy. He'd grown on me like a fungus. Granted, I didn't like the way he looked at Addie, but I reminded myself she wasn't mine in the first place. She was Calax's.

Not mine.

Fallon's head whipped towards the garage just as the door was pushed open. Elena ran in first, her coat wet from windward rain, but her skin surprisingly unharmed. I felt nothing but relief when I saw her.

Glancing over her shoulder, I strained to spot Addie and Tam.

Lilly was there. And Samantha. And the others…wait. Not all of the others.

Fallon turned towards her and said something. I wished I could hear his words, as Elena's face paled drastically. She looked exhausted, heavy bags under her eyes and cheeks stained from what appeared to be tears.

Calax's expression contorted with an almost incandescent fury, a mirror of Asher's. Fighting off my agitation at being left in the dark, I focused on Fallon just as he pressed Elena into the wall. His hand wrapped around her throat, and her eyes widened. Samantha charged forward, but stopped when Lilly put a restraining hand on her arm.

I knew Fallon could kill Elena. And he would, too, if Addie wouldn't have seen him as a monster. The man never hesitated to kill someone if his family was in danger, male or female. It was just one of the reasons why he was the respected and feared team leader.

Noting my quirked brow, Asher hurried to sign,

"The bitch left them there to die."

My body thrummed with a blistering rage. I'd never been the type to want to hit a female, but just then, I wished my fist accidentally connected with her face. She was a petty female driven by jealousy and lust.

Fallon said something else, something that made Elena cry, before he released her. Without a word, he stormed towards the garage and the cars.

"Come on boys," Asher signed, a cheerful smile on his face. The man was a closeted psychopath. *"Rain or shine, we have to get our girl back."*

"And Ryder and Ronan?" I inquired.

"They can take care of themselves," Calax interjected. His face was glacial, almost as if it were carved from stone. I wondered what Elena had said to cause all of them to behave so aggressively.

A problem for another time, I supposed.

Right now, I had to focus on saving my girl.

CHAPTER 11

*W*ell…

Getting held at gunpoint wasn't exactly how I'd planned to spend my day. No, I would've much preferred a repeat of today's earlier performance. The whole head-between-her-legs-as-she-moaned-my-name type of show.

Alas, the world was not so kind.

Instead of panicking as the barrel was pressed against the side of my head, I merely rolled my eyes and feigned indifference. Gun against my head? That was nothing.

So when the blonde bitch wrapped rope around my wrists and tied me against the wall, I continued to keep my face impassive. Ronan let out a string of creative curses before his sounds were muffled by a sock being shoved into his mouth. His eyes widened in disgust and horror, and he flashed them a glare that would've made any sane person piss their pants. Me? I tried to calm my erratic breathing as my mind brought me back to Liz's house.

My body, held captive beneath layers of ropes.

Her face contorted into a sneer.

Her cold lips…

I could feel the beginnings of a panic attack take root, but I quickly shoved them down. If there was one thing I learned at the academy, it was never to show fear. Fear was a reflection of your weakness, and the last thing I wanted to be was weak in front of these people. My stomach was a tumultuous mix of fear and desperation. However, anger also warred for dominance within me, and I knew that only one person, one brown-haired female, would be able to get my rage pacified.

Three girls and three boys. All similar in age. The blonde girl from earlier, two girls with dark hair, and three boys that could've been brothers. From what I garnered, the blonde girl was named Ali. The brunette was Amanda. The oldest brother, and the apparent leader, was Kai.

"I'll ask again," Kai said, leaning down so he was face to face with me. "Where are you camped out?"

Oh yeah. The assholes decided that they wanted to raid our "camp." They didn't believe me when I told them we were visitors from the deepest pits of Hell. To be fair, I wasn't lying. Elena's house was the equivalent to hell, and only Liz's house could compare.

The only good news was that they weren't killers. They didn't even want to hurt us. They were just six people playing the cards dealt to them by fate. The game was constantly changing, the rules fluctuating. One thing remained painstakingly clear—they wanted to survive.

"They're both cute," I heard Ali mumble, far enough away where she didn't believe I could hear. She glanced at me out of the corner of her eye. Amanda scoffed.

"Too dark. Not my cup of tea."

Figures. I was more of a coffee drinker myself.

The rope rubbed against my sensitive wrists, the pain increasing every second I was tied. My agitation must've been clear on my face, as Kai leaned down until his face was even closer to mine.

"Look," he said. "You obviously came from somewhere that has food, water, and other resources. I don't get why you won't just tell us. We should all stick together against those beasts."

Ronan, beside me, grunted, his words inarticulate due to the muffle. I couldn't help but snort myself. What did this man expect? To tie us up and then join us around a campfire? His idea had merit, but his execution needed some work. Bondage was more of Fallon's forte, if the rumors were true.

"Untie us," I snapped. "Maybe we'll talk after."

"Look, it's nothing personal, man." Another one of the men stepped forward, hands raised as if he were a criminal approaching a cop. He licked his lips and anxiously glanced at Kai the dick face. "We just had to protect ourselves before we talked to you. But we are sincere in our desire to join you."

This was getting fucking ridiculous. Addie was no doubt back by now and was getting worried. A worried Addie led to an insane Addie. Or at least more insane than she normally was.

A crack of thunder reverberated overhead. I'd seen the bloated storm clouds slowly inching their way to where we were. It would only be a few more moments before the sky opened up.

At a nod from Kai, the three girls pushed open the glass doors and waited outside, arms crossed over their chests.

"Stay with them," Kai ordered his brothers, and they followed. I watched in rapt fascination as Kai the dick face produced a pocket knife from his pants. It suddenly occurred to me why he'd sent them away in the first place. His hand trembled as he held the knife to my face, and in the blade, I could see my reflection.

Well shit.

He brandished the weapon with a clumsy swipe that suggested he wasn't familiar with how to properly wield it. Great. So I was going to bleed to death because some dumbass didn't know how to hold a weapon. Fucking peachy. His hand trembled as he pressed it against my neck.

"Come on, man. We have girls with us." The words were a pathetic plea.

I wanted to tell him that we did too, or at least one that mattered, but I kept my mouth shut. I had no idea what he would do with that type of leverage. Instead, I leveled an icy glare his way.

"Why don't you find an abandoned house or a store, hunker down, and live happily ever after. Have babies. Get an erection. I don't give a fuck what you do," I suggested through gritted teeth. Ronan hummed his agreement from beside me.

"Because people are savages, man. They'll try to take it from us!"

At that, I couldn't help but let out a bark of laughter. The fucking irony.

Kai must've realized how his words had been construed, as his frown deepened.

"We're not bad people," he insisted.

"No." I resisted the urge to roll my eyes. "You're just someone who holds knives to strangers' necks. Not bad people at all."

Kai's hand teetered dangerously close to an artery in my neck before he dropped the knife with a resigned sigh.

"Look, I just need to—"

I never did find out what he needed. One second, he was talking, and the next, he let out a strangled scream as a Rager jumped on his back and bit his neck. No, not a Rager.

A fucking Tommy.

Blood coated Tommy's mouth as he released Kai, and the man fell to his knees. His hand went to cover the wound while his eyes widened eminently.

"Fucking hell, Tommy," I cursed, eyes shifting from his bloodstained mouth to the fallen leader. With a shrug, Tommy wiped his mouth with the back of his hand.

"What? I saved you, didn't I?" The little asshole raised a brow and cocked his hip to the side, daring me to disagree with him. I had the distinct feeling that he would leave me here to die if I did anything but praise his holiness.

Fortunately, Tommy grabbed the knife that had clattered to the floor and cut my bindings before I could reply. Once freed, I scrambled to Ronan and pulled the sock out of his mouth. He immediately began to gag.

"Fucking asshole," he mumbled beneath his breath, his retching turning into dramatic dry-heaving. I patted his back and held his short-cropped hair away from his face.

"There, there, sweetheart," I teased mockingly. With his hands still tied, he could do little but glare at me.

Tommy was singing softly about being the "badass of the badasses," and Kai was moaning. Besides that, and the occasional crack of thunder breaking apart the sky, it was silent.

Which was why, only seconds later, the screams broke through the silence like the crack of a whip.

ADDIE

Don't panic.

I repeated those words in my head like a mantra, a chant, a prayer.

Don't panic.

I could see a dozen emotions flicker in Tam's gaze before it settled on determination. His jaw clenched so tightly, I was afraid it would break, he moved so that I was against the wall and he was in front of me. His hands pushed down on my shoulders, forcing me to my knees. Any words I wanted to say, any protests I wanted to make, were silenced by one look into his cold eyes. This wasn't the shy boy from before or even the confident man. He was a stranger, and for the first time since I'd met him, pinpricks of terror danced across my skin. My stomach plummeted at the predatory-like awareness in his gaze.

His hands moved from my shoulders and into my hair, pressing my face against the waistband of his pants.

The fuck…?

Before I could even raise an eyebrow, the bathroom door was kicked in and light from a flashlight momentarily blinded me. I flinched, immediately shifting to move to my feet, but one yank on my hair from Tam kept me on my knees before him.

Finally, Tam removed his grip with more callousness than I was used to from my sweet boy. He turned towards the newcomer, one hand moving to zip up his pants.

"Do you mind?" Tam asked coldly. I didn't recognize that voice, just as I didn't recognize his glacial expression. Was this an act?

Or was I finally getting a glimpse at the real Tamson?

I scrambled to my feet, peeking over his shoulder at the newcomer. Up close, I could see that he was entirely bedecked in black army armor. His helmet was off, revealing a strong jawline and dark hair. Wrinkles hinted that he may have been a few years older than us, but his body was the epitome of perfection, with muscles clearly accentuated through his dark clothes.

He leered in my direction, hunger dancing in his eyes.

"Who are you folks?" he asked, voice gravelly. Tam let out a bark of harsh laughter.

"She doesn't matter. I'm Tamson."

The way he dismissed me, as if I was the scum beneath his boot, brought back memories from my time with my father and mother.

The way they looked at me as if I was a disgusting insect.

The distaste in their eyes whenever I failed to meet their expectations of perfection.

The scowl on my father's face, seconds before he partook in a particularly gruesome beating.

My body tensed, and an incandescent fury filled me. After everything we'd been through…

Taking a calming breath in an attempt to pacify my rage, I looked at things logically. Tamson obviously had a plan. I had to trust him.

Trust.

Trust was following someone off a cliff with the promise that there was a net to catch you. Did I trust Tam?

As I studied his profile in the dim glow from the man's flashlight, I realized that I did. I trusted him implicitly and probably irrationally.

Lowering my head in submission, I took a tentative step forward so I was just behind his broad shoulder. Tam's hand snaked out to wrap around my waist. Possessive. Staking his claim.

"Say hi to the man," he drawled. When I didn't immediately respond, his hand came down on my ass. Not hard, despite the deafening sound, but enough to send desire straight to my core. You heard me right—desire.

What was wrong with me?

You would think that years of abuse would mean I had an aversion to that type of contact, yet all I could think about was him doing it again. And again. Maybe even harder.

"Hi," I mumbled, keeping my eyes averted. I couldn't see the man's face, but I heard his gruff laugh.

"You have that bitch wrapped around your finger," he said with what sounded like grudging respect. Admiration. Inwardly, I wanted to gag, but I managed to keep my face indifferent in response to his crude comment.

Tamson shrugged.

"Wasn't hard. Promised her protection in exchange for her obedience. Isn't that right, Flower?"

Flower? I much preferred Lil' One Punch to a name like Flower. For some reason, it evoked images of me skipping through a flower field. Yup. Totally not the badass impression I was hoping for.

"How did you know where we were?" Tam asked. He sounded both indolent and confident, as if he hadn't a care in the world. He drew me closer to him, his arms wrapping around my stomach. Creeper's eyes locked on the minuscule display of affection, desire once again making an appearance. He licked his chapped lips.

"I'm not an idiot like the others. I knew there was someone here with us." He shrugged. "Now comes the important question—what to do with the two of you?"

My body froze, and my heart pounded. I really didn't want to die now that I had so much to live for.

Tamson remained calm behind my trembling body. If anything, he relaxed even further at the man's words.

"Others? We've been wandering alone for a few days now. Maybe you could use an extra set of hands?" At his final statement, he squeezed my hips. Creeper's eyes latched onto where we connected. The way he looked at me...

Trust. I had to trust Tamson.

"Or we can make a trade," Tam continued. "I'm sure you have a bunch of supplies. Maybe even some weapons? I think we could come to an agreement."

My breathing was heavy, almost embarrassingly so. I told myself I had to trust Tamson, I had to believe in him, yet everything within me screamed at me to run. It was the fight or flight reaction I'd perfected since I was young. Tamson couldn't be serious. He had a plan. That was the only logical explanation.

Yet, as his grip tightened on my ribcage to the point of bruising, I felt the beginnings of doubt leak through my calm demeanor. The man was smiling at me, a malevolent smile that made me want to shrink in on myself. And Tamson? He was smiling back.

CHAPTER 12

ADDIE

The man led us to the same aisle where Tamson and I had initially camped out at. Our supplies, which we'd organized, were now shoved into duffle bags the assholes had brought. Three other men stood in a haphazard semicircle. When we appeared, their laughter cut off and six eyes burned a hole through my forehead. Tam's arm tightened around my waist marginally.

"Shawn," the largest one demanded. "Who are they?"

The man who had led us here, Shawn I presumed, gestured towards us vaguely.

"Tamson and his bitch."

I gritted my teeth together in a conscious effort to keep from screaming as fury ignited in my chest. Or biting. Both options were appealing.

The second man, this one with flaming red hair and dark eyes, appraised me calculatingly. The third glanced between the four of us warily. I couldn't define the expression on his face.

Shawn nudged Tamson forward, inadvertently dragging me along as well. I stumbled over my own two feet, only Tam's arm keeping me upright.

"Tell Greg what you told me," Shawn said. The largest man, Greg, raised a brow. It was surprisingly thin and delicate on his face, a contrast to his scruffy beard and mane of black hair. If I was in any other circumstance, I would've laughed. As of now, I could only hope that my word vomit wouldn't get me killed by unintentionally insulting the scary man's eyebrows.

"It's simple." Tam's calm words pulled me out of my thoughts. His body was relaxed, the underlying tension I'd seen only minutes earlier completely diminishing from his face. He looked as if he was in his element.

For the umpteenth time, panic began to take root, overwhelming even the anger.

It was a diminutive seed, barely beginning to grow into a full-blown tree, but it was enough to make my body tremble. The knife in my waistband had never felt so heavy. So damning.

"You have weapons. I need weapons." He shrugged. "I want to make a trade."

Greg's eyes moved slowly from Tam's face to my own. His eyes lit up, and his gaze did a slow perusal of my body. I felt dirty under his stare, as if someone had thrown a bucket of mud over my head. I wanted nothing more than to shower and rid myself of the disgusting sensation his mere gaze evoked.

"Would be hotter if she wasn't in those man clothes," he said after a moment of silence. "Why don't we see what she looks like without them?"

For the first time, I felt Tam tense underneath me. It was the merest flex of muscles, there and gone too quickly for me to be certain. His hand slowly moved up my ribs, to my neck, before roughly pulling my head to the side. Despite the initial sting, I didn't whimper. I wouldn't give any of them the satisfaction.

"Now now. Don't be hasty. She's still mine as of now." His nose brushed the sensitive skin of my neck, followed quickly by something wet. His tongue. It trailed down to my collarbone, alternating between tiny nips and kisses. My body instinctively leaned into his embrace. I told myself that I was acting, that I was playing a character, but I knew I was lying to myself.

"See how willing she is?" Tamson whispered, his breathing stirring my hair. His hand slowly released me, one finger at a time, and a shuddering breath escaped me. He was magnetic. It was impossible for me not to gravitate towards him.

The four men looked on with various expressions. Shawn and Greg regarded me with lust, Ginger looked annoyed, and Guy Four appeared positively horrified.

Tam slid into a lawn chair that had been brought out and pulled me into his lap.

"You know," Greg began conversationally. He too moved towards a chair opposite us. "We could just kill you and keep the bitch for ourselves."

A pounding resonated in my ears. My fingernails dug into Tam's legs. If he felt any pain from my grip, he didn't show it. Instead, he flashed Greg a cold smile. Perhaps a smirk would've been a better description. He looked positively devious and almost terrifying at that moment.

"You could," he agreed, and I mentally began berating him. You don't just tell the bad guy that he could kill you. I wasn't an expert or anything, but I was pretty sure that was a big no in the *How to Survive Psychos* handbook.

"Or…" he continued on, oblivious to my thoughts. "I can tell you where I keep my other willing ladies at. Fair trade. You get some. I get some." When the guys only looked at him, Tam nodded towards the glass door, where Bikini's body was still visible. The various cars still in the parking lot were beginning to corrode away. The paint chipped in irregular shapes, highlighting how acidic the rain actually was. How much longer until the rain broke through the roof of this store? How much longer until it made the cars unusable? I wasn't an expert on acid rain, though now I wished I'd studied it in extensive detail. That, and other natural disasters. From what I remembered during my brief course on environmental studies, acid rain impacted the immune system of an individual. It didn't burn away flesh. What exactly were we dealing with? And how would we survive an enemy we didn't understand?

All of my studies involving taxes and business law really paid off—said no one ever.

"She was one of my girls. I sent the others back a while ago, but I kept two with me for company," Tam was saying dogmatically. His hand leisurely stroked circles into my stomach through my shirt, a clear indication what he meant by the term company.

I couldn't help but feel disgusted by the way he used that dead girl as a prop for his twisted story. But at the same time, I couldn't help but note that I was still unaware of her name. Lacey, perhaps. Or Missy. One of those two.

The disgust turned inward, towards myself.

"She didn't make it," Tam said with another shrug.

Greg, surprisingly, turned towards Guy Four for confirmation.

"What do you say, Doc?"

The man anxiously fiddled with his glasses, pushing them back up his nose only to have them sink back down.

"Definitely died from the acid rain. Recently, too," Doc said. His eyes, once again, rested on my face. Unlike the lust and desire I could see swimming in the other three faces, he only regarded me with something akin to guilt and regret.

"So what do you say?" Tamson leaned back in the chair, his hand moving to my thigh. Even though the material of my pants, I could feel the heat his body emitted. His scent surrounded me.

Greg also leaned back in his chair, kicking his legs up to rest on a cooler.

"Let's make a deal."

∼

FALLON

If there was one thing I'd learned from my twenty-five years of existence, it was that I wasn't allowed to kill people without a reason. Elena? She gave me a reason. The bitch had the audacity to look me in the eye and tell me that I would be better off without Adelaide. Honestly, if the others hadn't been there, I might've snapped her neck. Female or male, no one was allowed to put my team into harm's way.

No one.

My hands were clenched over the steering wheel, knuckles white, as I maneuvered our van through the car cluttered street. For the most part, the town was deserted besides the occasional Rager. It reminded me of one of those post-apocalyptic movies where everything was left behind in a state of an evacuation. Houses chipped away by vandalism and inconsistent weather. Bodies loitering the street. Cars with their doors still opened after people had left in a haste. It was a gruesome sight, a sight that made my stomach drop and tighten. The dismal nature of the town was impossible to ignore.

I had one thought and one thought only.

Protect.

Fight.

Survive.

Calax turned towards me from where he sat in the passenger seat. Asher and Declan sat in the back, identical scowls contorting their faces.

"They're fine," Calax said. His low timber spoke the words with a sort of detached quality. He sounded as if he was merely reciting a fact, not assuring me that my family was safe. An involuntary snort escaped before I could stop it.

The brooding, angry bastard was comforting me. What had the world come to?

"She's fine. I'm certain of it." This was directed at himself, as if he needed the reassurance more than I did. The man's face was tight with an undefinable emotion, and his eyes had a feral glaze to them that hinted at an underlying tension. He was unhinged, a ticking time bomb just waiting to explode. We were similar in that respect.

Tick. Tick.

Boom.

"Holy shit," Asher muttered, pulling my attention back towards the matter at hand. I followed his finger and felt my eyes widen as well.

Holy shit was right.

There were Ragers everywhere. Walking. Attacking one another. Eating the remains of numerous dead bodies. I didn't know where to look. Their skin was beginning to deteriorate in some places and melt from the bones in others. The acid rain, which had the capability to kill a grown man, did not seem to deter them. If anything, it only gave them renewed vigor. Their faces vaguely reminded me of a cone of ice cream melting on a hot summer day...a fact that sent pinpricks of aversion and fear down my spine and to the soles of my feet. I would never be able to eat ice cream again.

I'd seen a lot of shit in my life. A lot of death. But this? This was something I couldn't even begin to articulate into words. I only hoped that Tamson had shielded Adelaide from this sight the best he could. No person could face such senseless death and desolation and remain sane. My heart hammered through my ribcage as I watched a Rager, dark hair dripping down its back and black veins crawling beneath its pasty skin, bite at the neck of a different Rager. Monsters. The whole lot of them.

I wondered if this was a sign from God. Had we really fucked up so badly that he resorted to making us mindless beasts? I thought of my own transgressions.

Father, forgive me, for I have sinned.

The list was endless. Murder. Theft.

Adultery.

My self-loathing reached a pinnacle. Wave after wave of despair threatened to consume me.

I'd never believed in karma before, but my perception of life and human nature was steadily changing. Bad things happened to monsters like me. It was a miracle that I was still alive and standing.

It was a miracle that I'd been able to fall in love, though what I felt did not classify as the traditional love. I was too battle-worn and hard to feel such a mushy emotion. What I felt didn't have a name, nor was it an exact science. It just *was.* A state of being, some would say. A sensation. A need to protect.

Shaking my head to clear my muddled thoughts, I moved farther and farther away from the assembled mass of Ragers, all clawing ineffectually at the retreating car. Even from this distance, I could hear their incoherent yells and pleas.

Savages.

Monsters.

A physical representation of my inner self.

CHAPTER 13

ADDIE

I'd gotten very good at reading people. At understanding each minuscule tick in their facial features. At watching and categorizing the way they moved their hands. Bodies told a story, and a lifetime of avoiding and fearing them made me an avid reader.

Lust. Anger. Fear. Sadness. Each emotion was carefully crafted on an individual, no matter how hard they tried to hide it. The slightest tightening of eyes here. The smile brewing there. The hair flip. The clenched fist. The Adam's apple bobbing. I sometimes wondered if it would be possible to decipher a person's entire life story based solely on their expressions and gestures.

Were they abused as children?

Were they unloved?

I prided myself in my ability, in my power to see past apathetic fronts.

But Tamson? I couldn't read him.

His posture was noticeably relaxed, but at the same time, his hand was clenched into a fist. Not a tight fist, but a fist all the same. His eyes were wide and sincere, earnest almost, but his lips were pulled down. His body was an epitome of contradictions, each one prohibiting me from getting an accurate read on him.

All I could do was watch from my position in his lap as he joked and conversed with the men before us. Conversation steered from girls to sports, and from sports to lives before and after. I listened with rapt interest as they divulged their life stories. Doc, no surprise, was an actual surgeon they picked up a few days ago. According to Shawn, they were on their way to Paradise.

A place where the monsters and storms couldn't reach those inside.

A place where we no longer had to live in fear.

A place where we could not only survive, but live.

I could see curiosity pique in Tamson's eyes as he listened to their tale of the supposed holy grounds. I, too, filed the information away for later.

"So…" Greg took a long drag of his cigarette, eyes once again focusing on me. I fidgeted at the intrusiveness of his stare, and Tamson put his hands on my hips to steady me. For some undefinable reason, tiny licks of pleasure erupted where he touched me. I knew that he wasn't entirely unaffected as well, if the hardness pressing into my back was any indication. "What are your specialties?"

Specialties?

"Well, Flower here—" Tamson began, but cut off when Greg raised a fist.

"I think the girl can speak for herself."

I was suddenly aware that I had every eye on me. I met Tam's impassive gaze, and the only indication he sensed my unease was the slightest nod of his head.

Specialties.

As a sex worker.

So you see, this is where I ran into a problem. I was horrible under pressure and had a tendency to babble when at a loss for words. Verbal train wreck.

"Wow. That's a loaded question. Okay…um…I'm very good at DP. And I just learned that it's *not* a fizzy drink. Imagine my surprise when I asked for a DP and I get freaking beads shoved up my hole, and not the good hole. Who needs to prepare anyways? And why do guys even like it? What if I were to take a shit or fart while the dick was in there? It would turn into a dip-shit. Oh, and I'm also good at licking, apparently. Like if you have blue, icicle balls, I can lick them for you. And I'm—"

Tamson, who'd been pinching me to get me to shut up, finally put a hand over my mouth.

Dammit, Adelaide.

Why do you have to go and open up your big mouth?

"Well damn," Greg huffed out in a laugh. Tamson indolently draped an arm over my shoulders. The other was still wrapped snugly around my waist.

"This is why we don't have the girls talk."

Though I knew his words were for Greg's benefit, they settled in my stomach heavily. It was a statement equivalent to what my dad had always told me. Girls were made to be seen, not heard. I repeated to myself that Tamson didn't actually feel that way, that he respected my opinions and enjoyed my sometimes crazy rants. He wasn't my father. He was merely a character at this moment.

My mind, unbidden, drifted to a day only a few weeks earlier.

Ryder sprawled himself on my bed.

"Stop moving," I scolded, picking up his foot with one hand and steadily applying the nail polish with the other. I was sitting awkwardly near the edge of the bed, the immense cast over my leg prohibiting me from getting any more comfortable.

"It tickles," he said, jerking his body yet again. I wanted to retort that nails couldn't be ticklish but held my tongue. It was a miracle he'd allowed me to paint them in the first place.

"I don't want red nails." Ronan was standing over my shoulder, watching me beautify his brother with undivided interest. I chuckled at the disgust in his voice, and my chuckling ascended into full belly laughter when he added, "I want green. Like my hair."

"Then you'll really be a leprechaun," I pointed out gleefully. It was a nickname I'd given

him when we first met and one that he took to heart. The fact that he smiled almost reverently at the name now made my stomach soar.

"What about you, Tam?" I asked. Tam sat on the leather chair in the corner of my room. His hands rapidly flew over the keys on his phone, whatever he was doing holding his entire attention. "Tam!" I repeated when he didn't respond. He glanced up, startled, before setting his phone down beside him. I couldn't help but wonder who he was talking to and if it was a girl. I didn't know why jealousy bucked me like a bull at the mere thought. Pushing the feeling down, I flashed him a smile.

"Sorry." He ran a hand through his hair, the strands becoming even more bedraggled than before. He had deep bruises beneath his eyes as if he hadn't slept in days. "I got distracted."

"Texting a girl?" I teased. Did he hear the note of jealousy in my voice? At my words, his face darkened, surprise giving way to unreadability. Just as quickly, he ducked his head, and his signature blush spread up his neck.

"Tam doesn't text girls," Ryder said in a mock conspiratorial whisper. Tam's blush deepened.

"Doesn't believe they're worth his time besides a quick fuck," Ronan added. I knew that the boys were only attempting to tease him, but their words made my stomach plummet even further until it practically fell through the floor. "He hasn't texted a girl back yet."

Conversation veered to a storm that had hit the west coast and the cancellation of their favorite sporting game—I didn't know the difference between balls and nets and sports names. Mercifully, they didn't bring up Tamson's strange behavior.

I never did find out who he was texting. All I knew was that my phone buzzed later that night, just as the moon peeked through the boughs of trees. I turned towards the phone, believing it to be Calax or Ryder or Ronan, but was stunned to see Tamson's name blinking at me on the screen.

TAMSON: *You still up?*

I WAS PULLED out of my thoughts by Tamson's hand tangling in my hair. I groaned at the contact, pleasure warring with pain. Pleasure, unashamedly, won.

"She could be fucking beautiful if it wasn't for that scar on her face," Greg sneered, pointing to the long scar etched across my face. The blemish was the remnant of my time with Liz. Time when she tortured both me and Ryder for her own twisted pleasure and amusement. Self-consciously, I placed my hand to my cheek as if that could somehow cover the permanent scar. It was still red and raised and ugly, but it was gradually disappearing. With time, it would become nothing more than a pink mark marring my skin.

"She's perfect," Tamson snapped, the first break in his normally lackadaisical front.

Greg opened his mouth, no doubt to protest or call Tam out on his uncharacteristic, almost possessive, behavior, when a van crashed through the storefront window.

CHAPTER 14

ADDIE

*E*verything seemed to happen in slow motion. Time was suspended—seconds turned into hours and hours turned into years. I could see it all, one diminutive piece at a time. The puzzle remained blurry, and I struggled to capture and hold all of the many facets provided to me.

I saw the truck barreling through the large window, glass shattering in thousands of pieces. It reminded me, oddly, of the rain still releasing its anger on the world. The sky was falling, so it only seemed fitting that the building would fall as well.

I felt Tamson's warm body cover my own. Shielding me from the onslaught of glass particles and the wayward rain carried in by the wind.

I heard someone let out a scream of anguish, quickly muffled.

I smelled something pungent, something that assaulted my senses. Did the rain have a smell? I would almost describe it as rotten eggs, horribly pervasive.

"Adelaide!" a familiar voice roared. I dared a peek over the top of Tamson's shoulder, stunned to see a familiar male staring at me from across the store. Fallon's normally immaculate hair was highly disarrayed. His eyes were just as desperate, as wild, as feral. The man looked positively unhinged, and an irrational surge of fear made itself known in the recesses of my mind. It was similar to how I felt when Tamson had treated me like coveted cattle.

The intensity of such an emotion frightened me, as did the lunacy of it. It took me a moment to pinpoint the origins of my fear. I didn't fear for myself, since I knew Fallon would never hurt me, but instead, I feared for everyone else in the room, Tamson included. Fallon was a lion that wasn't just out for the hunt, but for the kill. An avenging angel in the flesh.

He didn't seem to notice, or care, that wind brought in torrents of rain, burning his skin. Nor did he notice the man that had fallen, the only one without a name. He'd been closest to the window when it shattered, and the rain had begun to burn through his skin. Red, bloody streaks marred his face. With sickening satisfaction, I realized that he was still alive. The cry of pain must've come from him.

Doc was sitting nearby on the floor. He'd dived when the car arrived, barely missing being hit. Greg and Ass Face—I couldn't recall his name for the life of me— were nowhere to be seen.

The car doors were pushed open, and three more familiar figures stepped out. Asher, like Fallon, barely resembled the sweet boy I'd come to care for. His eyes were too wild, his hair too disheveled, his lips too pursed.

Calax and Declan surveyed the scene with matching expressions of distaste. After noticing I was fine, if not slightly crushed beneath Tamson's lean frame, Calax placed his hands into his pockets and drawled, "You really know how to make an entrance, Sarge."

Tamson lifted his head slowly at the voice, his eyes locking on mine. A few shards of glass hung precariously in his hair like diamond beads. Fortunately, none had reached his face, though I doubted his back had experienced the same leniency.

I couldn't help but remember the time I'd thrown myself over a body as well. Calax's body. We'd been back at the resort, and a tornado had ravished the area. He'd fallen unconscious, and it was instinctive for me to save him. To put his life above my own.

I hadn't realized before that my reasoning had been selfish. I'd loved him, though I would've never admitted it, and it was common sense to save his life at the expense of my own. The thought of living without him was unbearable.

The fear I'd once felt towards Tamson dissolved completely as we maintained eye contact. An inexpressible emotion clogged my throat. Forgiveness. Acceptance. Something else. Something deeper.

"Let's go!" Fallon called in his standard, no-nonsense voice.

My eyes remained latched onto Tamson's as if he were my lifeline. My savior. I supposed that, in a way, he was.

Dozens of emotions flittered in his own eyes, there and gone too quickly for me to get an accurate read on.

He scrambled to his feet, reaching down and extending a hand to me. I took it with bated breath. It felt as if everything depended on this one moment. I wasn't just grabbing a hand, but something else entirely. Something inherently sweeter.

I grabbed his hand as if I were lost at sea and he were a rope, guiding me to shore. I grabbed his hand as if I were dangling thousands of miles above land and he was the only support in sight.

I held his hand, even when Greg rose, an ugly sneer on his face as he realized our betrayal.

I held his hand as he raised something—something small and black and undeniably familiar.

I held his hand as Greg pulled the trigger on the gun and a loud *pop* resonated in the air. There was no way to describe the sound. I'd heard many guns go off before, but nothing like this. It seemed to shatter my delicate senses. Correction—it seemed to shatter my delicate sensibilities.

I held his hand until suddenly...
I wasn't.

RYDER

There was an old book I'd found collecting dust in my foster mother's bookshelf. The spine had been creased with age, and the print and image on the cover were faded. At one point, there might have been something that resembled a dragon, but the design now favored a dark smudge against the red background. I didn't know if the book had been used excessively or not enough, though the dust was a strong indicator of the latter.

I'd asked her why she had the book. It stood out against the shiny, glossy covers and the more subdued matte designs. She waved her hand dismissively, bringing the nub of her cigarette back to her lips.

"I wrote it." That was all said with calm indifference, as if she were merely reciting that the sky was blue. A fact. I stared at the woman I'd called mom for the better part of my life. Gray hair coiled in tight curls. Too much red lipstick. Eyeshadow that ranged from midnight black to emerald green. Larryanne wasn't a bad foster mom, as far as foster mothers could go. She was crass and impulsive, but I had the sense that she genuinely loved me. At first, I'd been bitter that Ronan had been allowed to stay with our birth mother while I'd been shipped halfway across the country, but that resentment was gone now. After all, I hadn't known he existed until he showed up at my doorway demanding money for drugs.

Larryanne wasn't my mother, but she was the closest I ever had to family at the time.

I remembered her house more vividly than any other foster family I'd lived with, mainly because it was located in the middle of fucking nowhere. The whistles of freight trains flew by one after the other for miles over prairie lands, brushing the rough, dry tips of corn stalks, filling up the blank spaces of country roads, and whistling around cold, steel silos, until they slammed against the vinyl siding of her home and into my ears. I could never sleep, due to the constant buzzing of noise.

Anyway, the woman once wore a diaper for a week because she wanted to go to a music festival and not worry about porta potties. She even robbed a restaurant once, though she'd never been caught. I imagined she wouldn't have been granted her fostering license if that little tidbit of information had become known. She was an enigma, my foster mother, but I loved her.

But her as a writer? A published author?

That was fucking hilarious.

The disbelief must've been evident on my face, for she swatted me with her hand.

"Don't give me that look, boy," she said. Smoke drifted up my nostrils from the cigarette now held between her two fingers. "I had an idea. Some characters are never able to have their stories told. I was determined to change that."

I didn't know why I thought of my dead foster mom as I stared at the bodies on the ground. My skin was red and blotchy from the rain. I'd tried to save who I could

—the girls, Ali, Amanda, and No Name, as well as the two boys. But by the time I'd dragged two of them inside, the rain pounding relentlessly against my bare skin, they'd all been dead.

Dead.

Five people whose stories would never be told. Five people who had their life snuffed out in a span of a second. All I could do was stare at their blotchy, bloody skin.

One of the girls had still been alive. Only for a second, but it was enough for me to see her face twisted in agony. As I watched, helpless, the life bled from her eyes.

Kai let out a scream.

For as long as I lived, I would never forget that sound. He'd lost his brothers. His friends. Hell, maybe even his girlfriend.

If I were to lose Ronan or Addie or any of the others…

Shaking my head, I focused on the sight before me. Ronan was attempting to restrain Kai. The man was positively enraged. The timid guy who'd threatened me with a shaking hand was nowhere in sight. In his place was a prowling tiger.

"Let me save them! Let me go!" he screamed, bucking against Ronan's arms. I'd only been able to "rescue" the one who was still breathing. Still moaning. And even that word, rescue, wasn't an accurate description. She'd died, despite my efforts.

Dead.

Just like Larryanne.

Just like those characters that never had stories written about them. The side characters. The woman in the background in the movie. Everyone had a story, but only a select few were heard.

"They're dead," Ronan was saying. "If you go out there, you're just going to die as well."

"Then let me die!" Kai screamed.

I remembered the fear I'd felt when the rain first began. When the screaming began. Instinctively, I'd run outside.

My entire life has been devoted to helping people. Why would I change who I was now? I'd winced when the first droplet of rain hit my skin.

Coming to the decision quickly, I'd pulled up my hood, tugged the sleeves down until they covered my hands, and run into the damning rain. The stench of burned flesh saturated the air so intensely, I could physically taste it.

All of that effort had been for nothing. Five people, five strangers, were dead. And all I had to show for it was more scars. More pain.

More death.

Ronan decked Kai over the top of his head after a particularly brutal struggle. The man fell in an undignified heap, his head ricocheting off the tiles. When I quirked a brow at Ronan, he merely shrugged.

The rest area was silent besides the rain. Thunder crackled, the sound almost malicious, and lightning flashed in the darkening sky. Ronan came to stand beside me, eyes focused on the window as well. I didn't know if he was staring at the bodies or the sky's vivid light show.

"Do you think they're okay?" He paused, his hands snaking up to fiddle with his lip ring. It was a bad habit he'd had for as long as I knew him. That, and chewing on his nails. "Do you think she's okay?"

"Addie?" I asked. I was unsurprised that he inquired about her specifically. He was in love with her and had been for a while. Even an imbecile couldn't help but notice the wistful glances he threw her way when he thought no one was looking. It didn't bother me, his feelings for her, just as it didn't bother me that he wasn't the only one. Addie needed all the protection she could get, and she more than deserved all of the love we could offer her after having to live without it for so long. I wanted that for her, just as long as I remained a crucial part in it.

Besides, we'd all shared girls before. Granted, there had never been feelings involved, but this situation was different. The *world* was different. Conventional went right out the window the second the first tornado had struck the resort and an elfin girl put her life on the line for one of our own.

"Addie's fine," I said. And I believed it. She was probably back at the house by now, getting babied by the others. She'd more than likely threatened castration at least twice by now. She was an innocent badass—an epitome of contradictions.

"She's a fighter," Tommy piped in, echoing my own thoughts. His voice was subdued, no doubt traumatized by what he'd witnessed, but the pride seeping through was unmistakable. I'd nearly forgotten about him, but I was grateful he was safe. The asshole was growing on me.

"As soon as the storm breaks, I can run to the car and pull it up," Ronan said. Always self-sacrificing. I bit my lip to keep from retorting. Now was not the time to conjure up an argument. He would risk the storm to save me, save us. I both hated and loved him for that.

"And what about him?" Tommy asked. I didn't have to look to know that he would be gesturing towards Kai.

Ronan and I exchanged an eloquent glance. We may not have been brothers for long, but the bond we'd forged surpassed years of shared childhoods.

"We bring him back with us. Let Fallon decide what to do with him."

Fallon always knew who was friend and who was foe. Who was a threat and who only had the potential to become a threat. A sixth sense, he called it. I had no doubt if Fallon deemed Kai as dangerous, he wouldn't hesitate to leave him for dead. Or kill him himself.

"So we wait?" Tommy asked.

I nodded stoutly. Already, I was itching to get back to Adelaide. To run my hands through her brown locks. To kiss her plump lips. To hear her talk about nonsense. To be with the woman I loved more than life itself.

Patience. I had to be patient. I was no good to Addie dead, despite the fact that I wanted to brave the storm and risk being burned to get to her.

My body throbbed at the thought, phantom pain making itself known from the many wounds on my skin. Fallon was going to shit a brick when he saw the condition I was in. Addie was going to murder me as well. Tag team murder. Who knew?

"We wait," I replied to Tommy.

CHAPTER 15

CALAX

I heard my first gunshot when I was seven.

My dad had decided I wasn't man enough for his liking and sought to remedy that. At the time, I hadn't understood what he'd meant. I watched sports, catcalled girls, and even had my first sip of alcohol. What else was connoted by that term?

He'd roughly grabbed me from my bed, hand an iron vise, and dragged me towards the rusty pickup truck already idling in the driveway.

"Today," he'd said in an imperious voice I'd learned to hate, "you will become a man."

There was something in his eyes, a sort of male smugness, that made me bristle. We drove down many twists and turns, across sweeping fields, until we parked in front of an immense forest.

I remembered being frightened by how tall the trees were. They towered over me, the sunlight just barely penetrating the darkness created by their canopies.

My father placed a calloused hand on my shoulder. He hadn't bothered to tell me where we were going, so I was still dressed in only a tank top and pajama pants. The morning air chilled my sensitive skin, and wet dew drenched the legs of my pajama bottoms. Still, I kept my chin set domineeringly high and trained my eyes straight ahead. I could be a man for my father.

I had to be.

With a loud smack of his bubblegum, he thrust something into my hands. I staggered under the unfamiliar weight, my hackles rising as I considered the long, brown object. I'd never held one before, though I'd seen Dad cleaning it out on the kitchen table occasionally.

The rest of that morning was a blur.

I vaguely recalled scrambling to keep pace with my father as he pushed branch after branch away from his face. Twigs snapped between my feet. No matter how hard I tried, my lumbering frame could not be as stealthy nor as quiet as my father's.

I remembered the doe's face seconds before he put a bullet through her head. So innocent. This was an animal unaware of the dangers plaguing the world. She merely stared at us, muscles tensed as if she was unsure whether or not she wanted to flee. I mentally begged her to.

Run, I wanted to say.

And then the gunshot…

I would never forget that sound. The way it reverberated through the forest, brushing against the needles of pine trees and into the empty burrows beneath my feet. The sound was more than just a loud boom—it was terrifying. It seemed to symbolize death. After all, what was the point of a gun if not to kill?

I thought all that as I watched Addie pause. Her hands went to her stomach, eyes widening in shock. Blood cascaded through her fingers, staining the white of the ratty old T-shirt.

The moment that gun went off, my world stopped.

And then promptly ended.

"No," I whispered, unable to tear my eyes away. She staggered, barely kept upright by Tamson's arm.

Fallon let out a roar. A scream. A cry of anguish. Before I could even blink, the man with the gun was dead. I wouldn't have been able to tell you what killed him. A knife? An arrow? Another gun?

Tamson was running towards us, Addie held tightly in his arms. Blood. So much blood.

And when her eyes met mine, I once again thought of that deer. *Doe eyes*, I thought somewhat incoherently. They shone with an inner radiance and light that had always been able to soothe the darkest recesses of my mind. In her eyes, now, I saw something else, something akin to acceptance.

The truth hit me like a freight train. I would've preferred that, would've preferred anything besides this unbearable pain as my heart shattered into thousands of pieces. I knew my mind would soon follow.

She was dying.

The girl I loved, my reason for living, was dying. And from the shuddering breath escaping her bloodstained lips and serene expression, I realized that she knew it as well. She knew it, and she accepted it. The fight had already drained from her body.

"Grab him!" Tamson was screaming. "Grab him!"

I didn't understand what he was saying, what he meant. I had a singular focus, and that focus was on the girl still bleeding in his arms.

Asher, thank God, must've understood what Tamson was talking about, as he lunged for an unfamiliar male and roughly shoved him into the back of the van.

It was that movement that spurred me back into action.

No. No. No.

"Baby," I cried, following both her and Tamson into the van. He placed her gently down, using a backpack as a makeshift pillow. His shirt was off and pressed against her open wound.

Dimly, I was aware of the car speeding away, jostling us.

"Be fucking careful!" That was Asher.

"Fix her," Tamson sneered, eyes beseeching. He had a gun out and aimed at the unknown man.

"I don't have the proper supplies," he placated, hands held up as if he were fending off a dangerous criminal. I supposed that, in a way, he was. There was nothing more dangerous than a man in love. We were desperate. Our tiny hold on humanity had snapped the second that bullet pierced Adelaide's stomach, and our instincts now reverted back to those of cavemen.

Protect.

I grabbed her cold hand in both of mine.

"You're going to be okay, baby girl. You're going to be okay."

My hand trembling, I brushed her hair away from her cheek. She let out a pained gasp, blood trickling in the corner of her mouth.

"You can't give up, baby. You need to fight. You need to fight, baby girl."

Her hand was so cold, it almost felt as if I was holding an icicle.

Please be okay. Please be okay.

I'd never been an overly religious person, but just then, I sent a silent prayer, a silent plea, up to the heavens. I would give anything for her to remain alive.

I'd made so many mistakes, but if she lived, I would strive to become a better person. I would fucking save the world. My soul? It was already lost without her. So if the goddamn devil himself wanted a sliver of it, I would happily offer it up on a silver platter.

I couldn't—I *wouldn't* lose her.

But when had God ever listened to me?

～

ADDIE

The kitchen was bustling with activity when I arrived. I spotted Asher first, flipping pancakes on the stove. He was shirtless, his abs accentuated by a light splatter of golden hair dipping down his delectable V. An apron was around his waist, and he hummed a tune beneath his breath.

"Hey, handsome," I said, sneaking up behind him and wrapping my arms around his waist. He startled, a reaction I was beginning to realize was common with these men, but instantly relaxed when he realized it was me. His hand dropped the spatula to hold both of mine, still around him.

"Hey, beautiful."

I nuzzled his back, inhaling the scent that was uniquely Asher's. Copper, almost. Like blood.

"It smells delicious." I inhaled deeply. "And I'm not just talking about the food."

"That was horribly cheesy," Calax drawled from where he sat at the table, sipping his coffee. I'd never understood his love for that dark liquid. Sure, I was a coffee drinker myself, but I always needed to add milk and sugar.

I crinkled my nose, and he merely smirked, bringing the cup back to his lips and taking a long sip. Damn. The way his lip connected with that rim…

I never thought the act of drinking coffee could be seductive, but I never had seven boyfriends before.

"Quit eye-humping Calax, Kitten," Ryder said, gracefully moving into the kitchen. He offered me a chaste kiss on the cheek before sitting down across from Calax, next to Ronan. It was Ronan that turned towards me, his standard white tank top boasting the intricately designed white unicorn.

"You can eye-hump me anytime." He wiggled his eyebrows suggestively, and I giggled, releasing Asher to perch on his lap. His hands immediately wrapped around my waist.

"Is breakfast ready?" Tamson ducked into the kitchen, Fallon and Declan directly behind him. All three men stopped and kissed my forehead, my cheek, my lips. I was surrounded by their love, as soft and as soothing as a moth's wing caressing my spine. I'd never realized it was possible to feel such an emotion. This elation. This happiness that surpassed anything I'd ever felt before.

All I'd ever wanted was to be loved and to love someone back. With them, I had everything I ever wanted. For years, I was told I was undeserving of love. The mere aspect of it was an elusive fantasy, a fairy tale that was whispered in the dead of night. When my parents talked about their own relationship, I'd begun to believe that love was a horror story.

And now?

Now, my entire mentality had changed.

God, I was one of those girls in a romance movie—a swooning, drooling heroine. Was that what love did to a person? I found that I didn't care.

I needed more. I needed *all* of the love.

Overcome with emotion, I turned to meet the eyes of each of my men.

Calax, the first man who'd stolen my heart. The enemy who became my lover. He saw my walls as a challenge to overcome, not as a stop sign.

Declan, my childhood best friend. The person who saw beyond the front I built around myself. The man who loved me unconditionally, despite the years that had passed.

Fallon, the brooding team leader. He hid behind an apathetic front, but those little moments when his eyes softened or his hand played with my hair demoted him from intimidating to approachable.

Ryder, my flirty boyfriend. We'd forged a bond that others couldn't even begin to comprehend. An unbreakable bond made entirely of steel—steel that was forged from shared trauma.

Ronan, the man who hid his pain behind a wide smile. The man who forced a laugh when I knew he wanted nothing more than to cry. He had the world pressing down on his shoulders, and that pressure repeatedly threatened to bury him alive. He didn't know how strong he actually was.

Asher, my sweet friend. My confidant. My attentive lover. He regarded me as if I held the moon in my hands. Would I ever be worthy of his unconditional, irrevocable love?

And finally, Tamson. The man that was two sides of the same coin. Shy and timid. Assertive and confident. Our relationship was built on trust. And I did trust him. Both sides of him.

"I love you," I said, my throat clogging. "I love you all."

"We love you too," Fallon said, speaking for the group. I knew he was telling the truth. Love emitted from their smiles, their warm eyes, the very pores of their bodies. I could die of contentment, surrounded by the men I loved and who, for some reason, loved me in return.

Movement over Calax's shoulder captured my attention. My eyes widened as a familiar figure glided into the room. I glanced anxiously from face to face, but no one seemed to notice anything out of the ordinary.

Ryder was throwing food at Ronan, and Calax was teasing Asher good-naturedly. Normal. Everything appeared normal, at least on the surface.

But...

The girl had brown, chestnut hair that cascaded down her shoulders. Her eyes were trained on mine, an unreadable expression darkening her features.

"Who are you?" I whispered. The men faded away until only she remained. Only *I* remained.

"You have to choose." The girl—the girl with an uncanny resemblance to me—took a step forward.

"Choose?" I parroted mechanically.

"You have to choose. Live. Or die."

CHAPTER 16

ADDIE

I had an extremely slap-able face. It was funny the things you noticed about yourself when you should've been focused on anything else.

Full bottom lip. High cheekbones. Chiseled jawline. Brown curls framing a cherubic face. She wore a hi-low black dress that dipped low, revealing a swath of golden skin and considerable cleavage. A white collar and matching white cufflinks provided much needed elegance to the scantily-clad attire. At least, those were my mother's words the first time I'd worn it. A simple pearl necklace completed the outfit. There were no scars distorting her face. No bruises.

No pain.

The contentment radiating from her like warm sun beams was almost tangible.

God, I really did look annoying. It was no wonder Elena wanted to punch me. Repeatedly. With a sledgehammer. And a baseball bat. A metal one. Or did a wood one hurt more?

"You're rambling," she said. "We always did get carried away." The girl chuckled, and I finally pulled my attention away from her sexy body and focused on her words.

"We?" I quirked an eyebrow reproachfully, unable to stop my gaze from skating over the petite figure. She really did look like me, but there was something different in her eyes. A sort of glacial coldness and loneliness that had long since diminished since forging my relationship—or was it relationships?—with the guys.

Shrugging, she ventured a step forward.

"I am you. You are me."

A sudden chill swept over my body, down my spine, and into the soles of my feet. Darkness pierced the kitchen, so suddenly that I scrambled to my feet.

"Where am I?" My arms wrapped around my waist, but it did little to fight off the frigidly cold air. Was there a window open? That was the only explanation I could conjure up to explain the steep decline in temperature. My breath came out in puffs.

Smiling serenely, the other me extended a hand. "Come, I'll show you."

I remained still, indecisive. I wished that the guys were here. God, how I needed their strength. Mustering up what little courage I had, I accepted her hand. Her smooth fingers and palm caused me to jump. In the days since everything had gone to hell, my own were covered in blisters and unhealed callouses. I couldn't even remember a time when my hands were that soft.

She led me through the front doorway and into the street.

Snow drifted down, blanketing the grass and skeletal tree branches. A blighted sun hung high in the sky, hinting that it was already midday. Despite the cold air, the sight was peaceful. Tranquil. Almost beautiful.

"Where am I?" I whispered, spinning in a circle. I extended my hands to catch the wisps of snow. It was something I used to do when I was younger, and I supposed the habit hadn't stopped with age. Mother had called me childish and told me that catching snowflakes was for babies. She seemed to have forgotten that I was only six when she first started reprimanding me.

"Do you remember this place?" the other me countered beseechingly. I tried to tamp down my irritation at being ignored, instead focusing on her words.

"Should I?"

"Think, Addie. Think."

I was such a condescending asshole at times.

Ignoring her, I focused once again on the fluffy snow, faded street signs, and white painted buildings. One in particular captured and held my attention. Foreboding dug its penetrating claws deeper into my spine.

The dilapidated house with its wraparound porch and chipped siding was familiar, almost eerily so. My face paled. I was looking at a ghost, both literally and figuratively.

Paint had long since flaked off, the white color resembling a muddy brown. Warped wood, nails protruding from the rickety staircase, beams with no support. It was a disaster just waiting to happen.

And it was also my happy place.

"I used to visit Ducky here," I whispered. I didn't know whether to be awed or stunned. Legs shaking, I took a step closer. "It was during winter vacation. He didn't have school, and there was a padlock on the gate surrounding the playground. We couldn't meet there. One day, we went exploring, and we stumbled across this abandoned house."

I stepped up onto the deck of the bungalow, being extra mindful of the loose nails.

"I'd completely forgotten about this place." Turning towards the other me, I added, "We only stayed here for a couple weeks."

And they had been some of the best weeks of my life. It had been Ducky and I against the world. In the small house with plastered walls and deteriorating wood, I'd never felt more alive. Mansions had nothing on this place.

For those few weeks, this had felt more like home than anywhere else.

As I watched, enraptured, two figures meandered out of the surrounding forest.

The young girl was wearing a hat that I knew belonged to the boy. His own brown hair, longer than hers, was intricately plaited away from his face.

Younger me and younger Ducky.

Both of our cheeks were red from the cold, but identical smiles brightened our faces. I remembered that time. A time when I was so happy, it didn't seem real. A time when I didn't feel the need to succumb to the pain that threatened to drown me.

Staring at her heart-shaped face, I couldn't help but note the three facets of my character. The golden girl, groomed by my parents to be the epitome of perfection. The innocent girl, naïve to the horrors this world had to offer and still holding on to hope that she would get a happy ending. And finally, the woman I had become. The woman desperately, probably irrationally, in love with seven men. The woman whose strength was unparalleled to the two pathetic girls before her.

For the first time in forever, I was proud of myself. There were so many trials I'd faced, so many monsters I'd fought, that at one point, might've had the power to tear me down. But I was so much stronger because of them. Better.

Elegant Adelaide released a heavy, wistful sigh.

"Do you remember being that happy?" she asked softly. Her eyes were trained on the two children now entering the desolate house. Ducky held young Addie's hand as if it were his lifeline.

Had he known how much I depended on him? He was wrong when he called me the sun. I wasn't. Not really. I was a darkness tarnishing everything in my path, but I relied on his light almost religiously. With him, I shone.

And damn if I didn't sound like a cliché.

Compelled by an undefinable force, I followed Ducky and younger Addie into the house, ignoring the other me's question as she had mine.

The inside was just as bad, if not worse, than the outside. The walls appeared to have crumbled years ago, cobwebs now decorating the banister and corners. Mildew and mold had corroded away what little remained of the wood. Floorboards, sporadically placed beneath my feet, were rotten. In some spots, they had completely deteriorated with age. The stench of stale water from leaking pipes and years-old mold assaulted my senses.

All in all, it wasn't the safest place for two ten-year-old kids to venture into, but it was all we had. All *they* had.

Surprisingly, or perhaps unsurprisingly, I struggled to identify with the little girl currently skipping towards the dusty couch. I couldn't find it within me to connect my historical identity with my current one. We were two separate individuals.

That girl wasn't aware of the darkness she carried. The darkness she craved.

In time, she would figure it out. It would take unbearable loss and helplessness before she recognized the seductive pulls of darkness, but she would. Of that, I was certain.

"You sure you're okay?" Ducky asked, kneeling beside her. My nose scrunched in disgust as I noticed the grit and other unsavory substances staining his knees.

Younger Addie began to tremble, eyes downcast. Her palpable fear polluted my lungs.

"No," she admitted, resigned. She glanced up at him from beneath her fringe of dark lashes. "I just don't understand why they hate me. Aren't parents supposed to love their children?"

I remembered this moment somewhat vividly. It was only hours after DOD had slapped me. Compared to some of the other beatings I'd taken and endured with a smile, this one was tame. Unfortunately, it left a nasty bruise on my cheek in the shape of a hand. Ducky had noticed it almost immediately.

Of course, he hadn't known, or even suspected, the extent of the abuse. I instead made it sound as if it were a one-time thing. A drunken fit. After arguing with him profusely, he'd agreed not to tell anyone. Hell, if I remembered correctly, we'd even made a blood bond for secrecy. Nothing was more sacred than the blood bond between two ten-year-olds.

"I understand," Ducky snorted in response to younger Addie. "My own parents hate me."

"Rick and Matilda?" I'd met his parents once before, and they seemed to adore Ducky. Showering him with affection. Baking cookies for him after school like the stereotypical suburban white mom. Watching football games on the couch. I'd been immensely jealous when I saw the bond between the three of them.

Younger Addie had a similarly perplexed expression on her face.

"No, not my adoptive parents. My birth ones," Ducky amended, and younger Addie leaned forward eagerly. It was very rare for him to talk about his life before he was adopted, and she eagerly grasped onto every fragmented piece he offered up about his past.

Though I already knew what he was going to say, I still leaned forward as well. Only Bitch Me didn't react, her expression impassive.

"My dad beat me all the time. Beat my mom. Killed my sister." He spoke without any inflection. Facts. I knew it was a mechanism he'd adopted long ago in order to survive. Conceal your emotions. Put on a front.

God, I'd completely forgotten about that. About him. About this moment. About this life-altering confession he'd so carelessly admitted.

It was the one and only time he'd ever mentioned it. Conversation steered away from depressing topics about abusive parents and into more fun territory. Namely, a cat younger Addie wanted to adopt.

Was I really so self-absorbed that I'd repressed this memory? This confession? Was it because I didn't want to deal with his pain along with my own? I couldn't answer that question, nor did I necessarily want to. All I knew for certain was that the memory hit me like a stack of bricks.

"Why are you showing me this?" I gasped, turning away from younger Addie and Ducky. The memory was almost too painful to witness.

Bitch Me—BM—shrugged. Or BM could stand for Bowel Movements. Either name was fitting.

"He was strong without your help, and he will continue to be strong. They all will. It's not like you've been the best friend or the best girlfriend." Her lips contorted into a sneer, though I couldn't tell if it was directed at me or herself. Or us. Damn. This was really beginning to confuse me.

"Why are you saying that?"

"Because I want you to understand that they will be fine without you. It may hurt for a little bit, like a pesky bee sting, but they will survive. So now you need to decide, for yourself, whether or not you want to stay or go."

Her words held a vague coherence. Memories, slightly blurred, pounded against my mind, demanding to be let free. There was something I had to remember, something important. Once I could recall that, I would better be able to understand the proposition BM was giving me. However, the memory faded like words etched into the shoreline. A wave would always come and eat them away.

I latched mechanically onto one of the last things she'd said instead of focusing on all of the unknowns.

"Y-You're wrong," I stuttered out. A breeze from one of the many broken windows sent goosebumps up and down my arms. I wrapped them around myself, both for warmth and comfort.

BM cocked her head to the side.

"I'm wrong? How am I wrong?"

"Declan will die." When she merely blinked rapidly at me, I hurried to explain. "He's allergic to bees. So if stung, he'll die."

CHAPTER 17

TAMSON

*O*nce the rain ceased, the sky became blood red.

Blood—a fitting similarity. The sky had opened up, released its deluge of tears, and left behind a blotchy, red-stained face. It was as if the earth was mocking me, mocking us. A physical manifestation of our own inner chaos. Turmoil. Pain. Agitation. The words were endless.

Words usually came easily to me. A product, I was sure, of the life I'd been thrown into. I once had to charm and seduce a rich heiress for a mission. Another time, I had to negotiate a hostage situation. Sarge once joked that eloquence was my middle name, but words weren't capable of mending Addie's flesh back together. No, for the first time in forever, words had failed me. No condolences, no placating sympathies, could save her life.

I cradled my head in my hands, tears that I would never shed burning behind my eyes. Like the rain, they wanted to release their torment onto the world. Also like the rain, the tears could be fatal. Not could. *Would*. If I started, I would never stop.

Sitting in the hallway outside Adelaide's bedroom door, I heard Doc's muffled voice as he said something to Sarge. Only our team leader had been allowed inside the room, overseeing the doctor's treatment of the girl we all loved.

Doc had incentive to treat her—if she died, he died. We died.

Everyone would fucking die.

Calax paced in front of me, his agitation and restlessness indisputable. The man was five seconds away from losing his mind. His entire body displayed his tension. The muscles flexed, the clenched jaw, the narrowed eyes, the hands curled into fists. He was terrifying—a beast in desperate need of a kiss from his beauty.

But a fucking kiss wouldn't be enough to wake her.

My team had always told me I was too pessimistic, too cynical. I wished I could refute their claim, but my mind kept replaying the moment the bullet speared her stomach. Despondent whimpers had escaped her blood caked lips, the sound threatening to haunt me until the day I died.

It should've been me.

That was the prominent thought battling for dominance in my head. It drowned out all others, even my fear and heartache.

Guilt.

Shame.

Love.

It should've been me.

It was no wonder she hadn't picked me—I hadn't even been able to protect her. She had relied on me, and I'd failed her. Like I'd failed my grandma.

I was such a fuck up. Like a parasite, I latched helplessly onto the only living, breathing entity in my life. My damn heart had claimed her as my own, completely ignoring the logical rebuttal from my brain that reminded me, repeatedly, of all of the reasons why she couldn't be mine. Did my heart listen? No.

And her last moments with me...

I'd been a monster. When she woke up—and despite my pessimistic nature, I'd be damned if she didn't—she would hate me for the way I treated her.

If she woke up...

My stomach clenched and tightened, threatening to expel the contents of my breakfast. How could everything change so suddenly? So drastically? So badly? Just yesterday, she'd been laughing over something Ronan said and baking with Asher. She'd been curled up with Ryder on the sofa in a whispered conversation and in Calax's embrace. She'd been teasing Sarge and practicing her sign language with Declan. She'd been putting a tentative hand through my own unruly red-brown curls, commenting on how soft they looked.

It was almost comical how quickly things could change.

Calax spun to face me abruptly, face pale and eyes wild. Unhinged. Despite his appearance, his gruff voice was uncharacteristically soft.

"I can't lose her."

I knew what he wanted.

He wanted me to tell him that everything was going to be okay, that she was going to open her eyes and smile up at him. But I couldn't. My own thoughts were running pervasive within my head, unattended, and I couldn't reel them back in. Instead of answering him, I stared stoutly ahead.

He couldn't lose her. I couldn't lose her. Fallon couldn't lose her. None of us could fucking lose her. The reality was, we *would* lose her. Unless Doc was some sort of miracle worker.

Why wasn't she fighting for us?

Why wasn't she fighting to come home?

I'd seen the fight drain from her eyes. She'd given up, both body and mind. For the briefest moment, I felt a stab of blistering anger. It burned a hole through my chest, like a branding rod. Just as quickly, the anger diminished to be replaced by something colder. She gave up because she didn't have faith that we would save her. She gave up because she didn't trust us.

Because of me.

Because I'd failed her.

Asher appeared from around the corner, a large duffle bag slung over his shoulder. Fallon had instructed him to go to the local hospital and gather all of the supplies he could as quickly as he could. Kill anyone who tried to stop him.

From the fresh blood darkening his blond hair, I concluded that he'd obeyed Fallon's orders.

"Grabbed random shit. Didn't know what I needed," he muttered. His eyes were in a perpetual daze. Ever since Adelaide had been shot, he appeared as if he was drifting through life. He couldn't even bring himself to put on his usual friendly, boy-next-door mask. No, in its place was a stone-cold killer. A hunter. An assassin.

Without a word, he pushed open the bedroom door, slipped inside, and shut it softly. I found that I couldn't bring myself to look up during that brief moment the door was open. I didn't want to see Adelaide lying pathetically in the bed, her brown curls damp with sweat, blood cascading from the gunshot wound in her stomach. Blood. So much blood.

I'd never considered myself queasy before. My job wouldn't allow me to be. But just then, I thought that I would vomit all over the carpeting.

I didn't know if I wanted to be sick or stab someone. Anyone.

Elena—the bitch—was lucky she'd left when she did. If we had come back to see her and her traitorous team, there was no telling what we would've done. People like her made me sick to my stomach. I couldn't believe that I'd once kissed that creature —a creature who believed it was acceptable to knock the crown off another woman's head.

I knew Addie, once she woke up, would be devastated by the turn of events. She'd considered Samantha and Lilly friends, if a bit too quickly in my opinion. Even Elena had wormed her way into Addie's heart. To know that they'd betrayed her, left her for dead? That wasn't something she could easily recover from.

Declan poked his head out of the room he was wallowing in, the damn black kitten held tightly in his arms. He seemed to have this misconstrued mentality that if he held the cat as close to himself as he could, it would somehow rouse Addie from her fatal slumber.

He raised an eyebrow at me, eloquently asking for any updates. In answer, I merely shook my head. I didn't have the energy to raise my hands to sign to him, nor did I even want to talk. My body felt weak and sluggish, a physical extension of my mind.

The front door opened and closed once again, and my body automatically tensed.

"Honey, I'm home!" Ryder called cheerfully. There was a sound of flesh hitting flesh, no doubt Ronan slapping his brother, and then a slew of curses, quickly muffled.

"What the fuck are you going to do with the body?" asked Tommy indignantly. My curiosity instantly piqued at that. Body? Where the fuck had they gotten a body?

My question was quickly answered when Ryder and Ronan came around the corner. Over Ronan's shoulder was an unfamiliar male with a shock of dark hair and pasty skin.

"Where's Fallon?" Ronan asked, hoisting said body further up when it began to slip. "I need to figure out what to do with this heavy asshole."

Tommy appeared from behind him. His sparkly pink glasses were noticeably absent from his pudgy face. He took one look at Declan, petting the squirming black cat, and then lifted his gaze to meet Calax's. Understanding dawned on his face, followed quickly by a shattering. That was the only word I could think to describe it. His entire expression *shattered*, as if he'd had his world turned upside down. As if a rock were thrown at a mirror. A pebble tossed into a once tranquil pool. He may not have loved her the way we did, but he considered her family. I didn't know which type of love was more dangerous.

Without his usual sly remark, he turned on his heel and stomped away.

Ryder and Ronan were slower to catch on, both of them engrossed with the body. Ryder was poking the man's cheek, attempting to stir him awake, while Ronan was bitching about the weight breaking his shoulders.

"Where's Addie?" Ryder asked, finally diverting his attention. His umber eyes, a strange golden color that seemed to flash yellow in the artificial lighting, widened. Before I could answer, he was already shaking his head in denial.

Ronan dropped the body unceremoniously, and it fell to the floor in an undignified heap.

"No," he whispered meekly. His attention was fixed on the closed door as if his eyes were somehow able to penetrate the wooden barrier and see the girl within. I didn't know how he knew she was in there. Sixth sense? A magnetic pull?

Before I could stop them—not that I wanted to—Ryder and Ronan shouldered their way inside. Once again, the door clunked ominously as it closed. It seemed to be an accurate metaphor.

The door closing.

Adelaide dying.

They were one and the same.

I resumed my customary position against the wall, knees pulled up to my chest and arms wrapped around both my legs. The position did little to hold myself together. My body was in shambles, but my soul had fallen to shreds the second the gun had gone off.

We weren't normal men, though.

We were hunters. Monsters. Dangerous individuals. If we were to lose our humanity, our reason for living, the entire world would pay.

There would be no survivors.

~

DECLAN

I couldn't just stand by and watch the woman I loved fade away. I wouldn't.

As the sun dipped beneath the boughs of trees and the sky turned a metallic violet, I hoisted my bag further over my shoulder. It held an assortment of supplies we had gathered—maps, canned food, and water bottles.

Nobody noticed when I slipped outside and made a beeline towards the truck. Paint was chipped away, both from the rain and from vandalism I suspected. Rust was beginning to form around the tires, a russet brown that contrasted greatly with the midnight black exterior. The corroding death trap wasn't an ideal form of transportation, but it was all we had. The van was in worse shape.

Nobody noticed when I stared once more at the house. It was dark. Only one room had candle flames flickering intermittently behind the closed blinds. I knew that an angel would be lying on the bed in there, fighting for her life.

Nobody noticed me leave.

Nobody, that was, except for Sarge.

By the time I slid into the driver's seat and started the car, he'd slipped into the passenger side. I jumped, startled, at seeing his shadowed profile.

Fuming with an almost incandescent fury, I reached up to switch on the car light. It illuminated the dark, heavy bags beneath his eyes and the white pallor of his normally tanned skin. His hair was wildly disheveled, slipping free of its usually immaculate ponytail. To be honest, the man looked as if he was inches away from death. He looked as if he should've been the one fighting for his life, not Addie.

The thought, once again, caused my hands to clench around the steering wheel, the veins bulging. Reluctantly, I wrenched them free and turned to face Fallon fully.

"What are you doing here?" I signed.

He gave me an exasperated look. It was the look I often received when I was a child, he'd first taken me under his wing.

"What are you doing here?" he countered, his hands moving rapidly in agitation.

I saw no point in lying to him. After all, he was perceptive enough to know I was leaving in the first place. I'd once joked he had eyes in the back of his head, but that was wrong. The man had eyes *everywhere.*

"I'm leaving." Shrugging, I reached into my pocket and grabbed a yellow slip of paper. Written in delicate script that we both knew belonged to Addie was an address—Nikolai's address.

Her brother.

Fallon's eyes narrowed into thin slits as he read what we'd all already memorized. According to the maps, it was just south of downtown Atlanta. Addie described the house as a tiny bungalow style more than a farmhouse. Thirty or so minutes away from the city.

I couldn't save Addie, but maybe, just maybe, I could save her brother.

"You're going after him," Sarge signed, and even I could see that it wasn't a question. He knew my intentions, but his apathetic front gave nothing away.

Instead of answering, I settled for a nod.

"Alone." Again, I knew instinctively that it wasn't a question. This time, I didn't humor him with a response, but instead leveled him with my best glare. Was he going to stop me?

There were many reasons I had to go to Atlanta.

Nik was one of those reasons. The other?

My father.

Sarge must've seen the resolution on my face, as his body sagged in defeat. His fingers tapped against the center console, hinting at whatever lurked beneath his seemingly impassive exterior. After a moment, he nodded and tugged his seatbelt on.

I was too stunned to do anything but blink at him. Noticing my dumbstruck expression, Fallon signed,

"I'm coming with you."

"No," I argued. *"You need to stay with Addie. She needs you."*

At the mention of her name, his entire demeanor changed and tightened. His eyes flared violently.

"I know she needs me." He ran a hand through his hair once more. *"But she would never forgive herself if anything happened to her brother. We're going to get him and bring him back to her. She would want to see him when she wakes up."*

The way he spoke…

It had only just occurred to me that he didn't perceive a future without Adelaide in it. That scenario just wasn't plausible in his mind. I had the distinct feeling that if something were to happen, he would live the rest of his life in denial.

The unfeeling icy asshole loved her.

He loved her just as fiercely as I did. As Calax did. As we all did. He would be willing to die for her, be willing to sacrifice us for her.

There was no changing his mind once he got like this. Addie was his world, and if he needed to save her brother to feel useful, then he would. We were a team. All of us. Live or die together.

And Sarge had chosen death.

Without another word, I put the car into drive.

CHAPTER 18

ADDIE

I really hated Bitch Me.

As she smiled at me, the epitome of smug bitch, I resisted the urge to deck her upside the head. Damn. This must've been what Elena and the others felt on a daily basis. No wonder they'd left me for dead.

Okay, that was a lie.

There was no reason for the way they behaved. I firmly believed that us women had to stand up for one another and protect each other. I didn't like using degrading terms to describe women, but Elena? She was a bitch. I could say that without guilt.

I was a bitch too, so no one could argue that I was being biased.

Without another word, I stormed out of the house and back onto the street. Snowflakes continued to flutter downwards, an ethereal combination of white and palest pink from the sun. I heard, rather than saw, BM follow me out. Almost instinctively, I turned back towards the house.

Younger Me was laughing at whatever Ducky said, her face alight with a childlike innocence and joy that had slowly corroded away with time. It was like the paint on a car—toxic influences diminished its beauty.

Inspecting their profiles through the dirty window, my mind wrenched me back to a day only a couple of weeks ago.

The pebble hitting my face pulled me from my slumber.

Bolting upright, I glanced anxiously around my room. Unsurprisingly, there was no one present, but that didn't stop unease from tightening my stomach. I'd been dreaming, though dreaming failed to accurately describe what I'd endured. A nightmare would've been a better description. I remembered the distinct taste of copper in my mouth. Blood. My blood. Or was it my parents' blood? I found that I couldn't recall. Try as I might, the dream slipped through my fingers. It was like trying to hold water for a long period of time—impossible.

There had been a shadow. A monster, perhaps.

And my men had been there...

Shaking my head to clear the remnants of my dream, I glanced once more at the pebble now lying beside me.

A pebble?

I didn't know why I thought I'd imagined that.

My confusion morphed into fear when a silhouette appeared in my bedroom. The moon highlighted a set of broad shoulders and an impressive, chiseled chest. He took a step closer, and I was able to see a shock of dark brown hair. Strong jawline. Arresting green eyes that saw into my very soul.

Quickly, I switched on my bedside lamp.

"Declan," *I signed.* "You scared the shit out of me."

He smiled sheepishly, the usual coldness I'd grown to attribute to Declan completely dissipating. In that moment, he looked almost boyish. Young.

"Sorry." *He chuckled, the sound sending delightful tingles straight to my core.* "I thought your window was closed. I was trying to be romantic. You know, throw rocks at the window and all."

My brain short-circuited at his use of the word 'romantic.' It conjured up images of him on one knee, a ring in his hand. A bouquet of roses.

But we'd never been a traditional couple, friends or otherwise.

Instead of rings, I got rocks hitting my face. Instead of roses, I got sly smiles and dark chuckles. His version of romantic varied considerably from my own. It was just one of the reasons why I loved him.

My brain rebelled at using such a word when describing my relationship with Declan, but then I instantly berated myself for my childish reaction. We were allowed to feel love for one another. We'd been best friends for years, and time had not lessened those feelings. There was nothing wrong with the emotion. The connotations had made it dirty. Wrong.

But society failed to realize that there were numerous types of love.

Romantic love.

Sexual love.

Familial love.

Platonic love.

Declan tapped my chin, garnering my attention. His expressive brows were furrowed.

"You okay?" *he signed, and I offered him a tentative smile. What would he think of me if he knew the direction of my thoughts? If he knew that I was thinking the dreaded "L-word," and not in a sisterly manner. No, the direction of my thoughts leaned towards the romantic-slash-sexual end of the spectrum.*

Great. Now I was thinking about sex. With Declan. In this bed.

And then I thought about Calax, my wonderful boyfriend, but instead of deterring me, I began to think about sex with both of them. Man, I had a secret kinky side. Three-ways. Four-ways. Freaking eight-ways. The sky was the limit. Correction—my vagina was the limit.

"How's your leg?" *Declan signed, nodding towards the black, heavy cast on said leg. I shrugged, unable to help noticing that Declan's eyes zeroed in on the swath of skin exposed on my stomach when my shoulders came up. My cheeks flushed.*

"It's seen better days. And worse days. And days in-between. Legs are annoying. I'm more of a fingers and penis type of girl."

He merely blinked at me, both because I'd forgotten to use sign language in my ramble and because of what I said. I silently prayed that I'd spoken too fast for him to read my lips, but when a delectable blush rose up his neck and to his cheeks, I knew that the gods weren't that generous. Damn my big mouth.

And my big, needy vagina.

All it needed now was a sign that said "Open for Business" in flashing, neon red lights.

Greedy, horny bitch.

"Let's talk about something else. I meant, sign about something else. Can you talk? I mean, I know you can, obviously. I heard you. Why don't you talk? Does your voice sound weird? Oh God, is that insensitive of me to ask? I give you permission to spank me. Damn. I have an unhealthy obsession with spankings. And whips. And chains. Hmmm...maybe it's just a phase."

Declan waved his hands vigorously in front of my face, and I paused in mid-speech. Mid-rant would be a more accurate description. Wincing, I dared a glance at him out of my peripheral vision. Instead of looking disgusted by my blurted confession, he appeared confused.

"I have no idea what you just said," he admitted without preamble. *Now my cheeks flamed for an entirely different reason.*

"Sorry," *I signed.* "I suck at this. Sometimes my thoughts run away from me, and my hands have trouble keeping up. Forgive me?"

A slow smile tilted his lips upwards. It caused delicious tingles to course through my body, as if I'd been shot by a bolt of electricity. Or a thousand bolts. Or a thousand bolts and a penis. Or a—

Down girl.

"Nothing to forgive."

The sound of a curse coming from outside made me jump. Declan's eyebrows furrowed.

"Everything okay?" *he signed, capturing and holding my attention.*

"Goddamn it. That was higher than I thought," a familiar voice muttered.

"Callie?" I asked breathlessly. Declan watched my lips move, his brow quirking, before understanding flickered in his eyes. Instead of looking angry at the intrusion, or even jealous, he turned towards the newcomer expectantly.

Calax's hands appeared first, gripping the sill, before his tall, muscular body was pulled through the window. He landed with a grunt on the ground, his dark hair disarrayed and dirt smeared on his high cheekbones.

"What are you doing here?" I squeaked. My eyes rapidly flicked from Declan, perched on my bed, to Calax, and then to the diminutive sliver of space between me and my ex-best friend. I had to have been breaking thousands of rules here. Rule Number 212: No Guys Besides the Boyfriend are Allowed in the Bed.

But Calax didn't seem perturbed at seeing Declan. Instead, he merely clapped him on the shoulder and came to sit beside me on the opposite side of the bed.

"You need to get some sleep," he said, a hand coming up to tenderly brush a strand of hair

behind my ear. I gaped at him, glanced anxiously at Declan, and then went back to gaping. Frankly, I resembled a lunatic fish forced out of water. Definitely not a sexy look on me.

Calax smiled smugly, but ignored my inquiring gaze.

"Get some rest, baby girl. We'll be here with you until you wake up."

When I just continued to stare at him as if he had a few screws loose, Declan pulled back the blanket and slid in beside me. Calax hastily did the same on my other side.

I found myself sandwiched between two very strong, very sexy men.

Oh god. The fantasy.

It was coming true, wasn't it?

I wasn't ready for double penetration yet. My butthole was too tight. I hadn't dared put a finger up there yet. What if I farted? What if I—

Calax's chuckle cut me off in mid-mental-rant.

"I'm thinking aloud again, aren't I?" I whispered against his broad chest. I could feel the heat emitting from Declan's warm body behind me. Before Calax could answer, Declan's arm wrapped around my waist, and his legs entangled with mine. It was such an intimate embrace that pinpricks of desire radiated throughout my body. I glanced at Calax, gauging his reaction, only to find his eyes on me, the heat in his gaze lighting a path.

"You were," he admitted. Before I could react, he brought his lips to my ear.

"And when I take you from behind, you'll be prepared."

Before I could reply—because really, what could I even say to something like that? —his teeth clamped down on my sensitive lobe. An instinctive moan of pleasure, of bliss, filled the air. Calax chuckled darkly.

"Goodnight, my love."

"Goodnight," I whispered breathlessly.

Held in the embrace of two men, I drifted off to sleep. Honestly? It was the best night of sleep I had in years.

"Are you just going to stand there with a dopey expression on your face?" Bowel Movements asked snidely, snapping me out of my reverie. I glared at the little bitch, wishing that I could punch her face…and then I realized that I was actually wishing to punch my own face.

Shit got confusing.

"I was thinking," I snapped. BM gave me an exaggerated eye roll.

"Wow. That's fascinating. You must be so proud of yourself."

Had I really been that condescending?

Had I really been that much of a bitch?

Yes. Yes I had.

Turning away from BM, I began to walk down the snow-covered street. The carcasses of tree branches grazed my face as I stepped off the path and into the forest the children had emerged from.

"Where are you going?" There was more disdain than actual curiosity in her voice.

"Away," I retorted back. Twigs snapped beneath my feet, the sound loud in the unaccustomed silence. I realized, somewhat vaguely, that the lack of sound was disturbing and unnerving. There should've been critters scampering to and fro. Leaves rustling in the cold winter breeze. Birds cawing from up above. Instead, I was met with a silence that slithered over my skin like a dark, sticky tar. I rubbed at my arms instinctively, as if that gesture could somehow fight the chill that had nothing to do with the cold.

"You can't run away from this!" BM called after me. I didn't even have to look to know that she would've been rolling her eyes. Knowing her—knowing *me*, her hip would've been cocked to the side with a hand on said hip. It was a standard pose I'd perfected when I was younger. The eloquent gesture communicated how many shits I gave. Namely, none.

"I'm not technically running!" I called back, very nearly tripping over a tree branch. I would like to give credit to my ninja-like reflexes for keeping me on my feet. My training with Fallon had most definitely paid off. "I'm walking."

"You always do this." Her voice came from just above my shoulder, and I flinched. Though her tone could almost be described as dispassionate, there was a certain coldness that thickened the air. Goosebumps erupted on my flesh.

"Do what?" I asked, though I didn't care. At this point, I wanted to get as far away from her as possible.

As far away from me as possible.

I was beginning to associate BM with the girl that I hated. The girl that I used to be. Weak and selfish and with this constant pressure to be perfect and to have the world behave perfectly as well. I knew that the weight on her shoulders was suffocating. I knew, because I felt the same way even now. This was a version of myself that hadn't survived such a drowning. She was still tumbling through wave after wave, unable to find that pocket of fresh air. Her features were hardened because of what she'd been through—no love, no companionship, no guys. A slave to our parents.

Briefly, I felt pity for her.

For me.

For the girl I used to be.

I remembered that existence. It had been...lonely. There was no other word to describe it. The loneliness was like a clamp on my heart, squeezing the life from me. I'd been dying ever so painfully, and I hadn't even noticed.

"You run away from your problems," Bitch Me was saying now, and any pity I felt for her instantly diminished. I spun on my heel so quickly that she staggered back a step. Despite being the exact same height, I felt as if I was towering over. With an imperious set to my chin, I spoke through gritted teeth.

"I don't run away from my problems. Not anymore. *You* do. And I'm not you. I changed...I'm better than I used to be." I gave her a once-over, my lips curling in disgust. I really had been a pathetic creature. Needy and undeserving of love. There were so many people I'd hurt, Ducky and Calax to name a few. My life was like a wrecking ball. Everyone in my path had paid the price, sometimes with their lives. "I'm better than you."

I had to give BM credit—she didn't cower away as I thought she would. Instead, she raised her chin and met my stare defiantly.

"You can say all you want, but I know the truth. You have feelings for all of them, don't you? All seven of them?" Something must've flickered in my face, guilt most likely, for she threw back her head in laughter. "Don't you think it would be easier to let them go? To stop stringing them along?"

Before she'd even finished speaking, I was already shaking my head.

"I'm not. Stringing them along, that is. I'm only with Calax and Ryder."

Bitch Me put a hand on her hip and tilted her head to the side. Brown tresses glowed in the waning sunlight, highlighting the strands of orange and gold. Damn, I was a hot piece of ass.

Not the time, Adelaide.

"Two boyfriends?" she said dryly. "And you believe that you're *not* stringing them along? That's low, even for you."

I didn't have to stand there and take her shit.

I knew what we had was unconventional, but it worked for us. I loved them, all of them, and they loved me. So what if it wasn't the traditional boy and girl romance? As I stated before, nothing about us was traditional. We were seven enigmas, seven tortured souls. We'd found each other when we had no one else, and faith intertwined our lives together.

There was no doubt in my mind that we belonged together.

All of us.

The realization sent me staggering back a step. I hadn't just included Calax and Ryder in that clump of people. I'd thought of all of them—all seven of them.

And me.

God, how had I been so stupid? It was so obvious that I wanted to scream.

I was in love with them. With Calax and Ryder. With Ronan, my sarcastic and sexy leprechaun. With Asher and Tamson, two of the sweetest boys I'd ever met. With the brooding Fallon. With my best friend, Declan.

BM smiled, no doubt coming to the same conclusion I had.

"You're only hurting them. If you loved them, you'd let them go."

Intuitively, I glanced over my shoulder. Seven distinct silhouettes stood in the forest. I didn't have to see any features to know who they were. The seven men who had captured my heart. The seven men who held that organ in their hands. The seven men who had the capacity to either build me up…or completely destroy me.

And I, them.

After all, love was a two-way street.

"Let them go," I parroted mechanically. My eyes slid back towards BM. With a soft smile, the first sincere smile I'd seen on her face since I met her in this shithole, she extended a hand.

"Come," she said softly. "End their pain. End your own pain. You'll be happier with me."

Indecision warred within me. I could hear the guys beckoning me to come with them. To allow them to love me. For me to love them in return.

But was that fair to them? There was only one of me and seven of them.

I wanted to run to them. Calax would hold me in his arms, offering words of comfort. Ronan would make a quip, and Ryder would respond with a sexual innuendo. Asher would berate both of them for their inappropriate behavior while smiling sheepishly down at me. Tamson would blush at the exchange, but a small smile, a smile reserved only for me, would grace his features. Declan would roll his eyes to the heavens. It was something he always did when he was searching for patience. And Fallon? He would glare at everyone present.

Except for me.

No, when his eyes met mine, they would flare with heat and something warmer. Something that I'd never seen on our fearless leader's face before. It would soften his features considerably, until the brooding male was almost entirely unrecognizable.

"This is for the best," BM assured me, no doubt privy to my inner turmoil.

"For the best," I repeated numbly. Her hand was extended towards me, tempting me, begging me to take it.

The guys were still behind me, calling for me. They wanted me to come home.

After a moment, I put my hand in hers.

CHAPTER 19

CALAX

She looked beautiful, even like that. Even with her face ashen and blood coating her skin. Even with death looming ominously over her body, threatening to take hold. I held her cold hand in my own and gently reached over to touch her cheek.

"Why isn't she waking up, Doc?" I asked, my voice unwillingly cracking. I would've liked to blame it on the lack of use the last two days, but that would've been a blatant lie. My emotions were running rampant within me. With no outlet, I had to settle for curling in on myself mentally like old, brittle paper.

Adelaide was injured, maybe even dying.

Declan and Fallon had left us with only a vague note promising that they would return.

The rest of us? We were barely holding ourselves together. Without our leader, Fallon, and our glue, Adelaide, we were lost puppies.

And then there was Tommy.

He'd locked himself in one of the spare bedrooms and hadn't come out. I wasn't even sure if he was eating, though Asher left a plate by his door every morning and night.

In a span of hours, the once modest bedroom had been entirely redesigned until it resembled a hospital room. An IV, a table full of scalpels and stethoscopes, adhesive bandages, and various painkillers, all courtesy of Asher.

I knew he and Ryder were attempting to get the generator up and running again, but the effort was futile. The thing was shot to hell and back. No amount of praying would fix the damn thing. Instead, we had to rely on the flickering glow from the sparse and unreliable candlelight. Lining the window sill. On the bedside table. Near the foot of the bed. It was a miracle that Doc was able to operate in the first place, what with his limited supplies and the scarce lighting provided.

The man looked tired. Weary. He hadn't left her bedside since this first began. Granted, we didn't really leave him much of a choice. A gun to the head was the only incentive he needed.

Addie would be horrified.

"I did all I could do," Doc responded. He leaned forward, resting his elbows on his knees and placing his head in his hands. Dark, prominent bags were evident beneath his hazel eyes. "Now it's up to her."

"What do you mean it's up to her?" I asked scathingly. Doc glanced up at me as if I were an imbecile. I just barely resisted snapping his thin neck.

We needed him alive.

For now.

After Addie recovered…

Well…

It would be in his best interest not to piss me off too much.

"She has to want to fight," he explained. "It's in her hands now."

"She's going to fight." There was no doubt in my mind of that. That was one of the things that I loved about her. And one of the things that annoyed the ever-loving shit out of me.

Doc startled at the conviction in my voice, his eyes flickering towards Addie's pale frame. I bristled at the disbelief in his expression. He didn't know her like I did. He didn't know that she would do anything for the people she loved, including fighting and winning against death itself.

"You should go get some food. And maybe find something to wash yourself off with." His nose wrinkled in distaste at the latter statement. "I'll tell you if anything changes."

I hesitated, gripping Addie's hand even tighter. I hadn't eaten in days, despite Asher's repeated attempts at getting food into me, and I hadn't washed myself off since…well…I couldn't remember when. My body was coated in a layer of blood, Addie's blood.

"You can send one of the others in here," Doc said beseechingly. "She'll be fine for the ten minutes you're gone."

Scrubbing a large hand down my face, I nodded in agreement. I was no use to Addie dead or weakened.

Without taking my eyes from the doctor, I stood and pushed open the bedroom door. Tamson sat in the entryway, eyes haunted as he stared at a blood stain darkening the carpeting. He only glanced up when I cleared my throat, eyes purposely avoiding the room—and consequently, the girl—behind me.

"I'll be back in a few minutes. Keep an eye on her?"

He hesitated, indecision disfiguring his features. I clenched my hands into fists and tucked them beneath my armpits. It was either that or punch him in the head.

"I know you don't want to see her like that. I don't want to fucking see her like that, but someone has to stay with her." Narrowing my eyes, I nodded towards where

Doc was watching our exchange with rapt attention. "Unless you want her to be alone with Doc."

At those words, his resolve strengthened, and he scrambled to his feet. Doc muttered something about "taking offense to that" behind me. Without another word, Tamson strode past me and slammed the door shut.

I winced at the sound.

Alone for the first time I could remember, I wandered aimlessly into the bathroom. Since the acid rain fiasco, we hadn't been able to use the stream to clean ourselves up. Instead, Asher had brought numerous packages of water bottles. I didn't like wasting such a precious resource, but the blood staining my hands felt just as acidic as the rain. I needed it off of me.

My tired eyes took stock of my reflection in the mirror.

Blood coated my black shirt and pasty skin. It had even found its way into my dark hair. I looked as if I had been through a war zone. How was I still standing?

How was I still breathing?

I was a soldier out on a battlefield with no purpose. No leader. No reason for fighting.

Sarge had abandoned us in our time of need. The man with all the answers, all the strength, had run with only a vague note explaining why and that he had a radio with him for quick contact.

Declan, my brother, had left us.

Everyone was fucking leaving us. Leaving me.

With more vigor than I intended, I pulled off the cap of a water bottle and dumped it on my head. The water was warm from being inside for so long, and it did little to lessen the blood on my skin. Instead, it merely turned the color pink. For some reason, I found that hysterical.

Fucking pink blood.

Addie would have a field day with that.

I conjured up images of her perfect, heart-shaped face. That fire in her eyes I'd come to both fear and love. The brown tresses that were just as soft as they appeared. The tenderness in her face when she told me that she loved me. *Me*. A beast. A monster.

My laughter contorted into heart-wrenching sobs. I gripped the sink until my knuckles turned white.

I couldn't lose her.

Not again.

I'd thought I had lost her once, and that pain had been unbearable. Now, I knew that she loved me. I knew what it felt like to be with her, to be loved by her, to taste her. She was a drug, and I was an addict.

Losing her would be the death of me. I wouldn't be able to survive such a fatal wound.

I'd lost everything and everyone in my life. I couldn't lose her as well.

My body sank to the ground, my legs unable to support my weight.

For the first time I could remember, I cried.

I cried for the little boy who'd lost his innocence. I cried for the family I never had. I cried for the girl I loved and lost.

It didn't completely diminish the pain I felt.

But it helped.

RYDER

"They'll be fine," Asher said easily, the katana sword cleanly slicing through flesh and bone. The Rager fell at his feet, a collection of sinewy, pale skin and black veins. He offered me a timid smile while simultaneously wiping the blood off on his jeans.

The blood of Ragers was not like normal blood. It wasn't red like you would expect, but instead a strange black color like molten onyx stone. It was as thick as tar and smelled something fierce.

"I don't want to talk about it," I mumbled, tossing a dagger into a Rager that was running towards Asher. The creature dropped like a bag of rocks, the copper handle protruding from its scalp.

"You do this a lot," Asher pointed out. He swung his sword in a swooping arc, effectively beheading three more Ragers.

"Do what?"

There was a reason I'd joined Asher on this supply run, and it wasn't to talk about my fucking feelings. No, I'd already decided I would keep them buried away. No amount of digging could uncover them.

The pharmacy we'd chosen to raid was a small mom-and-pop shop just at the edge of town. Since it wasn't a brand name, the building had been left alone during the initial riots and panic. The shelves were still lined with unopened medicine bottles and cans of food. The pungent aroma of stale milk and weeks old meat assaulted my senses.

I didn't know how the Ragers had gotten into this building, which had been padlocked shut. Perhaps they'd been in there when the virus initially hit. Perhaps they'd thought this building was a sanctuary—food, medicine, water, shelter. The essentials needed to live. To survive.

To flourish.

And now look at them—brainless monsters getting slaughtered.

There was a sort of sick, dramatic irony in that. My twisted mind wanted to laugh at the poetic justice.

Once the last Rager was taken care of, Asher turned towards me. The disgusting, black blood was plastered on his cheeks, staining his blond hair.

"Addie is going to be—"

"Don't you dare say fine!" I snapped, pointing a quivering finger at him. "Don't you dare fucking say it."

That was the last thing I wanted to hear—a false fucking promise. My insides convulsed, a strange combination of fear and an incandescent fury. I didn't need Asher to lie to me about something like that. No, we both knew that she wasn't fine. She was anything *but* fine.

And I wasn't man enough to be there with her.

For her.

She was dying, and I'd left her like a coward. I'd been selfish, unable to see her lying immobile on that bed. She'd once been such a vibrant flame, full of life, that it physically pained me to see her like that. My heart rebelled at the idea of losing her. The damn organ wouldn't listen to my logical brain. It held onto hope—that dreaded, evil emotion.

Hope was stupid. We built up these walls, these impenetrable fortresses made entirely of our mangled faith and hope. When hope faded, though, we were left with nothing but walls. These walls couldn't be broken.

So no, I didn't believe in holding onto hope.

Hope was for dumbasses.

The sooner I could accept the inevitable, the happier I would be.

But damn if my heart didn't pound against my ribcage, demanding me to stay strong. Adelaide was going to live. She had to, for my own sanity.

Without another word to Asher, who was regarding me warily as if I were a snake preparing to strike, I began to shove miscellaneous items into my bag. The monotonous movement allowed me to believe, if only for a second, that my life wasn't completely falling to shambles. That I hadn't only lost the girl I loved, but two of my brothers. For that brief moment, as sun slashed through the surprisingly clean window, I could pretend.

It was like being on stage. I was a performer, through and through. This was just another performance.

Asher, mercifully, changed the subject.

"There's a lot of them," he mused, indicating the Ragers. I grunted in response. "More and more." He paused, staring down at a decapitated body. I wouldn't have been able to tell you the gender. It could've been a female with a larger frame, or it could've been a male. It was disconcerting to see a body disconnected from its head.

I swallowed the bile that threatened to explode out of me.

"What measures do you think we can take to prevent it?" he asked, nudging the monster with his foot. "The infection spreading, I mean."

"I don't fucking care."

And I didn't. It no longer mattered to me if I lived or died. Became infected.

There was no point to any of it anymore.

Asher gave me a long look, no doubt questioning the sincerity of such an answer, before he sighed heavily. It was a resigned sigh. I wasn't sure if he agreed with my statement or just accepted it.

Silence thickening the air until it was almost palpable, we worked at loading the van. Like the rest of the vehicles, the acid rain had caused the exterior to rust and corrode away.

Ragers, faces hideously disfigured from the rain, roamed the street. Fortunately, they didn't pay us any mind, instead focusing on attacking one another.

Asher was right—these monsters were scary, but not in the traditional sense. There was no logical explanation as to why some people had been turned while others remained human. What attracted the worms to certain individuals? I was unsure if this question would ever be answered besides in vague theories and unconfirmed explanations.

"I love her too," Asher said, his voice breaking through the silence like the slash of a keen knife. I startled at his words, despite the fact that I'd already suspected as much. Before I could stop myself, I snorted. The sound was unintentionally malicious. I wasn't purposely trying to be a dick. Honestly. I was strung too tight, and it was only a matter of time until I erupted like a fucking volcano. Instead of lava, however, I would spew blood.

"Have fun loving a dead girl."

CHAPTER 20

DECLAN

We drove through the night, alternating sleeping in the passenger seat and driving.

It was impossible for us to talk. Sarge wasn't, by nature, a talkative person, and I had no energy to raise my hands. Instead, we sat in companionable silence. Moonlight spliced the upholstered seat, painting the car's interior in a soft, golden glow.

According to the map, we were still a few hours away from our destination. My fingers tapped against my knee as my unease strengthened and grew.

Was I making a terrible mistake by leaving Addie when she needed me? I didn't know, and I didn't want to fixate on it. Sarge expertly steered the truck down the backroads, avoiding the numerous stray cars with all of their doors thrown open and the occasional dead body. Ragers chased after us, hands curled into claws, before they quickly became distracted by one another. More than one fight broke out, a tangle of limbs and hair and blood.

So much blood.

Blood loss never seemed to deter them. If anything, it only seemed to spur them on. The grotesque sight was both mesmerizing and disgusting. I didn't know if I wanted to look away or continue watching.

The car suddenly slid to the side, balancing precariously on two wheels before skidding to a stop. I reached out, grabbing the oh shit handle. Wide-eyed, I turned to meet Sarge's gaze, but he wasn't looking at me. Instead, he was focused on something in the rearview mirror. Or someone.

I spun around with an almost blistering speed and came face to face with a familiar figure.

Chubby cheeks, tangled locks of hair, eyes currently narrowed.

Tommy.

And from the vein pulsing in Fallon's neck and his erratic movements, I figured he was bitching Tommy out. Tommy, of course, remained impassive if not slightly irritated. He crossed his arms over his chest and raised his chin defiantly. He didn't speak, but instead allowed Sarge to grill him. His face turned redder and redder the more Sarge droned on. I sort of wished I could hear what was being said. I imagined it was a lot of creative language and curse words.

Sarge turned his face towards the window, either too pissed to continue speaking or trying to restrain himself from murdering the little asshole.

I, however, kept my eyes narrowed on the little shit. He didn't cower under my penetrating gaze, but instead sat up straighter.

"Why are you here?" I signed. Tommy's eyes flickered to Sarge as he translated.

"I followed you, dumbass." The asshole exaggeratedly opened his mouth, each word overly pronounced.

"Why?"

I leveled him with a glare to stress that simple word.

"Because." He sneered at me, the expression contorting his chubby face. "I couldn't just sit there and do nothing."

"How did you know I was leaving?"

Only Sarge knew I was leaving, and that was because the bastard had eyes everywhere. But Tommy? How had he known?

Tommy rolled his eyes heavenwards. "I stalked you."

Well, okay then.

I would say I was surprised, but...

Fuming, I turned towards Sarge.

"What do you suppose we do about him?" I signed, aware that Tommy no doubt couldn't understand me and was getting annoyed. Added bonus, if I was being completely honest.

"Leave him to die," Sarge responded.

Tommy began to rapidly move his hands, a series of random gestures and dance moves. His middle finger made an appearance on more than one occasion. I rolled my eyes and ignored him. Hopefully, that irritated the little fucker.

"We can't leave him to die," I signed. Sarge blinked at me with the innocence of a wolf. When he just continued to stare at me, unperturbed, I hurried to add, *"Addie would be pissed."*

At that, he released a heavy sigh, his shoulders sagging. Once again, he'd admitted defeat in the name of Addie.

For Sarge to decide not to kill someone was real progress. Adelaide was rubbing off on him.

Tommy tapped my shoulder persistently, demanding my attention, and I reluctantly turned to face him. He smiled smugly, an imperious set to his chin.

"I know where you're going," he said. "You're going after Addie's brother, correct?"

When I didn't respond, Tommy took my non-answer as confirmation. His smile grew until it practically cut his face in half.

"Well, I want to come too. I need to do something with myself. I can't just sit around…" His eyes dropped, tears welling and cascading down his pudgy cheeks. He angrily brushed the stray tears away, the break in his brash front irritating him. With a shuddering breath, he met my gaze resolutely. "I'm coming. And there's nothing you can do about it."

Suddenly, Sarge's suggestion to leave him for dead didn't sound as bad.

Tempting, actually. Very, very tempting.

RONAN

She fit against my body perfectly.

Warm and soft, her body molding against mine. Lips cherry red. Eyes that never seemed to stick to one color but instead alternated between metallic violet and light blue. It all depended on where she was positioned in the sunlight. The sun was attracted to her, as it should be.

Like called to like, after all.

"What are you thinking about?" Her voice was thick with sleep. The raspy sound made my cock harden automatically.

"You," I answered softly. I tentatively brushed her hair behind her ear, allowing my fingers to linger on her flushed cheek. She was so beautiful that it physically hurt. An almost ethereal beauty. A beauty you would find in paintings, not in real life.

"Well stop thinking about me," she said with an embarrassed giggle.

How could I not think about her?

How could she not consume my every waking thought and be the star of all my dreams?

I tightened my arms around her, loving the way she felt in my embrace. I'd never believed in fate or soulmates, but my heart couldn't deny that Addie had been put on this world to complete my soul. With her, I was whole.

"I always think about you." I pressed my face against her hair, inhaling her unique scent. Peppermints almost, from the shampoo we'd stolen on our first supply run. I'd never associated that delicious scent with her before, but just then, it was all I could think about.

Who knew that peppermint could be sexy?

"Did you just sniff me?" she asked in disbelief, and I chuckled darkly.

"Yup."

"No shame."

"Nope."

I kissed the hollow of her throat, relishing her shiver of pleasure.

"I love you," I said softly. Sincerely. It was the first time I'd said those words to anyone outside of my family and brothers. I'd had dozens of girls, some of them I'd even considered as girlfriends, but none evoked such a reaction from within me. Love, for so long, was nothing but an elusive fantasy. It was something I would see in movies, hear about on television, watch couples wistfully through cafe windows. I'd never thought I would associate that word with me.

She was silent, no doubt lost in her own thoughts, before she responded.

"Why do you love me?"

The question took me by surprise. My arms loosened, and I pulled back to look at her. She was anxiously gnawing on her lower lip, eyes flickering from her feet, to the quilt on the bed, to the drawn curtains. Anywhere but my probing gaze. I gently tilted her chin up, urging her to meet my eyes. I wanted her to see the absolute devotion I felt for her. The love. I would do anything for her. Live. Die. Dismember.

"Why wouldn't I love you?"

She tried to pull her chin away from my hand, but I refused to let her go.

"You're everything to me and my team. Funny, smart, insane." I smirked at the last word, and she rolled her eyes. "I'll never get tired of listening to your inner ramblings. Or your stupid, perverted jokes. What makes it even funnier is the fact that you don't know they're perverted. I love you because you're too pure for this world, too good for someone like me, but yet you don't see that. You don't see the flaws in a person, only the good. You don't see what a fuck up I am, what fuck ups we all are. How could I not love you?"

Her lower lip quivered, and fresh tears sprang to her eyes. When the first tear fell, I leaned forward to catch it in my mouth. She shivered delicately beneath me, and that shiver gave me the courage to rewrap my arms around her and position her securely on my lap. She nuzzled the side of my face, her warm breath stirring the hair on my neck.

"I love you too."

It was the first time she'd spoken those words aloud, and my insides tightened. Fucking butterflies fluttered, demanding release. Before I could stop myself, I tilted her head up and pressed my lips against her own. She yielded immediately, her tongue slipping out to coax my own into submission. Licks of fire ran down my spine, from my fingers to my toes. My hands tangled in her brown tresses, pulling her closer. I needed her closer as much as I needed air to breathe.

Her hands grabbed eagerly at my shirt, pulling it up so we could be skin to skin. I groaned low in my throat. With a reverence I wasn't used to, she began to trace the dips and curves of my abs. The prominent V leading down my pants. Down and down.

Her hands were so cold, almost unhealthily so. It felt as if I was being touched by an icicle.

"Addie..." I murmured, pulling away. She needed to get warmed up. Perhaps I could start a fire...

Her face was pale, the shadows beneath her eyes pronounced. As I watched, horrified, blood dripped from her nose. Her ears. Her eyes. I screamed helplessly.

Where was Sarge?

Calax?

Ryder?

Why was I all alone?

A sob broke free as I held her dying form. Her head lolled to the side, the light leaving her eyes.

"No..." I whispered. "No. No."

"NO!"

I woke up with the word on my lips. Sweat drenched my skin and ran down my face.

Just a dream.

Just a bad fucking dream.

Gasping, I bolted upright and glanced around the darkened room. My heart was hammering, and my hands were shaking. Fear clamped my throat closed, strangling me. It had felt so real.

Her dying in my arms…

Shivers of revulsion rocked my body forward. I rubbed at the skin of my arms as if that gesture could somehow wipe away the remnants of blood from my dream. I yawned, stretching my taut muscles as sleep threatened once again to claim me.

Shouting from down the hall roused me further from my slumber. With a speed I didn't know I possessed, I jumped from my bed and hurried out of my room. I barely noticed that I was completely naked. No time for me to put on shorts.

I barreled through the door of Addie's room, fear snaking around my throat like an iron clamp.

"What's happening?" Calax was screaming when I entered. Tamson stood pale-faced by the door. Doc was standing over Adelaide, his hands on her chest as he began compressions. Her face was pale—as pale as it had been in my dream.

"No," I whispered.

Briefly, my mind flickered back to that old nursery rhyme I was told as a kid. Humpty Dumpty or whatever. But it was the equivalent to a fairy tale. It never reflected reality.

No number of horses or men…

…would put Addie back together again.

CHAPTER 21

I placed my hand in BM's.

Her smile was smug, predatory even, and her eyes possessed a voracious hunger, primal and carnal. I met her smile…and then roughly pulled her to the ground. She let out a gasp, and I twisted my body so I was on top of her. Jamming my elbow into the back of her neck, I hissed,

"I'm not leaving them." As an afterthought, I added, "Bitch."

She lifted her head up, lips curving into a feral sneer. I would almost describe it as a snarl.

Frankly, it was not a sexy look on me.

"So you're choosing to be selfish," she hissed. I pressed her face into the dirt, and she let out a cry.

"No," I answered evenly. "I'm choosing them. Always."

I could hear the men behind me, my men, coaxing me to come home. I would attempt to heed their call, even if it killed me.

"You bitch." Her face began to change and contort, becoming something entirely unrecognizable. Eyes turning a deep, garnet red. Teeth elongating. Nose protruding from her face. The change was so drastic, so sudden, that I staggered off of her, landing on my ass.

She towered over me, her features more monster than human.

Pain erupted on my calf as her claws dug into my skin. Hissing, I feebly kicked at the grotesque creature. I didn't even want to refer to her as BM anymore. No, there was no resemblance to the girl I once knew. I was staring into the eyes of the devil herself.

And she was furious.

"Unfortunately," she began, her voice a low growl that pulsated deep within me. It was a sound I'd never heard before, a sound that I only thought existed in movies. Goosebumps erupted on my skin that had little to do with the cold. She cracked her neck from side to side. "I can't let you leave."

Well…shit.

~

FALLON

The house was a cute bungalow style with a wraparound porch and hanging plants. A white picket fence greeted us as we drove up, further highlighting the homey feel the house was emitting. Two cars were in the driveway, the untarnished paint hinting that this area might've been spared from the acid rain. I wondered what storms they had faced. Earthquakes? Tornadoes? Floods?

"Well…this place looks fucking cozy," Tommy drawled. He pushed his head between the two seats and folded his arms on the center console. I didn't know how I hadn't noticed him before. The shit face had been unnaturally quiet where he'd sprawled himself out in the backseat. With the engine roaring and my own thoughts a mess, I hadn't even realized he was there until he'd showed himself. I really was losing my edge.

"Language," I said absently.

My entire attention was fastened on the closed window blinds. From what little I gathered, numerous houses on this street still had electricity. A small miracle, I supposed.

"Do you think anyone is home?" Declan signed.

Sighing heavily, I shrugged.

No, I didn't think anyone was home. The entire neighborhood was too silent. Too still.

Too dead.

The epitome of a ghost town. What memories haunted these streets?

Instead of saying all that, I slid out of the car and slammed the door shut. The air was warm, humidity making my shirt stick to my skin. My hair was matted to my scalp.

Mosquitos buzzed overhead, the sound deafeningly loud.

"Don't let them bite you," I warned Tommy while simultaneously signing to Declan. "We don't want to accidentally get infected."

Besides the worms and their origins, we still had no idea exactly how the virus was spread. I'd tried contacting my uncle but hadn't been able to get ahold of him. Or my father, for that matter.

Or Olivia.

I tried to make myself look as unimposing as possible, an unsurprisingly hard feat given my immense size and broad shoulders. The last thing I wanted to do was scare this family away. They didn't know me, and without Addie as a mediator, they would have trouble trusting our ragtag group.

Tommy shoved me aside and strutted towards the front door. I watched him, my brow creasing with a frown. He was an annoying little shit, but he was growing on me. I was beginning to think of him as a younger, albeit annoying, brother. Without waiting for me, Tommy rapped his fist against the door.

Rolling my eyes, I hurried to catch up with him.

"Nobody is answering." He paused, squinting at the doorway as if he would be able to see through it. "I'm going to break in."

"You are not going to—"

Before I could finish my sentence, Tommy kicked the door down.

Kicked the fucking door down, as if he was a badass action hero instead of a tweenager. Of course, he stumbled over his own two feet, fell to the floor on top of the broken door, and began cursing up a storm. Chuckling, I helped him up and brushed plaster and dust off of his shoulders.

"Careful, there," I said. He glared at me in response, eye twitching.

Literally, twitching.

The smile left my face as a pervasive smell pummeled my senses. My eyes watered, and I immediately brought my hand to my nose in order to stunt the overwhelming scent. I'd been around enough dead bodies to know what that smell meant.

"What the fuck is that?" Tommy gasped. I was too shocked to reprimand him for his crude language. The source of the smell was soon discovered as we moved farther into the small house. The living room, consisting of two floral couches, a flat screen television, and a water stained coffee table, was splashed in blood. It was everywhere, staining the walls and carpeting and tiny cherubic statue in the corner of the room.

Two bodies were lying on the ground.

My fear dissipated, transforming into something that resembled relief, when I noted that the two figures were both older. An aging woman, brown hair streaked with gray and white, and a wrinkled faced man. The woman had been dismembered, her arms disconnected from her body and her body separated from her head, the source of the excessive amount of blood loss I imagined. The man died of a gunshot wound to his head.

In his cold hand, he held a gun.

Tommy began to sob softly, and I immediately winced at the sound. I wished that I'd shielded him from all of the horrors in this world. He was too young, too innocent, to endure such tragedies.

"Wait outside," I said gruffly, venturing a tentative step closer. A broken photograph on the coffee table captured and held my attention. Hand trembling, I picked it up and surveyed the family smiling back at me. The man and woman, the same man and woman currently lying dead on the floor, had their arms around a little boy.

Brown, tousled hair. Emerald eyes. Red headphones around his neck.

His gaze was distant, not fixated on the camera but on a spot in the far distance. He didn't look uncomfortable, merely dazed. I remembered Adelaide telling me that he had autism.

"He's not here," Tommy said. His voice was a strangled gasp.

I frowned, listening intently.

Outside, a bird chirped. The day was peaceful, serene, and a contrast to the horror that had taken place inside of this house. It almost seemed to be mocking me, mocking the dead bodies. The slanting sunlight illuminated the scene like a giant spotlight. Tremors of revulsion ran down my body.

God, this was disgusting.

This *world* was disgusting.

It was easy for me to see what had happened. The blood was semi-fresh, maybe only a few days old, but there were no Ragers present.

The woman had been attacked. The man had freaked out and had committed suicide.

And Nikolai? He was nowhere to be found.

It occurred to me that he might've been dead, but I refused to believe it. I couldn't fail Adelaide now, not when she needed me.

Not when I'd already failed her once before.

I thought through everything I'd heard about this elusive Nik.

There were only a few things I knew about him. One, he was autistic. Two, he loved music. And three…

Nothing. I didn't know anything about him.

"Nik!" I bellowed. "Adelaide sent us!"

I didn't know what I was hoping. The door to be thrown open and Nik to come hurrying out? For him to pop his head over the couch?

"Nik!"

Tommy gave me a reproachful look, shouldering me out of his way. He cupped his mouth to amplify his voice.

"Nikky boy!" Tommy called. "Your crazy ass sister sent us! You know which one? The insane girl with brown hair? Talks to herself? Ring any bells?"

There was the sound of footsteps upstairs.

"Stay here," I instructed Tommy, though I doubted he would listen. Of course the little shit immediately ran up the staircase, ignoring my curses as I hurried to keep pace. "Damnit, Tommy."

We raced down the hallway, stopping in front of an open door to a bedroom. Spaceships on the blankets. Framed photographs on the walls. Everything was immaculately displayed, as if the owner had a keen eye for cleanliness. My eyes latched onto a small photo sticking out of the gilded edge of a mirror. The boy I recognized as Nikolai was staring down at an iPod. A young girl, maybe thirteen, had her arm wrapped around him, smiling brightly at the camera. She was so young. So innocent.

Adelaide.

Instinctively, I took the picture down and shoved it into my pocket. When Addie woke up, she would want this memory of her brother.

"Over here!" Tommy screamed, seeming to forget or ignore the fact that I was only inches away from him, and I turned towards where he was standing.

He was looming over a figure huddled in the closet. His hair was greasy, smeared with blood, and dirt streaked his hollowed face. It appeared as if he hadn't eaten in days, as his body was beginning to display malnourishment. His cheeks were sunken, and his skin was pasty.

Slowly, as to not scare him further, I crouched down to his level.

"Nikolai?" I asked softly. He was exactly as Addie described him, down to the red headphones. His eyes rested on my shoulder. "Addie sent us. Your sister sent us."

The only indication he heard me was the slightest twitch of his head. His hands twirled the black cord of his headphones, around and around his finger. They weren't plugged into anything, but I imagined he kept them on solely for comfort.

"We're not going to hurt you," I continued. Slowly, I reached into my pocket and grabbed out a beaded necklace. It was one Adelaide had worn frequently back at the resort. A gift from her father, she'd said. Nik's eyes widened in recognition. "My name is Fallon, and this is Tommy. Over here is..."

I paused, glancing around the room with narrowed eyes.

"Where the fuck is Declan?"

CHAPTER 22

ADDIE

The sun broached the horizon, painting the sky an almost metallic violet. I held the rock in a tight, white-knuckled grip, panting. The winter air stirred both my hair and the skeletal branches of nearby trees.

My eyes flickered from the blood, a surprisingly dark color, staining the rock to the person at my feet.

The girl.

Me.

Or at least the old me.

I found that I couldn't muster up enough strength to care as I smashed the rock against her face. With each hit, I could feel a piece of myself breaking. Leaving. The girl's face—my face—was distorted, grotesque almost, and held no resemblance to the girl she once was. She'd been slowly chipped away, each swing of the rock making her features entirely unrecognizable.

The rock clattered to the ground, my muscles loosening as my courage dwindled. Nothing could change what had transpired. Not the sun cresting the tree boughs. Not the birds balancing precariously on a low branch, mocking me with their silence. Not the air that seemed to get colder and colder as the seconds dragged on.

No, nothing could change what had happened. What I'd done.

The murder.

The massacre.

Darkness seeped through the edges of my vision like a black curtain being pulled closed. I could hear my guys, their voices the most beautiful sound in this god-forsaken forest, and I trudged forward.

I had to get to them.

I had to go home.

I had to.

All I could think about was BM's shattered, disbelieving expression as I'd pounded the rock into her face. There were no coherent thoughts in my head, no conscious thinking, besides the fact that I needed to return home to my guys.

Her face became even more unrecognizable with newly added bruises and bloody scabs, each hit tainting something in my soul simultaneous with the skin chipping away and the bones cracking. She wasn't the only one that had died that day.

I found that I had no regrets. I didn't like that girl, the girl I'd once been, and I was happy she was dead.

It was time to go home.

Snow flurried around me, water seeping through my thin leggings. Still, I trudged towards where my guys were silhouetted. They were calling my name, begging me to come home.

A large figure extended a hand—Calax, my rock, my protector, my best friend—and I gripped it with my own. Darkness clouded my vision, but I kept my hand firmly in his. I wouldn't let go.

I would never let go.

～

I BLINKED, attempting to articulate where I was and how I'd gotten there. Dim light broke through the darkness I was accustomed to. The product, I was sure, of multiple candles. I was lying in a bed, blankets pooled around my feet. And I was wearing...

Only my bra?

A slightly familiar male leaned over the bed. He had dark hair, an almost dirty blond color with black streaks, and a round, cherubic face. Memories came rushing to the forefront of my mind with an almost blistering speed, assaulting me.

The store.

Elena.

Bikini.

Greg.

Gun.

Doc.

That was his name, I recalled vaguely. Not his real name, but his title. He'd been in the store...

When Greg shot me.

"How are you feeling, Addie?" His voice was calm, soothing almost.

"W-Where's Tamson?" I stuttered, attempting to sit up. "And the others?"

"They're fine. It was you that we were worried about." His eyes darkened slightly. "Do you remember what happened?"

"Do I remember that you shot me? Yes, I have a rather vivid memory of that, thank you very much."

Face twisting, he folded his arms over his chest and scowled at me.

"I didn't shoot you. I saved your life."

"After you shot me," I pointed out helpfully. Really, the man should be grateful that I wasn't castrating him. Getting shot? Ten out of ten, would not recommend.

As if summoned by the thought, pain reverberated throughout my body.

Groaning, I catalogued my injuries.

My stomach burned with a sharp pain that radiated down my spine. My body as a whole was heavy, leaden, and tired. The combination was uncomfortable but not horrible. I could survive it.

Correction—I *had* survived it.

Blinking at the hideous stitches on my stomach, I diverted my attention back towards Doc. He regarded me with a clinical detachment common in most doctors.

"How am I alive?"

Because I should've been dead. I'd felt the life draining from my body as if I were a faucet turned on. Though I was scared of what was to come, I'd accepted death.

I would've welcomed death gratefully if it kept my men alive.

Doc pursed his lips, eyes once more landing on my stomach. It would scar, of course, but it only served to remind me of all I'd conquered. Death. Pretty badass, if you asked me. And what was one more scar to the inventory?

"The bullet was a clean in-and-out," he said after a moment of silence. "Once I was able to stop the bleeding, it was up to you whether or not you were going to pull through."

"Me?"

Before he could respond, the door was pushed open. Tamson stood in the doorway, the flames from the candles highlighting his sunken skin and disheveled hair. He paused when he took stock of me, his mouth opening and closing. In his gaze, I could see a multitude of emotions.

Shock.

Relief.

Pain.

Happiness.

Love.

It was the last one that caused my throat to close and tighten with an undefinable emotion. My heart fluttered, and my stomach churned. How had I not realized it before?

Tamson loved me.

And I loved him.

It wasn't the same type of love I felt for Calax and Ryder, but I was beginning to believe love was fluid. There was no set definition for it. Love was purposefully vague, designed to conform to each person's own interpretation.

I loved Calax and Ryder and Tamson.

And Fallon, Asher, Ronan, and Declan.

I loved them all so much, I thought my heart would explode. Break. These men had the potential to break my heart, just because I loved them.

"You're okay," I whispered. I tried to sit up, but Tam raced towards my bedside and put a restraining hand on my shoulder.

"Rest." His eyes roamed over my body, no doubt analyzing every injury. They stopped once they reached the protruding, jagged mark on my stomach. A forlorn expression darkened his features, there and gone too quickly for me to comment on. That was replaced by a certain reverence, a certain tenderness, that made tears well in my eyes.

I grabbed his hand in my weak one, stunned to feel it shake and tremble beneath my grip. His whole body quivered as if he'd been shot through with electric currents. One look into his eyes, and I could see decades of grief and pain from the few days— weeks? —I'd been unconscious.

With a sudden burst of courage, I reached a hand out and gently pulled him down to my awaiting lips. I didn't care that I'd been unconscious for days and that I hadn't brushed my teeth during that time. I didn't care that I was probably a disgusting mess. No, all I cared about was the man above me. The man who'd somehow stolen and kept a piece of my heart.

It was a slow kiss, almost as if he was mapping out my lips. He met me stroke for stroke but never tried to deepen it. It was the kiss I would've expected from old lovers. A kiss that had no reason to be rushed. A kiss that promised thousands of others.

I didn't hear the door open and close until a shadow loomed over us ominously.

"You're awake," Calax said softly. I broke free from Tamson, face burning, only to see nothing but relief in the giant's face. Ryder stood behind him, a similar expression on his own.

No jealousy.

No pain.

No betrayal.

Only relief and an immense happiness that I was alive. Acceptance. Love. I knew I shouldn't have expected anything else, but the confirmation was very nearly my undoing.

Calax reached me first, eyes tracing my features as if he meant to memorize them. Tears brimmed in his eyes, but his smile was radiant.

"Don't you ever fucking do that again. I will bring you back to life just to kill you myself." He moved to kiss my lips, but I turned my face away. When his eyes flashed with hurt, I hurried to explain.

"My breath is probably rancid. I heard that the government was thinking about using it as a weapon of mass destruction against the Ragers."

Rolling his eyes, Calax gently turned my face back towards his and brushed his lips against my own. If he died, he only had himself to blame. What romance novels and movies failed to mention was morning-slash-unconscious breath. It was a real, horrid thing. Trust me.

"Kitten," Ryder said, coming to stand on the other side of the bed. Tam graciously stepped aside and moved to stand near my feet. "Don't scare me like that. I'm an old fucking man."

He, too, pressed his lips to mine, not seeming to mind or care that I'd just kissed two of his best friends. Or that, you know, I was a disgusting, greasy mess of blood and sweat.

There was only love in his gaze.

Ronan stepped up next, expression unsure and almost shy. Timid. It wasn't an emotion I was used to seeing on my eccentric leprechaun.

"I'm glad you're okay, Princess," he whispered roughly. He lowered his lips to my cheek. The chaste gesture made my stomach flutter and heart race.

God, I loved him. I loved them all.

Ronan froze, eyes widening in his handsome face. Ryder began to chuckle, a relieved albeit terse sound. Raspy almost, as if he hadn't laughed in a while. I wasn't used to a somber Ryder, and I vowed to rectify that.

Before I could refute what I'd accidentally said aloud, Ronan's lips touched mine.

A graze of lips.

There and gone before I could blink. He rested his forehead against mine, eyes promising what would come.

"I love you too."

Asher came to stand beside Calax. He didn't have to say anything, as his eyes spoke volumes. There was a story in those blue orbs, a story that hinted at pain and darkness behind his happy façade. A story that narrated the life of a man that loved a girl.

I tried to convey my own feelings with an eloquent smile.

But...

There were two people missing. Where was Declan, my childhood best friend, and Fallon? A strangled sob escaped me at the realization. There was only one reason why they wouldn't be there with me, but I refused to believe it.

They couldn't be dead.

No. No. No.

"They're fine," Calax assured me, tentatively brushing at my hair. All of the guys were being extra gentle with me, extra attentive, as if I were cracked glass, one drop from being shattered. The attention was unnerving but not entirely unpleasant. "They left a note. They'll be back soon."

"And Tommy?"

Calax's eyes widened, and he whipped his head towards Ryder, who shrugged. Both of them glanced at Asher, who subtly shook his head no, and then they all turned towards Ronan and Tam. At their guilty expressions, indignation speared a hole through my chest. I was in love with a bunch of fucking assholes.

"Have you guys checked on him?" I asked, making sure to say each word slowly. All of the guys refused to make eye contact. "Where the fuck is my little psycho?!"

I tried to sit up yet again, but a sharp pain in my stomach prohibited such a movement. I hissed through gritted teeth and slowly lowered myself back down.

"About that..." Ryder trailed off at my murderous glare. "I love you?"

"Somebody go check on Tommy before I murder you all." Wincing yet again, I turned towards Doc. "And my stomach freaking hurts."

He nodded, a weary grin tilting his lips up.

"Yes, getting shot can do that to a person. You're going to be on bed rest for a couple weeks, maybe even months. I'll do everything I can to help make you comfortable."

"Thanks, Doc."

He quirked a brow. "Don't get me wrong. Greg and his buddies were sexist, kidnapping assholes, but the last thing I wanted to do was end up being the private doctor for you and your harem. If there wasn't a constant knife to my throat or gun on my back, I would've let you die." He shrugged unapologetically, and the twisted part of me appreciated his candor. The guys, however, would not appreciate such a sentiment. I turned towards them, now huddled near the doorway, to gauge their reactions towards Doc's announcement and caught a snippet of their conversation.

My eyes narrowed, and my voice sliced through the air like keen throwing knives. "What the fuck do you mean you have a prisoner?"

CHAPTER 23

DECLAN

*T*he prison was shadowed in the waning sunlight. Gray stones comprised the dull exterior, as well as the two, identical pinnacles on either side of the entrance. A separate building, this one surprisingly modern, stood a little distance away. A wrought iron fence greeted me as I walked up and stood beside a guard tower.

One glance through the small window confirmed that the guard was dead. His intestines were separated from his body.

The humid, Georgian air caused my clothes to stick to my skin. The pungent smell of decaying flesh permeated my nostrils.

An ominous warning was painted in blood over the entrance to the prison.

Beware of Zombies.

Frowning, I considered the dauntingly large structure with calculating eyes. From this distance, I could see figures moving erratically in the fenced-in yard. Ragers. A whole lot of them by the look of it.

I knew, without any doubt, that stepping through this gate would lead to my inevitable death. It was practically mocking me.

Indecision made me pause.

Was I ready to die? Was I ready to leave this world and the girl I loved?

The girl I loved who didn't love me in return?

I thought of the man inside of the prison, the man I was going to kill.

My father.

"Father" was too sentimental of a term to describe that horrid being. We were only related by blood and looks.

The last time I'd seen him, fifteen or so years ago, he had the same long brown hair I used to have. His belly had been large, protruding over the waistband of his jeans, and his eyes had been glacial. This was a man who hadn't seen warmth and certainly didn't know how to distribute it. He was cold, unyielding, and cruel. His fists always had to be pounding into a face, either my own or my mother's, and his lips spewed a constant barrage of poison.

The very last day I saw him, he'd been attacking my mother. Allison had been held tightly in her arms, the little baby blissfully unaware of what a monster her father was. Mother had tried to shield my sister the best she could, but the gesture was futile. One particularly hard hit from my father's drunken rage sent them both sprawling. Mother had obtained only a few bruises, but little Allison's head had ricocheted off of the hardwood floors.

She'd died on impact.

It was that memory, that image of her tiny face, that gave me the courage to move forward. I was going to die. It was something I accepted with an icy detachment. Fear no longer consumed me. Instead, it gave me the courage and strength to do what had to be done. That monster didn't deserve to live, either as a human or as a Rager. He was an insect—an insect I was determined to squish underneath my boot. For once in my life, I wouldn't be the victim around that man. That monster. I would be a fighter. A survivor.

I was going to join Allison and Addie in death.

Maybe, just maybe, that action could redeem me for failing her, failing them both, in the first place.

~

ADDIE

The boy they led into my room had dark, onyx black hair. A gag was shoved into his mouth, and his hands were tied behind his back. Whimpering, the man's eyes rapidly flickered from face to face.

"What the hell is this?" I directed my question towards Ryder, who was currently leading him into the room.

"*Who* the hell," Doc corrected snidely. I rolled my eyes but didn't humor him with a response. Folding my arms across my chest, I accidentally pushed my ample breasts up. I'd forgotten I was only wearing a lacy black bra that left little to the imagination. Calax subtly—read as totally not subtly—pulled my blanket up to cover me.

"This is Kai," Ronan supplied, waving his arm in Kai's direction.

"Why is Kai tied up with a gag in his mouth?" I asked. "It's not some kind of kinky sex game, is it?" Really, I had to get the important questions out of the way.

Ryder released Kai quickly, a grimace on his handsome face.

"Kitten, you're the only one I want to tie up."

Ignoring him, I said, "Get the gag out of his mouth." My body was heavy, and my eyelids continually threatened to close. The more I talked, the more my words slurred together. "What's happening to me?" This was directed at Doc, who was standing in the corner, arms folded over his impressive chest and a smirk on his face.

"That would be the drugs," he answered.

"Fucking drugs. Why'd you have to drug me? I'm sleepy. Why am I sleepy? Papa Jose would…" I struggled to maintain consciousness. There was something I had to remember. Something important…

"Repeat after me," I slurred. "We don't tie people up unless it's for a sex game. Tying people up is not nice. Drugging people is also not nice."

Vaguely, I realized that the drugs were probably the only reason why I didn't feel any pain. Instead of a blistering, searing pain, my body felt light and buoyant.

"In my defense, he tried to stab me." Ryder said this casually, shrugging his shoulders.

At his words, I saw red. Nobody—and I meant nobody—was allowed to harm my guys.

"Why is he still alive?!" I exclaimed. Kai's eyes widened in terror. Damn right he should be scared. I was a terrifying person when you threatened what was mine. "Bring him here, so I can kill the fucker."

"Ehhh…" Ronan began, while I could've sworn I heard Asher mumble, "So sexy."

"We need to radio Fallon. Let him know you're all right," Calax said gently. He seemed to be trying to distract me from my murderous tendencies. What. An. Asshole.

If you couldn't murder someone, what was the point of life?

And yes, I blamed my thoughts on the drugs.

"Can I take a quick nap first?" I asked, though the words sounded like a foreign language. Doc, of all people, chuckled. "Suck a dick, Doc."

"Already do," he retorted.

Before I could reply, darkness crept through the corners of my vision. I had one final thought before sleep consumed me. *When did Doc, that fucker, have time to drug me?*

~

I woke up to someone whispering my name. Peeling open my crusted eyelids, I stared up at Asher's handsome, boyish face. He held a dark, familiar object in his hand.

A radio.

"I've been talking to Sarge," he said softly. Without breaking eye contact, he pushed a strand of hair behind my ear. "I think it would be good if he heard from you."

The drugs must've been wearing off, as there was a dull throbbing in my stomach that seemed to reverberate throughout my entire body. Still, I smiled and extended a hand for the radio.

After quickly explaining what buttons to push, Asher ducked out of the room. The sky was an inky black, almost velvety in appearance. The candles had long since burned out, leaving only the moon as light.

My heart hammering, I pressed down on the button Asher had indicated.

"Fallon?" I whispered, my voice cracking. I released the button immediately, my breath bated as I waited for him to respond.

There was a crackle of static followed by a disbelieving gasp and then, "Adelaide?"

"I'm here." Tears formed in my eyes, and my throat closed up. Emotions, some of them undefinable, battled within me. My hand was shaking as I held the radio to my lips. "I'm here. I'm okay."

There was a gasp. Something akin to a sob.

Was Fallon crying?

More tears trailed down my cheeks and landed on my dry lips. I licked them away, tasting salt.

"I'm so… I was so fucking worried."

"I know." And I did know. There was nothing Fallon hated more than being helpless. Than seeing the people he cared about in pain. "But I'm okay. Are you okay?"

"I'm with Tommy and Declan," he replied. "I'll make sure they're okay. And then we'll come home to you."

"Do you promise?" I hated how weak I sounded. How vulnerable. At that moment, I was nothing more than a forlorn child wanting confirmation that she was loved.

"Promise. I'll always come back to you, don't you know that?"

This time, I couldn't keep the sob from escaping. I brought my fist to my mouth to muffle the sound.

"I love you, Fallon." The confession escaped me before I could reel it in. And surprisingly, I didn't want to.

There was silence on the other side.

"I love you too."

"But I—"

"I know. I know. And it's okay. We'll figure it out together. All of us. But I have to go now, okay? I'll see you soon. I love you."

The radio slipped from my fingers, safely landing on the bed. Tears cascaded down my face, but they weren't tears of sadness. No, they were tears of happiness. I couldn't remember the last time I'd felt such contentment.

Not even the pain in my stomach could diminish the elation I felt.

"Addie!"

The bedroom door was thrown open, and Calax stood in the entryway.

"I just finished talking with Fallon." I nodded towards the radio. "I'm going—"

"No time." Before I could protest, Calax scooped me up in his arms. I cried out as pain speared my stomach. "We need to leave. Now."

I bit my lip to keep from crying out, but there was no denying the urgency in Calax's voice. The fear in his eyes. The panic.

"What's going on?" I asked through gritted teeth.

Holding me securely against his chest, Calax turned to face the closed door. From behind it, I could make out growls and shouts, steadily growing louder.

"Ragers. A whole bunch of them."

CHAPTER 24

DECLAN

*J*couldn't move. My feet were cemented to the ground, my body coiled tightly like a snake preparing to strike. The sun had disappeared behind the gray prison wall, and moonlight took its place. It illuminated the prison yard and the figures with jerky movements and grotesque skin that continued to amble in the gated confines.

My hands trembled.

What it came down to was whether or not I was ready to die. The longer I stood there, debating my options, the more gray the world became. My courage ebbed simultaneously with the sun lowering. What had I been thinking?

I took a tentative step forward.

"Why are you in a bad mood?" I signed to Addie as she entered the kitchen. Sweat coated her skin in a glossy sheen, and a few stray curls escaped her ponytail. Even with the scar on her face from that bitch, Liz, she was still the most beautiful woman I'd ever feasted my eyes upon. It was impossible for me to look away, as if she had her own magnetic orb. I was lost in her gaze.

"Fallon is an asshole," she replied, her hands moving rapidly to hint at her own agitation. I snorted but didn't contradict. Sarge was an asshole. No one could deny that.

"Why is he an asshole?" My lips curved upward instinctively. She was adorable all pissed off, though I doubted she would agree with such a sentiment. Like a puppy.

"He's making me exercise." Her face twisted in horror. "I don't exercise. Ever." Her hands dropped as she absentmindedly began to ramble about the dangers of working out. I could've sworn her lips said, "It makes my boobs sag."

But I could've been mistaken.

She paused suddenly, her lips clamping into a tight line. Her eyes flickered to the doorway that led to the backyard, and something akin to fear flashed in her gaze. Before I could inquire, she had thrown herself underneath the table and sidled to sit between my legs.

I froze, peering down at her with wide eyes. With the way she was positioned...

I shifted uncomfortably, praying she didn't see how hard I'd become. Fortunately, she remained blissfully oblivious to my predicament as she put a single finger to her red lips.

Raising my eyebrow in confusion—really, I should've just expected as much from that crazy female—I noticed a figure move in my peripheral vision.

Sarge entered the kitchen, eyes narrowing.

"Have you seen Adelaide?" *he asked.* "She ran out in the middle of training. Claimed that her boobs had come undone, whatever that meant."

I didn't even have to look to know that Addie would've been shaking her head rapidly beneath the table.

"No," *I signed, nodding towards the old newspaper in front of me.* "I've been reading."

Sarge glared, as if doubting my sincerity, before he stomped away.

I waited until he was out of sight before pulling up the table cloth and peering once more at Addie. Her hand was over her mouth as she restrained a giggle. Her eyes were alit with mirth.

Briefly, she rested her chin on my knee.

"My hero," *she said, moving her lips slowly enough for me to read. At this point, I was pretty sure I had those things memorized. When I dreamt, it was about those damn plush lips. What I wouldn't have given to taste them...*

Keeping my face impassive, I nodded.

"Always."

Always.

I was such a horrible liar.

There was a name for someone like me. Narcissist. Selfish.

I'd broken my promise. I'd left her after I'd promised to always be by her side. Maybe I hadn't said it in so many words, but I'd meant it. She was mine. After years of forced separation, I would never leave her side again.

But...

Groaning, I pulled at my dark hair. The physical pain somehow diminished my mental one. More. I needed more.

I took another step towards the large structure, knowing that I was both literally and figuratively walking to my death.

A hand clamped down on my shoulder, making me stagger back. Stunned, I turned to meet Sarge's burning eyes.

The car headlights switched on, illuminating his face.

"I knew I would find you here," *he signed. I watched his hands move in rapt fascination.*

"How?"

Nobody knew about this place. Nobody. I'd made sure that this—he—had remained a secret. It was my burden to shoulder alone. I couldn't discern if it was embarrassment or shame. After all, what type of person wanted to claim relation to an abusive, murderous asshole? Would they think we were one and the same, cut from the same tree or however that saying went?

"Did you believe I wouldn't do my research on the team?" *was his simple answer.*

I scoffed.

Of course he would. He was Sarge.

Two figures in the car captured my attention. Tommy I recognized straight away, but he was talking animatedly to an unfamiliar boy wearing thick, red headphones around his neck.

Nikolai.

He had the same bone structure and hair color as Addie.

I turned back towards Sarge.

"You found him? He's all right?"

His face softened as he nodded.

"He is. And I heard from Addie."

At those words, my body tensed. I scarcely believed it. Addie was dying. I'd seen the life drain from her eyes, had held her cold, icy hand in my own. Was he saying…?

"She's okay. Addie is okay." He took a step closer. "And she wants us to come home."

Addie was okay.

A weight from my chest was lifted at those words. It was as if I could finally breathe again, finally live.

Helplessly, I glanced once more at the prison. Sarge tapped my shoulder, redirecting my attention back to him. His eyes were very near pleading, something I was unfamiliar seeing on the apathetic team leader.

"She needs you. The team needs you. I know what you're thinking. I know that you want to get revenge on your father, but we both know that walking up there is a death sentence. Addie is waiting, and she loves you. Don't break her heart like this."

Tears blurred my vision.

Loved? She loved me?

Surely, Sarge was mistaken. She loved Calax and maybe even Ryder. Not me.

Never me.

It was a fantasy I used to have, though I never believed we would be the traditional couple. I had too many demons, too many jagged edges. She, on the other hand, was a bright fucking light. But I would've been the first to admit that if she was the sun, I was her shadow, following her to the end of the world like a diligent pup. Sometimes, when the darkness was too much for people to handle, they craved the light. It was a selfish mentality but undeniably true. I needed her because she was the light to my tarnished darkness.

I'd been horrible to her when we reconnected. It became clear that we behaved the worst to the people we loved because we knew they would never leave us. But god, she had come so close. More than once. With her, it felt like I could fall and always have someone at the bottom catching me.

"When have I ever lied to you?" Sarge snapped, easily reading the indecision and disbelief on my face.

Before I realized what was happening, I collapsed against him, sobbing. It wasn't a manly cry by any means. Oh no. It was a collection of snot and tears and gasps. Sarge remained rigid, unsure how to comfort me, before awkwardly patting my back.

I cried for Addie and all she'd endured.

I cried for my mom, choosing to live a life on the streets to feed her addiction. She'd chosen drugs over her own son. Over me.

I cried for my baby sister, whose life had been snuffed out too early.

And I cried for myself. The realization came crashing down on me, the onslaught bordering the precarious line between pain and relief.

I couldn't do it. I couldn't sacrifice my life for a twisted version of vengeance.

I'm so sorry, Allison.

Everything became simple. Black and white instead of a thousand shades of grey.

I was choosing Addie, as I'd done countless times before. And maybe, just maybe, she'd chosen me back.

ADDIE

Calax's arms were iron vises around me as he set the radio into my lap. I gripped it tightly in my hand. Distantly, I was aware of a screeching coming from outside the house. The sound was getting louder and louder with each passing second.

"They're here!" Ryder stood in the doorway, eyes wild and face ashen.

"What's going on?" I asked, anxiously glancing from face to face.

"Some asshole is driving a police car with the sirens blaring," Ryder said through clenched teeth. "It led the Ragers right to us."

Fear paralyzed me, sparking down my spine and to the toes of my feet.

"Who would do such a thing?" Either someone was an idiot or...this was intentional. But who? Questions assaulted me, but I knew now was not the time to get answers.

"Ronan and Asher are collecting more supplies from the hospital," Ryder informed us as we moved down the long hallway and to the staircase. "We'll meet them there. Tamson is starting the car. Doc and Kai are with him."

"Weapons?" Calax asked, hurrying his pace. The siren was just outside our house now, the sound very near deafening.

"None with me," Ryder replied briskly. Before anyone could say anything else, there was the sound of a window shattering. Fine particles of glass flung through the air, a few keen shards nicking my skin.

A Rager crawled through the window.

Its body held evidence of the recent surge of acid rain. Peeling skin, darkening to a sickly red color. Hair leaving its head in clumps. Brittle bone appearing at intermittent intervals throughout its body. It...or was it a he? His genitals were on full display, somehow demoting him from a monster to a human.

Ryder lunged, slamming into the Rager's deformed body and taking them both to the ground. His fingers dug into the creature's neck, loose skin breaking until the brittle, offset white bone was revealed. I turned my face into Calax's chest, resisting the urge to vomit, as the putrid stench of blood bombarded my senses.

The creature writhed and bucked beneath Ryder, but he held firm, never once removing his hands from the Rager's neck.

With a sudden burst of strength, the Rager shoved Ryder off of him. Blood and skin dribbled down his face as he leaned over my lover.

"No!" I screamed, voice a mere rasp. At the noise, the creature's feral gaze whipped in my direction. There was nothing remotely human in his red, pinprick eyes. He was a shell of a man. The monster had completely overtaken him. I was wrong in my initial assessment. Not a he. An it.

Ryder used its distraction to slide out from underneath, crawling towards the door. There was an ugly gash in his chest that hadn't been there before, but otherwise, he looked relatively unharmed.

"Shit," Calax murmured, arms tightening around me. He took a step backwards, eyes locked on the creature…

Until a rough hand grabbed at us from behind. Calax let out a curse, shielding my body more firmly with his own. The new Rager clambered through the broken window, clawed hand snaring Calax's shirt. Another one appeared over her shoulder, this one just as grotesque as all the others. More and more were invading the house, circling us like we were prey and they were the hunters. I supposed it wasn't an inaccurate analogy.

There were too many of them.

Too few of us.

I could hear the car start from nearby, and I prayed that Tamson had made it to safety. It was a futile prayer, but a prayer nonetheless.

"We need to go!" Ryder shouted. He stood behind the throng of Ragers, fists raised as he prepared to fight.

But there were just too many. Swarming us. Surrounding us. Gnawing at us. Calax let out a scream as a Rager bit down on his arm, blood spewing from his mouth. I gagged at the pungent copper scent.

I could see the exact moment that he came to the same conclusion I had. His brow had been furrowed, but just then, it smoothed over. His eyes turned warm as they traced my face.

"I love you so much, baby girl," he whispered, brushing his lips against my forehead. I trembled in his arms, the realization that we were going to die drowning me. I wanted to check out, to mentally leave this horrible place, but I couldn't leave Calax alone. At the end, we only had each other.

The rest of the world fell away—the Ragers' inarticulate cries, Ryder's scream of agony, the car engine only a wall away. Nothing mattered but the arms of my first love.

We'd survived so much together. Our lives were forever interwoven. He held a piece of my heart in his large, calloused hands, and I held a piece of his. They may have been broken individually, but together, they became whole.

"I love you too," I whispered, knowing that those would be the last words I ever said. I could only hope that the others would forgive me, forgive us, when all was said and done. Hopelessness settled over me, over us, like a death shroud. My heart was beating so rapidly, it sounded like a snare drum in my ears.

Steely determination crossed Calax's face, and his arms tightened around me. Before I realized what was happening, we were moving.

The Ragers clawed at us, their fingers gnarled, keen knives. Calax bellowed in agony, but still he continued to trudge forward. Before I could blink, before I could beg, I was flying through the air. That was the only word I could think to describe it.

My body soared, slamming into Ryder's a few feet away. Agony speared my stomach as my stitches came undone, and blood seeped through my new shirt.

And...

"Calax!" I screamed, scrambling to my feet. Ryder immediately picked me up bridal style, turning towards the doorway.

But I still saw.

I saw the Ragers converging on a fallen figure, tearing through his flesh. I saw the tip of his brown boot, now soaked with blood. I heard his anguished screams as the monsters ate away at his flesh.

"Calax!" I screamed hysterically. Ignoring the pain, I bucked against Ryder's hold. Pounded on his chest. Sobbed. Begged. "Calax! We have to get Calax! We have to go back!"

His face was pained, tears forming in his golden-brown eyes. He finally met my gaze, even as he carried me farther and farther away.

"There's nothing we can do," he whispered.

I refused to believe that. Calax needed me, needed us. He had to be okay. He just had to. The alternative was too horrible to even consider.

I was screaming, agony piercing my chest as my heart broke into thousands of pieces. I struggled futilely against Ryder's hold, Calax's screams still haunting me.

No. No. No.

"Calax!" I screamed into the night sky. "Calax!"

Darkness crept along the edges of my vision. Blood soaked through my hands that were now resting on my stomach. I didn't care about the pain. When more Ragers ran towards the house, bypassing both Ryder and me, I realized that Calax wasn't coming out.

"CALAX!"

Darkness consumed me.

CHAPTER 25

ADDIE

*T*here was a lake I used to visit.

Perhaps 'lake' was too strong of a term for the diminutive pool of water. Big enough to fit the occasional speedboat. Small enough where you were easily able to see the opposite shoreline. It glistened in the sunlight, tiny crystal beads, and gently crested against the grassy shoreline. The air had been thinner there. Fresher. With the serene water rippling in tandem with each passing boat, I'd felt nothing but tranquility standing on the shore. Grass tickled my toes, and my hair carried in the breeze.

Couples often visited this particular shoreline. Dancing in the firelight. Kissing. Laughing.

Free.

Just like the water.

It was one of my happy places, that lake, with the throng of trees and rows of immaculate mansions stretching the shoreline. The beach had barely any sand. Instead, grass and dirt greeted my bare feet. It was this image, this calm pool of water, that helped me fabricate my mental garden, the garden I'd created inside of my mind in order to survive.

My mental garden was actually a combination of many locations. The old house I'd visited with Ducky. The pond behind Calax's apartment building. The schoolyard.

I went there then as Ryder held me tightly in his arms, shielding my body with his own. I barely processed when he laid me down on the backseat of the car, screaming directions up to Tamson. I heard Doc's voice, and then felt hands press down on my bleeding stomach. I felt that all before I drifted away.

In my garden, there was a simple stone bench beneath a white painted archway. Flowers and vines climbed up the sides, intricate patterns that combined perennials with blood red tulips and purple violets. The odd combination was almost ethereal in beauty.

Peace.

I felt peace in my garden.

But all good things couldn't last.

As I watched the frosted waves, I became aware of a figure moving to sit beside me on the stone bench. His body emitted heat, and I yearned to sink into his embrace. I hadn't even realized I was cold until I came face to face with a human furnace.

"What are you doing here?" Calax asked softly. I absently brushed my fingers over a silky rose petal. It was beginning to wilt and decay. Everything had an expiration date.

Everything died.

"It's better in here than out there," I responded. The real world. My own personal hell.

"So you're just retreating?" he asked in disbelief.

"Are you dead?" I countered.

His face turned contemplative. His hand snaked up to rub at his scruffy jaw.

"You keep me alive," he said after an agonizingly long moment of silence. I snorted.

No, I had most definitely *not* kept him alive.

"I like this place," I said, changing the subject. "You're here with me."

"Always."

He leaned forward, resting his elbows on his jean-clad legs. I was once again struck by how handsome he was. With his shock of dark hair framing an arresting, chiseled face, he was the epitome of perfection.

And he was mine.

"Why did you sacrifice yourself for me?" I whispered, the words catching in my throat. I tried to hold back the sob that threatened to escape. "Why?"

That was the question for all things in life—why?

Why did Calax have to die?

Why did I have to live?

Why? Why? Why?

"I don't want to live without you." These words were a broken plea. Salty tears dripped down my cheeks. Pain. Pain everywhere. All I'd ever known was pain. I'd hoped I could leave my love behind like breadcrumbs for him to follow home. But what if love wasn't enough? Love couldn't conquer death, no matter how much we wished otherwise. We could weave stories of friendships and families, of love and pain, but there was always something that trumped it. The ominous death hung over us like a bloated storm cloud threatening to expel its contents.

"I know, baby girl. I know. But you're going to have to wake up now. The others need you."

"No!" I answered instantly, clutching at his large bicep. I wanted to mold my body into his. I wanted us to become one. "I'm not leaving you."

"Don't let my sacrifice be in vain. I love you too much for that. Wake up."

I was sobbing now, unashamed by my show of emotion. How did he expect me to go on? To pretend that everything was okay, and I wasn't falling apart at the seams? This was how you could die while still breathing. A broken heart hurt worse than thousands of gunshots to the stomach.

Calax cupped my face tenderly and pressed his lips against mine. It was a slow kiss, different from any other I'd ever experienced before. I trembled once in his arms.

"I love you," I whispered.

"Wake up for me."

Wake up.

Wake up.

And I woke up.

EPILOGUE

CALAX

*V*oices.

Some indistinct murmurs. Some louder.

None of them were hers.

"The girl here?" This voice sounded just over my head.

Was I dying? Was this death?

"That's a negative. Look at this fuck. Is he still alive?" Somebody touched my neck.

"Barely. Think we should have Michaels check him over?"

"If he knows where the girl is…"

The voices trailed off, and I mercifully drifted back to sleep.

~

I AWOKE to someone touching me. Poking me.

Pain. Agonizing pain.

A scream escaped my lips before I could smother it.

"Shut him up, will ya?"

My eyes were blurry, barely able to focus, but they did latch onto a figure leaning over me. White lab coat. Gray hair. A doctor.

And behind him?

Two masked figures.

One a lion. One a plain white mask with red eyes.

I struggled to hold onto consciousness, but it pulled me under. Frankly, it was better than the pain.

So much pain.
Pain.
Darkness.

BONUS SCENE

Fuck! Fuck! Fuck!

I could hear the footsteps getting louder, taunting me. A form of cruel, cruel torment. The pounding of my heart seemed to echo around me as I waited with bated breath for the cacophony of noise, for the men to realize we were here and rage at us.

What would they do to Addie?

Think, Tamson. Think.

An idea occurred to me with the intensity of a whip striking at the skin of my back. A rock settled in my gut at the knowledge of what I had to do.

It was inevitable we would be discovered, but maybe...

Maybe I could reason with them. Play their sick game.

I clenched my jaw tightly before spinning towards Addie, moving her so she was flush against the wall. Hating myself a little more with every passing second, I pressed down on her shoulders, forcing her to her knees.

Please forgive me.

Confusion and fear splayed across her face, clear for everyone to see. Fortunately, it would help sell the story, though my stomach twisted into thousands of intricate knots with the knowledge that fear was directed at me.

But I was good at hiding my anguish, my pain. Great at it, even.

Bile rushed up my throat like lava in a volcano, just waiting to erupt, as I tangled my hands in her hair and pressed her face to my crotch. My cock instantly hardened —a fact I hated myself for—as she stared up at me through thick, sooty lashes. The fear on her face transformed into confusion, though she didn't pull away. She didn't fight me.

Just on time, the bathroom door was kicked in and the room became engulfed in bright yellow light from the newcomer's flashlight. Addie flinched, struggling to get to her feet, but I kept my hands in her hair as I surveyed the man who found us, willing my face to remain cold and indifferent.

The only way to save Addie's life was to pretend I hated her, that my heart didn't beat solely for her. That I didn't love her fiercely, intensely, with every bit of darkness and light within me.

The man was dressed entirely in black armor, a similarly colored visor obscuring his features from view. He slowly removed his helmet, revealing a face hardened by age and this new, dangerous world we'd found ourselves in. Maybe, at one point, he'd been a good man. A husband and father, perhaps, but there was now nothing but malicious glee in his cold, dark eyes.

Hungry eyes.

Fuck.

He stared at Addie as if she was something to be possessed, as if he could hunt her down and claim her.

But if there was one thing I knew about predators…

There was always someone bigger, stronger, faster, deadlier.

This time, that person had to be me.

I removed my grip from Addie's disheveled hair, making a show of zipping up my pants.

"Do you mind?" I demanded, glaring at the newcomer. My tone could've been hewn from pure ice.

I could hear Addie scrambling to her feet behind me, and then I felt warm air on my neck as she stared at the intruder. Her breath hitched, but I willed her to stay quiet. Submissive.

He leered in her direction, hunger dancing in his eyes, and it only exacerbated my rage. I could already see all of his twisted desires, and the need to protect Addie was the only thing keeping me remotely sane at the moment. All I wanted to do was wrap my hands around the man's neck and squeeze, which was a strange sensation coming from me. I'd never been the violent type before.

But maybe this world had changed me as well, made me into something, *someone*, I barely recognized.

"Who are you folks?" the man questioned, finally peeling his gaze away from Addie. He probably saw how close I was to breaking his neck.

I huffed out a bark of laughter. "She doesn't matter. I'm Tamson."

Don't pay attention to her. Don't notice her.

Focus on me.

Addie tensed behind me, but I willed myself not to react. I had to pretend that she didn't matter, that she was just another whore, or else this man would really take an interest in her. Already, I could see him dismissing her as nothing more than a used-up slut.

Good.

If he knew that I loved her…

Horror, darker than sticky tar, infiltrated my system, sluicing through my veins.

I couldn't let that happen. I would die before I allowed him or any of his friends to touch her.

Addie must've come to some sort of conclusion. Out of the corner of my eye, I watched her lower her head and take a tentative step closer.

Good girl.

Was it wrong that arousal flooded my system at her submissive posture? Probably, but I was suddenly bombarded with ideas for the bedroom. There weren't many girls who liked to be dominated the way I preferred, and the thought of Addie—

Focus, Tamson.

I snaked an arm out to wrap around her waist, the move decidedly possessive.

"Say hi to the man," I instructed her in an indolent drawl. When she remained silent, no doubt confused as fuck, I slapped her tight ass. Not hard, despite the deafening sound, but enough to have my cock twitch and to get the point across.

Play along, Addie. Just for now.

But please don't hate me.

"Hi," she mumbled, keeping her eyes averted.

The man laughed gruffly. "You have that bitch wrapped around your finger," he noted with approval. Maybe even a little admiration and jealousy.

And I'll have your intestines wrapped around my finger when I kill you.

I shrugged, trying to ignore the violent direction of my thoughts.

"Wasn't hard. Promised her protection in exchange for her obedience. Isn't that right, Flower?" I didn't wait to see if she acknowledged me, instead addressing the man once more. "How did you know where we were?" I tightened my arm around Addie almost imperceptibly as the old fucker licked his chapped lips.

"I'm not an idiot like the others. I knew there was someone here with us." He shrugged. "Now comes the important question—what to do with the two of you?"

Addie froze once more, and though I wanted to calm her, comfort her, I couldn't risk him seeing. Instead, I forced my body to relax and flashed the man a smile. Maybe if he thought I wanted to join their group...

I sifted through idea after idea before deciding to play to his ego, to ask for help, to make him think I wanted to join his sick group.

"Others? We've been wandering alone for a few days now. Maybe you could use an extra set of hands?" I squeezed Addie's hips, drawing his attention to my hand on her flesh. I hated the way he looked at her, but I had to sell it. I had to get him to somewhat trust me, a stranger, if I was gonna get us out of here. "Or we can make a trade," I continued. "I'm sure you have a bunch of supplies. Maybe even some weapons? I think we could come to an agreement."

And just as I expected, the man grinned, believing that I didn't care about the woman in my arms, that I'd be willing to sell her to get what I wanted. That trust...

It would make him weak. Stupid.

Just the way I wanted.

Hook. Line. And sinker.

THE MONSTERS WE HUNT

TOGETHER WE FALL BOOK 4

PROLOGUE

CALAX

The dream started off as it always did.

 I sat on the bed in my apartment, my back against the headboard, as indecipherable voices reached me.

Shutting the book I was reading, I moved stealthily towards the door. The voices were louder now, but their words were still indistinct.

"Hello?" I asked. Slowly, with bated breath, I pushed the door open and stepped into my living room.

My heart was hammering inside my chest, each heartbeat threatening to be my last. That was what fear could do to you. It was an all-consuming, all-encompassing type of terror. A double-edged sword waiting to fall. A mosquito sitting on your bare arm but never biting. Nails scraping against a coffin seven feet under.

"Hello?" I repeated.

Was it *them*? I didn't want to see them, see their masks. They were the prime instigators of my fear, though I would never admit that aloud. Instead, I shoved it in a box under lock and key and buried said box miles beneath cement.

"Callie!" a familiar voice cooed. The fear dissipated instantly, a flame being blown out, and I found that I could breathe again. The clenching of my heart ebbed as suddenly as it had arrived. My lungs, which had once been unable to take in air, now greedily lapped up all the air they could.

Hearing her, seeing her, was like stepping in front of a fire after days in a blizzard.

Addie's brown hair was cascading around her shoulders, and her eyes twinkled as if she was in the know of a secret.

The scar from her confrontation with Liz still marred her beautiful face, but she was whole and alive. It was all I could ask of her.

"Baby," I whispered reverently, scooping her into my arms. Her head nestled beneath my chin, and I held her tighter, my arms iron vises around her tiny, slender frame. "I miss you, baby." My voice was a hushed murmur.

"I know."

"I love you so damn much. Do you know that?"

I needed her to hear it, to understand, to feel the love that seemed to seep out of my every pore.

"I love you too." She nuzzled my cheek with her own. "And that's why you have to hold on. You have to fight, Callie. Fight for me. Fight for us. I'll come for you."

"Promise?" I hated how my voice broke, the tiniest of trembles that hinted at what I wanted to remain hidden behind an apathetic front.

Her smile was sincere, reaching her eyes, when she gazed up at me through her fringe of black lashes.

"I promise. You own me, Calax. Heart, body, and mind. You're mine, and I'm yours."

Mine.

That word reverberated through my head long after I woke up.

~

IT WASN'T OFTEN I felt pain.

They tried, but I'd learned how to bury it. The pain, that was. Bury it beneath layer upon layer of sand and cement until it was nearly unrecognizable.

But pain? It crept up on you when you least expected it. That monster lurking beneath your bed, waiting for the moment you fell asleep.

"Where is she?" This was his only question. Never *"How was your day, Calax?"* or *"How are you feeling?"*

The demand, the question, would float through one ear and out the other.

I would stubbornly face the wall, eyes fixated on my reflection in the mirror. My hair was greasy and disheveled, and a beard covered the lower half of my face, a tangled mane.

It wasn't often that they allowed me to bathe, so I was sure I smelled something awful.

The pain that had once dominated me had since diminished. They put me through surgery after surgery after surgery until I was sure I resembled Frankenstein's monster.

They said it made me whole, but without Adelaide, I was a broken man. A shell of who I once was. A statue that had been dropped one too many times.

But I never told them. They could hurt me, they could cause agonizing pain, but my lips never spilled the secret they so desperately desired.

They might have saved me, but that didn't ensure my loyalty. Only one person had it, along with my heart and soul.

Until the day I died, the day they killed me, they would never get any information about Adelaide.

CHAPTER 1

ADDIE

*I*f I were a superhero, my power would be accidentally crushing balls.

How did one accidentally crush balls?

Talent, my friends. Pure, undiluted talent.

"Shit!" I cursed, scrambling towards a kneeling, groaning Asher. His hands were protectively cupping the front of his pants, eyes anguished. "I meant to aim for your head."

"How the fuck did your fist miss my head and hit my dick?"

Well, when he put it like that…

"I'm sorry, Ashy," I cooed, taking a step towards him. His blond hair, now shoulder length, glinted in the waning sunlight and highlighted the fireworks of lighter blue in his eyes.

At my gentle tone, his head snapped up, and his expression softened.

"I'm not mad, sweet girl. I'm just…in pain." He dramatically rolled onto his back, legs and arms sprawled. I moved to lay beside him and rested my head on his chest. His arm wrapped around me, holding me close.

The house we'd found ourselves in was a small, bungalow style building with decaying hanging plants and shrubs riddled with bugs. While it wasn't aesthetically pleasing, it had two fences blocking it from the outside world, protecting us from the monsters roaming the streets.

It had been three months since we'd left Elena's house. Three months, one week, five days.

An eternity.

Three months, one week, and five days since I'd last seen three of my men and Tommy.

Calax, with his broad shoulders and cropped black hair, his rough and surly exterior contradicting the gentle giant underneath.

Declan, my childhood best friend and one of the men I loved.

Fallon, the appointed leader of our group.

Tommy, the boy I'd deemed as my younger brother. He and Nik held that role in my heart.

Gone. Missing.

Dead.

I didn't want to start thinking of that, of them, because I knew if I did, I would start spiraling into a pit of depression, an abyss of despair.

Rolling over, I leveled Asher with my best glare.

"Again."

"Again?" He rolled onto his elbows, the movement causing his shirt to roll up. I'd chosen not to be intimate with any of my loves until we were all reunited, and they respected that decision. However, Asher was making it quite difficult.

His muscles were more defined from our long and extensive workout sessions. With his light blond scruff and golden hair, he was almost too handsome for his own good.

"Sweetheart, we've been doing these drills for a few hours now. You're exhausted."

Even before he finished speaking, I was already fisting my hands and bouncing on the balls of my feet. Asher watched me warily. Cautiously.

"You can't keep working yourself this hard," he continued. "It's not good for you."

"What's not good is being a liability. Being weak." My stomach twisted at that word. It had been my weakness, my inability to fight, that caused me to be kidnapped by Liz, Ryder's ex-girlfriend. It had been my weakness that caused me to get shot, leaving behind scars that went far beyond the one on my stomach.

And because I'd been shot, we'd been trapped in Elena's house when the Ragers arrived.

Killing Calax.

Tears burned my eyes, the mere memory equivalent to a knife twisting in my heart.

The world had ended, ravaged by natural disasters and zombie-like monsters, but Calax's death had been the thing to end *me*.

Asher was saved from responding by the back door opening and closing.

"Kitten, it's time for dinner," a melodic voice said.

Ryder leaned against the porch railing, the epitome of calm.

The man was beautiful, sexy, with dark skin and cropped black hair. Tattoos lined his muscular forearms, currently bare with his red tank top.

"We'll be done in an hour, then we'll head in," I said, turning back towards Asher. I heard Ryder's heavy, resigned sigh.

"Addie, no." Asher's cadence, from his voice to his face, was stern. When he got like that, there was no talking him out of it.

Reining in my irritation, I snapped, "Fine."

I knew I was being a bitch, a brat, but I couldn't stop myself. Ever since that fatal night, when I witnessed Calax getting swarmed by Ragers, my emotions were too raw. Too real. I was a semi truck powering ahead at full speed, never stopping, even with a brick wall fast approaching.

And Fallon and Declan...

The two of them had taken an improvised trip, but we had no way of getting in contact with them when we had to hastily leave. The one radio we'd owned had been left behind...and destroyed.

We'd waited for weeks in the town for them, but they never arrived. Either we'd missed their return, or something had happened to them. I prayed that it was the former.

Maybe they were fine. Maybe they'd found another girl to love, to cherish, to protect. I would be fine with that if it meant they were alive.

After the allotted time had passed, we'd traveled to Nikolai's house to try and find them. Instead of my lovers and little brother, we found a massacre of dead bodies and bloodstained walls.

Did it make me a horrible person that I felt relief when I realized not one of those bodies belonged to the people I loved?

It was on our way back, retracing the trail to Elena's house and leaving cryptic messages for the guys to find, that we found the enclosed house with distressed wood and a dilapidated roof. Still, it protected us from Ragers and the elements.

Shouldering past Ryder, I entered the sparsely lit kitchen. There was no electricity, so we had to rely on candles.

Ronan's broad, bare back was illuminated in the flickering flame. He had lighter skin than his half-brother, Ryder, a light mocha. He, too, was covered in tattoos, the most prominent one being a white unicorn on his chest.

His back was to me as he sang beneath his breath, dancing to a tune only he could hear. He poured something into a bowl and spun in a circle before reaching for a spice jar on the rack.

I watched him silently for a moment, aware that both Asher and Ryder were struggling to hold in their laughter. After a moment, I said, "You're such a dork, Ro."

He spun wildly, eyes widening, before a teasing grin crossed his handsome face.

"Yes, but I'm your dork, Princess."

I hated when he called me that.

I may have been a princess in his eyes, but I wore a crown of prickly thorns and my kingdom was a graveyard.

Still, I flashed him the smile I knew he wanted to see before wrapping my arms around him. He hugged me back immediately, bending down to kiss my forehead with a loud, exaggerated smack.

"Gross."

The deadpan voice came from behind me. I knew, without even looking, that it would belong to a man in his mid-thirties with dark hair and eyes that seemed to be perpetually amused.

"Crawl out of your anthill, Doc?" I asked with feigned sweetness.

Ignoring me, he stepped farther into the kitchen and peered at the bowl in front of Ronan. His nose crinkled in distaste, skin between his brows furrowing.

"Ew."

With that proclamation, he sat at the table like the condescending asswipe he was.

Doc was, as the namesake suggested, a doctor who'd saved me after I had been shot. Of course, he was halfway behind it. He'd been part of the rival group who's member had shot me before we kidnapped him.

Yup. Kidnapped.

We were apparently doing that now.

Speaking of kidnapped victims…

Kai stepped into the kitchen, stretching his arms over his head.

Honestly, I didn't know what Ronan and Ryder were thinking when they brought him here. They'd claimed it was momentary insanity.

"Morning, ladies," he chirped. Yup. He was one of those people, you know the type—always happy and smiling and stabbing people.

"It's seven at night, dumbass," Ronan snapped. My green-haired leprechaun was not a fan of Kai.

"Semantics."

He moved to the table and sat beside Doc, two outsiders staring through a glass window at the rest of us. Only, after three months, they weren't outsiders. Not anymore. They weren't a part of my "harem," as Doc so eloquently liked to point out, but I didn't hate them. Doc and Kai were the two older brothers I never had and never knew I wanted.

And of course, I didn't miss the looks they sent each other when they thought no one was looking.

"Dinner is served, *ma chérie*," Ronan said, placing the bowl on the table. It appeared to be some type of cold stew and a loaf of bread. In the world we lived in now, it was the equivalent of a five-star meal.

Smiling at his over-the-top antics, I surveyed the room once more.

"Where's Tamson?" I asked. His red-brown hair was noticeably absent.

When no one replied, I felt panic unfurl in my gut.

"Guys, where is he?" My hands gripped the back of the dining room chair, painfully aware that not one of the guys was making eye contact with me.

"He went on a supply run, Princess," Ronan said soothingly. He took a step forward, but I automatically stepped away.

"By himself?" I hated how my voice came out as a screech. "No! He can't be by himself! What if something happened to him? What if he doesn't come back? Oh god…"

I collapsed onto the ground, my legs unable to keep me up, to keep me balanced. The world was spinning, rotating on its axis, and I couldn't hold on. The ground continually opened its gaping maws to swallow me whole, dragging me into the dark abyss I knew awaited a broken, rotten girl like myself.

"Addie, he'll be fine," Ryder said, trying to comfort me, but I shoved his hand away. They always did that—comforted me—as if their entire world hadn't also been destroyed at the same time mine had.

They were brothers in the truest sense of the word. Kinship and fidelity was a choice, one they made, and they'd created ties that could not be severed by the sharpest of knives. While some may have looked at their team as a burdened obligation, a weight on their shoulders, my men saw it as an opportunity to make a family, a family they'd lacked. Falling in love with me only fortified that bond instead of breaking it apart.

Losing Calax, Fallon, and Declan was just one of many tragedies. Our lives were a myriad of them.

I knew they could feel their lost brethren's absence as keenly as I could.

I hated how often I fell apart, how grief had shattered the last of my sensibilities. I needed my men with me, all of them, or else I would lose myself completely. I couldn't fathom a world without them in it, but unfortunately, I had to.

Every. Single. Day.

I was sobbing, whispering inarticulate phrases, when strong arms wrapped around me. Without even opening my eyes, I knew the man holding me was Tamson.

"It's okay," he whispered into my hair, voice hoarse. "It's okay, my love. I'm sorry I'm late. I'm sorry."

And I continued to cry, arms wrapped around his waist, as indecipherable apologies escaped my lips. Apologies for being weak and desperate. Apologies for reverting back to the scared little girl they'd met at the resort.

Apologies for forcing them to love a broken girl.

TAMSON

After her heartbreaking sobs receded and she descended into unconsciousness, I remained holding her. In the months since Calax's death, her body was thinner, weaker, despite the many hours she spent fighting. She never ate, barely slept, and could only last a few hours at most without one of us with her.

We didn't mind, but we hated how this was slowly breaking her, chipping away the girl we loved more than anything else.

"She asleep?" Asher asked, voice tired.

"Yeah." I kept my voice low so as to not wake the sleeping beauty. She needed sleep desperately if the bags beneath her eyes were any indication.

"She's getting worse," Ronan mused, running his fingers through his green-tipped hair. The bastard had found a can of hair dye during one of our supply runs and had insisted on maintaining the green streaks. For Addie, who had a strange fascination with his hair. He, of course, was willing to oblige. Anything to see that smile on her angelic, heart-shaped face.

Addie's behavior was troubling, to say the least. She was consistently cloaked in a shadow of pain and grief. Her haunted eyes were a testament to all she had endured.

"It's depression, dumbasses." Unsurprisingly, the cocky voice came from Doc. At his words, all of our heads snapped in his direction. He was languidly leaning back in his chair, sipping a mug of cold coffee. If he was perturbed by our undivided attention, he didn't show it.

Ryder's voice was scathing when he spoke next. "We know what the hell it is. What can we do to help her?"

"Euthanasia might be beneficial," he drawled. And that did it. Before we could stop him, Ryder charged towards the doctor, hands extended as if he meant to strangle him. Kai stood up automatically, and both Ronan and Asher moved to restrain the prowling beast that had replaced our friend. Ryder's eyes were positively livid, a monster emerging from the dark depths.

"Say that again. I fucking dare you," he hissed darkly. He bucked once against the hands holding him back before reluctantly moving to kneel beside Addie. His hand gripped hers as if she were his life preserver while he was adrift at sea.

Doc sighed heavily, folding his hands over his stomach. "There's not much you can do, boys," he admitted seriously. "Before the world went to shit, I would've recommended a therapist and some medicine, but now? Just continue loving her."

Ronan released a humorless laugh. "That's what we've been doing, asshole. But she's still hurting, still grieving, and nothing we do can stop that."

"You're right," Doc agreed, surprisingly amicable. "That girl there is a volcano seconds from exploding. Right now, she's merely spitting out tiny bits of lava here and there. Nothing that can destroy a town or kill a community. But soon, that volcano is going to erupt and everyone will be a casualty. It's not going to be pretty."

Asher's nails dug into his palms as he faced down the devil himself, the bane of our existence. I didn't care that Doc had saved Addie's life once upon a time. He was an asshole through and through. No amount of pretty, poetic metaphors and comparisons would change that fact.

"Fine. Ignore my ramblings. I only had, like, ten plus years of medical training, but it's fine. Ignore the truth of what needs to be done with that girl of yours and watch what happens. It's not you she's going to hurt in that inevitable explosion, but herself."

I was seething, a red fog obscuring my vision. If I didn't have Addie in my arms, I would've lunged towards the pompous asshole and tore his tongue out of his mouth. What he was implying…

I knew Addie was hurting, hurting deeply, but she wouldn't resort to physically harming herself, would she?

The mere thought had me tightening my arms around her tiny form, almost imperceptibly.

Without another word, I gracefully rose to my feet, still holding Addie. Her head was tucked beneath my chin, and I couldn't help but pepper a couple of kisses on her forehead.

Moving swiftly, not trusting myself to stay in the same room as Doc McStuffins without maiming him, I stepped into my bedroom and placed Addie on the bed.

She looked so peaceful when she slept. Regal, almost. A princess—no, a queen in the flesh. She hated when Ronan used that nickname because she no longer saw herself as someone worthy of carrying a crown. She often compared herself to a prickly thorn, and a part of me wanted to agree with her.

But like with anything as beautiful as a rose, the pain inflicted was worth the inevitable end. I would hold a thousand thorny stems just to feast my eyes upon her beauty.

I removed her shoes and socks rhythmically, lost in my own thoughts.

I hated to see her hurting. She'd always been an abnormally strong woman, but there was only so much she could take.

Had this finally been her breaking point?

No, I couldn't believe that. She was still walking and smiling. Laughing and teasing. Her episodes were getting less and less frequent with time.

And her pain now didn't compare to the month directly following Calax's death and our other two members' disappearances. It didn't even scratch the surface.

My heart gave a painful throb when I visualized her sobbing into her pillow, terrible, desperate sounds that pierced me like thousands of knives.

My own grief clogged my airway, my lungs, but combined with hers, it was almost unimaginable.

Shaking my head to clear the memory, I pulled back the blankets and crawled in beside her. She made a happy sound, immediately curling her body around my own.

"We'll get through this," I promised resolutely. I pressed my lips to the crown of her head and allowed them to linger. "We'll all get through this."

CHAPTER 2

ADDIE

*L*ight streamed through the open window, burning my eyes. It highlighted the human-sized indent, still warm, beside me. The body it belonged to was noticeably absent, but I didn't allow panic to claim me as it had last night, especially when a lilting, raspy laugh ascended from the kitchen downstairs.

He was safe. They were safe.

I repeated that mantra in my head as I rolled out of bed, grimacing at the dirty clothes still on me from yesterday.

My panic attacks were getting worse. I'd never considered myself a needy, clingy girlfriend, but now the mere thought of being away from my men for an extended period of time sent me into a raging panic. The turmoil unfurled in my stomach, a tumultuous mixture of trepidation and anxiety. I'd already lost so much.

My brother. My parents.

Calax, Declan, and Fallon.

I wouldn't survive anything else. I knew that as surely as I knew my first name.

Frowning, I grabbed a change of clothes from the dresser and moved towards the bathroom. There was no running water, but one of the guys, probably Ryder, had carried up five buckets of rainwater. The cold water bit at my skin like keen knives, but it felt good to be clean.

After scrubbing myself thoroughly and using the water on my hair, I stepped out of the shower and grabbed my fluffy, white towel.

Only to realize that I wasn't alone.

Ronan sat on the bathroom sink, preoccupied with one of the radios we'd uncovered. We had hoped to use it to get in contact with our missing teammates, but none of us knew how to get to a frequency Declan and Fallon would be able to hear on their radio. Instead, we used the radios to communicate with each other when we were scavenging supplies or traveling to the next town over. Kai and Doc both had one as well. Mine was always on my bedside table unless I was leaving the house.

"We're going to have to make another supply run today, Princess," Ronan said, still staring intently at the grey box in his hands. "Go to the usual spots before the next storm...whenever the hell that may be. We wanted to give you a heads-up. Ryder will stay with you, but we'll check in every hour and be home tonight before dinner."

"I want to come with," I said automatically.

His eyes flickered upwards with almost lazy disinterest, no doubt to reprimand me, when they froze. That lazy disinterest turned into smoldering heat, need, and want, all wrapped up in an enticing package. He swallowed, his Adam's apple bobbing.

"Christ, Princess, why don't you have a towel around you?"

I shrugged nonchalantly. "You distracted me."

His eyes ravenously traced my every curve. The supple mounds of my breasts and peaked nipples. The shaved hair down below. The water running in rivulets between my breasts and down to my stomach.

"Shit," Ronan cursed. He did nothing to hide the prominent tent in his pants.

I would've been the first to admit that I wasn't sexually on the same page with all of the men. With some, I'd done nothing more than share a few stolen kisses. With others, we'd touched each other in our most intimate spots. It wasn't because I didn't want to, I did, but I knew that different men needed different types of affection.

I hadn't even kissed Ronan yet, and I knew I needed to rectify that situation.

Crossing the distance to him, I stood in front of my tattooed, green-haired leprechaun.

"You're so beautiful, Addie," he whispered reverently, and I melted. I stood on my tiptoes, my eyes traveling over his high cheekbones and dimpled cheeks. With bated breath, I closed the distance between us.

The second my lips would've touched his, Ronan backed away. His eyes were wide, wild, feverish, but his voice was clear.

"Are you sure?"

"What?"

Self-consciousness reverberated through me. I'd just thrown myself at Ronan, a man who admittedly had his fair share of females, and he'd rejected me. I never thought I would feel vulnerable with any of my men, but standing naked in front of Ronan, I wanted nothing more than to turn into a liquid puddle under his penetrating gaze.

"It's just..." He agitatedly ran a hand through his hair. "You've been so sad, baby. I don't want our first kiss to be something you'll regret."

"You think I'll regret kissing you?" I couldn't keep the hurt out of my voice.

"Shit! That's not what I meant." He stared at me for a long moment, love and warmth emanating from his eyes. Still, all the love in the world couldn't pacify my roiling emotions.

I felt like such an idiot.

"Get dressed and come to your room," he said finally. With one last glance in my direction, carefully perusing every inch of my bare skin with his heated eyes, he stepped out of the room and closed the door behind him.

Alone.

I felt nothing but numb. That numbness clambered from the tips of my fingers to my heart, squeezing it in iron claws.

Rejection.

It was an emotion capable of killing you.

Robotically, I dressed in a pair of leggings and a sweater. My hand trembled as I combed through my brown tresses.

I was an idiot. An absolute idiot.

I had stupidly assumed that Ronan felt for me the way I did him, but when had he ever said anything about having feelings for me like that? When had he ever given any indication that he wanted to kiss me?

He watched once, when Ryder ate my pussy, his hand stroking his brown cock. Maybe it was a one-time encounter. Maybe he'd lost himself in the moment.

Tears burning my eyes, I stepped out of the bathroom and into the connecting bedroom.

The first thing I noticed was that all of my blankets had been removed from my bed. The second thing I noticed was that those same blankets had been haphazardly thrown over chairs and my desk to create a makeshift fort.

My throat closed with emotion, the fort reminiscent of the one I'd made for Ronan so many months ago.

The man in question poked his head out, smiling sheepishly up at me.

"In this fort, the outside world doesn't exist. It's only me and you. You and me. Us against everything." Lowering his voice melodramatically, he added, "Enter if you dare."

This time, the tears that sprang to my eyes were the product of an entirely different emotion.

"You remember," I whispered, crawling in after him. There was a single candle flickering in the center of the fort, and I momentarily feared Ronan would knock it over and set the house on fire.

"I'm not going to light the house on fire, Princess," he said, snorting amusedly.

I blushed. Even after all these months, I still had a tendency to say my thoughts aloud. A way to cope with past trauma, my therapist had told me. An inherent part of myself.

"In this fort, there are no secrets, do you understand?" Ronan asked me, eyes reproachful. I bobbed my head decisively.

No secrets. I could do that.

"Is there something you want to ask me?" I questioned.

"Maybe." Shrugging, he reached for my hand and tugged me onto his lap. I went willingly. "I just want to know that you're okay."

"Truthfully?"

"Always."

I exhaled a deep, pent-up breath, one that I felt like I'd been holding for years and years. "I'm not okay, Ro. I don't know if I'll ever be. It hurts, constantly. Every little thing is a reminder of what I lost. And I know, I *know*, that they would want me to be happy, but I don't know how I'm supposed to be. It feels like I'm disrespecting their memory by smiling."

It was the first time I'd voiced my fears out loud.

Ronan kissed my temple. "You have it wrong, beautiful, but I think you know that. Calax would fucking kick my ass if he knew that I was allowing you to mope. He loved you more than anything, and he would want you to be happy. He would want to see that beautiful smile of yours and know that you are loved and in love. I know it's hard, but all we want is for you to be happy. Not fine—I don't think that's possible after what you've been through—but happy. Could you try? For me? For us? For him?"

He didn't have to clarify for me to know who the "us" and "him" he was referring to was.

I wanted to tell him I understood, that I would try, but the words got lodged in my throat. We were in the fort of honesty, and any agreement would be the exact opposite of that—a lie.

How could I be whole, or even pretend to be, when two pieces of my soul were missing and one was dead?

"Can I ask you something?" I whispered back.

His body twitched at my obvious avoidance of his request, but he gave me a nod.

"Why did you reject me in the bathroom? Do you not want to kiss me?" I waited for his answer, breath held, but he remained silent. The only indication he'd heard my question was the tightening of his fingers on my waist.

Of course, that was when awkward Adelaide came out to play. And awkward Adelaide liked to talk about random shit.

"Is it because I kissed your brother? Because I don't regret it. I kissed Calax too. And Tamson. And I said the L-word to Fallon. Oh gosh. Do you think I'm easy? Because my vagina is not a hussy, despite contrary evidence. The sign officially says 'closed for business.' Unless your name is Fallon, Calax, Ryder, Ronan, Declan, Tamson, or Asher. If that is your name, then the doors are open. Well…not if that's your name, because I'm sure there are plenty of men with names like Ryder and Asher. What I'm saying is, not just anyone is allowed access to the water slide, if you know what I mean. My vagina is a coveted dessert. A la cremé pussy milk. Is that a thing? Hmm…now that I'm thinking about it, all vaginas should have a name. And since mine is a shameless hussy when it comes to you guys, I'm just going to call my pussy Elena. Or is that weird? Can I name my vagina after your ex-girlfriend?"

"I'm just going to stop you now," Ronan said with barely contained laughter. My face paled when I realized what I'd said.

What. The. Fuck?

"I want to say sorry," I began slowly, "but I can't remember what exactly I said, so you aren't getting an apology. I can give you anal instead."

He choked on air.

"Wait. Do girls not offer to give guys anal?"

"Addie, just stop talking." His hand snaked up to cover my mouth. Instinctively, my tongue darted out to lick the blistered skin, and goosebumps rose on his muscular arms.

"Shit, woman, you're going to fucking kill me." He took a deep breath, nuzzling his face against my neck. I canted my head sideways to give him better access. "I don't even know where to begin after all that, but to start off, you're not fucking naming your vagina Elena. Elena is going nowhere near your...girl part."

"Isn't that every guy's dream?" I mused, chuckling silently at his inability to say pussy. "To watch two girls together?"

Before I'd even finished speaking, Ronan shook his head vehemently. "No."

"No?"

"You're ours, Princess. Only ours." His voice was a growl, eyes uncharacteristically cold. I couldn't help but squirm in pleasure at the possessive, carnal hunger in his expression. "No one else can touch you. Which leads me to my second point."

"Which is?"

Suddenly, so suddenly that I squealed, Ronan rearranged me so that I was straddling him, one leg on either side of his muscular thighs.

His eyes entrapped me, holding me hostage, but I was a willing captive.

"You're mine, Addie. You have been from the first stupid ass joke, you just didn't know it yet." He leaned forward until his breath fanned over my lips. "Addie...I thought you realized it already. I love you, crazy girl. I love you so damn much that it terrifies me. I open my eyes, and all I want to see is you. I close them, and you're a part of every dream I have. I love you. I fucking love—"

I crushed my lips to his, reveling in his moan of pleasure. My hands curled around his neck, pulling him even closer to me, as his own hands tangled in my hair. He kissed me with a feverish intensity, the euphoria in the air nearly palpable.

It was Ronan who pulled away first, pressing a sweet kiss on the corner of my lips.

"Lucky Charms?"

"Yes, Princess?"

"I love you too."

He pulled me towards him once more, and our lips and tongues eagerly resumed their dance. This time, it was me who pulled away, breaths sawing in and out and heart hammering.

"You love me?" Ronan's voice was a hushed murmur. A whisper. A breath of air, as if he could scarcely believe that someone like me could love someone like him.

Didn't he see how wrong he was? How beautiful and gentle his soul was, lighting up the darkest pieces of me?

How could I not love him?

"I love you," I whispered. I punctuated that statement with a kiss to his temple. He trembled underneath me, as if my tenderness unraveled him. "I love you so freaking much."

My lips lowered, landing on his chest. His unicorn tattoo.

"You haven't told me why you have this," I murmured, replacing my lips with the pad of my finger. His eyes watched my hand on his inked skin with rapt fascination.

"My tattoo?" he asked for clarification, and I nodded.

"I haven't told anyone this before, not even Ryder."

"No lies in this fort, remember? Only truth."

His anguished eyes met mine. "When I was sixteen, I got a girl pregnant."

Whatever I'd expected his words to be, it wasn't *that*, and I was taken by surprise.

I pulled away from him so I could see his face fully. Those glorious amber orbs of his were filled with unshed tears.

"I wasn't in a relationship with the mom, Ali, but I was good enough friends with her. We decided to keep the baby." He took a deep, shuddering breath. "I didn't love her or anything, but I was willing to put my life on hold for her and our baby."

My hand continued to idly trace the unicorn on his chest. I knew, innately, that this story wouldn't have a happy ending. Wasn't that why we connected the way we had? Two broken souls grasping for each other in the monotonous darkness? Two tragedies desperately searching for relief?

"What happened?"

"Car crash," he answered brokenly. "She was seven months pregnant."

My heart broke for him, the girl, and his unborn child. I knew that pain could leave thousands of invisible scars on a person's soul.

I wiped at a tear cascading down his cheek.

"I understand," I whispered.

"Do you?" The question wasn't accusatory, but curious.

"I got pregnant when I was fourteen," I admitted softly. His eyes widened, and his strong arms tightened around me. "My dad made me...he made me..." I couldn't finish my sentence. The pain was too raw, an open wound in the beginning stages of scabbing. I didn't know which part pained me more—the fact that I was in that position to begin with, or that I'd had my choices ripped from me.

"Was it...?" Ronan's face was red with rage, no doubt knowing the hideous truth behind this story.

I nodded. "A business associate of my father's."

A man three times my age.

A man who wouldn't take no for an answer.

Dozens of emotions flitted across Ronan's face—anger, sadness, agony. At the end of the day, there was nothing either of us could do to change the past. We could only look at the future and grasp it with two hands.

Placing my head back on his shoulder, I outlined the unicorn with my pointer finger.

"Would you want kids?" I blurted out before I could stop myself.

The man only just confessed his love to you, and you're already asking him to be your baby daddy. Smooth, Addie.

He made a surprised noise in the back of his throat. "I would love kids," he admitted at last. "And...I think you would make an amazing mother."

My heart, which was beating rapidly from my impulsive question, stopped.

Me? A mother?

The thought filled me with both dread and excitement. My mother hadn't won any mother of the year awards, so I didn't have a good role model to follow. However, I knew I would never be like my parents. I would never harm my kids the way they'd harmed me. I would never discard them or make them feel unloved.

Would that make me a good mother?

Chuckling humorlessly, a futile attempt to diffuse the tension soaked air, I added, "And I won't name my vagina Elena. I'm thinking Buttercup. What do you think?"

CHAPTER 3

ADDIE

I brandished the knife in front of the dead Rager's face, a smug and admittedly sardonic smile on my face.

"You've been…knifed." Frowning, I turned towards Asher, who stood beside me, his favorite crossbow slung over his shoulder. "I need a better catchphrase."

"Catchphrase?" he asked, wiping the blood from the arrow on the hem of his shirt. His eyes glinted with feral amusement. The sick bastard enjoyed killing Ragers, stabbing knives in their heads, cutting off limbs.

"When I kill people," I explained lightly. The Rager at my feet was ugly. Red, blotchy skin. Milky, sunken eyeballs. A head that canted to the side in death.

"You plan on killing a lot of people, sweetheart?" he asked amusedly.

I shrugged. "Maybe. I have a lot of pent-up aggression. Maybe it'll manifest as murdering people."

"Psycho."

I stuck my tongue out at him in response.

"It's not psychotic if you admit it's psychotic. Then the word psychotic loses meaning. Thus, it's perfectly sane," I pointed out smugly. Asher merely blinked his beautiful, large eyes at me.

"I'm going to pretend I understood that."

Around our feet, half a dozen Ragers littered the asphalt. Their sightless eyes stared up at the cerulean sky peppered with wispy clouds. I wondered if they'd felt any pain before death claimed them. I wondered if they'd felt my dagger slicing through skin and bone.

Ragers were the product of a horrific organism that had ravaged the nation. It took the form of a black parasite, a disgusting worm-like creature, that appeared when global warming melted the ice caps. The parasite affected both the hypothalamus, which regulated the basic biological drive related to survival, and the limbic system, which dealt with fight or flight. The parasite caused you to fight, constantly, with a rage-like mentality. A rage that was almost primitive in nature.

Nobody was prepared for the world to end. Not me, not my family, and not the seven boys who'd come to mean the world to me. For weeks, we'd been on the road traveling to Atlanta to save my younger brother, until Fallon and Declan decided to play hero and save him themselves.

One would think we would've been relieved at finally being able to hole up in one place for an extended period of time, but all we felt was a pronounced loneliness without the missing three pieces of our collective soul.

"Look, I'm just saying, I'm not against killing people for the people I love. You guys, Mof, Tommy..." My voice choked on that final name, another scab getting picked open. I placed my hand against my chest and rubbed at the skin, as if that gesture could somehow soothe the organ thumping erratically underneath.

Tommy was my pseudo-son, my younger brother in all ways but blood. And god, I missed him. So damn much, it was almost painful. His presence had always been the balm to my twisted soul.

He was as broken as I was, hastily glued back together in jagged ways. But his spirit called to mine, his misery an echo of my own. We both understood pain, were intimately familiar with it, and somehow, we'd found each other in this new world.

Asher, easily able to read my emotions, graciously changed the subject. "Your cat attacked the curtains last night. Completely shredded them."

"Aw. He's such a good kitty," I cooed, the first real smile touching my lips. The black cat had been my companion since this whole shit fest—shest—had started. I would've been devastated if anything happened to the little bugger.

"He's a menace to society," Asher countered, but his lips twitched upward. They were always attempting to get me to smile. It was almost as if my smile chased away the storm clouds. As if they lived in constant, monotonous darkness that was only broken apart by my laugh. Their own rare smiles would grace their handsome faces, as if my own was contagious.

And I loved them for it, even if a part of me wondered if I could ever truly be happy again. Happiness was fleeting, I knew. As fleeting as lives. The thin string could be cut by a keen blade in seconds.

One of the Ragers on the ground twitched, head canting to the side and milky, sunken eyeballs roaming over my body. I launched myself at the creature, dagger raised, and stabbed him directly in the forehead.

"Yippie-kayak, motherfucker," I whispered darkly.

Nailed it.

Pulling myself off the ground, I found Asher staring at me with a decidedly amused, albeit quizzical, expression.

"What?" I asked in mock defense. "You're just jealous of my sexual prowess."

He snorted but didn't contradict my claim. No surprise. I knew I had sexual—and murderous—appeal far beyond my time.

Now that the threat had been eradicated, we made our way inside the small, dilapidated pharmacy. The walls were bleached from the sun and corroded by acid rain, but the roof remained firm over our heads. Broken windows and graffiti adorned the exterior. The interior was just as depressing, with shelves made out of distressed wood, shattered glass, and overturned tables that had once housed appliances. It was apparent the store had been ransacked one too many times.

Still, we knew better than to leave any store—and in particular, any pharmacy—unchecked. There was always a hidden treasure lurking in their depths, like a bottle of valuable medicine overlooked by someone who may not have known what they needed. Needle and thread. Adhesive wraps.

Food.

It didn't surprise me that Asher was knowledgeable about medicine, immensely so. Apparently, he'd planned to go to medical school before this entire shest started. Asher was kind and compassionate, and he loved helping people…just as much as he loved hurting them.

Well…hurting people who harmed me at the very least.

My blond-haired boyfriend was a little psychotic.

Wait a damn minute. Back up. Retreat. Abort mission. Boyfriend? Was Asher my boyfriend?

Shit. Shit. Shit.

"Boyfriend?" Asher poked his head up from where he was bent over, surveying a fallen display shelf. His eyes burned hotly, like a banked fire was hidden beneath the depths. One look in his eyes told me that he *liked* the idea of being my boyfriend. No, not liked it.

Loved it.

His smoldering gaze held me, ensnared me, and I was helpless to look away. Not that I wanted to. I couldn't imagine ever looking away from him. It wasn't just because he was handsome, beautiful even, but because he was the one who'd saved me. The one who'd refused to look away.

My parents were bad people. Like, mafia-level bad. They took their anger out on me in the form of fists and kicks. Breaking my spirit one wrathful word at a time. Destroying me until I was nothing but skin and bones.

The people around me knew what was going on, knew the extent of my parents' abuse, yet they'd turned a blind eye to it because they were afraid of *his* eyes being on them. My father. The man who quite literally had gotten away with murder more times than I could count.

But Asher had held my stare. He hadn't turned away, hadn't swiped it under the proverbial rug and pretended it didn't exist. No, he'd faced it head-on without a second thought.

And…and I loved him for it.

Maybe that made me confused or ornery. Maybe it made me a selfish bitch. How many guys was I allowed to love? Surely I'd reached my quota by now.

Ryder and Calax were okay with sharing me, with being in a relationship with me, but would they be okay with me adding others? There was no denying I had feelings for all seven men, including brooding Fallon.

Maybe Elena was right. Maybe I was a slut.

A hoe.

A whore.

"Stop it," Asher said fiercely, hinting that I may have spoken those private thoughts out loud. "There is nothing wrong with you."

"Isn't there?" I countered demurely. "I'm in love with seven men, Asher. There is most definitely something wrong with me."

It took me a moment to realize what I'd unintentionally confessed. I wanted to backtrack, to deny, but there was no use. I couldn't even hide it from myself anymore.

"Love?" Asher's voice was shaky, chest heaving.

While a part of me wanted to cower, I raised my chin imperiously and met his eyes. I could only pray that Ryder and Calax would forgive me. That Ronan would. And Fallon, Declan, and Tamson.

All men that held a piece of me.

With them, I felt complete. I felt whole and beautiful, as if I hadn't been broken by my parents and the world itself. Asher had always held one of those pieces, from the very first time we'd made eye contact in the restaurant and I'd accidentally called him Gorgeous.

"Yes. Love." I meant for my voice to sound confident, but it wavered towards the end. I was suddenly terrified. What if I confessed my feelings for him and he didn't feel the same way? What if he left me?

After all, everyone I'd ever loved had left me, either by choice, death, or things beyond our control.

Ryder had been taken by Liz.

Calax had been attacked and killed by Ragers.

Fallon and Declan had never returned from their trip to Atlanta.

Who was next?

Still, I steeled myself, braced myself, metaphorically closed the shutters against the oncoming hurricane.

"Asher, I love you."

His breath caught. Slowly, as if approaching a cornered beast, he ventured a step towards me.

"Say it again," he whispered, pupils dilated.

"I love you."

He was directly in front of me, his hands clasping my shoulders. His fingers flexed, tightening and then loosening on the bare skin my tank top revealed.

"Again."

"I love you." Feeling bold, I wrapped my arm around his neck and played with the blond hair there. He shuddered at my touch, eyes imploring me silently. For what, I didn't know.

"Addie, sweetheart," he groaned softly.

"I love you." My hand tightened in his hair, and his chest vibrated with a growl. The look in his eyes now was a carnal hunger, a desperate need. And love. It softened his face exponentially.

"Adelaide." Something in me tightened at hearing him use my full name. "I love you."

And then he crushed me to him. I groaned as our lips met, desperate for more, but Asher seemed determined to take his time and savor me. His lips moved slowly against mine, and despite my repeated attempts to demand entrance, he refused to open up. Instead, he peppered light kisses over my lips before lowering them to my jawline. I instinctively tilted my head, granting him better access.

When he pulled away, his eyes were hooded.

"Sweetheart, I want to show you how much I love you. Will you let me?"

I nodded, feverish to feel his hands back on me, his lips meshing with my own. Asher complied immediately to my wordless request, his mouth devouring mine once more. This time, he didn't hesitate to open for me, his tongue tangling with mine. He tasted like peppermints, and I never would've thought something as insignificant as his taste could send heat straight to my core.

My hips began to gyrate against him, need churning low in my belly. I needed him to touch me, to help me fend off the emptiness, to show me that he loved me as wantonly as I loved him.

If there was one thing I knew about Asher, it was that he loved to please. He wasn't like the others with intense foreplay.

No, he proved his love by giving me exactly what I wanted.

His hand pulled down my pants and panties in one go, and his finger sheathed itself in my wet heat. I groaned, bucking against him, but his other hand went to my hips to hold me in place.

"Asher…" I moaned. Begging him to…do what exactly?

Fortunately, Asher heard my plea and added a second digit alongside the first. He began to stroke me, softly at first, and then faster as my moaning intensified.

"So fucking beautiful," he murmured, reclaiming my lips in a heated kiss.

A third finger joined the other two, pinching my clit.

"I'm going to come," I warned him breathlessly. Not that I cared. It just seemed like something you were supposed to say.

Or at least that was what porn had taught me.

I didn't expect my confession to cause Asher to stop, and I nearly cried in disappointment when he removed his fingers.

Honestly, at that point, I was thinking of reneging on the whole love thing.

Asher dropped to his knees, and before I could ask what he was doing, he put his mouth on my clit. And sucked.

My knees buckled, and I might have fallen if Asher's hands hadn't been on my ass, steadying me. Really, he was quite *handy*. Get it? Handy?

Not the time to make jokes, Addie.

He chuckled against my clit, and that vibration sent me over the edge. I gripped his shoulders helplessly as I tumbled over, Asher's name a cry on my lips in the silent store.

Asher lapped me up, devouring me, until I finally reemerged on solid ground.

"Oh my god," I whispered reverently, curling my fingers into his blond hair. I pulled him up and kissed him fervently, tasting myself on him.

But I wasn't selfish. I wanted to return the favor and then some.

Pulling away, I met his dazed eyes and dropped to my knees.

"What are you—"

Before he could finish his question, I unzipped his pants and freed his rock-hard erection. Pre-cum glistened on his mushroom tip, and my mouth watered. Eating me had made him so incredibly hard, so ready.

"You don't have to," he whispered, but his hands were tangling in my brown hair. Pulling me towards him. Needing me.

And I didn't want our relationship to be one-sided. I loved him, and I wanted him to know that.

"I know I don't have to," I whispered, licking the tip. It tasted salty, decadent, like the forbidden fruit in the Garden of Eden. "But I want to. I love you, Asher."

"God, I love you. So, so much."

His words cut off on a groan as I took him completely in my mouth. I'd never given a blowjob before, never trusted someone enough to give him that piece of myself, but I'd watched enough videos and heard enough stories to realize how it was done. Asher wasn't that thick, but he was long. The longest I'd ever seen before.

For a moment, I worried I wouldn't be able to take him all. Cupping his balls, I ran my tongue over his veiny underside, and he made a strange sound in the back of his throat. I wanted to take him even deeper.

I swallowed him whole, hollowing my cheeks. He began to whisper my name, the heady scent of his arousal permeating the air.

"Addie..." he groaned, moving his hips to fuck my mouth. There was one technique I wanted to try, something one of the maids had gossiped about with her friends.

I began to hum around him.

His explosion was sudden, his cock jerking in my mouth before his seed spilled. He continued to move his hips erratically as he released himself, and I swallowed everything up eagerly. It didn't taste the best, but it was *Asher's*. A part of him.

I wanted to do that for him.

"Shit, Addie," he murmured, pulling himself out of my mouth. My tongue snaked out to lick away the remaining cum dousing his cock, and his eyes fixated on that. He noticeably gulped. "That was so sexy."

"It was?" I whispered, suddenly feeling insecure. Did he like it? Did I do it well? Obviously, he liked *something*, if the load he'd expelled was any indication. Still, self-consciousness ribbed me.

"That was perfect, Addie. You're perfect." He reached out a hand, legs shaking, and pulled me into his arms. Both of our pants were still around our feet and cum still dribbled down our legs, but the embrace was as perfect as Asher claimed I was. Him and me against the world, in a cocoon of our own making. I felt safe and loved and protected. All of my previous fears and worries...well...they didn't quite abate, but they no longer consumed me. The hurt was there, but so was this feeling of completeness and elation.

"I love you," he whispered against my hair, and I felt my lips curve up in an answering smile.

"I love you too."

A few minutes later, we found ourselves cleaned up and loading up the vehicle. Asher wore a dopey grin on his face, and I knew my own expression mirrored his. We were two people in love and had somehow found each other in the chaos of this new world.

We deserved to be happy, to smile, despite the shit we'd faced. I refused to allow myself to feel guilty for loving Asher, for sharing a part of myself with him.

He was right—the others wouldn't want me to stop loving, stop living, because they were no longer with us. I could practically see Calax's glower as he called me out on my shit. Fallon would merely stare at me, his narrowed eyes saying more than a thousand words.

At the thought of our missing leader, my eyes flickered to the store across the street. It was one of many stores we'd painted symbols and coded words on in order for them to find us.

A crown—a symbol the guys associated with me—and numbers.

Coordinates, Ronan had told me. An address would give our location away to looters.

My lips pursed as I stared at the black paint. Over the numbers, someone had drawn a penis, effectively obscuring the coordinates from view.

Assholes.

But that wasn't what gave me pause. My eyes fixated on the image above the crown. The letters.

A black cat was painted over top of the crown, MOF capitalized directly above it. And above *that* was a series of numbers similar to the ones we'd initially painted.

Coordinates.

"Ash," I whispered, fearing my eyes were playing a trick on me. A horrible, horrible trick. When Asher continued to load up the van, oblivious, I touched his shoulder and raised a trembling finger to point in the direction of my hastily drawn cat. "Ash."

He followed my gaze, and the cans he'd been holding dropped. Neither of us paid it any mind.

Only a few people knew about my cat, conveniently named My Only Friend or Mof for short.

And if Asher, Ronan, Ryder, or Tamson hadn't written that…

"It's them," I whispered, scarcely able to believe it. "They're here."

CHAPTER 4

CALAX

I hated the smell of blood.

There were very few things I hated… Well, that was a lie. I hated a shit ton of stuff.

Slow walkers, fucking picnics on the beach, painting…oh, and assholes who liked to beat the shit out of me.

My head was tossed backwards with the force of the blow, but I kept my grin firmly in place. It seemed to piss the assholes off—the knowledge that they couldn't break me. They could try, but I had something they only wished they had.

Literally.

"Where is she?" Punch. Blood drizzled down my chin, the taste of copper heavy on my tongue. The man, whose name I'd discovered was Gabriel, pulled his fist back once more.

"Enough," a soft, sensual voice said, followed by the clacking of high heels. Bitch stepped into the room they had designated as mine, arms folded over her chest. Of course that wasn't her real name, but it was the name I'd given her in my head.

Addie was apparently rubbing off on me.

The dumb bitch had tried to seduce me when I first arrived, as if a mediocre face could ever turn me against Addie. As if any face could turn me against my love. A part of me thought she was still pissed that her feminine wiles hadn't worked on me or some shit like that. Either way, she loved to be present for my "interrogation sessions."

Read as torture sessions.

They may have healed me from the Ragers' attack, but they were determined to break me. What they failed to realize was that I was unbreakable.

Fucking assholes.

"Are you going to tell us where she is?" Bitch asked, kneeling to face me. She tried to look sympathetic, but it came across more like a grimace. She moved to touch my face, but I jerked away. Blood rushed to my ears, the movement causing my head to pound, but it was worth it to see the shock on her face. That shock was quickly replaced by a blistering anger, hot enough to destroy this room.

She pulled her hand back and slapped me square across the face. This time, I barely even moved, refusing to break eye contact with the horrid woman. I wanted her to see me when she inflicted pain. I wanted her to see the resolve in my eyes, the determination.

I would die before these bastards got their hands on Adelaide.

Through the metaphorical grapevine, I'd discovered that these were the assholes that had helped Liz kidnap Ryder and Addie. The deal had been simple—Liz could have her fun with them, but Addie was not to be killed. Harmed, yes. Mutilated, also yes. But killed? That was a hard no by the powers that be.

I still hadn't garnered why. Why Addie? What did they want with her?

Turning away from me, Bitch looked up at Gabriel.

"He's here," she said. Each word was clipped, acid practically *oozing* from her pores. Aw. She was still pissed that I'd rejected her. Poor bitchy thing.

And then her words registered.

I focused on their conversation fully, eagerly lapping up every snippet of information they seemed so inclined to share.

"Shit." Was I mistaken, or did Gabriel look worried? Whoever this "he" was scared the shit out of both Bitch and Gabriel. He probably should've scared me as well, but instead, I felt something that resembled relief. Maybe I could finally figure out what the hell was going on.

The only conclusion—Addie's parents were looking for her. It would explain the manpower, their penchant for violence, the fear emanating from my two tormentors. I just couldn't figure out why. Were they that desperate for a punching bag?

The thought of her vile parents getting their hands on my girl filled me with rage unlike anything I'd ever felt before.

I would die before they even caught a glimpse of her.

Gabriel, after one more ineffectual punch at my face, hurried out of the room to greet this mysterious person. Bitch remained for a moment longer, hands clenched into fists at her sides.

"This all would've been easier if you would've accepted my offer," she said snidely, and I couldn't help but snort. As if I would forget Addie and fuck her instead.

She was lucky I didn't name her Dumb Bitch.

Kind of pathetic she had to resort to blackmail and bribery in order to get laid, if you asked me.

When I merely glared at her, trembling with barely suppressed rage, she huffed and stomped out of the room.

And then the waiting game began. I knew, as surely as I knew that the sky was blue, the grass was green, and Adelaide was fucking crazy, that the big honcho would come check in on me. Maybe throw a few punches himself. Oh, he wouldn't want to.

Not at first. He probably would've preferred for his identity to remain a secret, but desperation made men do strange things.

And this man? He was desperate.

So I waited.

ADDIE

Sunlight penetrated the kitchen, catching on dust particles floating stagnant in the air. My nerves were frayed, tension peaked, as I waited with bated breath for the guys to finalize the plan.

I'd wanted nothing more than to charge into the identified house, guns blazing—well, vagina blazing—but Asher had insisted we consult with the others.

Make sure it wasn't a trick. After all, there were still people after us, after me, for reasons unknown.

I tapped my foot impatiently as Ronan and Ryder talked over the map. The coordinates on the wall led to a small neighborhood only an hour away.

I was desperate to see Fallon and Declan again, to see with my own eyes that they were okay.

I wanted to hold Tommy and hear him reprimand me for swearing. Ironic, considering he swore every other word.

And Nik...

There had been no indication at my brother's house whether or not he'd been rescued by the others. For all I knew, he could be...the D-word. I didn't want to even mentally think it, as if thinking it would somehow make it true.

The clenching in my heart grew until it was nearly unbearable. Run to them. Run to them. Run to them.

"You okay, Kitten?" Ryder asked, pulling me into an embrace. I softened against him instantly.

"No," I admitted hoarsely. "What if it's not them? What if it's a trap? What if they've already left? What if they're injured or...you know. The other thing. The D-word. What if they don't want to see me? Oh god. They probably found a bunch of beautiful models and fell in love and had babies and—"

"Shh." Ryder put his finger to my lips, and I broke off in mid ramble. I knew my fears were valid, but I also knew they were illogical, at least the last few. Fallon had confessed his love to me during our last conversation, and I knew Ducky felt strongly for me too. I didn't know if that strong feeling was the same love I felt for him or something more platonic. Either way, I knew they would be waiting for me.

It was decided that Kai and Doc would remain behind and hold down the fort, so to speak. I wouldn't be surprised if they grabbed all of our belongings and ran.

After a quick goodbye, we began the hour-long journey to the neighborhood.

I didn't remember what was said during the drive. All I remembered was a restless energy pushing me forward.

By the time night fell, we'd arrived in front of a tiny brick home. Candles flickered through the front window, but I couldn't make out anything inside. Not that we were that close. Always on the side of caution, we chose to park a few houses over, the headlights off and the running car silent.

"We'll go first," Ronan said, indicating his brother and himself. Ryder nodded his head, eyes already trained on the unassuming house.

I opened my mouth to protest but quickly closed it. I'd learned it was futile to argue with them when they got in macho, protective mode.

As one, the brothers slipped out either side of the car, stealthily moving towards the house, practically blending in with the shadows. They were good, I would give them that.

"Addie," Tam began gently. "You're shaking the whole car." He put a restraining hand on my leg to stop the fidgeting limb.

"Sorry," I whispered back. "I'm just so fucking nervous I might piss my pants."

"No pants pissing is allowed in my car," Asher said sternly. His lips twitched to show me he was joking. "Pants shitting is allowed though."

"Weirdo." But his words had the desired reaction from me. The tension abated from my body as suddenly as it had appeared. I trusted Ronan and Ryder to find our men, the two missing parts of our family, and bring them back to us.

I had to believe that they would still be here. I had to. The alternative was too awful to think about.

I watched in rapt fascination as Ryder and Ronan disappeared around the back of the house, shadows eating them up, swallowing them whole.

I could feel each heartbeat pounding against my rib cage. It wasn't the standard *ba-dum*, but a flurry of activity as thousands of butterflies threatened to break free. I couldn't quite understand this emotion.

It wasn't hope, not really, but something else. Something deeper and more intense that caused goosebumps to pepper over my skin. My leg moved anxiously, jerking up and down, up and down. My unease seemed to be physically manifesting itself, and I couldn't stay still, couldn't breathe.

My mind conjured up images of Fallon and Declan.

Fallon's golden-brown hair pulled back into a low ponytail, his eyes trained intensely on me. It had once been unnerving to have that undivided attention on me, but now I couldn't imagine life without it. Without him.

Declan's brown hair, longer on the top and shorter on the sides. The perpetual smirk etched onto his face. Those eyes of his that tracked my every movement.

"They'll be here," Tamson said, glancing at me from the driver's seat. I didn't know if he was trying to convince me or himself.

I willed myself to calm down, but my heart continued to battle with, race against, my thoughts.

Deep breaths.

In.

And out.

In.

And out.

In.

The passenger side door opened, and I was wrenched out of my seat, dropping uneremoniously onto the asphalt. I scrambled to my feet, but rough hands jerked me against a soft chest. Tamson shouted, unbuckling and crawling over the center console. Asher was already out of the car, gun raised and aimed at the intruder.

I felt something cold press against my neck.

A knife, I realized dizzily.

I was so damn tired of being held at knifepoint.

"Lower your weapons," a voice said coldly. It was low and raspy, but the feminine lilt was undeniable.

Another figure emerged from the shadows, pointing a gun at Asher's head. My blond-haired lover tensed, but he refused to lower his own gun. The tension in the air was almost palpable, waves of electricity setting my skin ablaze.

Tamson didn't have a weapon, but his fists were raised. Tam was a skilled mixed martial artist, and I had no doubt he would be a deadly foe against even the worst of weapons.

"Drop your knife," Asher countered. Dark. Deadly. Dangerous.

Sexy.

Not the time, kinky bitch.

A third figure marched forward, and Tamson shifted his attention to him.

"Lower your fucking weapons," the new man said gruffly. He had a hint of an accent in his voice, but I couldn't discern from where.

Asher, Tam, and I all exchanged looks as we weighed our options. On one hand, I trusted my men's skills to get us out of this situation. On the other, I wasn't sure even Asher, as skilled as he was with a gun, could put a bullet in between my captor's eyes before the knife cut skin.

The fight didn't drain from their eyes, both men were too proud and pissed for that, but Asher reluctantly lowered his gun to the ground as Tam dropped his fists. They practically radiated rage, an incandescent flame burning hotly beneath the surface. The flame would lead to an inferno, a wildfire, I knew, if we didn't get out of this situation.

But I was tired, so damn tired, of being the damsel in distress. First Liz, and then the asshole who shot me. Never again.

As the woman holding me loosened her arms, deeming the threat as over, I pushed my body back, remembering in vivid detail all of the training sessions I had with my guys. The back of my head rammed into her face, and she let out an anguished cry, dropping her knife.

In the span of seconds, I had the knife picked up and pressed to her throat. A strange sound emitted from the back of her throat, a combination of amusement and horror, as I dug the keen tip into her fleshy neck.

To the strange men—and from their bulkier builds, I determined they were, in fact, men—I said, "Lower your fucking weapons."

They resisted at first, eyes flaring defiantly. From this angle, I could see that they were older, probably in their mid-thirties. Their gazes flickered from me, to the knife, and then to the woman I was holding. As one, they dropped their weapons to the ground.

Asher and Tamson immediately picked them up, aiming them at the two men's heads.

"Funny how the tides change, isn't it?" I whispered darkly into the bitch's ear. She growled in response.

Yes, funny indeed.

CHAPTER 5

FALLON

I loved Tommy, I honestly did, even if he was a little shit.

Groaning at his antics, I watched as he paraded through the store, a Rager's head balancing precariously on the tip of his sword. Yes, a sword.

The asshole needed to know how to defend himself, and at least with a sword, he couldn't accidentally shoot me. Stab me, yes, but I'd learned to maintain my distance from him when he had it out.

"It's getting late," I said stiffly, exchanging a glance with Declan. His hair had grown out, scruff covering the lower half of his face. Dark bags settled beneath his eyes, only heightening his sickly pale skin. The man looked as if he was inches away from death. The strain ate at him in a way I tried to suppress.

Tried being the important term.

"Grab your bag and let's go," I instructed, and Tommy's face fell with disappointment.

"But…"

"And leave the damn head."

This time, there was a definite pout on Tommy's face. Damn sociopath.

Like us, the last few months had changed Tommy, and not entirely in a good way. While his baby fat had all but diminished, his eyes had a haunted look that hadn't been there previously. Sure, there was no denying that the little guy was fucked in the head, more so than even us, but the shadows had steadily receded with the light that was Adelaide. Now that she was gone? They came back with a vengeance.

My throat closed up, emotion clogging my airway.

Don't think. Don't think. Don't think.

I repeated that in my head until her face all but disappeared, swept beneath the metaphorical rug. Oh, I would for sure think of her. Later. In the safety of my own bedroom behind lock and key. There, I would allow myself to feel her absence as intensely as a blade stabbing through my chest. The only saving grace was the fact that she was alive and with the others.

They would look after her, protect my love with their own lives. It was moments like this when I was immensely grateful she had six other people who loved her. Six strong, passionate men who would move heaven and hell for her.

But they were wrong about one thing. They wanted—hell, half of them had even promised—to move mountains for her, but she didn't need that. Not really. Adelaide had the strength to move her own mountains, as long as enough people believed in her.

The thought of my love made my heart thump wildly in my chest. The last few months had been hell. No matter where I went, what I did, everything reminded me of her. I couldn't even look at a damn cat anymore without wanting to burst into tears.

Normally, I would've been scared at what others might have perceived as the loss of my masculinity, but I knew better. I was more of a man with her in my life than I was without it. The second I found her, and I *would* find her, I would fuck the shit out of her. Love her completely. Worship my queen.

The thought had my cock twitching in my pants.

Yes, I would show her what it was like to be loved by me.

If only some asshole hadn't scribbled over the coordinates...

She was here, somewhere, and I would search for her for the rest of my life. I knew Declan felt the same. He woke up every morning exactly at five and began his futile search, scouring neighborhoods, inquiring with other travelers, marking walls with a code only the others would understand.

We slung our bags over our shoulders, each containing an assortment of cans and clothes, and headed for our van. Dusk had fallen, painting everything in a light gray and a raspberry red. The town we'd looted was silent, still. Dead bodies littered the sidewalk and street.

The ride back was silent except for Tommy's constant chatter as he discussed a few comic books he'd found in the grocery store. He knew Nik would love them.

We were fortunate enough that Tonya and Davis, good people, were willing to watch Nikolai during our trip. Normally, I would've been hesitant about entrusting Nikolai in the hands of strangers, but I trusted them with my life. We'd found them when we were at our lowest, and they, along with Tonya's brother, Jared, had taken us in and given us food and shelter.

We chose to stay in a house next door to them in an abandoned neighborhood. Not our preferred choice of home, but it was safe and cozy, albeit empty.

An hour turned into two, and that turned into four. By the time we pulled up into our tiny, nondescript picket-fenced house, everything was plunged in darkness. Crickets chirped in the distance, and moonlight painted everything in a pale white.

Tommy snored in the backseat, and Declan absently stared out the window. Suddenly, his brows furrowed, the skin between them creasing. He patted my arm to get my attention.

I moved to turn on the interior light so I could sign to him, but he shook his head vehemently, pointing at something in the distance. No, not something. A car. Idling a few blocks over.

"Shit," I cursed, scrambling out of our own car. I hastily grabbed my gun out of its holster and checked to make sure the safety was off.

"What's going on?" Tommy asked groggily, voice laden with sleep.

"Stay in the fucking car," I hissed, though I doubted he would listen. Tommy seemed to have the mentality of breaking all my rules and then asking for forgiveness later. Sort of reminded me of Adelaide. It was no wonder the two got along like peas in a pod.

Declan appeared at my side, his own gun raised. Silently, I pointed towards the wall beside the door, and Declan immediately pressed himself against it. Moonlight illuminating my face, I began to count backwards from three silently. When I got to zero, I kicked down the door, and Declan ran inside, gun raised.

I followed after him, painfully aware that Tommy was behind me carrying his sword, the little shit.

There was the sound of startled gasps, a cry, and then I ran face first into Declan's broad back.

"What the fuck?" I roared, despite knowing he wouldn't hear me. I finally glanced over his shoulder, my gun held firmly in my hands.

The first thing I saw was Tonya, Davis, and Jared all tied up to our dining room chairs, gags in their mouths and expressions positively livid.

And then I saw...

My mouth opened, closed, and then opened once more.

Asher and Tam stood behind them, each holding a gun and pointing it at their heads. Ronan and Ryder sat on the couch opposite them, their eyes comically wide as they stared at us.

Lastly, my eyes rested on the most beautiful person in the world. My light. My love. My fucking queen.

Her gaze was bouncing from me to Declan and then to Tommy, unsure of who to focus on. Those beautiful blue orbs of hers were bright with unshed tears. The knife she was holding clattered to the floor.

Time slowed and then stood still.

Only one word left my lips, a desperate plea. I almost pinched myself in fear that I was dreaming. It would not be my first Adelaide dream.

"Addie?"

～

ADDIE

There was a feeling you got when you knew your life was going to change astronomically.

Where you were standing in a darkened room, unaware of your surroundings, and suddenly, a light was flipped on. The change was instantaneous. The darkness receded to be replaced by...well...everything. Everything you didn't know you were missing.

As my gaze volleyed back and forth from Fallon's piercing eyes to Declan's wide ones to even Tommy's haunted ones, I knew this was my moment. My change. The moment when everything was flipped sideways, upside down, and through a damn twister.

I didn't know who moved first, but suddenly, Fallon's arms were around me. His face buried in my hair as he inhaled deeply, body shaking.

I'd seen the big man pissed before, scared even, but never anything like this. Never as if the entire world had shifted and he was hanging on to the edge by only the tips of his fingers.

He was whispering into my hair, and I could've sworn I heard the words "my queen" repeated like a mantra.

Suddenly, I was ripped away from Fallon and turned to face Declan. Ducky. Tears fell from his eyes, softening his features. He pulled me to him, holding me close, as if any second, I would slip through his fingers like fine grains of sand.

He rocked me back and forth in his arms, not releasing me even as Fallon rejoined us, his hard body resting against my back. His lips moved to my neck, light kisses creating a decadent pathway.

Soon, we would be putting on a nice show for our prisoners.

And I wanted it. I wanted *them*. The need was nearly more forceful than anything else, a train with no brakes barreling towards a cement wall.

But...

I wrenched myself reluctantly from Fallon and Declan's arms, stepping backwards to orient myself. Phantom tingles raced up and down my arms as my skin remembered the feel of theirs pressed against mine.

"Tommy?" I whispered hoarsely, brokenly, glancing towards where I had last seen him. My heart froze when I saw he was no longer there.

Until he walked through the front door, his hand clasped with a younger boy with light brown hair and large headphones around his neck.

"He was staying next door with the neighbors. The neighbors you, by the way, tied up and assaulted," Tommy said dryly, but there were tears of relief in his eyes and a wide smile on his face.

Nikolai glanced up at me, eyes widening slightly, almost imperceptibly, before he ventured one step forward.

Now, I couldn't keep in the desperate sobs that escaped me. My brother. My little brother.

Standing in front of me.

Alive.

Unharmed.

Safe.

I knew he hated physical contact, but I couldn't stop myself from lunging at him, arms encircling his thin waist. He stiffened immediately before hesitantly holding me back. That stunned the hell out of me, but I was too lost in my own emotions to focus on that novelty.

"Nik," I sobbed into his hair. His arms left my waist, but he didn't pull away as I clung to him, crying.

I cried until my eyes were red and raw. I cried when Fallon and Declan both crowded me, as if they couldn't bear to be separated from me even for a moment longer.

I even cried when Tamson and Asher sheepishly released our prisoners.

Somehow, those tears turned into a drowsiness, dark curtains being drawn closed. I was aware of someone holding me to them, my body being lifted like a bride entering her new home.

And then, I was aware of nothing.

CHAPTER 6

ADDIE

I woke up surrounded by two sexy, warm bodies.

Peeling open my crusted eyelids, I turned sideways on the bed and stared first at Fallon's sleeping face. His golden-brown hair was out of its customary ponytail, cascading in loose curls around his face. His lashes, twigs of ebony, rested on his tanned cheeks.

Peaceful. That was the only word I could think of. In sleep, he looked serene, the harsh planes of his face softening exponentially.

His hair was longer than it had been when I'd last seen him, but the skin on his face was smooth.

Unlike Declan's.

I turned towards the second male, breathing in his pine scent. Like Fallon, his hair was longer. Light scruff covered his arresting jawline, and I yearned to rub my fingers over it.

What had happened during those months apart?

As if he could feel my eyes on him, Declan's lashes fluttered, and I was suddenly greeted by eyes as familiar to me as my own. They were the eyes of my childhood best friend, Ducky, and effectively ensnared me. Held me hostage.

Hand trembling, Declan curved his palm around my jawline, and I twisted my head to kiss the tender skin.

For a moment, we only stared at each other. The rest of the world fell away.

Him and me.

Me and him.

Us against the world.

Shifting slightly on the bed, I held my hands up so I could sign.

"You're here," I both said and signed. "You're really here."

Declan pressed a kiss to my shoulder like he couldn't help himself.

"Nik?" I continued when he glanced back up at me. His hands reluctantly left my skin so he could reply, movements rapid.

"He's fine. Promise. He's spending the night in Tommy's room."

It made my heart happy, ecstatic, to know that the two of them were getting along. I loved them both.

"He's a good kid," Declan signed, eyes warming as he spoke of my brother.

"The best," I agreed. My body moved closer to his, the tips of my breasts brushing his chest. He inhaled sharply.

For a moment, I felt a brief stab of insecurity. Doubt. Had he missed me like I'd missed him? I supposed what I was really worried about was whether or not he felt the same way for me as I did him. I didn't know if I would survive if he rejected me. Did that make me greedy?

"Did you miss me?" I whispered vulnerably.

Our noses were touching, and his eyes flickered from my lips to my eyes and then back to my lips. I was no longer able to sign, my hands pressed between our two bodies. Still, I knew he read my lips.

For a moment, there was only silence.

And then he crushed my lips to his.

It was a gentle kiss, our lips moving together with a tantalizing softness. It was a kiss that spoke thousands of words. And when I opened my eyes, it was to see him staring at me with love and need. Desire. Lust.

Any and all fears diminished as quickly as they came.

I deepened the kiss, and he released a low moan. I took the opportunity to slip my tongue in his mouth, tangling it with his. His hands moved to my ass, cupping it, and I instinctively rocked against him. Licks of pleasure burned my veins, setting me aflame. I could feel him growing hard, his cock pressing against my stomach and twitching beneath his sleep shorts.

A throat cleared behind me, and Declan and I pulled apart. His cheeks were colored, and I knew mine were as well, but not for the reasons he may have been thinking.

I was...turned on at the thought of Fallon watching us kiss. Watching me gyrate my hips against Declan's leg subconsciously. Hearing my moans, my pleas, my need for my men.

Feeling wanton and needy, desperate, I turned on the bed and pressed my lips to Fallon's. He didn't seem to care that I was just kissing Declan, his brother. He didn't seem to care that I'd kissed all the members of his team.

No, Fallon grabbed the back of my head, fingers tangling in my hair, and kissed me like I was his and his alone. Those lips of his dominated me, seared me. They were rough and brutal, everything I expected from our team leader. There was no denying the possessiveness of his kiss, his hands, his legs tangling with my own.

I was *his*.

His hands kneaded my breasts, and I was practically trembling beneath his ministrations.

Another pair of lips moved to my neck, and I mewled at the dual sensations.

"You like that?" Fallon whispered hotly against my lips. He pulled back so he could stare into my eyes. Gauge my reaction.

All I could do was nod with a helpless whimper. I'd been without Declan and Fallon for far too long. I needed him, needed them, in a way that left me trembling.

"I need you." I turned so I could face Declan. He was sitting up on the bed, his shirt off and the sculpted planes of his chest on display. His breathing was heavy, chest rising and falling as his eyes desperately took me in. "I need both of you. I love you both so much." My voice cracked with emotion, with the rawness of my feelings.

Declan's eyes darkened at my admission, and before I realized what was happening, he had me pressed down on the bed, his lean body covering mine.

He kissed me harshly, enthusiastically, as one hand grabbed both my wrists and held them over my head.

When he pulled away, both of our faces were flushed red and our lips were swollen. Declan closed his eyes, lashes fluttering over his high cheekbones, before he reopened them and stared down at me with something akin to determination.

"I love you." His voice was raspy, but there was no denying the words. The words he'd spoken aloud. For me. Only me.

Tears blurred my vision, but I ignored them, freeing my hands from his and pulling him back to me. He came willingly, eagerly, his body fitting perfectly against mine.

No more words needed to be spoken as I used the heels of my feet to take off his shorts. My mouth watered when I realized he'd gone commando beneath the loose-fitting basketball shorts.

I wanted to memorize him. See every curve and dip of his delectable body. Feel him. Taste him. Kiss the scars on his chest.

Before I could do anything, Declan ripped my shirt straight down the middle. He made a move to do the same thing to my bra, but I put a restraining hand on his bicep.

"Bras are fucking expensive," I told him, arching my back so I could reach behind me and unhook the lacy white fabric.

"It's the apocalypse, sweetheart," Fallon said gruffly, but there was no denying the amusement in his voice. "You don't have to pay for bras anymore." He leaned closer so his teeth caught on my earlobe. Nibbling once, he added, "I'll steal you every fucking bra in the world."

Awww. If that wasn't the most romantic thing I'd ever heard.

Slipping the straps off my shoulders, I raised my hips so Declan could pull off my shorts and panties. Soon, I was bare to them.

I was sure they'd seen dozens of other girls before, but they both looked at me as if I were the only girl in the world. As if I didn't have scars, some of them still hideously raised and a dark red color, marring my stomach. As if I was loved and treasured and the only thing they needed in life.

"Do either of you have…?" I trailed off, cheeks pinking. I'd had sex before, but never with someone I truly cared about. Never with someone I loved. While I wanted to feel them inside me, skin to skin, I knew we weren't ready to bring a child into this world.

Not yet.

Fallon chuckled and reached into the bedside table drawer, grabbing out a condom.

Something like jealousy pierced me.

"How many girls do you bring up here?" The jealous remark escaped before I could stop it.

Fallon surprised me by laughing.

"Addie, I don't think you realize how much we fucking love you. There's only you for us." He pressed a soft kiss to my tender lips. "Only *you*. You own us, baby girl. Heart, body, and soul."

Declan, oblivious to the conversation happening around him, rolled the condom over his thick length. I never would've believed that something as simple as putting on a condom would be sexy, but my mouth watered.

Heart, body, and soul.

Hearing it confirmed made my heart pound. They were mine as surely as I was theirs.

Turning away from Fallon, I gripped Declan in my hand and lined him up with my wet entrance. He hesitated, only briefly, before sheathing himself fully inside me.

I groaned, loving the way he felt inside me. As if we were two puzzle pieces connected together. As if we were one.

I didn't know who started rocking first, but soon he was pounding into me, hips slapping against me with each thrust.

"Declan!" I screamed.

Fallon's warm mouth moved to my breasts, tugging at my nipple with his teeth. His tongue swirled over the beaded tip, and the combined stimulations were very nearly my undoing.

Declan leaned over to take my lips in a bruising kiss, seemingly unconcerned that his chest brushed against Fallon's hair.

He relentlessly fucked me, made love to me, as his tongue prodded the seam of my lips.

I cried out against his mouth, my orgasm only seconds away.

Sensing how close I was to that pinnacle, that cliff, Declan grabbed my legs, placed them over his shoulders, and began to fuck me earnestly. This new position caused the tip of his dick to brush against my clit. Fallon moved his mouth to lick, suck, and bite at my neglected breast. I weaved my fingers in his hair, holding him to me.

"Declan!"

My pussy squeezed his cock, milking him for all he was worth. Declan grunted, his cock twitching, before he exploded inside me.

On and on it went, like fire exuding from me in waves. The orgasm was unlike any I'd ever felt before.

Even after he was done, my body shook with the remnants of pleasure.

He killed me.

Death by orgasm.

Declan chuckled darkly, all smug male satisfaction.

"That was fucking amazing." I groaned, completely sated, and he pressed his lips to mine once more in a chaste kiss.

"I love you," he signed, a brilliant smile etched across his face. My own lips curved at his infectious happiness.

"I love you too."

But he wasn't the only man I loved.

Turning, I faced Fallon with half-lidded eyes. He remained on the bed with us, though he'd moved to a sitting position. His arms were folded over his bare, muscular chest, and there was an obvious tent in his pants.

I moved to take care of him—it—the way he'd always taken care of me, but he grabbed my hand in his, gentle but restraining.

"No, my love."

My brows furrowed, lips twisting down.

His eyes softened as they caressed my face.

"I love you. Never doubt that. But there are some…things in my past. Things I need to tell you before we take this next step." He leaned forward and rested his nose in my hair, inhaling deeply. "God, I missed you."

I knew there were secrets he was keeping from me, but I couldn't find it within me to care. I had my two men with me, my two missing pieces, and for a moment, I was at peace.

The rest of the world could wait. I wanted to hold on to this tiny slice of heaven for a moment longer.

CHAPTER 7

DECLAN

There was no greater feeling than holding the woman you loved in your arms. As my arm tightened once around Addie's thin waist, I marveled at how lucky I was to have found her. Again. Not many people could say they ended up with their childhood sweethearts.

Reluctantly, I untangled myself from Addie's sleeping form, pulled on my pants, and made my way downstairs. Fallon, who'd left only a few minutes before me, was standing by the coffee pot with his muscular arms folded over his chest. His eyes were intent on Ryder as he discussed all that had transpired during our absence.

Ronan and Asher sat at the dining room table, sipping coffee from their mugs. Tamson was volleying his gaze from Fallon to Ryder as the two talked. I didn't see Calax anywhere, but knowing the ugly bastard, he was probably still sleeping.

"Morning," I signed, moving to the coffee machine and pouring myself a steaming cup. Through some miracle, we'd come across a battery-operated coffee pot. I hadn't even known shit like that existed, but it was a blessing in disguise. I needed the bitter liquid to survive the day.

I turned, shocked to see all eyes were on me. Fallon's were curious, while the others' were wary.

"Is she still asleep?" Ronan signed rapidly. His dark brow was furrowed.

Frowning, I nodded once and took a sip of the blistering hot liquid. It soothed my throat and warmed my cold hands.

Ronan exchanged an undefinable look with Asher before nodding once and walking upstairs where Addie slept. I lifted a brow at their odd behavior.

It was Tamson that spoke, pushing his reddish-brown hair out of his face. "She gets nightmares if she's alone for too long."

Nightmares?

That was new.

Sarge must've been thinking the same thing, as he set down his own cup of coffee and took a step closer. He looked intimidating as fuck in the flames of the candles, all sharp edges, broody scowl, and barely contained power.

"What's going on?" he asked. I imagined his voice would be dark, clipped.

Once more, the guys leveled one another with that same look. I could feel my never-ending patience splintering. Seemingly on the same wavelength as me, Fallon pounded his fist onto the table.

Ryder's face was grave when he spoke next. I might've believed he was impassive if his eyes hadn't tightened, pain emanating back at me from his umber gaze.

"Calax." His lips moved slowly though his hands remained pressed down on the tabletop. Normally, the guys were more considerate when speaking to me. Whatever he had to say was obviously bad enough if he couldn't even sign it.

I braced myself for the words I knew would change my life.

"He's dead."

I froze, muscles bunching together as pain and grief consumed me. The coffee mug slipped from my fingers and shattered. The world was spinning rapidly, wildly, and I desperately grasped the back of the chair in order to orient myself to my new reality. A reality without Calax in it. Without his customary scowl and the warmth that seeped into his eyes only around us and Addie. The protective way he cared for each and every one of us.

My best friend.

My brother.

I swayed, and Asher rushed forward to help me sit down. Numbness encased me, overwhelming even the pain. Oh the irony. Who would've thought numbness would be stronger than grief?

Out of the corner of my eye, I took stock of Fallon's expression. He was standing there, eyes staring at something on the far wall. His face was apathetic, and not even I could derive anything from his facial features. His Adam's apple bobbed as he swallowed deeply.

"What happened?" he asked.

I turned my attention towards Ryder to read his lips. I needed to know, to understand. Pain grasped me in iron claws, refusing to release me.

"We were at the house." Ryder wouldn't meet either of our gazes. "After Addie got off the radio with you…" He nodded towards Fallon who remained immobile, rooted to his spot against the granite countertop. "Something happened… I'm not sure what…but there were suddenly Ragers everywhere. He was carrying Addie, but they were surrounded. He sacrificed himself for her."

Tears marred Ryder's face as he recollected the memory. His agony was almost tangible, and I knew the pain was reflected in my own eyes. Hearing what had happened…

While I'd stubbornly decided my own life wasn't worth living…

I leaned over, dry-heaving. Someone patted my back sympathetically.

My heart broke for my brother doing what we all would've done—protect the person we loved more than anything. A part of me wanted to hate him for leaving us, but I knew I would do the same in a heartbeat.

Something mingled with the grief. Gratitude, I realized.

I sat up, blinking tears out of my eyes. Suddenly, all of the men froze, eyes widening. As one, they rushed towards the staircase, taking the steps two at a time. I followed along behind them helplessly, wondering what they'd heard to cause such an immediate reaction.

That question was answered as we piled into Addie's room. She was curled in Ronan's arms on the floor, tears dripping down her face as she sobbed.

Oh Addie...

I focused on her lips moving as she cried out something. No, not something. A name.

Calax.

I wanted to be strong for her, but I couldn't. Collapsing to my knees, I crawled towards her and took her from Ronan. I needed to feel her in my arms, to know she was alive and well. Only when she was settled firmly against me, her tear-stained face resting in the crook of my neck, did I allow my own tears to fall.

Pain washed over me in a tidal wave. Losing someone you loved did things to you. Changed you intricately.

We were strong, I knew that, but I also knew how death could alter your entire perspective on life. What if Calax's death was the one thing we couldn't come back from?

The six of us had lost a brother, and Addie had lost the love of her life.

That wasn't something any of us could just bounce back from. Memories would haunt us, our dreams would warp reality, and the slightest reminder would send us barreling over the edge.

As my tears fell harder, I realized the rest of the men had subtly exited the room. Even Fallon.

I worried about him the most, even more than Addie.

He considered himself the leader of our group, the brain. Addie may have been the heart and the glue that held us together, but Fallon—or Sarge as we so lovingly called him—was the one we looked to. The one who'd always protected us. How would he take this? How would he compartmentalize his grief?

All I could do was hold Addie a little tighter, a little closer, and hope that would be enough for now.

But I knew it never would be.

~

ADDIE

The Ragers were closing in on us. So many.

"Addie!" Calax called, his voice tight with agony. I searched for him desperately in the sea of blotchy faces and milky, sunken eyeballs.

"Calax!" I cried, cupping my mouth with my hands. When there was no reply, I raised my voice to be heard over the cacophony of grunts and growls. "CALAX!"

But I knew I wouldn't find him.

"Calax!"

I woke up with his name a scream on my lips. Desperately, I patted the bed beside me, but it was empty.

I was alone.

A strangled sob escaped me as I searched the darkened room for any of my men. Where were they? Were they gone? Dead?

I couldn't breathe past the tightness in my chest.

A scream built in my chest, tears simultaneously streaking my cheeks. I staggered out of bed only to trip over my own two feet and land in a puddle on the ground.

"Shit! Addie!" A worried, familiar face entered my clouded vision, and I clutched at Ronan's arms desperately. His considerably larger body folded around mine, rocking me back and forth. He whispered in my ear, comforting words about how they were all safe, how much he loved me, how he would never leave me.

I was distantly aware of a new set of arms pulling me away. I recognized Declan's scent immediately, burrowing myself further into him.

I didn't know how long we sat there, both of us crying, but it was long enough for my body to ache with shooting pains.

With a gurgling sound I couldn't quite recognize, I pulled myself away from Declan. His face was red and blotchy, the fauxhawk I admired so much hanging limply in his eyes. Almost absently, he brushed at the disobedient hair.

"You know?" I signed. There was only one thing that could cause such pain in his eyes. He nodded slowly.

"Are we...are we going to get through this?" I continued. He didn't answer right away, instead leaning forward to brush his lips against my forehead. I trembled at the connection, the feel of him. When he settled back, his arms still wrapped loosely around my waist, his eyes were determined.

"We'll try," he croaked out.

That was all any of us could do—try.

CHAPTER 8

*T*he next day, I found myself sitting across the table from Nik and Tommy.
Their shoulders brushed as they leaned forward, Tommy's expression inquisitive while Nik's was blank.

"I missed you both," I said at last, breaking the long silence we'd found ourselves in. I reached across the table to capture each of their hands. "So, so much."

Tommy sniffled, wiping away a non-existent tear.

"Don't do that shit again," he cursed, squeezing my hand. "Or else I'll spank your ass." His cheeks paled when he realized what he'd said, expression contorting into one of disgust. His nose crinkled. "Not the way your boy toys spank you, dear god. Yuck."

I snorted. Trust Tommy to bring a smile to my face, even with my uncharacteristically demure mood.

"Love you, Toms," I said, flashing him a smile. "Even though you were the one who left in the first place."

He feigned hurt. "Hey. I resent that. I was trying to be the hero and all that shit!"

This time, it was I who gave his hand a squeeze. "I'm just glad you're okay."

"Fucking peachy. Peaches and pears and applesauce."

Rolling my eyes, I turned towards Nik. I noted that his free hand was gripping Tommy's on top of the table. My brows rose at that, especially since I couldn't remember the last time Nik had initiated contact, but I didn't comment.

"And how are you, Nikolai? How have they been treating you?"

He shrugged his shoulders, face burning.

When he didn't answer, Tommy barged into the conversation yet again. I could tell Nik was grateful when his lip curled upwards minutely. "Jared's teaching me how to use a sword!"

That was…terrifying.

"That's great!" I lied with a cheeky smile. Tommy, always able to see through me, rolled his eyes.

"I don't just stab people without reason, Addie. I'm not a stab first, ask questions later type of person. That's more Fallon's style." He leaned forward then, voice dropping to a conspiratorial whisper. "I like him. And Declan. You have my blessing to date them."

Easygoing banter continued between the two of us, with even Nik listening and nodding along to our conversation. My cheeks hurt from how wide my smile was. It felt…right.

Having Nik and Tommy back in my life was a much needed balm to my tattered heart. It didn't fully heal the broken organ, but it helped keep it together. The pain was no longer unbearable.

Overcome with emotion, I cut Tommy off in the middle of his speech about flying tomato cans and bikini Ragers.

"I love you both," I choked out. Tommy's eyes widened at my admission before his lips curved up in a soft smile and crinkled the skin around his eyes.

"I love you too. Even if I do question your taste in men," he said.

Nik didn't say the words back to me, but his smile was luminous when his eyes met mine.

I had my two brothers back, and I'd thank God every day for that gift.

~

THE NEXT FEW days were a flurry of introductions, plans, and reunions. Every night, I found myself nestled between at least two of my men, if not more. There was never a lack of kisses, cuddles, and orgasms. It seemed as if Declan especially was attempting to make up for lost time.

Only Fallon seemed hesitant to do more than kiss me, but I never pushed him. He would tell me whatever he kept hidden when he was ready.

At night, we found ourselves convened around the dining room table. Some were sitting, but the majority of us were standing, our elbows on the table as we surveyed a map of the United States. Red marks marred the crinkly paper.

"What about this?" Fallon asked gruffly, finger tracing a highway near the east coast. Before he'd even finished marking his desired route, Davis was already shaking his head.

"Wouldn't work. A tsunami hit the coast a month ago. Wiped out a good chunk of homes and roads."

Tonya sat beside her husband, though her eyes occasionally flickered towards Fallon's ass on display in his tight-fitting jeans. Not that I blamed her. My men were fine specimens.

I wasn't even jealous of her blatant ogling. I didn't care that she had her eyes on him because I knew *his* eyes would only ever be on me.

Despite that, I liked Tonya and her crew. Davis was quiet, the gruff protector persona reminiscent of Calax, and Jared was funny and charismatic. Tonya herself was a good companion. She'd willingly given me some birth control she had collected, a morning after pill, and a box of condoms.

"Sheathe it before you reap it," she'd said with a wicked glint to her eyes.

"I still vote we head west," Jared interjected now, turning towards Fallon.

"Do you truly believe paradise exists?" my rough leader asked. His lips were pulled down into a tight frown.

Jared chuckled, but the sound was hollow even to me, a person who didn't know him that well.

"You, my friend, are a pessimist."

"Or I'm just realistic," Fallon countered. Ryder, sitting on one of the wooden kitchen chairs, clapped his hands to garner their attention and stop their bickering.

"What's this I hear about paradise?"

I could see the others leaning in as well, expressions varying from curious to cautious to excited. The latter was mainly worn by Ryder and Ronan.

Fallon sighed heavily.

"It's folklore. A story about a place where the storms can't reach and Ragers can't attack. Something that doesn't exist." With the last statement, he stared pointedly at Tonya, Davis, and Jared.

"People have seen it," Davis insisted. He forked his fingers through his dark hair, nearly down to his shoulders. Jared, on the other hand, had buzzed hair, so blond it was nearly white.

Tamson leaned forward, his palms pressing down on the oak table. "Where is this supposed paradise?"

The three of them exchanged uneasy looks. Tonya shifted uncomfortably from foot to foot.

"We actually aren't sure."

Asher raised an eyebrow, folding his arms over his chest. "Not sure?"

Jared once more broke in, raising his hands placatingly. "We only know what's been said at outposts."

This time, it was me who couldn't remain silent. "Outposts?" He'd spoken as if it was capitalized, as if it was equivalent to a name or a title. As if it was supposed to be "Outpost" instead of "outpost." Despite the normalcy of the word, goosebumps erupted on my arms and legs, and the hair on the back of my neck stood at attention. Fear skated down my spine, and I leaned further against Declan.

"There's a dozen of them around the United States now," Tonya explained, eyes lingering on the minuscule space between my body and Declan's. No doubt, she wondered about the unconventional relationship between me and the others. There were six of them and one of me, but we weren't shy about showing our affection. Exchanged kisses, lingering touches, cuddles on the couch.

"They were once run by the US military, but now they're more of a safe spot for travelers." Davis took over the explanation, eyes fixated on the chipped paint of the wall. "They offer food, a place to sleep, entertainment in the form of…um…services."

Not wanting to interrupt him, I shook Declan's shoulder. Once I had gained his attention, I signed, *"What does he mean by services?"*

His cheeks went red, and my stomach dropped.

Oh.

Oh.

"You didn't buy any of these services, did you?" I continued, hands trembling with each sign. I worried my lower lip between my teeth.

Declan's eyes widened in horror, and he shook his head vehemently.

"No, never! Fallon wanted to break the hand of the girl who dared to touch him." He chuckled darkly at the memory, but my mind was fixated on the fact that some gorgeous girl had touched *my* man.

Who knew I was so possessive? Geez.

Why don't you just pee on all of them already?

A ball of lead tangled with the nerves in my stomach. *"I wouldn't blame you if you did. We were separated. And even now, I'm dating all of you and you're only dating me. How is that fair?"*

I wanted to vomit at the mere thought of them with another woman, but I was determined not to be selfish. Were we even in an exclusive relationship? My heart ricocheted, drowning out even the roaring in my ears.

Declan stared at me for a long moment. Before he could reply, however, a soft patter of footsteps echoed from the living room, stopping in the kitchen.

Nikolai was dressed in too large pajamas, rubbing sleep from his eyes. For the first time in forever, he didn't have his large, red headphones around his neck. His sleepy eyes tracked all who was in the kitchen before resting on Tonya.

"You want some water?" Tonya's voice was…doting. The type of voice a mother would give a son. This time, jealousy *did* spear my chest as I watched their exchange. The easy way Tonya walked up to Nik, wrapping her arm around his shoulders. The tentative smile that touched my little brother's face. The hushed thanks as he took the proffered cup from Tonya's hand.

I pressed the palm of my hand to my chest.

Shit. That hurt.

"What are you doing up, Nik?" Tommy asked, languidly stretching in the doorway.

Tommy and Nik had a relationship I couldn't quite understand…one I wasn't sure *they* understood. They were almost always together, and I knew they slept in the same bed. Even now, their fingers brushed as Nik walked back towards the bedroom with his water and Tommy remained with us.

"What are we talking about, heathens?" Tommy plopped himself onto the counter, legs dangling.

"Paradise," Jared drawled.

"Before we do anything, we have to stop back at the house and pick up Kai and Doc," Ronan butted in, glancing at the others. Declan's brows furrowed, and an almost incandescent fury darkened Fallon's face.

"Who the hell are they?" he asked harshly, and I could've been mistaken, but it almost sounded like he was jealous. His eyes flickered to me sharply before looking away. His jaw was clenched so tightly, I was afraid it would break.

"You remember Doc," Asher said, a small smile evident in his voice. He, too, had seen the jealousy on Fallon's face. Always the perceptive one. "He treated Addie for her injuries. They spent *a lot* of time alone together."

Fallon's eyes darkened further.

"And Kai... Well, let's just say it involves adult kidnapping," Ryder added. His white teeth gleamed as he smiled. "I know he and Addie are really close. They sometimes have sleepovers together."

Fallon looked positively murderous, enraged, seconds away from getting in his car, driving to the house Doc and Kai were held up in, and cutting off both their dicks.

Not that Ryder had lied, necessarily. Kai and I *did* have sleepovers. Sometimes I needed a break from all the testosterone with...more testosterone. At least testosterone that didn't constantly kiss me and treat me like breakable glass. I needed Kai to call me out on my shit and be my friend. God only knew how badly I was lacking in that department.

"Oh, calm down," I said, patting Declan's arm reassuringly and flashing Fallon a shit-eating grin. His eyes narrowed when he realized we were teasing him. "They prefer sword fighting, if you know what I mean."

"I like sword fighting!" Tommy piped in with a large smile, happy to contribute to the conversation.

"That was...oddly disturbing," Ronan mused, shuddering.

"Before we do anything, I want to have a funeral. For Calax," I said resolutely. My lower lip trembled, and fresh tears welled in my eyes. Still, I willed them back. I had to remain strong. Calax would've wanted me to.

"Of course, Princess."

"We'll have it tomorrow, Kitten."

"Whatever you need."

What I needed was Calax, but that would never happen.

That night, I cried until my face hurt and my throat was raw. But crying couldn't numb the pain in my chest, my head, my soul.

Only a dead man could help me.

If some people dreamt of sugar plums and fairies, I envisioned handsome men with soft smiles and whispered words of love. For the first time, I fell asleep with a smile on my face.

CHAPTER 9

CALAX

*I*f there was one saving grace to being a prisoner, it was that I had an actual room and bed.

Until...I didn't.

My body was throbbing from a particularly bad beating, and I couldn't see out of my left eye. I imagined I looked like shit.

What a shest, I groused, my lips tilting upwards at my unintentional use of Addie's favorite word. Apparently, it was a combination of shit and fest. A shit fest.

It was evident they didn't know what to do with me. It had been months since I'd last seen Adelaide, and they knew as well as I did that the team would never stay in one location for too long. It pained me to know I was nothing but bait. Even the "interrogations" were just a pathetic excuse to beat the shit out of me.

But they needed me alive, at least for now, to lure Addie to them when they found her.

They'd removed me from my small room and deposited me in an even smaller space, resembling a cell, a few days ago.

Stereotypical villains much?

Gray, stone walls encased me, coldness permeating the air. Iron bars separated me from the walkway, and dried blood stained the walls and floors.

What type of building was I in that had a damn prison in the basement? A fucking medieval dungeon? The pungent scent of copper reached my nostrils combining with decaying flesh.

I was dirty, sweaty, and probably smelled something fierce. Still, I kept a small smile on my face as I tossed rocks at the bars, attempting to land one in an abandoned bucket a few feet away.

I pumped my fists in the air when the rock finally settled where I wanted it to.

"They're going to break you, you know," a scratchy voice said from the cell beside me. I jumped, since I hadn't had known anyone else was around me. I'd inventoried the cells when I was first brought down, but the voice was coming from the direction opposite the doorway.

"I'd like to see them try." Smirking through the pain running rampant through my face and body, I picked up another handful of rocks and resumed my methodical throws.

Fortunately, there was a hanging bulb in the sparsely lit hallway. I might've gone insane—well, more insane—if I was plunged in absolute darkness.

"What's your name?" the stranger asked. He coughed violently, as if his voice was unaccustomed to speaking for such an extended period of time.

Frowning, I considered my options quickly. While the guys upstairs knew my name and identity, I didn't trust my fellow prisoner. For all I knew, he could be working with the assholes who'd tortured me daily. The less he knew about me, the better.

"Callie," I decided on at last, my heart warming at the nickname Addie had given me. That and "Big Guy" were her two favorites.

Addie…

The stranger chuckled, effectively pulling me out of what might've been a riveting daydream.

"Okay. Let's pretend I believe that. Why are you here?"

My suspicions only grew. Here we were, shoved in cages, and the man wanted to focus on the past, not on a plan to escape.

When I remained stubbornly silent, tossing rocks into the bucket, he released a weary sigh.

"You can call me Doug," he said. Another cough rattled him.

"Doug," I repeated blandly. "And is that your real name?"

"Is Callie yours?" he retorted.

"No."

There was no use lying.

He chuckled darkly. "You're smart, kid. Don't trust anyone."

"Even you?" I couldn't help but ask, twisting my body so I faced the cement wall. Another laugh escaped him.

"Especially not me."

Another bout of silence settled between us. Despite the many aches and pains in my body, I couldn't find it within me to sit still any longer. Jumping to my feet, I paced the small confines of my prison.

I needed to get out of there.

That one single thought ran rampant within me, racing even my heart that was currently battering against my rib cage. Oh, I'd tried. Thirteen times to be exact.

Ten of those times had been after I'd woken up from my surgery and discovered Addie wasn't with me. The last three times had been after an extensive session with Asshole and Bitch. Every time, they caught me. Every time, I was punished.

Hell, the farthest I got was a few steps away from the door before men jumped on me.

Maybe an ally would be good in this shithole.

"Why are you here?" I asked, breaking up the monotony of silence.

For a moment, I thought Doug wouldn't answer. When he finally spoke, his voice was raspy, as if sandpaper had been used on his vocal cords. "Used to work with them."

His admission had my hands balling into fists, eyes narrowing. Anger thrummed through me.

"I don't even have to look at you to know you are glaring at me." He chuckled harshly. "Discovered my wife was fucking the head honcho. I confronted him, he lost his shit, and I've been here ever since."

"And your wife?" I asked absently.

"Probably still fucking him."

Silence.

"What about you?" Doug questioned.

My voice was soft when I replied, "I fell in love."

He waited, probably expecting me to say more, but I kept my lips pursed in a thin line.

"Well, there's your problem," Doug said, his voice reminding me of an old wise man children talked to in storybooks. "Falling in love only leads to pain. But falling in hate? That's when you fucking win wars."

∼

ADDIE

We held the funeral in the fenced in backyard. It was a beautiful day, the sun brilliant in the cloudless sky. Fitting, I supposed, for a funeral. I wouldn't have been able to handle it if the clouds opened up, releasing a torrent of rain.

I had dry eyes. It only made sense for the day to be too.

Fallon had crafted a wooden cross beneath the single tree. Carved into the smooth wood was Calax's name.

Calax Griffin.

My eyes traced each letter until they were etched into my memory.

There was no body for us to bury, but it wasn't difficult to imagine my beautiful Calax resting beneath layers of dirt. Was he happy? Safe? Would I see him again when I died?

The numbness I'd felt initially after his death cloaked me now. All I was capable of was rapid blinking as I focused on the cross.

Calax's entire life, summarized in these few short minutes, represented by a haphazardly carved symbol.

I remembered when Tamson and Asher had searched for his body. It was difficult, since the house had still been infested by Ragers, but they'd done it for me. Unsurprisingly, their search was futile.

There was no body to be found. The Ragers had destroyed him so completely, so seamlessly, that nothing but bones and dried blood remained in the hallway.

Blood.

Like a dam cracking, I exploded. Sob after sob escaped me as I fell to my knees. Dirt collected on my bare knees, the black skirt of my dress riding up, and pebbles embedded themselves into my hands.

I felt warm arms surround me, and Fallon's deep timbre whispered soothing, nonsensical nothings into my ear. Another body met the first, and I stared into Tamson's eyes.

"It's okay, Addie. Let it out. Let it out."

"It hurts," I cried out. My chest felt as if it were exploding, and my heart battered against my rib cage, the pain excruciating.

The guys alternated holding me, brushing my hair out of my face, and dabbing at my eyes. Each of them cried with me, cried for their fallen brother.

Pain.

Pain everywhere.

It was *unbearable*.

They said there was nothing you couldn't survive, but those people had obviously not lost someone they loved.

It was like running a race with no definitive ending. Your lungs burned, legs ached, but still, you ran. Tears dropped from your eyes at the strain, but you never let up. It was that crippling disappointment when you reached where the finished line should've been and you saw nothing but forest. Alone. You were alone, running an endless race. The cycle continued until the pressure became too much, and you succumbed to a fit of despair, succumbed to death.

I was running repeatedly in a never-ending cycle, but the second I would've reached Calax, he disappeared like a damn mirage. I needed him like a drought needed rain. Without it, the land would die.

I would die.

There were no words to encapsulate the pain, the anguish, as I curled in on myself like yellowing paper and cried. Fallon spoke softly to the cross, to Calax, but his words were lost to me.

I was dimly aware of a new pair of arms, a smaller set, wrapping around me. It was enough of a shock to startle me out of my stupor. Glancing up, I met Nik's dark eyes. He blinked at me, eyes shimmering with unshed tears, before he resumed his cautious holding. His hand limply patted my hair, the touch hesitant, but it was enough for me.

I held my little brother tighter against me, crying into his hair.

"I'm so sorry, Calax," I whispered. "I love you."

CHAPTER 10

ADDIE

We set out the following night, me, Fallon, Ryder, and Asher in one car, while Nik and Tommy rode with Declan, Ronan, and Tam in another. Tonya, Davis, and Jared drove separately in a beat-up pickup truck with dirty, unwashed windows, russet brown siding, and beer bottles scattered on the backseats.

Ryder drove in our vehicle, a van, while Fallon took the passenger seat. Asher and I sat in the middle section. The back was full of supplies—everything from medicine they'd collected over the months to clothing and food. As Fallon had stridently stated to our team and newcomers, we would not be coming back.

Of course, that set me off all over again. Calax may not have died in the nondescript, neighborhood home, but his memory was laid to rest there. Fallon assured me we would continue paying tribute to him. Some cheesy shit that went in one ear and out the other.

Still, that did not quell the grief that threatened to bury me alive in the proverbial ground, like Calax's body should've been in the proper burial he'd never gotten.

I blinked away the sudden onslaught of tears, focusing on the rolling, somewhat familiar, landscape.

By the time we pulled into the house we'd been staying at, the sun had lowered, painting everything in palest green and pink.

"I'm surprised they're still here," Ryder murmured, nodding towards the candle flickering in the window. My smile broadened when the front door was roughly pushed open and Kai emerged, dressed in pajama bottoms and a white shirt. His eyes widened when he saw me.

"Holy shit! We thought you guys were dead or something." Eating up the distance, he pulled me into his arms.

Fallon, behind me, took a threatening step closer, eyes narrowed.

"Hands off the merchandise," he said darkly. I snorted, lifting my head from Kai's chest but not releasing him.

"Merchandise? Seriously?"

His scowl turned into a sheepish smile. Instead of a proper apology, he grunted.

Fallon, I realized, really only spoke two languages—grunts and growls, the double G. It was his preferred form of communication. Sometimes, I wondered if he'd been plucked from the Stone Age.

His scowl returned. "You said that out loud."

"Not sorry," I sang, finally releasing Kai. "Fallon, this is Kai. Kai, this is Fallon and Declan. My boyfriends. And over there is Tonya, Davis, and Jared."

Fallon and Declan both straightened imperceptibly at the introduction and title. Their chests puffed out as they extended their hands.

Oh yeah. They liked being introduced as my boyfriends.

We quickly explained the plan to Kai and Doc before retiring to our rooms. Tonya, Jared, and Davis remained in the living room, and Tommy and Nik took a guest room.

My men surprised me by all piling into my room, Tam and Ronan dragging in two spare mattresses.

"You're all sleeping in here tonight?" I asked them, moving to the adjoining bathroom. I left the door open as I brushed my teeth using a water bottle, mint toothpaste, and a toothbrush we'd found inside a gas station.

Watching them get ready for the night felt so...mundane. As if we'd done it hundreds of times before. A tiny thrill went through me.

Because...*ohmygawd, we were doing couple stuff.*

All of them except Declan looked over, laughing, and my cheeks flamed.

"I didn't mean to say that out loud," I admitted.

"But you did." Ryder's sultry smirk was firmly in place. "Because we're a couple doing couple things. A...very large couple."

"A very large couple would imply that all of you were doing couple things," I retorted smartly. "And I don't see any of you kissing."

Ryder wiggled his eyebrows suggestively, a mischievous gleam in his eyes I recognized all too well, before he lunged across the bed and grabbed the back of Tam's head.

Oh my god.

I stopped breathing. Literally stopped.

Their lips moved closer, closer, closer...

The second they would've been touching, a soft knock sounded on the door.

"Addie?" Tonya's familiar voice said through the wood. "Can I talk to you for a minute?"

"Fucking dammit!" I cursed, slapping my hand on the marble bathroom countertop. I leveled Ryder and Tamson with my best glare, both men blinking innocently at me. "You two, don't even think about moving."

With one last wistful glance in their direction, I marched to the door and wrenched it open.

"What?" I growled. She blinked at me wordlessly.

But the girl deprived me of an orgasm and would receive no sympathy from me. I knew where that kiss would lead…and my poor vagina had been neglected for too long. A solid day, the horror.

Her blinking increased, and muffled laughter reached me from behind.

"Shit. I said that out loud, didn't I?"

"Just about your sexual frustrations," Ronan called, amusement thick in his voice. "Are we not taking care of your needs, Princess?"

"Don't Princess me," I snapped. "My vagina is empty of cock, and you're all to blame. When I come back, you better be naked and, like, kissing or something."

More laughter.

Poor Tonya looked as if she was seconds away from fainting.

"But we all want to kiss you, Kitten, and only you," Ryder cooed. "So when you get back, I'll be more than willing to rectify the situation."

"By kissing Tamson?" I pleaded, finally glancing back and batting my eyelashes. He'd moved back to the bed, his dark chest and tattoos on display. When he saw me looking, he rolled his eyes.

"Maybe. If you're good."

I would be the best damn girl in the entire world if orgasms were the reward. Placing apples on desks type of good. Hell, I would even clean my damn room.

Totally willing to kiss ass…well…at least their asses.

Tonya's face paled further, and more laughter drifted to me.

Before I could accidentally speak my thoughts again, I hurried out of the room and shut the door.

We walked in awkward silence towards the kitchen until Tonya broke it, fiddling with the hem of her shirt. "Sorry for interrupting."

"Oh, don't worry about it. You only interrupted what was probably going to end up being the sexual fantasy of every girl who has ever lived. No biggie. They're one in a million."

I tried to be empathetic, but when her eyes went wide, I realized I may have put my foot in my mouth. Again.

Were orgasms and sexual fantasies not normal girl talk?

Gossip Girl had lied to me.

The kitchen was dark, illuminated only by the moon glowing through the fluttery blinds. Tonya moved swiftly to a candle, lit it, and then pressed her back against the wall, watching me.

"So…what did you want to talk to me about?" I asked lightly. In all honesty, I was curious. No girl had ever pulled me from a potential orgy before to have a top-secret conversation.

Was this…?

Was I finally living a normal life?

The thought made my heart ricochet in my chest, and I flashed Tonya a blinding smile to put her at ease.

However, she wasn't looking at me. Her long, nimble fingers were once more fiddling with the hem of her shirt.

"It's about Tommy and Nikolai," she said softly. Panic churned in my stomach instantly, and I found myself taking a trembling step towards her.

"What's wrong? Are they okay? Where are they?" I asked, firing off the questions in rapid succession. My turbulent, panicky thoughts were only soothed by a tiny smile pulling up Tonya's lips. Surely she wouldn't have smiled if something had happened, right?

"They're fine. Safe. Sleepy." She waved a hand dismissively. "I just...I need to address something with you."

I wait with bated breath.

"They love you dearly. Anyone with eyes can see that. They think the world of you, and I know you think that of them." I could tell there was a "but" coming with that. Tonya took a shuddering breath, turning her back towards me and placing her hands on the counter. "I've gotten to know them the last few months. Care for them. I may not be their mother or their sister, but I do want to remain a part of their lives."

Her words were...not what I expected.

Spinning towards me once more, I was shocked to see unshed tears glimmering in her eyes.

"I lost my child, my little girl, when this whole shit show started. She was with the babysitter while I was at work. A nurse. And...look...I know those boys aren't my baby, but I love them. I'm going to stay in their lives, whether you want me to or not. I mean, I know I'm nothing special to them and—"

I cut off her ramblings by placing my hand on her arm.

"You don't have to apologize, and you don't need to ask for my permission to remain in their lives. That's their choice. But...I see the way they look at you. They love you, and I would never say no to more people loving my family." I paused, considering my words. "Unless you're talking about loving my guys, then we'll have a problem."

Her eyes sparkled when she smiled, and I was struck by how beautiful she actually was, with her curly black hair and brown skin.

"I have one man to deal with. I don't need more." She leaned forward to whisper conspiratorially. "But seriously, six? How do you keep them all straight? I'd be forgetting their names. And they're all okay with it? And stay exclusive to you?"

I smiled, popping my hip against the low kitchen table.

Finally, we could begin the much needed girl talk.

WHEN I ARRIVED BACK in my room, I was disappointed to see all my men already asleep. Tamson and Ryder shared my bed, an Addie-sized space between their two muscular bodies.

In the cover of darkness, I shimmied out of my shorts but left my shirt on.

Crawling across the mattress, I settled between the two warm bodies, Tam's arm immediately encircling my waist.

I snuggled against him, my back to his front, and sighed in contentment.

Dark eyes, barely visible in the scarcely lit room, stared back at me.

"You're still awake?" I questioned Ryder, reaching a hand out to intertwine our fingers.

"How was girl talk?"

"Good." I smiled. "Once we got the hang of it, I told her about all my orgasms."

His chuckle was dark, delicious. Sinful.

"I'm glad. They seem like good people."

"They are. I'm happy Nik and Tommy have them." I shifted closer, still keeping my body against Tam's. "But…why are you guys asleep?"

"We waited up for you, but you took too long," he responded with another low, sultry chuckle. I pouted. "Another day, Kitten."

"So…have you ever, like, kissed a guy before? One of them?" The thought made my heart pound, my breath catch, and heat pool between my thighs. I couldn't deny that the visual was enticing, mouthwatering even.

"Does that make you hot, Kitten? Thinking of us all with you? Kissing each other to pleasure you?" His voice turned low and raspy, and that blaze turned into an inferno. I gulped, entranced by his umber eyes.

He continued, "I'm not gonna lie. I don't think any of us have ever kissed a guy, nor do we really want to. *But* I can't deny the thought of you watching, salivating, touching yourself…" He trailed off, body shaking with a shudder. "Fuck, that's sexy."

"You like that?" I whispered, trying to mimic his low, seductive cadence. "You like thinking about me putting my fingers into my pussy? So turned on by you that I can't think straight. My fingers tweaking my nipples."

He groaned, breath hitching.

"Do you have any idea what you do to me?" he asked, voice breathless. "Do you?"

Ignoring Tam's arms still around my waist, he cupped my ass and pulled me against him. His throbbing cock touched my stomach through his basketball shorts. I released a tiny whimper.

"I want to bury myself so far in you that you forget both our names." He leaned forward to nip my lower lip. "Soon, Kitten, I'll make you mine completely."

"I'm already yours," I whispered, throat closing with emotion. "I love you, Ry. So much."

"I love you too." He pressed his lips to my forehead in a chaste, tantalizing kiss.

"And you're okay with…all this?" I waved a hand to encompass the "this" I meant. Namely, five other men sleeping in my room.

"I'm not gonna lie and say I don't want you all to myself, but they love you and you love them. I can't fault any of you for that. My brothers deserve love, as do you. And you're capable of it. I see how you love—with your entire heart and soul. I know your love for all of us is ten times more potent than the love of one normal female."

I closed the distance between us and pressed my lips to his. He tasted sweet and minty from the toothpaste.

The kiss was over in seconds, but it left delicious tingles in its wake.

"Sleep, my love. We'll finalize our plans tomorrow. Decide if we're staying or finding this supposed paradise."

"Do you believe it exists?" I asked meekly. "Paradise?"

"I don't know. But I think we're going to find out."

CHAPTER 11

ASHER

By mutual consensus, we agreed to travel to the nearest outpost and ask around about the alleged 'paradise.' Fallon had made it clear that we would not partake in a wild goose chase. If the outpost led to a dead end, we would bunker down in a fenced in home.

The drive was relatively uneventful. Besides a splatter of acid rain and a couple dozen Ragers, we ran into very little trouble.

The heat, on the other hand, proved to be a problem. It crept up on us with the force of a freight train. The sun sat high in the sky, but it felt like it was mere inches from my body. Even with the air conditioning blowing, sweat coated my skin. It was blistering hot, almost to the point of making you feel sick.

Half a dozen water bottles littered the ground of the backseat. Addie was insistent on Tommy and Nikolai staying hydrated. She herself was *not* covered in sweat, cheeks and forehead red. Definitely dehydrated.

After she shoved another water bottle at Fallon, I placed my hand on hers gently.

"Sweetheart, don't neglect yourself by taking care of us. You need to drink too."

She made a face at me, but complied when I handed her a second bottle of water.

Up ahead, the van that Tonya, Davis, Jared, Kai, and Doc were driving slowed to a stop.

"Stay here," Fallon instructed gruffly. With a pointed look at Ronan sitting beside him, the two exited with their guns loaded.

The car idled on the road, and Addie took their absence as an opportunity to lean forward, pressing her face to the vents.

"So. Hot," she moaned dramatically. Ryder, sitting in the middle row of the car beside Nik and Tommy, wiggled his eyebrows suggestively.

"Yes, you are."

"Language!" Tommy spat out, and Ryder frantically gripped his chest, the dramatic asshole.

"I didn't even swear!"

"Sexual innuendos are the same as swear words."

"Look at you. Using big words," he teased, and Tommy's glower deepened.

"Look at you. With your nutsack removed and fed to Ragers."

"No nutsacks are being removed," Addie said absently, still staring intently at the vent. Cold air blew her brown hair back, and she moaned.

That sound made blood rush to my cock, and I shifted uncomfortably. The memory of Addie's lips around my erection...

I was barely able to contain my own moan.

Fallon and Ronan returned to the car seconds later, faces somber.

"What's up?" Tam asked. He and Declan sat behind Tommy, Nik, and Ryder. We were fortunate to have found a van that both ran and fitted all of us in a used car lot. An eleven passenger.

"Ragers. Probably at least fifty of them up ahead."

"Shit," I breathed. Instinctively, I inched closer to Addie as my eyes scanned the horizon.

Their forms were minuscule, silhouettes in the blinding sun, but it reminded me eerily of a wave approaching the shoreline. In this case, the wave was full of flesh-eating monsters.

"Is there another way to the outpost?" Addie asked. We'd been planning on driving to the one a few hours east of Atlanta, in a town I couldn't remember the name of, but now I wondered if that was even possible.

Paradise or not, Fallon would never do something that could cost us our lives.

"We'll go around it," our leader said resolutely. It was this behavior alone that had caused us to nickname him Sarge—a drill sergeant and a play on his last name all in one. He knew what he wanted and cupped life by the metaphorical balls. "It might add a few hours to our trip, but I'd prefer that over..." He trailed off ominously, his hand clenching the steering wheel.

I heard the words he didn't say. *Couldn't* say.

Over another death.

Memories of Calax bombarded me, assaulted me, but I brushed them away. I would've been the first to admit that I wasn't as close to him as some of the others had been. I was reserved, soft some would say, while he was hard edges and pene-trating eyes. If it wasn't for our team, we would've fallen out of sorts years ago.

If it wasn't for Addie...

I glanced towards the brunette sitting beside me, eyes scanning her surround-ings in rapt interest. Her brow puckered as it always did when she was deep in thought.

"I'm so happy we're stopping," she muttered to no one in particular. Another quirk of our girl. "I need to shit."

Ronan snorted, and Ryder cracked up behind her. Her cheeks pinkened, but she held her head high.

My girl was crazy, but then again, so was I.

I glanced at my brothers, and I knew they were thinking about the conversation we had the other night while Tonya was talking to Addie.

Fallon nodded once to show he understood, and my lips quirked.

If Calax's death taught us one thing, it was that life was too short. We needed to hold onto the little things while we could. Grip them for dear life.

And those big things? Like the ones we loved above all else? We needed to show it to them constantly.

And tonight, we would do just that.

~

CALAX

"You are a horrible singer," I quipped, resting my head against the cool stone of my prison.

Doug chuckled but continued to sing loudly, horribly out of tune.

"You're just jealous of my gift!" he cooed.

Gift.

What he had was a weapon that could be used for mass destruction.

His song was interrupted by the sound of a door opening and closing. Doug immediately ceased his singing.

Standing up, I moved to the bars and gripped them firmly. It was rare we would see our prison guards more than once a day. They would arrive periodically to deliver us food and sometimes dump out our chamber pots.

Yup. Chamber pots.

A fucking bucket I had to squat over to take a shit.

The click of heels was the only indication it wasn't our usual stone-faced guard. A second later, Bitch appeared alongside Asshole. Her blonde hair was, as always, impeccably straightened and cascading to her shoulders. Her cold, dead eyes flickered to me and my gaunt, skinny form. Her lips twisted in disgust.

"You look horrible."

"Not trying to impress you, sweetheart," I drawled.

Ignoring my snark, Bitch turned towards Asshole with a raised brow. "He'll need a shower before he meets with..." She slyly cast her eyes in my direction, thin lips pursing. Meets with who? "I'll wash him."

Fuck, no.

"You'll do no such thing," Asshole sneered. "You're still my wife, and that's crossing a fucking line."

"Trouble in paradise?" I asked teasingly, my lips twitching at the accidental relationship reveal. Bitch glared at me hotly, but Asshole kept his attention firmly on her.

"You may have been rejected by your last boyfriend, but that doesn't give you the right to be a cheating bitch. Look all you want, but don't fucking touch."

She sniffed haughtily. "Fine. It's not like I want to touch him anyway. He smells disgusting."

"It's shit," I piped in helpfully. "You know, from the lack of soap and water after I drop a mean one."

If it was possible, and I didn't think it physically was, she looked even more disgusted. Her face turned a shade greener.

"Step away from the door," Asshole instructed me, and I complied. I was too weak, too tired, to do anything else. The lack of food was beginning to weaken me. But still, I was the good boy who moved without question. Listened. Obeyed.

Like a fucking dog.

Asshole procured a set of dangly keys and placed one in the bronze lock. When the bars were pushed open, Asshole grabbed my arm roughly and pulled me out. My knees buckled, but he kept his arm firmly around my shoulders to keep me steady.

"Come on."

"Where are we going?" I asked roughly as we moved to the exit. I tried to peek into Doug's cell, but it was too far away. Only shadows greeted me.

Asshole shoved my shoulder roughly, and I fell to my knees. High heels appeared in my vision as Bitch crouched down. Her pinstripe skirt bunched upwards, revulsion filling me as she purposely tried to flash me her disgusting pussy.

"You have a meeting, Calax. And he won't be as generous as we've been. Either you help us find Addie...or we kill you. Simple as that."

CHAPTER 12

ADDIE

I was submerged in darkness.

It wasn't a normal darkness you would get when stepping outside at night. Not the inky gray as stars peppered the sky and the moon hung suspended overhead. It wasn't even the dark you get when you step inside a windowless room, turn off every light, and wait with bated breath.

I couldn't put my finger on how it was different, only that it was.

This darkness felt as if I was trekking through feet of black tar. The blistering hot air made sweat drip down my neck and my hair cling to my scalp.

"Hello?" I whispered into the obscurity. "Is anyone there?"

Silence greeted me, as pronounced as the darkness itself. My stomach somersaulted as I took a tentative step forward. I strained my eyes, desperate to see anything other than the pitch-black darkness.

"Anyone there?" I repeated, and my voice echoed back at me.

Anyone.

Anyone.

Goosebumps pebbled on my skin at the ominous sound reverberating through the darkness. I couldn't even see my hands mere inches from my face.

Trudging through what felt like snow, I became distinctly aware of a voice calling my name.

A voice as familiar to me as my own.

"Calax," I whispered, spinning rapidly.

The darkness receded as a single spotlight illuminated my tall, surly lover. The mere sight of him caused my heart to ricochet. My chest was as taut as a laundry string spanning between two buildings.

He looked exactly as I remembered him. His dark hair grazing his eyes, sculpted cheek-bones and jawline, muscular body that rivaled all of my other lovers. His eyes, though, reflected a tenderness he only reserved for me. I melted under his stare.

"Callie," I whispered hoarsely. Reverently.

I didn't just love the large man. I adored him. He was my first love, the first person who'd looked past the superficial façade to the broken soul underneath. He'd held my heart with both hands, exhibiting a tenderness I never would've imagined from someone like him.

For so long, I'd hated him. But my hate was only a front for the true way I felt about him. He wasn't safe or easy. He made me feel with an intensity that left me breathless. Fear, anguish, love. They all became woven together.

With him, I was alive.

And I loved him. I loved him so damn much, it was almost a physical, excruciating pain to see him now. My heart catapulted out of my chest when he flashed me a blinding smile—the same smile that often remained hidden behind scowls and frowns.

"Baby."

"I miss you. So fucking much."

"Then come get me," he countered. I froze in my pursuit to him, head tilting curiously to the side.

"Huh?"

"Think it through, baby. Did you see a body?"

His words evoked memories from that horrible night. The Ragers converging on us. Calax's pleading, anguished eyes meeting mine before he was completely devoured. The snap of my precarious sanity.

"I saw you die," I whispered, emotion jamming my airway.

"But did you?" he asked mockingly. The same no-nonsense voice I'd fallen in love with. He never allowed me to wallow in self-pity. He saw my bullshit and immediately called me out on it.

"Cut the crap, Bitch," I retorted, reverting to the childish back and forth banter we used to have. His lips curled.

"Don't call me a bitch, Mega Bitch."

"Don't call me a mega bitch, Extreme Asshole Bitch."

We shared soft smiles, the tension of the last few months draining from my body. Talking with him again, teasing him, being with him...

The ache that had grown in my chest didn't entirely alleviate, but it did lessen.

"You know that cheesy saying? About how a person is always alive because they live in someone's memories and blah blah blah?" I asked, venturing a step forward. "They're right. I'm here with you, aren't I?"

"And you can be with the real me if you looked," he responded dryly.

Dream Calax was as big of a dick as Real Calax.

"You're dead."

"No, I'm not. Why else would your subconscious dream of me like this?" he countered with a devilish grin.

"Because I want it to be true so badly. I want you to still be alive. I miss you. I need you. I can't breathe without you," I lamented. Tears sprung to my eyes.

His own features softened. "Didn't I promise I'd never leave you? Never. I'll love you forever, baby. Forever."

His form began to shimmer around the edges, disappearing before my very eyes. Desperate to touch him, kiss him, show him how much I loved him, I broke into a run.

But the darkness returned with a vengeance, once more obscuring Calax from view. In the abyss, I began to scream and cry.

"Calax!"

~

I AWOKE WITH A START.

"Wake up, sleepy head. We're here," Asher said softly, brushing my sweaty, tangled hair out of my face. I blinked the sleep away, glancing warily around.

The darkness had descended, painted with stars and a crescent moon the palest shade of gold.

"How long was I asleep?" I asked drowsily. Moving slowly, I tested each of my taut muscles. After being cramped in a car for hours on end, it hurt to move more than a millimeter.

"Half a day," replied Asher easily. "We're stopping for the night. Jared and Fallon already cleared the building."

The building was actually an elegant hotel complete with balconies lining the sides and intricately trimmed wood. The beige color was offset by darker ornaments decorating the windows. At five stories tall, I recognized the building as being owned by a competitor of my dear old daddy.

Funny how things turn out.

Taking Asher's hand, I marveled at the inside complete with a three-tiered chandelier, a fountain currently devoid of water, and leather chairs on either side of a large fish tank.

My heart lurched uncomfortably at the dozens upon dozens of dead fish floating at the surface of the water.

Still, there was no denying the elegance and opulence of the lobby. Even in the midst of the apocalypse, it was gorgeous.

"This place is fucking beautiful," I cooed, peering around the purple and green themed lobby. The colors, oddly enough, didn't clash. The light green made the room softer while the deep purple captured your attention.

The inside was hot, but nothing compared to the heatwave outside. Sweat still prickled at my skin, but it was no longer unbearable.

"The others are upstairs already," Asher explained, tugging at my hand. We moved in silence towards a grand staircase in the far corner of the lobby.

"Asher?"

"Yes, sweetheart?"

"Is it possible that Calax is still alive?"

Asher stumbled up one of the steps, gripping the golden banister to right himself. Wide-eyed, he turned towards me. I hurried to elaborate.

"We never actually saw a body, and we left before... Well, he was still alive when we left." My throat closed at that statement.

Did he think we'd abandoned him?

I knew he'd told us to leave, but saying something and doing something were entirely separate things.

Did he actually expect us to leave, or did he assume we would come back for him? Save him?

Refusing to go down that road, I focused back on Asher. The skin between his brows was creased as he carefully considered his answer.

"I know you want him to still be alive. Heaven only knows I do too. But, sweetheart, there's no way he could've survived that. Not without immediate medical help. I'm sorry." And I could tell he *was* sorry, and not just for Calax's death.

For bearing the news that he was never coming back.

I knew it, I honestly did, but something in my heart stopped me from believing it completely. Was it foolish to hold onto hope?

Yes, very much so.

That hope would inevitably shatter, and I would be left with nothing but pain. For now, I would clutch my hope, my fractured heart, close to my chest. I refused to succumb to the despair yet again.

That hope would keep me sane, I knew, in the coming weeks.

"Come on." Asher tugged at my hand. "We have a surprise for you."

"Surprise? What is it?"

He turned his head, a tremulous smile on his face. "If I told you, it wouldn't be a surprise. But first, you need to speak with Fallon."

"Fallon?" I asked, blinking. "Why?"

"No idea. Maybe it's another surprise."

I had the feeling I was in for a surprise all right, but not necessarily a pleasant one.

As we walked, I made outrageous guesses about the surprise.

"A sparkly dildo on a unicorn?"

"The USA swim team?"

"A girlfriend for Mof?"

My cat was currently with Tommy and Nik in whatever room they were holed up in. It seemed as if I had been betrayed by the black critter.

Word of advice? Never trust a cat.

I spun out of Asher's embrace before dramatically swooping back in. I rested my chin on his shoulder and smiled up at him.

"Is it a hot orgy?"

His cheeks flamed deliciously.

Before he could confirm or deny, he stopped in front of a door on the second floor.

"Fallon's in there. We'll see you after, all right?"

"Sir, yes, sir." I saluted, wiggling my hips.

Wiggling. My. Hips.

Sometimes, I wondered what was wrong with me.

Asher smiled kindly, not commenting on my awkward dancing, before knocking on the door. A moment later, Fallon answered, face solemn. That wasn't uncharacteristic. Our team leader was a moody bastard.

"Heard that," Fallon muttered.

"Me, Fallon. I grunt." I lowered my voice in an admittedly poor impersonation of the man before me. It had the desired reaction—his face softened instantly, and a small smile touched his face.

Pecking Asher on the cheek goodbye, I followed Fallon into a candlelit room. It had a single king-sized bed, a desk, a television on a stand, and a connected bathroom.

It was the bed Fallon sat on, twiddling his thumbs anxiously. It was shocking enough to see Fallon in a setting as mundane as a hotel room, but seeing him nervous? That was something I thought I would never see.

"You wanted to talk to me?" I asked, suddenly timid and unsure.

Was he breaking up with me?

Could he even break up with me when we were never officially dating?

Think of the children. What would we tell them?

"We don't have children, Addie." His lips twitched.

"I meant our nonexistent children. Obviously." I waved a hand dismissively before joining him on the bed. Immediately, he grabbed my hand and began to play with my fingers.

That was *not* something you would do if you were planning on breaking up with a person, right?

"I'm not breaking up with you," Fallon said quietly. His entire attention was riveted on my lean fingers. His hand engulfed mine, skin a few shades darker than my own pasty coloring.

Tension I hadn't even known I'd been carrying seeped out of me. My shoulders visibly relaxed, and I shifted closer to Fallon.

"So…?"

He took a deep, shuddering breath. His eyes snapped closed, and his hand went to pinch the bridge of his nose. I might've believed he was annoyed with me if he hadn't suddenly opened his eyes, allowing me to glimpse the anguish and fear.

Worry slammed into me. "What is it? What's wrong?"

"I'm going to tell you something, but I'm afraid you'll hate me." His voice cracked at that. The unbreakable Sarge, the commanding leader, was scared.

He was…broken.

"I'll never hate you."

Another deep exhale left his chapped lips. His hand tightened over mine.

"I was engaged."

His words were biting, fast, nearly inarticulate, but I heard them as if he'd screamed.

"What?" I asked, blinking at him.

"I was engaged until two weeks after I met you."

His words made my breath leave me. My heart ricocheted up a notch inside my chest. *Thump. Thump. Thump.*

"What?" Honestly, at this point, I was surprised I was capable of saying anything.

"Her name was Olivia," he said softly. Absently. He didn't look up from where our fingers interlocked. "My uncle and father thought it would be a good match. She was the press secretary's daughter, beautiful, witty…but I never loved her. It felt as if I was going through the motions day after day. Almost as if I were in darkness my entire life. I knew I should've loved her—hell, I wanted to love her—but I couldn't. Not even the others knew about her. Oh sure, they knew I was seeing a girl, but they don't know how serious it had become. At least, on the outside.

"I'd just proposed to her when I was called to the resort to save my team after a tornado struck. At the time, I'd been doing research about a human-trafficking ring. Olivia had been with me...so I proposed. It felt like something I was supposed to do, you know? I was dating this girl, had been for two years, and she'd confessed her love to me. I said it back, because what else was I supposed to say?

"And then I visited you at the hotel with Ryder, and you were in that damn wheelchair looking so fucking beautiful, and it was like a light being flipped on.

"I got to know you, started to fall in love with you, and I realized I couldn't lead Olivia on. I called her that day and ended things."

His breathing quickened, hand tightening around mine to the point of pain.

"I left a girl in the middle of the fucking apocalypse, Addie. Of course, I didn't know it was the apocalypse at the time, but still. What type of man does that? Not one deserving of you, that's for damn sure. I left her, and I didn't think twice about it. She's probably dead by now, and that fucking hurts. I may not have loved her like that, but I did care about her. Does it make me heartless?" His voice lowered to a raspy whisper. "Do you hate me now?"

Slowly, I untangled my hand from his and placed it on my lap. I needed to process what he'd just told me.

Fallon had been...engaged.

To a girl.

And he chose me over her.

His words tumbled through my mind, like a gymnastics routine I couldn't quite keep up with. Tears lingered in my eyes.

For the first time since I'd met Fallon, I understood him.

Sure, I'd always loved him, but love didn't necessarily equal understanding. For so long, he'd kept an impenetrable barrier between the two of us. Secrets grew around that wall like flowers in a garden.

Today, he'd trusted me with his deepest secret. Trusted me to love him and handle it.

But what if I couldn't?

Fallon had left that poor girl for me. What if he met someone new and did the same thing again? What if he left me for some blonde bimbo?

I knew I wasn't thinking logically, but the fear remained.

And what of that girl? He'd just *left* her. I knew he didn't love her and people break up all the time...but why me? What made me so special?

I barely understood my own thoughts.

"Please say something." Fallon's voice was choked. "You're the only girl I've ever loved. The only one I *will* love. I can't do this without you."

The raw sincerity in his voice nearly unraveled me.

"Fallon..."

"I love you." He grabbed my hips desperately, positioning me on his lap. He trailed open-mouthed kisses over my shoulder and neck. "I love you. Please don't hate me. Please don't leave me. I love you."

It was only then that I understood. Fallon acted as if he were made of cement, but that wasn't true. He was actually crafted from glass and one wrong move could break him. How had I never noticed it before? Fallon—Sarge, our leader—was broken.

"Fallon." I captured his head, my palm resting on his cheek, and turned his face towards mine. Tears glimmered, unshed, in his eyes. "I will never hate you. What you did...yeah, it was pretty shitty. Breaking up over the phone in any circumstance is shitty, but you didn't know the world was going to end. No one can blame you for that. I'm not mad at you. At all. I'm confused, yes, and hurt that you didn't trust me, but we'll get through this. I love you. I trust you. You fell out of love. Or maybe you never truly loved her to begin with. Only you can answer that, but either way... Fallon...that's normal. Just...just don't fall out of love with me, okay?"

"Never." He pressed his lips to mine in promise.

And I knew then that what we had, though unconventional, was forever.

CHAPTER 13

ADDIE

We walked hand in hand down the hall to another room. The tension between us hadn't completely abated—I hated being lied to more than anything—but we both knew it wasn't the end for us. Not by a long shot.

My nerves were haywire as we stepped inside a room similar to the one Fallon had been in. King-sized bed, a television mounted on the wall, two tables flanking the bed. Asher and Tamson sat on the bed, whispering to each other, while Declan leaned against the wall. Ronan and Ryder were resting on the two chairs positioned in the corner of the room. All five of them glanced up when we entered, eyes zeroing in on me with a heat and intensity that left me reeling.

Declan signed, *"Did you work everything out?"*

Only when we both nodded did the tension drain from their shoulders. I hadn't even realized how stressed they'd been, how worried. I didn't know how much they knew about Fallon's secret—from his explanation, next to nothing—but they'd obviously sensed the life shattering news he'd planned to drop.

"I'm happy I don't have to kill you for hurting my kitten," Ryder joked, but it fell flat. The room was still amped up with a thickening tension. Ryder tried to smile, but it appeared more like a grimace. Ronan shifted from side to side.

Were they…?

Were they nervous?

"What's going on?"

Newton's Third Law of Physics or whatever—when your boyfriends were nervous, you get nervous as well. Fact.

I grabbed a strand of my brown hair and fiddled with the ends. It was in desperate need of a cut. My split ends were getting split ends.

"We have something we want to ask you," Tamson began softly. His cheeks, as usual, were a bright crimson. When I met his eyes, he ducked his head with a sheepish smile.

"Yes?"

Oh god. Is this it? Are they breaking up with me?

"No!" Ronan said quickly, hands raised as if fending off an attack. "The exact opposite actually."

He exchanged a look with Declan who nodded. Fallon moved from behind me to stand beside Tamson and Asher, both of whom had risen from the bed. Ronan and Ryder joined the line of solid muscle. A sexy wall I wanted to climb like a rock wall...

As one, the men dropped to one knee.

I couldn't breathe, couldn't think, couldn't even hear over the erratic pounding of my heart. It thrummed against my rib cage, but instead of a soothing song, it was a cacophony of noise.

Tears pooled in my eyes, and like a protagonist from a cheesy eighties movie, I put my hand over my mouth.

My entire life, I'd dreamed of someone loving me enough to want to spend eternity with me. To see six men who'd never knelt for anyone, six men who personified strength and love, on one knee for me? It was only a testament to how much they loved me.

It was Declan who produced a tiny, velvety box. With bated breath, he opened it to reveal a ring straight out of my dreams.

The band was silver, glinting like starlight in the candle glow. The center of the ring consisted of a shimmering amethyst stone surrounded by seven diamonds.

The tears in my eyes cascaded in a steady torrent, and I was helpless to stop their steady flow down my cheeks.

"We love you," Ryder said softly. The usual playful banter was gone from his voice. In its place was a tenderness and love that caused my heart to lurch.

"And it's only going to ever be you," Ronan added. I was stunned to see tears in his eyes.

"You brought me out of my shell," Tamson chimed in. His voice was quiet but sure. "Showed me love, even when I was at my lowest." His eyes tightened with pain, and I knew he was thinking of the confrontation that had caused me to get shot. He'd acted cruel, crass, and had treated me like a whore. It had all been an act, but I knew he was haunted by his actions, despite my own forgiveness of them long ago.

"You're our world," Asher added simply. The tears were falling in earnest now down my face, and Asher flashed me a small smile. It was a smile he'd perfected, a smile he reserved only for me, a smile that made me feel comforted and warm and safe. Seeing that smile was coming home to a roaring fire and hot chocolate after trekking through a snowstorm for days.

Fallon grunted. He didn't like to show his feelings, especially in front of others, but our conversation reverberated through my mind. He loved me.

I glanced lastly at Declan. Ducky. My oldest friend. His brow was furrowed in concentration as he opened his mouth, and slurred, beautiful words escaped.

"Will you marry us?"

Time seemed to slow as I stared at my six lovers and the ring. All different. All perfect. All mine. I knew, innately, that there was supposed to be a seventh on one knee before me as well. Like a mirage, I visualized Calax on the other side of Fallon, his gruff face uncharacteristically warm. My gentle giant. My enemy.

My best friend.

He nodded his head once, encouraging me to follow my heart.

Like any mirage, he vanished in a cloud of gray smoke.

The ring was a perfect representation of our relationship. As unconventional as being the lover of seven—six men was. The gem in the middle was my birthstone, and the diamonds that sprouted from it like the legs on a spider represented each of my guys.

They hadn't forgotten Calax, even though he was no longer with us. They knew he would always hold an irreplaceable piece of me.

"Yes," I whispered softly. And then louder, "Yes."

The guys converged on me, kissing any bare skin they could find. I felt so loved in their arms. Safe. Protected.

My loves.

My boyfriends.

My soon-to-be husbands.

Mine.

~

TAMSON

The others retired for the night to the rooms nearby, each pressing a kiss to Addie's lips. While we'd all agreed we wanted to see where the group aspect of our relationship went, we knew now wasn't the time. She was still fragile, still hurting, and despite her strength both physically and mentally, it wasn't the time to test her.

Her eyes remained locked on the ring as she stripped out of her clothes. Declan had been the one to find the ring during his separation from Addie. When he'd showed it to us, we all knew that it was now or never. We loved her, and we wanted to spend the rest of our lives by her side.

It didn't bother me that I would be sharing my wife with five other men. They weren't just strangers, but my best friends. My brothers. They could protect her when I couldn't, could offer her stuff I never could.

Heat rose to my cheeks as I took in her creamy, voluptuous body. Her breasts barely covered by the scrap of material she called a bra. Her panties that showed more than they hid.

My cock was suddenly unbearably hard.

"This is a dream. A freaking dream. Am I Cinderella? Am I going to wake up at midnight and find myself back with my parents at the resort?" she murmured to herself.

Watching her stand there in her bra and panties, hand extended as she looked at the ring, I'd never been so turned on in my life. The ring was a symbol of our forever. Of the fact she was ours, mine, and we were hers.

She didn't seem to know how fucking beautiful, how sexy, she truly was. I was intoxicated by her presence, lost in sensations only she had ever evoked from me.

Her head tilted in my direction before dipping lower. I didn't even have time to cover the obvious tent in my boxer briefs—what I usually wore to bed—before she raised a single eyebrow.

Spinning completely, she placed both hands on her slender waist.

"Tamson," she said softly. Sultrily. Huskily. The noise sent heat straight to my cock. The beast was standing at attention, waiting for my command. "We haven't had time to be together, just the two of us." She took a step closer, and I could've been mistaken, but I would've sworn she added an extra sway to her hips.

When she pressed her lips to mine in a teasingly slow kiss, I thought I would come in my pants.

Still, I clenched my hands into fists to keep from touching her.

"Addie..."

She must've heard something in my voice, as she pulled away abruptly and her eyes flashed with hurt. I hated that I was the one who did that to her. Again.

"I want you, my love. More than anything. But..." I rubbed a hand down my face.

"But?" she pressed.

"I don't think you're ready for me."

At that, her eyebrows rose in what appeared to be a challenge. "Are you super big? Because my vagina is fully equipped to handle big cocks, let me tell you. This isn't my first rodeo, cowboy."

I frowned. "No...I mean yes, it's big... I mean... Look, I don't want you talking about any cocks near you or inside you that's not one of ours. Got it?" My tone turned unintentionally authoritative, but the mere thought of someone kissing her, loving her, *touching* her, made me see red.

Her breath hitched at my voice, eyes flaring with desire and carnal hunger.

My own breath caught at the wanton expression on her face. Addie had *liked* when I commanded her. My skin heated, a blazing inferno growing inside me, and my balls clenched painfully.

"I'm not like the others," I said slowly, carefully, gauging her reaction. She tilted her head to the side curiously but otherwise didn't react. Face flaming, I added, "I like control."

"Control," she repeated.

I nodded once. "Being in control of your pleasure and my own. What I like to do requires a certain level of trust—"

"I trust you," she interjected, and my lips curled.

I wanted to resist, but she was standing before me like some decadent treat. A forbidden fruit.

Her eyes were hooded with desire, her thighs rubbing together to alleviate the tension, and I knew there was no denying her.

What my queen wanted, my queen would get.

"At any time you want me to stop, say so," I told her hoarsely. The whimper she released was music to my ears. "Now, be a good girl and get on the bed."

With a coy smile on her lips, Addie did as instructed.

My eyes trailed over her perfect form, those heaving breasts just begging to be sucked, the wetness seeping through her panties.

"You're so wet for me," I murmured huskily.

That small hand of hers trailed down her stomach and towards her pussy. Before she could touch herself, I draped my body over hers and kissed her senseless. That same hand fisted in my red-brown hair, tangling the strands.

I allowed her to. For now.

Soon, she would learn what she could and couldn't touch without my permission.

"Do you trust me?" I whispered against her mouth. Chest heaving, she nodded. "I need words, Addie, or else this isn't going to work."

"Yes, I trust you," she rasped. Nodding seriously, I moved from the bed, ignoring her cry of protest, and grabbed two of my clean shirts from my suitcase. They weren't ideal, but they would have to do until I could get adequate supplies.

My breath left me at the thought of Addie in a sex store with me.

Shit.

Returning to the bed, I raised both of her hands above her head and used the first shirt to tie them together. My good girl didn't struggle.

I'd feared, with her past, she would be hesitant about being tied up and dominated. I may have loved this type of sex, but I loved Addie more. I would've been more than willing to give up this control in order to be with her.

But having her at my mercy...

Fuck me. This was every fantasy I'd ever had come to life.

"You need to rely on your senses," I told her as I used the second shirt as a makeshift blindfold. "Your hearing." I caressed her cheek with my lips before moving to her sensitive earlobe. Nibbling once, I sat back, watching her. Her lips were parted as she panted. "Your smell." I leaned back down to lick from the tip of her nose to between her eyes, stopping before I reached the blindfold.

"Tam..." she moaned, gyrating against my hip.

"Touch." I grabbed her dainty hand and brought it to my mouth, swirling my tongue over each digit before taking her thumb completely in my mouth. My eyes locked on the ring declaring her as ours, and I couldn't stop myself from planting a soft kiss to the stone. "And finally, taste." My tongue prodded her lips until she opened for me. I took her tongue between my lips and sucked, reveling in the low moan emanating from her chest.

Releasing her, I sat back once more, positioning my body so I was on top of hers. Usually, I would've taken my time, teased her, brought her to the precipice of pleasure before sending her stumbling over.

But she wasn't any girl. She was *Addie*. The love of my life. The love of my fucking existence.

I needed her, craved her, too badly for extensive foreplay.

Heart hammering like a schoolboy with a crush, I unhooked her bra straps. With her hands still tied together, it was impossible to remove it completely, so I allowed the fabric to settle just above her wrists.

Fucking glorious. Perfect.

Palming her heavy breasts, I allowed my thumb to caress her beaded, light pink nipple. Hungry for her, I ducked my head and took one in my mouth. She groaned my name, hips moving, as I devoured her breast. My other hand worked the other tit, kneading the tender flesh.

Planting kisses in the crevice between both breasts, I whispered, "Usually, I would take my time. Worship your body, my goddess. My queen. But I'm not going to last much longer if I'm not inside you. Do you want that, baby? For me to be inside you? To feel how much I love you?"

"Yes," she whimpered.

Smiling softly, I pretended to cup my ear, despite knowing she couldn't see me. "What was that?"

"Yes! Fuck me, Tamson! Show me you love me."

My hands moved to remove my boxer briefs and her own pesky underwear. Tired of the bra, I ripped it from her body, ignoring her half-hearted cry of protest. I quickly placed a condom over my throbbing cock. "Who do you belong to?"

"You."

Abruptly, I grabbed her now bare ass and spun her around, positioning her so she was on her elbows and knees. My hand curved around her ass cheek before I pulled back and slapped it. Not enough to hurt, but enough to leave a red handprint on the creamy white skin.

"Fuck, Tam," she moaned, thrusting her hips. I immediately leaned forward to kiss the red mark, soothing away the sting.

"Tell me you love me," I whispered darkly, backing up so I could line myself up with her wet entrance. My cock settled at the edge of her wet folds, waiting.

"I love you," she cried out. "So fucking much."

That did it. I thrust into her with one, smooth stroke—a stroke that belied my experience. She felt so fucking good. Heavenly.

"Fuckkkk," I drawled out, pounding into her. I curled my hand around her throat, pulling her backwards until my chest was aligned with her back. The new angle allowed me to go even deeper. I rolled her nipples between my fingers as I fucked her. "Do you know how much I love you? Can you feel it?" I demanded.

"Tamson!" Her pussy clenched around my cock as she exploded around me. I continued fucking her through her release, even as my own balls tightened and I orgasmed like I never had before.

We both collapsed in a sated heap on the bed, skin slick with sweat. I removed the condom and tossed it in the garbage before settling back in beside Addie. Gently, I removed the blindfold and the restraints.

She cuddled against me, her head on my chest, and I pressed a kiss to her hair.

"That was amazing," she stated, voice awed.

I tried not to feel smug, but...she'd said it was amazing and I was only a man.

"I didn't hurt you, did I?" I whispered, rubbing at her wrists.

"Not at all. I'm not gonna lie, I didn't think I would enjoy something like that, but..."

"But?" I asked, scarcely believing what I was hearing.

"But I loved it. I wouldn't love it with anyone else, I don't think, but there was something so incredibly sexy about seeing you dominate me like that. Breaking out of your timid shell. I fucking loved it."

My heart swelled with love for this woman.

"So you would want to do it again?" I asked hopefully. She laughed.

"Or ten more times." Her smile was mischievous. Smiling as well, I pulled her into a feverish kiss.

"I can arrange that."

And so I did.

CHAPTER 14

*W*e arrived at the outpost three days after my engagement.

Engagement.

My stomach still fluttered like thousands of butterflies were rapidly batting their wings. I never thought I would fall in love with one man, let alone seven. My parents had severely tarnished the concept of love for me. What might've been depicted as beautiful in romance novels and movies held nothing but painful memories to me.

I saw how love could be twisted, warped, until it was barely recognizable. Mom and Dad had claimed to love each other, yet they punched, hit, and scratched until blood was drawn. Faithfulness? That was a fucking joke.

My definition of love was skewed because I'd grown up with the idiotic mentality that to love was to be weak. The comfort a child should've gotten from her parents was noticeably absent in my early years.

Crying led to a slap in the face.

Innocent hugs contorted to perverted gropings.

Now, I had six soon-to-be husbands, and I was constantly cocooned in warmth and love. It was surreal.

"You can't stop smiling," Asher pointed out as a daunting, large school came into view.

Deciding for honesty, I said, "Tamson tied me down and fucked me a few nights ago, and I'm engaged. That's something to smile about. And I'm thinking about anal too."

Silence.

"Holy shit, Kitten," Ryder said with a gasp.

"Actually," I continued contemplatively, "I wasn't thinking about anal, but now I am. Hmmm. Would any of you be down for that?"

Six hands quickly rose into the air, and I couldn't contain my chuckle. Even Fallon, who was driving, had one hand raised.

My mood was buoyant, bright, and I felt like I could conquer anything.

According to the faded sign, the building was a high school in a nondescript town. It was surprisingly modern, with elaborate archways, brick siding in all directions, and a new fence sprouting from the ground like jagged, silver teeth. A guard post was situated in front of the gate opening, made up of roughly hewn logs and a single window. A young guard stood inside, a gun strapped over his chest.

More men guarded the length of the fence, their eyes turned curiously but not suspiciously towards our car as we pulled up.

Our caravan consisted of only two large vans. Tonya and her crew, Kai and Doc, and my brother and Tommy were in the second vehicle.

Fallon rolled down the passenger window, and Asher flashed a kind smile.

"How many in your party?" the guard asked stiffly, eyes roaming over each of us. It rested a moment longer on me, and the heat I was accustomed to seeing in men's eyes flared in his. It was different than the way *my* men looked at me.

It didn't hold any love or warmth or affection. It was pure, undiluted lust.

I stiffened instinctively, and Declan tightened his arm around my shoulders. I recognized the gesture for what it was—possessiveness.

"Seven in this car. Seven in the other," Fallon supplied, voice tight with an unnamed emotion. Only someone who knew him as well as I did could see the crack in his impeccably placed apathetic mask. He didn't like the scrutiny of the guard.

After a quick inspection of both cars—checking for bombs, Tamson told me quietly—he waved us through with a scathing warning about being on our best behavior and leaving all weapons other than a knife in the car.

We parked in the full lot and, as instructed, left our weapons in the car. I could tell my men didn't feel right about it, but they didn't complain. Whether it was trust or blind faith, I couldn't discern, but we walked into the building with only our hidden knives.

Despite their lack of weapons, I knew my guys were a force to be reckoned with. Their bodies *were* their weapons.

I pushed my way through the guys until I was standing between Nik and Tommy, the latter of which held a surprisingly content Mof in his arms. Slinging my arms over both of their shoulders, I asked, "How are my two favorite men doing?"

Tommy, of course, took that as an opportunity to cast a smug look behind him. Nik just shrugged his shoulders.

"Hot as balls," Tommy complained, turning back towards me. "I'm sticky and gross and have an itch where an itch should never be."

The heat wave was still at full blast, the sun damning overhead. It had gotten to the point where I wasn't even sweating. My skin was sticky, yes, but the combination of the heat and my lack of water made me dehydrated. Stupid, I knew.

I just needed to be sure the people I loved were okay before I began taking care of myself.

"That car is fucking cramped," Tommy added, ignoring Fallon's gentle reprimand for bad language. I leaned forward to rub my cat behind the ear, but he hissed, claws extended. Tommy glared at me as if it were *my* fault my cat was a traitorous bastard. My. Fucking. Cat. Damnit.

"At least it's better than the last car," I pointed out, pulling my hand back to my chest after leveling Mof with the stink eye. "That one was a sauna."

We went through cars quickly in the apocalypse, though that was entirely incidental. They either got destroyed, stolen, broke down, or we needed an upgrade to accommodate more people. Instead of the three cars we'd started with, we now had two.

"When we get inside, it's going to feel like a clubhouse," Fallon explained to the group. "Or a skanky bar. Usually, these places have a makeshift cafeteria you can eat at in exchange for weapons or…other services." Clearing his throat, he continued doggedly, "There's also rooms they allow you to spend the night in. Usually, you don't have to pay a fee, but you're often sharing with a few others. I'm hoping with a group this big, we'll all be put together."

"The most they'll allow you to stay is a night," Declan took over, hands moving fluidly as he signed. I was surprised to see both Tommy and Nik staring at his hands with something akin to understanding. Did they pick up sign language during our months apart? *"Sometimes two, but that's pushing it."*

"This isn't a hotel or a safe haven," Tonya cut in, eyeing the approaching building grimly. "This is a place designed to stop at on your way to your destination. A rest area."

Nodding my head once to show them I understood, I stepped through the glass doors and into a small entryway with ceramic tiles, a reception office, and what looked to be an abandoned art studio, complete with dried paint, fallen paintbrushes, and half-finished paintings.

Guards eyed us as we entered but nodded towards what appeared to be a cafeteria.

It had been entirely remodeled. What had once been a serving line was now a makeshift bar with a half dozen bar stools in front and a collection of alcohol lining the shelves behind. Tables cluttered the rich gray carpeting, each one occupied with people of all ages.

I watched a woman only a few years older than me saunter from one table to the next. She wore high heels that would've tripped me up in seconds, a corset that pushed up her ample breasts, and shorts that resembled a pair of cheetah dotted panties.

She lifted her eyes when our group entered, and light entered them. Putting an extra sway to her hips, she sashayed over to where we stood.

"Fancy seeing you again," she purred, brushing a red-painted fingernail down Fallon's bicep.

Seeing you again?

Icy dread slithered down my spine.

When Fallon didn't immediately push her off him, my breathing turned uneven.

"Abigail," Fallon said at last. "Let me introduce you to my fiancée, Addie."

He turned towards me, and his hard eyes immediately softened. Moving away from her sensual touch, he wrapped an arm around my waist. The tension drained from me just at his proximity, his touch seeping warmth into my frigid skin.

"Addie, this is Abigail. I met her at the other outpost."

Abigail twisted her lips, which were annoyingly bright red and plush, into a pout. She was all curves and beauty and sensuality while I was…not.

"You were a lot more fun when she wasn't around," Abigail whined, flashing me a smug smile. I went ramrod straight, body jerking like electricity shot through my veins.

"When he rejected you?" Tommy asked, full of snark. When Abigail's eyes narrowed, Tommy added, "I don't like the asshole either, but don't even think about lying or spinning the truth. Or else I'll kick your ass, female or not. You propositioned both Fallon and Declan. They sent you away."

By the time Tommy had finished his tirade, Abigail was red in the face.

I had to give the girl credit—she composed herself quickly and turned towards Ronan and Ryder.

And then the bitch did what I least expected. She popped out a boob.

Yup. Suddenly, I was face to face with a cherry red nipple. Oh god. That was unnaturally red. My guess? Some type of infection. Would it be weird if I asked Doc to look at it?

"So, boys, what are your names?" Her voice took on a husky cadence.

Ronan and Ryder pointedly looked away from the escaped tit.

As one, they said, "Taken."

"Taken as well," Tamson said softly, face bright red. I couldn't tell if it was embarrassment or anger, but either emotion pissed me off.

Who did this bitch think she was flashing her sagging tits like a fucking flag on a pole?

Ryder and Ronan snorted, hinting I might've spoken out loud, and even Fallon hid his laughter behind a well-placed cough.

Abigail's face went beet red as she sputtered.

"Now listen here, slut, I don't know—"

She broke off when Asher was suddenly in front of her face, eyes cold but smile oddly sardonic on his handsome face. Damn if the combination didn't turn me on.

"Don't speak to her like that ever again. Do you understand me? And don't waste your time. Our answers will always be no, do you get that?"

Her face was turning redder as the seconds dragged on.

"Not always," she protested, but Asher cut her off with a glare that could blast ice to smithereens.

"Leave, Abigail," Fallon said darkly.

I thought she was going to protest again, but she was smarter than I'd initially given credit for. After one more fondle over her breast, thumb flicking over her nipple, she retreated with an angry grunt.

Tommy, from behind me, whispered, "If that's a girl's boob, I think I'm gay."

The poor kid sounded traumatized. All I could do was pat his back sympathetically and awkwardly promise that not all the boobs in the world were like that.

Parenting for the win.

Less than an hour later, I found myself on one of the barstools, a bottle of Coke in my hands.

Tonya's group had retired for the night, along with Tommy and Nik. Kai and Doc had snuck away to do…whatever it was they did. Probably not play Scrabble.

My men were spread out on the floor, each talking with a different group. Fallon wore a large albeit fake smile as he talked to a group of middle-aged men. Asher was nodding earnestly a few tables down to whatever an older woman was saying. Tam sat only a few seats away but was engaged in conversation with a smartly dressed man and his significantly younger wife. A younger wife who kept giving Tam fuck me eyes, much to my displeasure. Ryder and Ronan were together, and their group included, unfortunately, others like Abigail. More than one scantily-clad female tried to touch them. One even went so far as to sit on Ryder's lap before he unceremoniously dumped her on the ground.

Of course, he apologized and helped her back up, but the message was clear—off limits. The working girls steered clear of my men after that.

Declan sat a few stools down, reading the lips of the animated bartender. He couldn't reply, so he settled on making dramatic hand gestures that had the older man in hysterics.

All six of them would glance at little old me periodically, and whenever a man would get too close—or worse, proposition me—one or all would jump to their feet.

I prepared for another repeat of the "possessive and protective" show as a warm body slithered up beside mine. And yes, I meant slithered. Most of these men were snakes, offering me food in exchange for sex or entering the outpost with another girl and still asking for my room number.

Disgusting.

Heaving out a sigh, I prepared myself for a minute of senseless flirting followed by "bitch" or "slut" when I rejected him.

The next words, however, caused my breath to leave my lungs.

"Hello, Adelaide."

Spinning, heart in my throat, I met the dark eyes staring down at me, penetrating my skin. It took me a moment to recognize where I knew him from. When it came to me, goosebumps exploded on my arm and my tiny hairs stood on end.

Enzo.

I'd first met him months ago, before the whole world went to hell. He'd been the son of one of my father's business partners and a masochistic dick. With olive-toned skin and a shock of dark hair, Enzo might've been traditionally handsome, but I knew about the beast that lurked under the surface.

The man had tried to kiss me, tried to rape me, and he might've done it if I hadn't fought back. Hell, before my men barged into my life, I might've been a passive participant.

The good girl.

His dark eyes speared me, roaming over my skin. I was fully clothed in a tank top and shorts, but he made me feel naked.

"It's nice to see you again," Enzo continued, a tremendous smile on his face.

"You too." I tried to infuse sincerity into my words, but it was hard. Nearly impossible.

And where were my guys?

A sly glance showed Declan staring intently at the bartender's lips as the jovial man spoke. Out of my peripheral, I spotted Fallon with his back turned.

I couldn't see the others from this angle, and I wasn't about to announce their locations to Enzo. We had no idea if it was my parents coming after me, but it was logical to believe so. Who else would want me so much they would hire mercenaries to kidnap me?

Couldn't they just find another punching bag? Wouldn't that save them the hassle? I supposed it was too much to hope for. Evil didn't think logically. They saw things in black and white.

"You look beautiful, even after all this shit." Enzo moved to brush a strand of my brown hair out of my face, and I trembled in revulsion. That only made his eyes flare brighter, but whether because he mistook my disgust for want or because he knew I feared him remained unclear.

"You too."

Yeah, real coherent, Addie. Real smart. Tell the crazy man you hate that he's beautiful. Ten out of ten. Good survival instincts.

"You still do that thing? Speak your thoughts out loud?" He snorted. "I suppose it's impossible to take the crazy out of the girl."

He leaned closer, and the stench of stale beer assaulted my nostrils.

His voice was a hushed murmur. "I've been thinking about you. Our kiss. The salty taste of your skin. When I'm fucking other girls, I'm thinking of you."

What. The. Fuck?

"What the fuck?" a high-pitched voice echoed. Fear skated down my spine.

Tommy stood behind my barstool, hands on his chubby hips. His large glasses were sliding down his nose, and he used one finger to push them back up.

"Who the fuck are you?" Enzo asked, and to my relief, he sounded more amused than annoyed.

"I could ask you the same thing. What you just said… That's nasty, man. Fucking nasty. You watch your tone, boy. Do you speak to your mother with that dirty mouth? Don't make me wash your tongue with soap." Ignoring Enzo's flabbergasted expression, Tommy turned towards me. "And what are you still doing up? It is past your bedtime, missy. Don't make me start a scene, because I will."

Too late for that. Everyone in the general vicinity was turned towards us as Tommy's voice rose in volume. Declan's face was glacial as he slid from the barstool. I could see Fallon meeting Tam and Asher, all three walking towards us with deadly calm faces. Ryder and Ronan, however, did not exude the calmness of my other four lovers. They had always been passionate, always been hotheads, and this was no different. Red-faced, they pushed the throng of people aside, intent on getting to Enzo.

Enzo, seemingly unperturbed, flashed me an indolent smirk before sliding off the barstool.

"I'll be seeing you real soon, Addie. Real fucking soon."

And with that, he disappeared down one of the many hallways.

CHAPTER 15

RYDER

*W*ho did that fucker think he was?

Barreling forward, red-faced, all I could see was his hand on *my* girl's shoulders. Twirling a piece of hair around his finger. Addie seemed oblivious, eyes wide in her beautiful, dewy face.

When Enzo disappeared down the hall, she remained staring after him, mouth agape.

"Kitten," I moaned, grabbing her shoulders and pulling her into a hug. Her body was limp, flaccid against my own, shock coursing through her like electrical waves. "Are you okay?"

I was distantly aware of Fallon barking orders at Asher and Declan to follow Enzo. Ronan moved so he was behind her, hands resting gently on her shoulders.

"I'm fine. I just… What was he doing here?" she groused, peering up at me from beneath sooty lashes.

I'd recognized the fuck waffle the second I laid eyes on him.

Enzo Angelo. Son of Julius Angelo, a known gun provider on the black market.

We hadn't investigated Julius in depth, since our targets had been Addie and her parents, but we knew enough to be wary. To stay clear.

To have Enzo here…

It was only bad fucking news.

"We need to leave," I sniped at Fallon, pulling my face away from the crook of Addie's neck and resting my chin on her head. She remained huddled against me, tiny tremors reverberating through her body. Addie spoke before Fallon could.

"We can't," she said softly.

"What do you mean, Princess?" Ronan asked softly. His eyes emanated a certain warmth I'd only ever seen when he was around our woman.

"If Enzo knows anything about my parents and what they're after, he'll tell them where we are, right?" Before we could agree, she plowed on. "I trust you guys to protect me. If we stay, we might be able to finally end this. Once and for all." Her gaze captured each of our own, imploring us to see things the way she did.

In her mind, this was a chance to end things.

In ours, it was a chance for her to get injured or killed.

Nothing was more paramount than her safety. Nothing.

But Fallon's face was drawn tight, a frown marring his gruff features. I recognized the look in his eyes—consideration.

Ronan read it at the same time I did and straightened, thick muscles bulging in an attempt to look more intimidating.

"You can't possibly be thinking of staying?" my brother asked in disbelief.

"She has a point," Fallon conceded. "If Enzo isn't involved, then the worst that happened was meeting up with a pervy fuckboy. If Enzo is involved, then we might be able to stop this. Cut the monster's head off. Confront them."

Addie wiggled against me, and I reluctantly released her, kneading her ass once. She jumped, glaring at me over her shoulder, but I merely winked at her. The normality, the banter, was something I craved.

She moved to Tam and wound her thin arms around his waist. His cheeks turned bright red, but he hugged her to him as if afraid she would disappear in thin air. I wasn't jealous or even upset that she left me for him. Obviously, she read something on his face that hinted he needed her more than I did at the moment.

"Fine," I bit out. "But we're all staying together the entire night. And at least two on guard at all fucking times."

"Agreed." Fallon nodded once.

Before I could place my next request, Declan and Asher reappeared on the edges of our makeshift huddle, faces red with anger.

"He's gone," Asher spat out, the normally cheerful smile replaced by a brooding scowl. His eyes were cold, glacial in his face, reminding me once more that behind the boy-next-door façade, Asher was a merciless killer.

We followed him to a room, but when we entered the room, he'd already snuck out a back exit, Declan signed.

Fallon nodded as if he'd suspected as much.

"Okay, let's head to our room. Us seven are sharing one opposite Tonya and the others. We'll discuss more there."

We all nodded, recognizing we were garnering the attention of stragglers and their way too curious ears.

We moved to a hallway that once housed the classrooms but had now been reverted to sleeping chambers. Each door had two windows stacked in a vertical alignment overhead, allowing some semblance of privacy.

Reaching our designated room, Fallon stopped me with a hand on my shoulder.

"Would you and Ronan mind talking to the others?" He nodded towards the room across the hall. "Tell them what happened, but also tell them not to worry."

Frowning, because the last thing I wanted to do was deal with virtual strangers when I could've been with Addie, I gave a brisk nod. What the leader wanted, the leader got.

Fallon said a few words to Ronan, who nodded just as stiffly, hanging back to let the others past him. My brother gripped Addie's arm lightly and whispered something that had a smile blending with her tears. Those tears exacerbated my rage.

No man, no person, was allowed to make her cry.

Not anymore.

"I don't fucking like this," Ronan seethed once the door was closed. "We should be with her."

"Agreed, brother."

We moved silently across the hallway, stopping at the door opposite. My hand froze on the handle.

"She's going to be okay, right?" I asked Ronan quietly. After everything I'd been through, everything I'd dealt with, I needed a win. Addie was my fucking win.

Ronan clasped my shoulder. "She's strong-willed. Resilient. She's going to be okay."

His words shouldn't have relieved me that much, but they did. The tension drained from my shoulders, and I threw him a large, jovial smile.

Shaking off the last of my melancholy, I shoved open the door.

Surprisingly, Tonya, her brother, Jared, and her husband, Davis, were nowhere to be found. Neither were Kai and Doc. Tommy and Nick sat next to each other on a small sleeping mat, seemingly engaged in an intense conversation.

When they spotted us huddling in the doorway, neither of them blushed in embarrassment. Instead, Tommy raised one eyebrow and Nik glanced down at a colorful magazine.

"You need something, assholes?" Tommy asked, all snark.

Ignoring his sass, something he had a surplus of, I asked, "Where are the others?"

"Fucking, probably." He said that so crassly, so casually, that Ronan snorted in amusement beside me. That was coming from the same boy who was terrified of a girl's boob. When we didn't reply, Tommy continued slowly, as if speaking to an imbecile, "When a man and woman—or man and man or woman and woman—love each other very much—"

"Okay we get it," Ronan interjected, disgust twisting his features. "The last thing I want to visualize is them banging."

"Tonya and her husband left an hour ago. Her brother was supposed to stay with us, but he met a girl down in the cafeteria. Doc and Kai have been gone for hours."

My lips pursed. These kids should definitely not have been left alone. I'd be having a *long* talk with Tonya and the others later.

"You two staying out of trouble?" Ronan asked sternly, the playfulness all but diminishing from his eyes. I called it his dad face. Reserved for anyone under the age of fifteen.

Tommy rolled his eyes.

"Yes, bitch. Though…I'll be the first to admit this is the first time I'd been in high school." He sounded uncharacteristically sad just then. Wistful, almost. His eyes flickered to the teacher's desk still pressed against the wall. The rest of the seats had been removed, but that one desk remained, posters taped to the front announcing the school's musical production of *Peter Pan* and the theme for the senior prom—starry night.

"High school was fun," Ronan admitted. "But I always got in trouble."

"Trouble?" Tommy parroted, as if he didn't understand the concept. Ronan's lips twitched.

"You should've seen my senior prank. Or, pranks. I convinced the entire senior class to park in the parking lot sideways," he admitted unabashedly.

"I did something similar," I said with a chuckle. "Had half the class ride in on tractors."

"I released three pigs in the school," Ronan countered, turning towards me. "I wrote on them one, two, and four. You should've seen the teachers' faces as they tried to find the nonexistent third pig."

"I started a game of freeze tag. Some students were frozen for hours. Never made it to their classes."

"Well I—"

"Are you guys measuring dicks? Is that what this is about?" Tommy interrupted. Turning from my brother, I scowled at the little asshole.

"If we did, mine would be bigger."

"Oh please," Ronan said with a snort.

Indiscreetly flipping him off, I focused fully on Tommy and Nik. These two boys were important to me, I'd come to realize. I'd only just met Nik, but I already considered him a younger brother. And though he annoyed me like no other, Tommy was one too.

Infusing as much gentleness and sincerity into my voice as I could, I said, "As soon as we're safe and settled, we'll find you guys a school, okay?"

"We can even teach you ourselves," Ronan added.

"Like what? The art of killing with a smile?" Even his jest held no malice, an excited glint in his eyes.

"Nah. That's more Asher's specialty," Ronan quipped. "But, seriously. What do you say? Is that something you'll be interested in?"

Tommy glanced at Nik, who'd finally looked up from his magazine. No, not magazine. Comic. If those helped him connect with the world, I'd make sure he had a ton.

When Nik gave a subtle nod of his head, Tommy faced us once more with an exuberant grin on his face. It made his eyes twinkle and cheeks dimple.

"We'd love that."

"I'm glad. You're family now, you understand?" I said seriously. "And once you're a part of this family, you're a member for life."

God, now I sounded like I was recruiting for a creepy ass cult.

"A family?" Tommy's question was tentative, unsure, but his eyes were hopeful.

I exchanged a glance with Ronan, my brother. In the room opposite me, I had the love of my life and my other brothers huddled together. Here, I had Nik and Tommy.

With them, I didn't need anyone else.

"Family," I agreed resolutely.

A family I would kill to keep intact.

ADDIE

Enzo's presence had shaken me.

I would've never admitted to anyone in words how rattled I was, but they knew. They always knew.

The darkness was heady, blinds drawn tight. The heat, though combated by the air conditioning, was suffocating. The blankets the outpost had provided were pooled around my ankles.

Even in my thin tank top and shorts, I was burning.

I just kept seeing Enzo's face when I closed my eyes, and I finally admitted to myself the truth.

He would've raped me if he'd gotten the chance.

I recognized the lust in his eyes. The desire. The need.

Next to me, Asher slept soundlessly, chest rising and falling.

The room was...silent. Deathly so.

Weirdly so.

Not even Fallon, a renowned snorer, was making noise, and I knew he was asleep. Hell, they all were asleep, even Ronan and Ryder, who were supposed to be on guard duty.

Something's not right.

Even as the thought came to me, I recognized the rightness of the statement. No way would all my men be asleep after the threat with Enzo. Unless they were dead or sick or drugged—

Drugged.

Horror filled me instantly, and I jerked upright in bed. Placing my hand on Asher's shoulder, I began to shake him.

"Wake up, baby. Wake up."

He slept on.

Pulling my hand back, I only had a second to register what I was doing before I slapped him across the face. Guilt and regret surged through me, but that contorted into horror when he still didn't stir.

"Fuck!"

Scrambling off the bedroll, I did the same to Fallon. Then Declan. Then Ronan and Ryder. Finally, Tamson.

Not one stirred.

Panic ran down my veins, clogged my throat, suffocated me. The darkness which had once been comforting now felt like keen knives stabbing into my chest.

I couldn't think of a curse word bad enough to encapsulate what I felt. Fuck bucket. Penis breath dog shit face—my personal favorite. Bloody tampon. Satan's flaccid dick masturbating in a pool of tears. Shit head asswipe.

Muttering under my breath, I procured a dagger from underneath my bedspread. A gift from Asher, my lovable psychopath. With bated breath, I pressed myself against the wall where the door would open.

And then I waited.

It took less than an hour for someone to tentatively push it open, broad shoulders filling the frame. Too large to be Enzo, that meant.

His head moved from body to body, and I could almost see the wheels turning when he didn't see mine.

I took that moment to leap from my hiding place, kicking the back of his knees. When he fell, a startled gasp escaping him, I wrapped my arm around his throat the way Fallon taught me. A chokehold.

And not the kinky type of choking either.

He was significantly larger than me, but I used my legs to cling to him like a spider monkey. His hands feebly pawed at my arm, nails digging into my skin to the point of pain, but I held firm. My other hand pressed the knife into his back, nicking skin.

"Don't struggle," I whispered in what I wanted to be a soothing voice but probably sounded more like a sociopathic murderer luring children to her van. Yup. I did not have a future career as a serial killer. Couldn't get the voice down.

When he finally passed out, large body toppling unceremoniously onto the tiled ground and head lolling, I whispered, "You've been…Addified."

Still needed a better catchphrase.

Before I could revel in my victory, rough hands yanked under my armpits and jerked me back. I yelped, flailing, as one hand released me only to move to my mouth. Gagging me.

I was fucking pissed.

New rule—no one but Tamson was allowed to tie me up or gag me. Hell to the no.

Quickly recalling my training, those formidably long days in the backyard covered in sweat, I threw my head back and connected with the cartilage of his nose. He didn't release me, but his arms did loosen enough for me to duck out of, spinning with the dagger raised. Before I had time to second guess myself, I swiped the blade where my attacker had been moments before. He danced out of the way before I could pierce skin.

A stinging slap had my head twisting to the side, cheek burning.

Okay, now *that* deserved a triple fuck sundae on the whole curse words scale. I really hated being slapped.

The man grunted suddenly, keeling over.

"Take that, bitch."

Tommy stood behind him, panting, a baseball bat clasped in his hands. And…was that a fucking sword on his back? I recalled him mentioning it vaguely, but hearing about it and seeing it were two entirely different things.

For one, how had he snuck that weapon inside the outpost?

Two, which one of my dumbass boyfriends had trusted him with a fucking sword?

And three…

Well, there were actually only two.

Before I could comment, Tommy swung the bat at the newcomer's head, and he fell unconscious.

"Fuck Declan sideways," I whispered, hustling back a step.

Tommy smiled, slightly sardonically if I was being honest. "You're welcome." His eyes flickered over the two unconscious men. "We need to tie them up."

"Tam might have handcuffs in his bag." I nodded towards where he slept, red-brown hair disheveled in sleep. While I kept my attention fixed on the two bodies, Tommy scrambled to collect the handcuffs, seemingly unconcerned why my shy lover would have handcuffs and/or rope in his bag. Nik stood in the doorway, cautiously analyzing the entire scene.

Tommy cried out, "There's a paddle here too. Can we use that during our torture interrogation?"

Oh sweet baby Jesus.

CHAPTER 16

ASHER

My head was still groggy as I leveled a glare that could burn ice at our two prisoners. Fallon had once told me I ran two temperatures—blistering hot or painfully cold. At the moment, I was hot.

A fucking inferno.

The assholes had drugged me, drugged my team, and had attempted to kidnap Addie. The rage thrummed through my veins like pinpricks of white-hot fire, growing, growing, growing, until everything in the general vicinity was ablaze.

Frankly, I wanted to beat the information out of Shit Head One and Shit Head Two. Only that would pacify my need for vengeance.

But my temper? That could be cooled by only one person, someone who needed me to be level-headed. To love and protect her.

Addie snuggled beneath my arm, head resting on my shoulder as she stared at Fallon's large back towering over the two men.

I pressed my lips to her forehead, silently offering her my comfort. I was proud of my girl for fighting back and winning against two men twice her size, though I wished she'd escaped unscathed. The Shit Head One sized handprint on her face only fueled my incandescent rage.

"You okay, sweetheart?" I asked, focusing on her and only her. The rest of the world fell away. Fallon, Declan, and Tamson demanding answers. Ronan and Ryder attempting to find Enzo. Nik and Tommy huddled together in the corner of the spacious room across the hall, under the watchful eye of Kai and Doc.

My family.

"Did you see, Ashy? I kicked their asses." She sounded so fucking proud of herself, practically preening. If she were a cat, she would've been strutting down the halls with her tail high and an imperious set to her chin.

"I'm so proud of you, my love." I squeezed her shoulder at the sentiment.

Suddenly, her body went stiff beside mine, unnaturally still. Tension coiled her muscles.

"What is it? What's wrong?" I whispered, my lips brushing her scalp with each word.

"If they capture me…" When she trailed off, I put a finger beneath her chin and tilted her face up to gauge her expression. She furrowed her brows, red lips curling downwards. "If it's my parents…I don't want to go back to them, do you understand? You have no idea what they'll do to me."

My arms tightened around her.

I had a pretty fucking good idea.

Before I loved her, when she was just a kind, slightly insane girl at the resort, I'd watched her parents implement a type of torture. They stripped her down as a form of humiliation and pressed her to the stovetop.

Her screams…

The smell of burnt flesh…

The whites of her eyes before she mercifully passed out…

It had haunted me for days. I couldn't sleep, couldn't think, couldn't breathe with the knowledge that she'd been tortured by the people who were supposed to love her. I knew that wasn't the only thing her parents did.

Rumor had it that men came to her room.

Bruises covered her milky white skin.

Slashes of a knife on her back.

Self-inflicted cuts on her arms and thighs.

Being in love with her only intensified the horror and rage. I would've felt anger for any girl forced to endure such torment, but knowing it was the only girl I'd ever loved?

I would die before her parents got their sick, twisted hands on her again.

"They're not going to get you, sweetheart," I vowed. Over my dead fucking body. Tenderly, I brushed a strand of brown hair behind her ear. Her sooty lashes fluttered closed, and she tilted her head so her cheek was pressing against my palm. Both of us reveled in the sensation of flesh on flesh. My thumb caressed her full bottom lip, soothing strokes against the sensitive skin.

When she reopened her eyes and focused her glorious orbs on me—a color that wasn't quite blue but wasn't quite violet—I lost myself. I could wander through her gaze for an eternity.

Her words pulled me out of my bliss, a metaphorical bucket of water dousing me.

"If you can't save me, kill me."

The world stopped. Time stopped. Everything fucking stopped. If it wasn't for my heart beating erratically beneath my rib cage, I might've thought I was dead. My mind replayed her sincere words, but try as I might, I couldn't comprehend them.

She wouldn't have asked me to…?

"Addie." Ronan's voice was aghast. I hadn't even heard him enter. He brushed a hand through his green-tipped hair and dropped to his knees. "You better not fucking mean that."

She was already nodding her head before he'd finished speaking.

"I do, Ro. If they capture me, and for some reason you know you won't be able to save me in time, I want you to kill me." Her pleading voice had garnered the attention of the other men in the room.

"Don't fucking talk like that," Fallon snapped, glaring at Adelaide. She pursed her lips stubbornly.

"I don't want to be used as a toy, a prop, a tool. I refuse. The things they do..." She broke off, voice choked. My heart broke for her, for her childhood, for the woman before me who was both so incredibly vulnerable and yet incredibly strong. "I refuse to." She met each of their eyes before seeking out my own. "I know you kill, Asher."

She couldn't possibly be asking me what I thought she was asking.

"Not you," I rasped out. "I won't fucking kill you. How can you ask that of me?"

Because I wouldn't want to live if something happened to her. A world without Addie in it was not one I wanted to be in. Insane thinking, maybe.

And if it was by my own fucking hand?

I may have been a killer, but what she was asking of me made me ill, nauseous, my stomach curdling like weeks old milk.

Beneath all that, I was devastated. How could she think I'd agree to something as awful as that? Did she doubt my love for her?

"No. Absolutely not. No fucking way."

She must've seen the resolve in my face, as she turned her pleading eyes onto Fallon. He continued to glare at her, possibly too angry to speak. Ronan and Ryder had similar stony expressions on their faces. Tamson refused to meet her gaze, but Declan did. And held it.

I prayed to God that it wasn't assent I saw in his eyes.

One thing became clear as I held her trembling body against my own.

If she ever did come into contact with her asshole parents, it wasn't them we had to worry about.

I knew never to underestimate Addie, and one thing was clear—she would do whatever it took to free herself of her parents.

Even at the expense of her own life.

ADDIE

I knew they wouldn't understand.

How could they?

They didn't have to endure year after year of endless torture. The slap of a hand. The fist pelting your chest, stomach, and face. Burn marks on your arms and legs. Unwanted hands grabbing at you, undressing you, touching you.

And because they didn't understand, they had no fucking say. Now that I knew freedom, happiness, and love, I could never go back to the half-life I'd been living. A life where men who weren't my fiancés touched me. A life where one misspoken word led to a thousand bruises. A life where happiness was fleeting and pain was a guarantee.

No more.

Asher's arms were constricting around me, but I nestled even further into his embrace. I knew my request had hurt him deeply, and I sought to rectify the situation.

Tilting my chin, I pressed light kisses to his jawline, down the slope of his throat, and back to his cheek.

"I love you," I whispered. "I'm so sorry."

"You're not sorry if you're still considering it," he responded harshly, turning his head moments before my lips would've touched his. Instead, I kissed his clenched jaw.

"You have to understand—"

"I don't fucking understand. I can't live without you, do you get that? So I don't want to hear this crap again."

He sounded so angry, so livid, that tears sprung to my eyes. I knew why he was mad of course. I would've been furious too, if the person I loved asked of me what I did of him. At the same time, I thought that he, of all people, would understand.

Instead, it was Declan who held my gaze and gave a subtle tilt of his head. I couldn't tell for sure if it was agreement, but it was enough to cause hope to surge through me.

A freaking demented type of hope, but hope all the same.

"Asher, I know you wouldn't hurt me, and I shouldn't have asked that of you. I'm sorry. I'm just scared, okay? Terrified of what would happen when I'm back in those monsters' hands—"

"That's not going to happen," he snapped, cutting me off.

"But I love you, and I can promise you that I'll try my hardest to come back to you. Always. We're forever, you and me. Me and them."

I could feel the tension physically leaving him as his shoulders drooped. He desperately, helplessly, began to kiss my cheek, my neck, and finally my lips. It was a slow, languid kiss, but through every sensual stroke of his tongue, I could feel his love for me like a physical caress.

I wasn't completely forgiven yet, but I was pretty damn close.

Our moment was interrupted by Ronan's belligerent voice. Unlike Asher, he was still pissed at me.

"Guys…" he warned.

Twisting my head, I met a startling pair of narrowed green eyes and a malevolent smile that made the thin hairs on the back of my neck stand up.

One of the prisoners was awake.

CHAPTER 17

ADDIE

*A*side from his mossy green eyes shot through with golden flecks, the man was unremarkable.

Large nose on a small face, crooked teeth stained yellow, a cleft that made it look like he had balls on his chin. Still, the man exuded power and strength, even tied up. I didn't know how. He wasn't overly muscular, nor did he have battle scars on his face. There was just something about him, something that caused my heart to clench in terror.

Fallon wasted no time. "Who sent you?"

The man surprised all of us when he dropped his head back and laughed. "Fallon, Fallon, Fallon. Aren't you tired of babysitting a bunch of children?"

Fallon jerked back as if he'd been physically slapped. Coming from a man who'd spent his life hiding behind an impassive front, that reaction said it all.

The man wasn't supposed to know his name.

"Who are you?" he asked again, composing himself. Once more, he took a threatening step closer, looming over the prisoner with a venomous look in his eyes. I would be cowed, fearful, at being on the receiving end of such a look. I had to give the man credit—he had more balls than I ever had, even when I was a fake boy named Lil' One Punch.

"Call me Garrett," the man answered easily. Too easily. There was no doubt in my mind that "Garrett" was a fake name.

"Well, Garrett," Fallon sneered, Garrett's name sounding like poison coming from his lips. "How do you know my name? Who sent you?"

"So many questions." He tsked disapprovingly. "Have you figured out nothing yet?"

"I figured out that I want to cut off your balls, shove them so far up your ass that they're coming out your mouth in a demented form of anal, and then feed your cock to a gorilla," Ryder deadpanned.

Garrett gave him a scathing glare that quickly turned curious. "Young Ryder. And is that your brother, Ronan?"

Both men tensed under his scrutiny. I didn't blame them. It was unnerving to be the focal point of such a dangerous man.

A man who I'd taken out with my bare hands. Not trying to toot my own horn or anything…

But a pat on the back for me.

Badass status achieved.

Finally, the man turned to me. His gaze trailed up and down my body, obvious interest flashing in his eyes. Asher moved behind me, possessively wrapping an arm around my waist. Garrett's eyes latched onto that, not missing a thing.

"And the girl of the hour herself! Adelaide! Or is it Addie?"

"It's nothing to you," Ronan snapped.

Declan moved to stand on one side of me, and Tamson on the other. With Asher at my back, I was fully encased in the warmth of my men.

Garrett's eyes glimmered in the artificial lighting. Real lighting, not the flames of a candle. The outpost was fortunate to have a generator for electricity.

His lips tilted upwards.

"Is she that good of a fuck, or are you guys—" Before he could finish his statement, Tamson lunged forward and punched Garrett straight in the face.

The crazy prisoner merely laughed, spitting out blood from his mouth.

"I take that as a yes. A good fuck."

Tamson surged forward again, fist extended, but Fallon held him back, seemingly reluctant to do so. He whispered something to my red-headed lover that I couldn't hear before releasing him. With a huff, Tamson smoothed down his shirt, met my eyes, and blushed a deep red. I held out my hand for him, the one Declan wasn't gripping in a steel vise, and Tamson took it, squeezing once.

Once more, Garrett followed our interaction with amused eyes.

"Who's your friend?" Fallon continued the interrogation, changing tactics. He nodded towards the blond-haired man still slumped forward in his seat.

"Friend?" Garrett blinked his eyes innocently. "I don't know what you're talking about."

"Lie," a small voice said from the doorway, and we all turned.

Nik's eyes tentatively flickered from face to face while Tommy glowered at Garrett. Behind them, Kai and Doc pushed their way through, confused and bored respectively.

"You okay?" Kai asked, peering down at me with concern.

"I'm fine," I assured him. I didn't know Kai that well, but he'd comforted me more than once after everything that had happened. He was a good friend, a good break from my numerous boyfriends.

Doc moved towards Garrett, eyes cynical.

"What are you doing?" Fallon demanded of him.

"I want to make sure he's not bleeding out in that tiny head of his," responded

Doc dryly. It was only then I noticed he was carrying a doctor's bag. "Not that a brain bleed would be a bad thing…"

"You a doctor?" Garrett asked gruffly. Suspiciously.

Doc shrugged. "Eh."

"The other guy was the one I hit in the head," Tommy piped up, sounding too damn proud. Aww. My little boy was turning into a man. "Addie strangled this asshole."

Yes, I did straighten and puff out my chest. Proudest damn moment of my life.

Garrett's eyes narrowed.

"I let her do that," he said casually.

I snorted. "Sure you did."

After Doc did a quick inspection of Garrett, deeming "he would live," Fallon renewed his interrogation with vigor.

I moved away from my men to sit on the floor beside Kai. The day had been physically and mentally draining, and I was beyond tired. Pulling my knees up to my chest, I wrapped my arms around both of them.

"Who sent you?" Fallon questioned.

"I don't know," Garrett intoned.

And then, voice soft, Nik whispered, "Lie."

"You sure you're okay?" Kai whispered, pulling my attention away from the interrogation.

"I'm exhausted," I admitted. "In pain. My body hurts. And I have the worst fucking wedgie known to mankind. Like the thing is halfway up my anus by now, but it would be weird to start picking in public."

Kai nodded slowly. "I can…relate to that?" He posed it as a question.

"Feels like a bunch of anal beads rammed up there," I murmured. "But, like, fabric anal beads. Is that a thing? Hmmm. I should ask Tamson. He'll know."

"That's disturbingly amusing."

"Like the anal beads rammed up my butt," I replied seriously.

The expression on Ronan's face when he walked over to join us? Priceless.

A gurgling noise interrupted whatever he was going to say. That was followed by a low moan, a grunt, and then a "what the fuck?"

The second prisoner was awake, blinking rapidly as he attempted to orient himself to his surroundings. He almost reminded me of Asher, with shoulder-length blond hair, darker than my fiancé's, and high cheekbones. However, he was more muscular, with shoulders of a linebacker and appeared to be nearing his thirties. Blond scruff dusted his jaw.

Alarm flickered across his features when he finally realized where he was.

"Yeah, you're fucked, bro," I pointed out helpfully, and his eyes dropped to me. Widened. Practically bugged, like a life-sized cartoon character.

"Addie…" Fallon reprimanded quietly, pinching the bridge of his nose.

"Yeah, yeah. Leave the interrogation to the professionals. I remember." I waved a hand in the air dismissively. "But I'll have you know, I can be a great torturer. That paddle Tamson has? Yup. I can spank his ass to next year."

Tamson narrowed his eyes at me, even as his cheeks turned crimson. "No."

"Torture is my jam," I continued, ignoring him. "Like, if the prisoners are peanut butter, I'm totally the jelly. Wait. That made more sense in my head."

My rant was interrupted by Kai putting his hand over my mouth. All six of my men sighed in relief. Even Doc, the traitor, smiled.

Frowning, I pulled Ronan down on the other side of me and cuddled into his side. He physically relaxed, shoulders slumping and a deep breath escaping.

"I'll ask you again," Fallon said, low and deadly. "Who sent you?"

"Your mom," Garrett sneered, and Fallon nodded towards Tamson. Without preamble, my normally shy and timid lover punched the man square in the jaw.

"I'll ask you again—who sent you?"

"I told you. Your mom."

Another punch.

Asher, through it all, had been inching closer and closer, knife extended. His vibrant blue eyes flickered to me.

"I don't want her here to see this." His voice was quiet, soft, meant for Fallon's ears only, but I heard him as if he'd been yelling. When I tried to meet his gaze, he looked away, throat bobbing as he swallowed harshly.

Suddenly, I was terrified I'd broken something irreplaceable between him and me. The mere thought had my heart hammering inside my chest, the erratic pounding muting the roaring in my ears. If he hated me…

I didn't know what I would do.

Acquiescing with his request, despite everything in my body begging me to stay, I moved unsteadily to my feet. Ronan came with me.

"Nik, Tommy," I said, nodding. Tommy looked furious he had to leave, but Nik quickly staggered to his feet and followed us out.

"It's going to be okay, Addie," Ronan said reassuringly, but his words only made me run cold. Addie. Not Princess.

I really fucked up.

"Yeah," I agreed with a wan smile. Hell, a practically non-existent smile.

An earsplitting scream sounded from farther down the hall, and Ronan immediately angled himself in front of Tommy and Nik. I appreciated that more than he would ever know. There were times I needed saving…and times I preferred others were saved in my stead.

A familiar figure barreled towards us, gasping. Blood ran down his dark face in rivulets.

"Jared?" Ronan said, but despite knowing the man, his body did not relax.

Jared's desperate eyes raked over our group.

"Ragers," he gasped out. "Inside."

It seemed that he, too, had picked up my nickname for the zombie-like monsters.

"What?" Ronan snapped, and I knew his thoughts mirrored mine. How did they get past the guards and guns? How had we not heard anything?

When another scream reverberated down the hall, Ronan and I exchanged a grim, uneasy look.

One thing was certain—the infestation, the parasite, had been released inside.

CHAPTER 18

ADDIE

*R*onan all but dragged us back into the room, one hand clasped firmly around my upper arm and the other grabbing Nik's hand. Nik grabbed Tommy's hand, and Tommy reached for Jared's.

The sight before me was…gruesome.

I'd known it was going to be, and in some ways, I'd prepared myself for it.

But the amount of carnage done in such a short period?

Bile rose instinctively in my throat as I stared at Garrett's already puffy and red face, the color before it bruised, with long and hideous gashes curving down his neck. His blond-haired partner hadn't fared any better, with cuts on his face and a finger bent at an unnatural angle.

Just as quickly as the pity and guilt came, I dismissed it in a hurricane of anger. These men would've killed my men and kidnapped me, of that I had no doubt. They didn't deserve any emotion from me except for rage.

Asher glanced up from where he was hovering his knife inches from the meaty flesh of Garrett's cheek. Trails of tears smeared the older man's face, a shocking feat in itself. This man had laughed only minutes earlier. Now, he looked as if he was unraveling at the seams.

Fallon's face went stark white when he caught sight of me, and he threw Ronan an accusatory glare.

"I thought you were—"

"We have a problem," Ronan interrupted, voice terse.

Declan moved to stand beside me, interlocking his fingers with my own. There was comfort in that simple, eloquent gesture. I knew I wasn't alone.

"Ragers," Jared explained briskly. His terrified eyes flickered once more to the door, and I couldn't tell if he wanted to charge into the melee headfirst, guns—knives —blazing or run in the opposite direction. Which reminded me…

"Jared, where is Tonya? And Davis?"

When he didn't answer, his desperation suddenly made more sense.

"They wanted some alone time," Tommy offered, voice uncharacteristically subdued. He was squeezing Nik's hand until they were both white, veins bulging.

"We'll find them," I reassured, but I was beginning to question if I was giving the boys false hope.

As always, Fallon was quick to put on his metaphorical leader cap.

"Okay, Tamson and Declan, you'll take Hopper. Keep him in his cuffs." He nodded towards the blond. Hopper. Hmm. Another fake name, I presumed. "Ronan and Ryder, take Garrett. We'll head straight to the van. No stopping. No detours."

"What about Tonya and Davis?" I asked immediately. I didn't know the two that well, but what I did know was that they both cared for Nik and Tommy something fierce and vice versa. As such, they were family.

And I protected my family.

"Our priority is getting everyone to safety," Fallon said solemnly, but his eyes flickered with guilt. "Tonya and Davis know to head straight to the van. They wouldn't want us to search for them." He nodded towards Tommy and Nik, the barest tilt of his head, but I knew he was right. If the situation were reversed and I was the one away from the group, I would want them to continue on without me. Get the boys to safety. And I knew Tonya would want the same.

"We need to go after them," Tommy protested when I grabbed his hand. It was smaller than I remembered, thinner. When I tugged, he tugged right back, breaking free. Tears shone in his eyes, and his lower lip quivered. Still, he was a fighter, a survivor, and he refused to let even a drop slip free.

"Tommy, we can't."

Ahead of me, Jared and Fallon had opened the door to the room, knives extended as they checked the halls. The prisoners were still tied up, still cuffed, and they rested heavily on my men's shoulders.

"Then I'll go by myself," he said immediately. Stubbornly. He made a move to do just that, but I grabbed his shoulder and dragged him to a halting stop. He flashed a scathing, white-hot glare over his shoulder. Hatred seeped from his eyes. My throat closed, breath stuttering, before I closed my eyes.

When I reopened them, the hate-fueled glare hadn't left his face.

"Think of Nik," I said softly, hands raised as if to show him I meant no harm. I loved him. He had to know that I would do whatever it took to protect him.

Even sacrifice Tonya and Davis.

Did that make me horrible? Maybe. But in a world of dog eat dog, man eat man, I refused to cower. I refused to be prey when I had the capacity to be a predator. Life had made me cold, numb almost, to certain aspects…the inevitable end, for one. Life ended, simple as that.

But I'd be damned if that life was one of my men or one of my younger brothers.

"Nik needs you to remain levelheaded," I continued soothingly. Tommy's resolve began to wane, eyes flashing towards my younger brother. Nik's headphones were once more on his ears, blocking out the rest of the world. He didn't seem scared or upset or even annoyed. His eyes were blank as they swept over our makeshift group of psychos.

"Fine," Tommy bit out. With one last blistering glare in my direction, a glare that hurt more than a thousand gunshot wounds, he moved to grab Nik's hand, whispering something to my younger brother that I couldn't hear.

I grasped Declan's hand tightly and allowed him to pull me into the hall. I was relieved to see Ronan and Ryder positioning themselves in front of Tommy and Nik.

The screams were louder now, barreling at us from down the hall.

A moment later, a Rager appeared from around the corner, running at full speed towards us. My heart lurched, nausea making my stomach somersault, when I recognized the man staring back at me.

Well, the man before the parasite disrupted his normal brain waves.

It was the bartender Declan had been talking to yesterday. Only now, black lines curved up his face and bare arms, almost like thousands of tiny snakes slithering beneath his translucent skin. His blood red eyes, a product of popped blood vessels, zeroed in on our group. His mouth opened, and indistinguishable words escaped his cracked, bloody lips. The man had bitten off his own tongue.

With a flick of his wrist, Asher's knife was lodged inside the Rager's throat. He sputtered, black blood foaming around his mouth, but continued to limp towards us. His head was canted precariously to the side, blood and pus oozing from his opened wound. He opened his mouth, jaw cracking, and something black crawled out of the abyss of blood-soaked teeth and severed tongue.

The parasite.

It left his opened mouth, dropping unceremoniously onto the floor. At the same time, the Rager's eyes glazed over, and he collapsed, dead. It seemed as if his wounds finally caught up to him now that he didn't have the parasite propelling him forward.

The worm was…insignificant. Tiny and black, the length of my pinkie finger but thinner. How could something so tiny end the fucking world?

It was the first time any of us had seen the parasite, the worm, out of its host. All we could do was stare with varying expressions of disbelief. We knew where the parasite came from, and we knew it could infect both humans and animals. But we'd never seen one in the flesh.

Was it just a mindless creature, latching onto the nearest host and corrupting their mind, or was it a cognizant being?

"Nobody move any closer," Fallon hissed. He glanced over his shoulder once to make sure we obeyed before the damn hypocrite tentatively ventured a step towards the worm. He raised his boot, preparing to squash it, when the creature uncoiled from the ground like a striking snake.

And like a snake, it lunged forward, too fast for Fallon to contain.

The worm hit my bare leg, sharp incisors breaking skin, before it burrowed inside of me. I dimly heard a cry of anguish, a scream, someone grabbing my waist, another squeezing the life out of my hand.

But all I could focus on was the parasite's inky black form climbing up my body, visible underneath my pale skin.

Infecting me.

My eyes shot on the dead Rager.

Soon, that dead Rager would be me.

FALLON

I'd never known true fear before. Not when my father and uncle used to beat me. Not when my mom ran away with a man she met online. Not when my bitch of an ex lied and told me she was pregnant.

But seeing that parasite enter Addie?

Icy fear skated down my spine, unlike anything I'd ever felt before. It couldn't even be called terror, as that word failed to encapsulate what I felt.

She held her hands out in front of her, staring at her skin as if she expected it to change and contort any moment now. We'd never seen a Rager turn before. Would it take days? Hours? Minutes?

Crashing pulled my attention away. It was accompanied by a cacophony of growls, screams, and snarls. A hoard of Ragers were descending on us. Some were slower, the knives in their legs and bodies impeding their gait, while others were running.

"We have to go!" I shouted to be heard over the noise. I sounded strident, in charge, like I knew what the hell I was doing. Inside, I was a fucking mess. I was fumbling through a forest blind, and the one fucking light might've been...

No, I refused to believe that. The parasite had left the previous Rager. That meant it could leave Addie too before it corrupted her brain. Electrocution. Loud noise. I would try just about anything.

I couldn't lose her.

We couldn't lose her.

"Go!" Addie screamed, shoving Asher's shoulder. She took a trembling step back as if she was prepared to jump into the throng of mindless monsters. As if she'd sacrifice herself if that meant we could escape unscathed. But frankly, I wasn't in the mood for her hero shit.

In one long stride, I was in front of her, and in the next moment, I had her over my shoulder in a fireman carry.

"Fallon!" she screamed, pounding at my back. "I can't go with you. It's not safe!"

Ignoring her, I tossed one of my throwing knives at one of the encroaching Ragers. It landed right between his eyes, hitting his brain, and he fell to the ground, dead. I wondered if the parasite died with the host.

Or if it would just find a new victim to exploit and inevitably kill.

All the way to the van, we mindlessly stabbed and killed, only stopping once for Tommy to grab the damn cat. Black blood coated me—my hair, my clothes, and my skin. Claws gorged the skin off my arms, but the pain was a welcome relief. It somehow filled the emptiness consuming me.

I didn't know how we made it to the two vans. Tonya and Davis were already in one, and they looked relieved to see us. I registered that distantly, as well as Tommy throwing himself into her arms as he cried, sobbing Addie's name inarticulately. I found myself driving, and I mechanically pulled the van out of the parking lot.

I was on autopilot, moving but not living. Breathing but not thinking. Existing but not feeling.

A Jeep pulled out in front of me, and I slammed on my brakes. I heard a curse—Addie—and my entire body froze at the sound. My hands were gripping the steering wheel so tightly, my knuckles were white.

The Jeep was accompanied by a dozen more similar vehicles, and men in armor all piled out. I recognized them immediately.

United States Army.

"Fallon," Addie whimpered.

I didn't speak as they surrounded our van, roughly pulling us out one after another. I didn't speak when they shone flashlights in our eyes, surveyed our bodies, sneered in our faces. I didn't speak when they reached Addie and alarm coated their faces. When Ryder and Ronan screamed, lunging for them, and Asher buried a knife in a man's throat. I didn't speak when two soldiers gripped each of Addie's arms and dragged her kicking and screaming away.

When Tamson ran after the retreating vehicles.

When Asher released a strangled scream.

When Declan began to cry.

When Ryder got into my face, screaming obscenities at me.

When Ronan stared blankly ahead, almost as if he couldn't determine up from down, left from right.

It was too much, too fast.

Failure.

I'd failed the person I loved the most. Failed.

Failed.

My head was foggy, my legs unable to support my leaden body, and I collapsed.

CHAPTER 19

ADDIE

I was going to die.

That realization settled bone-deep within me. A heady, suffocating sensation.

Either my death was going to be at the hands of the parasite or the burly army men who'd kidnapped me. Honestly? I preferred the latter. There was something immensely intriguing about dying with my morality intact.

Well...what was left of my morality, at the very least.

Sometimes I wondered if the greatest monsters were the ones who looked human.

They didn't tie me up, and I wondered if it was because they underestimated my sense of survival or overestimated themselves. I sat nestled between two men, our thighs touching. With my men, that connection would've caused pinpricks of desire to shoot up and down my back. Now, all I felt was revulsion.

I debated, briefly, fighting back. Having them put a bullet through my head and ending my suffering. Or soon to be suffering. The vindictive side, the side I previously coined as Bitch Me, wanted the parasite to corrupt my mind and destroy all of these men. Rip the flesh straight from their throats. Bathe in their blood.

Bitch Me might've had psychopathic tendencies.

"It's a damn sauna in here," one of the men groused, wiping sweat from his brow.

"It's my fault," another injected. "I'm just too damn hot for you."

The guys laughed, and my heart tightened. Their banter reminded me of my men.

Men I missed more than anything in the world. I hadn't even been able to say goodbye to them, tell them I loved them.

Before...

Before I died.

Those three words curdled in my stomach. At the same time, I was grateful I wasn't around my men or brothers. They would hesitate to do what had to be done... they would hesitate to kill me.

Sacrifice.

I'd used that word when referring to Tonya, but I knew it applied to me as well. I was willing to sacrifice anything and everything for the people I loved, including my own life. It was insignificant in the grand scheme of things, wasn't it?

I just wished I could say goodbye, at least once. Tell Fallon I loved him and forgave him. Joke with Tamson until his cheeks burned crimson. Cuddle with Asher, my constant supporter and the man who grounded me. Joke with Declan, my best friend, and repeat what we did on that bed so many nights ago. Flirt with Ryder and hear him call me Kitten. Build a fort with Ronan.

Fight with Calax. Call him my nemesis. Tease him until he glowered.

Love him until he smiled.

There were so many things I never got to do with them. Our wedding, for one. Children even. It had all been snatched away from me.

The rest of the drive was silent, the men solemn minus the few glances they snuck at me. Then, I could see disbelief and surprise in their eyes.

When would I turn? What would it feel like?

Would it be a gradual progression of sanity, or would I completely snap?

What felt like hours later, we pulled into a large, industrial-like building. Or buildings. Dozens of them littered the large expanse. A fence bordered it, bright yellow signs warning us that it was electric. The barrage of cars pulled up to a guard tower. Unlike the one at the outpost, this one towered over the ground, official-looking men in armor manning it. The driver stopped at a video monitor and stared into the camera. After a moment, the gate whooshed open and the rest of the cars filed in.

I spotted hundreds if not thousands of men hurrying to and from each building. The majority were male, but I spotted a few females as well. Each carried a large ass gun.

That did *not* bode well for me.

When the car stopped and I was pulled into the bright sun, one of the men gaped at me.

"So it's true," he breathed.

I didn't bother acknowledging him.

With two men flanking me, we traveled down a winding trail bogged down with weeds. Some were growing strong while others were trampled. The trail took us away from the main cluster of buildings and to a smaller one, resembling a ware-house in appearance.

The terror I hadn't felt moments before appeared with a vengeance. I dug my heels into the ground in an attempt to stop our momentum.

"Come on," one of the men growled, pushing me forward. "We don't want to hurt you."

"Aren't you going to kill me?" I asked. It would make sense. I had the parasite running rampant within me, and it was only a matter of time before it impacted my logical thinking. Unless…

Unless the government wanted me for nefarious reasons.

Dissect me? Experiment on me?

The possibilities were endless.

We entered a door big enough to fit three of us walking side by side comfortably.

The inside showed nondescript silver walls, a collection of computers unattended, and hallways expanding in either direction like a six-legged spider. It was one of those halls the men led me down, their hands loose on my elbows. This should've been the time I fought back. Kicked ass and took names.

But I was tired, so damn tired, of fighting a losing battle.

I wanted to sleep for a thousand years and wake up when this whole nightmare was over.

"If you're not going to kill me, what are you going to do to me?" I asked bitterly. Before anyone could reply, a large figure stepped in front of us.

Nothing about him was significant or memorable. Blond, shaggy hair. Nose too large over lips too thin. A mole on his cheek.

"You're a tough girl to get ahold of," he said, and there was an undercurrent of something in his tone, something I couldn't place. A darkness, almost. An anger that was personal.

"Do I know you?" I asked.

He smiled sharply, showcasing two rows of shark-like teeth.

"I met you before." His smile grew. "You and your boyfriend. You might not have seen me. After all, I did hit you from behind."

His words instilled fear deep within me, sort of like being dunked head first in the Arctic Ocean.

Another epiphany assaulted me then.

These men…

They worked for my parents.

~

RONAN

I didn't know how that scraggly cat was still alive. Honestly, I would've thought it'd be dead by now.

I'd never liked cats. Kind of prissy creatures, if you asked me. Needy and bitchy and willing to claw off your face if the need arose.

Still, my hand fisted in the black cat's fur, freshly cleaned thanks to Tommy. Mof. My Only Friend.

Addie always had a penchant for dramatics. It was one of the things I loved about her. She couldn't just be normal, not my girl. She had to be extra. Instead of a ten she was a one hundred.

"Are you fucking listening to me?" Ryder screamed in my face, his hands moving to my shoulders and shaking. I blinked up at him. Everything was hazy, the sort of feeling you would get if you were high. My mind was just as blurry, unable to connect any of the pieces, any of the words floating to my ears. Distantly, I was aware of Fallon falling. Asher screaming as he stared at the now flat tires of the van. The assholes had shot them, I remembered. And then...

My mind latched onto Addie the last few moments I'd seen her. The parasite slithering under her skin. The fear widening her eyes. The tears streaming down her cheeks as the men dragged her to the car.

The acceptance as the door closed, cutting her off from us. She knew, as did I, that there was no surviving. No escaping. No coming back from the parasites that plagued our world.

"Say something!" Ryder screamed, spit flying from his mouth. When I remained silent, staring impassively over his shoulder, his fist rounded back and punched me square in the jaw. Fire exploded in my face, but the pain had a strange numbing quality. It didn't completely pacify the agony of losing Addie, but it definitely helped.

I brought my hand up to rub at my tender jaw. Ryder was staring down at me, his breathing heavy, and I stared right back.

I wanted to tell him that I was sorry and I loved him. He was my brother in more than just blood. I also wanted to tell him that she was gone. As good as dead.

But he knew.

I could see the acceptance in his eyes, but also the steely determination. We both knew it was a losing battle.

But we would fight for her anyway.

"We need to go after her," Ryder said. His words were strident, intended for everybody, not just me.

Fallon had moved to his knees, head lowered. He didn't react to Ryder's proclamation besides the slightest tightening of his back muscles.

"Did you hear me?" Ryder screamed, rounding on our leader. I knew better than to kick a wounded dog when he was down, but Ryder was more impulsive than me.

Fallon remained immobile. If his back hadn't been rising and falling steadily, I might've believed him to be dead. It was unlike him to completely break down.

But Addie...

My throat clogged with emotion, some of which I refused to recognize. Grief, for one. What good was it without action? Mixed with it all, interwoven like the finest strings of a tapestry, was heartache.

And that fucking killed me.

"Get up, you ugly bastard! Get up!" Ryder was screaming, garnering an audience, but he didn't care. His face was red, and his hands were fisted. Asher said something to him, too low for me to hear, and Ryder responded with a punch to his face.

You get a punch, you get a punch, and you *get a punch,* I thought, a hysterical chuckle bubbling in my chest. Dammit. I was losing my mind.

Asher didn't even flinch when Ryder's fist connected with his face. His expression was carefully blank. Guarded. A fortress that no one could demolish.

My chest tightened, lungs burning.

How would we come back from this?

How *could* we?

Before I could voice my fears out loud, Fallon exploded. That was the only word for it. One second, he was kneeling on the ground, and the next, he'd charged to his feet with a roar. The sound reverberated through me.

Hundreds of emotions flashed in his piercing eyes. Grief. Pain. Anguish. Anger. Denial. And then determination. It hardened him, changed him, and I knew he would never be the same. Hell, I doubted any of us would be the same. Our scars ran soul deep from slap after slap to the face. It wasn't something we could bandage.

"We'll get her back," Fallon said resolutely. His teeth were clenched so tightly, I was afraid his jaw would break. His eyelashes feathered over his cheekbones, and he took a deep, calming breath. "We bring her back, even if it's a body."

His words made icy fear skate down my spine.

A body.

Addie's body.

Ryder turned his face away from mine with an anguished sob.

No, we would not be bringing home a body.

And if we did, the world would fucking burn.

CHAPTER 20

They led me through a maze-like sub-basement and into what looked like a sterile hospital room. The heady scent of bleach and other disinfectants permeated the air, so potent that it was almost suffocating. The white walls, white bedspread, and white tiling made the room unwelcoming instead of cozy. Inhabitable, as if no one had ever stepped foot in it before.

A severe looking woman handed me a thin, scratchy hospital gown before leaving with the rest of the men. Leaving me alone.

The full truth of my reality hit me then.

Alone. I was alone and dying, away from my men. Soon, I wouldn't be able to even recognize them as the parasite infected my mind. I wouldn't be able to recognize myself.

My breathing was erratic as I mechanically slipped out of my clothes and into the uncomfortable gown. It fell just below my knees, opening in the back to reveal more of me than I liked.

I caught a glimpse of myself in the mirror and frowned at how...sickly I looked. My face was abnormally pale, devoid of the usual red splotches on my cheeks. Dark shadows accentuated how tired I actually was. My hands went to my face, touching the skin. How long until my eyes turned red? Until my hair fell out in clumps?

How long until the Adelaide I knew and loved was gone?

Because the second my mind was gone, the second I attempted to harm another human being, I wouldn't be Addie anymore. I may have still had a body, had a heartbeat, had a brain, but the girl I knew would be long dead.

I was terrified.

I allowed myself to realize that, embrace it. I was terrified I would never see the men I loved again. Would I see Calax in the afterlife? I supposed that was one bright spot in this monotonous darkness.

A knock on the door had me jumping ten feet in the air, heart racing.

Quickly, I moved until the backs of my thighs met the hospital examination table. The last thing I wanted to do was show a person who wasn't one of my guys my ass.

Instead of the nurse from earlier, I was greeted by an older man in a white coat. His hair was gray and receding, and beneath the coat, he wore an impeccably ironed business suit. His no-nonsense demeanor and penetrating eyes allowed me to see that he meant business.

"Adelaide," he said stiffly, gliding into the room. You could tell a lot about a person by the way they walked. Some people slouched, almost as if they wanted to disappear into the floor. Others kept their chin up and eyes straight ahead. Some had a bounce to their step, and some moved as if weights trailed behind them.

This man walked with purposeful strides, an imperious set to his chin. His keen eyes seemed to be aware of everything—every breath and twitch, every heartbeat and thought. Those were eyes that saw it all.

I squirmed, moving to sit down and kick my feet. I knew he could see through my feigned nonchalance, but if I was going to die, I didn't want to be cowering. Scared. Pissing my pants.

Because, let's face it, I was tempted to take a massive dump right then and there. Some people shook when they were scared, others shitted themselves. Guess which category I fell into?

"Call me Addie," I told the man.

His lip curled as he glanced down at his clipboard.

"Okay, Adelaide, do you know why you're here?"

"Because I was kidnapped?" I said dryly, my feet swinging back and forth over the edge of the bed. "Now, are you going to tell me your name? It's only fair because I told you mine. That's usually how communication works, you know. Tit for tat. Or is the saying tat for tit? Honestly, I don't know why we have to talk about tits in the first place. I have seven boyfriends, and only they are allowed to talk about my tits. I hate that word—tit. It makes me sound like a teenage boy going to second base for the first time. Other words I hate—boob, moist, and penis. Like, why a penis? Why not death bringer? Turkey sausage? Skin pickle?" As I mused, the man's—I refused to call him Doc—face went carefully blank. He slowly placed his clipboard on the counter.

"Are you done now?"

"Naming penises? Declan's—that's one of my boyfriends, FYI—is definitely a pleasing sword. I need to do more research before I name the others."

Yes, I was babbling. My tendency to speak my mind became more prominent when I was nervous. Or scared. Or...nervared.

Another Addie original word. I'd fight anyone who said differently.

"When did the Arctic enter your bloodstream?" the man with no name asked, picking up his clipboard and holding a pen over it. My brows furrowed.

"Arctic?"

"The worm." He spoke as if he was speaking to an imbecile. "Named after its origins in the ice caps. How long ago did it enter you?"

"Um…an hour or two ago." My hand began to scratch at my arm. Was I hallucinating, or was there something crawling beneath the surface?

He nodded solemnly.

"May I?" He held up his stethoscope, and my face twisted in distaste.

"Do I have a choice?"

"No."

At least he was honest.

~

THE NEXT HOUR was the equivalent of a doctor's physical. He tested my reflexes, checked my blood pressure and temperature, and jotted down what seemed like hundreds of notes. When he was done, I'd been poked and prodded more times than I cared to admit.

I was tired and hungry, but at least I learned the old doctor's name. Deth.

Dr. Deth, ironically pronounced like death. By the time we were done, he was more animated than I thought possible. He practically smiled, which seemed to be a normal person's version of bouncing off the walls and partaking in orgies.

"Incredible," he murmured, staring at a vial of my blood he'd drawn. "Absolutely incredible."

"Um…thanks?"

My voice had his head snapping up, eyes narrowing. For a long moment, he merely considered me with keen eyes. Seemingly coming to some unknown conclusion, he nodded and gestured me forward.

"Come," he said, moving towards the door. I moved to follow him before freezing, hands going to my opened gown.

His lips twisted down further. Honestly, I was beginning to think he only had two expressions—a glower and a frown. Maybe he was just immune to my sparkling personality.

With a heavy sigh, he nodded towards my discarded clothes.

"Change."

"Yes," I replied. Apparently, we were speaking one word at a time.

I waited until he exited before pulling off the gown and stepping into my pants. I quickly donned my shirt. While Deth didn't give off pervy vibes, I didn't want to test my luck. I'd seen how some of the men at the compound had looked at me—as if I were meat prepared to be devoured. The last thing I wanted to do was add fuel to the fire in a society where perpetrators were victimized and actual victims were blamed.

Deth was waiting for me outside my door when I exited. Immediately, he began to walk down the long hallway.

"Are we meeting up with my parents? Hideous people, both of them. There are some people you want to see dead, and there are some that you want to cut up into pieces, castrate with a rusty spoon, and feed their entrails to stripper penguins. Guess which category Dear Old Dad and Mommy Dearest fall into? I'll give you a little hint—it's not the first one. Sure, a death would be nice, but torture sounds much more amusing. Does that make me a horrible daughter? Wanting pain and suffering bestowed on the people who tortured me for years? Hmmm…I don't really need to be on Santa's nice list. Not that I ever got presents, mind you. I think my mom got an STD from my father one year, but that's the extent of gifts. Wait! Christmas when I was twelve. I got a stuffed bear because DOD was trying to impress a fellow business man. Took me to a Christmas party and pretended to be a doting father. Afterwards, he stole the bear from my hands and sold it for crack. You'd be surprised by the things you can sell for crack, especially around the holidays."

We stopped in front of a large window displaying a hospital room similar to the one I just came from. Same uncomfortable looking bed, white painted walls, and freshly mopped tiles. A young man was lying on the hospital bed, arms and legs strapped to each post. His body shook with sobs, barely audible pleas leaving his lips.

Horror filled me, and I brought a hand to my mouth. Tears stung my eyes.

"Why are you showing me this?" I whispered. Was this what my future held? Strapped down like a prisoner and crying?

"Don't waste your tears on this man," Deth said harshly. "He was an inmate at the prison a few towns over. Murder, first-degree."

The door to the room opened, and two men entered. Each one wore white biohazard suits and masks. A silver cylinder was gripped tightly in one of the men's gloved hands.

"Watch," Deth instructed. Unbidden, my eyes turned back to the scene. My brain screamed at me, warned me to look away. It understood that what I was about to see was going to be gruesome. Disgusting. Horrifying. Yet, I couldn't move, utterly captivated.

The biohazard man unscrewed the lid and held it over the sobbing, trembling man. A black worm crawled over the edge before dropping onto the man's bare stomach.

"Please, no! Please! I have a family! I have children!" But the man's pleas fell on deaf ears. Without another word, the two men in white exited out the door they came through. The final clank of the door shutting was ominous. Damning. The tiny hairs on my arm stood up.

The man, the prisoner, was screaming and thrashing, eyes fixed on the worm crawling over him.

As I watched, transfixed, the worm lifted its upper half before plunging down, burrowing itself into his skin. The man let out a cry of agony, the worm slithering, growing, beneath his skin.

I watched the path the parasite made—up his neck and cheek, across his forehead, and finally disappearing behind his shock of dark hair. My stomach churned, threatening to expel the contents of my last meal. I wrapped my arms around myself as if that could somehow hold the food in.

And then, it happened.

The man's eyelids shut, and when he reopened them, his eyes were red as the blood vessels popped. White foam exploded from his mouth, and his body convulsed. A sound that wasn't entirely human emitted from his mouth. A feral growl. A scream. I could only describe it as a combination of the two.

It was too much. Hands on my stomach, I turned away from the gruesome sight. Deth's lips curled into a sneer as I vomited, tears burning my eyes. Only when I was sure that my stomach was empty did I turn back to the death doctor and his beady eyes.

"Why did you show me this?" I whispered hoarsely. I used the back of my hand to wipe the remnants of vomit from my mouth. I felt disgusting. All I wanted to do was shower and then sleep for an eternity. My body shook as fear rode me. Instinctively, my eyes flickered to the skin on my arm. White scars adorned each of my wrists, intermingling with savage looking burn marks. Was the parasite, the Arctic, slithering just beneath my skin?

"The longest it took for the parasite to corrupt the mind was thirteen minutes and twenty-two seconds," Deth said. He began to lead me back down the hall, in the opposite direction of my room. I followed along behind him feeling helpless. Small. Vulnerable. An insignificant, pesky bug just waiting to be squashed beneath his boot.

"And?"

"And." He turned back to stare at me, a white eyebrow raised. "It's been hours, and you're still normal. Well, relatively normal."

"I don't understand," I said honestly. We stopped at a nondescript door at the end of the hall. There was no placard announcing what, or who, I would find inside.

I pictured my father sitting on a leather throne, a bottle of whisky in one hand and his favorite cigar in the other. I pictured his feet kicked up on the desk as he reclined, but when I entered, he would drop his feet to the ground and take a threatening step towards me.

My hands were sweating, shaking, and I swore my heart was beating irregularly fast. I could barely see through the terror, barely think. I was suffocating on my own fear.

Deth didn't bother knocking, instead pushing the door open without preamble.

I shoved my hands into my pockets as if that gesture could somehow quell the shaking. Nope, didn't work. Still felt like thousands of bolts of electricity were coursing through me.

I slowly lifted my eyes to face the figure in the room, and my breath left me in a swooping exhale. I physically staggered back a step, hand rising to cover my chest. My heart.

It couldn't be...

"Fallon?"

CHAPTER 21

ADDIE

On closer inspection, I saw that it wasn't Fallon, but a man who looked like him. An older man with gray and white peppered throughout his hair. His tawny skin held an array of wrinkles—around his eyes, the corners of his lips, and drooping down his cheeks. He was how I imagined Fallon would look like twenty years from now.

This man must've been a relative.

He smiled when he caught sight of me, muscular arms extending as if he intended to pull me into a hug. Instinctively, I shivered, backing up a step.

He may have looked like Fallon, or at the very least an older version of him, but he wasn't. I couldn't afford to have my guard drop for even a second.

I didn't know who he was or what he wanted, but he obviously worked for my parents. That in itself was bad fucking news.

"Addie!" he said jovially, a smile severing his face in two.

My teeth gnashed together, and my hands curled into fists.

Who was he, and what did he want?

He tried to wear a mask of benevolence, but I could see something lurking just beneath the surface. A coldness. A flash of malice in his eyes. A curl of cherry red lips. Everything about him did the exact opposite of his intended reaction. Instead of ease, I felt fear slither up my spine like a striking snake.

"Who are you?" I demanded, crossing my arms over my chest. I tried to look badass, nonchalant, as if I wasn't dying and hadn't been kidnapped by cruel army men. Fake it till you make it.

"Please, have a seat," Not Fallon said, ignoring my question and gesturing towards a leather seat in front of his desk.

When I hesitated, Deth pushed my shoulder and sent me toppling forward. I glared at him. Asshole.

My body was tired, and my head was still reeling from all I'd witnessed. With heavy reluctance, I perched myself on the leather chair. The seat was cold against my bare arms, scratchy as well.

The least he could've done was invest in a comfortable fucking chair.

"I've been hearing a lot about you," he said, steepling his hands on top of his chest. His own chair swayed side to side as he stared at me, eyes intent and penetrating.

"All good things, I hope," I drawled out, the cliché saying slipping from my mouth before I could stop it. I had a moment of panic, a blistering type of pain. Would he mistake my humor for flirting? Why did I live in a fucking world where I had to be cautious of each and every word that left my mouth?

He surprised me by throwing back his head and laughing. The sound sent goosebumps up my arms, and not the good kind. These were the type of goosebumps you received watching a horror movie and knowing the main protagonist was going to die. You still rooted for her, but you were mentally judging her stupidity at entering the dark, abandoned hall weaponless.

"Who are you, and what do you want?" I repeated. I half expected my father to creep into the room at any moment. He was a snake, a monster, and I had no doubt he'd sharpened his fangs in preparation to strike. My prolonged separation from him should've made me less terrified, but it hadn't.

I'd gotten a taste of freedom, and I was determined to hold on to it. The prospect of being back under my father's dauntingly heavy thumb was terrifying.

"Forgive my poor manners. My name is Lucian." He extended a hand over the desk, and I eyed it warily for a long moment. With bated breath, I took it, half expecting my entire body to shrivel up and die from the contact.

But…nope. Nothing. Not even static electricity.

I didn't bother giving him my name. The asshole already knew it and probably knew every little thing about me.

"I'm going to cut right to the chase, Addie. You're a very special girl."

I snorted. This was already off to a great fucking start. My father called me special seconds before he hit me. My mother called me special when she sent slimy men up to my room. I hated that word and the connotations behind it.

Ignoring my interruption, he leaned forward, eyes eagerly tracing my features. "Let me explain. You're special, Addie. Your blood is special."

"I don't understand what you mean," I gritted out, but that unease in my chest was unfurling, growing, until I was practically choking on it like a large ass cock.

"Your blood has the cure. Your blood could save this entire world."

Oh, fuck.

～

CALAX

My muscles were coiled as I pressed my face against the steel bars.

I'd been waiting, saving my strength, allowing my body to heal. It had been agony, to say the least, but now I was ready. Now, I would fight back.

My mind had been in a hazy sort of numbness since the meeting…weeks ago. My stomach was somersaulting repeatedly, twisting and turning and clenching.

They had intended for me to turn on Addie, to do what was right, but they'd severely underestimated my devotion to her. Their words only cemented my resolve to break free of my prison.

So I waited, biding my time. Playing the good prisoner, the good man, the selfless one.

I ate when they said eat, and pissed when they said fucking piss. The darkness encroaching on the edges of my mind was held at bay. The mere thought of Addie propelled me forward, convinced me to fight a little longer, a little harder.

I would live to see my baby again.

"You're thinking too hard," a voice rasped from down the corridor.

I would've been the first to admit I had a soft spot for the little bastard. It was either him or silence, and that silence threatened to lead to insanity. All in all, it wasn't a very hard decision.

"Shut up," I griped, hands tightening on the bars. I heard the telltale creak of the door opening followed by the patter of footsteps. In the cell next to me, I heard his sharp intake of breath, the noise he always made when *she* came to feed us.

He'd told me she had once been his wife. Beautiful and vibrant, grasping the world by its metaphorical balls and squeezing tightly. She'd chosen our captors over him and had paid greatly for her decision.

Her face was nearly unrecognizable, riddled with slashes from a knife. Her body was thin, so thin I could see her collarbones and hipbones. The gauzy white dress she wore was sheer and did little to protect her from the harsh chill of the dungeon.

Her eyes remained downcast as she slid a plate of food through the bars. I resisted the urge to grab her pasty white skin and demand she release me. Demand she break me free. The need was almost unbearable, but I wasn't a monster. I wouldn't hurt an innocent woman in my quest for escape.

When she reached Doug's prison, she faltered only barely. Her lip curled into what was probably a sneer but was so disfigured, it could've been a smile. With a flick of her wrist, she tossed the plate through the bars. I heard the thump of food on the cement flooring, and Doug's signature growl.

"Bitch," he murmured to his estranged wife. She bared her teeth at him.

Without another word, she turned on her slippers and sashayed out of the prison. The heady scent of piss and vomit and blood was enough to make anyone run.

"She dumped your food again?" I asked Doug. It was our go-to conversation starter. She would come at least once a week, throw his food, and then huff away with an imperious set to her chin. We never talked about consequential stuff, like our lives before we were prisoners or our goals for when we escaped.

I didn't trust him, and he didn't trust me. Oddly enough, it worked for us. I didn't need a best friend or a brother, only a companion. Someone to hold the weight of the world when it became too heavy.

"Dumb bitch," Doug groused, and I heard him shuffling around. Probably picking up his fallen meal.

Glancing down at my plate, I saw that they had made a sandwich with turkey and cheese. An apple, slightly brown, was sitting beside it. The meal didn't look artistically pleasing, but food was food and I was starving.

"What do you have?" Doug asked.

"Sandwich. Apple. And…what looks to be a fudge brownie."

He growled. "Stupid bitch gave me tuna fish and moldy cheese."

"Still holding a grudge, I take it?" I asked in amusement. Grudge was the understatement of the century. The woman was *murderous*. Their history was full of pain and bloodshed, that much was clear. I would've needed a large glass of bourbon and a psychology degree to unravel their entire relationship.

"Still planning your escape?" he countered, and this time, it was my turn to growl.

He called it a fantasy, a dream, a wistful thought. More than once, he'd laughed in my face. He was resigned to his fate. Hell, he expected it. Live and die down here and all that shit.

When I told him why I needed to escape, why I needed to fight, he laughed harder. A full belly laugh that had my hands clenching instinctively.

This man had never been in love before, had never cared for someone so fucking deeply, he'd have been willing to do anything for them. He saw emotions as a weakness, and I imagined it was because he'd been burned one too many times. He had a wife that hated him and kids who loathed him. He didn't understand my need for light because he'd lived too long in the darkness.

"Yes," I answered briskly, turning back to my meal. The meat, thankfully, was not moldy. It actually tasted pretty damn good, if I was being honest. I was practically salivating by the time I came to the brownie.

"You're an idiot," Doug quipped. His voice was muffled, as if he was speaking with his mouth full.

"I need to get to her. She needs me, especially now."

Now more than ever, though I didn't tell him that. What I'd discovered, what I'd been told…

Tremors reverberated through my body, and my heartbeat rose exponentially. I could feel it pounding against my rib cage.

They couldn't get to Addie.

My hands were shaking as I brought the brownie to my lips and bit down, immediately assaulted by the rich, gooey goodness.

And something hard.

I choked, sputtered, and removed the object from between my teeth.

"What the hell?" I whispered, glancing at my palm.

"What? Did you piss your pants again?" Doug droned. "I told you it's not that big of a deal to use the chamber pot. It's only a little unsanitary. I'm sure your ass will only get a mild infection."

"Shut the fuck up, Doug." My voice was high in wonder, taking the bite out of my words. I held the bronze key up to the scarcely lit hallway.

Not just any key, but the key to my prison.

"What the fuck?" I repeated. I held my breath as I brought the key to the lock. I was at a precipice just waiting to fucking fall. Every breath was wheezing, horrible gasping noise.

"What's going on?" Doug exclaimed. He sounded closer. I imagined he was huddled against the bars, attempting to peer out.

There was a clicking noise as the key turned, and the lock clattered to the ground. I held my breath as varying emotions battled for dominance. I settled on disbelief.

Was this a trap?

Was this a way to test my loyalty?

"Did you just…? Let me out, man." Doug's voice took on a pleading quality.

Ignoring him, I opened the door the rest of the way and stepped into the hallway. The cement was cold beneath my bare feet, colder than even the floor of my cell. The light was dim, barely breaching the far corners. The door out of the prison, the door to my freedom, sat in front of me.

Waiting.

Trap or no trap, I would never have another opportunity like this. It would be worth the beating to just claim I tried.

"Let me out!"

"Sorry, man." I took a tentative step forward. "I need to get to her and soon. But I'll come back for you."

Maybe.

When had I turned into such a heartless bastard?

Doug's laugh was humorless.

"And you still think I'm a spy?" he asked, and I shrugged my shoulders, a gesture I knew he didn't see.

"No. But I don't know your physical condition or what you did that would require them to lock you up. I can't take that risk. As you always told me, it's every man for themselves."

Another laugh wheezed through his lips. Surprisingly enough, this one was heavy with amusement.

"I'm surprised you took my lessons to heart. I don't blame you. I don't deserve to see the light of day." His voice lowered with self-loathing. "But can you do me a favor?"

"What?"

I was bouncing on the balls of my feet, antsy to escape. To go to her. To cradle her beautiful face and see with my own eyes that she was alive and well.

And then, I'd hide her from the rest of the world like the selfish asshole I was.

"Make them pay."

I smiled cruelly into the darkness. I was a sight to behold I imagined, covered in blood, sweat, and grime. A monster just waiting to be unleashed. A monster prowling the forests, hunting its prey.

"Already planning on it," I replied darkly.

With a deep, shuddering breath, I stepped up to the door and pushed it open.

Either freedom or death awaited me. At this point, I would take either one.

CHAPTER 22

CALAX

I pushed open the door, cautiously glancing in both directions. I hadn't needed to worry, though, because the door merely led to a steep wooden staircase. The distressed wood pressed in on either side of me, making me feel boxed in. Suffocated. It smelled of copper and sweat.

I debated briefly going back for Doug. It might've been good to have someone in my corner, someone who knew his way around the compound. And while those were solid reasons to bring him, the seedling of distrust continued to grow in my stomach. He would as soon stab me in the back as he would watch it.

No, I had to do this alone. Maybe, when I found Addie, I would come back for him.

But probably not.

I masked my footsteps, but it was tiring work. My hand clenched the slivered wooden railing. The food had reenergized me somewhat. Combined with the adrenaline, I felt like I could do anything.

Burn this fucking place down.

When I reached the top of the stairwell, I paused, pressing my ear to the wood. Nothing but silence greeted me from the other side, and I released a breath I hadn't realized I'd been holding.

Slowly, ever so slowly, I pushed open the door. Inch by fucking inch.

Thankfully, it glided silently open. Before I could even check the hallway, ensure it was empty, a knife was pressed to my throat.

I froze, heart thumping, and with bated breath, turned towards the person who dared to threaten me. It wasn't a guard. It wasn't even Bitch or Asshole. Instead, standing in her drab white dress with scars distorting her face, was Doug's wife.

For a long, excruciating moment, we merely stared at each other. I didn't want to hurt her, but I would. I implored her with my eyes, begged her, to look the other way.

Don't make me hurt you.

Finally, she bobbed her head slightly and twisted the knife so the copper handle was extended to me. I stared at the weapon for a long second, too long, before gripping it and testing its weight.

It would do little against a gun or even a sword, but it would have to do.

"Thank you," I whispered hoarsely. She opened her mouth and then closed it abruptly. Still, during that brief moment, I could see something pink and jagged twitch.

Her tongue.

Her severed tongue.

What did the bastards do to her?

It only solidified the fact they could never get their hands on Addie. I needed to leave here and find her. Warn her. Protect her.

Keep the truth from her.

The woman lifted her hands and made exaggerated gestures. I tilted my head to the side, attempting to understand. Was she trying to help me find the exit?

She blew out a breath and grabbed my arm, tugging. My feet remained cemented to the ground.

Did I follow her?

Trust her?

What alternative did I fucking have?

"You lead me to the exit, you got it?" I said to her, voice dark. "I need to get out of here."

In answer, she tugged on my arm again.

"If you're leading me to a trap, I'll kill you," I warned. Probably not the smartest idea to threaten the woman who was saving me, but I was desperate.

Another tug.

Another long, penetrating slash of eyes. Her gaze branded me.

I nodded, moving my feet to follow her.

Death or freedom.

Death or freedom.

~

ADDIE

"What exactly are you saying?" I whispered, gaze focused on my hands as they twisted the hem of my shirt. The fabric was dark against my too pale skin. Tiny threads dangled precariously from the hem, seconds away from unraveling completely. I focused on that, only that, and it allowed me to pretend my world hadn't changed completely in the span of seconds.

"You called me Fallon when you first saw me," Lucian said softly. He moved from his seat, perching on the front of his desk. His long legs indolently kicked outwards until they were touching mine. I winced at the contact, pulling my own body farther back into the chair. "My nephew does look a lot like me. Granted, I'm a more stunning version."

He tried to smile, tried to make it reach his eyes, but it failed. Epically.

"Nephew?" I parroted, my mind latching on to that one word.

Suddenly, my conversation with Fallon and the others came back to me. The reason they knew so much about the parasite and the natural disasters. The reason they were at the resort to begin with.

Fallon's uncle had been the Secretary of Defense.

"I see the wheels turning," Lucian said brightly. "I see my nephew spoke of me?" He stepped even closer, and behind me, Deth ventured a step towards me as well. I felt surrounded, enclosed. Only the high-backed leather chair kept their bodies from touching mine. "I was employed by our president, God rest her soul, when she was first elected three years ago. Unfortunately, President Ali was infected near the beginning of the outbreak, and her vice president, Reiyna, took over. The country wasn't aware, what with the lack of internet and cable." He smiled, almost as if he believed he'd made a joke.

A fucking joke about the end of the world.

"Soon, she was dead as well. Actually, the entire cabinet fell. Except for me. I knew very powerful men, you see. Like your father."

His words were the equivalent of a bucket of ice water being poured over my head. My body went rigidly straight. I could hear each heartbeat, but the rhythm was irregular. I was so fucking terrified.

How could he still affect me the way he did? How could I still innately fear a man who'd been absent from my life for months?

Full body shivers jolted my body forward, and I brought my hands up to my face. A throbbing headache was forming behind my eyes. I reluctantly dropped my hands and faced the man who wore the face of my lover.

"You see, Adelaide, the government was aware of the Arctic long before it was freed. We studied it. Tested it. Experimented on it. Some of these experiments, I'll admit, were not sanctioned by the United States government. Sometimes, we have to do immoral things for the sake of billions. Money and power have a lot of pull in the world, you know? Your father was more than happy to accept a handsome paycheck for his services."

My entire body was cold, numb. I couldn't look away. God, I wanted to. The need to divert my eyes was driving me hard, but something in me rebelled. I needed to hear what he had to say. Every last horrible word.

"Your father experimented for years. We provided him the worm, he used his connections, and we gave him money. His favorite test subject? His daughter."

The air whooshed out of me. Even before he'd finished speaking, I was shaking my head.

"No, you're wrong. I would've remembered. You're wrong—it wasn't me."

"But it was." He smiled to take the sting out of his words. I glared in response. "Your father masked it as normal abuse. Don't you remember the drugs he injected in you? The doctors he made you see?"

I continued to shake my head rapidly.

"You're wrong! You're fucking wrong!"

Even as I said that, a memory assaulted me.

I shivered against the cold, pressing my leg closer to Ducky's. The silver gated fence was against our back, the school's playground in front of us.

"Are you cold?" Ducky asked softly. Only his head moved to stare at me. We were shoulder to shoulder, and tiny bolts of electricity reverberated through me at the connection.

"Freezing," I admitted. Without a word, Ducky removed his oversized coat and draped it over my shoulders. I zipped it closed, inhaling the flowery scent that was uniquely Ducky.

His long brown hair was braided, cascading over his shoulder. I yearned to run my fingers through it. Touch it. Would it feel as soft as it looked?

"You don't come around as much as you used to," Ducky said. He'd tried to keep his voice impassive, but it broke halfway through. He was hurt, devastated.

Didn't he know that I would rather be here than anywhere else? Did he know how much he meant to me?

My fingers interlocked with his, and I squeezed his hand.

"You know I love our time together," I whispered.

"More than anything?"

"More than anything." I smiled, and his answering one was luminous. I practically melted when he directed it at me.

The shrill ringing of the school bell announcing recess as over broke us apart. We both jumped, heads snapping upwards.

"I need to go." He sounded so sad, so despondent, as his head turned towards the front door of the school. Children were teeming near the entrance, waiting for the teachers to let them in.

I yearned to be one of them, one of those students. What would it be like to be a normal child?

"See you tomorrow?" Ducky asked timidly. He blinked at me through his thick fringe of lashes.

"Always."

I waited until he was lost in the sea of kids before I ambled to my feet, wiped dirt off my dress, and headed back in the direction of my home. Well, my home for now.

Daddy moved us monthly, it felt like. This home was the farthest from the school I'd ever been, a penthouse at the top of one of his hotels.

The walk back was quiet, interrupted by only the intermittent chirp of birds and the songs of crickets. It was peaceful, serene, and I resisted the urge to spin in a circle like a fairy-tale princess.

I stopped near the largest oak and removed Ducky's jacket, folding it up and putting it in a chest I always kept at the base of the tree. I was beginning to acquire quite the collection of his clothes. His pants, too long for both him and me. His tee shirt I wore after I spilled chocolate on my own. His sweatshirt. And now his coat.

I smiled softly, emotions I'd never felt before warming me from the inside out.

Finally, the hotel came into view. It was an impressive structure, even my ten-year-old mind could see that. Roughly hewn logs gave the hotel a rustic feel. Balconies sprouted from each room, black rails freshly painted. The doorman, a sweet guy named Nate, smiled when I entered and nodded his head.

"Good morning, little miss."

"Good morning."

He never asked me where I went so early, before the sun fully crested the tree boughs. And more importantly, he never tattled on me.

I moved into the spacious lobby and smiled at the front desk worker.

His smile faltered, eyes widening in alarm, just as a rough hand grabbed my little arm.

"Where have you been?" Daddy sneered, dragging me towards the elevator. I struggled futilely, but it was no use. I was no match for him.

"I took a walk," I lied easily. He would kill me if he discovered the truth.

"Every morning?" he countered darkly. The elevator was empty, and he all but shoved me into the tiny box. I fell onto my hands and knees, a sob being wrenched from my throat.

"I'm sorry, Daddy."

"You should be."

My fear only grew when he pressed the button for the basement, not the top floor. Only one thing was in the basement. The elevator descended, and it felt like I was traveling to hell.

Was this when he finally killed me? I was a bad, disobedient daughter. I wouldn't blame him.

The elevator beeped, and the silver doors slid open. I was still on the ground, but Daddy grabbed my arm and dragged me to my feet. I could either follow helplessly behind him or risk my arm being dislocated from my body.

The basement was empty, both the walls and ceiling made up of gray slabs of stone. He led me towards a familiar room where a familiar man stood over a hospital bed.

Dr. Whitelock was my doctor when I was younger. He reset my broken bones, stitched up my cuts, and provided me makeup to cover up my extensive bruises. All of this was done with an apathetic detachment.

At least he didn't smile.

I hated when they smiled.

"You know you need to be punished," Daddy said sternly. Tears welled in my eyes, and my lower lip trembled. I knew I needed to hold them in. Daddy saw tears as a weakness, a sign of emotion. He told me that tears made me look like a pussy.

"Yes, Daddy."

Eyes downcast, I pulled myself onto the hospital bed. I heard the clatter of equipment as a wheeled tray was pulled up. On it was an assortment of machinery I didn't know the name to. I recognized a stethoscope and a thermometer, but it was sitting next to a vial and needle and what looked to be a silver, spindly spider made out of machines.

Dr. Whitelock took the needle and vial and held it over my arm. He glanced towards Daddy for confirmation.

"I don't want to have to do this, but you need to learn your lesson. You need to be punished." He tentatively, almost sweetly, brushed my brown hair behind my ear. "Do you understand, sweet girl?"

"Yes, Daddy."

With a sigh, Daddy nodded towards the doctor.

The needle jabbed into my skin, and I was consumed by pain. The pain was blistering, running up and down my veins. I thought I was going to die.

I wanted to die.

Finally, I passed out.

CHAPTER 23

*M*y head pounded in tandem to my heartbeat. It didn't just beat, it *galloped*. Hurtling through the fucking forest while the rest of the world fell apart in shambles around me.

Instinctively, my hand moved to touch the skin where the doctor had injected me so many years ago.

What had been in that vial?

The cure?

The parasite?

Something else entirely?

Lucian watched me, but I couldn't quite read the expression on his face. I would've almost described it as triumphant before he carefully masked his features.

"I see recognition in your eyes," he said pointedly. His hand moved to gently pat my arm, and it felt like a molten brand on my skin. It took significant willpower not to pull myself away and then feed his balls to alligators. Why my mind immediately went in that direction, I didn't know. Apparently, I had a morbid fascination with the removal of testicles.

And people said I was psycho. Please. If you didn't have at least one fantasy about castration, then were you really living?

"I don't know what you're talking about," I lied, but even my haughty tone couldn't stop the terror from ricocheting through my body.

"I think you do." He stood, running his hands down his pants suit. "Did you know you have O negative blood? Otherwise known as a universal donor."

His abrupt change in topic had me reeling.

I wordlessly opened my mouth, closed it, then opened it once more. My hands were clammy, and my throat felt like cotton.

"What does that have to do with anything?" I asked with more bravado than I felt.

Pound. Pound. Pound.

My heart was so fucking loud, it could've had its own soundtrack. It sounded in my ears, my neck, my wrists, almost as if my entire body were made out of diminutive hearts with the same erratic heartbeat.

"Deth." Lucian nodded his head towards the doctor, and the older man grabbed my elbow and hoisted me up. I didn't bother struggling, despite the revulsion I felt at his touch. Lucian trailed behind, hands clasped behind his back.

He looked so much like Fallon, my heart began to ache for an entirely different reason. But while Fallon's eyes gazed down at me with love and awe and worshipful reverence, this man's eyes were cold and cruel. Mocking. He seemed more likely to lick away my tears with a malicious cackle than to comfort me. Probably got a boner from female tears.

Heaven only knew Deth did, the evil twat. Evwat—another Adelaide original word.

We moved back into the hallway where men and women armed to the teeth roamed the halls. They nodded respectfully towards Lucian when we passed.

"The men who helped Liz kidnap me…were they soldiers?"

I didn't know why the question was so important to me, only that it was. Fallon… he was a soldier. A man who'd done right by his country, serving it the same way he'd done everything else in his life—with his entire being.

But those men…

The cowards who'd hidden behind masks and had helped Liz torture Ryder by taking him for her…

They didn't deserve that title.

My stomach was a clamorous combination of anger and fear when I thought of the man who'd smirked at me, dragging memories to the surface I'd longed to keep buried. I wanted that man, that stranger, to die. A man whose name I didn't even know.

What had this world done to me?

"Mercenaries for hire," Lucian explained. "You'll be surprised what people will do for a quick buck. And what makes it even better is that we don't need to give them an explanation. We say jump, and they ask how much."

"So people don't know…"

That I have the apparent cure in my body.

That I might be able to save the lives that others deemed as lost.

"The last thing we want to do is cause a panic. Mass hysteria. As I said before, anyone could be bought. And you, my dear Adelaide, are in high demand."

I hated that he talked about me like a fucking dog toy in a shop, something available for purchase. And maybe that was Lucian's problem—he didn't see me as a human, only as someone who could potentially save the world.

Would I behave any differently if I were in his shoes?

He saw me as a commodity. Valuable, yes, but only for the supposed blood that ran through my veins. He wouldn't hesitate to kill me if it was my life versus the world.

Not that I blamed him.

Choosing to live would be utterly selfish and repulsive.

"Your father kept you from me for a long time. Hell, we didn't even know the cure was in his own daughter. He made sure to kill everyone on the team. The doctors, the scientists, the poor middle men who happened to get caught in the wrong place at the wrong time. He claimed he'd never found a cure…until he came crawling to me a few months ago with news about you. News and proof. But then the asshole lost you." Lucian tsked. "The man could run an empire, but couldn't keep track of one rowdy young girl? Imagine my surprise when I heard you were with my nephew."

He paused in front of another wooden door, immaculate carvings adorning the frame. Without pause, he pushed it open, and I was forced to peel my eyes away from the beautiful woodwork.

Down numerous twisting hallways we went, one stride of Lucian's equaling two of my own. Deth remained silently at my back, a harbinger of death.

Finally, we stopped in front of an elevator.

"Get in," Lucian demanded, nodding towards the silver box. Memories of my father assaulted me. Was he still here? Waiting for me?

Holding my breath, I pressed my nails into my palms and stepped into the tiny enclosure. The doors slid shut silently, and elevator music drifted from the speakers. It was a surprisingly peaceful song, a direct contrast to my storming emotions.

When it pinged, we moved as one down another hallway and into what appeared to be a torture chamber. I'd never seen one outside of movies, but it was exactly how I would've pictured it.

A simple wooden table was in the center of the room, holding an assortment of tools. Clamps, chains, and what appeared to be whips. Iron manacles hung from the ceiling, connecting themselves to a young man.

No, not a man.

A Rager.

"Yes, a Rager," Lucian whispered, hinting that I may have spoken that thought out loud. Hearing a man as put together and sophisticated as Lucian use my crass term for the infected made me feel oddly validated.

The Rager was thrashing against his chains. The red irises had expanded completely, swallowing the pupils until they were twin chips of garnet. The familiar black veins protruded from his translucent skin, withering and twitching. Alive.

He lunged for us, head canting precariously to the side, but the chains kept him restrained. Thank God.

The last thing I wanted to be was Rager kibble. I was sure I tasted horribly. Well, maybe not my lady bits. I'd heard that those were quite tasty, actually. But the rest of me? Nasty.

"Begin the demonstration, please," Lucian instructed to the three people who'd entered the room behind us. They all wore similar biohazard suits and masks, faces obscured.

With practiced movements, they circled the snarling Rager. The monster's head whipped from one person to the next, unable to keep his attention on any one individual. When he was distracted, white foam exploding from his mouth, one of the scientists lunged forward with a syringe of red liquid.

My blood.

The Rager released a roar of agony, head tilting back as he cried to the heavens. As one, the three scientists stepped back and behind Lucian. I wanted to look at them, to question how they were okay with all this, but the Rager held my entire attention.

He was twitching, jerking, convulsing. Spit flew from his mouth, and his red eyes rolled back in his head. Pitiful moan after moan left his lips, the sound gurgled through the white foam still erupting from his mouth.

Instinctively, I took a step back.

This wasn't experimentation.

It was fucking torture.

Finally, after what felt like hours, the man's head lolled downwards, chin resting on his chest. I brought my hand up to my mouth to smother the gasp, the sob, that threatened to escape.

Another low moan left the Rager's mouth, and his head lifted. Lifted. Lifted.

Until I was staring at a pair of mossy green eyes in a face devoid of blemishes. He blinked rapidly, seemingly coming out of a daze.

"What? Huh? Where am I?" His voice was drowsy, weary, and his lips were pressed into a thin line. Still, he was alive.

And human.

Human.

The events of the day finally caught up to me. Lucian's confession, my own distorted memories, the proof of what my blood could do.

Too much.

Too much.

Too much.

My eyes rolled back in my head.

I wasn't even sure if I hit the ground before unconsciousness consumed me.

~

CALAX

I followed her down hall after hall, and the farther we went, the more disoriented I felt. My head was already aching, brain fuzzy, from…well…everything. Torture and starvation did that to a man.

"Where are we going?" I growled out in a hushed whisper. "If you're fucking with me…" I trailed off ominously, but I honestly wasn't sure how to finish that statement. My moral compass prohibited me from hurting her, but I would be fucking pissed.

She placed a single finger to her lips and shushed me.

Finally, we stopped in front of a door that resembled *every other fucking door on the hall.*

When she nodded for me to enter, I eyed her warily. This was a woman who'd given me a key to escape, had fed me, had been nothing but kind to me. While I knew I should've trusted her, the logical part of my mind wondered if she was leading me to a trap.

Surely she wouldn't have saved me just to kill me?

Unless she was a psychopath…which I could totally see. Yup. Did not want to go into that room.

When my feet remained stubbornly planted on the ground, she gave my shoulders a firm push.

Of course, it did nothing to me. I may have been weak and frail, my muscle mass nothing like it used to be, but I still towered over her in height alone.

But still…

If trusting her could earn me my freedom, could lead me to Addie…

Releasing a heavy breath, I entered the room.

My mind catalogued it all. It appeared to be a bedroom with purple silk drapes, a barred window, and a plush bed, with bedding in a similar shade of purple, adorned with dozens of throw pillows. Two nightstands flanked the bed, one holding a single lamp and the other carrying a picture frame. On closer inspection, I saw that the standard prototype picture hadn't been removed. In black block letters, were the words "insert photo here" over a portrait of a smiling family.

The room hadn't been lived in.

"What—" I began, but before I could articulate my thoughts, the bedroom door was slammed closed.

I let out a roar, charging forward like a fucking rabid dog. I was practically foaming at the mouth, my anger and frustration potent.

I didn't trust easily. Hell, I could name on one hand the number of people I trusted. I didn't know if I was more angry at myself or her. My brain had warned me against trusting her, but my damn heart had only been thinking of Addie.

I tried the knob half-heartedly, despite already knowing it'd be locked. I could ram it down, but what were the chances someone would hear me? Would they allow me to live?

Holding my breath, I pressed my forehead against the wood. It was cold beneath my skin, the chill seeping into my very core.

My mind automatically focused on Addie. My light. My salvation. My love. She'd saved my life more times than I could count when I was a prisoner. Whenever I wanted to give up, give in, sink into the inevitable abyss of oblivion, I heard her voice. Calling to me. Comforting me. Assuring me of her love.

"Callie, hang on."

"Seriously, Big Guy, quit being a pussy and fight back."

Her words had helped me, saved me, woven together the jagged, tattered remains of my wounded soul. Through it all, she'd been beside me. Every torture session. Every flirtation from the evil, conniving bitch. Every moment when my own thoughts became my worst enemy.

I knew, without a doubt, she would help me get through this now. I just had to hang in there, plan an escape, and then I'd hold her in my arms for all of eternity.

Easy.

Voices reached me from the other side of the door, coming closer with each heartbeat. I glanced in both directions quickly, debating whether or not I should slide under the bed before deciding on the closet.

Such a fucking cliché.

Hiding in the closet from an evil governmental group who tortured me and wanted to kill my girlfriend. Honestly, you couldn't make this shit up.

I'd just shut the closet door when the bedroom door was pushed open, and voices reached me.

No, not voices.

One voice.

It was music, pure music, and it caused my already erratic heartbeat to pick up speed. I felt simultaneously ecstatic and terrified as her sweet voice filtered to me in my hiding place. Tears burned my eyes, and I didn't stop them from cascading down my cheeks. The salty taste hit my tongue, and I covered my mouth to silence my sobs.

Was I dreaming?

Hallucinating?

Were my days of pain and torture and sleep deprivation and hunger finally catching up to me?

Was I going mad…again?

But no, it was her sweet voice permeating the air. Slamming into me. Killing me ever so sweetly.

I closed my eyes briefly as she sarcastically wished her captors a good night and then threatened to skin their penises.

Addie.

CHAPTER 24

I stared through the binoculars so intently that a headache erupted behind my eyes.

When Tamson had rejoined our group, sweating profusely from his run, he led us to the building he'd seen Addie's car disappear into.

Tommy and Nik had stayed with Tonya, Jared, and Davis at a house a few miles back. Doc and Kai had elected to come with us. Addie had worked her way into their hearts as well, even though Doc would deny any attachment to the slender brunette who made up my entire world.

I recognized the warehouse-like building. Before the Ragers and the storms, before the world went to shit, it had been an army base. It was comparatively smaller than others across the country, but Uncle Lucian had run it with an iron fist before he'd been promoted. I myself had spent more days than I could count in there, both as a boy and a man. Running through the maze-like subbasement much to the frustration of recruits. Wielding my first gun. Partaking in extensive training exercises. Training unruly soldiers.

Most of my career had been inside those four gray walls.

What the fuck was going on?

Were we wrong? Was it not Addie's parents kidnapping her but someone else entirely?

I would kill everyone inside if there was a hair out of place on my beloved's head.

I told myself repeatedly that she was fine. Probably scared and angry, but fine.

I deluded myself into believing that the parasite hadn't entered her bloodstream, wasn't slowly corroding the mind of the girl I loved. A diminutive part of me, hidden beneath miles upon miles of misguided hope, knew that she would be either dead or changed by the time we got to her, but I refused to believe it. I would lose my sanity.

Instead, I focused on what I would have to do to bring my girl home. *Our* girl.

The front entrance of the base would be impossible to breach. Guards with guns manned it twenty-four seven. The fence was electrified and impenetrable.

But the back entrance...

Security was lax, rightfully so. A hoard of Ragers, at least one hundred of them, mindlessly stood in the road leading to the gate's entrance.

As such, the men and women inside were cocky, relying on savage monsters to protect their building.

Well, they'd learn to regret that decision when we stormed the fortress and rescued the princess, so to speak.

Tamson, who was peering through the second pair of binoculars, lowered them.

"I counted one hundred and twenty-two," he said, nodding towards the hoard of Ragers. I lowered mine as well.

"Same."

"What's the plan?" Kai interjected. The young man was bouncing from foot to foot, his nerves beginning to overtake him. He wasn't a fighter by any means. When Ryder and Ronan met him—and eventually kidnapped him—he'd been meek and scared of his own shadow. Of course, the brothers were known for over-exaggerating their stories. I believed this one had swords and dragons in it.

"Kill the Ragers. Enter through the back once Ryder cuts the power. Have a team near the front detonate the bomb for a distraction." I spoke in my no-nonsense voice, as if I truly believed this plan would go off without a hitch.

But even my contingencies had contingencies. There was plan A and plan B all the way to plan fucking Z.

The basic principle? Save Addie and fuck shit up.

Kai swallowed audibly, and Doc put a comforting hand on his shoulder, squeezing once.

"And how do you expect to get through the flesh-eating monsters?" Doc asked dryly. "If we're sacrificing someone, I vote Ronan." When Ronan whipped his head in the doctor's direction, momentarily shaken out of his stupor, Doc shrugged unashamedly. "What? You're my least favorite harem member."

"Dick," Ronan murmured, but the word held no malice. He was too fucking tired to verbally spar with the other man.

"No distractions. No virgin sacrifices or whatever...though you won't find any here." I chuckled humorlessly, scraping my hand over my light hair. It was getting longer and in desperate need of a cut. Even my ponytail couldn't contain the silky strands completely. "We don't want to clue the men and women inside to what we're up to. We kill only enough Ragers to get through."

As I spoke, I put a silencer on my gun. We'd chosen to use a variety of weapons, each fitting our strengths. Ronan carried twin daggers, while Declan had a sword. Asher had both daggers and swords, his body covered from head to toe in weapons. Tamson would be setting off the bomb as soon as we radioed him, and Ryder would be in charge of cutting the electricity from a nearby plant the assholes had left severely under protected.

I turned towards my men, my family, and met each of their gazes firmly. I wanted them to see the sincerity in my eyes and hear my raw anguish.

"This is dangerous as fuck, and I would not blame any of you for turning your back on the mission. Addie wouldn't blame you either. Hell, she would probably spank our asses for putting ourselves in harm's way. You guys can go back to the safe house, and no one would think less of you." I flicked a glance in Doc's and Kai's direction so they knew the final statement included them as well.

"Fuck no," Ryder seethed. "We're a family. Live together, die together."

Ronan nodded his head in silent support, and Asher smiled cruelly. His eyes were cold in his face, any traces of warmth absent. Declan and Tamson nodded as well.

"Oh, what the fuck," Doc muttered. "We're in."

"Let's kill some Ragers," I responded darkly.

Hold on, Addie. We're coming.

ADDIE

As my mind raced, so did my heart, anger, fear, and frustration vying for attention. Battling for first place.

The implications of what we'd discovered could alter the world as we knew it. Hopefully for the better.

I wasn't optimistic. Every person had an agenda, a reasoning for their actions, an end goal that didn't necessarily line up with the good of the world as a whole.

Oh sure, people could make empty promises, slather balm on a wound, offer bandages, but what options did we have to fix this fractured world? What role did greed play in Lucian's experimentation?

I rapidly sifted through my thoughts as Deth led me to a door.

"We had this prepared for you," he said curtly. I offered him a closed-lipped smile, my teeth gnashing against each other.

So they'd been expecting me for a while. Noted.

"I hate you," I told Deth seriously as I stepped into the room. The first thing I noted was the silver bars on the window. Fucking peachy.

Ironically enough, one of the last things Lucian said to me was, "You're not a prisoner."

Snort.

"I'm going to circumcise your dick," I continued, leveling a glare over my shoulder at Doctor Deth. "Slash it off with all the blades I keep hidden in my hair. Yup. You heard me right. Maybe I'll wait until the blades are rusty and *then* circumcise you. You'll be awake, of course, and aware of every slash of my knife against your penis. Feel my wrath, motherfucker." Only when he shut the door, effectively caging me in a prison that apparently wasn't a prison, did I call out, "Have a good night!"

I could be a real classy bitch, taking the high road and all that.

Frowning, I made an immediate beeline for the bed, intending to crawl under the covers and sleep for an eternity. My hopes for sleep were interrupted by a clattering sound emitting from the closet, almost as if someone had run into an entourage of hangers.

I froze, muscles tensing and back straightening.

Someone was in the room with me.

"Hello?" I placed my bare feet on the carpeted floor and ventured a tentative step closer. "Don't make me cut off your dick. Or boobs. Either, or. I don't discriminate."

Another step.

And another.

And another.

The closet door was wrenched open, and a tall male stumbled out, eyes watering.

"Addie," he breathed.

I gaped at the figure who was both painfully familiar and unfamiliar. A face I memorized. A face I saw every time I closed my eyes. One of seven thoughts that kept me going, kept me breathing, when the darkness encroached on the edges of my mind.

His dark hair was longer, falling to his shoulders in disheveled, greasy tangles. A rough beard covered his angular jawline. His cheeks were sunken, pale, almost as if he'd been starved for months with no sunlight. His body fared similarly. While he was still tall, still large, he no longer held the muscle mass I remembered.

Fuck.

I was hallucinating.

Again.

"Oh fuck," I said out loud. Maybe I was finally succumbing to the madness?

At least in insanity, I could be with Calax.

Positive thinking.

CHAPTER 25

ADDIE

"Not again," I groaned, scrubbing a hand down my face. "Not a-fucking-gain."

The Calax hallucination took a trembling step towards me, wobbling like he didn't know how to use his legs. His arms were extended, and his lower lip trembled.

Now I knew for sure I was hallucinating. The Calax I knew and loved never cried.

I waved him away dismissively.

"Shoo," I said. "Go back to the corner of my mind where you belong."

"Addie." His voice was raspy, harsh, and sent tremors up and down my arms. My flesh erupted into goosebumps. How could his voice unravel me so, crumble the carefully constructed walls I'd erected around myself? Damn Fake Calax.

"My memory got this right," I whispered hoarsely, taking a step backwards. "Your voice. I would recognize it anywhere." Stepping closer, I grazed my finger over his neck, pulling away his hair as I went. He trembled almost delicately at my touch. "And right here. You have a mole. I noticed it before, but I didn't say anything. You should probably get that checked out. You don't want to get skin cancer."

"For fuck's sake, baby—"

Tears flooded my eyes.

"Callie used to call me baby," I cried. His gorgeous golden-flecked eyes widened in his face as something akin to realization twisted his features. He cursed under his breath and stomped towards me, eating up the distance in two long strides.

I'd to lift my head to maintain eye contact, but I refused to look away for even a second. He might've been a figment of my imagination, but he was still Calax. My mortal enemy. My archnemesis. One of the loves of my life. He was a mirage of water after I'd been traipsing through the desert for days. A sight so sweet and beautiful, yet so sinfully deadly. Looking at him, seeing him, was like balancing precariously on a sharp sword. One wrong move, and you would impale yourself, blood dripping down the keen blade.

But fuck if it wasn't the sweetest way to die.

"Addie, baby, listen to me." Fake Calax put his large hands on my shoulders. I stared down at the splatter of golden freckles on his knuckles. They weren't as pronounced as I remembered them being. And there, on the back of his hand, was a tiny white scar. I never knew what he'd done to get it. "I'm here, baby. I'm fucking here, and I'll never leave you again."

He moved so our foreheads were pressed together. His hot breath fanned against my face, smelling vaguely of mint.

"Your breath smells good, Fake Calax," I blurted out. "Like minty chocolate."

"There was a sink and a toothbrush in our prison cells. And I just ate a brownie," he said softly.

"Prison. I don't like that word. It just sounds kind of…weird. Like, who the fuck says prison anymore? Actually, don't answer that. I know a lot of people say that word, even though I think it should be banned. Maybe I'll talk to the president, Fallon's uncle apparently, about removing it from the dictionary. A prison-free country. Hmmm…I could get behind that."

Before I could say more, could ramble more, Fake Calax's chapped lips were devouring mine. I froze, heart racing, even as my hand snaked up to fist in his hair, tugging on the silky strands.

I'm making out with a hallucination.

"I'm real, baby. I'm not a hallucination," he murmured against my mouth, greedily pushing his tongue inside when I made a noise of protest. His warm lips moved to my neck, sucking and lapping at the skin. "What did you tell me so many months ago, when I thought you were dead? That you were a real girl. Well, I'm a real guy, and I fucking love you. Please come back to me, Addie. Don't leave me. I need you." His voice broke, quivered, and his lips against my skin turned desperate and needy.

"Oh fuck, Callie, I missed you so much." It took all of my self-control, all of my effort, but I placed a hand on his chest and shoved. Like the real Calax, he stepped back immediately, though his eyes flashed with hurt and frustration. "I love you so damn much. And I miss you. And I want you to be real, I want you to be real so badly, it's a physical pain, but you're not. I saw you die. The memories haunt me, but I know what's real and what isn't. And I wish you were fucking real and alive and in this prison with me, but you're not. Calax, I love you. I love you so fucking much."

My legs couldn't support my body, and I collapsed to the ground, the carpeting softening my fall. Calax dropped to his knees and took my face in his hands, eyes emanating love and tenderness. He kept me tethered to the world, to the here and now.

"I'm real, Addie, and I'll prove it to you."

His lips once more claimed mine.

CALAX

She was here. In the flesh. Alive.

In my arms.

It was every dream I'd had in the dank, suffocating cell below the earth. Hell, it was every dream I'd had before the apocalypse even started.

Her warm body melded to my own as if she were made for me, and I for her. Everywhere we touched, we dissolved into each other. Ours kisses ratcheted up a notch in intensity until we were practically inhaling each other. Breathing each other in.

Her tongue darted out to tangle with my own, and I moaned deep in my chest.

"I'm here, baby. I'm alive, and I love you. I won't leave you ever again." My hand tightened on the bottom of her shirt, tugging at the thin material. "Please don't leave me."

"Callie…" she moaned, reclaiming my lips in a heated, possessive kiss. My body was on fire, a reaction only Addie was ever able to evoke from me. "Please be real. I need you to be real."

"I'm right here. I'm real."

I was suddenly desperate. We were close, but I needed to be even closer. I needed to feel her lips, her warm body pressed against my own. I needed us to be skin to skin, nothing prohibiting us from connecting fully. The months we'd been apart…

I didn't want to think about those days. The darkness that threatened to consume me. The light that only illuminated my cell when I thought of Addie and her sly smile.

"But you're not real," she sobbed, even as her lips descended my neck. I arched my head back to grant her better access.

"You're so fucking infuriating sometimes, you know that? But I love you so fucking much. Even when I want to kill you."

Our teeth clashed together once more as I curved my hand around her waist and lowered us both horizontally on the ground. She stared up at me with wide eyes glossy with unshed tears. I hoped she could see the love I felt for her in my own. The devotion. I nipped her plump bottom lip, pulling it with my teeth.

For the first time, I captured and maintained eye contact with a girl as I stripped my shirt off, tossing the disgusting material in the corner of the room. At least my body was clean from the shower they'd allowed me to take just the night before. Small blessings, I supposed.

But Addie either didn't notice or didn't care as she made a sound in the back of her throat, eyes roaming over my body hungrily. I felt a brief stab of self-consciousness.

My body was nowhere like it used to be. My once defined abs were non-existent, and my skin had lost its tan. Would she think I was ugly?

As quickly as those thoughts came to me, I swept them beneath the proverbial rug. Addie loved me. I knew that, always had, and she wouldn't care if I had horns sticking up from my head and scars distorting my face. She cared about me, the man beneath it all, and loved me unconditionally in spite of my flaws. My blemishes told a story of all I'd survived, and I knew she understood that.

That self-consciousness was nothing more than my depression talking, yelling, inside me. With Addie here, in my arms, I was able to ignore the insistent voice.

"You're beautiful," she whispered in reverence, fingers trailing over my shoulders and down my chest. She paused when she got to my stomach. I knew the skin there was red and ragged, the flesh torn and hastily stitched back together again.

"From the Ragers," I lamented, my mind whirling, transporting me back to that night. I could still feel the phantom teeth digging into my skin, claws embedding themselves in my stomach, bodies piling on top of me until I thought I would suffocate.

And then...

Gunfire. Merciful gunfire. The sound had reverberated through the room until it drowned out even the cacophony of snarls. I'd assumed it was my team coming back to save me, coming to put me to rest, and I'd wanted to reprimand them for their foolishness.

But it hadn't been them, and I didn't know whether to be grateful or horrified.

"It's hideous," I whispered as her finger traced a particularly deep and jagged scar. Goosebumps followed the trail of her finger.

"It's a part of you," she said firmly. Her eyes flickered up, towards my face, and I was stunned to see tears suspended on her eyelashes. "You're here. You're really here."

"I'm here." I captured her hands in both of mine, tugging them to my chest.

"Please don't leave me." Her voice was a cry, a plea, and it fucking gutted me. I did that to her, not her parents, not Lucian, not the assholes who kidnapped her. Me.

I knew mere words wouldn't pacify her, so I pressed my lips to hers again. We always did better when we were kissing. Each sensual nip of her teeth on my lip, flick of her tongue, spoke louder than a thousand words.

She broke away to pull her shirt over her head before pulling my lips back to hers. My hand covered her entire back, my fingers digging into the velvety soft skin. Still kissing her, my hand inched upwards until it fingered the claps of her satin black bra. There, I hesitated, pulling back slightly to gauge her reaction.

We'd kissed before, confessed our love, declared our relationship status, but we hadn't gone any further...and not because I didn't want to. I wanted Addie fully, every crazed and deranged piece of her. Every flaw and every perfection.

When she nodded, I unclasped the bra and watched as she slipped it down her arms. I swallowed, eyes flickering over her body.

There was a scar on her belly, similar to the one I had on mine. It was red in some areas and white in others, marring her perfect skin. No, not marring it. Somehow, the scar made her seem even more beautiful.

My gaze lifted higher, taking in her luscious, heaving breasts. They were easily a handful, if not more, and her perfect pink nipples were already peaked.

"You're beautiful, baby," I whispered in awe.

"Even the scar?" Her brows scrunched together as she stared down at her body. Her hand poked the discolored skin.

"Especially the scar."

"Okay, good. Because I'm pretty sure it looks like a penguin giving anal to a giraffe. Please tell me I'm not the only one who sees it? Ryder says I'm being ridiculous and asks how I would know what that looks like. Or maybe the scar looks like a massive duce that couldn't get flushed down the toilet. Or maybe—"

I leaned down and captured her nipple in my mouth. My tongue flicked over the sensitive bud as she moaned, arching her back. Tiny hands tangled in my hair, keeping me in place. I could easily break free if I wanted to, but for the first time in who the fuck knew how long, I was exactly where I was supposed to be.

I licked a circle around her nipple before grazing my teeth over the peak. When I moved my mouth to her other breast, I lifted my hand to fondle the one I'd neglected, twisting and pulling the swollen nipple.

"You drive me fucking crazy, girl. I don't know if I want to fuck you or kill you half the time."

She groaned as I bit down, hips bucking beneath me. I was getting so fucking hard for her.

"This is why we're enemies," she panted. "So the angry sex is so much hotter. Like Romeo and Juliet...without the whole suicide thing. Fuck, we can be Bonnie and Clyde. If they weren't criminals, of course. Not that I'm against a little healthy murder or anything—"

I released her breast with a pop, resting my chin in the valley they created.

"Why don't we just be Addie and Calax?" I suggested, staring up at her. Her cheeks were red, eyes hooded with lust, and fuck if that wasn't the most arousing sight in the world.

"Addie and Calax," she repeated with a serious nod. Her hands moved to my sweatpants, tugging down the material. My boxer briefs went with them, and I stood to kick them both to the side before dropping to my knees once more. Kneeling in front of Addie naked, I didn't feel vulnerable or self-conscious. There was a potent amount of heat in her gaze, yes, but also love. I could've drowned in the heady sensation.

She crawled on her hands and knees, tits bouncing, and flicked her tongue out to lick the pre-cum on my tip. My cock jerked, as desperate for her as I was.

"Fuck, baby. I need you."

"You have me," she purred sultrily. I honestly didn't think she realized she was doing it. She was naturally a sensual creature, exuding raw sexuality, and she wasn't even aware of it. Men everywhere stared when she entered a room, and women wanted to be her. She could be wearing tattered shorts and an oversized shirt and she'd still be the prettiest, sexiest, girl in the room.

Her mouth slid down over my shaft, sucking and licking. I growled, grabbing her ass. My girl had been practicing.

Strangely enough, the thought didn't make me jealous. If anything, I felt relieved she had people looking after her when I couldn't. And not just strangers, but my brothers. I knew they would love and protect her as completely as I did.

Her warm mouth continued to tease my cock, and her hand reached to cup my balls, kneading the flesh.

My cock ached with the effort to keep from coming, but I'd be damned if I didn't come inside her.

Grabbing her hair, I pulled her off my cock and grabbed at her pants and underwear. I wanted to appreciate her body, take my time, but I knew I wouldn't last.

No, I would save that for another day.

I briefly thought about a condom seconds before I sheathed myself in her wet heat. I knew I should care, but my body rebelled against my mind.

She seemed to be on the same wavelength as me.

"Are you clean?" she asked, and I nodded. The second I devoted myself to her, the second I realized she was the one, I'd had myself tested.

And fuck if it didn't feel amazing touching her skin to skin.

I waited a minute for her to adjust to my size before moving my hips. Once. Twice. Three times.

Gripping her hips, I fucked her relentlessly, earnestly, my hip bones slapping against her skin. Her pussy fit like a glove around my cock.

It felt so fucking good. Better than good. I could die inside of her.

"Baby…" I groaned.

"Fuck."

Her hands were on my ass, kneading the flesh. Pulling me closer. Closer. Closer. I could never be close enough.

I lowered a hand to play with her clit as I continued to pound into her. This was both lovemaking and fucking, as aggressive as my relationship with Addie has always been.

"Calax!" she screamed, pussy clenching around my length. My balls tightened, fingernails digging into her skin as I pistoned inside of her.

"Fuck!" I shouted through my orgasm. She trembled in my arms, hand creeping up to brush at my sweaty hair.

"You're real," she whispered. I twisted my head to kiss her palm.

"I'm real."

Her eyelids fluttered closed, a single tear cascading down her cheek.

"Calax, I love you."

"Love you more." I pressed my lips to her forehead. "Sleep, my love. I'll protect you."

I'll always protect you.

The day had no doubt been long and draining. We would have to debrief and discuss everything that had transpired, but at that moment, I was content with holding her in my arms. Listening to her heartbeat. Feeling her bare chest rise and fall.

We may have been prisoners, but we were together.

And that was all that mattered.

CHAPTER 26

RONAN

*M*y lungs ached as I plunged my dagger into the Rager's grotesque forehead. Black blood sputtered as his eyes rolled back in his head. He fell to the ground, unintentionally taking a second Rager down with him. This one was a female, but both of her legs had been cut off, and she was forced to crawl across the ground.

If she was alive, I was sure she would hate it. Hate herself. Hate what she'd become.

It was a relief to kill her. I was putting her out of her misery, allowing her soul to rest in peace.

Blood covered my hands and face. My clothes. My pants. It coated me like a second skin. I wanted to scrub it off, wash the darkness that tarnished my skin, but I couldn't. The fight wasn't over.

I was fighting based on instinct only. My mind was on my princess, but my body mechanically tore through the monsters. The Ragers. For the first time, I was the hunter.

We weren't killing them all, just enough to clear a path towards the fence. Fallon was using it to his advantage—he would lead Ragers towards the fence and smile with grim satisfaction when they were electrocuted.

Again, I tried not to think of the people we killed as human. They weren't. Not anymore. They were monsters through and through, unredeemable and deadly. They would not hesitate to sink their claws and teeth in our skin if the opportunity arose.

The way they had done to Calax.

With a ferocious roar, my vigor renewed, I lunged back into battle.

A demented part of me didn't care whether I lived or died. I knew that my princess had long since succumbed to the worm. The virus. The whatever the hell it was. Logically, I knew it couldn't be a virus, but my mind still viewed it as such. I'd never been a science guy. That was more Tamson's field.

I wondered if we could keep Addie with us. Lock her in a basement, perhaps. Or a cell.

How fucked up was that?

But, no. She wouldn't want to live her life as a monster. She would choose death without a moment of hesitation. Hell, she would even welcome it.

Tears slid from my eyes as I fought through the Ragers, finally reaching the silver door in the gate.

"How much longer?" I called to Fallon. He stealthily moved away just as half a dozen Ragers ran towards him. Their bodies convulsed, screams tearing from their lips as they were electrocuted.

Fortunately, their sounds of anguish were nothing new. The Ragers were known to fight amongst themselves. No guards would come running to check on the noise, except the ones on rotation. And we still had twenty minutes before they were scheduled to arrive.

"Soon," Fallon said. We were relying completely on Ryder infiltrating the plant and being able to shut down the electricity. The whole plan depended on it.

While we waited, we fought. It was a grueling battle as the time trudged on. Seconds turned into minutes…though it felt like hours. My arm ached from repeatedly slicing down Ragers. Sooner or later, we were going to get too tired to continue. Already, my body was heavy with fatigue, a leaden sensation intermingling with the ball of nerves.

Come on, Ryder.

I trusted my brother implicitly. I knew he would get this job done.

"What did the Rager say when it crossed the road?" I asked Fallon, sidestepping the claw of an incoming Rager. I couldn't see the rest of my brothers, but I heard Asher's grunts from within the throng. Declan was supposed to be back-to-back with him. Kai and Doc were fighting nearby, but their strength was waning. They wouldn't last much longer.

I wouldn't last much longer.

"Come on, Sarge. What did the Rager say when it crossed the road?"

Fallon kicked his foot out, catching a monster in its stomach. It—she—staggered before righting itself. Herself.

I didn't want to humanize them, give them names and stories. I was content with them being nameless, faceless monsters we were tasked to kill. Disposable. Garbage. It was easier than thinking of them as humans with families and loved ones and lives that had been snuffed out. At the same time, it was becoming increasingly harder for me *not* to see them as humans, especially since Addie…

"Fine," Fallon said with a sigh. "What did the Rager say when it crossed the road?"

Before I could respond, there was a large *pop*. Simultaneous with the noise, every light in the facility went dark. The cackling of the electric fence died as well.

"Ryder fucking did it," I murmured. To Fallon, I asked, "Is it off?"

"There's only one way to find out." Without a care for himself, he sauntered to the gated door and swung it open. When he didn't, you know, die, I released the pent-up breath I hadn't realized I'd been holding.

"Did you have to be so fucking dramatic?" I asked Fallon, racing after him. We didn't know how long we had until the generators kicked in. My guess? Only a few more seconds.

Declan and Asher ran in after us, followed quickly by Doc and Kai. Declan had a nasty gash on his forehead, and Asher was favoring his right arm, but other than that, the two were unscathed. Kai and Doc were similarly fucked up. Hideous bruises under each of their eyes, cuts and scars, and shredded clothing. Kai was holding his stomach, grunting in pain. No doubt, the man had broken a rib.

Made me feel kind of bad for kidnapping him and dragging him into this in the first place. Oh well. Let bygones be bygones and all that shit. My new motto—what would Addie do? And Addie would most definitely justify that kidnapping, crazy bitch.

Only seconds after we were through the fence and the door was shut, the generator kicked in and electricity once more came to life. I could hear it crackling, the sound oddly malicious.

"Ryder fucking did it," Asher said, running a hand through his shaggy blond hair.

"Never doubted him," I said.

Fallon removed the radio from his pocket and pressed down.

"Tam? We're ready."

Tamson's muffled voice came back. "Roger that."

Before I could catch my bearings, before I could orient myself, a booming explosion sounded from the opposite end of the building. It reverberated through my body. Made my ears ring.

"Let's go get our girl," I said, rubbing my hands together like an evil mastermind. Again, what would Addie do? I was determined to live by that motto, and my girl was just crazy enough to laugh like an evil witch at a moment like this.

As we sidled up to the wall, eyeing the guards who hadn't run in the direction of the explosion, Fallon leaned over to whisper, "What did the Rager say?"

"What?" We moved into the heavy shadows of the building, hidden from the blighted sun covering everything in its blistering rays.

"What did the Rager say when it crossed the road?"

I held my bloody knife more firmly in my hand. My eyes were slitted as I considered my prey. Four muscular men carrying semiautomatic rifles. These people *were* human, yet I considered them just as monstrous as the creatures roaming outside the fence. What type of people kidnapped an innocent girl? My girl? They were all monsters in my mind.

"Fuck if I know," I answered Fallon. "I didn't think that far ahead. I'm pulling an Addie and telling jokes without a punchline. Come on. Let's kill some fucking monsters."

ADDIE

I traced invisible patterns onto Calax's chest, my fingernails grazing his nipple.

"I can't believe you're alive," I whispered. My eyelids were heavy, sleep seconds from consuming me, but I was afraid to close my eyes. I didn't want Calax to be nothing more than a dream. I didn't want to open my eyes only to discover I'd imagined the entire encounter. No, I was determined to keep my eyes open no matter what. I didn't want him to disappear like a mirage.

"Baby..." He pressed his lips to my forehead.

"What did they do to you, Callie?" I didn't want to know the answer.

"It doesn't matter. We're together, okay? And we're going to get through this."

I moved my fingers to the smattering of hair on his chest, pulling it through my fingers. Suddenly, his hand grabbed mine, a pensive sigh escaping.

"What's this?" His thumb traced my engagement ring.

Voice quiet, I said, "I think you know what it is. Seven stones for my seven loves."

"You still love me? Even after I abandoned you?"

I couldn't believe what I was hearing. My nails dug into his chest, probably to the point of pain.

"Of course I love you, you big idiot. You're mine, just as thoroughly as the others are. Unless, of course, you don't want to be mine..." Tears sprang to my eyes unbidden. What if he no longer wanted me? What if too much time had passed and our good memories had been tarnished by bad ones? I wouldn't survive. No, that was a lie. I could survive because I knew he was alive and well, but a tiny piece of me would die forever.

His arms tightened around me before he released me with a sigh. "Don't be fucking stupid, baby. I love the shit out of you. It's always been you, and it'll always be you. I'm not as romantic as the others, but fuck. When this is over, I want to be able to call you my wife. To have you call me one of your husbands. Normally, I would fucking serenade you with candles or some shit, but you'll have to settle for this—us naked in bed after we've both been kidnapped. Addie, baby, will you marry me and make me one of your seven husbands? Enemies for life and all that."

I snorted, even as fresh tears sprang to my eyes. Happy tears. He loved me. He wanted to spend his life with me, even if it meant he had to share me. And more importantly? He saw a future outside of these walls. A future where we weren't hunted, where the world wasn't being submerged into the fiery pits of hell. He saw a happy ending, and fuck if I didn't melt into a puddle.

"Yes. Fuck yes. I'll marry you, Callie. You're mine, now and forever." At my proclamation, my ownership of him, he pulled me into a long, passionate kiss. It only reconfirmed what I already knew—I was his as surely as he was mine.

We became silent once more, my hand once again resuming its tracing of his soft, sweaty skin. Why were guys always so much sexier after sex? Not that Calax wasn't sexy normally, but damn. He looked good with a post-sex flush and his hair disheveled.

"Did you know what they told me? Calax, my blood holds the *cure*. We might be able to stop this. I might be able to save the fucking world." It felt surreal even to say, as if I were looking through a distorted funhouse mirror. The girl I saw wasn't me. At the very least, it didn't feel like me. The Addie I knew was gone.

Calax tensed beneath me, and I lifted my head to read his expression. His jaw was clenched so tightly, I was afraid it would break, his teeth gnashing together. He shook with barely suppressed rage.

"Baby…"

I gave him a look. *This* was why we were mortal enemies. He thought of me as fragile when I was anything but. If I didn't love him so much, I might've hated him.

He took a deep breath, arms tightening around me. They were iron bands. I couldn't break free, even if I wanted to…which I didn't. I was content to stay in his arms for the rest of my life.

He was alive.

He was safe.

And he loved me.

I may not have believed in happily ever afters, but it felt like I was one step closer to having my own. I just needed to find my other six men.

And, you know, not dying would be an added bonus.

"Lucian lied to you," Calax bit out scathingly.

"Huh? No, Big Guy, I saw my blood work. I saw it save that Rager—"

"He didn't lie about that. Your blood *is* able to expel the worm, but you only have a ten-minute timeframe."

He was making no fucking sense.

"Calax—"

"Once the worm, parasite, Arctic, enters your bloodstream, you have ten minutes to inject the blood. Actually, you have nine minutes and forty-seven seconds. Anything after that, and your blood would do nothing. The Rager you apparently saved? I have no doubt he was injected with the parasite mere seconds before they administered the blood. He was a demonstration. And if he was to get infected again by the parasite, they would need to inject *another* dose of blood into him. Addie… baby…maybe they'll be able to study your blood and create a cure or an immunity, but at the moment, Lucian only wants to use you for profit. He wants to rule the fucking world, and what better way to do that than selling the blood someone needs to carry on them at all times? Only you have an immunity. Your blood isn't capable of giving others the same permanent immunity, at least from what I gathered. And, baby, Lucian plans to drain you completely."

His words slammed into me like an aircraft carrier being shot out of the air and hitting land. A proverbial explosion followed that declaration.

I was numb, shaking, replaying Calax's words in my mind and comparing them to what I knew of Lucian.

My blood…

If what Calax said was true, it would be turned into a product for sale. A hot commodity.

Not the savior of the human race.

The rich and powerful would buy my blood in spades, since it wouldn't grant them an immunity and they would need to inject themselves each time the parasite entered their bloodstream. The normal, everyday human would suffer exponentially.

Wars would start.

All because of my blood.

"Shit," I whimpered, the full implications choking me. And not in the kinky way Tamson would.

Nausea swirled in my stomach, and I just barely threw myself off the bed before I vomited. Calax was there in an instant, pulling back my long hair and wrapping it around his wrist. I threw up until I felt like I was empty, both mentally and physically.

"What the fuck?" Calax stuttered, and I glanced at him in surprise. He wasn't looking at me, however, but at my vomit. Fucking gross.

On closer inspection, I saw something mixed in with the tawny color. Something black and flaccid.

The worm.

The dead worm.

"*That* was fucker inside me?" I hissed, barely resisting the urge to pick it up and crush it between my fingers. That might've been a little overkill.

Get it? Overkill? Because it was already dead? Sometimes I cracked myself up without even realizing it.

"I think we know what happens to the Arctics who enter your bloodstream," Calax mused, voice tight with disgust.

Before I could reply, the lights flickered once before we were plunged into complete and absolute darkness.

CHAPTER 27

*I*t lasted only a moment. A second later, artificial lighting once more illuminated the quaint bedroom.

"Get dressed," Calax said sharply, already depositing me on the opposite side of the bed. I nodded, not trusting myself to speak through the sudden surge of emotion. If you'd asked me what the emotion was, I wouldn't have been able to name it. A strange combination of fear and anger and a love so heady and encompassing, I could drown in it, swept away in a Calax wave.

We'd just finished getting dressed when the bedroom door was pushed open. Two familiar figures stood in the threshold, and I immediately looked away, unnerved by their gazes.

One was Enzo. His dark hair was brushed to perfection away from his face, and he was meticulously groomed in a form-fitting suit and white cufflinks. A red tie completed the look. Beside him was the man whose name I didn't know. The one who'd revealed himself to be Ryder's and my kidnapper.

Both of them flashed me identical smiles. Identical in the fact that it made my hackles rise and blood turn cold. An almost incandescent fury burned within me, an inferno waging a war in my chest. My hands were claws by my sides, and I wanted nothing more than to scratch at their smirking, cocky eyes.

Neither of them seemed shocked to find Calax in the room with me. Instead, Enzo clapped his hands together and took a step forward. Calax moved behind me, resting his hands on my waist.

"Gabriel," he hissed at the second guy, the sound emanating from low in his throat. A growl, almost. It vibrated through me.

"Calax." The scum of the earth nodded at my fiancé, lips twitching as he fought to hold back a smile. "I see you moved up in life." His gaze flickered around the room before resting pointedly on me. His eyes landed on my feet before slowly, languidly, moving upwards. The asshole paid extra attention to my breasts before finally making eye contact.

Calax vibrated with barely contained fury. He sort of reminded me of a can of pop after you shook it, waiting for the inevitable explosion once you opened it.

"You done now?" I drawled, trying to show both Calax and this Gabriel Anus Hole that I wasn't bothered. On the contrary, I was. I was *extremely* bothered. The man, the stranger, looked at me as if he had every right to. As if my body was for his eyes and his eyes alone. It was that sort of delusional mentality that saw rapists being acquitted for their crimes.

"We have places to be, people to see. Let's go, sweet Adelaide," Enzo cooed in a singsong voice.

"I'm coming with her," Calax responded darkly. One glance over my shoulder showed his face just as dark. Livid. Shadows haunted his eyes, shadows our love-making hadn't entirely been able to displace.

Something clicked then. An ah-hah moment that made me feel like an idiot for not noticing sooner.

When Gabriel and Enzo turned back into the hall, I stood on my tiptoes and pressed my lips to Calax's ear.

"Is that the asshole who hurt you?" I whispered, not fully recognizing my own voice. He didn't have to say anything for me to know, for me to be certain. At this point, I couldn't demarcate where he ended and I began. I wanted to say we were two peas in a pod…but that was unsexy as fuck. To put it simply, we understood each other better. When our bodies joined, the last barrier between us had collapsed. It solidified our bond in a way no one could understand. Hell, I wouldn't be able to articulate it, even if I tried.

So I knew exactly what Gabriel Anus Hole had done to him. I could sense Calax's embarrassment and guilt. Resentment. Fear. Anger.

I was fucking livid.

Before Calax could stop me, I jumped on Gabriel, clinging to him like a spider monkey. This time, I *was* able to claw at his eyes with my fingernails. He let out a curse, twisting this way and that in an attempt to dislodge my body from his. Instead of helping, Enzo threw back his head in laughter.

Laugh it up, bitch. I'm coming for you next.

Honestly, I was a little terrified of my own thoughts.

I put pressure on his windpipe with my arm, as Fallon and Tamson had taught me, and his hands came up to claw at my skin.

"You hurt Calax?" I screamed in his ear. "I *kill* you."

Yup. Totally not a psychopath.

"Baby," Calax said softly, but he sounded amused. And a little turned on, if I was being honest. Still, when his hands gently grabbed my waist, pulling me off Anus, I came willingly, purring like a contented cat.

Gabriel fell to the ground, eyes wild. Enzo continued to laugh, and I struggled against Calax's strong arms, determined to get to my next victim.

I should open up a new business—Dicks Be Gone.

The goal? Cutting off the dicks of rapists, murderers, and kidnappers.

I could probably get a few posters made...

"Apologize, you little bitch!" Gabriel seethed, that cock-sucking ballsack lube face.

"Bitch is a completely unoriginal nickname," I mused, tapping a finger on my chin. "Like, it technically means a female dog, and I personally think dogs are cute and fluffy. Wouldn't it be worse to be called an alligator or something? Like 'you little alligator' or maybe even a spider. I hate spiders. They're all creepy and crawly and have eight legs like some kind of horror movie monster. Seriously, why would God create a monster? Oh wait. He made a lot of monsters. You, for one."

Apparently, Anus Hole didn't like my speech. He charged towards me, hands extended. It was Enzo, of all people, who put a restraining hand on his shoulder and held him back. They whispered something to one another, too soft for me to hear.

I rested my head on Calax's shoulder while he peppered kisses across my scalp and forehead. In his arms, the rest of the world could just go right ahead and fuck off.

"Come," Enzo said at last, stepping back from his little dick friend. Gabriel was glaring at me, and I might've been scared by the anger in his eyes if I'd actually believed he could hurt me. But no, he was just Lucian's little bitch. And yes, that time, I felt bitch was used in the correct context.

Lucian bossed Gabriel around as if he were on a leash. Under his thumb. He could say whatever he wanted about me, but I wasn't the one thoroughly pussy-whipped. Or, to put it in better terms, cock-whipped. We all knew pussies were stronger than cocks.

Calax set me on my feet and straightened my clothes before interlocking his fingers with my own. After a quick, reassuring squeeze, we followed Enzo and Gabriel down the hallway and into a familiar hospital room.

Deth was washing his hands in the sink while Lucian leaned languidly against the wall, arms crossed over his muscular chest. His face lifted into a smile when he caught sight of me, and his eyes glimmered.

I didn't trust that smile for one damn minute. Now that I knew the truth, the reality of what type of monster he actually was, I wanted nothing more than to ram my boot into his nuts. The nut-cruncher was back at it again. The—wait for it—nutcracker.

Pretty proud of that one.

"What do you want?" I asked tersely. Calax was pulled as taut as the strings on a guitar. I wanted to reach out and comfort him, touch him, but I knew he wouldn't want to show any signs of weakness. No, he would have to fight whatever inner battle he was facing alone. At least for now.

"Calax! Welcome!" Lucian spread his arms wide in a swooping gesture. Calax didn't answer, face set in stone. It could've been carved from granite with how hard it was. Each line etched into his skin was as hard and unforgiving as his penetrating gaze.

Unperturbed by Calax's lack of response, Lucian patted the hospital bed. A white, scratchy sheet was already pulled over the leather. It wrinkled when he touched it.

I focused on that, only that, and the rest of the world fell away.

Lucian was talking enigmatically, making elaborate gestures with his hands, but I paid him barely any mind. Deth added something, tone low and dark, but it went in one ear and then out the other.

I was in a predicament. Morbidly, I wished that Calax had never found me, that he'd escaped this prison hellhole. At least then, I would've been able to refuse their offer without Calax's life being dangled in front of my face like a tasty morsel. It was both the sweetest, most tempting gift and the worst possible scenario. They had something they could use against me, something that would make me comply. And I would. Eagerly. Without preamble. I would sacrifice my life one hundred times over if it meant Calax got to live.

At the same time…

Was what they were doing really that bad? They weren't looking for a cure, no, but a quick fix. And their experiments *would* save lives. At the same time, the already shit world would fall further into shambles as the powerful fought to procure my blood. I had no doubt in my mind that if my blood could do all that, it could also be used for finding a cure. A vaccination.

But these men wouldn't be working to uncover that. No, their reasons were purely selfish, driven by greed.

Fuck.

If they killed me, if only they had access to my blood, I was condemning the world to a life of haves and have nots. The rich would prosper while the poor suffered. The powerful would thrive at the demise of the weak.

"What do you want from me?" I repeated. My throat was scratchy, like sandpaper had been rubbed over my vocal cords.

"To save the world, of course!" Lucian's smile was almost sincere. If I didn't know any better, I would've believed him. All it did was piss me off.

"That's such fucking bullcrap, and we both know it. My blood only works if it's injected in a ten-minute timeframe after the worm enters the bloodstream. And even then, it works only once. You're trying to create a fucking monopoly off my blood. You're trying to rule the world." My voice rose with anger until I was practically seething by the end. Red coated my vision as icy anger coursed through my veins. I felt like I could burn the world with my fury. Destroy it.

Destroy him.

Lucian didn't even flinch after I confronted him. To be honest, his expression didn't change at all. A smile remained firmly etched in place, and his eyes continued to glow.

I remembered reading about psychopaths and sociopaths during one of my online courses. I was obsessed with studying them, learning everything there was to know. For the longest time, I'd believed my dad was one. Now, I just believed he was a sadistic asshole intent on destroying me.

Anyway, sociopaths were incapable of feeling emotions such as regret and remorse. However, they were skilled at mimicking them.

And Lucian? I was beginning to believe he was one, especially when his brows furrowed and lips turned downward. It was the eyes, though, that had me staggering into Calax's chest. They contained that same glimmer, same spark of amusement, that was evident when he smiled.

"I don't want to help you," I whispered.

"Sweet Adelaide…" Lucian tsked. "Sometimes, you don't have a choice."

Calax made a strangled sound in the back of his throat, and I spun in his arms, eyes wide. His own were dazed, staring at a spot over my shoulder, and his hands dropped from where they were rubbing my neck. The color had drained from his face, and it was only when he turned, horror carved into every feature, that I saw Deth standing beside him, holding an empty syringe.

A startled scream lodged in my throat.

No. No. No. No.

The skin on his neck shifted, something crawling just beneath the surface. No, not something.

An Arctic.

The parasite.

Deth had just injected Calax with it, and I felt my entire world stop. Icy terror skated down my spine, filled up my lungs, churned the contents of my stomach.

"No," I whispered, but I didn't know who I was pleading with.

Lucian's smile was large in his face. Too large.

"Sometimes," he repeated, stepping closer, "you don't have a choice."

With jerky, desperate movements, I threw myself onto the bed. The blanket was scratchy against my bare legs, but a twisted part of me reveled in the pain. The discomfort.

I just got him back.

That thought repeated on a loop in my head. Over and over and over again. It was all I could think about, all I could focus on. I just got him back…and I was losing him all over again. This was staring down the barrel of a gun and knowing you were going to die. You saw your inevitable end laid out before you like a welcome mat. Hell, a part of you even *welcomed* the relief only death could bring.

Something salty touched my chapped lips. Tears, I realized blankly.

"Do what you want with me," I whispered to Lucian darkly. "But save Calax."

A tiny piece of me broke that day. A piece that no number of bandages or thread could fix.

I would never forget the moment Calax's eyes turned a vibrant red. When his skin shifted and contorted right before my eyes. When he stared at me, eyes looking right through me. When he snarled and lunged, only being restrained by five guards with guns. When the ropes were tied tightly, mutilating his skin. When he hissed at me, called me names, threatened me, all in a guttural voice.

I supposed a part of me always believed our love could survive the transformation. That a part of him would still remember and love me.

I was a fucking idiot.

I didn't just break that day in the hospital room, the pungent smell of bleach assaulting my senses.

I died.

<h1 style="text-align:center">CHAPTER 28</h1>

ASHER

e moved as one into the compound. It didn't take long to find a group of guys and disable them. Only when they were rendered unconscious did we strip them of their clothes and weapons.

The black uniform with the angel wings crest and breastplate was uncomfortable. The one I put on was a size too small, the sleeves stopping just before they reached my wrists. The pants themselves ended above my ankles, and the stainless steel boots made my toes curl awkwardly.

Sarge unstrapped the rifle from the fallen soldier and slung it over his own shoulder.

Once more, we moved through the crowded halls.

It was surprisingly easy to blend in. In a compound this big, not one person knew every other person. So for a group of large guys to roam the halls, chins tilted upwards imperiously? It was just another day on the job for them. We received no second looks besides the initial passing glance. A nod here. A crude joke there.

Sarge played his part surprisingly well. Laughing when cued, smiling at the other men and women, walking with purposeful strides.

It also didn't take long to find a man who knew about Addie.

"That sexy bitch?" he purred, palming his cock through his pants. I lunged forward immediately, Ronan's hand on my shoulder the only thing holding me back. I hated the way this man, this stranger, talked about her. I knew my eyes had turned scarily cold.

A lot of people believed I was a psychopath. I knew that wasn't true, but there were times I felt my grip on sanity loosening, unraveling. Those times were brief and far between, but I was terrified of the moment when the thread completely unraveled, revealing the broken man underneath. I was an enigma, I knew. I would give the shirt off my back for the people I cared about but not hesitate to stab the people I hated. I blushed when I saw boobs, but laughed when face to face with a dead body. I hated cursing out loud, especially around Addie, but my thoughts were a chorus of "fucks" and "shits."

"Where is she?" Sarge asked darkly. He took a menacing step closer, towering over the smaller man and looking intimidating as fuck.

The soldier's eyes narrowed suspiciously. "Why do you want to know?"

One second, we were standing in the hall, and the next, we were in a tiny alcove. Fallon pressed his arm against the man's neck, cutting off his air supply.

"Where is she?" His cadence changed. Gone was the smiling soldier roaming the halls, and in his place was a prowling tiger. The man was thirsty for blood, and soon, it would be difficult to differentiate between friend and foe.

"Fuck, man." The soldier's eyes were comically wide in his face. "Ground level. Room two-fourteen."

Fallon released him as quickly as he'd grabbed him, and the man dropped to his knees, limp and pliable.

The man's eyes wandered from Fallon to a radio on his belt buckle. The movement was almost imperceptible. If I hadn't been looking intently, I would've missed it.

The second his fingers would've touched the radio, I lunged forward, hands wrapping around his neck. With one twist, his neck was snapped and he fell to the ground, dead.

Kai gulped, glancing away with disgust, but the others didn't even bat an eye. Doc actually smiled cruelly.

"Where are we now?" I asked Sarge, straightening. I stepped over the body without a backwards glance.

"Basement. We have to go up a floor," Fallon growled. He leveled a stern, eloquent look at each one of us. "We only kill if necessary, but Addie is our priority, understand?"

Declan and Ronan nodded their heads decisively. Fallon didn't even bother looking back at me. He knew I wouldn't hesitate to kill if I had to. I wouldn't shy away, hide behind the others, or fear the throwback of a gun.

I did what I had to do.

~

RYDER

There was a lot you could do with a pretty face. A wink here. A sly smile there. A touch of the shoulder. I never went any further.

I was a changed man. A *taken* man. Before, I wouldn't have hesitated to use my body to get what I wanted, to gather information. Twist and contort people to fit the mold I needed them in.

Everything changed after Adelaide came into my life. Kitten. I would never, not ever, do anything to hurt her.

When I entered the plant, the woman there had taken one look at me...and swooned. Expectantly so. My hair may have been disheveled, dirt and soot might have covered my cheeks, but I knew I looked good. I told her my name was Darrin and that I was lost. I told her I stumbled upon this building with its bright lights and the few guards pacing the entrance.

She'd believed me, since I played my part as one would play a guitar.

Her hand had rested on my shoulder, my arm, my stomach, and each time, I had to physically stop myself from flinching. Wincing. Despite the fact it didn't go any further, it felt like a betrayal, and I hated myself.

But no. I knew the gain outweighed the loss. Allowing this woman to touch me was just one step closer to getting Addie back.

Of course, the woman didn't expect me to blow up the building.

A grim smile lit up my face as I wandered across the woodsy path bogged down with weeds. Behind me, flames licked at the building, a kaleidoscope of reds and oranges and even a deep blue.

I'd allowed the woman to live, obviously. I wasn't a monster, but I made it quite clear she should run as fast and as far as she could. My leniency and compassion only extended so far.

With a swagger to my step, I stopped beside Tamson, who was huddled behind a bush, facing the compound. Now that I'd destroyed the initial source of power, the immense building had to rely on a generator. At least that was what Fallon remembered from his time as a soldier and trainer. The front entrance was in similar disarray to how I'd left the plant.

Tamson had expertly deployed his bomb right at the front entrance, between the two guard towers made up of roughly hewn logs. The men and women were running, searching, hunting, their guns raised.

But Tamson was fast. He'd always relied on his body more than other things. While the guards and soldiers went in one direction, chasing after the supposed bomber, Tamson stealthily ran in the opposite direction. His light footsteps barely broke any twigs or leaves. Barely left an indent in the forest floor.

No one would know to go after him, especially after he'd left a noticeable trail in the opposite direction minutes before the explosion.

"They're in there right now," I said, scanning the silver building with a curled lip. "They" were my brothers and Kai and Doc. I was furious, livid almost, when the guys instructed me to go to the plant and shut off the power. I felt as if my skills could be used elsewhere...particularly saving my kitten. But Fallon had a point. I was a skilled engineer. A skilled charmer. A skilled...bomber?

Damn. That made me sound crazy.

Either way, it was done.

"Do you think they're okay?" I continued, but what I really wanted to ask was, *"Do you think she's okay?"*

Tamson didn't answer, eyes fixed straight ahead. After a moment, he glanced at me and rose from his crouch. I followed him mechanically, my body moving while my mind wandered.

I'd always been the optimist of the family. It was my job, the one thing I was good at besides fucking answers out of females. But now, I didn't feel optimistic. Not one fucking bit. I'd seen the worm enter her bloodstream, watched the light flee her eyes as terror replaced it. The damn girl knew she was going to die. Knew…and accepted it.

My heart beat something fierce in my chest.

Fucking damnit. I couldn't lose Kitten. Not now. Not after everything we'd been through.

On silent feet, Tamson led us to the back gate where Ragers swarmed. Some of them were attacking one another, their hideous faces appearing almost deteriorated in the waning sunlight. Over two dozen were lying on the cement, dead. Black blood puddled around their bodies.

"How do you feel about giving them a little help?" Tam asked softly.

"What do you propose?" I raised a brow, and in answer, Tam held up the remaining grenade. The bastard held it without care, without fear, without any self-preservation. Crazy son of a bitch.

A cruel grin curved my lips upwards.

"What if this backfires?" I questioned, shocking the shit out of myself by being the voice of reason. "What if it harms our guys?" And our girl.

"Oh please." Tamson snorted. "They took out over thirty Ragers while a hundred more looked on. This will serve more as a distraction than anything else. Something for the soldiers to focus their guns on."

My smile widened, knowing he was right and feeling a sick sort of vengeance and satisfaction.

I released an admittedly deranged laugh.

"For Addie?" I asked.

"For Addie," he agreed with a decisive head bob.

He smiled darkly before expertly throwing the grenade at the gate. It took only a moment for it to explode like a red-hot firework.

A gaping hole in the fence remained.

A gaping hole that the Ragers were running through.

Tam and I exchanged another cruel smile.

Fallon wanted chaos…and chaos he got.

CHAPTER 29

ADDIE

A sort of numbness overtook me. Surrounded me. Engulfed me like the arms of a lover. The room felt almost swelteringly hot, unbearably hot, and sweat beaded on my forehead.

Voices.

They reached me, but I couldn't quite grasp what they were saying. It was like trying to hold back the waves in the ocean, pushing at the cresting water with your arms extended—impossible.

Growls. Voices. More growls.

Something sharp jabbed into my skin—a needle, I realized blankly. I felt no pain as the blood was drawn. Honestly, I didn't think I even would've been able to. It was like my body had shut down, inch by excruciating inch. Soon, my damn heart would stop beating in my chest, and I would succumb to the darkness encroaching on my vision. The sweet, merciful darkness.

Everything was too much. My senses were on overload. Each sensation, each touch, each voice, was the crack of a whip against my bare skin. Not painful, but demanding. I imagined it would be similar to standing in a crowded room naked, feeling eyes on you but not being able to cover up.

Displayed.

Ridiculed.

Empty.

So I did what I did best.

I went to the place all broken girls and boys go to when reality gets too difficult. My retreat. My oasis. My mind.

My garden.

Behind my closed eyelids, it was exactly how I remembered. Carefully planted roses and tulips intermingled with the shrubbery and manicured grass. There were no weeds, no clouds. Nothing but a bright sun shining down on my own, personal paradise.

I walked down a stone trail, stopping at a white gazebo erected from the ground. Flowers twined themselves into the wooden siding, and a single gray bench, ornately detailed with carved flowers and vines, was directly beneath it.

It was there I sat, relishing in the sunlight and warm breeze. In my garden, it was never too hot nor too cold. The weather was positively perfect, somehow balancing a calming heat and a light wind.

It was safer in the construct of my own mind. Nothing could hurt me there. Death couldn't reach me, and life didn't feel so fragile.

"You'll be okay, Addie," Tommy said softly, and I glanced towards the left side of the bench. He sat beside me, his fingers interlocked with my own. "Do you need me to kick any asses?"

I felt pressure on my thigh, and I turned to the right. Nik sat on the opposite side of me, his familiar pair of red headphones around his neck. His eyes weren't on me, but love and warmth emanated from his body in soothing waves.

"You guys are my brothers, my family," I whispered. Tommy squeezed my hand.

"And you're ours."

Before I could respond, they vanished into the air.

"How many bikinis do you have?"

The male voice, though familiar, made me jump a foot in the air. I pressed a hand to my heart to calm the racing organ. Snort. As if a hand over my skin could do anything besides provide false comfort.

Ronan moved up the path, his hands in the pockets of his basketball shorts. His green-tipped hair was tousled, unruly, almost as if he'd run his hands through it. He smiled deviously at me.

"Bikinis?" I parroted, confused as to where this weird as fuck conversation was going.

His voice raised in a poor impersonation of a Valley girl. He twirled a short strand of hair dramatically around his finger, kicking his leg out.

"You need one for masturbating in," he said in that high-pitched voice.

"One for dangling your toes in…" I whispered.

"One for flaunting in the hallways. But that one can*not* get wet. It's made of solid gold."

A tiny smile flitted across my face. This was almost the exact conversation I'd had with Ronan when I first met him.

His face changed, contorted, and blond hair and tanned skin took his place.

"Hi, Gorgeous," I said in a hushed murmur. Emotion clogged my throat.

"What can I get for you?" Asher asked with a large, beautiful smile.

I glanced down, stunned, to see a table bedecked in a white tablecloth in front of me. A glass of champagne and a plate of fettuccine alfredo adorned it.

"Thank you, Ash," I said, grabbing a fork to eat my meal.

"Anything for you, sweetheart," he replied reverently. There was the sound of a chair being pushed back, and I glanced up from my alfredo. Ryder sat across from me, the sun highlighting his dark skin and abundance of tattoos.

"What might your name be, Kitten? Something as gorgeous as you are, I suppose." He winked a golden eye at me, and I involuntarily snorted.

"So fucking cheesy, Ry."

"So fucking cheesy," he teased. I narrowed my eyes.

"Quit copying me."

"Quit copying me."

"Stop it, Ryder."

"Stop it, Ryder."

"Go choke on air."

"Go choke on air."

"You guys are both children," Calax snapped, and I spun on the stone bench. Leaning against the gazebo, strong arms crossed over his chest, was my handsome giant. A familiar glower was etched across his face.

Moving like a lion stalking its prey, he positioned himself in front of me. The table and Ryder were both gone.

"Hi, Callie. How is my archnemesis doing?"

"Addie," he growled.

"Sorry, Big Guy, I don't respond to growls. Use your words. Or else I'll kiss you. That's the ultimate sign of hatred."

A grunt behind me had me spinning around once more.

"Oh, look at that! If it isn't the King of Grunters."

Fallon responded with a—you guessed it—grunt.

Before I could respond, he pressed his lips to mine and ravaged my mouth in the way only he could. His hand fisted in my hair, the slight sting being soothed away by tiny presses of his lips to my own.

Fallon didn't need words to communicate with me. Didn't need fancy mono-logues or dramatic speeches. Every heated touch, every caress of his eyes, every stroke of his tongue spoke louder than a scream.

A throat cleared, and I reluctantly tore my mouth away from Fallon's.

Tam's cheeks were a dark red, and his eyes flickered from his shoes, to my swollen lips, and then back to his shoes.

"I'm sorry for making you uncomfortable," I whispered, leaning forward to squeeze his arm. He captured my hand with his own, tangling our fingers together.

"You're the only thing in this world that *doesn't* make me uncomfortable."

"I'm a thing?" I blurted, realizing that my big mouth had ruined our romantic moment. Fuck me.

Actually, that was a pretty good idea. I was sure we could use the vines for some ropes…

Before I could make that suggestion, Tamson disappeared like a cloud of smoke.

Soft lips pressed to the side of my head, and I turned towards Declan expectantly. Only, it wasn't Declan, at least not the one I remembered. Instead, it was a young boy with abnormally long hair and eyes that seemed to stare into my soul. One quick glance down confirmed I was wearing a white dress with my hair in pigtails. Ducky's face changed once more, features hardening and elongating. His hands moved to sign, and I focused on his fingers in rapt attention.

"*I. Love. You.*"

Heart swelling, I repeated the motions back to him. I'd just crossed my arms over my chest for love when he, too, disappeared.

My heart ratcheted up a notch when I realized I was all alone.

Clouds, dark gray and bloated, covered the sun until everything was encased in darkness. The flowers began to wilt in their own bug riddled refuse. The gazebo shattered, and I barely dodged the collapse, landing on my butt in the weedy grass.

My paradise, my mind, was falling apart.

As if to further emphasize that point, the clouds opened up and released a torrent of brutal rain. It stung everywhere it hit, the coldness so intense, it could've been molten lava.

"No!" I screamed, spinning in a wide circle. I searched the darkness for my men, for Tommy, for Nikolai. But I was alone.

All alone.

"No!"

CHAPTER 30

CALAX

J wouldn't have been able to tell you what being a Rager felt like.

It was mere minutes, but it felt like a lifetime. A lifetime of hurling insults at the woman I loved. Of growling and snapping, a carnal need rising within me to eat and claim and fuck. The scent of blood permeating the air.

And a red-hot, blistering rage consuming me. It was an inferno running rampant within me. A volcano. It was a rubber band pulled back so tightly, all you could do was wait for it to snap.

I was aware of it all. Or at the very least a primal part of me was. It sort of reminded me of staring through a window on a cold winter night, snow covering the ground, drooping tree branches, and the murky window pane. Yet inside, you could see a roaring fire, a tray of hot chocolate, and the fluffiest fucking blanket imaginable. You pounded relentlessly on the window, desperate to get in, but no one responded. The wind continued its relentless assault on your body as snow pelted your face.

My muscles felt sore and heavy, and I rolled my shoulders back. Fuck.

It was almost like coming out of a deep sleep, this change. I blinked, readjusting to the piercing artificial lighting and the inarticulate voices. The first face I saw was Deth leaning over me, a tiny flashlight in his hand. He shone it in one eye and then the other, murmuring something beneath his breath. A brown-haired woman, similarly dressed in a white lab coat and wire-rimmed glasses, jotted something down on the clipboard she was holding. Lucian must've left at some point, the long-haired asshole nowhere in sight.

"Where's Addie?" I asked dizzily. My head pounded something fierce. "Where is she?"

Ignoring me, the doctor grabbed a stethoscope and attempted to place it on my chest. I batted it away with a scathing glare.

"Where. Is. She?" I asked darkly, barely recognizing my own voice. You could take the Rager out of the man, but you couldn't take the man out of the Rager. Or some deep shit like that. Honestly, I'd save the dramatic sayings for Asher.

With a roll of his eyes, Deth nodded towards something behind me. No, not something. *Someone.*

My breath left me, and I stumbled unsteadily to my feet.

"Baby…"

Her eyes were glazed, staring blankly at something on the wall. Something no one else could see. Numerous contraptions were hooked up to her. What looked to be an IV jutted from one arm, while the other one held a bag of red liquid. Her fucking blood.

They were treating her like a fucking animal. My rage burned hotly inside of me, just waiting for an outlet. Instead of destroying this godforsaken world, I fell to my knees and took her hand in mine.

"I'm here. You're okay. I'm okay. Addie, baby, please look at me." Those eyes didn't even blink, didn't light up with love, didn't even acknowledge my existence. Fuck. "What did they do to you?" I whispered, my voice cracking

"We didn't do anything," Deth said sternly. He glided over to stand on Addie's other side, checking the heart monitor and other vitals. "Her own mind did that. Fragile thing, I'll tell you."

"Don't fucking talk about her like you know her," I hissed.

"But can you deny it?" He clucked his tongue. "Either way, it makes my job easier."

I rose from my crouch, preparing to beat him dead, when something cold pressed to the back of my head. I froze even as my anger notched up another step.

"Don't fucking move," Gabriel hissed. "You may be a successful experiment, but you're still a dead man if you try anything."

"Fucking asshole," I sneered, not bothering to turn around towards the smug ass face and gun I knew I would see.

"Sit." He used the gun to point to the chair I'd vacated. My body rebelled, wanting to stay with Addie, but I moved without complaint.

"Where's your girlfriend? The little bitch?" I asked snidely. Gabriel moved so he was in front of me, features flaring with anger. Apparently, he could call her a bitch all he wanted, but the second I did, he got pissed. Noted.

Enzo, who was leaning indolently against the wall, snorted out a laugh.

"He has you there, Gabe," he said with a chuckle. "How many of us has she fucked? Or at least tried to?"

"Shut up," Gabriel snapped venomously.

Before Enzo could retort, a loud siren emitted in the room. The noise was piercing, like a scream, and made me wince. I brought my hands to my ears, anxiously flicking my gaze to Addie. She remained oblivious to the screech breaking my eardrums. Those wide eyes stared sightlessly ahead, the juxtaposition making my head spin.

Fuck, baby.

Red lights flashed simultaneously with the blaring screech of the siren. Both my ears and eyes attempted to adjust to the change.

"What's that?" I asked, but the men ignored me. Deth backed against the wall, hiding behind his female assistant, while Enzo and Gabriel lifted their guns.

The two exchanged long looks before Gabriel inched forward, using one hand to open the door.

He'd just swung it open when the Ragers merged on him like maggots on a decomposing body. He screamed, falling backwards, as the monsters ate away at his flesh. His mouth opened in a silent scream as slowly, almost agonizingly so, his stomach was torn to shreds by the Ragers.

"Fuck!" Enzo shouted, firing at the creatures. More and more were filing in, their faces grotesque, heads canted to the side, garnet-colored, sunken eyeballs emanating such rage and hunger.

I was like that.

I had been one of them.

The realization momentarily cemented my feet to the ground before I came to my fucking senses and lunged towards Addie, pulling her to my chest. I held her like a baby, and I supposed with her mental state, she was just as fragile as one.

It didn't take long for the Ragers to pull Enzo down as well, gnawing his leg off his body. I felt no sympathy for him or Gabriel. The monsters got what they fucking deserved.

There was a feminine scream, and the assistant fell as well, disappearing beneath the mound of Ragers. Her clipboard clattered by Deth's feet, the doctor cowering in the corner of the room.

Deciding quickly, I lunged for the weapon around Enzo's shoulder. He screamed, eyes begging me to put him out of his misery as the Rager pulled out what appeared to be a rib.

Only seconds later, the light faded from his eyes as he succumbed to his injuries.

I didn't pay him any heed, attempting to balance Addie and the gun.

But I couldn't just leave…

Not yet…

I fired at an incoming Rager, and he collapsed.

"Help me!" Deth begged desperately. "Help me!"

I moved towards him, and I saw his body physically sag in relief. That relief lasted only a moment when I ignored him, grabbing the clipboard off the ground and placing it on Addie's chest, before moving towards the exit.

I fired once, twice, three times, until there was a path big enough for us to fit through. I twisted my body protectively around Addie's, the memory of the last time I'd done that haunting me.

Still, it was worth it. I would die one hundred deaths before I allowed one fucking hair on her head to be hurt.

"Help me!" Deth cried. "I can help! You need me if you want a fucking cure!" His screams were hoarse, becoming more indecipherable the longer he yelled.

I laughed maniacally, glancing in both directions down the hall. It was a bloodbath, Ragers and soldiers fighting. Gunfire rang amongst the screams and growls.

I didn't need him. Not really. I had Addie and the fucking clipboard with all their notes. I wasn't positive, but I hoped this information could help someone find a cure. Maybe.

In all honesty? I didn't give a fucking shit.

"You need me!" Deth screamed again, but his voice broke off, turning into a bloodcurdling scream. I didn't have to look to know the Ragers had descended on him.

Holding Addie tighter against my chest with one hand and holding the gun up with the other, I moved down the hall.

~

DECLAN

The room was an explosion of purple.

Not a bright purple, but a darker, more subdued color.

It decorated the bed and curtains, the carpeting, the hint of color on the accented walls. I should've been relieved that Addie hadn't been placed in a prison cell to die, but all I felt was a chilling numbness. Falling through a layer of ice into the cold water below. Drowning, the air rapidly leaving your lungs while your mouth opened in a silent scream, desperate for air.

Only minutes earlier, a red light had begun to flash intermittently. The first Rager we saw had been already dead, shot in the head. The second and third had been engaged in a fierce battle with a soldier.

I had no doubt in my mind who was behind this little assault.

Ryder and Tamson had been up to no good.

I knew the others were talking behind me, but I ignored them, trailing my fingers over the still warm bed. The blankets were twisted near the foot, almost as if someone had kicked them off in a hurry. I narrowed my eyes at the damning stain in the center of the bed, darkening the sheets.

A fucking stain.

My stomach clenched and tightened, dozens of possibilities running rampant in my mind. What had happened to Addie on this bed?

Nausea had me gripping my stomach and my eyes feathering closed. I didn't want to think about it, let alone imagine it. All I could picture was her body, flesh blue in death, lying helplessly on the bed as men ravaged her. Used her. Discarded her.

I turned my face away, breathing erratic.

One thing was for certain—I couldn't let my brothers see the stain. No doubt, they would fly off the handle.

Composing my features, I stepped into Fallon's line of vision. Immediately, he took up ASL as well as speaking normally.

"She's obviously been kept here. But why? Why provide her a comfortable bedroom? Why provide a dying girl clothes?" His expression crumbled, shattered, when he said "dying." Asher's jaw clenched so tightly, I was afraid he would break a tooth.

"Maybe this isn't just her room," Ronan suggested, a dark finger caressing the gilded edge of the mirror. I focused on his lips as he spoke. "Maybe someone else stayed here before her."

"Maybe," Fallon agreed. He didn't look convinced.

Shaking my head, I pushed past them and peered into the hall. A few bodies were lying against the far wall, blood splattering around their heads like a macabre halo. Two more were on the ground, limbs disconnected and thrown farther down the hall.

Fuck. It was a massacre in here.

Not all the soldiers had guns. Not all of them were trained for an enemy who couldn't be killed or incapacitated by a mere shot to the chest. Ragers kept coming for you, kept attacking, even when they were missing arms and legs. Even when you shot their chests, their legs, their stomachs. Only a direct hit to the head, the brain, assured their deaths. Or their hearts.

Everything else was just an annoyance, as these monsters didn't feel pain.

Without preamble, I moved down the hall, poking my head into each door as I passed. I knew my brothers were following behind me, rigid and alert.

I grabbed a gun off a fallen soldier, momentarily feeling a brief stab of pain when I caught sight of his distorted face. What was this man's story? Was he an active participant in Addie's kidnapping, or was he an innocent man attempting to do what he thought was best for the country?

I knew to some that we may not have appeared as the heroes, and I was okay with that. I didn't need to be a hero or walk on the side of good. There was such a fine line between good and bad, light and darkness. The definition changed and contorted depending on the situation, different facets of each blending together until everything was a murky shade of gray.

Let me make something clear—there were no heroes. No villains. Just two sides attempting to survive this chaotic world driven by entropy. An atom explosion, lighting everything on fire.

I embraced my darkness but celebrated my light.

Fallon placed a hand on my shoulder, and I paused, cocking my head to the side. Obviously, he'd heard something I couldn't.

A second later, his face went slack with shock, even as his muscles stiffened. Tightened. My confusion only grew when a pretty blonde woman raced around the corner, tears smearing her mascara. Her eyes widened when she caught sight of us before resting on Fallon. She cried out his name, arms twining around his waist.

Fallon's face could've been cut from granite. I wouldn't have been able to tell you what he was feeling, what he was thinking. He didn't hold her back, but he didn't push her away either. His mouth opened and closed and then opened again. Shaking his head, almost as if he was clearing his muddied thoughts, he shoved at her shoulder, and she staggered back a step.

Her eyes were wide with terror as she glanced fearfully at Ronan's gun, pointed her way, and then Asher's knife aimed at her throat. She noticeably gulped.

Friend of Fallon's or not, she was not leaving here without answers.

"Olivia," Fallon said, mouth twisting with that one name. "What the fuck are you doing here? What's going on?"

The girl, Olivia, began to cry, wiping at her eyes dramatically.

Her name sounded familiar, and I tried to pinpoint where I'd heard it before. The realization sent me staggering back a step.

Olivia.

Fallon's ex-girlfriend.

Correction—ex-fiancée.

I'd never met the girl before. None of us had. Hell, half of my brothers hadn't even known she existed, Fallon preferring to keep his personal life private. I only knew about her because he'd gotten drunk one night and complained.

I knew very little of their relationship. She was selected by Fallon's father and uncle because of her connections in the government.

Why the fuck was she here?

Fallon seemed to be on a similar wavelength, as he took a step closer, arms raised like a prisoner approaching a police officer. His lips moved rapidly—too rapidly for me to comprehend.

It was only then I saw her hand reach for the gun in her back pocket, Fallon oblivious. I opened my mouth to scream, to warn him, when Olivia lurched forward suddenly. She turned away from Fallon, towards me, and her hands went to the front of her white blouse. Blood stained the shirt, rapidly growing. Her eyes went white in the second it took for them to close, and she collapsed to the floor.

Fallon's eyes were wide, almost saucers. At first, I thought he was shocked and upset at seeing his dead ex on the floor, blood rapidly pooling around her. But then I realized his attention wasn't on her, but on something over my shoulder.

I spun, gun raised.

My breath left me in a whooshing exhale. Every nerve in my body came to life like a fire burning just beneath my skin. It was like a dream, and I was afraid that closing my eyes would rip it away from me.

Calax held Addie tightly with one large arm beneath her ass, while his other hand held a gun. His expression was grim, face haggard, as he stared at the dead woman.

"I've been wanting to kill that bitch from the first moment she laughed at me. The first time she slapped me. The first time she touched me without my damn permission." He glanced up then, and a sly smile worked up his lips. "Did you guys miss me?" Staring wistfully down at Addie, he added, "Miss us?"

CHAPTER 31

CALAX

 $\mathcal{M}$ y brothers...

I turned from face to face, memorizing them. Fallon's longer hair was hanging limp and disheveled around his face, dirt and blood streaked on his cheeks. Asher was similarly bedecked in blood and soot, the color staining his blond hair. Ronan and Declan moved to stand in front of the group, in front of Bitch, their mouths agape.

They stared at me as if I were a ghost. A painting come to life.

"What... How...?" Ronan sputtered, venturing a trembling step towards me. "How are you alive?"

"Long story. No time," I grunted out, but my damn eyes burned with tears.

"What happened? Is she hurt?" Fallon roared, the first to come out of whatever funk they were in. I understood the feeling all too well.

Seeing someone you loved standing in front of you, someone you thought was dead, was mind-boggling, to say the least. You couldn't differentiate between up and down, left and right. Your entire world was tilted, your reality skewed.

"She's in shock," I explained, handing her over to Fallon somewhat reluctantly. I didn't want to relinquish my claim. The feel of her in my arms, as if she was meant to be there, was addicting, my drug of choice.

Fallon brushed at her hair reverently, love, awe, and hope all emanating from his eyes. Addie continued to stare blankly ahead, her sooty lashes fluttering against her cheekbones with every blink. I wondered what was going on in that pretty, chaotic mind of hers. I sometimes wondered which one was the actual apocalypse—reality or our own minds.

I knew she struggled with depression. I knew that my 'death' had haunted her. Hell, her reaction to seeing me again said enough.

But I hadn't realized how precarious her grip on sanity was. How her fingers gripped the edge of the cliffside as rain and snow pelted her face and fingers. How she just wanted to let go and drop into the abyss waiting down below.

"I can't believe you guys are both alive," Ronan whispered. He moved to Addie first, stroking her cheek with the back of his hand, before moving to me. He gripped me in a fierce hug, and while normally, I would shy away from physical contact, I pulled him even closer.

"Your hair's gotten longer," I said hoarsely, ruffling the green-streaked locks. He sniffled.

"Your face has gotten uglier," he retorted.

"That's scarily true."

Ronan was replaced by Asher, who hugged me just as tightly. He was immediately followed by Declan.

"Where's Ryder and Tamson?" I asked, scanning the sea of faces desperately. If something had happened to them...

I would murder everyone in this fucking compound. That might be the knife that finally cut Addie beyond fixing. That might be the dagger that reopened all of her previously scabbed wounds, bleeding her out.

"They're fine," Fallon whispered, eyes flickering from my face to Addie's. I'd never seen such emotion on his face. It was a heady combination of hope and agony. "But fuck, I'm glad you guys are okay."

"Me too." I turned towards where Bitch had fallen, dead. "Sorry about your ex-girlfriend. But she was kind of a psychotic bitch with murderous tendencies."

"Fallon has a type," Declan signed with a small smirk, and Fallon laughed, a quick, sharp sound that seemed to bubble out of him.

"Fuck, I'm so sorry, Calax." Fallon's words were directed at me, but his face was pressed against Addie's forehead. "I didn't know you were alive, or else I would've come for you. I'm sorry that people I know...my ex..."

"And your uncle," I mumbled. His brows furrowed, a crease forming on his tanned skin.

"My uncle?" He exchanged anxious glances with the other men. "How far does this fucking go?"

"All the way to the top," I replied. But now wasn't the time to discuss all I'd learned. We needed to get out of here. Now.

"How do we fix her?" Ronan asked, peering down at Addie. She looked so small in Fallon's arms. So frail. So vulnerable.

"If I may?" a clipped voice asked. I turned towards the familiar male, eyes narrowing. It was the doctor from the store. The one who was present when Addie was shot, just before I arrived here.

What the fuck was he doing with my team? My family? Nobody else seemed bothered by his presence, Fallon going as far as to twist Addie towards him.

My temper flared momentarily. How could they allow this man near her? Sure, he'd saved her life, but it was only because he was under duress. A gunshot to the head was ample motivation.

The man next to Doc was also familiar, though I couldn't recall his name.

It was the man Ronan and Ryder had kidnapped from the rest area. After he'd *tied them up*. And now they were all making friendship bracelets?

What the fuck was happening?

"Don't kill me," Doc warned, meeting Fallon's eyes first before staring at each one of us in turn. When they settled on me, he raised a brow as if daring me to fight him. I scowled but consented with a nod of my head. I wouldn't kill him, though the idea was tempting…

That mentality changed when he slapped Addie. Hard.

Her head whipped to the side, brown hair flying, and a red mark in the shape of his hand remained on her cheek. Fallon growled, and Ronan and Declan lunged for him. Asher went as far as to cock back his gun, a malicious glint in his eyes as if he was savoring this moment.

Doc refused to cower beneath the combined stares burning a hole in his back. Instead, he backed up with a knowing grin.

"What…? Huh…? Where's my pizza?" Addie murmured groggily. She abruptly sat straight up, nearly falling out of Fallon's arms, as alertness flooded her. "Calax!"

"Shhh…baby…it's okay. You're okay. You're here, and we're all okay." I gripped her small, trembling hands in my own, and her glossy eyes met mine.

"You're no longer a Rager," she whispered, removing her hands from mine so she could stroke my face with the tips of her fingers. It felt like brush strokes, like she was the artist and I was her canvas.

"What the fuck are you talking about?" Fallon interrupted, and Addie squealed, staring up at him.

"Sarge?" she whispered, seconds before he plundered her lips.

"Hey, Princess," Ronan said softly, and she broke the kiss with Fallon to tip her face towards his. Ronan kissed her with a softness and reverence that was almost painful to look at. It felt like I was intruding on their private moment, and I wanted to both continue watching and look away.

"Sweetheart," Asher whispered, and he took her from Fallon's arms. His face had softened, melted, the cold man nowhere in sight. "How are you feeling? Do you need anything?"

Declan moved so he was in her line of vision and signed something. Finally, I *did* look away, allowing my brothers to have a semiprivate moment with our girl. I heard her ask about Ryder and Tam, voice a screech, and Asher reassure her they were alive and well outside of the compound. She asked about Nik and Tommy next, and my heart elevated at the knowledge the two were okay. That they were able to rescue her brother.

Turning towards Fallon, I gave him and Ronan a brief synopsis of all that had occurred. The men saving me and then torturing me. The questions about Addie. Her arrival. Her blood.

Their faces were abnormally pale after I finished the five-minute speech.

"So her blood has a cure?" Doc asked, his voice sounding way too fucking interested. I glared at him before handing the clipboard to Ronan, ignoring the doctor's inquisitive eyes.

"This is all the information from when they checked her over. Maybe from earlier. I don't know exactly what it is, but I thought it might be useful. Protect it."

Ronan nodded, no hint of teasing on the joker's normally jovial face.

Doc peered over Ronan's shoulders, scanning the information with heightened intensity. I wished I could speak nerd or doctor. To me, it appeared to be an onslaught of random numbers, symbols, and notes that made zero sense.

"We need to get out of here," the steely voice came from Addie, moving to stand in between Fallon and me. One hand gripped his while the other grabbed mine. Asher moved behind her, resting his hands on her shoulders.

"Agreed," Ronan said. "And then, Princess, I'm going to spank your ass for allowing me to believe you were dead." This last statement was accompanied by a flirty wink, but I could still feel the pain behind his words. The terror that had only just been alleviated.

"Yes please," Addie murmured, and Ronan's eyes flared with banked heat. He might not have been as open about it as Tamson, but I knew he sometimes enjoyed rougher sex. The number of stories I'd heard from him before he met Addie and settled down was mind-boggling. Like, how could you tie up both hands and feet to the same hook on the ceiling?

Declan signed, *"Enough,"* before reaching for Addie's hand and pulling her away from us. Fallon and I exchanged an expressive look, a look that made words unnecessary, before flanking Declan and Addie on either side. Asher took point, and Ronan brought up the rear. Doc and Kai trailed behind us, deep in conversation.

I didn't trust them one bit, but at the same time, I didn't know them. A lot could change in three months. Loyalties, for one, though mine had always been and always would be with my family.

If my team trusted these men, then I'd put my hostility aside...at least until we emerged from the compound victorious.

Asher fired off a rapid round of bullets at a barrage of Ragers racing towards us. Each one hit expertly in their foreheads, and they dropped dead. Addie made a strange sound in the back of her throat, half a gasp and half a sob. I knew she was imagining me as one of the Ragers. *My* body hitting the floor in a puddle of black blood. *My* eyes rolling into the back of my head.

Lucian had messed her up. Deeply. His sick, twisted games had changed something in her mind, something that might take years to heal.

We turned at a fork in the hall, and I momentarily startled at seeing a familiar woman face down on the ground. The woman who'd saved me from the prison and led me to Addie. I didn't know who she was or what her story was, but I owed her my deepest gratitude. She definitely didn't deserve to die.

I turned my head away before my wayward gaze could capture anyone's attention.

We moved as a unit, a team, a family, down the blood soaked halls. I kept a continuous eye on Addie as we weaved through the labyrinth-like basement. Hall after hall. Door after door. Rager after Rager. A few soldiers ran past us, but none of them paid us any mind. Why would they? For all they knew, we were a team ambling these halls and attempting to survive, the same as them.

A door captured and ensnared my attention. Simple, with accentuated wood and a dark knob.

Simple…yet familiar.

I hesitated, weighing the pros and cons of my decision.

I hadn't realized I had stopped until Fallon tugged at my arm. "What's going on?"

"I know someone down there," I said softly, nodding towards the door. Down there, the moldy basement covered in dust with the smell of piss and blood permeating the air, had been my home for the last couple months. The man in the cell beside me had been my…well, not my family, but an acquaintance. I didn't like him, but he'd been the one constant during the weeks of torture and starvation. The weeks when my body wanted to succumb to the darkness pressing in on all sides of me like a moving box.

"What?" Addie turned towards me, the skin between her eyes creased in confusion and her pouty lips puckered.

"Get Addie out of here," I told Fallon. "I'll be right behind you."

Because I knew I couldn't leave Doug. That wasn't the type of man I was and wasn't the type of man I wanted to be.

Fuck, when did I develop a conscience? I blamed it on a certain brown-haired beauty currently glaring up at me.

Doug was wrong about one thing—love was the only thing capable of winning wars.

"No fucking way in fuckity fuck," Addie cursed, lunging towards me. Her tiny hands were fisted, and she pressed them against my chest. Her eyes pleaded with me, implored me to see things from her perspective. "We're not separating ever again. Any of us. We'll go with you. It'll take, what, five minutes to enter and exit? We do it as a fucking team. Don't make me revoke your lover privileges and make you public enemy number one…because I will. Don't test me, Callie."

I couldn't say no to her, not when she was staring at me with large, watery eyes. Not when her hands smoothed over my chest, kneading the material of my thin, cotton shirt. Not when her teeth worried the plump skin of her lower lip.

No, I was a damn sucker for her.

Breaking eye contact, I turned towards Sarge with a question in my gaze. He nodded once, expression cut from stone.

"Five minutes," he said at last. "In and out. Then we're getting out of here. No questions asked, got it?"

We all murmured our assent before lifting our weapons and pointing them at the door.

As we opened it and stepped down the musty smelling staircase, I couldn't help the snort that escaped me.

"Home sweet home," I murmured to no one in particular.

The cells were exactly as I remembered them. Five on each side, totaling ten. A single hanging bulb illuminated the stone walls and floor.

The key I'd used was still in my cage, and I grabbed it out of the lock.

"Is that you?" Doug asked, voice breaking on a cough. "Did you come back for me?" Another cough.

I opened my mouth to respond, but immediately closed it when I saw Addie running in the direction of the cell. Her face was pale in the scarce lighting, eyes wide. Fallon called her name on a hiss, but she ignored him, stopping when she was directly in front of Doug's cell.

Her voice breathy, she whispered, "Dad?"

CHAPTER 32

The man staring back at me was undeniably my sperm donor. The man who'd tortured me for years. Beat me.

Sent men to rape me.

His hair was longer than I remembered, cascading down his face in straggly, greasy strands. A multitude of bruises covered his face, curving up his jawline and to his cheekbones and then to his two, piercing eyes.

Eyes that were staring at me just as intently as I was staring at him.

"Addie…" he whispered, just as Calax screamed. Literally screamed, his voice a hoarse growl. He lunged towards the bars of the cage, banging his fists against them.

He looked more beast than human. More *Rager* than human. His eyes were slitted, and his lips were pulled back from his teeth in a ferocious snarl.

"You…" Calax pointed a finger accusingly at the man cowering in the corner of his cell. "You…lied…to…me." Each word was physically pulled out of his mouth. Wrenched from it, an unintelligible growl.

"I didn't lie," DOD said, but his eyes were fixed firmly on me. Watching me. Assessing me. I felt like I was on display in a cage, his eyes slicing at me until I was bared to him. "I didn't know who you were. I didn't know you knew my daughter."

"So your name is Doug now?" I asked, lips curling into a sneer.

Dear Old Dad smiled softly.

"It was the only name I could think of in the moment." He shrugged before glancing at the key in Calax's hand. "Are you going to let me out?"

"Why did you do it?" I asked. My voice was quiet and subdued, barely recognizable. Demure, almost. All I needed now was to lower my head in submission, and I would be the perfect, obedient daughter. How did seeing my father revert me back to *that*? The female who was scared of her own shadow?

But that girl was dead. Gone. Swept away. Buried miles beneath cement.

I wouldn't yield to my father's commands, not anymore.

"Why did you experiment on *me*, your own daughter? Why did you hurt me? Why *didn't you ever love me?*" My voice rose to a scream as tears streamed down my face. The pain... It fucking hurt. It was unimaginable.

I'd grown up hearing stories about parents who loved their children. Adored them. Cherished them. My reality was completely different. I'd never known the loving touch of a mother braiding my hair back from my face. A father teaching me to drive a car. I'd lived my life in the shadows so they could flourish in the light.

How could a parent do that to their child? Their own flesh and blood?

When Dad didn't answer, I continued on doggedly. "Was it money? Was that why you experimented on your own daughter? Risked my life? Is that why you sold me out to your business partners? Is that why you hit me? Do you just hate me or some-thing? Answer me! *Answer me!*" My hands balled into fists, and I slammed them once, twice, three times against the bars. He didn't flinch, didn't react, at my rage.

I wanted him to explain it to me. Offer me an excuse for his behavior. Tell me why I was tortured beneath his hands, the hands that were supposed to love me.

At the same time, I knew that evil didn't always have an explanation. Their reasonings were not explicitly clear. Why did the Devil tempt Eve? Evil was just as chaotic as this newfound world we'd found ourselves in. There was no rhyme or reason for my father's actions. He was just evil, plain and simple.

"Addie..." He released my name on a long exhale.

"Don't say my name."

"Look, what do you want me to say? Sorry? Is that what you want? I could give you a thousand excuses, but none of them would be the truth. You see me as the enemy, but don't you realize how much stronger you are now because of me? I taught you how to take a hit and dish one right back out. I taught you when to fight and when to submit. I taught you loyalty. Everything you are today is because of me!"

"Everything I am is because of *me!*" I countered on a scream, thumping my chest to emphasize my words. "I needed a dad! I needed someone to love me and care for me and protect me! Why didn't you? Why didn't you ever love me?"

"Because I didn't want you to begin with!" he replied. We were both breathing heavily. At one point, he must've stood and meandered towards the bars. He pressed his forehead against the metal, chest heaving. I was distantly aware of my men inching closer, guns raised, but most of my attention was fixed on my father. "I never wanted a child. I knew I couldn't handle one, not in my line of work. But your mother was persistent." I wanted to ask where my mother was now, but I knew if I interrupted him, he would clam up. I wanted—no, needed to hear his story.

"We had a baby girl. Beautiful." His tone turned almost wistful, but I knew it was a lie. He was an expert on faking emotion. "She was beautiful, and I knew we would do great things together."

"And then you grew up and learned to hate me," I whispered. It wasn't a question.

"I saw the value in you," he countered. "I knew I would never be a doting, loving father, so I used you for a different reason. I gave your life a purpose, a meaning.

Mine to do with as I pleased. To use. To trade. To experiment on." Ignoring the guys' growls, he pressed his face against the bars. "I learned to be a father the only way I knew how. Just because it's not normal or conventional doesn't make me any less of a dad. Our relationship has always been different—"

"Don't call what we had a relationship," I seethed. "I'm not your daughter any more than you are my father. I hate you. *Hate* you. I didn't think that was possible. I didn't think I was capable of hating anyone, but you? I hate you. *Loathe* you. And I think a part of you hates me as well. I don't know why. Do I remind you of your own shitty childhood?" I released a humorless laugh. "I don't know and I don't care. All I know is that I hate you and I'm done with you. No more hiding in your shadows…no more. I'm the fucking sun, and I'm not going to allow you to smother me any longer. I'm not a puppet you can use and discard. I was your *daughter*, but now? I'm nobody." I took a wobbly step away from the bars, away from my past. It would no longer haunt me. I would no longer *allow it* to haunt me.

"Addie…" he warned darkly, and goosebumps skated down my spine just hearing my name on his lips. "I'm your father! I made you!"

"You destroyed me!" I took a deep, shuddering breath in an attempt to get my emotions under control. I needed to keep them under lock and key, at least until we made it out of here. Only then would I allow myself to fall apart. "You took an already broken girl and ripped her to shreds. You could never love me, not the way I needed you to. You saw me as something to use, something that was yours. But I'm not. I never have been, and I never will be. I belong to myself."

"You belong to those men," my father retorted with a sneer. "You're their whore."

Asher growled low in his throat, taking a step forward, but I reached out and placed a hand on his chest to stop him from charging towards my father. I loved it when they fought my battles, but this one? It was *mine*.

"You're wrong," I said slowly, succinctly. "These men belong to *me*."

I was about to add something about them being my whores but figured that would actually hurt my case. Points for me for keeping my mouth shut.

Turning away from the asshole, I gripped Ronan's hand tightly. "Let's go."

"Addie!" Dad called after me, just as Declan signed, *"Are you sure?"*

"I've never been more sure about anything in my life," I whispered. Asher moved to grab my other hand, and together, we walked back up the stairs. I could hear my father's screams behind me. His promises to be better.

Lies.

That was all he ever did. He wove his lies like a spider wove a web, each one intricate. I learned long ago I couldn't believe a word he said.

When we reached the hallway, my breathing was erratic and my heart was pounding against my chest. God, I wouldn't be surprised if I went into cardiac arrest. Too much had happened today, and I felt the weight of it on my shoulders like a cloak made of metal.

I pressed my forehead against the wall, attempting to get my breathing under control. Asher rubbed my back, reminding me to breathe and mimicking the motion. I watched the steady rise and fall of his chest, my own instinctively matching.

We left the door to the prison wide open, and not one of my men stopped the

Ragers from racing down into the dank, suffocating basement. Not one of them made a move to lift their guns when my father's screams reverberated up to us.

"My mother?" I asked no one in particular. It was Calax who answered, eyes bright with sympathy.

"I'm sorry."

I didn't know how to feel about that. Sad? Happy? Numb?

"She freed me," Calax added, his hand snaking up to rub my neck. His touch was soothing, calming, and I arched back against him. "She freed me and led me to you. I don't know why, and now we'll never know. Maybe she wanted me to save you. Maybe she wanted to redeem herself. Maybe she truly loved you."

"Or maybe she wanted to use you to hurt me," I added in a whisper. Calax squeezed my neck.

"Maybe," he agreed softly.

"We need to leave." Fallon's voice interrupted my turbulent thoughts. I knew he was right, but a part of me couldn't move from my spot against the wall. I didn't *want* to move.

The man below was a monster, but he was still my father.

And I had killed him.

Maybe it hadn't been my hand holding a gun, my knife hacking at his flesh, but it was my actions that led to his bloodcurdling screams.

The Ragers wouldn't be able to kill my father, not yet, not with the bars blocking them, but I knew it was only a matter of time before their combined weight broke down the cell...or DOD died of starvation. I didn't know which death was more satisfying. Perhaps it was neither. Perhaps it was my dad's terrified screams as he stared death in the eye and was forced to embrace it.

I gripped the hand nearest to me—Declan's—and held it like the lifeline it was. The life preserver bobbing in the tumultuous ocean. The only thing keeping my head above water.

"Addie," Fallon warned softly. He extended a hand towards me...a second lifeline. Still holding onto Declan's, I interlocked my fingers with Fallon's and allowed him to pull me down the hall.

We needed to get out of here. See Nik and Tommy. Kiss Ryder and Tamson. Well, *I* needed to kiss Ryder and Tamson. No one else. Unless my men were into that sort of thing...

"Yes. Out. Yes." Apparently, I was a robot now, only capable of speaking one word at a time.

We turned another bend in the hall...

And froze.

Fallon's body went rigid beside me, hand tightening to the point of pain around my fingers. I could see from my peripheral the rest of my men spreading out behind me. Kai and Doc moved too, though Kai held his gun as if it were a poisonous snake and Doc appeared slightly bored.

Standing in front of us, blocking the exit, was a wall of muscled soldiers bedecked in black armor and helmets. In the center, appearing like an avenging angel, was Lucian, his crazed eyes tracking our movements.

"Uncle Lucian," Fallon said. I knew he'd already been told about his uncle's involvement in all of this, but his words were breathed out in shock. Pain. Hurt. His uncle may have been an ass, but he was still family. Still blood. Fallon glanced at the man as if he was staring at a stranger. A stranger wearing the face of his uncle.

"Nephew," Lucian said tersely, but his eyes remained fixed firmly on me. "Hand over the girl, and we'll let you and your friends go."

Fallon moved a step closer to me as Declan pressed his body against my other side. I could feel a warm body against my back, but I didn't dare peel my attention away from Lucian to see who it belonged to.

"That's not going to happen," Fallon said gruffly in a tone that brooked no room for argument. Lucian sighed heavily, as if Fallon's answer genuinely pained him.

Lies.

Was that just an adult thing? Did they all have to lie, have to fake loving their family?

Or was it just an "us" thing?

"Then you'll die."

As one, the soldiers lifted their guns and aimed them at our chests.

Fuck.

I couldn't let this happen. These men, my men, couldn't die because of me. I absolutely refused. It might have been selfish...or it might have been utterly selfless.

Either way, my men would not shed blood for me.

"Wait!" I screamed, staggering a step forward. My legs wobbled, exhaustion and hunger creeping up on me. I just wanted to sleep and forget this whole day ever happened. Was that too much to ask for?

Well...that and orgasms. Orgasms were always nice.

"Addie," Ronan warned.

"You guys can't die for me. No. That can't happen. I won't allow it." I didn't meet any of their eyes as I spoke. My voice was hoarse from crying, tears dripping down my already puffy cheeks.

I attempted to pull free from Fallon's and Asher's hands, but their grips were like iron.

"Please let me go," I begged.

"No." That came from Calax, moving to stand on the other side of Fallon. "Live or die together."

"That's right, Princess." Ronan stood beside Declan, and Asher silently moved to take up residence beside *him*. An immobile line. A wall of muscle.

My heart clenched with my love for them...and my overwhelming terror.

"No! Fuck, no! That's not the way our story ends," I sobbed, desperately and futilely attempting to free myself. "I'm supposed to go down in a blaze of glory."

"So dramatic," Ronan mumbled under his breath, and Calax actually flashed a smile.

"Oh, what the hell," a sly voice said, and a second later, Doc and Kai joined the line of men. Kai looked scared, but his hands were steady on the gun. Doc held his chin up defiantly, nose in the air, as if he were the king, and Lucian and his men were the fucking peasants. Honestly, he looked pretty badass.

I only had a second to breathe, just breathe, before the soldiers began shooting.

CHAPTER 33

ADDIE

A body pressed against mine, forcing me to the ground. I tried to move my hands to cover my head, but they were firmly pinned against the rough wooden floors.

Gunshots rang all around. My men dived towards the nearest doors, flinging them open and using them as a makeshift cover.

A strangled sob left my mouth, and a pair of lips pressed against my forehead.

"Shhh…Addie. It's okay." Calax. He was the one on top of me, his body protecting mine. It reminded me of the time in the resort when the tornado had struck. I'd used my small, dainty body as a shield to protect Calax. I still had the scars from that day.

The day that changed my entire life.

The day new bonds, bonds I couldn't even have begun to imagine at the time, were forged. It solidified my relationship with the guys, deeming me as theirs and them as mine. Who would've thought?

"Callie…" I cried, but not from the pain. I was so fucking worried. Terrified. I could hear the gunfire, the screams, the curses, the snarls of approaching Ragers, but I couldn't lift my head from the ground. I had no way of knowing who was hurt. Who was dead.

And I had no doubt in my mind that not everyone would leave this hall alive.

Calax let out a grunt, and his body was ripped off of mine. I let out a scream, desperately searching his body for injuries, even as someone grabbed my hair. My breath left me when I finally caught sight of him. He appeared to be unscathed, his body held between two soldiers. There was a bloody wound on his head, but other than that, he was fine.

Pissed, but fine.

"No one move," Lucian said darkly, pressing a gun barrel to my head.

My men immediately froze, holding their hands up as if to prove they weren't dangerous. The soldiers, however, did *not* freeze. They lunged into action, collecting weapons and kicking my men to their knees.

I surveyed the damage despite the growing terror unfurling in my stomach. Asher was bleeding severely from his leg, but he didn't appear to be in too much pain. That could've been merely adrenaline, though. We would need Doc to look at it right away. Ronan and Declan appeared fine, but their faces were tightened in anger. Fallon, similarly, was nursing his shoulder, but like Asher, he managed to throw livid glares at the man holding me, as if the gunshot wound was nothing more than an annoyance.

"Is that how this is going to be, Uncle?" he asked, twisting the word 'uncle' until it was something ugly.

"I thought you were smarter than this, boy," Lucian retorted. He painfully gripped my shoulder, gun still pressed to my head, and pulled me farther down the hall. Away from them.

I continued my inventory of the men, but stopped short when I caught sight of Doc.

And Kai's dead body.

He was on the ground, head bent at an unnatural angle. Blood cascaded around him, a dark red color. A single gunshot wound was in the center of his forehead.

Doc let out an agonized cry, folding his body over his dead lover. Tears sprang to my eyes.

Kai was my friend. He'd stood by me, protected me, when no one would've faulted him for running. And these *men*, these monsters, had killed him. Snuffed the life out of him as carelessly as a candle flame being blown out.

My fault.

As quickly as that thought came, I brushed it away. Buried it.

The fault relied solely with the assholes holding their guns at my men and Doc. The asshole holding a gun to my own head.

That was where the blame laid.

"This girl," Lucian shook my shoulder to emphasize his point, "has the cure to this entire thing. She can save the world. For once in your lives, don't be selfish. Let her go."

I knew he didn't mean that final statement literally. He meant my memory. Their love for me. Let it all go.

"Selfish?" Fallon released a humorless laugh. "You want to talk to me about selfishness? You only want her for the power she'll bring you. The money. But this isn't the world we knew anymore, Uncle. Money can't buy you shit. Power can't buy you shit. You're going to get *exactly* what's coming to you. And then some."

"I'm sorry, boys. But we'll just have to agree to disagree on this matter." Lucian backed up another step. And then another. And then another.

A dead soldier was resting against the wall, a gun held loosely in his hand and blood dripping from a wound in his head. A recent death, probably caused by one of my men.

"You're right," a familiar voice said snidely. "Agree to disagree."

Lucian let out a grunt, pushing me to the ground, as Ryder shot him in the back. While a normal man would've toppled, I had determined Lucian was superhuman. Super…villain? Or maybe that was just a trait of all sociopaths. He turned, distracted, and aimed his gun at Ryder.

Then Lucian turned, dodging to the side and redirecting his aim as Tamson came around a corner, firing his gun. I scrambled on my hands and feet, crab walking backwards. My hand closed on the gun near the dead soldier.

Behind me, I was distantly aware of my men fighting against the soldiers. Screams. Gunshots.

There was an odd roaring in my ears, almost as if I were underwater. Slowly, carefully, I ambled to my feet. Lucian had his gun raised, aimed at Tamson. Another soldier was occupying Ryder's attention.

So I did the only thing I could do.

I shot once, twice, three times, four times, into the back of his head. The back of his head that looked so similar to Fallon's but would never be my lover's.

I shot until his body fell to the ground, dead.

And then I fell.

~

TAMSON

It was chaos when we arrived inside the compound. Absolute chaos. We'd expected chaos would ensue…but not to this extent. Blood painted the walls a vivid red, and dead bodies littered the halls.

Ryder took point, expertly moving down the twisting hallways. I followed behind him, my gun held loosely. I didn't need a gun to fight, though, unlike my brother. I much preferred to use my body, my fists.

"Fuck," Ryder cussed, voice a hushed murmur. When he held up a hand to stop me, I slammed to a halt, attention piqued. Over Ryder's shoulder, I took in the scene with rapt fascination.

A somewhat familiar man, a man I'd only met once or twice but who happened to bare a striking resemblance to Fallon, held Addie in his arms, a gun to her head. In front of them, on their knees, was the rest of our team. Asher, Declan, Ronan, Fallon…and Calax.

I blinked, wondering if I was imagining it. Did I hit my head?

Ryder inhaled sharply.

Because…fuck. This felt almost too good to be true. Calax was supposed to be dead, and Addie was supposed to be dead, and the entire world was supposed to be dead. But this? This felt like the start of a very good dream.

Except for the man holding a gun to Addie's head.

Red briefly engulfed my vision. My body tightened, icy rage skating up my spine. Anger like no other thrummed through my veins.

But I knew I needed to keep my wits together. Ryder wouldn't be able to, so I had to.

Tapping his shoulder to garner his attention, I nodded towards the hall to the left of the men and Addie. Without words, we moved into position.

"You're right," Ryder said cockily, but only someone who knew him as well as I did could note the slightest waver in his voice. "Agree to disagree."

Really, Ryder? Were the dramatics necessary?

The man grunted, cried out, as Ryder shot him in the back. I would only trust Ryder with that job. He'd always been an expert shot, and he needed to hit the far left side of the man's back, right below his shoulder blade. The one place that wouldn't hit Addie as well.

The man released Addie, and she fell to the ground, backing slowly towards the wall.

When the man turned towards Ryder, gun raised with a ferocious snarl, I stepped from the side hall I had disappeared down, materializing from the shadows.

I shot him until my gun ran out of rounds. Without preamble, I dropped that gun to the ground and pulled out a second one.

While I didn't overly like guns, I was damn good at using them.

Ryder was currently out of commission, partaking in a struggle with a soldier. Both weapons had been dropped to the ground, and he struggled against the larger man, ducking before the man's fist could connect with his face. Ryder wrapped his arms around the soldier's meaty middle and tackled him to the ground.

But my moment of hesitation had cost me.

The man, the man with crazed eyes and a feral grin, the man with a malicious twinkle that made me think of serial killers and monsters beneath the bed...he was walking towards me, gun raised.

I was briefly reminded of an old western show I used to watch. Two men standing in a small, dusty town, tumbleweed emerging from behind a tavern of roughly hewn logs. His eyes twitched, my eyes twitched. His hand pressed down on the trigger, my hand pressed down on the trigger. Only one of us would survive.

I didn't want to close my eyes, but at the same time, I didn't want to see the bullet enter my chest.

A second later, a gun went off. Multiple times.

My eyes widened, and I stared at the man's scrunched face. His mouth was agape, a soundless scream escaping his lips.

And then he dropped.

Addie stood behind him, holding the gun of the fallen soldier. Her eyes flickered to the gun, almost as if she didn't recognize the object she held. One second, she was standing, eyes widening almost imperceptibly, and the next, she fell to the ground beside the dead body.

I ran towards her immediately, afraid she would accidentally set off the gun.

"Everyone okay?" Fallon asked gruffly. The gunfire had receded, and I turned to see that the battle was over. Asher was hobbling on a bloody leg, and Fallon's hand was pressed against his bleeding shoulder, but they were fine. My family was fine.

A strangled sob came from farther down the hall, and I turned towards the distressed noise, anxiety creeping up on me like a psychotic killer.

Doc.

He was clinging to Kai's dead body as if his touch were capable of bringing the man back to life. But I knew, as did the others, that no number of horses or men would put Kai back together again.

"We need to go," Calax said, grabbing the doctor's shoulder.

"No!" He struggled against the giant of a man, tears streaming down his face. He looked as if he had aged *years* in a matter of minutes. His face appeared sunken, eyes unfocused.

"Doc," Ronan tried, crouching down on the other side of Kai. His eyes were sad as they flickered over the man. I wondered if he blamed himself. After all, he and Ryder were the ones who'd kidnapped him, brought him into our world. At the same time, it had been Kai's decision to remain with us. That was what made us different from the Ragers and the men and women operating this facility—free will.

"Kai wouldn't want you to remain here. He wouldn't want you to die," Ronan continued earnestly. "Fight. You have to fucking fight, Doc, because believe it or not, we need you. You're a part of this family now, and we don't leave our own behind."

Doc blindly stared at him. Stared at him…but didn't see him. I wondered if he even heard a word he'd said. He opened his mouth to no doubt protest when Calax whacked him over the top of the head with the butt of his gun.

"We need to go," he said briskly, grabbing the man and slinging him over his shoulder. He struggled slightly under the weight before righting himself and moving towards the exit. It was still surreal to see Calax standing in front of me, alive and well, but I would marvel at that later. Right now, we needed to get out of here.

I scooped Addie up and nodded towards the exit.

"Let's get the fuck out of here."

CHAPTER 34

I woke up twice during the car ride back. The first time, I found myself sprawled on the backseat, my head in Ryder's lap as his fingers combed through my hair. As if he felt my eyes on him, he glanced down, a small smile making his golden umber eyes twinkle.

"Kitten, you gave us quite the scare. Naughty, naughty girl."

"Are you going to punish me?" I drawled dazedly. Honestly, I was still half asleep at that point.

"I'll save that for Tamson. What do you prefer? Rope, chains, or paddle?"

"Why not all three?" I murmured, closing my eyes and inhaling his citrus scent. Before sleep could fully consume me, a loud, agonized cry came from the seat behind us. I attempted to look up, to see who'd made such a gut-wrenching, awful noise, but Ryder pressed his forehead against my own.

"Shh…" he told me, lips brushing against my nose.

"Kai!" I recognized the voice now, but I'd never heard it like this. Never like this.

Doc.

He sounded as if he was in *agony*, not just pain. If I were to have my spleen ripped from my body, then maybe, just maybe, I could've replicated such a noise. Actually, I was pretty sure I *did* make that exact same sound before, after we'd lost Calax. My agony had been almost palpable, settling heavily in the air like a storm cloud. I knew that my pain had drenched the others as well. My own melancholy rainstorm hadn't just remained above my head.

Ronan said something to Doc, too quiet for me to hear, but the man only released another wail.

The memory of Kai's broken body bombarded my senses. It was all I could see, all I could smell, all I could think of. Had he suffered? Or was it a clean death?

The world was so bloody unfair at times. There were never any winners, just losers and bigger losers.

I could feel my own heart twisting, breaking, as Doc's grief contaminated the air. It felt as if I'd lost someone I loved myself.

That pain, the heartache, pulled me under once again.

∼

THE NEXT TIME I woke up, I was in Declan's lap. He had yet to realize I was awake, so I took the uninterrupted moment to analyze him without self-consciousness. His fauxhawk had grown out, but his brown hair was still cut short on the sides with the hair longer at the top. Light scruff coated his jawline, and his body had filled out underneath the guard suit he still wore.

I couldn't believe I'd gotten him back. Gotten Fallon back. Gotten Calax back. The moment was bittersweet, tainted by Kai's death and Doc's grief.

Finally, Declan turned down to stare at me, face softening slightly.

I lifted my arms up—an awkward feat, considering I was lying with my head on Declan's lap—and signed, *"Hi, Ducky."*

"How are you feeling?" he signed back.

"Like shit. Like I was kidnapped by the fucking government and had gallons of my blood drawn. The usual."

He chuckled soundlessly.

Continuing on, I added, "But when we get home, you're feeding me pizza and chocolate cake. And then I'm getting a whole bunch of orgasms. In my humble opinion, getting kidnapped definitely calls for pizza, chocolate, and orgasms. And I don't even care where we have to get it! Well...except for the orgasms. I don't want just some random nobody plugging me with his electrical cord, if you know what I mean. But the pizza and chocolate cake? I'm pretty lenient. But Asher makes a pretty mean chocolate cake. I'll even lay an egg if you need me to."

Yup. I was rambling. It was an adorable quirk.

Declan shook his head at me, but his lips twitched, amused. The back of his hand brushed my cheek.

"I love you," he signed before cupping my face tenderly. Reverently. His lips brushed mine, as light as a moth's wing. A tease of a kiss.

The memory of my dream flitted through my mind. My garden. My men. Only this time, there were no storm clouds unleashing a torrent of rainfall. No decaying grass and weedy grounds.

"I love you too," I replied, and his answering smile was luminous. I would never get tired of saying—signing—those words. I knew they were true, just as I knew my name was Addie. I loved them with every fiber of my demented, fucked-up being, and I knew they felt the same. Who would've thought we would find each other in a world where happy endings no longer existed?

Well...

That wasn't entirely true. I was pretty damn sure my happy ending had only just begun. The ending of any book was amazing, but the road to get there? The trials and angst? That was what made our story, what defined our love.

We finally pulled up to a two-story house an hour's drive away. While the house itself wasn't familiar, the two figures standing on the front porch were.

I flung open the door and ate up the distance between us. My arms stretched wide, one looping around Nik's shoulders and the other holding onto Tommy. Tommy held me back immediately, but Nik remained rigid for a long moment. Finally, *finally*, he hugged me back...just as tightly as I hugged him.

"Fucking hell, Addie, you can't do this to me again," Tommy cried, burrowing further against me. He sniffled. "Or else...you'll be grounded! Don't test me, young lady."

"God, I missed you. I missed you both."

"We missed you too," Tommy said, and Nik tightened his arms around my waist.

Feeling significantly lighter, as if a weight had been lifted from my shoulders, I bounced inside.

We congregated in the living room, grabbing any chair we could find to fit our ragtag group. I was relieved to see Tonya, Davis, and Jared unscathed. The former procured a fucking tray of tea...yes, complete with tiny porcelain cups, a kettle, and a container of sugar. She acted as if she was greeting guests in the eighteen-hundreds.

My respect for her only grew.

Tommy, Nik, and I took the floral sofa, me settling between them. Asher sat on the floor in front of me, leaning back to rest his head in my lap. Doc had numbly checked over both Asher and Fallon and had declared in an impassive voice that "they'll live." The bullets, fortunately, went straight through. Both were required to wear bandages until they healed, and Asher was prohibited from using his leg for the foreseeable future.

Ronan and Ryder leaned against the wall, and Fallon stood in the entryway, always the sentry. Calax and Tamson pulled up chairs from the kitchen, while Declan and Tonya sat in the armchairs. Davis and Jared perched awkwardly on either side of Tonya.

I didn't see Doc.

"We need to talk," Fallon said gravely, resting his gaze first on me and then Calax.

And then began the long, drawn-out recap of everything that had occurred. Tonya's face went pale, and she looked as if she might vomit. After an hour of listening to Calax's tale, with me occasionally adding my own input, she silently excused herself.

"This is...a lot for her to take in," Davis explained to me when I raised an inquiring eyebrow. "She thinks of you as a sort of daughter...a younger sister. She hated that she wasn't there for you."

That was...surprising. And sweet. I guessed I assumed I was more like an annoying growth on her body she couldn't get rid of. Like a pimple you just had to wait to run its course. It made my heart immensely happy to hear that she had come to care for me in the short amount of time I'd known her.

"So what's next?" Jared asked, leaning forward and resting his elbow on his knee. "What are we doing with the information we received?"

All eyes flickered to Ronan. My green-haired leprechaun held up a clipboard splattered with blood. Still, the writing was undeniable.

Deth's.

"You stole that?" I directed the question at Calax, who nodded sheepishly. His eyes gauged my reaction, almost as if he was searching for condemnation in my gaze. Instead, I smiled brilliantly. "Thank you."

If we could use the research to save the world…

I would be remiss if we didn't at least try.

"Let me see that," Doc said from behind me, and I jumped, not having heard or seen him enter the room. His eyes were red and puffy, lips pursed, but the steely determination I always associated with the doctor was present as well. He strode purposefully towards Ronan and wrenched the clipboard out of his hands. His eyes quickly scanned the information, widening slightly.

"Can you do anything with that?" Fallon asked gruffly, his arms crossed over his chest.

"I'm a doctor, not a scientist. Believe it or not, there is a difference." His words were curt and felt like a needle popping my balloon of happiness. I physically began to deflate. His next words, however, made me straighten with interest. "But I might know some people who can help. Some of my Harvard buddies. Biochemists. Genetic scientists. Doctors. Smart men and women."

"We don't even know if these people are still alive," Davis snapped, and then winced when the word "alive" left his mouth. "Sorry, that was insensitive—"

"They're alive," Doc interjected, tone scathing. "I ran into one of them at the outpost. Apparently, he knows of a team searching for a cure. I don't know if this information will help, but it wouldn't hurt."

"They give you an address?" Fallon asked, a light brown brow raised.

Doc nodded.

"They would need this information and probably a vial or two of Addie's blood." When my men hissed, stiffening around me, Doc held his hands up placatingly. "Just to study. I won't even give them her name. For all they know, she's long dead." He turned his gaze towards me, eyes beseeching. "Addie, I trust them."

And he did. That much was clear to see in his eyes. The sincerity in his tone.

But did I trust *him*?

I rifled through everything I knew about Doc. He'd hurt me, yes, but he also came for me when he didn't have to. He was hard around the edges, jagged and crippled with a pain I understood all too well, but he was family now. Looking into his grey eyes, I knew he had our best interests at heart. He honestly believed these people, these friends of his, could make a difference in the world. I needed to do something I'd never done before—put my faith in him.

Before I'd even consciously come up with a decision, I found myself nodding. Fallon gritted his teeth, but he allowed me to make my own decision. After all, it was *my* blood. And if my blood could be made into a cure? If it could be turned into a vaccination in the long run? Who was I to say no?

Definitely not someone I wanted to look at in the mirror.

"Then it's decided," Fallon said succinctly, clapping his hands together. The resounding noise echoed in the room. "We head to the address Doc was given. Give them the clipboard and a vial of blood. Live a damn long life."

"Settle down," I added wistfully. At my words, Davis and Jared exchanged a long, potent look. It was Jared who spoke, clearing his throat and leaning even closer. His hands steepled together on his lap.

"We were talking..." Another exchange of looks, expressions indecipherable. "What about paradise?"

"We don't even know if it exists," Ryder pointed out.

"He's right," Ronan added. The two were leaning against one another...almost as if they needed the comfort. The reminder that they were both alive. I knew the brothers were close, but it had never been more noticeable than it did then. I could definitely see the similarities in their sculpted bodies and dark hair, though Ronan was a shade lighter than his half-brother. Feeling my eyes on them, they turned as one and winked.

I would *not* mind being the meat in that sandwich.

Jared cut off whatever he was saying and stared at me, brows furrowed. Ryder and Ronan broke into laughter, the mundane sound slicing through the remaining tension.

"Did I say that out loud?" I asked, wincing. Some things never changed.

"Of course, sweetheart," Asher said, reaching behind to pat my knee.

"Anyway," Fallon said, steering the conversation back on track. "We don't need this alleged paradise that may or may not exist. We could easily find a gated, abandoned house near the address Doc was given from his friends. Settle down. Start a life."

I was surprised to hear those words leaving my gruff fiancé's mouth. He wasn't the sentimental type by any means. Before me, I doubted he loved or cared about any female enough to start a life with her. Even his ex had been there merely for convenience and to appease his family.

"I agree with Fallon," Doc said tiredly. He moved to perch on the arm of the couch, beside Tommy. "Settle down. Forget this paradise. We can make our own."

"Our own paradise," I whispered, and the idea sounded so damn appealing, I was afraid my heart would stop. The organ was practically *bursting*, love emanating from it like fireworks. It lit up the darkness and chased away the shadows until it was the only thing I could feel. Could see. Could breathe.

Jared and Davis hesitated once more, but a strident voice interrupted whatever they were going to say. "We stay with them."

Tonya reentered the room. Her eyes were red-rimmed, but her expression was fierce. Determined. She looked as if she could take on a hundred Ragers by herself and still emerge victorious. She was the type of woman I admired, one I yearned to be. She exuded power and confidence as she stormed to the center of the room, keen eyes fixed on her husband and brother.

"We stay with them," she repeated, voice terse.

"Ton..." Jared trailed off at her expression.

"We're a family now, and we'll stay together. Paradise isn't a place. Not really. It's *us*. It's the people we care about, and the people who care for us. We have that here. Why would we throw that away?"

Her words made my eyes burn with tears.

Paradise.

Glancing from face to face, I realized she was right. Paradise wasn't a location, wasn't a full tray of food and a warm bed. It wasn't a roof protecting us from the storms or a fence keeping away the Ragers.

It was the family we made, the family we found.

Tonya, Davis, and Jared, all nodding with soft smiles on their faces.

Doc who was surveying the clipboard, the first sign of life entering his eyes.

Nik and Tom, my brothers in more ways than blood.

Declan, Calax, Fallon, Ryder, Ronan, Tamson, and Asher. The men who found me when I was at my lowest. The men who put me back together again. The men who loved me unconditionally, even when I was a little shit.

That was paradise.

CHAPTER 35

TWO MONTHS LATER

ADDIE

I stared at myself in the full-length mirror, smoothing my hands down my hips.

"Do I look okay?" I asked anxiously, and Tonya smiled at me in the mirror.

"You look beautiful." Her hands gave my shoulders a reassuring squeeze, and I couldn't help but admire her in the mirror.

Her dark curls were intricately braided away from her face. The form-fitting, teal colored dress clung to her like a second skin, the deep V-neckline showing a hint of cleavage. Bracelets adorned her right wrist, jingling with each move she made.

"You look okay," Doc drawled from the leather sofa. He, too, was dashing in a crisp black suit, white cufflinks, and a cherry red tie. His peppered hair was slicked away from his face.

It had been two months since we'd arrived at the small town in Kentucky where Doc's friends were staying. So far, they'd had no luck in creating a cure, but they were confident it could be done. Already, they'd replicated my blood and were working on distributing it across the nation. Small steps, but steps all the same. We couldn't cross an ocean until we started moving.

"Addie! Are you ready?" Before I could answer, Tommy pushed open the door and strode towards me. Nik followed behind him.

"You guys look so handsome," I cooed, emotion clogging my throat. They did. Both were wearing suits and ties, their hair artfully disheveled. For the first time, Nik didn't have his headphones around his neck.

"Damn right we do," Tommy said with a lopsided grin. "And you look beautiful."

I dramatically curtsied, batting my eyelashes for extra effect.

"Damn right I do," I joked, parroting his words back at him. He rolled his eyes, but his smile was wide when he extended one arm to me. Immediately, I linked mine through his, and Nik moved to take the other.

It felt right to do this with them.

When I asked, Tommy's eyes had glistened with unshed tears. Instead of answering, he merely nodded. It was the first time I'd seen him truly speechless. For as long as I'd known him, he'd been the type of man to scream when the rest of the world whispered. His silence was a testament to his feelings.

Nik had wrapped his arms around my waist and held on for dear life.

And he never needed to let go. Now that I had him, I was never letting him go. Either of them.

"Let's do this thing," I whispered, more to myself than anyone else.

"You got this," Tonya agreed.

"Don't trip," Doc deadpanned.

Ignoring them, I cracked my neck as if I were preparing for a fight. Yup. I had this. Badass extraordinaire ball-crusher at your service.

Despite my mental pep talk, my feet were cemented to the ground and my stomach was a block of lead mixing with my already jumbled nerves.

Fuck, I didn't have this.

Before I could run in the opposite direction, the doors were pulled open, and I took my first step forward.

The first thing I noticed was the beautiful church. I'd seen it once when we were picking out a location, but I hadn't seen it since, having been led in through the back entrance. Row after row of pews lined either side of the aisle, twinkling white Christmas lights adorning the wood. The vaulted roof steepled upwards, and each wall was made up of stained-glass windows depicting everything from an angel praying to Jesus on the cross. The sight was ethereal, beautiful, and made my heart pound even faster.

But the true beauty rested on a low stage at the front of the church.

My men stood in a line, hands clasped behind their backs. Each one wore a black suit that curved around their bodies to perfection. They were so damn beautiful, my breath literally caught.

And mine.

They were mine.

I hadn't even realized I started walking faster, desperate to get to them, until Tommy chuckled, yanking me backwards.

"Patience," he whispered to me, and Nik actually cracked a grin.

Nik had also changed significantly in the last couple months we'd all been together. He smiled more, for one. And he actively engaged in conversations with both me and my men.

And Tommy.

They both refused to admit anything, but I'd seen the way they looked at each other. I was stupid, not blind.

Wait...

Nik snorted.

"Said that out loud?" I asked sheepishly, and both of my brothers nodded.

Finally, my legs carried me up the short staircase and to my men. I chanced a glance at the audience, unsurprised to see Tonya and Doc had joined Davis and Jared in the front row. Tonya was desperately trying to wipe away tears, but they came quicker than she could wipe. Even Doc had a lazy smile on his face. Jared held my cat —well, a cat that I claimed as mine but who hated me in return. The cocky asshole was purring, content to remain in Jared's arms for all of eternity. Traitor. At least Mof was getting meat on his bones, the black cat no longer as scrawny as it once was. It was definitely my cat expertise. I was the cat expert…the cat whisperer.

Behind them were a few people we'd met throughout our stay here. Scientists, mostly, and the people working on creating a cure. Maybe they weren't the best choice. Maybe they weren't the smartest. Maybe there was another facility a few states over that was closer than them to creating a cure. Maybe.

But our world didn't run on maybes anymore.

I caught my reflection in one of the windows and smiled softly. The dress was long and as white as mountaintop snow. The top was intricately beaded, leading to a cascading skirt. My brown curls were pinned away from my face, and I wore a light amount of makeup.

I felt so damn beautiful standing up there with my men. So loved. They looked at me like they'd never seen another girl before, like they never *would* see another girl. It was me. And it was them.

It was us.

It was "I do."

It was promises of love, forever and ever. Through the good and bad, the fight and the win.

It was the tears and the laughs.

It was the trials and errors.

It was the "I love you" and the "shut the toilet seat."

It was perfect.

EPILOGUE

ONCE YEAR AND SIX MONTHS LATER

ADDIE

Ragers were still ugly.

Hideous, even. Time hadn't changed that little fact. Their grotesque faces were at the beginning stages of decay, and the smell wafting off of them was almost palpable. Their eyes were red, the color of ruby gemstones with how vibrant they appeared on their sunken faces, and their hair was falling from their scalps in clumps. Only one word could articulate these disgusting creatures—monsters. In the truest sense of the word.

They were the monsters you would see under the bed, elongated teeth and scales expanding down their bodies. You would see them beneath a staircase, lying in wait for their newest victim.

Fear. They evoked fear in you, a primal, tangible entity, seconds before you were devoured.

They were the face of evil incarnate. The asshole of the devil. Or Elena, the she-bitch who'd left me for dead.

And no, I wasn't being dramatic.

Geez.

As Asher cleanly sliced through the neck of the Rager, I admired his muscular form. Over the last year and a half, he'd bulked up in a way that made my vagina open for business. I could clearly see each muscle accentuated through the thin shirts he loved to wear. With his back towards me, I had a clear view of his ass. That was one asshole I loved to stare at. Asshole, as in his butt, not the man. Asher was intense, maybe. And probably psychopathic. But not an asshole. He just had a nice one that I loved to squeeze.

And not in the creepy way. Could assholes—and the loving of them—even be creepy? Like fingering an asshole? Was that creepy? Or normal? I knew that I loved fingers and other anatomical parts in my asshole. The guys, personally, didn't care for it. I made them try once or twice, but they said it felt too strange. Ryder told me that he much preferred his dick inside my asshole instead of fingers inside of his. Or other dicks. We tried that before, and all of the participants said it was too weird. Shame.

Okay. Stop. Thinking.

Asher was laughing, the only indication I must have spoken my thoughts out loud.

I still had a tendency to speak my mind. Literally. If I had a thought, you could bet your ass that it would be spoken out loud. Even after over a year in this apocalyptic hellhole, that one thing remained consistent.

The world fell to shambles around us, but good old Addie still spoke her thoughts aloud.

"Don't listen to me!" I shouted, just as another Rager raced forward, arms extended. Before it could converge on Asher, it was shot in the head.

Ryder blew on the barrel of the gun, eyes sparkling with amusement.

Ryder was the dark to Asher's light, at least in looks. While Asher's light blond hair was now hanging down to his shoulders, Ryder kept his black hair cropped short. Asher's skin was pale, while Ryder's was dark as night. Two entirely different men in both looks and personality.

Two entirely different men who made my heart kickstart.

I hadn't realized how desperately I could love someone—or multiple someones—until these men barreled into my life like a freight train.

My story started off pretty damn normal, if I did say so myself. Rich, mafia-like, abusive parents. A quarter of a billion dollars in my trust fund. A life of luxury in a fancy resort.

Completely normal.

My new normal? Slicing the heads off Ragers while cackling malevolently and planning my next orgasm.

We'd gifted my blood over a year ago to a group of scientists, but so far, they hadn't found a cure or vaccination. I hadn't given up hope yet. With Doc leading the team, I knew they would get it done. It might take ten more years…or it might take ten more minutes. Either way, I had faith. Until then, we just had to survive.

Fallon pulled his dagger out of a Rager's pinprick red eye. I'd given him the dagger for his birthday, and he hadn't been without it since. I even heard him whispering to it from time to time, as if it were his own baby.

Yes, this new world made him psycho, but he was my psycho. They all were.

I had a crossbow as my weapon of choice. My men had gotten it for me as a gift for our wedding—an intimate event where we just sort of talked, exchanged rings, and then had large group sex. It was then that we tried out the whole butt thing—or *hole* butt thing.

How did I put up with seven husbands? Lube. Lots and lots of lube. And I fed them. And petted them. And sometimes took them out for walks, depending on my mood.

"Put the supplies in the van, and let's get moving. I don't want to stay here longer than necessary." Fallon clapped his hands together, seemingly indifferent to the tar-like black blood coating his hands from the Rager he'd just killed. Ryder wordlessly handed Fallon a cloth and a bottle of water, and our leader worked on cleaning himself.

Ronan, who was driving the van, leaned his head out the window.

"Hurry the fuck up."

Ronan's dark hair was tousled, longer on the top than the sides now. When I first met him, back when he infiltrated the resort I'd lived in, the spiky tips were green. They had long since grown out, but I'd been on the lookout for green dye.

Nostalgia purposes, of course.

When he saw me looking, he flashed me a cheeky smile and a wink, and my own lips reflexively turned up. He had that way about him, a way of innately demanding attention from anyone who looked directly at him.

It was just one of the many reasons why I loved him.

I blew him a kiss, and he pretended to catch it. Fallon flickered his eyes between the two of us before rolling them. Still, he was smiling.

According to Tamson, I was the only person alive who could make Fallon smile like that. He took broody to an extreme. I once said that Fallon made brooding sexy...and that resulted in multiple eyerolls from the rest of the guys. They just *wished* they could brood and grunt like Fallon.

Shielding my eyes from the blinding sun, I looked at the modest building we'd decided to raid. It had once been a restaurant, but the glass was littered on the side-walk and paint was beginning to peel. The entire face of the building had been ravaged by atrocious storms and vandalism. Still, it had been an oasis after five hours of futile searching. The kitchen was, surprisingly, still fully stocked. It was one of the few places that hadn't been completely ransacked.

While most of the food was spoiled, we did happen to come across numerous gallons of water and canned goods.

I hadn't been invited to go on this trip. My husbands were...protective, to put it mildly. They much preferred me hidden away behind impenetrable fortresses. Unfortunately for them, the rest of our team was on a separate mission a few towns over, and no one wanted me to be left alone.

I tried to tell them I was perfectly capable of protecting myself—after all, I wasn't nicknamed the Ball Crunching Bitch for nothing—but the guys were stubborn.

"Princess..." Ronan pinched the bridge of his nose. "No one calls you the Ball Crunching Bitch."

"Stop listening to my thoughts," I countered, moving to sit on a crate.

"Then stop speaking your thoughts out loud."

To prove that I was a badass, I grabbed my dagger out of its sheath and began to absently pick at my nails with the sharp blade. I'd seen Asher do this once or twice before, and he was the epitome of badass.

"You're going to cut yourself, baby," Fallon said, swiping the blade out of my hand before I could even blink. He eyed me disapprovingly, and I squirmed, feeling prop-erly chastised.

"I just want to be of use." I knew I was whining, but I couldn't seem to stop myself. They'd been treating me with kid's gloves ever since The Announcement. And yes, that was meant to be in capital letters.

"Don't fucking pout," Fallon warned. When I continued to stare at him, he scowled, running a hand through his disheveled light brown hair. "I said don't fucking pout."

"Is Kitten giving you the face?" Ryder ran up beside Fallon, casually dropping his elbow onto the other man's shoulder.

"What face?" I questioned.

"The face that makes us want to start wars for you," Ryder said casually.

"The pouting face!" Asher called from where he was cleanly slicing off the last Rager's head.

"I don't make...pouty faces." I scrunched my nose.

"You're making it now," countered Ryder with a small smirk.

I tentatively reached a hand up to feel my lips. They were, in fact, pursed into a perfectly pouty frown. Whoops.

I smoothed my expression into one of impassivity.

"No pouty face," I deadpanned. While Ryder threw back his head in laughter, Fallon merely quirked a brow. I met his hooded stare defiantly, not pouting like a boss. "I want to be helpful."

"You know why you can't," he said. It was always the same argument with him. Every. Single. Freaking. Time. He was beginning to sound like a broken record.

"I just don't understand why I'm always kept shielded. I know how the world works. I know it better than anyone. You guys have always been protective, but ever since The Announcement, you haven't even let me out of your sight. One of these days, I'm going to sneak out, and you'll only have yourself to blame."

When Fallon's stare turned glacial, Ryder began to laugh harder.

"You know that if you ever try to leave us, Fallon and Asher will quite literally tie you up and put you in the basement," he said, wiping tears from his eyes. "And the rest of us would be more than willing to help."

In confirmation, Asher winked. He was dripping in Rager blood, dead bodies around his feet, and a scar marred his face. Ryder wasn't fucking kidding.

Why did that thought get me so turned on?

"You like that?" Fallon whispered, dropping to his knees before me. "You like knowing that you're ours, just as we're yours?"

Ryder moved to sit on the ground beside me, legs outstretched and eyes heated. Asher continued watching, moving to grab a discarded, clean T-shirt and wiping at his face and hands.

Fallon's fingers were tantalizingly soft as they climbed up my jeans. Over the material, he began to rub my suddenly throbbing pussy.

"Don't ever fucking say that you'll leave us again," Fallon continued darkly.

I wanted to tell him that I was his—theirs—forever, but all I managed to do was moan. The girl who couldn't stop speaking transformed into the girl who could only grunt and make weird noises. What was this world coming to?

Fallon's hand trailed up to the waistband of my jeans, and he undid the snap and zipper. Eyes trained on me, with a look that promised both pleasure and punishment, he shimmied the pants off my legs. Ryder moved behind me and pulled my shirt over my head.

Dressed in only a mismatched set of bras and panties, I closed my eyes, head lolling back.

"Look at me," Fallon demanded. My eyelids snapped open.

His own eyes emanated a voracious hunger, both primal and carnal. The heat in his gaze made me whimper.

"Who do you belong to?" As he spoke, his fingers resumed their gentle strokes over the dreaded fabric. I really should start going commando.

When I didn't answer, arching my hips into his awaiting hand, he stopped. His fingers were a hairsbreadth away from my dripping pussy. Ryder hovered over my breasts, tongue snaking out to lick his chapped lips.

"Tell your husbands who you belong to."

My eyes flickered upwards. Ronan was still leaning out the car window, but his eyes were dark with lust. Asher freed himself from his pants. As I watched, he began to stroke himself.

"You guys," I breathed, wiggling. I was desperate for them to touch me, to love me, to make me theirs so completely. I needed their hands and lips on me. I needed it more than I needed anything else in my life.

"Names," Fallon said gruffly. His own cock made a large tent in his pants, and I preened, glad I was affecting him the way he was affecting me.

"Fallon. Ryder. Ronan. Asher. Tamson. Declan. Calax."

Lust permeated the air.

Before I could beg, my bra was discarded, and Ryder's lips devoured one of my aching nipples. I gasped at the sensation of his tongue swirling over my beaded bud.

My eyes closed instinctively, wave after wave of pleasure threatening to drown me. Ryder's hand tweaked my other nipple, molding it into a sharp point.

"Eyes open," Fallon demanded, and I obeyed instantly. He stood above me, his pants discarded and his large cock on display. His was definitely one of the longest and widest, a single vein running down the side. I reached out immediately, eager to touch it the way I knew he liked me to, but he stopped me, hands creating vises around my wrists. He grabbed the edges of my panties and *ripped*. Fucking panty destroyer.

In one sure stroke, he sheathed himself within me. I gasped, adjusting to his girth, before I began to move my hips. He leaned down to capture my lips in a bruising, heated kiss. There was no denying the possessiveness as his tongue tangled with my own. He wanted me to know who I belonged to. Who *he* belonged to.

He began to rock inside of me, hands tangling in my brown curls. My own hands were tangled in Ryder's short hair, keeping his face on my breasts. Abruptly, Fallon broke the kiss and turned my head to face Ryder's cock, now free and erect.

"Suck him off, baby girl. Show me who you belong to."

Without having to be told twice, I wrapped my lips around Ryder's length and used my hand to cover the distance my mouth couldn't reach. He hissed, hands tangling with Fallon's in my hair.

If there was a grading system for blow jobs, I would easily give myself a gold motherfucking star. Having seven husbands and only one vagina really taught you how to be creative.

I released his cock with a dramatic smacking noise. My tongue licked down his side, grazing my teeth over the sensitive skin the way I knew he liked. When I reached his balls, I took one in my mouth immediately, marking it with my saliva.

Ryder let out a curse.

I prepared to take him back in my mouth when Fallon began to pound into me harder, fucking me mercilessly. Earnestly. Possessively.

Quickly, I took Ryder back in my mouth, sucking him off in tandem to Fallon's punishing thrusts.

"I fucking love you," Ryder moaned. His hands fondled my breasts, now swaying.

My eyes lifted, my gaze landing on Asher. His hand erratically moved over his own cock, and sweat beaded on his forehead. His eyes were fixed on me, flickering from Fallon's cock pounding in and out of my pussy, to my bouncing breasts, to my lips around Ryder's length.

It was the look in his eyes, the intense combination between want and desire and love and need, that sent me spiraling over the edge. My pussy clenched around Fallon, and he roared as his own orgasm overtook him, his cum dripping down my legs.

I hummed around Ryder's length, and he jerked his hips. That was the only warning I had before he came in my mouth. I lapped it up eagerly, finally releasing him with a reluctant moan.

For a moment, we remained there, a panting, sweaty heap of nerves and lust. It was Asher who broke the stillness, grabbing a shirt out of his backpack and gently cleaning me up. At this point, we were going to run out of clean clothes. Stupid Rager blood and orgasms. Well, not stupid orgasms. Happy, happy orgasms. Fallon placed his now flaccid dick back in his pants.

Once I was cleaned, Asher helped me back into my clothes, planting gentle kisses on my bare skin in the process.

"I love you," I whispered softly, too quietly for the rest to hear. The smile that appeared on Asher's face was bright.

"I love you too," he replied, brushing his lips against my own.

"I am fucking wrecked! I don't think I can walk!" Ryder dramatically stated, lying on his back on the asphalt. His cock was still out of his pants, saluting the world.

"Stop bitching," Ronan snapped. "If you're going to take a hot as hell blow job for granted—"

"For granted?" Ryder peeled open one eye, meeting my gaze with a sultry grin. "That was one of the best moments of my life. Granted, every day is the best of my life since Addie came into it."

Rolling my eyes, I allowed Asher to help me up. "So fucking cheesy."

"But you love it."

"Put your damn dick away," Fallon snapped. It was Ryder this time who rolled his eyes, but he immediately shoved his cock back into his pants. I could've sworn I heard him mumble something about all the other guys being jealous.

Ryder *did* have a rather nice cock.

Definitely something that would cause jealousy.

"Shit!" Asher cursed suddenly, redirecting my attention. His hands were providing a makeshift visor for his eyes as he stared up at the sky. Following his line of vision, a curse escaped my own lips.

He wasn't just staring at the sky. No, instead he was staring at the green-tinted storm clouds coming in off the horizon.

It had taken over a year of research to detect what each cloud meant. Which ones brought acid rain. Which ones would bring thunderstorms. The green-tinted ones *always* released a torrent of acid rain. Always.

And it was heading straight towards us.

"Addie, get in the van!" Fallon shouted. Asher took my hand, propelling me forward. I staggered over my own two feet but followed, sliding into the backseat. The rest of my men followed me, our supplies forgotten.

"Shit," I mumbled, rubbing at my bare arms as Ronan quickly drove out of the parking lot. Ryder put his arm around me, and I cuddled into his chest.

"Shit is right, Kitten. Shit is right."

THE RAIN WAS RELENTLESS, pelting the roof of the van. Bloated storm clouds rolled in off the horizon, carrying with them gushing rain. The air inside the van was stifling, the tension almost tangible, but still, we drove on.

We passed a group of Ragers screaming in outrage, their grotesque bodies paying heavily. Each new onslaught of rain further decayed their mangy skin and obliterated their tattered clothes. The rain, while horrifying, was also a blessing. The number of Ragers decreased significantly after each storm.

"What's the plan?" I asked, leaning forward to rest my arms on the center console. Ronan was still driving, and Fallon, of course, had claimed shotgun. Asher and Ryder sat on either side of me, both touching me in some capacity. Asher was stroking my hair, while Ryder was tracing patterns onto my thigh.

"There's an outpost a few blocks over," Fallon said, surveying the aged map. We'd added information about surviving cities, outposts, and government bases.

I'd been to a few outposts before with my guys…and I hated them. A lot. They were always crawling with prostitutes and scantily-clad women desperate for protection. I knew my guys would never cheat on me, but it didn't ebb the jealousy I felt when the women threw themselves at *my* men.

The nights always ended with epic angry sex. Well…angry on my end. I was pretty sure the others were more confused than anything.

Not that they complained. The kinky shits liked it when I tied them up and possessed them so thoroughly, mind, body, and soul.

"What's with the face?" Ryder asked seriously, giving my shoulder a soft squeeze.

"Pouty face?" I cocked my head to the side, cataloguing my features in the rearview mirror. Yup. No pouty face.

"No, this is your someone-is-about-to-die face," Asher chimed in.

"I'm just thinking about all of those girls," I murmured bitterly. Honestly. There was never any other option with these men. They demanded absolute honesty from me, and I expected it in return. It was what allowed our unconventional relationship to not only work, but thrive.

Ryder's brows furrowed adorably, the slightest crease on his dark skin that always appeared when he was confused.

"What other women?"

Fallon had swiveled in the passenger seat to face me fully, and even Ronan was casting me anxious glances, as if questioning my sanity.

"The women at these outposts," I groaned out, hating how oblivious they were. "They practically throw themselves at your feet. They need to realize that you're mine. My cocks, dammit! My men!"

I stomped my foot like a petulant child, and Ryder's lips quirked. Asher turned away from me, body shaking with laughter.

"Are you jealous, Kitten?" Ryder asked, caressing the side of my face. I reached for his hand and interlocked my fingers with his. I always loved how safe I felt with Ryder, how small he made me feel when his hand engulfed mine entirely. The contrast of our skin. The tiniest white scar by his thumb, a product of this new life we'd found ourselves in.

"I wouldn't say jealous…" I drawled. "I mean, I know you guys are mine and I'm yours. And I know you'll never look at these other women, but fuck, it's annoying! I really need to make signs that say 'Property of Adelaide.' It's kind of sad, really, how pathetic these women are, thinking they actually have a chance." I leveled each of the men with my best glare. "Mine," I growled.

Impulsively, I dug my fingernails into Ryder's thigh. "Mine."

That did it.

They threw their heads back in laughter. Ronan even had to pull over to the side of the road, his body shaking as tears dripped from his eyes.

"God, do you have any idea how much we fucking love you?" Ryder said between fits of laughter. "Hot damn. Is that why you tie us up?"

"I need to remind those bitches who you belong to," I said with a huff, crossing my arms over my chest.

Fallon met my gaze, his dark eyes holding mine hostage. It was impossible to escape the intensity of his stare. Falling in love with Fallon was like falling into a black hole, an endless abyss.

The beauty, however, was worth all of his darkness.

"And you obviously never notice the attention you receive at these outposts," he said curtly, eyes penetrating through my skin and seeing into my very soul.

"Me?"

I thought through every interaction, but my mind latched on to our last encounter at an outpost. Namely, Calax tied to my bed as I rode him relentlessly while Tamson and Declan were forced to watch. Good times.

"All of the guys stare at you as if *they* actually have a fucking chance." Ronan's voice was uncharacteristically bitter as he began to drive once more. His knuckles whitened as he clenched the steering wheel.

"Both guards and travelers alike flock to you," Ryder added. "I want to kill everyone there."

"Stab first, ask questions later," Asher said cheerfully. The damn psychopath began to clean his knife on the bottom of his shirt, smiling sincerely.

Tears blurred my vision, and I sniffled, brushing them away.

"So you guys all get murdery too?" I asked weepily. "We get murdery together? I love you all so much."

"Honestly, I thought you were so possessive and loving while we're there to set *our* minds at ease, not your own." Ryder shrugged. "You're our entire fucking world. We proved that to you time and time again."

Fallon's heated eyes continued to hold mine, promising punishment for my irrational jealousy. Punishment in the form of ropes and spankings.

Heat swarmed low in my stomach, and I squirmed uncomfortably. Fallon, seeing what his expression look did to me, turned towards the windshield, smiling smugly.

Asshole.

His lips twitched once more, the only indication I'd spoken out loud.

Time moved slowly, gruelingly slow, as I stared at the back of Fallon's head, listening to my men converse half-heartedly. It was so…normal. So right. This was how it was always meant to be, how love was meant to be. And Fallon? He had a good back of head.

"We need to get in contact with the others," Fallon said abruptly, interrupting Ryder's long-winded spiel about the best way to hide a body.

I half wished I'd paid attention to that conversation instead of eye humping Fallon. Oh well. Hopefully, the body in question wasn't anyone I knew.

At Fallon's words, I eagerly raised my hand into the air.

"Me! Me! Me!"

Rolling his eyes with a slight smirk, he handed me the black radio.

"You press down on the—"

"Yeah. Yeah. Yeah." I waved my hand dismissively, interrupting Ryder's pointless instructions. I was the Badass Ball Breaker. I knew how to use a damn radio.

"Not a Badass Ball Breaker," murmured Asher. I shushed him.

After assuring myself that the radio was already switched to the designated channel, I pressed down on the button. The static receded instantly.

"Badass Ball Breaker to Giant and the Peeps. Badass Ball Breaker to Giant and the Peeps."

I took my thumb off the button and waited. At first, there was nothing but static. Finally, Calax's wary voice came through.

"Am I Giant?"

"Of course." I rolled my eyes. "In more ways than one."

Silence.

"Fuck, baby. You really know how to boost a man's ego."

I didn't know *how* I boosted his ego when I'd merely been talking about his big head. Maybe he misconstrued my words…?

Realization slammed into me with the force of a semi truck. Oh. His cock. Yeah, that was giant too.

"So does that mean Tamson and Declan are the Peeps?" Calax continued, amused. "I don't know how well they'll take that."

"Well, it would've been a mouthful to say Quack and the Ginger."

Ryder snorted, laughter dancing in his dark umber eyes.

Silence.

"What the fuck?" Calax asked. I could picture his eyes widening slightly, almost imperceptibly. No doubt, Tamson would be signing the conversation to Declan. All three of my men would be staring at the radio with a quirk to their brows and amused expressions.

"Because Declan's nickname is Ducky. Quack. Get it? And Tamson has reddish brown hair?"

I waved my hand dismissively, a gesture I knew they couldn't see, and gave Asher an eyeroll. Did they really want me to spend hours explaining their nicknames? You didn't see me bitching about being called Kitten and Princess and baby.

Granted, I loved those nicknames, but they didn't need to know that.

"Okay, we're getting off topic, Callie." I leaned against Ryder and placed my feet on Asher's lap. Asher immediately untied my boots and began to massage my feet. I very nearly moaned at the contact, the press of his palm against my sensitive arch.

"Where are you?" Fallon called back.

There was static before Tamson's voice came through. I smiled slightly, envisioning my timid lover. At least to the outside perspective. In the bedroom, he was as dominant as Fallon, if not more so. More than once, he'd tied me up and tortured me endlessly with hints of pleasure. His hot breath against my core, whispering my name and how much he loved me. His tongue licking the thin fabric of my underwear, never touching me where I wanted to be touched.

"A few hours north of the home base," Tamson answered Fallon, jerking me out of my reverie. I flushed when I realized where my mind had headed, my nipples sharp against my shirt. Ronan smirked at me in the rearview mirror, privy to my perverted thoughts. He, too, enjoyed foreplay with Tamson. They never did anything sexual with each other, but they both enjoyed tag teaming me and taking me to the pinnacle of pleasure—Tamson in charge of my punishment, and Ronan in charge of my reward.

It was a partnership I never knew I'd needed until it happened.

"Where are you at?" Tamson questioned.

"Forty minutes south of the home base," Fallon answered briskly. We never revealed our exact location on the radio, on the off chance that someone was listening in. Tam had assured us numerous times that the radios were secure, but even he was cautious, especially when it came to my safety.

"Acid rain over here," Ryder filled in, leaning towards me.

There was another long, pronounced silence. I could practically feel the tension from the others, hundreds of miles away.

"Everyone safe?" Calax asked roughly.

"I know you're really asking if Addie's safe," Ryder said dryly. He clutched at his chest. "I'm wounded."

"*Everyone* is fine," Fallon cut in, casting me a pointed look. I stuck my tongue out at him in response.

Calax let out a noticeable breath of relief. My gentle giant was always worrying about me, always seeking new ways to protect me. He'd argued profusely when Fallon had suggested we separate, three of the guys heading in one direction and four heading in the other with me. Calax had nearly blown a nut when he discovered he was in the former group. Ever since The Announcement, he'd refused to let me out of his sight.

I remembered that haunted, broken look in his eyes seconds before I left with the others. As of right now, it was just a crack, but I knew from experience that the crack could turn into a fissure. From there, he would shatter, and all hell would break loose.

"I miss you so much, baby," Calax murmured. I imagined his face was bright red, never one to outwardly admit his feelings.

"Aw. I miss you too!" Ronan cooed, and Fallon whacked him on the back of the head.

"I would totally do some hot radio sex," I said casually. "But the others might be a little weirded out. So when I see you guys tomorrow, I'm going to give you all blow jobs, okay?"

"Okay, baby," he said, humoring me.

I recognized Tamson's sultry chuckle.

"I love you all," I continued, my voice catching. I'd never felt such raw, carnal emotion before. These men reverted me to a primal beast, where all I wanted to do was love them with every fiber of my being. And fuck them. For some weird, undefinable reason, they'd decided I was worthy of their love in return.

"Love you too, baby," Calax said gruffly.

"You already know how much I love you," Tamson added. There was another stretch of silence. "Declan says he loves you too. And to wear the nightgown when we come home. What nightgown is he talking about?"

My lips tilted up reflexively. One caveat of having seven different relationships was having certain things that belonged to only one of my lovers, whether that be emotional or physical. With Asher, for example, we would stay up for hours talking about anything and everything. He made me feel alive and loved, and I, in return, reminded him of his humanity. With Tamson, I allowed him to dominate me in the bedroom while he ceded his control to me outside of it.

And with Declan, my childhood best friend, I had the lacy black nightgown that showed my nipples and pussy. It was our kink.

"Nothing," I said, smiling softly.

Ryder and Asher eyed me suspiciously, but didn't ask me to elaborate. They knew I did certain things with only some of them. It was a way to keep our group and individual relationships separate.

"Be safe," Calax said.

I directed my attention to the radio, wishing upon all else that I could see them. Their tender, almost reverent, expressions. The red-brown curls shielding Tam's freckled face. The muscles bulging in Calax's arms. The intense stare Declan always wore. The way his eyes fixed intently on my lips.

"Always. You too."

"We'll be home tomorrow," Fallon added. "We don't want to drive in this weather longer than we have to. There's an outpost a few minutes from here."

"Understandable," Calax said begrudgingly. "But be careful. All of you. See you tomorrow."

With a resigned sigh, I handed Fallon the radio, and he placed it back in his backpack.

"You'll see them tomorrow, Kitten. No reason for that sad face." Ryder wrapped his arm around me, hugging me tightly. Sometimes, it felt as if he wanted to meld our bodies together, to make two become one.

"I just worry," I admitted with a helpless shrug.

Whatever Ryder was about to say was interrupted by Ronan slamming on the brakes. We'd pulled up in front of an immense building, two guards blocking the entrance. This outpost was located in the remnants of a football stadium, the vaulted roof able to withstand the storm and the metal gates manned by men with guns.

"Let's get this party started," I murmured dryly.

Four manly chuckles greeted my less than enthusiastic statement.

"THEY TOTALLY LOOKED AT YOUR ASSES," I mumbled stubbornly, tossing my backpack onto the ground of the cubby we found ourselves in. It had once been a food stall, but the outpost owners had removed all of the equipment and replaced it with torn mattresses.

The owner, a kind, younger gentleman named Derrick, had originally offered us two rooms, but my men had disagreed. They wanted us to stay together.

As we'd walked the long halls, the rain pelting the vaulted roof and lightning flashing overhead like a giant spotlight, I couldn't help but note the sultry stares of the women present. One had purposefully dropped her notebook, bending down to give my men an ample view of her cleavage. Another had the gall to offer her services to Asher, who looked ready to tear her head off. The final straw occurred when a blonde bimbo placed her hand on Fallon's arm with a tinkling laugh. If looks could kill, or at least penetrate skin and bones, I was sure her manicured hand would've fallen to dust. Fallon had merely glared at her offending fingers with an almost incandescent fury until she removed it with a muttered apology.

"Did you see the way Derrick looked at you?" Ryder countered with a grin.

"He was nice," I protested.

"He wanted what's ours," Fallon said briskly. He moved to light the few candles adorning the perimeter of the room. There were some outposts that had generators for electricity, but this was not one of them.

"I love it when you get all possessive," I said idly, unzipping my backpack and pulling out my nightshirt. It was a bright garnet and fell to my knees, the name of some obscure band sewn across the chest. It was Ronan's old shirt, and I knew he loved it when I wore his clothes.

Ronan, who was leaning against the moldy wall, flashed me a grin. "You're wearing my shirt, Princess. I believe I have the right to be possessive."

Sticking my tongue out at him, I pulled my shirt over my head, reveling in the four sharp intakes of breath as I revealed my pale skin and lacy black bra, before slipping into my nightshirt. Honestly, they acted as if they hadn't seen me naked only... oh...two hours ago. Needy shits.

"I'm sorry," I mumbled, moving to sit on one of the cots and absently running my fingers through the frill of the quilt. "I don't know why I'm acting so jealous and shit. I was never like that before…before, you know, The Announcement."

Asher placed a hand on my thigh, lightly squeezing.

"It's hormones, sweetheart. Completely understandable."

"Hormones suck ass," I grumbled. Absently, I placed my hand on my stomach. "Everything about being a woman sucks ass. Periods? Sucks ass. PMSing? Sucks ass. Like, who would want to bleed out of their vaginas?" I tapped a finger against my chin, pondering the questions of the universe. "Remember when we watched that vampire movie at the one military base? And he wanted to drink her blood? Well, what would happen when she was on her period? Actually, I'm sure a lot of those females were on their periods. Wouldn't the vampires go all murdery? All bitey? I mean, all that blood…"

Cue four rather confused faces. Actually, appalled faces would be a better description.

"Well…that just killed the fucking mood," Ryder said petulantly, but his eyes betrayed his amusement.

"What mood?" I teased. "I wasn't trying to seduce you motherfuckers."

Ryder crawled towards me on his hands and knees, eyes half-lidded with heat. Want. Need. This voracious hunger that made my nipples harden. "Stripping down? Talking about our baby inside of you? The way you're ours so completely? I don't know what else could possibly be more of a turn-on."

I made a strange sound, a combination between a moan and a mewl. My entire body was coiled tightly, a snake preparing to strike, and Ryder was my victim. The need to memorize the feel of his shoulders, the fullness of his lips, to trace the tattoos snaking down his sides with my tongue was almost overwhelming.

Ryder leaned closer, lips inches from my own…

Before he was abruptly pulled back by Fallon.

"Later," he said fervently. His eyes flickered to mine over Ryder's shoulder, and the blistering heat in them was nearly my undoing.

"Later?" I asked in disbelief. Instinctively, I opened my legs. "Why not right now? Why not right this damn moment? In the vagina." Pouting, I spread my legs even farther, feeling oddly like a kickass gymnast.

Damn. I don't know how much longer I can hold this position.

Asher coughed to cover his laugh.

And I just spoke out loud. Again.

Another laugh, this one from Ronan.

And again.

"Ryder and Ronan," Fallon instructed, ignoring my outburst. At this point, he was used to my random ramblings. "Go to the medical wing. Ask for prenatal vitamins. We're getting low."

The brothers nodded seriously, the lust dissipating from their eyes. With a kiss on both of my cheeks, they hurried out the door. Fallon then turned towards Asher.

"I'm going to meet with Derrick. Discuss trading. He seems like a good guy, if a little oblivious to when a woman is already taken, and he would be a good ally to have. Stay with her."

Grabbing the back of my neck, Fallon pulled me into a bruising kiss. His tongue just barely touched mine before he pulled away. I made a sound of protest which he purposely ignored. Without another word, he strode out the door, slamming it shut behind him.

"Alone at last," Asher teased, joining me on the bed and lying back, holding his arms open.

Contentment surrounded me like a warm blanket, and I burrowed myself inside of it. Smiling, I cuddled against Asher's strong chest, and he wrapped his arms around me from behind, holding me closer to him. He planted tantalizingly soft kisses on the skin behind my ear.

Being with Asher was like coming home after trekking through an atrocious snowstorm. The wind howling, the snow assaulting my face, the water seeping through my pants. Once I entered the house, warmth emanated from a lit fire and the smell of baked cookies wafted from the oven, the smell orgasm inducing. Home. Asher felt like home.

"How are you feeling?" he asked softly. He pushed up my shirt, resting his hands on my bare stomach.

"Horny. Pregnant. The usual." I shrugged nonchalantly, but my stomach was a tumultuous mixture of excitement and apprehension.

"You're worried," Asher stated. It was never a question with him. He knew me better than I knew myself at times, able to read me like an open book.

Sighing heavily, I grabbed one of his hands and began to play with his fingers. The monotonous gesture distracted me, if only for a moment, as I got my thoughts together.

"Are we doing the right thing?" I whispered. His fingers were long and thin, white scars adorning them like rings. "Bringing a baby into this fucked-up world?"

Asher remained silent, stroking my stomach and allowing me to confess all my deep-rooted fears.

"Will I even be a good mother?" I continued. "My own parents were shit, and the last thing I want… Well, I don't want to be like them. I want to love my baby the way I never was. I want…" I trailed off, tears surging in my eyes and distorting my vision.

"Are you done now?" Asher asked, not unkindly. He removed his hand from my stomach to stroke my hair. I nuzzled my face into his neck, breathing in the distinct scent of the cologne he'd used in the car. Citrus, maybe, mixed with engine grease and gasoline. It wasn't a smell I would've usually associated with my sweet husband, but it was becoming more and more common from all the cars we stole and gas we siphoned.

"I just don't know if the universe picked the right person to mother this baby," I confided.

Asher was silent for a moment, his fingers massaging my scalp. When he finally spoke, his soft voice broke through the silence like the slash of a whip.

"There's a lot we don't know, a lot we don't understand. This world…it's big and terrifying. We don't know what tomorrow will bring, so we have to focus on today. Can I be honest with you?" He didn't wait for me to respond, though he knew my answer would be yes. Always. "I'm scared too. I think we're all scared. We're bringing this vulnerable being into a fucked-up world, and I'm terrified. Of a lot of things.

"What if something goes wrong during childbirth? What if we lose you?" His voice broke, and his hands tightened imperceptibly around me. "And then we have to think about this baby we're bringing into the world, this baby we're destined to love and care for. *Our* baby. Addie, my love, you're not alone in this. This baby has seven fathers who would die for it. I have no doubt in my mind that you will be an amazing mother. Adelaide, you are the epitome of love. Love and compassion and everything good and bright in the world. I love you so fucking much."

Tears blurred my vision. Somehow, in a matter of seconds, Asher was able to pacify months of insecurities and despondency. He took the weight I'd been carrying and shouldered it selflessly.

"I love you," I whispered, arching my neck. My lips crashed to his, a clash of tongues and teeth. It wasn't gentle, but it wasn't rough. It just…was. Pure, undiluted feeling.

Asher spun me so that my back was against the mattress and he was leaning over me. His eyes were fixed on me as his tongue mingled with mine. His arousal pressed against my stomach as his lips moved to my neck, kissing from my jaw to my collarbone and then to my breasts, still covered by the red sleepshirt.

Without preamble, he pulled the shirt over my head, baring my bra-clad breasts to him. The old me might've shielded myself, felt self-conscious and keenly aware of all the scars and bruises. The largest one was on the center of my stomach from a gunshot wound.

But there was no pity or disgust in Asher's eyes. Only love so intense that my hips bucked beneath him. He didn't hesitate to remove my bra, dropping it to the ground beside us.

His hand cupped my aching breast, rolling my nipple between his thumb and forefinger.

"I love you so much," Asher whispered, ducking his head to kiss me.

He helped me shimmy out of my pants—sans underwear, thanks to Fallon earlier —before pulling off his own shirt and pants. My mouth dried when I noticed he was commando, his impressive cock aimed at my chest. He gave my breast another quick squeeze.

"You're beautiful," he said softly, awestruck.

Removing his hands from my breasts, he cupped my cheeks tenderly, kissing me once more. In one quick thrust, he sheathed himself inside me. I groaned, adjusting to the length of him, before moving my hips.

His eyes held mine as he moved with me, and my hips arched upwards, while he pounded into me earnestly. Sweat coated his forehead, and I leaned up on my elbows to lick it away.

His balls slapped against my ass with each thrust, and I knew I was seconds away from shattering. My eyes rolled back in my head as his fingers flicked my clit.

The orgasm shattered through me so hard that I saw stars. A strangled scream escaped my parted lips as wave after wave of pleasure coursed through me. I was tumbling head over heels in an ocean, each new wave pulling me back under. I was drowning, but it was the sweetest death possible. I wouldn't have been able to stop it even if I wanted to—which I didn't. It was the equivalent of standing in a storm and trying to stop the rain with your bare hands.

Asher let out a roar as he exploded inside of me, my pussy tightening around his cock.

Thoroughly satiated, I leaned back, and Asher collapsed on top of me. His blond hair tickled my cheeks as he repeatedly kissed my neck.

"Well, well, well." The amused voice came from the doorway. I hadn't even heard anyone arrive. "Looks like we missed all the fun."

Raising my head, I met Ryder's smoldering gaze. Ronan and Fallon stood beside him, arms crossed over their muscular chests and pants tented.

Ronan smirked when he caught my eye.

"Are you up for round two, Princess?"

Ronan's lips attacked mine before I could answer, claiming me. Branding me. Marking me. We fit together seamlessly, his strong hand coming to squeeze my breast and flick my nipple.

Asher had moved behind me, his hand on my waist and his lips on my neck. I could feel him hardening once more against me, that kinky shit. If there was one thing I'd learned about Asher, it was that he loved to watch. He loved the prospect of the others filling me, planting their seed in me, loving me.

"Getting ready for round two as well?" I asked my sweet boy with a grin, breaking away from Ronan's bruising lips. Asher chuckled against my neck.

"I don't think I could ever have enough of you." His fingers brushed against my ribs with the delicacy of a butterfly's wing. The way he made me feel with just a simple touch...

Love sometimes seemed too inadequate of a word. My heart *burst*. It shattered, creating seven new hearts in its place. Each heart belonged to one of my men. I'd seen it in movies, read it in books, but I hadn't believed it was possible. Giving your entire heart to a man sounded like a cliché.

Until I fell in love and realized how true it actually was.

"And *I* think you guys are wearing too many clothes," I quipped, my gaze roaming over my men. Ronan smiled cheekily before removing his shirt and sliding out of his pants. He kept his boxer briefs on, a noticeable bulge in the front. Leaning forward to kiss him once more, I cupped his cock through the material. He groaned against my lips, hands tightening in my disheveled, sex mussed hair.

I didn't even have to look up to know that the others were getting naked as well. But I did anyway. I needed my hourly dose of male cocks. One glance confirmed both Ryder and Fallon in all their naked glory, cocks already erect and in their hands. I practically salivated at all the silky skin on display.

There was something arousing about a man's dick. The contrast between the soft skin and the hard muscle in my hand. The pre-cum at the tip, just begging to be licked. The thought that I could make a man fall apart with just the lightest of tugs.

I felt a sudden surge of anxiety at the prospect of being with all four men at once. Maybe anxiety was too strong of a word, but my stomach was a tumultuous mixture of fear and desire. It was irrational, of course, especially since this wasn't the first time I'd been with more than one man at the same time. It was, however, a reminder of one of our last group sex sessions...and how it had ended up.

With a freaking unexpected bun in the oven.

Fallon reached down and grabbed a handful of condoms out of his bag, and my eyes fixed on that.

"Is that a me thing or a you thing? Because if it's a me thing, I need to practice putting it on your dicks. I don't want to screw this up and get pregnant again. Do I unwrap it? Twirl it around my finger? Fit it on like a hat?" I rambled, even though a small part of my brain recognized I'd put a condom on my men over one thousand times. Me? Dramatic? Please.

Desperately, I glanced over my shoulder at Asher, who was watching me with bemused eyes.

"Somebody grab me a damn pickle!" I shouted in panic.

Fallon chuckled darkly, pulling my attention back to him.

"No, Addie. You don't have to worry about putting the condom on. I can do that. But I don't understand why you're so insistent on us wearing one when *you're already fucking pregnant.*"

Trust me, man. I didn't know either. I blamed it on the hormones making me irrational. I supposed Tonya's lessons about wrapping it up like a Christmas present stuck with me, even a year and a half later.

"But there's four of you... Where are you all going to fit? I only have..." Lifting my fingers, I began to count. "Three holes. Shit. Are we doing double penetration? WHERE IS MY PICKLE, DAMMIT?!"

There were no ifs, ands, or buts. I needed to practice. The last thing I wanted to do was cleave my ass in two. I already had a hole...

I chuckled at my own joke, and four groans accompanied the thought I must've said aloud.

Their loss. I knew I was hilarious.

My smile fled from my face when Ryder knelt beside me, turning me to face him, his glorious cock on display.

"What hole will that fucking monstrosity be going into?"

Would Fallon be down for some anal action?

Because it sure as hell wasn't going in mine. I didn't know why I was so anxious, since I'd been penetrated in my ass before, but tonight, I felt especially worried. Damn pregnancy hormones and irrational fears.

Before I could voice my concerns, I felt lips press against my naked spine, tantalizingly soft. Hands wrapped around my chest, kneading my aching breasts. Long fingers tweaked my nipples, and I arched in the contact. Heat settled in my core.

"I'm going to bury myself inside of you," Ryder whispered huskily, still holding my gaze as Asher worked me like a damn guitar.

"Like a casket?" I asked innocently. "Because that makes me think of dead bodies, and I don't know about you, but the last thing I want is a bunch of moldy Rager penises poking at my body."

Cue four simultaneous groans.

Apparently, talking about death and caskets and moldy body parts and Ragers wasn't sexy.

Noted.

Asher moved out of the way, content to sit on the sidelines, while Fallon moved to kneel behind me. Using my juices, he slid a finger into my ass. I shuddered, the full feeling nearly overwhelming me. I felt off-kilter, unable to decipher left from right.

Leaning forward, Asher began to help Fallon lube my ass, his finger unintentionally, or perhaps very intentionally—though I knew that wasn't true, but a girl could hope—brushing against Ronan's cock. I was so aroused, I almost felt physical pain.

Ryder turned my head to the side to kiss me once more, just as Ronan slammed his cock into me. I gasped against Ryder's mouth.

"You ready, baby girl?" Fallon purred. Before I could answer, I felt his hard cock brush my back entrance.

I needed him in me. I needed all of my men in me, surrounding me, making me theirs as thoroughly as they were mine.

I made a pathetic noise, wiggling my ass to get Fallon where I wanted him to be. Ronan cursed at my movement, fingers digging into my hips.

Slowly, ever so slowly, Fallon moved inside of me. I felt stretched, so incredibly full. Pain erupted with such intensity that I cried out before it diminished and was replaced by pleasure. Licks of fire raced through my veins.

It was Fallon who set the pace, slamming into me. Kinky, authoritative bastard.

Ronan placed his hands on my shoulders, meeting Fallon thrust for thrust. They worked my body like an instrument, knowing exactly where to touch me, where to kiss me, when to unravel me. I was a ball of yarn in desperate need of falling apart. These men held the thread in their capable, experienced hands, tugging.

Abruptly, I shattered, the orgasm seeping through every pore in my body. Stars danced in my vision as wave after wave of pure pleasure took me over that precarious edge I'd been tiptoeing around.

Ronan came first, crying out against my shoulder. His body shook from the force of his orgasm. It didn't take long for Fallon to explode as well. My name was a scream on his lips.

Reluctantly, they pulled themselves out of my trembling body and moved to clean themselves up. I felt sated and spent, the sort of feeling you would experience after running a marathon. I wanted nothing more than to curl into a ball and cuddle with my loves until the sun broached the horizon.

But there was still one thing I had to. One more person I had to show my love to. He had been so patient, his eyes emanating nothing but love as he watched me fall apart between his brother and leader.

Crawling on my hands and knees, I pressed a kiss against Ryder's muscular chest. He moaned, falling backwards immediately on the mattress.

I knew that my position allowed the other three a clear view of my pussy, a mixture of all of their fluids combined with mine on display.

I felt a finger brush against my swollen nub before a mouth descended. With my position, I couldn't see who was devouring my clit, tongue and teeth scraping against the sensitive skin.

"You have been so patient," I murmured against Ryder's chest. A cry tore from my throat as a second pair of hands kneaded my tender breasts. "Tell me who you want."

Ryder's breathing was loud, an echo of my own.

"You," he whispered.

"Me?"

I swirled my tongue over his nipple, reveling in his sharp intake of breath. My nails scraped down his chest, even as I moved my lips upwards, my tongue licking at his skin with my ascent. Across the tattoos and scars on his chest. To his jugular vein. To the light scruff on his jawline. I purposely skipped over his lips, much to his dismay, and settled on nipping at his high cheekbones, his dimples, his earlobes.

The mouth against my aching core abruptly pulled away, as did the hands on my breasts.

Slowly, keeping my eyes locked on Ryder's, I sank onto him. His long lashes fluttered closed, lips parting in a breathy exhale. To see a man like Ryder fall apart beneath me was empowering. There was no denying his love for me, his need for me, as he surrendered himself.

When we came together, we didn't fuck. It was much more tender than that. It was two people desperately in love coming together. I didn't know where he ended and I began.

His hips bucked under me, the sounds of flesh hitting flesh filling the now silent room.

"I love you," he whispered, eyes opening with wonder. Wonder and awe, as if he was unaware how someone like me could be here with him. I would never understand his reverence towards me. If anything, I should've felt that about him. About them.

A person like me didn't deserve to have a happy ending. Yet, somehow, I did. I had seven incredible men who, for some inexplicable reason, loved me. I had a child on the way. I had a home and family. I had everything I never knew I needed, never knew I wanted.

As I exploded one last time, I couldn't help but smile. The universe had finally earned my forgiveness by giving me these men. The world could fall apart—hell, it already had—but with them by my side, I knew I could do anything.

They were mine.

I was theirs.

Together, the darkness wasn't too much for us to handle.

BONUS SCENE

ASHER

The pharmacy was small and dilapidated. The walls were crumbling in most places from the storms, but those that remained were covered in graffiti and bleached from the copious amount of sunlight streaming in through the broken windows. The shelves were hanging precariously from the wall, most of them empty of anything of value.

As someone who'd planned to go to medical school before the world turned to shit, it didn't surprise me that I'd been assigned to collect medical supplies. It did overjoy me, however, when Addie asked to tag along.

Addie, who was currently mumbling to herself, replying to some inner thought she must've had. So freaking adorable.

"Wait a damn minute. Back up. Retreat. Abort mission. Boyfriend? Was Asher my boyfriend? Shit. Shit. Shit."

"Boyfriend?" I lifted my head up at her words, a surge of male satisfaction rumbling through me like bolts of lightning. Why did the thought of being Addie's boyfriend make my cock so unbelievably hard? In my mind, we were practically married. Any titles were just a formality at this point. But the thought of her considering me her boyfriend...

Fuck, yeah. I *was* her boyfriend, whether we agreed upon it or not. I didn't even care if that made me a possessive, psychotic asshole.

Addie was mine.

Ours.

And I fucking loved it. Loved her.

As I held her stare, willing her to see the love emanating from my own gaze, I saw a dozen different expressions flit across her beautiful face. Confusion. Fear. Horror...

"Maybe Elena was right. Maybe I was a slut. A ho. A whore," she mumbled, once again oblivious that she was speaking out loud.

"Stop it," I told her fiercely, hating that she perceived herself like that because of the cruel words of jealous women. I didn't give a damn about what others thought of our unconventional relationship, but I knew it bothered her. A lot. And anything that bothered her, bothered me. "There is nothing wrong with you."

"Isn't there?" she countered, lowering her eyes demurely. "I'm in love with seven men, Asher. There is most definitely something wrong with me."

She thought there was something wrong with her? I—

Finally, my brain processed her words, and my legs grew weak. All I could do was stare at her with wide eyes, willing to carve my heart straight from my chest and give it to her on a silver platter if she asked me to.

"Love?" My voice shook as I was assaulted by the enormity of my emotions for this woman. My obsession and need.

From the first moment I saw her in the restaurant, that haunted look in her eyes present, even as she tried to smile, I knew she was made to be mine. Now and forever. I claimed her, and I'd kill anyone who tried to take her from me.

Addie tilted her chin up and met my gaze, her own eyes now defiant as if she'd come to some sort of conclusion.

"Yes. Love." Her voice quivered on that final word, almost as if she was hesitant. Afraid that I wouldn't reciprocate her feelings. Didn't she know that my world revolved around her? That I was completely and utterly obsessed? She took a shuddering breath, rolling her shoulders back, and said, "Asher, I love you."

My breath caught in my throat, and I swore my heart stopped beating for a few seconds, sitting suspended in my chest like a meteorite preparing to strike. My entire life…

Everything led up to this moment.

"Say it again," I whispered, unsure if I'd ever heard anything sweeter.

She blinked at me, her beauty never failing to leave me out of sorts. "I love you."

I dropped my hands to her shoulder, loving the way her silky smooth skin felt beneath my rough palms. Fingering the strap of her tank top, I tightened my grip, wishing I could meld my body with hers. Disappear inside of Addie and become one.

"Again," I demanded, my voice breathless.

"I love you." Something sparked in her eyes, and she wrapped her arm around my neck, playing with the blond hair there. I trembled at her touch, desperate for more of her. I needed her in a way I'd never needed anyone before. A way that was primitive and feral. Somehow, she replaced all of my broken pieces with jewels and gold.

I needed more of her.

Always more.

I was desperate for it.

"Addie, sweetheart." I groaned low in my throat.

"I love you." She tightened her hand in my hair, and my chest vibrated with a low, primal growl.

Fuck, I loved her.

And I would spend the rest of my life showing her how much. Those three simple words weren't nearly enough to express how much she meant to me. Our love…

It transcended time itself. We were the type of love that poets wrote about. I would kill and die for her, all without a second thought. She was the air I breathed, my moral compass, my reason for living in a world that was constantly against me.

I held her stare, willing her to see the sincerity in my eyes. The truth in my words.

Because I wouldn't want to survive the apocalypse if she wasn't there beside me.

"Adelaide, I love you."

And right then and there, in the abandoned, desolate pharmacy, I showed her how much.

THE CHRISTMAS WE SHARE

TOGETHER WE FALL BONUS STORY

CHAPTER 1

ADDIE

*N*ote *to future self—don't ever, not ever, grab a Santa suit you found in an alleyway between a strip club and a Walmart.*

I stared at the heavy fabric with barely veiled disgust. The red suit was twice as big as my body and lined with fur. Black buttons adorned the center, climbing from the bottom of the suit to the neckline. The outfit was completed with a large red cap leading down to a white puff ball.

Inhaling deeply, I smelled the distinct stench of cigarettes, cum, and something coppery. Probably blood. Maybe Santa got ran over by a reindeer or however that song goes.

"Addie," Fallon grunted from the doorframe. I quickly, futilely, tried to hide the depressing costume beneath the bed. Of course, I felt like an idiot immediately after because there was no way in hell he hadn't seen it when he entered.

My husband's eyes were narrowed into thin slits. He was the most intimidating of my husbands, preferring to communicate in grunts and moans instead of actual words. I called the language Caveman. With his light brown hair pulled back in a low ponytail, scruffy beard, and muscular frame, he could've been a caveman.

Ride me like a dinosaur. Bang me with your club, oh Great Caveman.

Fallon's eyes widened imperceptibly—the only indication I'd accidentally spoken out loud. Again. Honestly, I thought all of them were used to it by now. It only got weird when I said that shit in front of the kids.

Awkward.

Fortunately, they were too young to understand what it meant, thank fuck.

"I wanted to do something special for Christmas," I said with a pout, nodding towards the rancid smelling Santa suit permeating the air. Fallon scrunched his nose in distaste.

"Do you know how many diseases you can get from that?" he asked. When I didn't immediately answer, choosing instead to sulk in silence, he released a heavy sigh. "Addie, we can have Christmas if you want. You know we'll do anything for you."

"Really?" I asked, wiping away an invisible tear. I wasn't actually crying, but I realized early on that the tears got me what I wanted. Ryder blamed my sex appeal. Apparently, it was impossible to deny me.

When Fallon nodded once, jaw clenched tightly, I let out a squeal and threw myself into his arms, kissing every available space of skin on his face. He grunted, but his arms tightened around me marginally. The surly asshole could act like he hated the attention, but I knew he secretly loved it. Fallon was a romantic at heart. I had no doubt that if this wasn't the apocalypse, he would've been watching rom-coms while crying over the dismembered corpses of his enemies.

Oh yeah. The world had ended. Probably something I should've mentioned earlier. Natural disasters, viruses, and zombie-like creatures I dubbed as Ragers.

But hey, at least I had seven sexy husbands and four beautiful children. Maybe the world ending was the best thing that ever happened to me.

～

I FOUND Ryder in the living room with Charlotte and Caspian on each knee. The twins were identical in appearance, with auburn hair highlighted with gold and black strands and emerald green eyes. We weren't entirely sure who the biological father was for these two. Tamson, perhaps, or even Calax. It didn't matter, though. All of the guys loved and cherished them as if they were their own.

At two years old, Charlotte was already a bubbly ray of sunshine. I swore her smile could light up any room. Caspian, on the other hand, was quieter than his energetic sister. He watched us all with eyes that seemed to see everything and give nothing away.

Both kids looked up when I entered, a large smile blossoming on Charlotte's cherubic, beautiful face.

"Mommy!" she squealed, wiggling in Ryder's vise-like grip. With a weary chuckle, Ryder placed our daughter on the ground and watched as she scrambled towards me. She was capable of walking short distances. Anything farther, and she would face-plant on the ground. It wasn't because of her age—my daughter was just a clumsy fuck. When she was within reach, I scooped her up and took her into my arms.

"Hi, my little angel," I said, kissing her chubby cheek. She giggled, immediately pulling on my brown locks.

"Daddy Ryder was reading us a story," she proclaimed with a self-indulgent grin. I ruffled her auburn curls.

"Attempting," Ryder said, still holding Caspian. "The little devils keep talking over me."

Charlotte rolled her eyes.

"Your story was boring." She glared at the picture book Ryder had discarded when I entered as if it had personally offended her. "I like Daddy Asher's stories better."

I knew Asher had been reading the twins *War and Peace* before bed each night. I hadn't realized that she'd actually been listening.

Ryder muttered something inarticulate beneath his breath—something about Asher being a kiss-ass. I gave him a look at his language, and he smiled sheepishly, blowing me a kiss.

Even after all these years, Ryder was still capable of making my heart pound. He was sexy, there was no getting around it. With obsidian skin covered in tattoos, buzzed black hair, and broad shoulders leading down to a tapered waist, he was every girl's bad boy, rocker wet dream.

And he was mine.

Still holding Charlotte, I moved to plant a chaste kiss on Ryder's plush, unbelievably soft mouth. His eyes heated exponentially, a promise of what was to come the second we were alone. My body wouldn't get impregnated by itself, you know. This vagina needed cock, or else it got prickly. Literally.

Smiling softly, I peered down at Caspian. His own smile was tentative, soft, but it made his entire face light up like a candle was lit beneath the surface. I sometimes wondered if Caspian had autism like his uncle. I wouldn't know until he was older, though. Either way, I loved him with my entire heart.

"How's my handsome man doing?" I asked, kissing his forehead.

"Good," Ryder answered, and I shot him a look.

Charlotte giggled, slapping at my arm until I deposited her on Ryder's lap beside her brother.

"She wasn't talking to you, silly!" Charlotte exclaimed. "She was talking to Caspian!"

My daughter was abnormally smart for her age, already able to speak coherently and in complete sentences. Doc suggested we test both of their IQs, but a mother always knew—my children were geniuses. Be jealous.

"Wasn't talking to me?" Ryder put his hand on his chest in mock horror. "But I'm the most handsome man!"

"No, you're ugly!" Charlotte tittered, and even Caspian offered a timid grin. The kids had been spending way too much time with Doc.

"I'm going to go see if dinner's ready," I told Ryder. "And once the kids are in bed, we're going to have a family meeting."

His eyes flashed with concern, but he nodded, a brilliant grin crossing his face when he stared down at our two babies. With one last kiss for all three of them, I headed to the kitchen where Ronan and Asher were preparing dinner.

We had a schedule for household chores, but Ronan and Asher were by far the best cooks. We once put Calax on the cooking rotation and… Well…let's just say that no one left the bathroom for days. And we weren't even having an orgy, so I could say with certainty that it was a big disappointment.

Ronan was dancing to music only he could hear, while Asher watched on with an amused, albeit confused, smile. Two pots were boiling on the stove—we had to cook quadruple the normal amount. Feeding seven guys, one hormonal female—me, if you were wondering—and four kids required a shit ton of food. Sometimes my brother, Nik, and his boyfriend, Tommy, came to visit. Sometimes Doc stopped by. Other times, Tonya and her husband took over our tiny kitchen.

But tonight, it would just be us.

"Something smells delicious," I purred, dancing over to where Ronan was shaking his sculpted ass. I wrapped my arms around his muscular waist and pressed a soft kiss to his neck. Goosebumps immediately erupted on his dark skin, and I couldn't stop the giddy smile from cleaving my face in two even if I tried. Ronan was Ryder's half-brother and just as handsome. Like his brother, he was covered in tattoos, the most prominent being a unicorn over his chest.

"Stop sniffing me, woman," Ronan jested, setting down the spoon he was using to stir before grabbing both my hands. The position pulled me even further until my front was pressed snugly against his back.

"You're too sniffable," I countered. And because I could—it was in our vows and everything—I leaned forward and licked a trail across his shoulder blades. Thank fuck for tank tops or else that would've been weird.

He shivered delicately, tsking beneath his breath.

"Naughty, naughty girl. I'm going to have to punish you." His voice was low and raspy and had the desired reaction. My panties? Completely wet. Flooded.

Ronan and Tamson were the only two of my husbands into…um…alternative sex. Sometimes they would explore my body together, Tamson commanding and us obeying like a well-oiled machine.

The thought of a punishment…

My mind flashed to the one room of the house we kept under lock and key. It was where we put our toys. I made the mistake of saying that in front of Maya, our eldest daughter, and she immediately demanded we show her. I'd calmly stated I would show her when she was older, to which Calax had punched a wall and Fallon had turned bright red with anger in response. I pitied the man—or men—who tried to date my daughters. Some girls had to deal with one overprotective and slightly psychotic father. My kids had to deal with seven.

"I'm feeling neglected," Asher said with a teasing grin. I glanced over my shoulder to see his eyes burning with banked fire. His blond hair, slightly longer than usual, was ruffled. Asher was model handsome—the stereotypical boy next door male. Quarterback of the football team. Class president. Modeling gig to earn some extra cash.

Except my boy next door? He was a little bit of a psychopath. With me and the kids, he was nothing but gentle and kind, warmth emanating from his bright eyes. With everyone else? The man could be a scary motherfucker. He would not hesitate to rip you apart with his bare hands if you dared to hurt his family.

"Ash, get your cute ass over here," I said, still clinging to Ronan like a spider monkey. Asher smirked at my antics but complied with an easy grin. A moment later, his hard, chiseled body was pressed against my back, the evidence of his arousal poking me. Being the sweet wife I was, I gyrated against him, eliciting a soft moan from his throat. Ronan chuckled.

"Definitely need to punish her," Asher said breathlessly, agreeing with Ronan's earlier statement. I felt lips brushing against my neck, pushing aside my mane of brown curls.

"Fuck, Ash…"

"Don't forget about me," Ronan whined, spinning around and pressing me further against Asher. Caged in between my two males was a kind of exquisite torture. Heaven. Absolute heaven.

"Maybe it can be your Christmas present," I said with a sly smile. "I'll wear nothing but wrapping paper—"

"Mommy!"

The three of us scrambled apart like our asses were on fire. A second later, the kitchen door was pushed open and Maya ran in. Declan and Calax trailed behind her.

Maya was no doubt Asher's biological daughter, though like with the twins and the baby, all of the guys treated her as their own. Her golden hair hung just to her waist in thick, beautiful waves. Her face was perfectly symmetrical, and her emerald green eyes were framed by abnormally long lashes. She was going to be a heart-breaker when she grew up.

And her dads would be ball breakers if any person was foolish enough to stare at her longer than a second. Nah. I wouldn't even give it a second. The poor boy would last less than a millisecond before he was attacked. In the future, of course. Maya was only six years old. She still had centuries before she had to worry about dating.

"Hey, princess," I said, scooping her up. Her small hands immediately grabbed at my hair, braiding the silky strands.

"Guess what?" The little girl was practically vibrating with excitement and energy. A beatific smile made twin dimples appear on her cheeks. But when your daughter smiled like that…

You should be scared. Very, very scared.

"What?" I asked, casting a glance at her sheepish fathers. Well, Declan was sheep-ish, ducking his head. Calax merely met my stare with a quirk of his brow, daring me to say something. Alas, he was right—my lips were meant for something better. Namely, wrapped around his cock.

It was official—the apocalypse had turned me into a shameless hussy.

"Daddy Calax allowed me to kill my first Rager!" she said enthusiastically.

My eyes narrowed at the man in question. "He did, did he?"

"Daddy Ducky gave me his favorite sword. Taught me how to swing it! Isn't that cool?"

I swiveled my gaze to land on my second idiotic husband. "He did, did he?" Without another word, I placed my daughter into Asher's waiting arms and stomped towards Idiots One and Two.

"Now, baby, let me explain—" Calax began, but I cut him off with a series of rapid gestures. Declan's eyes followed my hands as I signed… Well, let's just say it wasn't appropriate for young kids to hear.

Declan had lost his hearing as a child, and while he perceived it as a handicap, I saw it as something amazing. For one, our entire family knew a language that not many people did. For two, he was able to rely on his enhanced other senses. I was pretty sure Declan was capable of sniffing out Ragers from miles away. And no, I wasn't exaggerating. Sheesh.

"You guys are on Santa's naughty list," I finished at last, both speaking and signing to emphasize my frustration. And to think, I wanted to wear a sexy elf costume to celebrate the holidays tonight.

Not. Fucking. Happening.

They could cuddle with their coal for all the shits I gave.

CHAPTER 2

$\mathcal{W}$e reconvened in the living room after the kids were put to bed. I found myself curled up on Tamson's lap as his hand absentmindedly rubbed soothing patterns on my leg through my leggings.

Fallon stood at the front of the room, always the unofficial leader. I couldn't help but admire how sexy he looked in his tight jeans and pressed shirt. Every muscle was clearly accentuated. His light brown hair, highlighted with gold, was pulled back into a low ponytail.

"We called this family meeting because Addie has something she wishes to share with us," he began, and suddenly, I found myself the center of attention of seven sinfully hot men. My lady parts did a mental dance at their heated stares, but I warned myself to remain calm.

Even though I want to ride the cock train—

"Addie," Tamson said through a cough, shifting uncomfortably. I felt his hardness growing against my ass. "You're speaking out loud again, love."

"Well, shit. Sorry. I just see cocks, and my vagina opens for business. She's a kinky hussy, that one. And yes, I'm speaking as if my vagina is its own separate entity. I mean, why can't it be? She likes to eat just like any person. But I suppose her appetite is a little more...elaborate than normal. I mean, how many people can claim they feast on cocks? Well, seven cocks. She likes them," I babbled.

Cue seven blank stares.

"Shit, Kitten," Ryder murmured, readjusting himself in his pants.

"That dirty mouth of yours is going to get you in trouble," added Ronan, eyes glinting with amusement and banked fire.

"The good kind?" Being the bitch I was, I rubbed myself against Tamson's rapidly growing erection. His hands landed on my waist in an attempt to still me.

"Adelaide," he warned darkly, and his voice sent flutters straight from my stomach to my pussy.

"Can we get back on topic, please?" Fallon crossed his arms over his chest, but his eyes were alight with amusement. He leaned against the pillar separating the living room from the kitchen.

"Oh. Right. Back on topic. Because that's what mature women do." I nodded my head seriously. "So, as some of you may know, it's getting close to Christmas." I flickered my gaze from one male to another, attempting to gauge their reactions. I saw a wide display of amusement, confusion, and lust remaining from my comments earlier.

"And...?" Asher asked, not unkindly. When I glanced at him, he offered me a soft, encouraging smile.

Clearing my throat, I lifted my hands to both sign and talk at the same time. Declan was skilled at reading lips, but I tried to make things as easy for him as I could. Fortunately, I'd been skilled in sign language since I was a young child.

"I want to celebrate Christmas," I admitted. "A Christmas tree, presents, the whole shebang."

Why did it feel like I was confessing to murder? Was I really so nervous about how they would react? I felt my insides twist in half a dozen knots.

For a moment, the men were silent as they digested my words. Calax, of all people, imploded the silence with a gruff, "Fine."

"Yeah?" I asked, snapping my eyes up. And up. And up. And up. Calax was a giant.

"Of course, baby. Anything for you."

Tamson's hands tightened imperceptibly on my waist, warmth migrating from where our bodies touched and settling in my chest.

"I'm in. I want our children to enjoy the best life possible," he whispered wistfully, and I offered him a soft smile in return.

"Hell yeah!" Ronan cheered, and Ryder was quick to echo his brother. Declan and Asher both nodded with timid smiles on their handsome faces. As one, we all turned towards Fallon.

He stood domineeringly over our group, his face harshly masculine. A savage kind of beauty, one reserved for predators and monsters.

But he was my monster.

"I'll take a group to get the Christmas tree tomorrow," he conceded with a roll of his eyes. But his lips? Those were most definitely curved into a cocksure smile. He could pretend to act growly and pissed all he wanted, but there was nothing he wouldn't do for me and his family. Hell, I was pretty sure I could convince him to wear the Santa Claus costume.

Hmmm...Mr. and Mrs. Claus. I was sure that was a kink waiting to happen.

~

I AWOKE to soft lips trailing up my neck. Instinctively, I arched it to grant the kisser better access.

With a contented hum, I turned onto my side, lips parted to claim the lips of my mysterious visitor, when a hand slapped down on my ass. I released a startled yelp as my eyes popped open.

Tamson's hooded gaze met mine, his glasses discarded and dark red hair wildly disheveled. Tam was the nerd you loved to read about in romance novels—timid on the outside, but dominant in bed. The only difference? Tamson was very, very real.

"You think you can get away with teasing me?" he whispered, his hand curling around my ass cheek.

"Teasing?" I gasped as he ducked his head and suckled on the sensitive skin of my shoulder. "I don't tease. I just… Oh fuck, don't stop. I'll have your babies."

"You already had my babies," he pointed out, smiling down at me. While his smile was glorious and everything, I wanted his lips on my skin again, damnit!

A second set of hands tugged at the waistband of my sleep shorts, pulling them down. My arousal ricocheted up a notch. I hadn't realized there was anyone else in the room.

Our house was immense. It had to be with seven husbands, one slightly psychotic wife, and a bunch of kids. We'd decided unanimously to have one big room that fit all of us. However, we each had a room of our own if we needed space.

We never used those rooms for sleeping.

Despite that, our schedules were so chaotic and hectic that we were never all in bed at the same time. We always had one man on patrol, another two visiting the local medical center and Doc, and two more making supply runs. I never knew who would show up in bed with me.

The mysterious hands removed my panties as well, leaving me naked from the bottom down.

"You were naughty," Tamson continued, resuming his stroking. A moment later, his palm smacked down on the bare skin of my ass. I released a startled mewl, arching against him, and his hand immediately began to rub the sting away.

"Am I on Santa's naughty list?" I murmured huskily.

Because, yeah, I never said I was good at the whole dirty talk thing.

I think the worst time was when I mentioned Ronan's nickname, Leprechaun, and asked if his cock was magically delicious.

He was laughing too hard to continue fucking me.

Tamson's rough façade cracked briefly as he smiled before he quickly masked it with a serious expression.

"Right on top."

I felt lips kiss the bottom of my spine and then my ass cheek. I jumped again, a pathetic sound leaving my throat.

Oh, I can be on top, all right…

"Be a good girl, and suck my cock. Maybe I'll let you have an orgasm." The man behind me helped me to my knees, and Tamson wasted no time unbuttoning his pants and pushing them to his knees. His cock sprung free, dripping with pre-cum.

"Or you can just be a good husband and give me one anyway," I suggested, even as I licked my lips.

"That's not the way it works, Princess," Ronan whispered, licking a pathway up my spine and pulling my shirt up in the process. I hadn't worn my bra to bed, and my breasts hung free, nipples already peaked. Tamson's eyes heated as he leaned down, his tongue swirling around first one nipple and then the next. His teeth grazed the sensitive nub, the combination of pleasure and pain nearly taking me over the edge.

Would it be weird if I said, "Ride me, Santa?"

Too kinky?

Damn. Now I wished I'd insisted that one of them wore the Santa outfit.

"Hands and knees," Tam ordered, and I complied easily. Honestly, he could ask me to lasso him and I would do so with a smile. I not only loved these men, but trusted them. They knew my body better than I did, and they were capable of bringing me to the precipice of pleasure before I stumbled face-first off the cliff.

Before Tam could instruct me further, my tongue darted out to lick the slit of his cock. His familiar, salty taste awoke every nerve within me. I wanted to taste more of him—*all* of him.

"Fuck," Tam cursed, hips jerking forward. I smiled wickedly at my sweet lover before taking him completely in my mouth. There were a few things I'd learned about blow jobs. First, you had to hollow your cheeks and breathe through your nose. Oh, and not gag. I imagined it wouldn't be sexy to have vomit on your cock. "Ronan, reward my good girl," Tam bit out.

Ronan didn't need any more encouragement before he entered me from behind. It took me a moment to adjust to his length, but soon, I was eagerly moving my hips.

"I didn't say you could stop sucking," Tam snapped, and I realized my lips had left Tamson's cock. That just wouldn't do.

"You're so tight, Princess. So perfect. My perfect wife," Ronan murmured, fingers tightening on my hips.

"Does she feel good?" Tamson asked roughly, and Ronan released a pained whimper in response. One hand fisting in my hair to slow my movements, Tam continued, "Do you like his big cock filling you? Does it feel good?"

I believed I muttered something inarticulate around his girth. Probably along the lines of, "Fuck me faster, motherfucker, or else I'll castrate you and feed your severed cock to Ragers."

With Tamson's hand in my hair, I couldn't move my head, but I could move my mouth. My tongue snaked out to lick the sensitive skin of his cock, and Tam released a startled curse.

After that...

It was a flurry of rapid thrusts, hums, and curses. Ronan pounded into me from behind, his balls smacking against my clit with each thrust. Tamson's eyes closed in bliss as he fucked my mouth. One of these days, I was going to demand complete control of my red-haired lover. For now, I allowed him to do what he wanted with my body.

We climbed up the cliff together, and we jumped off together as well. My orgasm liquefied my veins, and white-hot pleasure cascaded through me. Ronan came a moment later, his cock growing inside of me as he released his seed.

Tam, always the showoff, held off for a few more erratic thrusts. When he came, he exploded with the force of a tsunami. From experience, I knew to swallow every last drop and lick away the cum remaining on his semi-hard dick.

We collapsed on the mattress, sweaty and sated.

"I love you guys so fucking much," I whispered. One would think time would diminish the feelings I felt for these men, but that couldn't be further from the truth. Each and every day, I grew impossibly more in love with them.

"I love you too, Princess. More than you could ever know," Ronan whispered, placing my head on his chest. He indolently traced circles on my bare shoulder.

"You're my entire world," Tam confessed, wrapping an arm around my waist. He must've stripped off the rest of his clothes after our tryst. His bare stomach pressed against my back as he tenderly kissed my shoulder. "I love you. And I love this family you gave me."

I fell asleep in the arms of two of the men I loved most in the world. Visions of sugarplums danced in my head.

And cocks. Lots and lots of cocks.

You can take the ho out of the girl, but you can't take the girl out of the ho. And me? I was a shameless hussy when it came to these men. I owned my sexuality.

You would too if you had men at your beck and call that looked like models and were smart, funny, and sweet. I hit the vagina jackpot.

CHAPTER 3

ADDIE

The tree had seen better days. It was taller than an average tree, nearly brushing the ceiling, with keen pine needles. However, the trunk was beginning to deteriorate and the needles were turning an ugly shade of brown. Still, it was better than nothing.

"It's harder than you think to find a Christmas tree during the apocalypse," Calax muttered. My giant had brown stains on his cheeks and pants. Black dirt was embedded beneath his fingernails.

"Thank you, Callie," I whispered, pushing up to the tips of my toes to kiss his plush lips. His rough stubble brushed against my chin and cheeks as we deepened the kiss. Too soon, a throat cleared behind us, and we reluctantly broke apart.

"As much as I hate interrupting," Declan signed with a cocksure grin. *"Asher found some decorations."*

And *that* was how we spent the evening. Golden tinsel was sewn across the tree, glistening in the sunlight. An assortment of silver and red bulbs were also applied, names etched into the sides. Apparently, there had been an Ali and Dennis in this house before we occupied it. Poor folks. Probably long dead by now.

"Mommy! Mommy! Can I put the angel on top?" Maya pleaded, bouncing from foot to foot. My little beauty was bedecked in an ugly Christmas sweater displaying Rudolph. Combined with her Santa hat and elf shoes, she was too cute for words.

"If you're careful," I said, nodding towards the ladder. Before she could take a step on it, Fallon scooped her up and held her. She giggled, straining her tiny arm up to position the angel.

"How does it look?" she asked once Fallon deposited her on her feet.

"No fair! I wanted to do the angel!" Charlotte whined, stomping her foot. She turned towards Declan and began to rapidly sign. Her sign language was still rusty, but she was improving every day. Caspian, however, was already fluent. I had no doubt that my little man would turn into a genius.

Ryder was holding our youngest child—a newborn boy. His skin was lightly tanned, like burnt copper, and he had a splatter of dark hair on his head. My guess? Either Ryder's or Ronan's biological son.

"The house looks amazing, Kitten," Ryder said, shifting the baby from one arm to the other. Matthias was a perfect baby, and I wasn't just saying that lightly. This momma had gone through three other children. I knew my shit.

He barely ever cried, and for the most part, he behaved exceptionally well for an eight-month-old.

"It is, isn't it?" I turned to survey the room. The blinds were pushed back from the glass windows, allowing in a copious amount of light. Our living room was the biggest in the house, consisting of three couches, two tables, and a pool table against the far wall. I had no doubt the previous occupants had been rich as fuck. The entire area was decorated with tiny Santas, green and red tinsel, and elves. I had to admit— it *did* look good. Amazing, actually. It was almost impossible to think that the apocalypse was happening outside the walls of our safe home.

However, the barbed wire fence outside ruined the illusion of normalcy.

"We need to invite Nik and Tommy over," I began, ticking them off on my fingers. "Doc, of course. And his new boyfriend. Tonya, Jared, and Davis."

"Consider it done," Calax said, moving to stand behind me. His arms encircled my waist, and he pressed his lips to the top of my head.

"I'll give you oral," I replied seriously in a whisper. His eyes heated briefly, and his hand inconspicuously groped my ass. With a final pat, he released me and stepped back.

"I'll hold you to that, baby."

"Hold mommy to what?" piped in Charlotte. She was sitting on Maya's back on the couch, the older girl half-heartedly attempting to push her off. Caspian watched them with an amused, slightly curious expression.

"Nothing, little girl. I'll tell you when you're older," I sang, dancing forward and taking her hands in mine.

"No, you won't," Calax muttered under his breath, but I ignored him, pulling my daughter into a dance.

"It's Christmas!" I sang in a purposely off-key.

"Christmas!" Charlotte parroted, extending a hand to Maya. She took it with a smile.

As we danced around the living room, my men and Caspian looking on, I'd never felt such happiness. My entire life had been a pit of darkness and despair...until them. Until they slammed into my life and turned it upside down.

They not only gave me happiness, but a family. *My* family.

How did I get so lucky?

CHAPTER 4

ADDIE

I woke up at the ass crack of dawn, sneaking down the stairs. The generator was silent, so every light in the house was off. I had to rely on the moon illuminating everything in soft yellows and whites.

With bated breath, I pulled open the closet door beneath the staircase. It creaked on its hinges, and I winced, waiting for one of the many doors to open accompanied by a stampede of footsteps. When the halls remained silent, I released the breath I'd been holding and grabbed the brown bag shoved beneath my winter coat.

"What are you doing?" a gruff voice demanded from behind me. I jumped, just barely covering my mouth before I could release a startled scream, and spun to face the intruder.

Calax leaned against the wall, giant arms crossed and face shadowed in darkness.

"Jesus Christ, Callie, you scared the daylights out of me!" I placed my hand over my heart and narrowed my eyes. Unfortunately, the latter gesture was lost in the darkness obscuring us both.

"It's nighttime," he pointed out with a quirk of his lips. "Technically, I scared the nighttime out of you."

"What are you doing?" I demanded, discreetly trying to step in front of the brown bag. Okay, so maybe "discreet" and "me" didn't really go together. I'd be the first to admit I practically lunged to the side, placing one hand on the wall in an attempt at nonchalance.

Nailed it.

"You think I wouldn't notice you sneaking out of bed?" he asked, and I could hear the amusement evident in his voice.

"I was hoping my sexual skills wore you out last night," I deadpanned, my body flushing at the memories of Calax's large hands on my breasts as Declan pounded into me from behind. Asher had moved my hair away from my neck to kiss the skin there…

"What are you up to?" he asked, still sounding too damn amused for his own good.

"Nothing," I blurted. "Except for masturbation."

Damnit, Addie, that's *what you come up with?*

With a heavy sigh, Calax stalked forward, easily picked me up in his arms, and dropped me behind him.

"No! Don't look!" I whispered-yelled, jumping on his back and attempting to cover his eyes with my hands.

He froze underneath me, his body hewn from stone. "Is that… Did you get us presents? Did you get *me* a present?"

"Err…" Instead of answering, I pressed my lips to his neck and began to trail kisses up and down. Goosebumps erupted in their wake.

"Quit trying to distract me, baby," Calax grumbled roughly. I was pleased when his breath hitched ever so slightly.

"It's only a distraction if it's working," I whispered against his skin, my teeth grazing his earlobe. "Is it working?"

In the next second, he had me pinned against the wall, his large arms beneath my ass to keep me up.

"Nope," he said resolutely, but the scarce lighting allowed me to see the banked heat lingering just beneath the surface. "Now, baby, I thought we agreed that we weren't doing presents this year."

I snaked my arms around his neck, my fingers playing with the short hairs at the nape of his neck. He grunted, but his hands didn't release me. My unfaltering, loyal, reliable giant.

"I lied," I said unashamedly. His eyes flickered to the bag once more, and his lips set into a grim line.

"You even got the cat something?" he asked, voice heady with disbelief.

"Mof is a part of my family too," I protested, using one hand to cup his cheek and bring his face back to me. His stubble was scratchy beneath my palm, eliciting sparks of liquid pleasure. I had distinct memories of that stubble on other parts of my body…

Focus, Addie. Rein in the vagina. I repeat, rein in the vagina.

"The presents aren't that great," I assured him. "You guys wouldn't let me leave the house to go shopping." The last part was said on a grumble. Overprotective fools. "However, there are a lot of things I found in the storage room down in the basement. I think you'll like your presents."

"I thought we agreed on only getting presents for the children," Calax pointed out. The guys had gone to the store a few days ago to retrieve dolls for the girls, books, clothing, and Caspian's favorite toy cars.

"I'm an equal opportunity gifter," I responded seriously.

He made a face at me—a face I couldn't resist kissing. "Is that why you insisted on wearing all red to bed?"

"I'm Santa!" I wiggled my hips until he put me down. Striking a pose, I added, "A sexier Santa, but Santa all the same."

It wasn't the disgusting Santa suit I'd found in an alleyway. I wasn't that stupid. Instead, it was a red lace nightgown with white trim and a sweetheart neckline.

"Fuck, baby," Calax cursed as I lifted the hem of my dress, revealing a sliver of creamy white thigh.

"Yes, that's a good idea," I agreed. "Fuck me."

He grabbed my wrist and pushed me into the closet. I released a very girly giggle as he pushed me down onto the floor.

"Not on the presents!" I protested, kicking the bag away. "Now, show me that I'm a ho ho ho." Calax groaned at my rather amazing pun before doing exactly that.

Doc was the first to arrive, shrugging off his winter coat and boots. A younger man trailed after him, glancing anxiously at first me and then the seven men behind me. Yeah. I supposed we were intimidating to virgin eyes.

"Doc!" I exclaimed, wrapping my arms around his frail waist. He had lost a lot of weight in the last couple of years. Working tirelessly on a cure and coping with the death of his boyfriend nearly destroyed him. However, he was slowly regaining his appetite and signature smirk. The light hadn't completely diminished from his eyes.

"Uncle Barry!" a tiny voice squealed. A moment later, Maya flew down the stairs and jumped into his arms.

Yeah. Doc's name was Barry. It shocked me too.

"How's my favorite girl doing?" Doc ruffled her golden hair, and she giggled.

"But I want to be your favorite girl!" Charlotte protested from where she was being held by Declan.

"You guys are all my favorites," Doc relented, leaning forward to peck Charlotte on the cheek. He raised a hand for Caspian to high five, understanding my son's aversion to touch.

Turning away from them, I smiled at the young man still hovering in the doorway. "And you must be Gabriel. Doc has told me a lot about you." Gabriel was an attractive man with light brown hair, mossy green eyes, and twin dimples. Apparently, they'd met at the research facility and hit it off. Not only was Gabriel good looking, but he was a genius as well. Doc hit the jackpot with that one.

"You can call me Gabe," he said, extending a hand for me to shake. Ignoring the proffered hand, I pulled him into a hug.

"Sorry! I'm a hugger!"

"And she also has seven husbands," Fallon responded gruffly. "So keep your hands above the waist at all times."

I rolled my eyes at his possessive display, and Gabe's body rumbled with his laughter.

"Sorry. I only bat for one team." He patted my back once before releasing me.

"Back off," Doc added good-naturedly. "He's mine. You don't need anyone else in your harem."

I chuckled, reaching behind me to slap Doc's stomach.

"Oh, shut up."

Before he could retort, the front door opened once more and Tommy and Nikolai entered. I was across the foyer in less than a second, grabbing both of them into a vise-like hug. Tommy chuckled and smoothed down my hair, but Nik went rigid. After a moment, one of his arms wrapped around my waist to return the hug.

"I missed you guys so much. I'm so happy you were able to come."

"The guys been treating you okay?" Tommy asked gruffly, pushing me back to survey me. If I thought of Tommy as my younger brother, he thought of me as his younger sister. It was a weird relationship, but it worked for the two of us. Our bond only solidified when he began dating my brother. Nik needed someone like him, and they brought out the best in each other.

"The guys have been treating me amazing!" I said, winking. He made a face at my double entendre.

"Uncle Tommy! Uncle Nik!" Charlotte practically leaped out of Declan's arms to run towards us.

"Careful, Spitfire," I joked, stepping back so my daughter could smother my brothers in her love.

"Where's the baby?" Tommy demanded as Nik conversed softly with my daughter.

Tamson stepped forward holding our youngest son. Without preamble, Tommy took the baby from my husband and rocked him.

My smile was so fucking big, I was afraid it would get stuck that way. But...

Would that be a bad thing?

~

"Dead puppies! No, um, Christmas trees! No... Ragers pissing on the bodies of dead men!" Tonya jumped up from her seat and clapped her hands excitedly, growing increasingly more animated with each guess.

Asher, who was currently acting out the card for our game of charades, frowned. "How did you go from Christmas trees to Ragers taking a piss?"

"She's been spending way too much time with Adelaide," Jared grumbled, but he threw me a soft smile to lessen the sting of his words.

"Too much time with all this amazingness?" I reached across Nik to grab a chocolate chip cookie smothered in red and green frosting. Tonya had complained vehemently when she caught sight of the treats. Claimed they were too sweet and would kill me faster than the Ragers could.

Death by cookies. What a way to go.

"Well, what were you?" Tonya asked Asher, throwing her hands up in the air. Asher displayed his piece of paper that read "Christmas shopper."

Either Asher really sucked at acting or Tonya really sucked at guessing. I was too preoccupied with my cookie to watch.

"My turn! My turn! My turn!" Maya squealed, jumping out of Tommy's lap and racing to the Santa hat. With an excited giggle, she procured a slip of paper, her thin brows furrowing as she struggled to read the word.

"Do you need help, darling?" I asked, but she shook her head adamantly, golden locks swaying.

"No! I got it!" Her face twisted slightly. "I'm an angel!" she blurted.

Tamson released a heavy sigh. "Sweetheart, the whole point of the game is for us to guess what you are."

Maya nodded seriously. "Okay! I fly, and I have a halo."

"Without words," added Ryder with a grin.

My daughter pouted. Honest-to-God pouted. She really did take after me. She should consider using that pout the next time she tried to ask for a dog. Already, I could see the adults bending to her will under her puppy dog stare.

"She can play the game however she wants," Calax said gruffly, one arm wrapped around Caspian and the other holding Mof.

"Oh! Shit!" I exclaimed suddenly as something occurred to me. Before any of the others could question my eccentric but not uncommon behavior, I was racing towards the kitchen where a heavy cloud of smoke hung over the oven. "Shit. Shit. Shit."

Before I could grab an oven mitt, Fallon stealthily stepped in front of me and removed the tray of burnt cookies from the oven. Tears sprung to my eyes as I stared at the rock hard, charred remains of Christmas tree-shaped cookies.

"Addie," Fallon began, but he paused when he took stock of my expression. "Why the fuck are you crying?"

"Because I burnt the cookies," I whispered hoarsely. His brows pressed into a thin line as he surveyed me.

"And?"

"And?" I asked, laughing humorlessly. "And this is the first Christmas we've celebrated since the apocalypse began. The first Christmas as a family! And I just ruined it."

He took a tentative step closer and placed a hand on my shoulder. "You're being hard on yourself."

"Am I? Because I just burnt the second batch of cookies. We turned the generator on specifically for this, and I had to go fuck things up—"

"Hey!" Fallon cut me off, voice as domineering as always. He leveled me with a no-nonsense stare. "Don't talk about yourself like that. Everyone's having a great time, and the first batch of cookies was delicious. Love, it'll be okay. It's just cookies."

I wiped helplessly at the tears cascading down my cheeks. "I just… I just want this Christmas to be perfect, you know? We deserve it after all the shit we've been through. I even got a fucking Santa costume—"

"That cesspool?" His face scrunched comically in disbelief, and I couldn't help but laugh.

"It seemed like a good idea at the time." I shrugged helplessly. "Sorry if I'm being a little dramatic," I said, ignoring the quirk of his brow when I said "little."

"Go back to the living room," Fallon said suddenly, swatting at my butt. He had a faraway look in his eyes, but there was a tiny smile pulling up his lips.

"What are you planning?"

As eloquent as ever, Fallon merely grunted in response.

CHAPTER 5

ADDIE

*I*t turned out I didn't have to wait long to discover what Fallon was up to. As the kids played a card game with Nik and Tommy and the adults conversed on the couch, I became aware of the twinkling of bells. I whipped my head in the direction the noise was coming from.

"Oh my—" I began, covering my mouth to keep from laughing.

"God," Tonya finished, eyes wide.

The guys broke into laughter, quickly muffling it at my scathing glare.

"Ho! Ho! Ho! Merry Christmas!"

Fallon stood in the doorway, bedecked in the red Santa costume I'd stolen. What appeared to be pillows were pushed up his shirt, giving him the appearance of being thicker than he actually was. A white, scraggly beard hung from his face. Wait… beard? Where the fuck had he gotten a beard? I was almost one hundred percent positive that the Santa costume hadn't come with one.

"Santa!" Charlotte screamed, jumping to her feet and practically plowing Fallon over.

"Merry Christmas!" Fallon said in a deep, raspy voice.

"Is this really happening? Is Santa truly here?" Maya whispered to me in disbelief. She was bouncing from foot to foot, eyes trained on the jolly man. And I say jolly loosely. Fallon had never been known for his Christmas cheer, if you know what I mean. He was the Scrooge to my Cratchit, but I loved him just the same.

"Go say hi!" I replied, pushing her shoulder encouragingly. She didn't need to be told twice. In the next second, she was across the room and in his arms, chatting enigmatically about how good of a girl she had been this year.

My heart filled with warmth as I stared at my husband. Love for him nearly consumed me. How did I get so lucky?

"I can't believe he did this," Declan signed, moving to stand beside me. He shook his head with a wry grin on his lips.

"He loves me, and he loves his children," I replied. "He'll do anything for us."

Declan's eyes warmed as he pressed a kiss to my forehead. When he pulled away, I was surprised to see tears in his eyes. *"Thank you for giving me this family, Addie. I love you."*

"I love you too," I signed back, stepping onto my tiptoes to offer him a proper kiss on the lips. A throat clearing interrupted our moment. I turned to find Tommy glaring threateningly at Declan, and Nik smiling softly.

"Shall we open presents now?" my younger brother asked, twining his fingers together with Tommy's.

"Ho! Ho! Ho! That's a great idea!" Fallon exclaimed with forced cheerfulness. The kids released a whoop and moved to congregate around the tree. Before I could join them, Fallon grabbed my hand and pulled me to a halting stop. "And you…have you been a good girl or a bad girl this year?" he asked in a whisper.

I smiled coyly. "I've been very, very bad. I believe you'll have to punish me." I had the pleasure of watching heat flare to life in his eyes. Honestly, I was tempted to pull him into one of the bedrooms and leave the party for an hour or two.

But alas, I couldn't very well fuck Santa, now could I?

THE KIDS LOVED THEIR PRESENTS. A dollhouse for Charlotte, a bow and arrow for Maya—Calax was still on my shit list for that one—and a toy train for Caspian. My husbands had even remembered to grab presents for my little man—a new blanket, pacifier, and rattle.

Fallon had changed out of his Santa costume, arriving back down as I opened up my present from all the guys. I covered my mouth, tears filling my eyes.

"Is this…?"

"It's from all of us," Asher admitted sheepishly. "Do you like it?"

More tears slid down my cheeks as I stared at the thoughtful present my amazing husbands had gifted me. It was a collage of pictures taken with old rolls of Kodak instant print film—pictures of me and them, our kids, Nik and Tommy, Doc, and Tonya. The entire collection was displayed in an intricately carved frame. By the woodwork, I had no doubt Calax was behind it. He'd taken up the hobby shortly after we settled down.

"Thank you," I whispered hoarsely. "I love it. And I love all of you."

"Christmas is about family," Ronan said with a shrug, but there were unshed tears in his eyes. "We wanted to show you how important you and our kids are to us."

"Our entire world," Ryder agreed, squeezing my shoulders. Nik placed his hand on my knee from where he was sitting next to me. While his attention was on the bright red jacket we'd gotten him, I knew he was listening intently to our conversation.

"I love each and every one of you." I lifted my gaze to include the others, even

Doc, Tonya, Jared, and Davis. "You're my family… Which brings me to the final gift of the night."

"Final gift?" Calax asked, glancing up from where he was ogling the keen blade I'd found for him. Apparently, the previous owners of the house had been avid hunters. I found a bunch of treasures for my psycho men in the basement.

I took a deep breath and smiled at my family. My loyal and caring husbands. My beautiful children. My brother. And my dearest friends. They all stared at me with unabashed curiosity. Only Doc knew what I was going to confess, a sly grin playing on his lips.

"This family is going to expand even more," I admitted, bringing my hands up to reverently cup my stomach. "Because I'm pregnant. Again. No surprise, given that I have seven husbands. You all have good aim."

As my men gaped at me, momentarily struck speechless, Maya and Charlotte both ran and wrapped me in their arms.

"We're going to have another sibling?" Maya squealed, and Charlotte blinked her doe eyes up at me.

"Sister!" she said with a giggle.

"It could be a boy," I told her with a grin. A tug on my sleeve had me looking into Caspian's eyes. Without a word, he hugged me tightly.

"We're having another baby?" Ryder asked roughly.

I smiled at them over the tops of my kids' heads. They all appeared to be in varying stages of happiness, excitement, and disbelief. "You know my motto—the more the merrier."

With a laugh, my men surrounded me, holding me tight. Maya let out a squeal as she got squished. I leaned over all of them to kiss my baby's head in Ronan's arms.

Calax smirked at me, tears glistening in his dark eyes. "Merry Christmas, baby."

It was a merry Christmas indeed.

ACKNOWLEDGMENTS

Eeep! I honestly have no words to describe how good this feels. My first ever boxset! Woot! Woot! Did you know that this was the first ever series I published...and also the first one I completed? It feels like it was only days ago that I was working on Addie's story and trying to figure out how to publish it.

I would like to thank my family first and foremost. Without your love and support, I wouldn't be the author I am today. Thank you to my sister for convincing me to publish and then supporting me unconditionally afterwards.

I would also like to thank my editor, Meghan, for going back through this entire series and re-editing everything. You made this story something I'm proud of, instead of one riddled with errors. Thank you!

And finally, I would like to thank you, the reader, for joining me on Addie's journey. I hope you enjoyed reading her story as much as I enjoyed writing it. She's batshit crazy, but you just can't help but love her! She'll always hold a special place in my heart as my first ever published character and the craziest female I've ever written!

ALSO BY KATIE MAY

Together We Fall (Apocalyptic Reverse Harem, COMPLETED)

1. The Darkness We Crave

2. The Light We Seek

3. The Storm We Face

4. The Monsters We Hunt

Beyond the Shadows (Horror Reverse Harem, COMPLETED)

1. Gangs and Ghosts

2. Guns and Graveyards

3. Gallows and Ghouls

The Damning (Fantasy Paranormal Reverse Harem)

1. Greed

2. Envy

3. Gluttony

Prodigium Academy (Horror Comedy Academy Reverse Harem)

1. Monsters

2. Roaring

Tory's School for the Trouble (Bully Horror Academy Reverse Harem)

1. Between

2. Beyond (Coming Soon)

Supernaturalette (Interactive Reverse Harem)

1. Introductions

2. First Dates

3. Group Outing

4. Game Night

5. Exes

Kingdom of Wolves (Shifter Reverse Harem Duet)

1. Torn to Bits

2. Ripped to Shreds

CO-WRITES

Afterworld Academy with Loxley Savage (Academy Fantasy Reverse Harem)

1. Dearly Departed

2. Darkness Deceives

3. Defying Destiny

Darkest Flames with Ann Denton (Paranormal Reverse Harem)

1. Demon Kissed

1.5. Demon Stalked

2. Demon Loved

3. Demon Sworn

STAND-ALONES

Toxicity (Contemporary Reverse Harem)

Blindly Indicted (Prison Reverse Harem)

Not All Heroes Wear Capes (Just Dresses) (Short Comedic Reverse Harem)

Charming Devils (Bully/Revenge Reverse Harem)

Goddess of Pain (Fantasy Reverse Harem)

Demon's Joy (Holiday Reverse Harem)

ABOUT THE AUTHOR

Katie May is a reverse harem author, a KDP All-Star winner, and an USA Today Bestselling Author. She lives in West Michigan with her family and cat. When not writing, she could be found reading a good book, listening to broadway musicals, or playing games. Join Katie's Gang to stay updated on all her releases! And did you know she has a TikTok? Yeah, me either. Follow her here! But be warned…she's an awkward noodle.